Dreaming the Storm: The Storm Begins
Seeing the future: blessing or curse?
For Anne, only the number of survivors changes. Few or none.
Anne knows the truth. Only Evan believes.
Can they make a difference, together?

Joining the Storm: The Storm Builds
Etan loves his life in Chicago, far from his native mountains.
Alex loves the city that welcomes him more than his own family.
Both seek the missing piece to their puzzle.
Dreams and patterns. Restless and searching.
Then one snowy night sets their shared destiny in motion.

Into the Storm: The Storm Strikes
Iris's paintings scare most people. Especially the strange ones.
Even in her hometown of Maple Ridge, Virginia, her own peculiar
magic makes her an outsider in a town full of them.
Then Iris meets Gena, the first to understand.
Will they survive as nightmares come true?

Fighting the Storm: The Storm Breaks
Alex and Etan thought love, hard work, and their own peculiar
magic protected them from the end of the world.
Until heartbreak struck much closer to home.
Picking up the pieces brings new friends and new challenges.
Will the power of family bring them all through, together?

Storms of Future Past: Books One through Four

Copyright © 2019 by Kari A. Kilgore

All rights reserved

Published 2019 by Spiral Publishing, Ltd.
www.spiralpublishing.net

Book and cover design copyright © 2019 by Spiral Publishing, Ltd.
Cover art copyright © 2019 by SÃ¸ren Sielemann | Denis Tevekov | Joyfull | Ig0rzh
|Dreamstime.com

ISBN-13: 978-1-948890-15-1
Library of Congress Control Number: 2019945322

This book is licensed for your personal enjoyment only. All rights reserved. This is a work of fiction. All characters and events portrayed in this book are fictional, and any resemblance to real people or incidents is purely coincidental. This book, or parts thereof, may not be reproduced in any form without permission.

Additional copyright information for previously published material at the back of the book.

For Teresa

For fantastic support and encouragement that keep me writing.

And keep me always striving for the next level, just like you do.

STORMS OF FUTURE PAST

BOOKS ONE THROUGH FOUR

KARI KILGORE

SPIRAL PUBLISHING, LTD.

STORMS OF FUTURE PAST BOOKS ONE THROUGH FOUR

DREAMING THE STORM

BOOK ONE OF THE STORMS OF FUTURE PAST SERIES

KARI KILGORE

AUTHOR OF IN THE PINES AND RESTRICTED SPECIES

To Carolyn and Linda

For countless hours of friendship, learning, and laughter.

PART I

BEFORE THE STORM

When a country, a society, or an entire planet is hit with catastrophe, an event that changes everything from that point forward, humans are driven to try to find out why.

What have we done to deserve this?

How can we get back to normal?

And did anyone know this was coming?

That last one is more than idle speculation by the unaffected, especially if there *are* no unaffected.

The mistake people make, the wishful thinking that leads them to pursue The One Who Knew, is assuming such a person could have made any difference. That she could have done one thing that would have kept all the bad things from happening.

Or, more darkly, that this mythical person knew and decided to do nothing.

Prophets have risen up many times through the ages, claiming to have this gift of seeing the future. Whether certain ones could or not is a debate for another day. What's not debatable is the most common response by society: to condemn them as insane, with often horrific results.

Is it any wonder, then, that people who do know - who can *see* - so often choose to hide their knowledge and themselves?

Is it any wonder that knowledge frequently torments them in solitude until they truly are as insane as others assume?

The only salvation for one so cursed - through chance, divine intervention, or a quirk of genetics - may be one person to witness their visions. To share in the fear and hopelessness, the struggle and possibility. To simply understand and believe.

The seer lucky enough to find such a witness may not only be able to make a difference in the terrible things to come, but may indeed have the strength to do so.

Anne Fincastle was eleven years old when the dreams started.

Evan Griffith was too young at thirteen to understand how, as witness to her dreams, he would save her life.

Chapter 1

EVAN SQUEEZED his hands hard against his ears. He didn't want to hear any more today, not of anything. His clothes crowded close around him, scratchy and soft and smooth, making an even smaller room inside his closet. A room he finally felt safe in.

The black behind his closed eyes turned to shifting red. Someone had opened his closet door.

He pushed against the cold wall, shoes he'd tossed back here and forgotten digging into his backside. Rich scents of grass, dirt, and his own stale feet rose up at the movement. Maybe whoever it was wouldn't see him huddled behind the row of pants and jackets. Evan was afraid his legs showed, though. He should have put the rolled up sleeping bag and heavy winter blankets in front.

The light moved again, and Evan only squeezed his eyes shut until his eyeballs ached. He heard rising and falling sounds through his hands, closer and slower than the shouting. Someone was trying to talk to him. He should be polite and see who it was, but he just didn't want to.

A cold, damp hand closed over one of his and he flinched away. That hand was too small to be one of his parents. The voice was too soft to be either of them.

He risked barely opening one eye.

Gwen, that was his big sister Gwen. Still wearing her school clothes. Stripy pants so wide at the bottom that Evan didn't know how she could walk, and a shirt with ruffles all over. She leaned in close, her long pigtail braids swinging forward. He shifted his right hand the tiniest bit off of his ear. He could still hear the shouting, but not too bad.

"Come on, Evvie. It's time to go."

Evan shook his head and hid his face against his knees. He was almost four years old now. Too big to be a scaredy-cat anymore. But he was scared to death of walking through the house right now.

Gwen leaned so close he felt her warm breath on his cheek, so Evan lifted his hand away from his ear again. A ringing pop brought all the noise back into his head.

"It's okay. Mom will know where we are," Gwen whispered. "She told me to take you with me when this happens." He squeezed his eyes closed again and started to cover his ear. Gwen grabbed his hand. "I'm supposed to take you with me, so come on."

Evan opened both eyes then, wanting to tell her to go away and leave him here in his closet. He felt safe here. If he ran to his bed and got enough pillows to go with his clothes, he could bury his head enough to drown out the whole wide world.

Gwen's brown eyes were right in front of his, and she was crying. He'd hardly ever seen her cry. She was nine, and so much bigger than him that he thought she never cried anymore. She held out her hand.

"We're just going down the street to Mr. and Mrs. Fincastle's house. They'll know what to do. It's okay."

He lowered his hands so he could get up, but a loud shout from his Daddy made him jump and cover up his ears again. Gwen squinted up her face, then put both hands under Evan's arms and lifted him up. She grabbed his fuzzy tan coat with big wooden buttons he could fasten by himself off the floor and wrapped it around his shoulders.

He could tell by her mouth that she was asking if he was ready, but he didn't dare uncover his ears again. Evan nodded, trying his best to be brave and strong. He followed his big sister.

Gwen had on her own coat with long brown fringe hanging from the sleeves and her big denim bag full of school books slung over one shoulder. That bag scared Evan and made him wonder just how long they were going to have to stay at the Fincastle's house.

He stayed as close behind her as he could on the shaggy blue carpet in the hall and on the stairs, so close that he bumped into her when she stopped to open the front door. He thought he heard a crash coming from the kitchen, and Gwen whirled around and looked that way.

Evan was too afraid to look. Now that he was out of his safe closet and almost through the house, he just wanted to get away. Gwen was crying harder now, but she managed to get the door open and pushed Evan through in front of her.

"I'm sorry, Evan," she said, putting her arm around him when the door was closed. He finally lowered his hands all the way, curling his fingers against the freezing cold. But he could still hear his parents shouting inside.

That awful sound was the end of the world to him.

"We'll just go over there for a little while, and Mom will come and get us when things calm down."

"What if they hurt each other?"

This time Gwen didn't look sad or cry at all. She looked really, really angry. Her mouth turned down and her eyebrows made sharp lines pointing toward her nose.

"They never have before." Her mouth was a tiny, thin line now, like his Daddy's was sometimes. When she was mad, Gwen looked so much like his Daddy that it made Evan a little scared. "What Mom told me is to get away and take you with me, so that's what I'm going to do."

They walked just down the block and across the street, Evan holding tight to Gwen's hand. He stopped every few feet to look back over his shoulder. He couldn't hear his parents anymore, but he kept imagining he could.

"What are you looking for?" Gwen said.

Evan stared at Gwen, not wanting to upset her more than she

already was. Mist puffed out of her nose and mouth and her cheeks were bright red from the icy wind.

"What if they do hurt each other, Gwennie?" He didn't say what he was really thinking, what his belly was feeling.

What if daddy hurts mommy?

"There's nothing you can do about that, Ev. They're both grownups. Mom told me once that all I can do is stay out of the way. Now I'm big enough to get you out of the way, too."

Evan closed his eyes, trying to squeeze the tears back inside. Some part of him, a part too old for his mind and body, was crying out that he *could* do something. Not only that he could, but he *had* to.

If he let his parents fight and never did anything about it, whatever happened would be his fault. Evan's fault. He wanted to run away and never look back, and he knew in his bones that leaving them alone screaming like that could only make things worse.

Gwen started up the steps to the Fincastle's house, but Evan hung back again.

"What's wrong?" Gwen said. "We should go inside. It's not good to just hang around out here."

"Will Mr. and Mrs. Fincastle be mad at us too? For wanting to stay here?"

Gwen shook her head and pulled on Evan's hand.

"They never have been before. They're really nice. Don't worry. They know what to do."

Gwen reached up to ring the doorbell, and Evan kept himself from pulling her away. He didn't want to bother anyone. He'd be perfectly fine sitting here on the porch, hidden where no one could see him.

Not being seen made a lot of sense to Evan.

Before he could say a word, Mr. Fincastle opened the door. His big, warm smile went away when he got a good look at the two of them. Evan stared down at his bare, grownup feet poking out of faded jeans that were all strings at the bottom.

"Are you two okay?"

"Yes, sir," Gwen said. "We just need to… Can we stay here for a little while?"

Evan glanced up at the shaky sound of his big sister's voice. She hardly ever sounded scared, even less often than she cried. Mr. Fincastle opened the door wide and stepped back.

"Of course you can. Anne just went down for a nap, so walk quiet as a mouse."

Evan was confused for a few seconds, worried about just how quiet a mouse walked. He remembered a birthday party at Mr. and Mrs. Fincastle's house back during the summer. Anne turned one that day, but she hadn't walked very well at all. What Evan remembered best was how she'd laughed when she dug her small fists into the pink icing on her cake.

He did his best to tiptoe as he and Gwen followed Mr. Fincastle inside.

"Come on back to the kitchen, and I'll get you something to drink. Mom, we have company."

A television with wood all around was on in the living room, but no one was in there watching. Evan saw a man with a big nose and a blue suit talking, a man he'd seen a lot lately. The man waved his arms and said "Well, I am not a crook…" as Evan walked by.

Evan expected to see Mrs. Fincastle when he walked around the corner into the bright gold kitchen. The refrigerator and oven were the same pretty gold as the ones in his house, and the shiny floor under his feet was covered with stripes of brown, blue, and that same gold.

Instead of someone his mother's age, Evan saw an old, old woman sitting at the kitchen table. He blinked and nearly tripped over his own feet.

"Well hello there!" The woman was beaming, her whole face lighting up in a smile Evan couldn't help returning. Now that he could get a closer look, he saw she had gray hair like his own grandmother did, but her face looked smooth and young. Her eyes were bright, and as green and pretty as Mr. Fincastle's. "And who are these beautiful children?"

Mr. Fincastle turned away from the refrigerator with a bottle of what looked like orange juice. Evan hoped it was the same thing the astronauts drank instead. Mr. Fincastle was smiling, but he still looked sad.

"These are our neighbors, Gwen and Evan Griffith. They live just down the street. They're going to visit with us for a little while."

"Oh, I remember Evan now!" The woman held out her hands, and Gwen and Evan each took one. Her fingers were warm and smooth. "And it's lovely to meet you, Gwen. I'm Mary Fincastle, and this is my son, Mike."

Mr. Fincastle sat down with four glasses.

"I don't think you've met Evan, Mom. Dad was still alive the last time... Anyway, I'm sure you remember Gwen. She's been here before."

Mary Fincastle tilted her head, looking so much like a curious dog that Evan had to fight back a giggle. No matter how he felt, he didn't think laughing while his parents were yelling at each could possibly be a good thing.

"You do look familiar, Gwen," she said, smiling again. "But Evan is here a lot. He's just like part of the family."

"He sure is," Mr. Fincastle said. "They both are. Are you two hungry? I can make you a sandwich or something."

"No, sir, not right now," Gwen said, and Evan shook his head. "We just... Our Mom said we should come here."

Her voice had that trembly sound, and Mr. Fincastle seemed as upset by it as Evan was.

"Don't you worry, Gwen, not about one single thing. Want to come into the living room and watch television for a while? Time to change the channel anyway. I think we've all had about enough of Mr. Nixon lately. There has to be something better on."

The shows were very good, and before long Evan's eyes were trying to close all by themselves. He didn't want to act like a big baby in front of grownups, but he was really sleepy. He was still young enough to need a nap, no matter what else was going on.

The next thing he knew, Mr. Fincastle was picking him up.

"I'm sorry..."

"Shhh, don't be sorry for needing a nap. I could use one myself most days."

Evan put his arms around Mr. Fincastle's neck and laid his head against his shoulder. A nap really did sound good. He heard a woman's voice, a younger woman than Mary Fincastle, but he couldn't quite manage to open his eyes.

Mr. Fincastle put him down, and Evan felt something warm beside him. He turned toward that warmth and snuggled up close. The last thing he heard before he fell into real sleep was two adults laughing softly, and one baby girl breathing.

Her breath against Evan's cheek smelled as sweet as flowers after the rain.

Chapter 2

FIVE YEARS later

Rainy summer days were the worst as far as Anne was concerned. Much as she may daydream about it, she never was going to find a magic hallway inside her closet or a hidden trapdoor under the shaggy brown carpet in her bedroom. She'd only see the same pale blue walls, the same dolls and cars and picture books on the same bright yellow shelves, the same songs to sing to herself until she was bored to tears.

The pebbled white ceiling of her room sounded like a constant roar of water, or maybe like her mother was running the vacuum cleaner in the attic. The view of the sky through her windows looked more like almost bedtime instead of not even lunch time. The streetlight she could see through the branches of a maple tree was even on.

Anne didn't understand why Evan loved the rain so much. The only thing she loved about it was when he came over to play on stormy gray days like this.

Then the dolls and cars and bricks came to life like magic, with Evan helping figure out what the next story was until it really was nighttime and he had to go home. Anne didn't usually like the board games her parents played with their friends, but Evan even managed to make those giggly fun.

Anne pulled another skirt out of her chest of drawers, at least the fifth or sixth she'd tried on in the last hour. The others were neatly stacked one on top of the other on her bed. She wasn't sure why she kept changing into different ones. A vague idea of wanting to outgrow her Christmas gifts floated in the back of her mind. Wanting to grow up to six so she could start school just a little bit faster.

The pretty pink skirt with blue flowers and green leaves all over it joined the others in the disappointing fits-me-just-fine pile.

She pulled on a pair of last year's pink pajama bottoms that were indeed a little too small, missed in her mother's regular thinning out of her clothes for sad kids who didn't have any. Anne scrubbed her sock feet on the thick shaggy blue carpet, then touched the metal of her doorknob. Nothing. The trick her father taught her about making sparks with her fingertips only seemed to work when it was cold outside.

Anne pushed the door all the way open and poked her head out into the hall. The blue carpet covered the whole floor and all the way down the stairs, but the walls were a boring grownup white. She couldn't hear a sound in the whole house besides that rumbly rain.

Her mother had said she wanted quiet time for a couple of hours, and that Anne was old enough to entertain herself without help now. The idea that she was old enough for anything usually made Anne happy, but not this time. She wondered if she needed to be a day younger, a month? Or all the way back to her last birthday when she turned five?

Anyway, it didn't seem fair to her.

Even more unfair was Evan visiting family in a far away place called Virginia for ages and ages now that he didn't have to go off to school all day long. The thought of joining him in real school, where the big kids were, delighted and scared Anne at the same time. A few hours of kindergarten hadn't been all that bad. She kind of wished she could go to her school today, but she knew she really was too old for that school now.

At the real school, there would be kids of all ages and sizes, not just little kids like Anne. Evan said it was okay, but he was already seven. She was afraid he knew secrets she didn't know, something his big sister told him when she first went to real school. Gwen was a lot older than Evan, and Anne didn't have a big brother or sister of her own. Maybe that was something no one else could warn her about, and she'd just have to walk in and face it.

Anne jumped at a slow, rolling boom of thunder over her head. Her daddy had said rain all day long and maybe storms. If it thundered, he said she couldn't go outside no matter what because of lightning. No chance to get out or have something fun to do until lunch time.

She put her hands flat on her belly, scowling down at her fingers laced together. Nope, not even hungry. Anne thought she'd been up here for at least four or five hours, but she should have been ready for lunch by now. She shook her head and sighed.

Her mother hadn't exactly said Anne had to stay in her room, only that she had to stay upstairs and be quiet. There wasn't much she liked up here outside of her own room, but she stepped out into the middle of the hall anyway. From her door at the end, she could see a guest room door, a bathroom door, and her parents' door, all shut tight. Only her grandmother's stood open, and in the gloom Anne could make out a glowing light in there.

Anne grinned and headed that way, doing her best not to stomp and make noise. She'd been sure her grandmother would be having quiet time too, not sitting right up here alone herself. If Gemaw took a nap, she almost always kept the door closed.

Anne slowed just before the doorway, listening as hard as she could. Even noisy rain wouldn't drown out her Gemaw's snoring, so she must be awake and bored just like Anne.

"Gemaw?" she whispered, tapping her fingertips on the wooden door frame.

"I'm awake, sweetheart. Come right on inside."

Anne walked through her grandmother's open door, her eyes on the pile of cases in the middle of the room. She'd never seen such pretty bags, shapes and sizes she'd never seen before, and so many different flowers and colors. The ones her parents used, and her own, were plain, hard plastic blue rectangles with tiny wheels on the bottom.

"What is all this stuff, Gemaw?"

"Hello sweet pea! These are just my suitcases."

"They're so pretty. Where did you get them?" Anne touched the biggest case, a dark purple rectangle bigger than she'd ever seen, made of soft fabric.

"I got these when I first got married to your grandfather, a long time ago." She stood beside Anne, one hand on her shoulder. "My mother helped me pick them out special."

"What's this one for?" Anne reached for a round case sitting on top, made of that same purple fabric but with pink designs all over. Initials were sewn into the middle, small m, big F, small e.

"That one was supposed to hold hats, but it doesn't anymore. I put my socks in there, wrapped around all the pretty things you've given me that I don't want to break."

Anne looked around the room then, noticing the walls and shelves were bare.

"Are you going somewhere?" Her grandmother sat on the bed, smiling. It was neatly made, but her special pretty pillows were all missing.

"I'm going on a trip, but everything is going to work out just fine." Anne was drawing breath to ask where she was going when she heard someone out in the hall. Instead of her mother grumpy about her interrupted quiet time, her father walked in.

"What's going on, Mom?" He was smiling, like her grandmother, but his voice sounded strange.

"I just wanted to get everything packed up so it would be easier."

Anne's dad raised his eyebrows, then squatted down and hugged Anne.

"Hi sweetheart. Listen, can you go play for a little while? I need to talk to Gemaw, private adult stuff."

Anne started to argue that she was bored, that she'd come in here to have someone to talk to, but her father had a serious, don't argue look now. Her grandmother was still smiling and seemed happy, and Anne couldn't figure out why her dad wasn't.

"Just for a little while, Anne. Okay?"

"Okay, Dad. See you later, Gemaw."

He pushed the door around when Anne walked out, but he didn't quite close it. She scooted her feet all the way to her own doorway, tapping her non-sparking bedroom doorknob with her fingers. She was still bored and still wanted something to do.

Her dad said it was private, but he hadn't closed the door. She rocked back and forth from her toes to her heels, trying to decide. Playing out in the hall was still playing. She grabbed her favorite doll and her favorite car and walked quietly toward her grandmother's room.

"I don't understand what you mean, Mom."

"Karen has been so kind to me, for a long time now. This will be easier on everyone, Mikey."

Anne sat down and rolled the car back and forth on the carpet, trying to be quiet as a mouse like her dad always said.

"None of us want you to leave. Why would you think that? Karen hasn't said anything to me, not a word."

"Well no, I know she hasn't. But I don't want her to have to." Anne scooted a little closer, her hip dragging the doll along the wall.

"We all love having you here, Mom. Come on, let me help you put everything back. A little mouse out in the hall can help. Right, Anne?"

Anne froze, her face and her whole body feeling hot. How had he known she was out there? Her plans to crawl backward until she got to her own room dissolved when he pushed the door open. He had one eyebrow raised, but he didn't look really angry.

"Gemaw needs help unpacking her bags, Scoot. Want to join us?"

A couple of weeks later, when Anne got up, she saw her grandmother's door standing open. It was another weekend, so everyone could sleep as long as they wanted, but Gemaw was dressed and sitting on her bed.

The pretty cases were all in the middle of the floor again.

"Good morning, sweet pea!" Her grandmother was smiling, looking as happy as a little girl.

"Good morning, Gemaw. Where are you going this time?"

"I'm just going on a trip, nothing to worry about."

"Can I go with you? I really want to go."

Gemaw shook her head and patted the bed beside her. Anne climbed up and scooted close for a hug.

"You can't go on this trip, Anne, only me. You need to stay here until you grow up a little more."

Anne crossed her arms and sighed.

"That's not fair. I want to go on a trip, too."

"Don't worry, pea. You'll get to go on a lot of trips when you get bigger, but it will all work out just fine."

Anne jumped when her father spoke from the open door.

"Morning, girls. Heading out again, Mom?"

"Good morning, Mikey. Yes, it's almost time to go."

"Well, come downstairs and have breakfast first. We'll check the schedule and make sure."

Everything got put away again after breakfast, but Anne's grandmother didn't seem upset at all. She thought her parents were only pretending to be happy, though. They all went to the park that afternoon, and Anne almost forgot all about it. When she came downstairs to kiss her parents goodnight, they were sitting in the living room talking. The TV was on, but it was turned down low.

She took the stairs one at a time, quiet as a mouse.

"I haven't said a word to her, Mike, not a word."

"You know how she picks up on things. If you wanted her to move, you should have said something to me. I had no idea."

"Then she doesn't either, so let's just forget about it."

They were quiet for a few seconds, and Anne had decided to go back upstairs after all when her daddy spoke again. She had to listen really hard to hear his words.

"She kept saying it would be best, now she's saying it would be best for Anne. Where else would she be getting that, Karen?"

"I told you I didn't say anything, and I didn't. If you're determined to get into this with me right now, I'll tell you right now she might have a point. These things get harder over time, not better. It might not be best for Anne to see that."

Anne stood up, forgetting that she wasn't supposed to be listening at all.

"Mommy? You want Gemaw to leave?"

Her mother stood too, but she didn't move toward the stairs. Her face was bright red.

"Anne, I've told you about sneaking around and listening to grownups!" Anne drew back at her mother's shout. "You need to get back upstairs and go to bed, now!"

Before her father could say a word, Anne ran back up the stairs as fast as she could. After she cried enough to feel a little better, she heard voices coming from downstairs, loud voices. The TV must be on louder now.

Just as Anne was about to fall asleep, someone knocked on her door.

"Anne, sweetheart?" her mother whispered. "Are you still awake?"

"I'm awake, Mommy."

Both of her parents came in and sat on the bed, one on either side of her. When her daddy turned on the light, she saw both of them had red eyes like they'd been crying.

"I'm sorry I yelled at you, Anne," her mother said as she stroked Anne's cheek. "I was surprised you were there, but I shouldn't have yelled."

"Your Mom and I were talking," her daddy said. "Private grownup talk. You know what that means, don't you?"

Anne wished she could hide her face under the blankets.

"I know. I'm not supposed to listen. I'm sorry. I'll try to do better." Her mother scowled, but Anne caught her father's smile. "Can I ask you something?"

Her mother and father looked at each other, then back at her. "Sure, hon," her daddy said. "But it is bedtime, so not too long."

"Is Gemaw going away?"

Her father brushed back her hair and sighed.

"I don't know, Anne. She will someday, you know that. Like Grampaw did."

"Yeah, I know she'll be gone someday, but I mean is she going to live somewhere else."

"How would you feel about that?" her mother said.

"I don't want her to go," Anne said. "She makes me feel better when I have bad dreams."

Her father moved closer and Anne put her head in his lap.

"What do you mean?" he said. "When do you have bad dreams?"

"I have bad dreams a lot, not every night, but a lot. Gemaw comes in and tells me everything will be okay. Sometimes I go into her room, but most of the time she finds me before I even get up."

Her mother's face scrunched up for a second, but her daddy only had a little smile. His eyes looked sad instead of happy.

"Well, no one's going anywhere right now," he said. "Gemaw did that for me when I was your age too, sweetheart, but you can come to us if you have bad dreams. You know that, right?"

"I know, but I don't want her to go. Please? I really want her to stay here."

"Enough talk for one night." Anne's mother kissed her forehead, then stood and turned out the light. "We all need to get some good sleep, and we all need some sweet dreams."

After a couple of quiet days, Anne's grandmother packed up her pretty bags again. She did that more and more often. For a while, she and her daddy made a game out of it, seeing how fast they could help her put everything back, and her grandmother played along.

Anne knew the second when everything changed. Her daddy never had to tell her a word. His whole face and his body and his heart changed. Her grandmother never did seem to be upset or sad when they were helping her put everything away, but after getting more and more upset every time, her daddy gave up.

He didn't make her unpack anymore, and he didn't try to talk her into staying. Her grandmother just slept on the boring bed in the empty room, her cases all piled up in the middle. Anne was too scared about what her daddy giving up might mean to ask questions, but something deep down in her chest knew what would happen.

Her Gemaw moved out into a huge, scary building before Anne had time to turn seven.

She never quite believed the promise that everything was going to work out just fine.

Chapter 3

By the time Gwen went away to college when he was eleven, Evan didn't need to hide in the closet from all the shouting anymore. He knew how to take himself away when a really bad fight got going, either to Anne's house or just out into the yard most of the time. Gwen had told him to keep himself out of the craziness however he could, and she'd helped by leaving her bulky old portable radio and tape player.

Unless things got really bad, Evan could stuff a towel against the bottom of his bedroom door, turn up the music, and pretend he lived in a normal house without all the yelling.

Or at least a house where the yelling didn't happen quite so often.

Everything between his parents had been quiet lately, at least while he was at home and awake. A stretch of calm over an entire weekend was unusual enough that Evan was able to dig into his homework instead of having to go to the library or to Anne's house. Once he got comfortable at his rarely-used desk, he enjoyed the change of pace.

His usual pop music station from the city was on, but not nearly as loud as usual, and he even had the door and the window open. A warm early summer breeze floated the Major League Baseball curtains he'd gotten for Christmas into the room every few minutes. He was tempted to go out there and enjoy the day, but he was almost finished with his report for school. He wouldn't admit it to much of anyone, but Evan enjoyed writing history papers more than just about any other homework. This one about the mysterious Cahokia Mounds, a few hours south just outside of St. Louis, was one of his favorites so far.

A stack of library books and a couple of his encyclopedias sat on the broad, scratched surface of his mother's old desk, but Evan rarely needed to look back once he'd read about something. If it caught his attention, the facts seemed to stay in his mind forever without much effort. He swung his feet just above the ground, lost in the words and the thoughts that drove them.

Evan didn't notice the soft footsteps out in the hall or the knock on his door. He blinked at the sound of his mother's voice. He hoped he wouldn't have to go to the library after all.

"Hey Ev, can I talk to you a minute?"

Megan Griffith stood just outside the door, gripping the handle even though it hadn't been closed. She wore her usual jeans and a bummy t-shirt for a working around the house day, so she wasn't planning to go anywhere. Her dark hair was caught back in a loose braid, and her cheeks weren't red or blotchy like when she was fighting with Evan's father.

She smiled, but her eyes looked tight and sad.

"Sure, hang on," Evan said. "I'll be right there."

The strange knot in Evan's belly faded when he focused on the paragraph he was in the middle of writing, then came back full force after he closed his notebook. His parents hardly ever interrupted during the rare times he did homework at home, not with something besides the shouting. He tried to convince himself that whatever his mother wanted wouldn't be that big of a deal without much luck.

She waited in the bright, sunny kitchen, but she wasn't reading or cooking or working on anything else she usually did. She was pacing back and forth, and Evan would have sworn she was talking to herself. She didn't notice him at first, then jumped when he spoke.

"What's going on?"

"Oh, hon, you startled me."

Evan sat beside her at the round kitchen table, pale wood spotless and gleaming. The knot in his belly was bigger now. And it was twisting.

"Listen," his mother said. "I wanted to tell you. I'm going to Chicago to visit with Gwen for a few days."

"You're… When are you going?"

"I'm leaving tomorrow morning."

"But this is Saturday. I can't miss the whole week of school."

She looked away from him, rubbing the side of her face.

"I'm going alone, Evan. You'll stay here with your dad."

He reacted before he had a chance to think.

"No! I'm not staying here with him, you'll just have to wait."

"Don't shout, son, please listen to me. I need to get away for a little while, that's all. It might be good for the two of you to have some time together."

"Good? There's nothing good about me spending time with Hurricane Ed!"

Evan wished he could get the words back, and he could feel his cheeks burning. Gwen would kill him if she knew he'd spilled their secret name for their father. He risked a glance up at his mother, expecting her to be upset with him.

She had one hand over her mouth and her eyes were watering, but that wasn't an angry look. His mother was trying her best not to laugh and doing a rotten job of it.

"Evan, you shouldn't… You shouldn't say things like that. At least not where I can hear you." She took a breath deep enough to regain her stern mom voice. "It's just for a few days, son. You two will be fine."

Evan shook his head and stared out the window into the back yard, trying to keep from getting even more upset. He didn't like to spend a few minutes alone with his father, much less a few days. He was more comfortable with complete strangers. At least the strangers weren't always looking at him like he'd let them down somehow.

And the strangers didn't spend so much time either fighting with his mother or not saying a word for hours on end.

"We're not exactly the best of friends, Mom. I think he'd be a lot happier if you took me with you and he stayed here."

"You never talk to each other," she said, her voice barely loud enough for him to hear. "How could you possibly be friends? This might be a good chance to try."

Evan shook his own head but kept staring out the window. He didn't want his mom to see the tears in his eyes.

"Dad doesn't like me, never has. No matter what I do, I'm some kind of disappointment. There's nothing we can talk about."

"That's not true, hon, of course he likes you." The sound of her voice made Evan turn around. She didn't sound like she was lying, not quite, but she didn't sound sure of herself either. "You just need to get to know each other."

"Why are you so determined to go right now? Does Dad know? Are you even going to tell him?"

Evan ignored the whispery voice saying he was mad at the wrong person. He didn't particularly care about being fair at the moment. What he cared about was being dumped and left behind. His mother leaned her elbows on the table and held her face in her hands.

"No, I'll tell him. Don't say anything about it. I'll tell him tomorrow. I just need to get away for a little while."

"Yeah, away from me." When she turned to him, her blue eyes flashing, he knew he'd said one thing too many. For the first time, he didn't care.

"No, Evan, *not* away from you, but that attitude isn't helping. I'm not leaving you, and I'm not leaving your father. I'm taking a break, I'm leaving tomorrow, and that's all there is to it."

Evan's heart ran cold at the idea of her leaving his father. What if this little break or whatever is was turned out to be something she liked? That would explain why she didn't want him to say anything.

He had several friends with divorced parents. There were times when he didn't understand why she stayed with Ed, but he hadn't really considered the reality of anything else.

"Leaving Dad? Is that why you don't want me to say anything? Is that what's going on?"

She blinked and tried to hide it, but Evan saw tears in her pale blue eyes. He'd seen his own eyes in the mirror too many times to mistake that.

"I'm sorry. I shouldn't have said that. Telling him anything like this is my job, not yours. I just can't deal with the hassle tonight." She squeezed her lips into a line and took a deep breath. "You're not a kid anymore, Ev. You know things have been a little rough around here lately. We've both been busy at work, and everyone's trying to get used to Gwen being gone. This feels like a time to take a break."

"I might need a break too, did you think about that?" Evan wiped at his cheeks, but he knew he wasn't hiding a thing. "What if he decides to take it all out on me with you and Gwen gone? That doesn't exactly sound like a break to me."

She leaned forward and hugged him, and after a few seconds Evan stopped trying to get away. The stray tears had turned into real crying now, but he didn't try to stop. She stroked his hair, just like when he was little.

"Come on, it's going to be okay. There's no reason he'd want to fight with you. Gwen pushed him as much as he did her, and you never have. You can always go over to Anne's house, any time you need to. You've always done that."

Evan sat back, grabbing for a napkin before his nose started running.

"I don't think he'd like that very much, Mom. I wouldn't be getting away from the shouting, not with only two of us here. I'd be getting away from him. I'm sure he'd notice if I just walk out the door."

"Well, truth is that's his problem, not yours." She brushed the hair back from his forehead, something else she hadn't done in ages. "You'll be at school most of the time, anyway."

"When will you be back?"

"Sometime over the weekend, probably Sunday. I can talk to

Anne's parents before I go. I'd bet they'd be happy for you to spend some time with them on Saturday. Okay?"

Evan shook his head again, but inside he knew there was no point in talking about it anymore. She was going to go, and he was going to have to deal with it. Getting more upset and yelling wasn't going to change a thing. It never did between her and his father.

"I guess so. I'm going to go finish my homework." When he stood, she caught him in a quick hug.

"Thanks, Evan. We'll plan to go up together soon, just you and me. We'll leave Hurricane Ed here by himself and see how much he likes it."

PART II
DREAMS BEGIN

Chapter 4

ANNE OPENED her eyes inside a massive library, the biggest one she's ever seen, even bigger than the one at the university in the city. The wood and metal shelves stretched away in all directions as far as she could see. Even when she leaned her head back far enough to feel dizzy, she couldn't see the tops of them or the ceiling.

Only hundreds, thousands, millions of books in every shape, size, and color.

Well, stacked impossibly high and forever out of reach in what she was starting to suspect was a dream, they were still books. More than she could read in her life, in a hundred lives. Anne smiled and hugged herself, turning in a circle to look at as much as she could. She breathed in the warm, welcoming scent of all that paper without even a hint of the dust or sharp cleaners that made her eyes and throat hurt in a real library.

There was no door or checkout desk, not that she could see. A few scuffed and scarred tables were shoved together in a clear spot beside her, with green cushioned chairs poking up here and there. She walked on thin gray carpet that made her footsteps silent, running her fingers along the row of books closest to her.

Warm scratchy fabric. Cool slick plastic. Rough bumpy paper. None of the spines she touched had any words on them, only flashes of color and pictures she couldn't make out. They all had a feel to them, a hit of sensation. She didn't have to read the titles to know which books would be scary, sad, boring, or exciting.

Anne wanted to find something happy to read. She'd been feeling very unhappy lately, even in her dreams, filled with something she could only call dread. She couldn't say why, but asleep or awake, she was sure something bad is going to happen. She wanted to escape, just for a while.

A huge book caught her attention, almost too heavy for her to pull off of the shelf she has to reach up to. The book was almost as long as from her waist to the top of her head, but it didn't weigh nearly as much as she thought it would. She managed to get it down and stagger toward one of the beat up tables. Even with her arms wrapped around the warm, pebbly surface, Anne couldn't tell how this book would make her feel besides curious.

The book landed with a huge, echoing bang, but no one shushed her. No one else seemed to be in this giant building but Anne.

She stared at the book, wondering why this was the one she had to read. Bound in well-worn leather, dark brown and fragrant. She smelled the old, slightly uneven paper when she ran her fingertips across the closed pages, one of her favorite smells in the world.

There was no picture on the cover, but she finally saw writing. Two words embossed in heavy gold took up most of the space.

The Future.

Anne grinned, hoping she'd found a new science fiction book. That was her favorite thing to read by a long shot, that and fantasy. Anything with spaceships and robots and dragons and magic sent her right into another world, so deep that she wanted to stay there forever.

She lifted the cover, wanting to get a look at the table of contents so she could try to guess what the stories were about. Instead of single pages she could turn, half of the book fell to each side. In the middle was a screen as long as Anne's arm. She could still see the edges of the pages on either side, but a strange, tiny, flat TV seemed to be jammed inside somehow.

She wasn't sure how to read it, but she was even more curious than before. The outside still looked like a normal book. She ran her fingers all around the sides, but she couldn't see any way to make the book work. She hoped the battery wasn't dead, if it even had a battery like a flashlight or a toy. She finally touched the middle of the screen.

Anne drew back as the screen came to life. She couldn't see any images, but the black was illuminated, a brighter version of nothing. She put her ear close to the book and heard the faintest hum. She remembered how her Gemaw's old television had to warm up sometimes, but Anne was sure a tiny flat television like this didn't exist.

The screen finally lit up.

A swarm of bees, crawling all over honeycomb, in and out of the picture.

Anne jerked her hands away even though she was sure it was only a movie. Even in her dream, she knew the things on the screen couldn't hurt her.

She'd never liked bees since she got stung a few years ago, one of the earliest things she still remembered. That bee had been on the rim of the glass Anne was drinking out of, and it crawled up into her nose and stung her before she could react. The pain had been horrible!

Her mother and father both tried to tell her that was a yellow jacket, not a bee, but the damage was done. Anne didn't kill bees. She just did *not* want to be around them.

The image shifted down in a fast movement that made Anne dizzy to show the ground at the bottom of the hive. There were piles of bees, drifts of them, and all of them were dead. Anne didn't see a single one stirring now.

The movie pulled back, and now she saw two hives with dead bees.

The image doubled to four, then again and again and again until the whole screen was filled with piles of dead bees. Despite her fear, Anne was terribly sad. Even though she didn't much like them, she knew bees did a lot of good.

What had killed so many of them?

The next picture showed a small green plant with tiny purple flowers, rows and rows of them. The flowers were moving, changing. They came out, dried up, and fell off, over and over again. Nothing ever sprouted from them. They just died. Eventually the plant turned brown, then it crumpled into the soil.

The same thing happened with different kinds of plants, this time with white and yellow blooms. They looked healthy, but the flowers just shriveled up.

People stood in huge crowds, and these people weren't real like the bees had been. They looked like drawings that moved, like old cartoons Anne and Even watched sometimes in the afternoon.

The cartoon people watched the plants trying and trying to make fruit and vegetables, but nothing ever grew. The people were silent for a long time.

Now all Anne could see was that crowd of people, but they were shriveling just like the flowers. Each person got smaller and smaller, thinner and thinner, then they crumpled up and blew away.

When blank spots opened up in the crowd, they started shouting at each other, screaming, clenching their fists, drawings of blue veins standing out on their necks. Anne wanted to close the book and make the movie stop before someone got really angry.

She was too late.

One drawing woman pushed a man and he fell down. Then the whole crowd was fighting, punching and kicking and clawing and biting. Some of the people had guns then, and when they shot, whole groups of people puffed away into dust.

Anne needed to close the book. She needed to put it back on the shelf and run out of the library and never come back again. But she couldn't move.

The scene shifted again, and she saw a lake. Not a regular lake, not like the one she went swimming in sometimes.

This lake was inside a big metal circle, a giant one, and bunches of other little round lakes were all around it. Some kind of machinery worked away in the middle of the groups of round lakes, and she could see the water moving. It flowed from one circle to another, getting less cloudy and dirty and more clear and sparkling with every move.

A low, droning noise grew, drowning out the noise of the machines, getting closer every second. The camera tilted up, making her stomach roll. Anne wanted to shield her eyes from the harsh light.

An airplane flew out of the sun, a huge plane, bigger than she'd ever seen. It seemed to hang in the clear blue sky without moving. When it was overhead, the belly of the plane opened up and dust fell into the water.

In just a few seconds, the water in every one of those lakes turned from clear, cool blue into a sickly, diseased green. The machinery strained, then chugged, then it finally fell silent with smoke floating around it.

A little girl much younger than Anne, maybe only two or three years old, walked along the edge of the lake on a metal sidewalk. The lake held real water, but the little girl was a drawing just like all the dead people.

She stopped and lay down on her belly, reaching her hands into the foul water.

"No! Don't drink that!" Anne shouted, her voice echoing in the vast library. "Can't you see it? It will make you sick!"

The girl drank anyway, but before she could sit up she clutched her throat. She coughed and clawed at her neck, then that little girl curled up on the metal sidewalk. She turned to dust and floated down into the water.

Anne moaned as the camera drew back to show hundreds of children around each of those lakes, all curling up and dying.

And she saw hundreds of lakes, round metal lakes and real, outside lakes.

And she saw thousands of them, blending into rivers and seas and oceans.

Around every single one of them, piles of dust as high as the dead bees were shifting and moving. Fish floated up to the top of the real lakes, drawings of fish with Xs for eyes. The fish turned into dust too, cartoon dust that covered the real water.

Anne knew that wasn't dust. That was dead things, dead things the poisoned water had killed. The dead things made the poison worse.

The screen went blank for a second, and Anne wiped her eyes, hoping the horrible movie was over. She didn't ever want to come back to this library again.

Then she saw dots slowly lighting up and glowing, coming to life scattered around the screen. There weren't very many, not even twenty of them. Lines formed on the screen, and after a second Anne realized those were the lines of the continents. The dots were on the land.

She could see a few on each continent, and only five in all of North America.

Her fear drew back a little as her curiosity started to recover. What was she looking at? They weren't near any of the cities she knew.

"What is it?" she whispered.

The lines of the continents faded in the middle, right around the Atlantic Ocean, and words floated to the surface. Pale blue words.

Remaining Human Population.

Anne gasped. She knew enough from school to recognize the vast, empty stretches where great cities were supposed to be. Millions and millions of people weren't there anymore. Chicago was gone, and so was St. Louis. The single, pale dot of her town was the only thing left in the whole Midwest.

Anne closed her eyes and shook her head, then covered her eyes with her hands to make sure. That was enough. Whatever this book was, she didn't want to see anything else it had to show.

Not now. Not ever.

She stood, keeping one hand over her eyes, the other held out to make sure she didn't run into anything. She backed away until she felt the shelf behind her. She walked slowly, hoping she could finally find the door in this awful place.

Sometimes in her dreams, she could run and run without ever getting anywhere. Anne was afraid she'd go crazy if that happened now, if she got trapped in this horrible place. The kind of crazy that waking up wouldn't even solve.

When she'd taken about ten steps, she peeked through her fingers.

She *did* see the door, a long way off through the stacks and tables and chairs. She lowered her hand and walked as fast as she could. The walkway out of this row of books and tables was getting more crowded by the minute. More chairs, desks, and even tables were everywhere, and she kept having to push them out of the way.

When Anne got to the end of the row, she stopped. She didn't want to look. She didn't want to see any more.

She had to look. If she didn't, she felt like she'd get trapped in this dream forever.

She held on to the shelf with one hand and a table with the other, and she turned her head slowly enough that she heard her neck creaking.

The huge book was still on the table, but it was closed now. Anne let out a breath she'd forgotten holding. A worried voice inside her head muttered that she should have put the book back in its place on the high shelf, but she didn't care. As long as it was closed, she wouldn't have to see anything else inside of it.

When she turned back toward the door, the path was even more full of chairs. She squared her shoulders and started walking, moving things out of her way, climbing when she had to.

If she didn't have to look at that book anymore, she wasn't going to let a little thing like getting out the door scare her. Sweat ran down her face and arms and legs, and all her muscles ached, but Anne kept moving faster.

When she finally jumped over one last chair and grabbed the cold metal handle with both hands, tears joined the sweat on her face.

The door to the outside closed behind her with a bang.

Anne sat up, wild-eyed, desperate to make sure she was still out of the library. She could barely see, even when she blinked and rubbed her eyes. A blue glow, way too close to the horrifying dots on that

TV screen, washed across her hands and arms. About the time her heart stopped pounding in her ears, she finally recognized the ceiling and shelves of her own bedroom.

Her face and her whole body were covered in sweat, so bad she could smell it. The sky was still dark outside. The clock beside her bed, the source of the glow, showed she had two more hours to sleep.

Sleep that might very well include more nightmares.

"Forget it," she whispered, swinging her legs over the edge. "Not worth it."

She dumped her pajamas in the hamper in the bathroom, thinking she'd probably need to do the same with her sheets. At eleven, she was pretty sure she was old enough to start doing her laundry herself, if nothing else to stop her mother from deciding to donate or throw away Anne's clothes without warning.

Right now she had to get in the shower and get the stink of the dream off of her skin.

Anne turned the water up as hot as she could stand it, until steam was pouring over the top of the sliding shower doors. She stepped in, hissing when the spray hit her, but she didn't turn the temperature down. She wished she could stand to turn it up a little higher, beyond the immediate reddening of her chest, arms, and belly.

Maybe enough scrubbing and soap with that scalding heat would get the reek of that library out of her pores.

After washing every inch she could reach and rinsing her pink washcloth until her fingers got wrinkly, Anne decided to go ahead and wash her hair. Might as well get ready to go to school, even if she had to try to sneak a nap during her afternoon classes.

She'd never had a nightmare quite like that one, and she'd had bad dreams as long as she could remember. It hadn't felt like a dream at all, not really. Anne was sure if she pulled the clothes she'd been wearing in the dream out of her closet, they'd be covered in the same musty smell as that library. She decided to hold her breath and dump them into the hamper under her sheets just so she wouldn't find out the truth.

Scrubbing her hair hard with a towel, hard enough that she knew she'd be combing out knots and tangles, didn't quite drown out the low hum lingering in Anne's ears. The same hum that awful book had made. She attacked her teeth just as roughly and with too much toothpaste, listening as hard as she could to the scratching of the bristles.

Anne started humming to herself when she walked back into her bedroom, and that finally replaced the sinister noise in her head. Or maybe her tuneless song only covered it up, but she didn't care.

Her eyes went to the row of spiral-bound notebooks on the shelves above her desk. She often wrote down her strange or scary or disturbing dreams when she woke up, and the good ones she remembered sometimes too.

Evan had given her the idea not long ago, when they were talking about her Gemaw moving out. He'd said she could write them down and that might make her feel better. And if that didn't work, she could take the notebook and tell her grandmother the next time they visited.

Anne was surprised at how often just writing it down helped, and she'd taken a bunch to read to Gemaw over the years as well.

She shook her head, humming a little louder without realizing it. She didn't want to write this dream down. The captured words and images, black ink following the pale blue lines on the paper, would give an already too real dream even more weight and substance.

That felt a big step too close to making it come true.

Chapter 5

A HUGE, echoing boom kicked off the dream next time.

Anne stood with her back against the door to the library, and she knew without trying that the door wouldn't open for her, not yet. She didn't want to be here, not here. The same library with the awful moving book was the last thing she wanted to see.

Anne took a few steps forward, determined to control something before bad things started to happen. Everything was so much larger than before, so big that her mind cried at trying to understand. The rows still went on as far as she could see in every direction, and the shelves again stretched so tall she couldn't make out the top of them against an invisible ceiling. The building still *felt* bigger, somehow.

Maybe this library was as big as the whole wide world.

If that was true, what if she got lost and couldn't find the door again?

The same stinky sweat covered her body, and Anne felt drops running down her scalp under her hair. She knew she'd wake up from the dream. She always had, even from the worst nightmare.

Still, this had the disturbing hint of reality, like she could open her eyes a thousand times and never be able to leave this place.

Well, she'd just have to stay within sight of the door and find something else to read. Eventually the door would have to open.

Anne turned the opposite way from where she'd gone the first time, when she'd had to climb over a thousand chairs and tables to get away from the huge reference books that now looked much taller than she was.

She spotted a shelf full of picture books only a few steps away from the door. These were all small enough to hold in her hands, books for children. Several tiny, brand new tables and chairs sat on a rug covered with blocks of vivid colors, and a fake hot air balloon in the same colors hung overhead.

Anne was her full size and age of eleven even in the dream, a little too old for such things. But she felt safe looking at them.

Most of all, and no matter how old she was, she needed something happy to look at. A clammy, dark feeling that something awful was going to happen kept rising up from under her bare feet, creeping slimy and cold up her ankles.

Anne needed something good to make her smile, to make her feel warm and silly. Not more terrible movies from the book about the future.

She took one more step away from the door, deciding losing sight of it just for a second would be worth the risk. Stepping under the balloon and onto the warm carpet dulled the echoes of the vast space around her, like she'd walked into a safe little tent. She pulled a bright book out from the low shelf that didn't even come up to her waist, one she remembered checking out herself just a few years ago. It was one about the moon.

She'd driven her parents crazy asking them to read it and renew it until they'd bought her a copy. She moved around the knee-high tables until she could see the door, then sat in the much too small chair. Her knees felt like they were as high as her shoulders. Anne laughed, the sound echoing too much for inside her sheltered tent.

The noise escaped into the unseen roof and bounced around, getting louder for several seconds before fading away. She was afraid a thousand little girls were laughing, just out of sight where she couldn't see them.

Anne squeezed her eyes closed tight, knowing the doorway out of the dream still wouldn't work yet. She vowed to keep quiet, opened her eyes, and started to read.

The words didn't quite make sense, but the soft, pastel drawings of flowers and castles and sweet animals were just what she needed to see. She gradually forgot the door, the awful book on the other side of the library, and the gigantic space all around her.

Her feet again felt like they were sinking into cold, sticky mud, right through the cheerful carpet, but she managed to ignore that for a while.

A loud click from behind her made Anne jump. She turned and blinked at a gigantic old wooden television on a metal cart she hadn't noticed before. Her teachers sometimes rolled a TV into the classroom for them to watch, like when the space shuttle launched, but this one was way too big.

Anne recognized her Gemaw's old set, the one in a cabinet that was big enough to sit on the floor and still be waist-high on a grownup. That couldn't possibly balance on top of the thin metal cart, but in a room bigger than the whole world, anything could happen.

Anne could hear the wood creaking and shifting as the huge TV warmed up.

Remembering the way the book had turned itself on, the bad book, she tried to get up and leave. Once again, she was held tight, unable to move.

"No," Anne whispered, trying to force her gaze away from the screen. "I don't want to see any more."

The black screen exploded into shapes and colors, and Anne couldn't stop herself from letting out a small scream at the swarms of bees. Her voice echoed again, getting louder and louder until she clapped her hands over her ears to block it out. All she could hear then was her own racing heartbeat, and sweat ran down her back despite the cool room.

Everything on the screen was the same, at least until the people with the guns showed up.

The people suddenly didn't look like drawings anymore. They looked like real people.

This time when the bad people shot, the groups of the dead didn't just turn into dust.

This time they were covered in blood that sprayed everywhere, and they were all screaming.

Anne squeezed her hands tighter over her ears, but she could still hear them. The same thing happened to mobs of people by the big round lakes, the only thing Anne knew more about now. She'd looked in her encyclopedias, too afraid to go to a real library. The first things the giant airplane had poisoned were for cities to clean their water, to make it safe for everyone to drink.

This time when the little girl drank the green water, the real little girl, she didn't just turn into dust. She turned green herself, then her body started to swell and look rotten.

Like in the first nightmare, the camera drew back until Anne saw hundreds of children beside the metal lakes, all drinking and falling and dying.

Even in a dream, Anne knew she couldn't possibly be smelling those tiny rotting bodies, but the thick stench coating her nose, mouth, and throat told her otherwise.

Finally the carnage on the screen stopped, with the cool, blue words floating in the middle of the Atlantic Ocean. The dots on all of the continents looked the same, and the words floated to the surface.

Remaining Human Population.

"How many are left?" she whispered.

The blue words in the middle of the ocean shifted and rearranged themselves.

Less than one million.

Anne covered her mouth, trying to keep breathing now that the stink of death was clearing. She knew a world with over four and a half billion people, and now there were less than one million?

She needed to get out of here before she saw more, and before the chairs completely blocked her path. She managed to raise one shaking hand and did the simplest thing she could think of. She pulled the plug.

When the TV went dark, Anne started to cry.

~

ANNE SAT STRAIGHT UP in bed, gasping for air. That awful dream, the same one as before? Barely a week had gone by since the first one. She'd finally started falling asleep without being afraid of it coming back. As soon as she'd let her guard down, she was right back there.

"You sound as crazy as Gemaw," she whispered, rubbing her eyes. "Talking to yourself isn't much better."

She dumped her pajamas in the hamper again on her way to the shower. Getting up two hours early had gotten her through the day the first time, but she didn't want this to become a habit.

She'd heard about recurring dreams somewhere, but she'd never had one. Why did it have to be a nightmare coming back? Why not a *good* dream?

Anne thought about her grandmother as she scrubbed and tried to steam the awful scenes and smells away. Calling her Gemaw crazy made Anne feel guilty, but it didn't feel far from the truth.

Her dad's mother was very sweet and very kind, just as when she'd lived here and comforted Anne after her ordinary bad dreams. Gemaw also didn't seem to understand what was real and what wasn't. Gemaw's mind ranged through time, like everything was happening at once. She was eight years old, she was in her thirties, she was her current age in her late sixties, she was twenty.

All of that in just one short visit.

Anne's dad said Gemaw had always been different, kind of unusual, but this had gotten worse as she got older. Anne had heard her mother talking about it to her Uncle Walt once though, and she'd told a very different story. More than any of the other times Anne had listened in to her parents and their grownup conversations, she regretted hearing what her mother said about Gemaw the most.

Her mother said Gemaw had always been nuts, that she'd never been right in the head. That the worst decision she'd ever made was to let someone like that move in where she could affect Anne. And the best had been when she agreed with the old woman that it was time for her to go.

Anne couldn't remember Gemaw living anywhere besides with them before she'd moved into her group home, though Anne's dad said she'd lived in her own house about an hour away until Grandpa died. Anne didn't really remember her grandfather either.

She didn't mind visiting Gemaw at all. It was like watching an actress play out different roles all in one movie scene. The thought of a movie made her shudder as she turned the water off.

That dream had been bad enough the first time, when the people looked like drawings. It had been creepier that way, really. More eerie than gory.

Seeing real-looking flesh and blood people was so much worse.

Anne got dressed for school, deciding to start writing down what she did before she went to sleep. She was still too afraid writing the dreams down would make things worse somehow, and she'd never tell her Gemaw about such awful things, anyway.

If something she was doing made those dreams happen, she might be able to change her habits. Her father had warned her about eating weird things or watching scary movies before bedtime. Her mother didn't want her reading too much before bed, either.

Anne hoped her parents were right. She was afraid of never getting free of the end of the world library, and of what that might mean for her mind and her sanity.

Chapter 6

ANNE FELL TO HER KNEES, hugging herself, tears streaming down her face. Not again.

Please, *please*. Not again.

She was in the same library, the same one she'd been dreaming of for weeks now. Sometimes the building was normal sized, like the one she never went to in town anymore. Sometimes it was gigantic, big enough to hold the whole planet.

Lately it had been tiny, making Anne feel like the room had been built with her flat on her back, close enough to keep her from drawing a deep breath. Books no bigger than her pinkie fingernail lined shelves pressed all along her whole body, and the ceiling pushed against her nose and stomach.

None of that mattered, not once the movie started. Realizing she was dreaming didn't make any difference at all. The moving scenes showed up no matter where she went, and they were getting worse.

The black and green computer screen the librarians used had revealed hand to hand fighting with knives and bullet impacts from the guns, all in close-up nauseating color and detail.

The encyclopedias had changed the shriveling people into starving people, and they weren't just getting thinner. Their flesh wasted away and sores grew on every part of their bodies. Their hair and then their teeth fell out before they finally fell. Horses, cows, chickens, even dogs and cats, joined the horrifying scenes, drinking the poisoned water with the same heartbreaking result.

In the claustrophobic space compressing her entire body, the white ceiling tiles with tiny black dots transformed into a screen. Anne was forced to watch people eating poisoned food, sometimes the poisoned animals, then throwing up until blood came out, then parts of their bodies followed. That smell, forced into her compressed nose, was by far the worst.

Anne had written down and tried changing all of her bedtime routines, but nothing had helped. At least a few times each week, and sometimes every single night, she was in the dreadful library.

"I have to change something in here," she whispered, wiping her eyes. "I've tried everything else."

She got to her feet and looked around, but today every section in the regular sized building looked exactly the same. The children's section was gone, the computers were gone, even the TVs that seemed to appear from nowhere were nowhere to be seen. Shelves and stacks of books stretched away from her, all of them dull and grey without any writing on the spine at all.

Anne looked to the right, where she'd found the TV screen book. She hadn't seen it again after that first dream.

"Maybe that's the problem," she said with courage she did not feel.

She walked toward that long, scuffed up table, trying to ignore her shaking legs. She had to do something to get the dreams to stop. Her schoolwork was suffering from the lack of sleep. She knew that even here. Her parents kept asking her what was wrong, though Evan had given up after a couple of weeks.

She knew she wasn't fooling anybody just as well as she knew she couldn't explain this. And she was afraid this dream was going to drive her crazier than she was already feeling.

She saw the original book, *The Future*, on exactly the same high shelf where she'd first found it.

Anne pulled it out, managing to get it onto the table without too much noise. Her stomach was twisting inside of her before she even got it open. The same screen was there, and the same touch of her fingers activated it.

Maybe it would be different this time.

Maybe it wouldn't be the ever worsening nightmare that wouldn't leave her mind all day long.

When the swarming bees appeared on the screen, Anne cried out and sat back in her chair. She knew she wouldn't be able to move or look away. She never could do that here.

The scenes played out again, each just a tiny bit more gory and graphic. The starved people and animals and war dead were piled up and burned in giant pits, and the smell and sound and even heat rose all around her.

By the time the blue letters appeared, declaring the world population at less than five hundred thousand this time, Anne was swallowing convulsively to keep from throwing up all over herself.

This had to stop, please.

"When is this going to happen?" she said, her voice trembling. "Will I be alive then?"

The letters faded before scrambling all over the screen, moving too fast for Anne to read. She waited, afraid to see the answer but afraid to turn away.

If she blinked, if she looked away for just a second, she could miss it. She could miss her chance to know what was going to happen and when, and maybe her only chance to stop the dream loop. The letters finally stopped moving.

You will be long gone, Anne Fincastle.

Anne tried to breathe deeply to stop the tears that kept welling up into her eyes. So many people dead. So many animals. So many children. No water to drink, no food to eat.

Deep down in her belly, Anne was relieved she would never see it. At the same time, she was terrified, and anger knotted up her face and her muscles.

This thing knew her *name.* This thing knew the way into her *sleep*.

This thing *never* left her alone anymore, even when she was awake.

If the dreams started happening during the day, too, Anne knew what little life she had now would shatter into useless pieces.

"Can I do anything about it? Can I save them?" She paused, then shouted loud enough to hurt her own ears. "Why do you keep showing this to me?"

You are the only one who can stop it. You are the only one who must. If you fail to act, all of humanity will perish.

The letters faded, and the outlines of the continents were again bright and clear. A few scattered dots on each land mass showed the pitifully few humans left on the Earth. Anne closed her eyes for a second, but when she looked back, she was sure some of the dots were missing.

Yes, one just went out, somewhere in Australia. They were going out on the other continents too, one after the other.

When all of the dots in Australia were gone, the outline turned red.

Anne gasped. The people were dying, all of them were dying. She tried to close the book, not wanting to see any more, but the screen now weighed a ton. She couldn't move it an inch.

The dots continued to go out, all over Europe and Africa, in China and India, then throughout South America. Anne kept trying to close the book, sweating and straining with the effort. It still wouldn't budge.

She watched, helpless, as each continent went red, one after the other, even the islands all around the oceans turned crimson. North America was last, with the lights fading from the coasts inward.

"No! I don't want to see this!"

When only two dots were left on the whole planet, one in Illinois, where Chicago should be, and one to the southeast where Evan went to visit his family in Virginia, Anne could finally move the book. She dug her fingers under both sides and pushed as hard as she could.

The book closed with a tremendous boom, far louder than before.

The floor shook underneath her, and she heard the other books rattling on their shelves.

The awful movie was finally gone.

~

THIS TIME ANNE woke with tears running down her cheeks and her pillow soaking wet. On one or two other nights, she was sure she'd screamed in her sleep, so this could be called an improvement.

The clock showed three hours before the sun would even come up. Waking up so early on a Saturday made her want to cry even harder.

She was so, so tired. Every part of her ached with exhaustion. Good nights were getting so rare that they seemed like a distant memory, like some kind of good dream she'd had years ago. She staggered into the bathroom and turned on the light.

She thought she looked nearly as old as her Gemaw now, like she'd skipped over turning twelve and gone straight on to sixty. Her green eyes were puffy and red, and she couldn't pretend the dark circles under them didn't show anymore.

Too many people had asked her about that.

Evan had noticed before anyone else did, even before her own mother.

Anne wondered sometimes if Evan liked her, not like a friend but like a girlfriend. She wasn't sure if she wanted him or anyone else to like her that way. It seemed like an awful lot of trouble to the adults she knew.

And if she was losing her mind just like her grandmother, no one would want to put up with that, anyway,

She washed her face and went back into her bedroom. She didn't think she'd be able to get back to sleep, but maybe she could figure it all out if she tried yet again. Anne sat down at her desk and got out her notebook, her special private notebook. It looked like a regular spiral notebook, and that was exactly what made it safe.

She was old enough to know writing *Private!* and *Keep Out!* and *Do Not Touch!* would only draw her parents to it like a beacon. This way, no one had any idea what was inside.

She turned to the last page with writing on it, nearly halfway through. She hadn't done anything special before falling asleep, and that never seemed to make any difference anyway. The dream seemed to be random, even though she was getting less and less of a break from it.

Nothing seemed to cause it, and nothing seemed to keep it away.

That didn't make her feel better.

Anne drew a line under the last entry and started writing. She didn't note what had happened on the screen. She was still too afraid to do that, though she was running out of other ideas. She couldn't stand to try to remember it more clearly. Flashes of the dying and dead in her mind all day long were bad enough already.

She wrote down what she'd done in the dream, like she had the last several times. The one thing she hadn't done to try to change the pattern, the one thing she could think of to try, was just what she'd done tonight. Getting that original book down off the shelf hadn't improved anything.

All she'd learned was she was supposed to do something about it, and that even the survivors weren't going to last long. She put then pen down and rubbed her burning eyes, laughing under her breath.

"What am I supposed to do about a bad dream?"

As it turned out, she already had made the difference, at least for a little while.

The dreams stopped, but before a week had passed Anne would have welcomed them back. Now she was having visions, and not just at night.

She was having visions of the end of the world all day long. And the visions weren't just scenes like a movie, as awful that was.

Now Anne *lived* in the visions, she was part of scene. She heard the screams, smelled the blood and the fear. She felt the heat of the burning pits of human bodies.

More than Evan or her parents or her teachers were noticing something was wrong with her now. She knew she seemed to zone out and stare into space when she saw the visions. Evan had told her that, but she couldn't figure out how to stop them. At least with the dreams, she knew she'd be alone when they happened.

Now she never knew when a vision would hit her.

People on the street seemed to stare at her even when she wasn't having one, but before long Anne couldn't be sure about that.

Not once she stopped seeing the faces of people around her.

The first time it happened, Anne ducked into the girls' bathroom before anyone could notice. Her gym teacher, one of the few who took the time to make sure Anne participated in classes anymore, played the victim. Ms. Denton no longer had short curly blonde hair and a ready smile, or at least Anne hadn't seen that.

Most of Ms. Denton's head was missing, and part of her legs were, too.

Anne somehow knew a plane crash tore the woman out of life just as it tore her body.

She didn't have to fake throwing up that day, and for once she didn't hide the reaction. Her mother picked her up from school. Anne wasn't sure if staying in her room the rest of the afternoon kept her from seeing more.

Not until she left the house the next day and saw the faces of the dead everywhere.

Instead of a man walking into a store, she saw a soldier dying with blood gushing out of his belly. Instead of a little boy running across the playground, she saw a starving shadow of a human being, his head huge and his belly distended.

And worst of all, instead of a little girl walking into the kindergarten room she and Evan walked by on the way to their classes, she saw a skeletal, ill version of the girl, clutching and clawing at her throat as the water poisoned her.

Almost every person Anne saw turned into a death mask, some version of how they would eventually perish. She didn't know when it would happen, or even *if* it would happen, and she didn't care. She couldn't stand to see any more.

She kept her eyes down and hurried from class to class, then she rushed home and went upstairs to her room. Even her parents, even their faces were dead and cold and lifeless to Anne. She could hear them talking, but they looked like cold, badly made wax figures instead of people. She was grateful she couldn't see how they were going to die, but seeing them dead was bad enough.

The only person she could stand to be around was Evan. She could actually see his face, hear his voice, look into his beautiful pale blue eyes. He could talk to her, or at least talk at her, even though Anne could hardly ever manage to say anything back to him.

She was so glad he kept talking.

She felt bad for ignoring him, but she couldn't stand to be away from him or around anyone else. She wondered why she couldn't see his death or even her own in the mirror, but she was afraid to wonder too hard.

The last thing she could stand would be seeing his face disappear behind his particular version of the end.

After a month of the visions, she knew she had to talk to Evan about them. No one seemed to notice she never spent time with anyone else when she could possibly avoid it. But even with him walking beside her every morning and every afternoon, cheerfully talking nonstop the whole time, Anne was starting to get terribly lonely.

She hadn't really talked to anyone in so long, not since the nightmares first started months ago. And she'd realized that was the one thing she hadn't done to try to stop the dreams or the visions.

She hadn't told a living soul about them.

Maybe if she did that, maybe if she talked to her best friend in the whole world, the only friend who'd stayed by her side, the visions and the dreams would go away. Maybe if she brought it all out into the light, it wouldn't be able to torment her any longer.

She was so afraid he would start to look at her the same way other people had, at least back when she could see other peoples' faces.

She didn't know what she'd do if Evan stopped spending time with her, or if she started seeing his face disappear.

But she was too scared and lonely to keep it all to herself any more.

Chapter 7

Evan's nearly empty backpack banged against his shins every few steps, but he didn't bother slinging it onto his back. The early spring weather was just warm enough that it made him feel way too hot. As he walked toward home with Anne silent beside him, he enjoyed the hot sun on his face after a terribly long and cold winter.

He'd grown used to the sound of his own voice on these walks over the last few months, and the lack of any response from his friend. Evan talked about his day, all the trivial little details he was sure no one else in the world would want to hear. From the second he'd parted company with Anne that same morning, he filled in all the minutes and hours in between.

Each class, every conversation, even the thoughts that wandered through his mind when he was bored.

Once he ran out of daily chatter, Evan switched to the walk itself. He pointed out how the daffodils were lining the sunnier yards and driveways, joining the redbuds in an early show of color and new life. He mentioned how many trees held the first pink flush of budding, with only the stoic oak trees refusing to respond to false warm weather. A car that he didn't recognize passing them on the residential street made it into his comments from time to time.

Evan wasn't naturally given to so much inane conversation. He was far more likely to want to listen most of the time. But since Anne had started to withdraw over the winter, turning into a pale, barely there whisper of the friend he'd grown up with, Evan couldn't stand the silence between them.

It never occurred to him to spend time with someone else, someone who would talk instead of leaving him running his mouth constantly.

Because somewhere inside, he was afraid if he turned his back on Anne, she'd fade away into nothing. Evan was somehow even more afraid of sinking into withdrawal with her and disappearing.

He slipped his worn flannel shirt off as they walked onto a sunnier street, getting close to the park where they'd spent hours playing in happier times. Evan knew he was probably going to feel too old for such things in the fall when he started high school. He couldn't remember ever seeing kids that old in the sprawling public park, at least not near the playground equipment.

He sometimes saw them in twos or in groups huddled in the picnic shelters, surrounded by low conversation, loud music from giant silver boomboxes, or floating clouds of smoke.

The move to a new building wouldn't be all that far or dramatic once the coming summer passed and Evan joined those crowds of older kids. He'd even still be able to walk to school with Anne and have lunch with her, though his big sister Gwen told him that wasn't the best idea, hanging out with a middle school kid.

Evan nodded and let Gwen talk, but he couldn't imagine purposely avoiding Anne, either on this walk or in the cafeteria the middle school and high school shared.

Being in a different building than Anne all day long was going to be more than enough change for him.

They were just about to turn the corner toward their street when a low whisper startled him.

"I need to talk to you."

"What? Did you say something, Anne?"

Evan turned to look at her, certain he'd imagined hearing her voice. She hadn't spoken to him for what seemed like weeks now. She was looking right at him instead of at the ground, her green eyes wide and frightened. She slowed, then stopped. Anne fidgeted for a second, then grabbed Evan's arm.

"I need to talk to you."

She pulled him back the way they'd come, continuing on into the playground. Evan was too confused to do anything but follow. He watched her straight brown hair shifting over her shoulders, flat and lifeless as it had been for a while now. She kept pulling him past the redbud trees in full violet bloom and stopped beside the swings.

Anne kicked at the ground and stared at it too, not meeting Evan's eyes, for several seconds.

"Okay then, talk," Evan said, dropping his backpack. "You haven't said a word to me in ages."

Anne dropped her own backpack and sat on one of the swings. Her feet finally reached the dusty groove underneath instead of dangling above it, but she just sat there. Evan sat beside her, wondering what in the world he was supposed to do.

He'd been worried about her for a long time, everybody had, but she'd resisted everything he'd tried to figure it out. His constant chatter wasn't working, so he decided to be quiet until she decided to say something.

He didn't have to wait long.

"I've been seeing things, Evan."

He was relieved she was still staring at the ground instead of watching him. Her seeing him scowl when she finally started talking wouldn't help either one of them.

"Seeing things? I don't know what you mean."

"Dreams, like I always had, but worse," Anne said, her voice a little louder. "Visions. Nightmares. I don't know what to call them, but they're happening all the time now."

Evan stared at her, afraid to move. He didn't remember anything like that happening to his sister several years ago when she was eleven. He did remember some of the awful dreams Anne had told him about over the past few years.

Until she stopped telling him much of anything.

"What are you seeing?"

"The end of the world," she whispered, finally looking into his eyes. "I keep seeing the end of the world."

"You mean like in the Bible?"

"No, this isn't like that." Her eyes and mouth wrinkled, but not like she was going to cry. She stared over his shoulder for a few seconds before looking at him again. "This is people, people do it. At least part of it. The air is poison and the water is poison and nothing ever will grow anymore."

Evan blinked, casting around desperately for anything to say. All his words had left him, and most of his thoughts had too. All he had inside was fear.

"Is it something you've been reading? A book or something?"

"No, not a book, not a Bible, not a movie or a TV show," she said, her voice rising as she scowled at him. "It's not fake at all. It *happens*, Evan. It's going to *happen*."

Now Evan was starting to get a little mad to go with his fear. Was she just trying to prank him, to make him ask her stupid questions and then laugh and tell everyone? That had happened to him before. He wondered for a second if it was April Fool's Day, but that was a few weeks away.

Something in his gut told him Anne would never do that to him.

"Why do you… I don't want to hurt your feelings, Anne, but what makes you think this is all going to happen?"

"I can see they way it happens, and it already has. Remember I told you about the woman in the room across from my grandmother, where she lives? I started seeing her face hurting and blue, like she choked to death, for days before it she really did die that way. I never saw the body, but I heard my parents talking about it. That woman, she had food hidden in her room when she wasn't supposed to have anything crunchy. She choked to death, Evan."

"You didn't tell me all of that," Evan said. As unbelievable as this whole conversation was, he had to force his brain, and his heart, not to focus on her keeping secrets from him on top of not speaking for weeks. "Why didn't you tell me that when it happened?"

Anne stared at him, her eyes bright with tears nearly falling. He was afraid he'd already said too much.

"Would you tell anyone about this, Evan? About crazy dreams, about predicting when an old lady was going to die? If I'd said something about seeing her choke, maybe they would have found the food and stopped it, but I never did!"

Evan shook his head, the pain in her voice almost making him cry. He rubbed her shoulder, wishing he had the courage to hold her hand.

"You don't know," he said. "Maybe she had it hidden really well. Or maybe she would have just hidden more later. I'm sorry. This is visions, not just dreams? Or did you dream about her too?"

"No, I didn't dream about her. The dream is always the same, about the end of the world." She took a deep breath, her chin and lips quivering. "But now I can see the way everyone is going to die. Every person. People don't look like people to me anymore. They look like they're dead. And the same people look the same way, all the time."

Evan's stomach fell past his feet. He couldn't imagine anything more awful. No wonder she didn't look at anyone anymore. She was looking at him now, though, right into his eyes.

"What about me?" he said, his voice trembling. "How am I going to die?"

"You look normal to me." She nodded once. "You're the only one left. That's why I want to walk to school and home with you. To get a break from everyone and their dead faces."

Evan looked at Anne again, really looked at her, and he saw something about her for the first time. He knew she would never tell him something like this to trick him, or fool him, or scare him on purpose. Without having to ask, he knew she'd never told anyone else about this. Not her parents or a teacher or any other soul.

Anne trusted him.

She was scared to death, and she was still trusting him. Even if nothing she was saying made any sense to him, he couldn't turn away from her.

Not now, not ever. Evan's fear went deeper, driving cold through his whole body.

And his heart left the secure place in his own chest, something he hadn't even suspected it could ever do.

Evan's heart belonged to Anne from that moment forward.

"Okay, Anne. You see the end of the world. Tell me how it's going to happen. Maybe we can do something about it."

Chapter 8

Anne covered her mouth with her hand, trying to stop what had to be her hundredth yawn this afternoon. Her watering eyes blurred the drawing of one of the blue-ridged mountains Evan constantly talked about after his visits to Virginia. The sharp colorful pencil lines morphed into a shimmering watercolor, then back.

The thick crust pizza the teachers had brought in for lunch sat heavily in her belly. Anne was afraid she'd start burping up pepperoni even worse than her smelly garlic breath any second now.

Evan sat next to her, his elbow occasionally brushing against hers. He hated drawing, and at thirteen he was two years older than everyone else in the class. Every time she glanced at him, he was scowling and chewing his lip.

Knowing he was only there because of her stirred up warmth in Anne's chest.

No one else at school knew how often Evan and Gwen came to Anne's house when their parents were fighting. Less than when they were all younger, sure, but more than he'd want anyone else to know.

Evan was the only person on earth who knew about her dreams, and the only one she could imagine ever telling. Talking to him helped somehow, forced most peoples' faces to go back to normal.

Anne yawned again, shaking her head to try to wake herself up as the teacher started talking about distance and perspective. The freezing cold classroom raised chills on her bare arms and legs but didn't help her fight off an intense need for a nap.

Evan grinned at her, his pale blue eyes merry, then went back to his labored drawing.

He was too nice to point out how this mid-summer art class had been Anne's idea in the first place, but here she was falling asleep. He'd never do that, not when he knew how little she slept at night.

Anne's eyes drifted closed, her fingers dragging a purple pencil through the middle of her pale green mountain lake. The teacher's voice faded. She tried one last time to shake herself, to stop the dream paralysis from taking over. For a second, she was more upset about falling asleep in front of everyone than whatever the dream might turn out to be.

That feeling didn't last out her next breath.

A woman sat in a bright yellow kitchen, her face buried in both hands. This didn't look like the things Anne been seeing during the night: strangers starving and fighting and dying in lands she didn't recognize. The woman and the house looked familiar, and she realized they felt familiar too.

Evan's house, and Evan's mother. Evan said she'd been home all week with awful headaches she got sometimes.

Mrs. Griffith looked up, and her face was all wrong. Her skin was pale and tight, like her whole body was clenched up. Like her whole body was tearing itself apart.

Anne tried to scream, no longer caring if everyone in the classroom heard her, but the sound never reached her throat.

She couldn't watch this. She'd seen too many people die in too many different ways in her visions and nightmares. She knew the look.

Evan's mom picked up her coffee cup and got to her feet. She grimaced and staggered, trying to catch herself against the counter. She fell hard, the cup shattering around her. She didn't move anymore.

Anne was caught, frozen, unable to even try to scream again. The other deaths she'd seen play out in her mind had been gory and sharp and horrible, but none were even close to this.

She knew this woman.

Evan's mom had always been kind to Anne, and Evan adored her. They were so much more alike than he was like his moody sister or his scary father. Now something awful had happened to Mrs. Griffith, and Anne couldn't remember what was going to happen next.

Couldn't *remember*? That didn't make any sense, but it did feel right.

This didn't seem like a nightmare anymore, far in the future, surreal and too vivid. This felt more like a memory, but Mrs. Griffith had seemed fine when they'd left Evan's house that morning.

Was this happening right now?

The horrible image inside Anne's mind got a thousand times worse when it split into three. In each one, Evan's mom was on the floor, her black hair covering her face. Motion in all three at once made Anne's head hurt.

She knew, somehow she *knew* she had to pay attention to everything.

Evan's father Ed walked into the kitchen, dropped his black briefcase, and knelt beside his wife. He touched her throat right below her jaw, then sat cross-legged beside her. He started to cry, the first time Anne had ever seen him do that. Ed was much more likely to shout.

He sobbed, rocking and holding his sides. After what seemed like hours and hours, he slowly got up and walked out of the kitchen.

When he came back, Anne couldn't quite make out what he had in his hand. Something black and metallic. He sat down again, with the thing in one hand and the other on his wife's shoulder. He looked at her for a long time, then brushed her hair back from her face.

Her eyes, pale blue like Evan's, wide and staring at nothing.

Mr. Griffith leaned down and kissed her. He put the thing in his mouth, and just as Anne realized what it was, a crashing boom jerked his whole body. She remembered that sound too well from too many nightmares. He slumped forward over his wife's body, a dark red lake growing all around them.

The last thing Anne saw was Evan, walking into the room alone.

At the same time…

Evan found his mother. He shouted and fell sobbing to his knees beside her. Anne saw herself in this memory, walking into the kitchen, panting from running through the painful heat outside. When Evan turned toward her, his broken, terrified eyes made her want to disappear.

In that instant, seeing how her friend was falling to pieces, she understood why Mr. Griffith put the gun in his mouth.

At the same time…

The third memory was the worst, so bad that Anne tried to keep herself from seeing it at all. Evan got home after his father, but not so long after. He walked in to catch his dad getting the gun out of the hall closet beside the front door.

After staring at Evan for a long time, ignoring the questions, Ed Griffith's face turned hard and empty. He hugged Evan, something else Anne had never seen him do, then put an arm around him as they walked toward the kitchen.

Anne tried to reach out somehow, to stop them, to get Evan's attention, to make even one small thing change. In the end, at least she didn't have to watch. She only saw the kitchen door swing closed. Evan screamed a second before the crashing boom. She heard a second shot.

It was all over.

In the same instant, Evan's father got home alone. Evan got home alone. Evan walked in the front door and saw his father with the gun.

In the same instant, Evan's dad slumped over his wife. Evan fell to his knees beside his mother. Two gunshots rang out.

They were all memories.

They were all true.

None of them had happened yet.

"Hey, wake up!"

Anne jumped, focusing on the room around her, on the voice of her friend.

Evan.

He still didn't know, he didn't know anything. His mother was dead, but that was the least of it.

He was going to go home and his father was going to be dead, too. He was going to go home and find his mom, lying cold and still. He was going to go home, and his father was going to kill him, then kill himself.

Anne couldn't let any of those things happen. She couldn't imagine how she could stop them.

Anything she did might make the worst memory come true.

"Where've you been?" Evan said, waving his hand in front of Anne's face.

She blinked, then turned toward him. Her eyes were dazed, like she wasn't seeing him at all. Evan didn't think she'd met anyone else's eyes for months, not since she'd started having nightmares almost every night. She hardly ever looked at anyone besides him anymore.

He touched her arm.

"You okay, Anne?"

She gasped and finally focused on him. He started to move his hand, but she grabbed it. He was a little scared by the tears in her eyes.

"Evan," she whispered. "Don't go home."

"What? Why would I go home? We're here for another three hours. This crazy class in the middle of vacation was your idea, remember?"

She shook her head, still staring into his eyes.

"Listen to me. Evan, you have to listen to me!"

She let go of his hand, but before Evan could be disappointed, she was hugging him tight. His heart pounded, and other parts of him responded, too. Kids glanced at their table, looking confused or smirking, all of them younger than he was.

Before he could decide what to do, Anne whispered, her warm breath against his ear giving him goosebumps.

"Don't go home. Don't go home, please. Don't go home."

Evan forgot about all the other kids and the teachers too.

"Anne, you're scaring me. Come on, don't do that."

What Evan wanted to do was hold her as long as she'd let him. She felt so warm in his arms, so perfect, and her hair smelled like the sun. But he hadn't been lying about being scared. Anne knew how much he hated that. He held her shoulders.

"What's going on? We're supposed to wait here for your dad to pick us up. Why can't I go home?"

She wiped at her eyes, but the tears kept falling. One of the teachers was going to notice everyone looking in their direction. Evan was sure he needed to know what was upsetting her, even if he got both of them into trouble.

"Just stay here, and you can go to my house later." Anne was nodding, her words running together. "My parents never mind when you come over. That will be better."

"No, tell me what's wrong," Evan whispered when he wanted to shout. "Tell me now."

"Ms. Fincastle? Mr. Griffith? Is this class boring you so much that you must interrupt everyone else?"

Evan shook his head without looking at the teacher. He should just apologize, get back to work on his terrible drawing, and worry about all of this later.

Something in Anne's eyes warned every nerve in his body.

"Stay here, Evan," Anne said, her breath hitching in her chest. "Don't go home."

Evan stared at her, trembling starting in his belly and moving up to his heart and brain.

If he left now, he could make the walk in about ten minutes. Less if he ran.

That was exactly what he needed to do. He needed to run.

Another teacher spoke from right behind him.

"Both of you get back to work. Your parents paid good money

for you to learn something, not for you to cut up and disrupt everyone else."

His parents.

Evan's jaw dropped. Anne's eyes squeezed closed, and she was crying harder, her mouth turning down. He barely heard her, but she was still whispering.

"No, don't go home. Don't go home."

He grabbed his backpack from under the table and shoved the chair out of his way.

"Evan!"

He ignored her and kept walking. He made it out of the classroom and halfway down the hall before he started to run. Evan pushed the doors open with both arms straight out in front of him. The midsummer Illinois heat hit him like a suffocating blanket, but he kept going.

By the time he got to his block, he had to slow to a walk, grabbing at the cramp in his side. No one else was out, everything still and quiet in the terrible heat. He wiped sweat from his eyes and face and kept moving.

Evan imagined everything that could be happening, from a robbery to a fire to his sister coming home from college to throw some kind of fit. He saw no smoke, but he was still relieved when he didn't see fire trucks. His sister's car wasn't there either.

Evan's flesh felt like it was going to boil off his bones. No thief would possibly be out on an afternoon with the air over one hundred degrees and soaking wet.

Walking up his driveway, still pressing his hand against the sharp pain in his ribs, Evan didn't need Anne to tell him something was horribly wrong.

～

BY THE TIME Anne made it to the big double doors, Evan was gone. He'd been out the classroom before she could even grab her own bag. She groaned at the blast of summer air and fierce sunlight, making her head pound after the freezing cold classroom.

Keeping both of them inside was one of the reasons their parents had agreed to the expensive class, but Anne wasn't worried about that. She was worried about not being able to see her friend at all.

She started walking, but before she left the school grounds she was running. Evan was two years older, several inches taller, and much faster. She'd never be able to catch him.

The awful memories of Evan's father getting home first hadn't faded at all inside her.

What if Mr. Fincastle decided to go home early today? What if she hadn't seen hours later, but what was going to happen in just a few minutes? Anne felt like she was drowning in the humid air, but she kept running. She had to make sure.

Please, don't let it be one of the other memories. Please.

Anne was gasping by the time she saw Evan's house. There was no car in the driveway. She stopped with her hands on her knees. No car.

Mrs. Griffith parked around back.

Evan's father wasn't home yet, not unless he had walked for some crazy reason. He worked in the city, so that probably meant he wasn't here. He might not know yet, but he could still show up if Evan called him or called the police or an ambulance.

The memory of Evan's face in all three memories, his broken and haunted eyes, got her moving again.

EVAN TURNED the key in the lock, still listening for the imagined burglar. Cool air hit as hard as the hot air had, raising chills all over his sweaty body and making his head pound.

Too cold, it was way too cold with no one home. His parents always adjusted the thermostat when they were all out.

"Anyone here? Hello?"

He closed his eyes for a second, holding on to the door. He heard his mother's voice in his mind, warning him about coming into a cold house after running around outside. Warning him he could throw up or pass out and hit his head. His head was indeed swimming, his stomach turning slow, sickening loops.

He remembered how pale his mom's face had been that morning, even though she'd planned to go back to work today. He dropped his backpack and walked toward the kitchen, keeping one hand on the wall in case he got dizzy again.

"Mom?"

The house was silent except for the rumble of the air conditioner, straining to keep up with the heavy air outside. Something didn't feel right. Evan was covered in chills again, this time unrelated to the cold.

He wished he'd listened to Anne, that he was still beside her, failing miserably to draw anything even he could recognize.

He should have waited. He should have thought this through like his father constantly said, called home or either of his parents instead of charging in here by himself. He'd never even thought of stopping at the pay phone he ran by in the hallway at school. Now it was too late to leave.

His guts knotted up and he was afraid he was going to be sick after all. He pushed the kitchen door open.

"Mom!"

She was on the floor, broken pieces of her coffee cup all around her. Evan fell to his knees, not noticing the shards that cut into his jeans and his palms.

He didn't need to check her pulse or her breathing.

He knew.

"Mom, please!"

Evan rolled her onto her back anyway, and her head rolled with her. Pale blue eyes just like his were open and staring at nothing. Evan's breath caught exactly the same way Anne's had, and he reached out with a shaking hand, touching right under her jaw.

Her flesh was cold, so cold.

Nothing inside her was moving anymore.

Chapter 9

ANNE CLOSED the door to Evan's house quietly, not sure why at first. Then she knew.

Anne still saw all three of those memories; she *felt* all of them.

Evan alone. Evan's dad alone. Evan walking in on his father with the gun.

Mr. Griffith wasn't here yet, but disaster was still coming. She looked at the closet beside the front door. Evan had never mentioned his father having a gun, but that didn't matter.

Anne opened the door, blinking when the bright light came on. She stepped up onto a grimy tackle box. She closed her eyes, trying her best to focus on just one memory.

All three of them were still playing in her mind, still rushing toward her with devastating force.

She leaned up as far as she could, calf muscles cramped from running in the heat, grasping the doorjamb. Right there, she'd seen Evan's father reaching right there. Her fingers felt something heavy, like bumpy leather instead of the steel she'd seen. She stood on her tiptoes and got the whole thing into her grasp.

Anne held the handgun from her memory. The light brown leather holster, embossed with some kind of western design with a dark EG in the middle, covered it almost completely, but this was the same gun. She touched the cold, oily barrel.

In her mind, she heard the crash as it fired: once, twice.

She stepped down and closed the door. Anne let her backpack slide down onto her elbow and unzipped the biggest compartment. The gun made her bag way too heavy, but it fit. She zipped her pack up, then carefully put it down beside Evan's.

Anne concentrated on the images still screaming through her head. Evan turning his face up to her was clear and substantial, and her own tears started. The other two, the memories with the gun, felt a tiny bit lighter.

Maybe she was making some kind of difference after all. She took a deep breath and walked toward the kitchen.

When she reached up to push the door open, Anne felt an odd tingling. She stared at her hand, surprised she couldn't see tiny blue lightning racing over her flesh. Nothing like this had ever happened to her before, but it wasn't exactly scary.

She had a sense of anticipation, of completion. No matter what happened when she opened the door, it was going to be terrible.

But Anne knew it was going to be right.

"Evan."

He turned at Anne's voice, sinking back to sit on his own heels. She was as red and sweaty and overheated as he'd been a few minutes ago, and she was crying again.

"You knew about this?" he whispered, looking back into his mother's eyes.

"I saw...I saw this. Right now. I remembered seeing you beside her. I didn't know what to do."

"When?" Evan wondered at the blood on his palms, still not feeling the cuts. "When did you see it?"

"When I told you." Anne knelt beside him, avoiding the broken cup. "Not until then."

Evan looked up at her, into her lovely green eyes. She was shaking her head and crying harder.

"I couldn't stop it, it was too late, your mom, I mean, but I thought if I could stop you from coming home, it wouldn't hurt you so bad. I couldn't let this be even worse."

"Hurt me." Evan couldn't understand her words or his. He stared at his hands again.

"I'm sorry, Evan, I'm so sorry. I couldn't make it stop."

He turned back to Anne, his movements and his thinking painful and sluggish.

Something. He had to do something.

His mother was…

His mom, she was…

"Be careful." Anne held out her hands. "You're going to cut yourself."

"My mom," Evan whispered, unable to find any other words. "My mom."

"I know, Evan. I'm so sorry."

Evan finally moved, crawling toward Anne, desperate to get to her before something inside of him broke.

He could feel it, a dam overflowing and cracking down the middle, failing to hold back a torrent that would drown everything and everybody in its path.

He grabbed her around the waist and held on for dear life, wondering if he would still exist after the flood.

Anne sat beside Evan on the couch in his living room, trying not to stare at Mr. Griffith. He'd charged right through the house without saying a word, staying in the kitchen for a long time. He'd only staggered back out when the paramedics arrived with grim faces, soft voices, and a stretcher piled up with all kinds of equipment she didn't recognize.

Evan's father had paced for a few minutes, still without speaking. Anne was terrified he would walk right to that closet and look for his gun, even with her sitting there. He'd glanced at the door every time he passed by, but he made no move to open it.

Once he finally sat in his favorite recliner across from them, her fear only worsened. Mr. Griffith stared at the coffee table between them, as if he was deeply offended by the piles of books and magazines that were always scattered across the surface.

He was still wearing his gray jacket, but he'd loosened his tie and unbuttoned his white shirt. Anne had never seen him looking so bad outside of her own strange memories, his thick brown hair standing up and his face blotchy. He started asking the same questions over and over again as soon as he sat down, but that wasn't what bothered Anne.

Evan's father vibrated like a cartoon character who'd been hit on the head with a giant hammer. She was sure it was one of her visions, something only she could see. His clothes didn't move, and neither did his hair or the chair he sat in. But to Anne's eyes, his face, eyes, and hands shuddered and flashed, shifting before she could figure out what was real.

She saw the red face, the messy hair. She saw his face pale and white, his son's blood splattered across his cheeks and forehead. She saw his eyes rolled up and empty, much more blood and gore welling out the top of his head.

The gun was still too close. Anne hadn't done enough to change what was coming. But she knew Evan's father would stop her if she tried to get away now.

"Your class was supposed to last all day, wasn't it?" he said. "Why were you here so early?"

Ed Griffith had asked that question already. He didn't seem to be hearing or seeing anything around him. Anne didn't know if she'd ever be able to explain what she'd seen back in the classroom to Evan, much what she saw now. She knew she'd never be able to explain any of it to Mr. Griffith.

She was too afraid her jittery vision meant the gun was the only thing he *could* focus on.

"We were bored with the class, Dad," Evan said, trying again with the same lie. "We decided to come home. We were going to get something to drink because it was so hot. Anne's parents weren't there yet. Then I…I called you when I saw."

Evan's dad covered his face with his hands, shaking his head.

She couldn't understand why she still saw the memories that hadn't happened, any more than the unnerving appearance of him. The memories with the gun. She hoped those would fade away. At least his voice sounded singular, steady.

"You should have stayed at school, son. You were supposed to stay there all day. That was the plan." Mr. Griffith got louder with every word. "That was what you told me. I would have never wanted you to see this. If you wanted to come home, you should have called me."

Evan turned to Anne, tears running down his cheeks again. She wanted to hug him, but not with his father there.

"I didn't think about calling. We just left. I'm sorry."

"That's just it, Evan, you didn't think!" Ed Griffith shouted, clenching his fists and glaring at his son. "You never think anything through!"

Evan's face went white. Anne finally understood why he and Gwen called their father Hurricane Ed.

"I think it's time for you to go, Anne. Your mother…" Evan said, his voice breaking. He held his breath for a second. "Your parents are going to be worried."

"Maybe that's best," his father said, looking at the floor. "I shouldn't have shouted like that. We've got a lot to take care of before your sister gets home."

Anne didn't need the memories to know that was going to be awful. Gwen was as likely as Mr. Griffith to get angry when no one expected it, much more so than Evan or his mother were.

His mother *had been*. Mrs. Griffith would never *be* anything again.

Anne hated to leave her friend, but she wanted to see her own parents very badly.

She took Evan's hand and stood beside him. He squeezed hard enough to hurt her fingers, but she didn't let go. Evan picked up her backpack, but he didn't seem to notice the extra weight. Anne was afraid to say anything to stop him.

"Thank you for staying, Anne," Mr. Griffith said, still looking down. "I still don't understand why either of you were here so early, but I'm glad Evan wasn't alone."

"I'm sorry," Anne said to Evan instead of his father. "I wish I could do something."

All three of them jumped when the kitchen door opened.

"I'll walk you home," Evan said, and they left without looking back.

He didn't let go of her hand or say a word on the walk, two doors down and across the street. They sat on the swing on her porch, facing away from his house.

Anne didn't want to watch the paramedics wheeling his mother out. She didn't want Evan to see either. Neither of them spoke until the silent ambulance drove by.

"Are you going to be okay tonight?"

"I don't know, Anne. I've never had one of my parents die before." He looked at her for a second, then he hugged her hard. "Thank you for trying to stop me."

He was down the steps before she could say a word. Anne stayed where she was, staring at the oak tree beside her house, not wanting to watch him go back home.

She remembered now that Evan and his father were going to have a terrible night. It would only get worse when Gwen got there.

She kept waiting for the other memories to calm down, but they were still strong within her. The crashing boom echoed through her mind, and Anne knew she had to get rid of the gun. If she took it into her house, her parents would find it. They'd guess where it came from too, with Mr. Griffith's initials on the holster.

The early evening was still uncomfortably warm, but she grabbed her backpack and walked around to the garage to get her bike.

~

THE SAFEST PLACE she could think of, a huge row of dumpsters behind a strip mall, was only a couple of miles away. Anne was dripping with sweat by the time she got there. She'd only passed a few cars along the way, and no one else was out walking or riding in the damp heat.

The sky was still light, but no one was behind the stores either. There weren't any windows on this side, only a solid row of cinderblock and stacks of empty wooden pallets. Sometimes Anne saw teenagers back here smoking. Cigarette butts, empty liquor bottles and beer cans, and food containers drifted against the dumpsters. If any of the stores had cameras, she was sure no one bothered checking them.

She got off her bike and walked down to one of the huge bins for the grocery store. That would be a great place with so many bags jammed into it each day. She lifted the lid, wrinkling her nose at the rotten stench even when it was mostly empty. She got the gun and holster out, then she froze.

She'd seen more than kids smoking back here. She'd seen grownups, sad and dirty grownups, rummaging through the grocery dumpsters. No, she couldn't put the gun here.

She walked her bike past three more dumpsters until she got to one behind a department store that always had discounts and sales going on. When she raised the lid, Anne saw a bunch of hangers, packaging, and empty boxes. Not much worth digging around in.

This one didn't really smell bad, but Anne still held her breath as she reached in for a huge wad of plastic. She took the gun out of the holster and wrapped it up. By the time she was finished, the gun was only a stain in the middle. She tied some long, white plastic strips around the whole thing and dropped it into the dumpster.

Anne turned the holster over in her hands. Nothing would link it to Evan's father besides the initials, but she still didn't want to leave it here. If someone found this, that could lead right to the gun, and the whole thing might end up back in Evan's house.

She smiled, surprised she could with her heart breaking for her friend. She knew exactly the right place. She put the holster in her backpack and rode away.

Less than ten minutes later, Anne stood on a bridge outside of town.

The road didn't even have lines on it because no one lived out here. The pavement went on for another mile or so, then it was just a gravel farm road passing through endless rows of corn and soybeans. Anne knew it wasn't possible, but she and Evan had ridden far enough out there that she was halfway convinced the road never ended. It only branched off into dirt roads and kept going on forever.

The river beneath her flowed fast with recent storms. The holster wouldn't sink to the bottom to be found someday during a drought. It would float away, with any luck ending up in the next county before it ever washed ashore. Anne had a feeling the muddy water would take care of the initials long before then.

She braced her hip against the concrete rail and threw the holster into the middle of the river. It sank for a second, then resurfaced several yards away. She closed her eyes and counted to ten. This time it was only a pale brown blob, so far away she wouldn't have known what it was.

Anne sighed, holding on to the hot, pebbled concrete as her whole body sagged. Seeing the holster floating away was only part of it. The memories, the two awful memories, had shifted somehow. They didn't seem real anymore, like they were waiting right around the corner.

The images were still vivid and terrible, but they felt like dreams now, normal dreams instead of nightmares. No longer deep and heavy and threatening, the scenes of Evan's father and the gun were now light as campfire smoke.

Evan's mother was still gone, and his family was going to suffer terribly over that. Evan most of all. But everything had changed.

As soon as Anne saw Evan's house on her way home, she remembered all the things he would do and every word he would say to her over the next few months. She couldn't do a damned thing to stop it, or change it, or make it easier for him. All she could do was wait and listen when Evan needed to talk.

He would need to whisper and shout and groan and cry, and he would need to be still and silent for longer than he ever had. As bad as the long days ahead would be, she knew everything could have been so much worse.

Anne hoped remembering what didn't happen would give her the courage to go through everything that did.

Chapter 10

For the first time in her life, Anne was relieved when school started. Not because the classes were a little better than the year before, though they were. Having an art class and a music class made a huge difference, choices she finally had getting into middle school.

She didn't even mind getting up so early, not as long as she got to sleep in plenty of time. The whole summer seemed like an effort to stay up as late as she could for some reason, with her body in an ongoing rebellion.

That disruption did have benefits, with Anne noticing a few changes she'd started to despair of ever happening. A few stray hairs in her armpits and lower down. A hint that she may actually need a bra at some point in her life. Increasingly oily skin and a few pimples around her nose seemed like a small price to pay if she was finally going to grow up a little bit.

She glanced at Evan, walking beside her in silence, no longer filling in the space with chatter about how his school day had gone. They'd gotten into the habit of walking the path around the park near their houses a few times before going home this year. Anne didn't have to ask why Evan wanted to take the extra time.

Living with only Hurricane Ed wasn't getting easier with passing time.

Her friend seemed to have talked himself out over the past few months, trying to adjust to his new reality without his mother. Anne missed the constant updates, the peek into what she could expect in whatever grade Evan was passing through.

She missed his light and happy company. Knowing he'd probably felt the same when she sank into silence the spring before only made her feel worse.

Anne saw other changes in Evan, even though she saw him so often over the summer that it was hard to notice. His voice settled into a deeper range, and she'd noticed how much hairier his arms, legs, and armpits were when they went swimming. He was growing even taller now, getting stronger in his back and shoulders. Once in a while Anne wondered if he was growing hair she couldn't see, like she was.

She would never admit it to another soul, but spending so much time with her friend was the main reason Anne was relieved about school. The separation she'd dreaded, with Evan going to the high school building instead of the one she was in, gave her the distance she hadn't realized she needed.

They still walked to and from school together, like always, and they ate lunch together most days. But the hours and hours of listening to him, mourning with him, had taken a toll on Anne. She was tired in a way even the constant dreams last spring couldn't manage. She hoped she hadn't exhausted Evan by telling him about the dreams in the first place.

The dreams and visions left her in peace, at least for the moment. That weary part of her felt like it was slipping somehow, like the nightmares had only retreated after the living nightmare of Evan's mother dying. Anne was sure they lingered still, waiting to see if she would recover enough to hold them back.

"I had to talk to the counselor today," Evan said, startling Anne. "They pulled me out of gym class for it."

Evan looked at her, rolling his eyes. He kicked a rock out of the way.

"Ms. Fleming? What was she like?"

"A waste of time. I hated it."

Anne had seen Ms. Fleming watching her at the end of the last school year, when she started to have the awful dreams. That was one reason she'd tried so hard to keep her school work at some kind of reasonable level. She was sure Ms. Fleming was nice enough, but her constant smile made Anne nervous.

"What happened?"

"She gave me this big lecture all about how it was okay to be sad, that no one was going to think I was weak for that. Does she really think I don't fucking know I'm sad? My Mom died!"

Anne was surprised at Evan talking that way, but she didn't want to upset him even more. She'd heard plenty of older kids using that word, but she'd never heard it from him. She sometimes forgot that he *was* two years older.

Evan sighed, a harsh, painful gust.

"She spent the rest of the hour digging and digging at me, trying to get me to tell her about the day it happened."

"What did you say?"

"I didn't want to say anything, that's private. No one knows about that day but you."

Anne felt her own cheeks turning red at that. He was right. No one else knew what had really happened, and even he didn't know all of it. She didn't know if she'd ever be brave enough to tell him, especially about his Dad and the gun.

"I told her Mom had an aneurysm," Evan said, "and that was it. She kept asking who found her, who found her, and of course she already knew. Why else would she ask that to begin with?"

They walked on for a few minutes, and Anne had no idea what to say or do. Evan had talked about that day for hours on end, to her. He'd had plenty to say.

"I think she was trying to get me to cry, to see if I would or something," he finally said, watching a bunch of kids playing soccer. "Like that would prove I was doing better, if I could cry on command for her."

"Did you?"

"Of course not!" Evan glanced at her, his eyes and mouth drawn in. "I'm sorry, I'm not mad at you. But I wasn't going to tear up because she wanted me to. I just looked her in the eye and answered her questions. She finally let me go, but she wants to see me a few times a week."

"Why?"

"I'm guessing my father wants her to," Evan said, pushing his hair off his face. "He has to be the one who told her about me finding Mom. And that keeps him from having to deal with me now that Gwen's back at college. I guess it keeps me from having to deal with him, too."

"I'm sorry, Evan. I wish I could help."

"You do help. I would have gone crazy stuck in that house with the two of them all summer. And I do need someone to talk to, just not them or Ms. Fleming. You don't make me feel like I have to pass some kind of sadness test so I'll be normal. I just feel how I feel with you."

He smiled at her for a second, then he looked back at the path. Anne knew Evan was able to cry, and that she could too. She'd been afraid he'd never stop a few times over the summer.

"Dad could stand to find someone to talk to," Evan said. "He needs it way more than I do. I wonder if Dad's making Gwen see someone."

"Think she'll cry on command?" Anne said, trying to imagine either Gwen or Ed showing that much emotion that wasn't anger.

"She'd probably scare anyone to death who tried. I'd like to see that, though."

Chapter 11

Evan saw the trouble before Anne did. Gwen's tiny blue Chevette was in the driveway, earlier than she normally would be on a Friday. He hadn't expected her at home at all this weekend, so it couldn't possibly be good news.

Anne caught on before he had a chance to say a word.

"Looks like you can ask Gwen about the counselor."

"Yeah. No need to wonder. No need to wonder how my weekend's going to go, either."

Anne smiled up at him, but her eyes were more tired than anything. Guilt he'd been feeling more and more curdled in his stomach, guilt at taking up too much of his friend's time and energy.

"Will you be okay, Evan?"

"I'll be fine, don't worry. Crazy as they both are, they're my family, I guess. We have to get this worked out sometime. Maybe I'll see you tomorrow?"

She stopped, her body facing her own house, face turned toward him. Evan tried to keep his eyes on hers, but he kept watching her chew her lip. Just a little tic of hers, nothing she even noticed doing. But he never failed to notice when she did.

"Call me later if you need to," she said with the first real smile he'd seen all day.

Evan watched her run across the street, stop to wave from her porch, then disappear into her house. Into her typical, normal family. Mother *and* father, no dramatic older sibling, no shouting he could hear from down the street.

He hadn't forgotten Anne's dreams or her strange visions, and he certainly hadn't forgotten her somehow knowing what had happened to his mother. But Evan envied Anne's family more with every passing second.

Standing out here on the sidewalk wouldn't be the best way to meet his father coming home, especially not with his sister already inside. Gwen knowing what was going on before everyone else did might make things calmer for her, but Hurricane Ed never seemed to like surprises.

Evan didn't like *any* of this, but he walked the few steps home anyway.

Gwen met him at the door before he could even drop his backpack or take his shoes off. She'd changed her look again, with some kind of pale makeup and dark eyeliner to match her dyed black hair. Her ripped jeans and faded black t-shirt seemed fairly normal, but Evan would have bet his allowance that she wore stranger things when she was at school.

"Did he make you talk to a shrink?" she said, blocking Evan's path away from the door.

Evan ducked around his sister, noticing he was almost as tall as she was.

"Good to see you too, sis."

"Yeah yeah, happy family reunion and all. We'll talk later." Gwen followed him into the kitchen nearly on his heels. "Come on, before he gets home. Did you have to see someone?"

Evan grabbed a bottle of soda out of the refrigerator, hesitated, then got two glasses out. He only poured for himself, though.

"I had to talk to the counselor at school today," he said. "I don't know if she's a real shrink or not, but she sure thinks she is."

Gwen filled her glass to the rim with the rest of the soda. She crinkled the bottle slowly enough to make Evan want to scream before she dropped it in the trash.

"He made me see one, too. Or at least he made the arrangements with my advisor. This one's real, I guess. A real graduate student. Poor guy deserves better than me for his first time out."

Evan tried to stop it, but the idea of some poor almost doctor, barely more than a kid himself, trying to make Gwen cry on command got to him. He laughed with a mouthful of the bubbly dark liquid and somehow managed not to inhale or spit it all over the floor.

"I doubt Ms. Fleming was ready to deal with the mood I've been in lately, either."

They both turned at the slam of a car door outside.

"Hurricane warning," Gwen said, draining her glass and closing her eyes. "I'm sorry, Evan. I know you hate this kind of shit."

"For once, I'm glad to have the excuse to get into it with him. Don't worry. I'll let you take the lead."

The two of them walked into the living room, arranging themselves on the couch without having to say a word. Gwen sat across from their father's recliner, leaving Evan a few feet farther away. Angry as he was, Evan didn't mind the distance.

Telling Ms. Fleming he needed help, telling her anything about Evan's personal, private life, was a step too far for his father to take. If Evan was ever going to speak up about anything, now was the perfect time.

He felt that way for all of about fifteen seconds, until Hurricane Ed opened the door.

Ed Griffith stopped as soon as he spotted his children, one hand on the doorknob, face stony and emotionless. He closed the door and leaned against it, locking gazes with Evan.

"What a nice surprise," their father said, voice flat, face still not showing any emotion. "Two for the price of one. Good to see you, Gwen."

When Ed finally focused on his sister, Evan's whole body started shaking and sweat broke out all over him. Without raising his voice or even saying anything directly to him, his father managed to terrify him to the core.

Ed had never hit him, and as far as Evan knew, he'd never hit

Gwen or his mother, either. But even the promise of confrontation, a promise he was certain his sister was going to keep, turned Evan into a trembling mess.

"Great to see you too, Dad," Gwen said, as if she could read Evan's mind. "Can't say I liked the surprise you sent for me today all that much."

Mr. Griffith stowed his briefcase and jacket in the closet by the door, then took his time loosening his tie before he turned around or answered.

"Is that all it takes to get you to come home for a visit these days?" he said, glancing at Gwen and Evan in turn. "I'll keep that in mind."

He walked into the kitchen, as if everything was normal and no one was upset at all. Evan couldn't imagine his father missed the thick, painful air in the room, like someone had dumped dust full of broken glass into the vents. His own lungs resisted drawing as much as a breath.

"Relax, Ev," Gwen said in a low voice when he turned to her. "All part of the game. He's trying to piss us off enough so we'll give up. Don't let him."

She looked calm enough, no more upset than their father was. When Ed walked back in, carrying a glass of water instead of his usual evening beer, Evan forced his body to stay still.

"Looks like you both have something to say," their father said as he settled into his recliner. "Let's hear it."

"Are you seeing someone?" Gwen said. "A shrink, I mean?"

"Not right now. I talked to a psychiatrist over the summer. That's what they're called, Gwen. They're doctors. He's the one who suggested I get help for you two."

"Someone who never even met either one of us," Gwen said, her voice still as cold as their father's. Evan felt like his whole body was on fire. "This guy can just decide what's best without a word to either one of us. He must be good."

Ed's eyes flashed, but he still sounded calm.

"That would be *me* knowing what's best for you. In case you forgot, that's my job. Making sure you kids are okay. And that's what I'm going to do whether you like it or not."

"I haven't even lived here for two years! That's the part you're missing, Dad. I'm twenty years old, not a kid you have to walk across the street. Evan's not a baby anymore, either."

Evan drew back from his sister's shout. Far from being ready to face any of this, all Evan wanted right now was to run and hide.

"That so, Gwen? All grown up now, no need for me to bother myself with you as long as the university cashes my checks? How about you, son? Ready to set off for the big city yourself if I'm going to interfere in your life? The way, oh, I don't know, a father might do?"

Evan tried three times before any words came out. Gwen let him down by keeping her own mouth shut while he struggled.

"I don't need to talk to Ms. Fleming," Evan said. "I don't think she can do any good. All she wanted to do was try to make me cry."

Ed frowned and raised his eyebrows at the same time.

"Well, if she's no good, I'll find you someone who is. You can talk to my guy. But you're going to talk to someone. Both of you."

"Or what?" Gwen said, leaning forward. "Sounds to me like you're threatening to stop paying my tuition if I don't waste hours spilling my guts to some grad student. Gonna decide my major now, too?"

Evan's ears, mind, and body braced for the outburst of horrible noise he knew was coming. His father sipped his water, then lowered his chin before he answered in a normal voice.

"That's a choice you have, Gwen, to give up on the education your mother and I worked so hard for. Just quit and get a job as a waitress or a cashier. Throw all your potential away. I've never said a word about what you want to study, and as long as you work hard at it, I never will. But you're going to let someone help you through this."

"Why do you think neither of us ever talks to anyone?" Gwen said. "Do you really believe we don't have any friends? How do you think we got through all the bullshit around here *before* Mom died?"

"That's enough!" Ed slammed his fist on his own leg, but Evan flinched away. "Whatever happened before doesn't matter, not any more. All the ways your mother or I messed up are in the past. You want to drag that up someday in the future, be my guest. We're all going to have to adjust to right now, whether we like it or not."

"Or else, huh?" Gwen's voice broke, surprising Evan more than his father's shout had. "No matter what we might want."

"In this case, that's exactly right," Ed said. His tight voice and face reflected his anger. "Like I told Evan, if you don't like the person you're talking to, we'll find you someone else."

Evan's voice and mouth acted without consulting his brain.

"For how long?"

"I guess that depends on you, Evan. I think until the end of the year is a good start. Then we'll see. Just promise me you'll tell me if you need to talk to someone besides your counselor."

"I do talk to someone," Evan said, his voice not much above a whisper. The energy that pushed him to speak without warning had deserted him. "Every day."

Their father shook his head and sighed. "Yeah, that's part of the problem. She's kind of a weird kid, Evan."

"Well so am I!" Evan shouted, fists clenched, halfway standing. "You had your psychiatrist! I only got through the summer because of her!"

Heat boiled up from Evan's stomach, out through his whole body. This time he knew the effect his words would have, and he didn't regret a damn thing. He would have said more if Gwen's fingers weren't gripping his shoulder.

"You finished, son?" Their father's voice was calm again, but bright red spots against his tight, pale cheeks said otherwise. "Got more to say to me?"

"Listen, maybe we do need help," Gwen said in a sharp tone that didn't match her words. She didn't let go of Evan. "Maybe all three of us should go until the end of the year."

Gwen squeezed harder, pushing Evan back against the couch. Ed could have been a statue staring into his son's eyes.

Evan waited for the air to crack and shatter inside his lungs and against his skin.

"Will you talk to someone too, Dad?" Gwen said. "You're right, we all have to adjust. All of us."

Ed stared at Evan for several more seconds before he spoke.

"Sure, Gwen. If that's what it takes." He stood, holding his glass of water. Evan had never seen his father hit anyone, but he'd seem him throw plenty. "You kids need to think this through, think about what this has been like for me instead of just yourselves."

Ed Griffith turned away, stopping before he left the room. He spoke without looking back.

"I'll get the grill going for dinner. Think you can handle the rest?"

Gwen let go of Evan, but she held him just as firmly with her gaze.

"Sure, Dad," Evan said. "We can handle it."

Their father nodded and walked toward the kitchen.

Evan fell back against the cushions, his heart pounding in his ears and even his vision. The only thing he could feel in his whole body was the sharp depressions of his sister's fingers. The rest of him may as well have been floating a thousand miles away.

"What the hell, sis? Trying to break my shoulder?"

"Trying to keep the two of you from breaking each other's heads." Her eyes flashed exactly the way their father's did. "What were you trying to pull? You know what he's like."

"I wasn't trying to pull anything. He just… That was too much. You said I'm not a kid anymore. I have to stand up to him sometime, Gwen."

She shook her head, then stood and pulled Evan to his feet. He doubted he could have managed on his own.

"Maybe someday, sure. I don't like the way he looked at you, Ev. I've seen him angry more than I should have, but nothing like that. Do me a favor?"

Evan followed her into the kitchen. Ed stood in the back yard beside their waist high brick grill, staring into flames still far too high for cooking anything.

"Tell me what it is first," Evan said.

"Don't get into it with Ed, not unless you have to. Not without me here. Okay?"

"What am I supposed to do when he gets like that?" Evan turned the oven on. "Let him walk all over me? Or maybe ask if he can wait 'til you get here?"

"You know the answer." Something in his sister's smile irritated and embarrassed Evan at the same time. "Go the same place I always took you when things got bad around here. Sounds to me like Anne wouldn't mind any more than you would."

"Run off across the street for the next five years, huh, Gwen? Don't you think he'll notice if I just disappear?"

Gwen walked around the small table in the kitchen, lining up plates and silverware.

"If he knows where you are, he'll be fine. Give him a chance to cool down, and you do the same. That five years will pass faster than you think, kid."

Chapter 12

Anne caught herself staring at the huge maple tree outside her bedroom window, trying to count how many leaves were orange instead of yellow. Weeks of the school year passing and frost in the mornings surely sent the number into the thousands.

Her mind wandered to how she could create a formula to figure it out, if only she got an accurate count of one branch then counted all the other branches. Algebra was taking over her brain, not that her grades reflected that.

And daydreaming all evening about ways she could do better, how she could impress her teacher with her revolutionary new maple tree theory, would never get her homework finished.

She turned her desk chair away from the window, scooting the legs from one set of impressions in the shaggy blue carpet to another. Her mother and father talked about wanting to replace the carpet in the whole house sometimes, maybe with thinner carpet or even smooth linoleum.

Anne hated that idea, but she'd never figured out how to explain why to her parents without sounding silly. The thought of losing all the impressions of her, from her chair to her bed to the flat tracks in her room and in the hall where she always walked, felt like she could disappear from everywhere.

The room did change around her, usually in ways she wanted. The shelves were now a crackled red and black instead of yellow, and filled with more books, sketchbooks, and notebooks than toys. Posters of her favorite singers and movie stars had replaced the faded and tattered drawings from her grade school years.

Anne's mother still patrolled her closet and drawers, making sure clothing that either didn't fit or wasn't worn often enough went to girls who really needed it. Anne didn't care enough about her clothes to argue about that anymore, not that arguing had helped much when she was younger.

She forced her gaze back to the history book on her desk, searching for answers to an endless list of questions she had to turn in the next day. Just like the past few weeks, Anne's eyes started to drift closed within minutes.

Ever since the horrible dreams came back, she'd struggled to stay awake once she escaped from the discomfort of acting normal at school. Sometimes she stood with her books propped on a shelf to get as much done as she could. Sometimes even that didn't work.

She spent more time trapped in the awful empty library, forced to watch movies about the end of the world, than she could ever manage to spend on her homework. If only the dream would let her work on classwork in there, she'd have straight As like Evan always seemed to.

Anne had tried that trick, focusing on her studies, several times before she accepted that the dream was going to have its way with her no matter what. The routine and predictability of the nightmare helped a little with getting through it night after night.

One thing she was thankful for was she hardly ever saw the death masks over people's faces when she was awake anymore. Only when she was more tired than usual or upset about something else. She was scared the masks would come back like the dreams had, but not so far.

Anne jumped at a knock at her door, realizing her eyes had closed all the way that time, long enough that they were dry and scratchy.

"Come in."

Her dad opened the door, and she could tell from his face this wasn't going to be good. He was smiling a little, but his eyes were wrinkled in the wrong way.

"I know you're busy, got a minute to talk?" he said, standing in the doorway.

"Yeah, for a little while. I have a lot to do."

He sat in the chair beside the window, the chair Anne used for reading when she could stay awake for it. He kept glancing at her, then looking away. At the floor, at the ceiling, anywhere to avoid her eyes. She didn't think she'd ever seen him so jumpy.

"We were talking, your Mom and I…" He shook his head and looked right at her. "Anne, I'm worried about you. Your school work, and other things, too. You were having trouble before what happened to Evan's mom, but now it seems to be getting worse."

Anne's chest churned out what felt like enough jittery heat to keep her awake for days on end.

"I'm okay, Dad. I talk to Evan a lot, and that helps."

"I know that part, hon. His dad says that's really important to Evan. I'm glad he seems to be holding his own after such a rotten thing. I'm more worried about you."

Anne scowled, trying to imagine Hurricane Ed saying anything that nice about her. Whether Evan's father liked her or not, talking about what Evan had been through usually worked to keep her own father from worrying too much about her.

"Evan's dad doesn't like me."

"Well, I don't know about that." Anne's father rubbed his eyes for a second before he looked back at her. "What I'm saying, what I mean to ask is do *you* need someone to talk to? Someone older than Evan?"

Everything inside of Anne stopped, frozen solid and scared to death. This was exactly the kind of attention she did not want on the shaky state of her own mind.

"Someone at school, like the counselor?"

"No, Ed told me how Evan feels about that. He sees a doctor now, too. You know that. A doctor who knows how to really help with things like this. You can talk to me and your Mom about anything, like always, but someone with training might be better.”

Evan did hate going to the counselor at school, but he liked Dr. Lewis a lot more. Anne thought talking to two different people only made things worse for him, not better. She wasn’t sure a doctor would be any different for her.

“I don’t know what I would talk to a doctor about.”

“Anything. How you’re feeling, what happened to Mrs. Griffith, things at school, whatever you’re worried about. You can talk to her about the dreams you’ve been having too, if you want.”

Anne stared at her father as painful chills ran up and down her body.

He knew? He knew about the dreams?

“What dreams do you mean, Dad?” she whispered.

He reached forward and patted her knee. “I’ve heard you getting up in the middle of the night for months now, and your Mom has heard you crying. You look tired all the time, Anne, and you’ve been getting more quiet. Your schoolwork isn’t nearly what it was last year. Something’s causing you trouble. Maybe talking to a doctor will help.”

“I didn’t know you knew about the dreams,” Anne said, and now she was the one looking everywhere but at her father. “Do I have to go?”

“I’m not going to make you go, no,” her Dad said as he stood up. “Talk to Evan about Dr. Lewis if you want. But I am worried about you, hon. I’d like you to. I really do think it will help. Will you try it, just a few times?”

Anne looked down at her hands in her lap. If her parents knew about the dreams, they might know about the visions and the memories too. She glanced at her special notebook sitting closed on her desk. Maybe her father had figured out which one to read after all, or her mother on one of her prowls through Anne’s clothes and shoes.

Finally telling Evan about the awful things she saw, at least some of it, had made her feel so much calmer and less upset last spring. Maybe talking to a doctor would do the same.

If she could just get more sleep it would be worth it.

"I'll try, Dad. At least a few times."

Chapter 13

THE WAITING room for the psychiatrist looked more like a family living room than a doctor's office. They were inside a house with a yard instead of a brick office building like most doctor's offices. Two toddlers were even sitting on a thick brown rug over a shiny hardwood floor playing with a set of plastic blocks. Their clinking and loud giggling made Anne's shoulders more tense with every passing second.

The furnace was on too high, and the huge brass vent on the wall gave off a hot, dusty smell every time the floor rumbled and warm air rushed out. Anne's father had quickly shed his coat, jacket, and tie before he settled down to fill out a stack of paperwork.

Anne wondered how he could write so much about her, check off so many little boxes, without asking her any questions. She was grateful he didn't want to talk, though.

Across from the row of hard, curved plastic chairs where Anne and her father sat, a wooden staircase took up all the space above the vent. She hadn't seen anyone go up or down the stairs, but she heard movement above her head. Despite Evan's reassurance about Dr. Lewis, Anne wasn't looking forward to climbing up into the unknown with someone she'd never met before.

Her father flipped all the papers with his thumb, then tapped the stack against the brown clipboard to even them up. He gave all of it to the receptionist sitting in a little office hidden behind the staircase. Anne heard them both speak, too low for her to hear, before her father sat beside her again.

"Should only be a few more minutes," he said. "Do you want me to go with you? I don't have to, but I'd be glad to."

"Not this time, Dad." Anne closed her eyes, wishing she could take back the sharp sound of her voice. "I don't mind, really, but I guess I should go by myself today."

Her father nodded, and the worried lines around his eyes and mouth relaxed a little.

"I'll be right here if you change your mind."

The ceiling creaked again, then Anne heard two sets of footsteps. They were moving toward the top of that mysterious staircase. Unless Dr. Lewis was going to talk to those little kids, it was almost her turn.

Both of them stopped playing, moving quickly to put the bricks and all the other toys away. By the time Anne saw blue jeans and white tennis shoes coming down the stairs, the children waited, coats in hand. Dark green pants and brown loafers followed the tennis shoes.

"Anne?" the receptionist said, smiling with her eyes and her voice. "Dr. Lewis is ready for you."

Anne stood so fast her head swam for a second. Her father grabbed her hand and squeezed, but he let go right away. She smiled toward him, but she was busy watching for Dr. Lewis's face.

The jeans and tennis shoes belonged to a young woman, and the children chattered as they joined her in front of the receptionist. Dr. Lewis stood on the second step, leaning down far enough to peek at Anne. He had brown hair with gray at the sides, an almost all gray beard, and little round glasses. His smile and his eyes behind the glasses were warm, and most importantly to Anne, he had no trace of a death mask.

Dr. Lewis's office at the top of the stairs looked even more like a room in a regular house. A small desk was tucked behind the door, but there was a couch, a recliner, and three other chairs scattered around a big round rug with bunches of colors. A few more toys were in a box in the corner, and even more books than Anne had filled a whole wall of shelves.

The doctor waited for Anne to sit cross-legged in one of the chairs before he sat across from her.

"I'm Dr. Lewis," he said, shaking her hand. "So, Anne, tell me what's going on with you. Why are you here?"

Anne stared, not sure what she was supposed to say. Dr. Lewis was nice, much more friendly and honest-looking than Ms. Fleming at school.

But she kept thinking about how Evan hated talking to the counselor. He'd never been able to figure out what she was looking for or how to make the regular meetings stop. If Anne didn't handle this first one right, she might be stuck talking to Dr. Lewis for years.

"Um, my Dad wanted me to talk to you."

"Of course, that's how I usually meet new people," Dr. Lewis said, smiling. "But parents have usually noticed something changing, something that bothers them. They don't understand, so they come to me. I want to hear from *you*."

Anne opened her mouth, then she couldn't figure out what to say. She had too many secrets, too many things she kept to herself. She hadn't even told all of it to Evan. Well, her dad had mentioned the dreams. If he knew about those, Dr. Lewis probably did too.

"I've been having dreams," Anne said, staring at her the tips of shoes poking out under her knees. "Really bad dreams, for a while now."

"When did they start?"

"Last year, last school year, I mean. Before the summer."

"Are you still having them?"

"Yeah, but not as often. Did my Dad tell you about that?"

"He talked to me about that, yes," the doctor said, looking down at a folder in his lap. "But I want to hear from you."

Anne looked into the doctor's eyes, wondering what all she should say.

"I dream about… I dream about the end of the world. About people dying."

"What causes the world to end in your dreams?"

Anne blinked, once again unsure of what to say. Dr. Lewis had reacted the same way Evan had, not the way Anne had expected. Neither of them had laughed or said she was crazy. They both just asked how it happened.

Maybe she could trust this doctor, too.

"The bees die and people starve," she said, feeling shaky and hot. "Then there's a war, and the water gets poisoned."

"A lot of people are afraid of those things happening. Is the dream always the same, Anne?"

"Yes," she whispered. "That one's always the same."

"Have you read a book or seen a movie like that? Sometime before the dreams started?"

"No, nothing like that. I just saw the same thing in my dreams. It was like a drawing at first, but now the people look real."

"How often do you have these dreams?"

"Just once in a while at first, then I started having them every night," Anne said, catching a tear before it could get away. "They stopped for a while when I started writing them down. That and talking to Evan so much over the summer, I think."

The doctor nodded, turning a page in his folder.

"Yes, I know Evan. He's your friend?"

Anne smiled, a warm feeling in her belly pushing a little bit of her nervousness away.

"Yes, my best friend. He lives on the same street we do."

"Your Dad mentioned Evan's Mom too, that she died over the summer. That couldn't have been easy for him, or for you."

"No. We talked about it a lot. We talk about a lot of things."

"Does Evan know about your nightmares too?"

"He was the first person I told about it, before the summer."

"Have you talked to Evan about anything else? Anything that bothers you or upsets you, Anne, that you might want to talk to me about?"

This was the first time Anne felt like she shouldn't say anymore. Maybe she'd already said too much. The doctor looked the same, that part hadn't changed at all. He didn't have a death mask. Still, Anne was starting to get an odd feeling in her head.

Something in her mind was going to split, double or maybe even more. She was about to see another memory, just like the day Evan's mom had died and a few times since then.

"Nothing in particular," Anne muttered.

"It's okay, Anne. I'm not going to get mad or anything. Listen, I don't want to hide things from you. I know something happened the day Evan's mom died, something that worried Evan's dad and your dad too. Can you tell me about that?"

Now Anne's heart was pounding so hard she could hear it. She couldn't believe Evan would have said a word about her knowing something was wrong during their art class. He would never do that.

"Did Evan tell you that?" Anne said. "Did he tell you what happened that day?"

"I can't tell you what Evan and I talk about. Whatever he says to me is confidential, Anne, just like whatever you say to me will be. I won't even talk to your parents about the specific things, not unless I'm afraid you're going to hurt yourself. Okay?"

Anne nodded, a reflex, like shaking the doctor's hand when he held it out. If Evan didn't tell Dr. Lewis, someone else had to. But who? No one else knew.

Then she remembered the teacher standing right behind them then, telling them they needed to stop causing trouble. Mr. Adkins, that was his name. He wasn't one of Anne's teachers, not now, but he was the art teacher at the high school.

He'd still been standing right there when Evan and then she had run out of the room. He might have told Evan's dad. Or one of the other kids, they'd seen everything too.

"I just, I had a bad feeling that something was wrong. I tried to stop Evan from going home."

"How did you know that, Anne?" the doctor asked, looking into Anne's eyes. "What happened?"

"I don't know," Anne whispered. "I just had a terrible feeling. When Evan left, I followed him. We found his mom there, then he called an ambulance and Mr. Griffith."

She knew she was answering the wrong question, but she had to get the doctor off the track somehow. That was too much, too close to the truth. She had never even told Evan about the three different memories of his mother's death. She'd never told anyone, not one person.

Anne stared at Dr. Lewis, cold washing over her.

She had written it down.

She'd written the whole thing in her notebook. All of it. If her parents had read that notebook, if they'd told Dr. Lewis about what was in her notebook, it might already be too late.

"Are dreams and strange feelings all you have that's different, Anne?"

Anne gripped the chair arms, fighting her screaming need to get up and run out of the room. If her father hadn't been outside waiting, if she hadn't promised him she'd at least try, she would have done just that.

"That's all, and that doesn't happen much anymore."

Dr. Lewis looked at her for a long time, not saying a word. Anne felt sweat on her face, and she smelled her own armpits. The doctor's warm brown eyes and sensible glasses felt more like huge spotlights and microscopes, with Anne pinned like the frogs her class had dissected last week. She couldn't move, and she couldn't think.

"Anne, I'm not trying to trap you, and I'm not trying to hurt you. Your parents aren't either. We just want to see if there's anything going on we can help with. That's all. But to help, we need to know what's going on."

"Did you read my notebook?" Anne said in a shaky voice, staring at the thick rug on the floor. "Do you already know?"

"I didn't read your notebook. I wouldn't do that unless you asked me to." Dr. Lewis closed the folder and looked at Anne.

"But my parents did."

When the doctor was silent again, Anne leaned forward in her chair.

"You told me you didn't want to hide anything, Dr. Lewis. Did my parents read my notebook?"

The doctor sighed.

"Your father knows enough to be worried about you. Do you want me to ask him to come in and talk to you about it?"

The odd feeling in Anne's mind got deeper, like the twitching muscles she sometimes got around her eye. She closed her eyes for a second, and she was in front of the massive screen in the library. She didn't see three different things this time. She saw only one.

On that screen, Anne was in a building, white and cold and lonely. She was sitting in a room on a bed, rocking and staring at the wall. She only saw that single image, but it was jumpy. Her movements seemed to skip and catch like a broken videocassette, and a jagged noise roared all around her.

"Don't I have any choices?" she whispered.

"I'm sorry, Anne, I couldn't hear you."

The doctor's voice was soft, but Anne jumped. She was back in the office, but the empty white room still hung in her mind. Every other time she'd seen a memory coming, more than one thing was there. More than one way it could go.

Now all she saw, all she felt, was herself in that terribly empty room.

"Are you going to put me in a hospital?"

Dr. Lewis drew back and blinked, and Anne felt a tiny bit better.

"That's not what your parents or I want. We just want to see if we can help you through a rough time. That's all."

"What do you think is wrong with me?"

"I don't think anything is wrong," Dr. Lewis said. "This isn't like you have a bad cold or ear infection. We'll just talk and see if I can help. I think there are medicines that may help you sleep, and maybe help with the rest of it, too. If you want, I can bring your father in and we'll talk more about that."

Anne nodded, fighting not to cover her ears. The roaring, broken noise in the empty white room was all she could hear.

PART III

A MIND BREAKS

Chapter 14

Much as he hated the noise and chaos in the shared cafeteria, Evan still looked forward to his time there every day. The grade school kids with their shorter school day were already out of the way by the time he and everyone else in high school got to the vast, echoing room.

Harsh overhead lights with bumpy plastic covers, an entire wall of windows, and white tiled floors magnified every noise and movement. Rich, sometimes overcooked food smells suppressed his appetite more often than stimulating it. Evan brought his own lunch when he remembered to pack it.

He'd forgotten today, so he waited in line, hoping something edible would be waiting for him. He couldn't see Anne at any of the big round tables in the middle of the room or the rows of long tables along the walls. She usually sat far in the back, though, away from the chatter and bustle.

Evan found her at a lonely table against the back wall, sitting with her back to the crowded room. He never could stand to sit that way, with his back exposed, if he could avoid it. By the time he joined her, the rectangular, greasy cheese pizza was nearly as cool as his soda. At least he wouldn't burn his mouth.

"Hey Anne. How's your day?"

She glanced up from her half-finished hamburger, shrugged, and stared at the floor.

Evan was dying to ask her how her appointment with Dr. Lewis the day before had gone. He liked seeing the psychiatrist on Tuesdays a lot better than Ms. Fleming on Thursdays. Anything was worth cutting down the times he was pulled out of class to talk to the school counselor.

He didn't want to push Anne, any more than he wanted his father or sister to push him about his own appointments. After a few minutes of eating in silence, Anne covered the remains of her meal with a napkin.

"Does Dr. Lewis make you take drugs?"

Evan grabbed his napkin, trying to contain the bite of congealed pizza he'd almost spit out.

"*Make* me take drugs? My dad's more concerned with *stopping* me from taking drugs. What happened yesterday?"

"I guess he's not making me. Not yet." Anne poked at the white napkin with her fork, pushing it into the puddle of ketchup on her plate until the red bled through. "He wants me to, though. Because of the things I see."

Evan tried his best to keep his face still and calm. He'd known that day he was making a mistake, deep down in his gut and his heart. He never should have told Dr. Lewis about Anne seeing death masks. But he'd also believed the doctor's promise that he wouldn't tell anyone else.

"My parents read my diary," Anne said. "My notebooks. I was so stupid. I never should have written all of that down."

Evan breathed out as quietly as he could manage, trying to hold on while his body floated and sank at the same time. What he'd done still wasn't right. But the consequences he'd face for that would all be his own.

"They want you to take drugs for that? What kinds of drugs?"

"Dad called them anti-psychotic, but they both kept saying I wasn't psychotic. Dad doesn't want me to take them. I think my mother does."

The word drifted and crashed around Evan's mind, repeated over and over again in his father's voice with that one extra word. *She's a psychotic kid, Evan…*

"If they think you're going to hurt people like John Wayne Gacy or some other murderer, they're the ones who are crazy."

Anne smiled, only a brief shadow, but enough to make Evan feel a little better.

"That's what I thought, too. They had to tell me what it meant so they could tell me I don't have it." Her eyes meeting his were too bright, and her chin trembled. "But it means people who have breaks with reality. People who don't know what's real and what's not. How can they say that's *not* what I have?"

"*I* say that's not what you have!" Evan tried to keep his voice down, but several kids glanced their way. "What you saw about my mom was true. Didn't you tell me your grandmother knew she was going to have to move out? That was true, too."

Anne held her face in both hands. Evan was relieved she sat with her back to everyone else. She couldn't possibly see the people behind her, whispering to each other and giggling, then laughing out loud. Evan stared at every single one of them until they at least looked away.

"That's what I don't understand," Anne said. She reached across the table and dragged Evan's key ring around in a circle. "My dad said he didn't want me to take those drugs because of how they affected my grandmother. He said they only made her lots worse. But Dr. Lewis still thinks we should try it."

"He only mentioned antidepressants to me, the first couple of weeks. I know my father's been taking them, and Gwen might be. I probably should." Evan held his breath for a second, hoping he wasn't about to make everything worse for his friend. "Do you think the medicine might help, Anne? How do you feel?"

"It's not what I feel, Evan. It's what I see. When my parents started talking about it when we got home, I saw the library. The one from my dreams. The one with screens inside?"

She took a shaky breath.

Evan wasn't able to breathe at all.

"I saw my parents fighting over me taking the drugs," she said.

"Dad said he was afraid it would get worse. Mom said how much worse could it get? I saw you and me sitting right here, like now, but I couldn't move. You tried and tried, but nothing helped. I saw my Dad in the kitchen, with a bottle of pills with my name on it."

"I can help, Anne," Evan said, fighting the urge to take her hand. "You spaced out a few times last year, remember? I can get you out of that, every single time."

"That's not how it works this time. I haven't had any as bad as this will be. All three of those movies in my head ended in one place. I'm in some kind of hospital, worse than the place my grandmother's in. That doesn't change, no matter what.

"Then maybe I can go with you," he said, scared of the idea but more scared of losing her. "I've been having trouble too, and I'm sure Ms. Fleming would tell them I need to go. She can't figure out what else to do with me. Dr. Lewis already wants me to have drugs, too."

"You don't want to go there," she said, shaking her head. "It's for crazy people. Not for people like you."

"You're not crazy! Don't say that. Don't let them make you *believe* that."

He wanted to say that enough people were already saying it without her pitching in, but he didn't want to hurt her feelings. Of course she knew, she knew what people were saying about her.

Evan couldn't pretend it wasn't true about both of them, not with even more kids staring at them now.

"It's not exactly normal to have the same dream over and over again." Anne scooted her chair back, making a harsh scraping noise. "Or to see how everyone around me is going to die. Maybe if something like this happens, all of that will stop. Maybe I could be normal after that."

"How long?" Evan said, not bothering to hide how his voice shook. "How long do they think you'll be there?"

"They keep saying we don't want that, we don't want that. I don't think what they want matters. I can't tell from the visions. When I see myself there, I look the same way I do now. It might not be long at all."

Evan wished he was the one with his back to the room as tears spilled down his cheeks. The only time he'd been away from Anne for more than a day was on trips to visit family back in Virginia. He didn't want to imagine weeks or months on end.

Or years.

"Let me help, will you?" he said, scrubbing at his face with the greasy, tattered napkin. He was afraid his aching heart would stop inside his chest. "Even if it's all going to go bad, just let me help."

He clenched his fists to keep from grabbing her hand when she stood.

Anne stared at him for several seconds before she turned and walked away.

Chapter 15

THE DREAM CAME BACK before Anne's father even had a chance to fill the prescriptions, and the dream was so much worse. Something had changed.

Anne walked into the gigantic, echoing library, the same as before, but giant screens were everywhere now. The shelves held screens, dozens of oversized computers sat on every surface, and the walkways were choked with rolling TVs. Even the table tops and the ceiling were massive screens.

She froze, afraid to take another step. Seeing more people than she could count dying on one was bad enough. She didn't know if she would be able to stand watching on dozens of screens at once.

She closed her eyes, breathing deeply, then screamed as loud as she could. Instead of bouncing around the space and getting louder with every repetition, Anne's voice didn't make it past her own ears. She dug at her arm with her fingernails, hard enough to draw shiny black dream-blood, but she may as well have been tormenting a rag doll. She never even felt it.

Anne jumped at a sudden electronic pop and hum as all the screens powered on. As afraid as she was, not watching might be even worse.

All the screens were still dark, but they were activated. All of them, even the giant one overhead, came to life at the same time. Anne walked into the jumble of tables and chairs in the middle of the floor, the trembling in her body forcing her to sit down.

The whole room filled with images of swarming bees, and the sound was deafening. The sudden silence when the bees all died made her ears ring even worse.

Anne forced herself to keep watching, hoping desperately for some kind of change, any kind of difference in the dream. Agreeing to let the doctor try to help her had to change something.

She covered her ears against the screams of dying people, the roar of gunfire that shook the floor, and the droning airplane that made her bones vibrate. Anne cried out when the screens went blinding white.

All of the screens, every single one of them, showed her sitting on the bed in the hospital room. The roaring static noise was back too, loud enough to make her teeth hurt.

One Anne on the screen started rocking, and all the others followed, one after the other. They were all a little off, just a second or two, and the various movements made her sick. Anne focused on the screen closest to her, one of the rolling televisions.

All she could think to do was count, each time she saw herself rock forward on the screen.

One. Two. Three.

The static got louder, but she could still hear a new sound, one she hadn't heard in the doctor's office when this memory first came to her. Anne on the screen was humming, low and quiet, then higher and louder when she rocked forward.

Both noises got louder, the static and the humming, until Anne squeezed her eyes closed and covered both ears again.

"Stop!"

This time her voice came back to her, hundreds and thousands of times, louder and higher pitched every time. Just before all the glass in the library surely would shatter, including the hateful screens, every noise stopped.

After a few seconds, Anne thought the sound wasn't going to come back. She slowly moved her hands, and the room was silent.

All she could hear was the soft buzz of so many screens. She opened her eyes, not sure if she would still see the lost girl or the dying people.

Instead she only saw scattered dots on all of the continents of the earth. Cool blue words hovered in the middle of the Atlantic Ocean.

Remaining Human Population

Anne drew in a shaky breath. At least this part she'd seen before. She even nodded to herself when the dots started to disappear, first in Australia, then all across the planet.

When only the two in North America were left, one north and a little to the east of where Chicago should be, one around Virginia far to the southeast, the tense muscles in her shoulders started to relax. This was where the dream always ended.

She still had no idea what she was supposed to do, but at least it would be over for now. The same thing had happened here dozens of times over the past few months, then she had woken up. It was almost over.

The northern light went out.

Anne gasped, looking at every screen she could see to make sure she hadn't imagined it. By the time she looked back at the screen right in front of her, the southern light had gone dark too. North America glowed just as red as all of the other land on Earth.

She didn't want to know. She couldn't ask the question. But she knew she would never wake up until she did.

"How many are left?" she whispered.

Remaining Human Population: Zero

A larger word filled the entire screen, all the screens, blocking out all the land, all the people, everything that had ever happened in the whole world.

Extinction

Anne curled forward and wrapped her chilled arms around her stomach, trying to keep cold facts from finding a place to stay in her mind.

Everyone. Every person on the planet. All of them dead. Her Dad and her Mom and Dr. Lewis had all tried to tell her it was just a dream. Only a dream.

If that was true, why was her heart falling to pieces in her body? Why did she feel the failure and devastation in every part of her? Not just a general failure that she couldn't understand, but *her* failure.

Only she could have stopped it.

Only she had failed.

The sobs were strong and deep, starting in her belly and ripping their way out through her throat and mouth.

Anne didn't quite realize she was rocking.

Chapter 16

For the next couple of weeks, Evan tried to pretend everything was going to be okay. He went to classes, did his homework, did his best to stay quiet at home and out of his father's way. He walked to and from school with Anne, and neither of them spoke of her dreams or the medication he was sure she'd started taking.

Even when he saw the dark circles under her eyes, same as when the dreams were so bad before, Evan pretended.

He revived his habit of talking about nothing to fill in the spaces when Anne withdrew into silence. That was returning to a kind of normal, right? The way things had been before.

Back when his mother was still alive.

His grip on the delusion, fragile to begin with, nearly slipped a couple of times when Anne seemed to disappear right in front of him. She stared straight ahead, her face and her eyes blank and lifeless.

Evan managed to get her attention without anyone else noticing, touching her arm, talking directly into her ear. The relief each time was strong enough to let him pick up his imaginary armor and keep pretending.

Somewhere inside, an echo of Anne's glimpses of the future, Evan never really believed his own pathetic pretense.

This was nothing more than a waiting game. A game he knew he and his friend were going to lose no matter how badly he fought to deny it.

The game ended in the worst possible place and time, leaving both of them with nowhere to hide.

Evan barely heard his own voice at times like this. His running commentary about his morning classes blended into the general drone of conversation in the noisy cafeteria. He paused long enough to pop his last potato chip into his mouth and glanced at Anne.

He didn't need to ask to know she hadn't heard a word for the last several minutes. His friend had disappeared right in front of him.

"Anne? Come on, don't do this. Don't leave me here."

Evan touched Anne's shoulder, squeezing and then shaking her gently. She seemed to be looking down at her half-eaten lunch, but he knew she was really staring into space he couldn't see. She wasn't seeing or hearing him or anything else.

"Listen to me. You're at school. Wherever you think you are isn't real. I know you can hear me."

Just as they had during that art class the day his mother died, kids were turning to look at them. Evan saw them out of the corners of his vision. He heard the whispers, rising around the room like ocean waves, drowning out all the other conversations.

"You've got to help me, Anne," he whispered, squeezing her arm a little harder. "Everyone can see. They're going to take you away from me."

Someone walked toward them, and he didn't even have to look. He recognized the clacking noise of Ms. Fleming's shoes. Someone had certainly warned her about the new medication Anne was on, and the woman still watched Evan like a hawk.

The two of them would never be able to hide.

"She's going to catch us," he said under his breath, reaching up to touch her cheek. "Stay with me, please!"

"Mr. Griffith?" Ms. Fleming said from across the table. "Evan? Anne? What's going on here?"

"Nothing, we're just fine," Evan said, forcing himself to look at her. "Just give us a minute."

The counselor clacked around the table and touched Anne's cheek herself. She leaned down to look into Anne's face, then jerked back up.

"How long has she been like this?"

"She's fine," Evan muttered, closing his eyes. "She's going to be just fine."

"How long?" Ms. Fleming said, the sharp tone in her voice forcing Evan to answer.

"A couple of minutes. She's always come out of it before."

"This happened *before*?" she said, getting a tiny notebook out of her bag. "No one told me that. How long is she out of it like this?"

"Usually only for a few seconds," Evan said, touching Anne's shoulder again. "Never like this. Can you help me?"

Ms. Fleming waved toward someone in the hall. Evan didn't see who walked in, but the flat tap of the shoes sounded adult. He heard the word *catatonic*. The sound of those four syllables chilled every part of him.

The counselor finished her whispered conversation, tore a sheet from her notebook, and pushed the other person away. Evan finally focused on her.

For the first time, he saw what looked like real compassion in Ms. Fleming's face. This wasn't on any of the scripts she seemed to follow in her meetings with him. She also looked only a few years older than he was.

"I'm hoping someone will be able to help her, Evan. Can you stay with her for a minute? If she comes out of this, she might be disoriented."

Evan nodded. Anne usually was confused at first, then she got embarrassed. She still hadn't moved, even with all the motion and noise around her.

She'd told him this would happen. She'd tried to warn him.

Evan wasn't ready.

He didn't want to be ready for this.

"She sees Dr. Lewis," he said, still staring at Anne's unmoving face. She hadn't even blinked since Ms. Fleming got there. "Same as me. I should call her Dad."

"Would you do that, please?" Ms. Fleming said, glancing around the room before she raised her voice. "Everyone finish up and get ready to go. Your next classes start in a few minutes. Everything is under control here."

She was lying.

Evan knew it, everyone around them knew it. He couldn't imagine she was fooling anyone, not even herself. But he couldn't think of anything to do to stop it or change it.

After weeks of trying to make it all okay, trying to fix whatever was going wrong with Anne, Evan finally admitted to himself that he needed help.

She needed help he couldn't give.

He still couldn't imagine what he was going to do, how he was going to face the walk home without her by his side. How he was going to walk to school alone tomorrow morning, and for who knew how many mornings after that.

But some part of Evan was exhausted from trying to do all of it himself. That part had always suspected he was too young for this, too weak and inexperienced. Even Ms. Fleming looked scared to death.

No matter how hard he'd tried or how impossible the task, Evan knew he would always feel like he'd failed his friend.

Chapter 17

ANNE FELT her life grind to a halt.

The world continued without her.

The tingling in her body that warned her of a memory rose to a scream that wanted to drag her into nothing. Everything was a blinding glare of white. She heard Evan's voice, still chattering away, not aware she was frozen into her memory.

"Anne?"

Evan's voice could have been coming down a long, twisting tunnel instead of right beside her. That one word drew out, echoing, doubling back on itself until it sounded like dozens of boys were speaking at once.

Still she couldn't move.

Anne sat on a hospital bed in a cold, white room. She couldn't hear or smell anything around her. This was a trap, a horrible trap she might never get out of. The memory kept her body frozen, but her mind was thrashing, trying to break free.

"…wherever you think you are isn't real…"

She couldn't tell if he'd spoken those words five seconds ago or five hours ago. Every syllable, every sound drew out, stuttering from his lips to her ears.

Anne had given up a long time ago on trying to figure out if things were real or not.

All she could focus on any more was whether or not they were true.

"The drugs…" Anne-within said, the words echoing around the hospital room like Evan's voice had.

That part was true, deeply horrifyingly true. Something about those pills her father was so afraid of kept Anne from breaking out of the memory.

Evan touched her, squeezing her shoulder, but it felt like she was wearing a dozen thick winter coats instead of a regular shirt. His hand gave her an odd sense of pressure, but no warmth at all.

The tone of his voice changed. He was talking to someone else. Ms. Fleming.

Anne screamed inside her own head, trying to force some part of her body to respond.

"…catatonic…"

That was Ms. Fleming, and Anne knew exactly what that word meant. Her breaks from reality were so deep now that she couldn't hide them.

Evan couldn't help her, and he knew it. Everyone knew.

She didn't have to see Evan's face or even hear his voice. She could feel the change from wherever she was.

"No!" she screamed, her ears ringing. "I'm still in here!"

"Can you help her…"

Her friend, her dear friend who had never turned away from her. He was being pushed away, and he was going. She felt him disconnecting, pulling things she needed back into himself.

If she was going into that lonely hospital, and she couldn't see anything that could stop that now, she would be going without Evan's support. She herself had told him he couldn't go with her, and of course he couldn't.

Saying that to him and feeling the reality as he pulled back from her weren't even in the same kind of human experience.

Anne's heart pulled out one tiny sinew at a time.

"Evan! No! Please don't go! Don't give up on me!"

Anne's throat grew raw with screaming. Anne's throat was perfectly calm as her body stared at the table. Everyone around her got up and shuffled out of the cafeteria, trying to see as much as they could on the way.

Evan sat still, touching her shoulder. Anne willed every part of her, every ounce of her body to try to move, to twitch under his hand. To cry, to scream, anything to let him know she was there.

"Evan. You should go on to your next class," Ms. Fleming said, her voice rising and falling like a terrifying fun house clown. "You don't want to see this."

"Yes I do!"

His voice was clear and loud, coming from her ears instead of down that narrow, dark tunnel. The last word continued on, getting lower the longer it lingered in her mind.

"Where are they taking her?"

Anne knew, she'd seen it, she was there now. She'd tried to tell Evan, but he hadn't believed her.

He never believed the bad things she told him until they came true.

"They have to get her out of this first. Then they'll probably take her to a hospital in the city."

She heard Evan's breath catch, the same way she had so many times over the summer. He was trying so hard not to cry.

He didn't always make it, no matter how hard he tried.

"I'm going with her."

"No, that's out of the question. Her father is going to meet her at the hospital, and you need to stay here. In fact, you need to be getting to your next class."

"She can't go alone! She won't understand what's going on if she wakes up alone. I know what to do when she comes out of this."

Anne started rocking in her hospital room, leaning forward, over and over. The springs on the hard bed squeaked, grating on her nerves. She hummed, trying her best to drown out the noise.

She didn't have any choice about rocking. Her body did it without asking.

Her body stayed frozen, staring at her half-eaten lunch.

"Listen to me, Evan. The doctors know what to do for her. They've been doing this for years. They understand what's wrong and how to help."

"No, they don't know," Anne moaned, rocking harder. "They don't understand. All they can do is make it worse!"

The screen was back in Anne's head, three scenes active and moving and changing.

Evan sat beside her motionless body, head in his hands, shoulders shaking. Ms. Fleming stood behind him with her hand on his back. The paramedics, the same two who had helped Evan's Mom, walked into the cafeteria.

Anne sat on the bed, rocking and humming, light glaring off of the white walls all around her. And the world slowly ground to a halt as billions of people died of starvation, poisoning, or war. Anne kept rocking, but she was crying now.

The dots scattered all over the continents started to go out.

Evan tried to hold on to Anne's shoulders, but Ms. Fleming and one of the paramedics pulled him away. He stood watching them for a second, then turned and slowly walked away.

The last light, the last surviving human population, went dark.

"Evan! Please don't leave me! Everyone is going to die!"

Anne's voice echoed off of the brutal white walls, forcing her to rock faster. Her voice got rougher, her throat more painful.

Anne wondered about losing her voice inside of her own mind. She knew a sore throat in the real world would eventually go away.

Would she ever get her voice inside back again?

The paramedics carefully lifted Anne, making sure to hold her head steady. They put her on the gurney and covered her with a blue sheet. One of them reached under the gurney and grabbed huge straps with metal clasps. She wrapped them around Anne's body, catching the ends and pulling them tight.

Anne wasn't sure why the woman bothered with that. She couldn't feel her body, much less move it. She didn't care to move it anymore.

Evan had walked away from her. Everyone was dead. Moving her body was the least important thing she could imagine.

Rocking was all that kept Anne aware and in the world. If she stopped, even for a second, she could slip back into that awful nightmare. Watching so many people die, over and over again, knowing there was nothing she or anyone else could do, pushed Anne down into a dark pit she could not find the bottom of.

She considered letting go to see just how deep it went. Maybe once she finally found the bottom, she wouldn't have to see anything anymore.

Ms. Fleming walked with the paramedics to the cafeteria door, and Anne was surprised to see she was crying. She never would have imagined that, not over her. All the counselor ever did was smile at Anne, not cry.

"If she wakes up… When she wakes up, tell her Evan is thinking about her," Ms. Fleming said, then she turned and walked away.

The paramedics rolled Anne out into the bright sunlight. She wished one of them would remember to close her eyes. That light hurt, and her pupils didn't seem to be getting smaller. Going blind in her body wouldn't give her mind any relief. Losing her eyesight wouldn't break the screen inside her head.

She only saw two scenes now. The third had gone black when Evan walked away from her.

Anne rocked in the hospital bed, her humming getting louder with every motion forward.

The map of the world showed nothing but red, all of the land on the planet dead and empty.

The gurney bumped the back of the ambulance, shifting Anne's body against the thick straps. The paramedics didn't notice that any more than they'd noticed her eyes. With a shove, they rolled her up into the small space.

Ms. Fleming had told Evan they'd be taking her downtown, to a hospital downtown. Anne didn't know where they would want to put someone like her. Her grandmother lived out near where Anne and her family did, not in the city.

Was she too young to stay with her grandmother? If she couldn't be with Evan, her grandmother might be all right. At least she'd have someone to talk to, someone who never looked at Anne like she was crazy.

"Have her parents been notified?" the man driving said.

"The counselor said he would meet us there." The woman sitting beside Anne finally pushed her eyes closed. "Poor kid. What do you think happened to her?"

"Probably drugs. Seems to get all of 'em now, no matter where they live."

Anne felt like laughing instead of sobbing or screaming, though she still couldn't move her body.

Yes. Finally someone could see what was going on, even if he was saying bad things about her, the wrong things.

The drugs. Her father had been right to be afraid of the drugs, but now the damage was done. It hardly mattered if Anne never moved her body again.

Everyone was going to die.

Evan had walked away from her, and they were all going to die.

Getting better felt like too much work.

Anne let go and slipped into the void inside.

Chapter 18

Evan blinked when the afternoon sunlight hit his eyes. He realized he'd stepped outside of the high school, onto the stairs heading to the front lawn. Same as he did every day. But when he got to the sidewalk today, he turned left to walk home alone instead of right to meet Anne in front of the middle school next door.

He shook his head, trying to remember the last few hours. He couldn't say it passed in a blur. A blur would be something, anything he could recall.

Evan's afternoon had passed in a blank.

One foot in front of the other was all he could concentrate on now. He had to trust his feet and the rest of his body to get him home.

"Evan."

Evan wasn't totally sure he'd actually heard that voice out in the world, the one he heard most inside his own head. Well, second most, behind Anne's.

"Back here, son."

He finally noticed he'd walked right past his father's sensible blue sedan. His dad was standing by the driver's side, elbows on the roof. Evan hadn't even noticed. He'd walked right past the entire afternoon without noticing after they'd taken Anne away from him.

"What are you doing here?" he said without thinking of how it sounded. "I mean, I'm glad to see you."

He headed back toward the car as his father got back inside. This was long before he should be home from work. Evan couldn't remember his father ever picking him up from school. His mom used to, but she'd worked in town, not so far away in the city.

Hurricane Ed dropped Evan and sometimes Anne off in the mornings, before they were old enough to walk or in bad weather. Never in the afternoon though.

"I heard what happened today," his father said when Evan shut the door. "I wanted to make sure you're okay."

"Oh." Evan looked down at his hands. "I've been better."

"Do you understand what happened? I know you're not a baby anymore. You're a damn smart kid. Problems like this aren't easy for anyone. Might be a good thing, though."

"No, I don't understand," Evan said. "I don't think it's good, not at all."

His father sighed as he started the car. He seemed to do that when he didn't want to say what he was thinking, as if that could fool anyone.

Evan had caught on a long time ago.

"She was sick, son. Same thing as last year, but worse. She wasn't getting better here, she was getting sicker. Maybe where she is she can finally get some help."

Evan squeezed his eyes closed, willing himself not to cry. He was in high school now, way too old to cry, even when his heart was tearing into a million pieces. He wanted to shout, to scream the words circling through his mind, without worrying about who could hear him or what they would think.

She doesn't need a hospital. She needs me! She kept me from going crazy after Mom died. I can't let her down. I'm the only thing that keeps her calm anymore, and I'm not with her!

"She's not sick, Dad. She's confused. She's not crazy."

"No, no one is saying crazy, Evan." His father's fast words and red cheeks told another story. "But she was unhappy. I know you could see that. I know you want her to be happy."

Evan looked out the window, and the tears got away from him. Of course he wanted Anne to be happy. That was one of the things he thought about most, how he could possibly make her happy.

He hadn't been able to for a while now, and that was keeping *him* from being happy anymore.

"Can I at least go see her?" Evan whispered.

"Maybe in a while. Not right away, no. She needs to think about getting better right now. You need to focus on your schoolwork."

"How long will she be there?"

"No one can say with these kinds of things. I hope she'll be there as long as she needs to be. She's young, so there's plenty of time."

Evan didn't have to ask who his father was thinking about. Anne's grandmother. He barely remembered her living with the Fincastles, and he'd visited her with Anne a couple of times.

He loved spending time with Anne's Gemaw. He knew she had to stay in the group home where she was, though. She'd been there a long, long time.

"Who told you about what happened?"

"Mrs. Fincastle called. She's worried to death about Anne, but she wanted to make sure you weren't too upset."

That was something else Evan didn't have to ask about. He'd overheard the conversations his father and Anne's mother had sometimes. Both of them were scared Anne would end up like her grandmother, even though Anne's father wasn't at all like that.

Evan hadn't been scared of that until today.

"Did her father go see her?"

"They're both probably there by now."

"Did Anne's mom say how she's doing?"

Ed parked in their driveway and turned to look at Evan. His eyes and mouth seemed pinched in his face. He took a deep breath.

"She didn't know when she called me. They probably won't know anything for a while. Now, I have to ask you a hard question, one I know you're not going to like."

Evan turned toward Anne's house for a minute, not wanting to hear whatever it was. The day had already been hard enough.

Both cars were gone, and the house looked empty and abandoned. He finally turned back toward his father.

Evan was sure he wasn't going to like the question either. His churning stomach matched his shaking hands. At least he wasn't numb anymore.

"Was Anne on some kind of drugs, son? Was she drinking or doing anything like that?"

Evan was horrified to have to bite his cheeks to keep from laughing. Drinking? Drugs? Who did his father have Anne mixed up with?

And if Ed thought she was doing those things, what did he think of his own son?

"No, Dad, she wasn't on anything. As far as I know, she's never had a drop of alcohol. The only drugs she's taking are the ones Dr. Lewis gave her. She's afraid of those."

His father blinked and leaned back a little, raising his eyebrows.

"Afraid of them?"

"She's been afraid they would make everything worse. She's been afraid of going to the hospital for a while. She was right about both."

Evan barely got the words out before he was crying again, turning away but not before his dad saw.

"I know this is a lot for you to handle, especially after… after the summer. There's nothing anyone could have done. If the drugs were making it worse for her, the doctors will figure that out, too."

Evan wiped his eyes before he turned back to his father. Ed Griffith looked years older than a few months ago, the day he'd come home to find his wife dead and his son and the odd neighbor girl there waiting for him.

The lines around his eyes and mouth hadn't been there before, and dark circles under his eyes never seemed to leave now. Several grays glinted in his thick brown hair.

Evan didn't want to cause him any more trouble. He was also terribly worried about his friend.

"Will you tell me when you hear anything?"

"Of course I will. Come on, we better get ready for Hurricane Gwen. She'll be here in a couple of hours."

Evan finally did smile, and his belly twitched with concealed laughter. He wasn't sure whether the nickname suited his sister or his father more. Or who would be more annoyed by it. Hurricane Ed put one arm around Evan for a second, the closest he got to a hug these days.

"You can talk to your sister about this, too, you know. She might not always show it, but she likes you most of the time. She likes you a hell of a lot better than she likes me."

Chapter 19

ANNE WAS CONFUSED by the noise at first. That didn't sound like the echo of the library where she'd been trapped for what seemed like years. That sounded like it came through her ears, her real ears.

She'd given up on her real ears working a long time ago.

"Anne, hon, I'm here."

The scent washed over her then, not just in her nose but all over. The dry aroma of thousands of books in that library and the warm, acrid scent of all the screens had numbed her sense of smell. Now smells overwhelmed everything else.

Her own skin, sharp citrus cleaner, something made with chicken, maybe, and… and something so familiar, so welcome, that it made her eyes and jaws ache. A musky smell and a flowery one, and just underneath, a faint, almost vinegar trace.

"Dad?" she whispered, her voice strange and rough. "Gemaw?"

"Yes, sweetheart, we're both here," her father said, tears in his voice. "We're both here. Everything's going to be all right."

Anne tried to open her eyes, but everything was too harsh and bright. The library was always dim unless all of those screens were on. That light wasn't like this though. That light was cold and blue. What she saw behind her eyelids was more warm and yellow.

Warm. Yes, warm, she could feel that light against her face.

Warmth like the sun, but it was too much for her eyes. She turned her head a little, rolling against softness, like a pillow. That was better.

"We're right here, and we're not going anywhere." A woman's voice. Her grandmother's voice. "You just take your time."

Anne opened one eye a tiny bit, and though it was still so bright, she could manage. She opened the other one a little and saw white walls. She wasn't surprised by that. She'd been seeing those same walls for weeks now, since long before she'd gotten trapped in that library.

This didn't seem like one of her dreams or one of her visions. She felt her body in the bed now, felt both of her hands. She didn't have to see to know who was holding each one. Her right was almost engulfed in both of her father's big hands, and her left in the dry, papery grasp of her grandmother.

"How long?"

"Three days," her dad whispered.

Anne forced both eyes open so she could see him.

Three days sounded like a miracle to her. She would have believed three years. Or thirty.

She'd wandered every corner of that damned library, looking at every single book on the shelves. She never found a door that opened. Only more books than she could count.

Some of the books were blank, only more screens. But she'd found and read dozens of books trying to keep herself sane, waiting for the awful movies to start up again all around her. Anne couldn't remember all of the stories in the books right now, but she hoped she'd be able to someday.

Her father didn't sound nearly as relieved as she felt. He sounded like three short days had been an eternity.

"Three days isn't that long, Dad," she said, her voice still raspy but stronger.

He laughed, and tears filled his eyes. Anne was amazed at how green his eyes were, at how much her grandmother's were just like his. She felt like she hadn't seen such a vivid color for a lifetime.

Her father looked awful, almost as bad as Evan's father had the day Mrs. Griffith died. His face was puffy and his hair stood on end. She wondered if he'd slept at all in those three days.

"Well, it might not have been that long to you, sweetheart," he said, wiping his cheeks. "But it's been a while for us."

"Are you hungry?" her grandmother said, not sounding nearly as upset. "They brought you lunch a little while ago."

Anne blinked and focused on the table beside the bed. A silvery dome sat on top of a tray. That was where the smell of chicken was coming from. A glass of water and a glass of milk made her throat ache. Her stomach was already aching.

"I'm starving. I haven't eaten in three days?"

That got her father laughing, and a second later Anne and her grandmother joined in. When she started to sit up, her Dad shook his head, still smiling.

"Hang on, let me raise your bed up."

He grabbed some kind of remote control, and the flat bed moved under her. In a few seconds, the bed was more like a giant recliner, and her grandmother rolled table closer.

"They've been feeding you," her father said, touching a shiny plastic tube that went into her arm. "I'd imagine you're ready for something solid."

"What happened to me?"

Anne had the fork in her hand before her Dad could uncover the food. Once the full aroma hit her, her stomach rumbled.

Three days? When you thought about three days without solid food, it did seem like a while. She ate tiny bites, trying not to go too fast.

"They think it was a bad reaction to the medication." He sat back and rubbing the back of his neck. "They've got you off all of it now. They said it would take a few days to clear out of your system."

"That happened to me, too," Anne's grandmother said, nodding.

"It did, Mom. That's one reason we knew to be careful with Anne."

Her father tried to hide it, but Anne saw his eyes. Not worried like before. He looked scared to death.

"What now?" Anne said, pausing to take a long drink of milk. "Am I going home with you?"

"Not just yet, no," her dad said, shaking his head. "With you having such a bad reaction, they want to make sure you're better before you come back home."

Anne stopped eating for a minute, staring at him, then her grandmother. They both looked perfectly fine, with no trace of the scary masks she'd seen on other people's faces. She didn't have any sense of a memory right now either.

Nothing hovered around her, and nothing seemed to be moving toward her.

The nightmares were another question that she wouldn't be able to answer until she went to sleep, but she felt better than she had for a long time. Her mind felt tired and foggy, as if she really had been asleep for days, but she wasn't afraid at that moment.

"I'm feeling better right now," she said, watching his face.

"I know, and I'm more relieved than you can imagine. What happened to you was pretty serious, hon. Everyone just wants to make sure you're okay."

He looked right into her eyes. He didn't seem nervous at all, just sad. Anne turned to her grandmother. Her face still had that small smile and her eyes were warm and merry.

"How long do I have to stay here?"

"I don't know," he said. "I'll talk to your doctors a little bit later on and try to figure it out, but we can't be sure yet. Don't worry about it right now. Just worry about getting better."

"Where's Mom?"

"She had to get a few things taken care of at work today, but she'll be here tonight. That's why I brought your Gemaw."

Anne didn't want to say it out loud, but she was much happier with her Gemaw there than her mother.

Anne hadn't forgotten her mother shouting that Anne needed the medication because she couldn't get any worse. She'd remembered that before it ever happened, but even knowing what was coming didn't let her avoid overhearing it in the first place.

She hadn't wanted to hear that, and not just because she knew it wasn't true. She knew she would get a whole lot worse. Her mother's words hurt so much she'd never mentioned it to anyone. Not even Evan.

Evan. He had to be scared to death too. His face the day she got trapped haunted her now that she was awake. And he was the only person in the world who made her feel more calm than her grandmother did.

"Can Evan come visit me?"

"Just immediate family for now," her dad said. "You need to get a little better first."

Anne ate for a few more minutes, thinking it was one of the best meals she'd ever eaten. It was just chicken and rice and vegetables, and not all that spicy, but the warmth in her middle was fantastic. She was wondering if they'd give her more when her father spoke again.

"What do you remember, Anne? About the day this happened?"

The fogginess had cleared with the food, but Anne knew she needed to be careful here. Telling the truth about her dreams and visions, or at least having the truth read from her notebook, got her on the medication to begin with. Only Evan knew she remembered things before they happened.

She didn't need a clear head to know telling her dad she'd remembered the day she got trapped for weeks before it happened wouldn't be a good thing.

"I remember going to lunch. Then I couldn't move." Anne pushed the table with the empty plate away. "I could still hear everything, but I couldn't say or do anything."

"Do you remember coming here?" he said, his voice soft.

"I remember them putting me into the ambulance, but then I think I must have fallen asleep. Everything got jumbled up once they put me in there."

So far she hadn't lied, and she hoped she wouldn't have to. Anne got so confused sometimes between the visions and the dreams and the memories that hadn't happened yet. The last thing she needed was to have to keep a bunch of lies straight in her mind.

"Do you remember anything after you got here?"

Anne thought for a second, trying to be honest again. She remembered being here, sitting up in this bed and rocking, humming to try to drown out the sound of the springs. But she didn't know if that had really happened or not.

That might have been one of the false memories, like the ones she'd had about Evan's father. She couldn't think of a way to ask without having to answer a bunch more hard questions.

"I don't really remember anything, Dad," she said, draining the last of her water. "I might have had some dreams, but I'm not sure. Have I been asleep the whole time?"

He closed his eyes for a second, and his eyebrows wrinkled toward his nose.

"I think today is the first time you've been all the way awake," he said slowly. "You weren't really asleep, but I don't think you knew where you were. That's one thing the doctors will talk more about when you're ready."

She knew then that the memories had been the truth, even if she hadn't experienced them directly. She *had* sat in the bed, rocking and moaning, going over the different memories over and over and over again in her head. She didn't remember anyone being in the room with her, but she was sure at least her dad would have been.

"I'm sorry I upset everyone so much," Anne said, drawing her knees up against her chest. "I didn't mean to."

"Don't you dare apologize for a damn thing," her grandmother said in the loudest voice Anne had ever heard from her. "Every last one of us does the best we can, sweetheart. If we're not hurting someone else on purpose and we keep trying, we're on the right path. Don't let anyone *ever* tell you different."

Her father blinked and smiled at his mother, then he leaned forward and hugged Anne hard.

"She's right, hon. You don't have anything to apologize for. You just think about getting better."

Chapter 20

Evan's bedroom felt like a bomb shelter to him sometimes, especially on the weekends. Even more so when his sister was home. He kept the door closed more often than not, usually with the radio on.

Same as when his mother was still alive, the volume changed depending on what was going on in the rest of the house.

The curtains and bedspread decorated with her beloved St. Louis Cardinals rather than the home state Cubs or White Sox was probably a little young for Evan. But so far he wasn't willing to let that much of her fade into the past.

He'd carried one of the framed photos of the two of them upstairs not long after she died. Evan-at-ten grinned into the camera, his mom kissing his cheek, her own cheeks rosy and happy. If his father noticed the picture's new home on Evan's nightstand instead of the living room wall, he hadn't said a word about it.

More books than anything crowded the shelves, spilling onto the floor recently. In contrast to the little boy sheets, the walls held maps ranging from ancient explorer's fantasy versions with dragons hiding in the oceans to modern, colorful images from airplanes and satellites.

Evan never could decide if he loved history or science more. He wanted to learn everything about both.

Regular bomb fallout from Gwen and Ed or not, Evan was starting to wonder if he stayed in his room way too much since Anne left. That feeling of withdrawal, of retreat, bothered him more than he admitted to Dr. Lewis or Ms. Fleming.

Nothing else made sense to him right now, though. Evan decided as the weeks passed that as long as he kept his grades at top marks, whatever he did to get through was fine with him.

Not even an hour after Evan settled down in Ed-free weekend peace to read, Gwen's voice pulled him out of the story.

"Let's go."

Evan looked up, surprised to see his sister standing in his doorway.

"Go where?"

"I'll tell you on the way," she said. She plucked his book out of his hands and closed it.

"I was working on something," Evan said, not sure if he should be annoyed or excited.

"It's Saturday, you dweeb. Much as I think they should, I doubt they assigned you *Dune* for ninth grade English. Come on, we haven't got all day."

Evan got up and grabbed his jacket, deciding on excited.

"What's your big rush on a Saturday, Hurricane Gwen?"

Gwen rolled her eyes, but she walked out the door, Evan close on her heels. She looked as much like their father as he did their mother, with her light brown hair and eyes. She acted a lot more like Ed, too.

Evan had often felt like he and his mother were calm ports in the storms that constantly tore through their family until Gwen left for college. Now he had to try to keep himself safe and out of their paths. And he'd lost the only person in the house who could see just how much alike Gwen and his father were without getting offended by it.

"Well, even though you know I hate it when you call me that, I'll still take you with me."

She ran down the stairs and out the door faster than Evan could keep up. By the time he locked the front door, she was already in her cramped, beat up blue Chevette. She had it started and in gear before he could close the door.

"Seriously, what's the hurry?"

"Hurricane Ed's only out for a few hours." She rested her hand on his cracked vinyl seat as she backed out. "We have to be home before then, or at least back in town."

Evan's head bounced off of the seat when she shifted into drive while the car was still going backwards, the same way his father did. With only a quiet protest from the transmission, they headed out.

"Here, you're good at navigation," Gwen said. "I think I know where this is, but help me keep an eye out."

She handed him a wrinkled piece of notebook paper, the edge ragged from the spiral binding. Evan absently pulled the twisted scraps of paper off as he stared at the scrawled lines, squinting in an effort to read his sister's writing.

When he deciphered directions leading into Chicago, with the ninth floor as the final step, his belly twisted. He could only think of one reason they'd be taking a forbidden trip that required extra secrecy.

Gwen was downright fidgety, looking in her rear view mirror, checking her watch, looking all around them until they were on the interstate heading toward the city. She took a deep breath then, and Evan wondered if she knew how much she even sounded like Hurricane Ed.

"Okay, enough with all the mystery, Gwen. Where the hell are we going?"

She accelerated around three cars and got back into the right lane before she glanced at him.

"I talked to Anne's father this morning."

Evan's heart leapt. Anne had been gone for three weeks now, and he hadn't even spoken to her over the phone. All his dad would tell him was she was doing better, and Evan hadn't seen her parents around.

"What did he say? How is she?"

"She's doing a lot better, Ev. They've cut way down on her

medication, and she seems to be pretty stable now. He said she's been hoping you would visit her."

"What? Dad told me just last night she can't have visitors yet! I've been asking him every day!"

Evan knew how loud his voice was in the cramped car, but he didn't care.

"That's exactly why we're going to see her right now. You know I normally try to stay out of these things, but this is just too much of an asshole move by Ed. She's been having visitors for a couple of weeks now."

"Goddamn it," Evan whispered, looking out the window to hide his tears once again. "Did Dad know that?"

"Mr. Fincastle told him as soon as he knew. He's been spending a lot of time taking his mother to see her, that's why he hasn't been around."

"Why didn't Dad tell me? Why?"

Gwen shook her head and glanced at Evan again.

"He's had a bug up his ass about Anne since Mom died, you know that. I don't understand why. I always thought she was a sweet kid. Her parents couldn't have been better to you, or to me. They kept us safe when Mom couldn't. Probably kept us as sane as we are."

"Did Ed tell you Anne was there? That she was with me when I found Mom?"

Gwen hummed low in her throat.

"Let me guess. He decided you both did something wrong. He never told me you were both there. He said you called him, but he didn't mention Anne at all. I'm glad she was with you."

"Dad thinks she's crazy, just like her grandmother. And I think Anne's Mom does too, or at least she's afraid of that."

Gwen snorted.

"Yeah, Ed and Anne's Mom are a lot alike that way."

"Did Mr. Fincastle tell you what's wrong with Anne? What happened to her?"

Gwen was quiet for a while, pretending to study the signs over the highway. They had sixteen miles before they had to exit. She was just stalling. Evan's heart pounded, and sweat sprang up all over his body.

"They're not sure, Ev. They think she did have a bad reaction to the medication, and getting her off of that has helped a lot. But they're not sure what's causing the nightmares or the rest. Has she ever told you much about what's going on with her?"

Evan glanced at his sister out of the corner of his eye, wondering how much he should tell her. She'd been home more often on the weekends since their mother died. Even though that too often led to sparks between Gwen and Ed, Evan knew she was worried about him.

She'd never tried to be his mother, not once. He was grateful she seemed to be turning into his friend. Gwen wasn't likely to side with their father, either. She never really had, not as long as he could remember.

"She told me about the dreams last summer," he said, now looking at the road ahead of them. "She has nightmares about the end of the world. She has for a long time now."

Evan hoped she wouldn't ask him any more. He felt strange about telling her that much.

"And they put her on medication just a few weeks ago," Gwen said, almost to herself. "Well, I'm no psych major, but if stopping the meds helped, maybe it's not anything permanent. And you're not going to catch it even if it is. A visit will do both of you good."

"Thank you, Gwen," Evan said, tears building up again. "Thank you for taking me."

"You're welcome, Ev. I'm sure I don't have to tell you not to mention this to Hurricane Ed. He gets on my last damned nerve, but he's paying for college. If he stops, I'll have to move back home."

"And no one wants that."

Traffic grew heavier and slower as they descended into the city, gray and silver towers rising to block out the pale sun. Evan tried to keep up the conversation, but the closer they got to the address on the paper he was now smoothing against his leg over and over again, the more nervous he got.

He'd tried to convince himself years ago that he didn't really like

Anne that way, not like a girlfriend. Even after she'd trusted him with her secret, he'd tried to deny it.

On the worst day of his life, the day his mother died, Evan had given up fighting how he felt about Anne. That was his one bright memory from that awful day, that whole awful summer. He didn't know if she felt the same way, and he wasn't sure what he'd do if he did know.

The thought of seeing her after almost a month turned his whole body into a manic swarm of butterflies.

"Ready, Ev?"

Gwen's voice jerked him back to the present. They were in the depths of a run down parking garage, an endless sea of cars stretching into the gloom. They'd gotten into the city faster than his father ever did, or his mother. No surprise with his sister driving.

Evan was surprised to catch himself wishing he had those extra few minutes to calm himself down. His heart raced and his palms were sweaty, and he knew his pale face wasn't hiding one tiny bit of the flush climbing up from this throat.

"Yeah, let's go."

Evan's feet never touched the ground as he followed Gwen across cracked, filthy concrete and iridescent puddles. The stink of exhaust and rubber coated the back of his throat.

By the time the dingy fake wood elevator door opened, he was afraid to look at his sister. If she saw how he was feeling, he was afraid she'd tease him for being such a baby and take him right back home.

He stepped forward and jabbed the cracked and stained button marked nine before she could.

Gwen set a quick pace along speckled yellow tiles in an endless white hallway, then stopped in front of window set into the wall. Silver wires crisscrossed the glass, and a grouchy looking woman wearing pink hospital scrubs stared at something on her desk.

As soon as Gwen pushed a glowing button between the window and a gray steel door, the nurse looked up. Her warm smile transformed her face and everything around her.

"We're here to see Anne Fincastle?" Gwen said, sliding her

driver's license through a gap at the bottom of the glass. "Gwen and Evan Griffith."

Evan held his breath, hoping neither of them would ask him any questions. He was afraid his voice would come out in a squeak if it came out at all. The nurse checked Gwen's driver's license against a printed list, then pushed it back through.

"Anne will be happy to see you," she said, winking at Evan. "Come on back."

She touched a buzzer under her desk, and the door to their left clicked. The silence in the hall dissolved into a chorus of beeping, ringing, and low conversation. A shorter hall, this one pale green with bright, cheerful paintings all along the walls, stretched back to a room that looked like the teacher's lounge at Evan's school.

Several doors with windows at the top were closed, with only a few standing open. Evan wondered which one Anne was behind, even as he seriously doubted his legs would carry him that far.

"What do we need to know before we go back?" Gwen said.

Evan watched the nurse, trying not to miss a word she said. The last thing he wanted to do in his whole life was make anything worse for Anne.

"Just talk to her, act normally," the nurse said. She handed each of them a yellowed plastic holder with Visitor on a blue piece of paper inside. "She's doing a lot better. Not quite ready to leave us yet, but don't feel like she's going to fall to pieces. Both she and her father have mentioned you, young man."

Evan managed to smile back at her, but he couldn't hide how badly his hand shook when he took the badge.

"Anything we shouldn't talk about?" Gwen said.

"Well, we're not quite sure when she's going home, so don't bring that up. She's worried about her school work, too. We've been telling her she'll have all the help she needs with it when the time comes."

"I'll help her," Evan said, his voice far too loud.

"I figured you might," the nurse said, smiling, and now his ears burned. "She's in room seven, and her door's open. Just go on back. Visiting hours go until eight pm, so you have plenty of time."

"Thanks," Evan finally said in a fairly normal voice before they were too far away.

Now his feet felt like lead and concrete. Everything was too loud, especially his pounding footfalls. The shaking had moved out from his hands through his entire body.

Before Evan was ready, Gwen stopped in front of the fourth door on the right. The room beyond was narrow, nothing visible but another of those silver-laced windows. His sister's smile made his face hotter when he didn't think that was possible.

Gwen looked like she knew a secret Evan couldn't even guess at.

"Here," she said, taking the badge out of his hands. "You're going to be just fine. I promise I won't spy on you or bother you. And everything is between us."

Before he could say a word, Gwen knocked on the door. Someone called out, a voice Evan hadn't heard in a thousand years. His sister walked him forward, her hand a gentle pressure between his shoulders.

Evan's pounding heart stopped.

Anne was there, she was right there, sitting at a wooden desk by the window. Hair clean and shining in the sunlight, falling in loose waves past her shoulders. Her face curious and unafraid. She looked more vibrant and alive than she had for a long time.

Anne was more beautiful than anything he'd ever seen or imagined.

"Evan!"

She jumped up and ran over to him, hugging him so hard he was sure he felt his spine crack. He squeezed back just as hard, breathing in her sweet scent, trying to make it part of his own body. His heart lurched into life again, and he knew she would feel it beating against her own.

"Anne," he whispered, unable to say anything else.

Evan would have been happy to pass the rest of his life in her arms, no need for anything or anybody else on the entire planet but the two of them. He didn't remember anyone else was in the room until Anne spoke, her breath against his ear sending hard chills all over his body.

"Gwen, thank you for coming."

It took every ounce of strength and courage he had, but Evan managed to let go. He didn't want to be rude to his sister, but more than that he didn't want Anne to let go first. She smiled at him, wiping her eyes with her sleeve, then stepped forward and hugged his sister.

She didn't hold on to Gwen for nearly as long.

"You look great, kid," Gwen said. "I'm happy to see you."

Before Evan could gather enough of his wits to move, Gwen picked up a light, spindly plastic chair and carried it toward the door. She glanced back at him with that same secret smile before she stepped out into the hall, but he didn't care one bit about that now.

"Come sit down, come talk to me," Anne said, grabbing his hand. "I haven't seen you in forever!"

"Forever and a day."

PART IV

EYE OF THE STORM

Chapter 21

Ordinary routines. The daily grind. Boring repetition.

The things most people complained about turned into the anchors for Anne's sanity. The doctors in the hospital in the city told her that, over and over again while she was there.

Look for the normal. Look for habits you can depend on.

Hour after hour at first, then day after day.

Worry about longer than that later. Much later.

The hospital kept a routine for patients for a reason, they said, and too many people forgot that after they went home.

At first, Anne thought that advice was crazier than she felt during those weeks away. She kept a long list of what she would do to break the monotony as soon as she walked out the door.

Stay up all night instead of getting up early. Eat hamburgers for breakfast and pancakes for dinner. Wear her clothes backward and inside out.

That was before the anxiety and fear she never expected hit her, right after the doctors said she could go home in a week. Anne's imagination twisted her silly ideas then, turning them into a trap instead of salvation.

Years ago her mother had scolded Anne for a sour expression, warning her that her face would freeze that way. Anne didn't quite believe that any more, but she was terrified her habits would do the same thing if she messed everything up on purpose. What if she threw up if she tried to eat her meals in the right order, or broke out in a terrible rash if she put her clothes on the right way? Or what if she forgot how to put her clothes on at all?

Anne surprised herself by spending that last week making new lists in her mind and on paper.

Anne's List of Boring Routines.

The other change in those last few days in the hospital would have made her mother proud if Anne ever figured out how to tell her about it. She studied her face in the metal mirror in her room any time she was alone, making every expression she could think of. Months of experience seeing all those death masks gave her more to choose from than most people.

She was determined to find Normal Face. The expression she could manage to hold onto no matter what she saw around her. What she felt inside her. The perfect arrangement of her features that didn't shout *blank*, or *anxious*, or worst of all, *crazy*.

Anne wanted less attention, not more. The best way she could think of to make that happen was to appear relentlessly *normal*. Hour after hour, day after day.

She knew she had it when the nurses, doctors, and even other patients started saying how great she looked, how healthy and happy. Her parents agreed, and her teachers did too once she got back to school.

Anne held Normal Face so carefully in place that her muscles felt funny when she tried to relax her features.

She practiced doing that at least once a day, though, making whatever expressions she could think of when she was alone. As much as Normal Face helped her get through the days and even *feel* normal, she was still a little worried about her face freezing that way.

The only person who didn't seem totally fooled by Normal Face was Evan. Anne caught him staring at her, brow wrinkled and a tiny frown on his own face.

Instead of scaring Anne, like anyone else catching her would have, knowing her friend saw through her made her feel better. In the middle of all her new routines and habits, she was glad this one thing hadn't changed.

Another thing that hadn't changed was the effect her smile, her honest and real smile, had on Evan when she caught him staring. His answering grin, and blush, made them both feel better.

No matter what everyone else seemed to think, Anne knew Normal Face wouldn't last forever.

THE STRANGEST REFUGE Anne found in her ordinary routines over the next four years was visiting Dr. Lewis. She couldn't quite drop Normal Face, no more than she could anywhere else but with her grandmother or Evan. But her psychiatrist seemed immune to constant worry about Anne, at least during their appointments. Relief from the stress of someone else's expectations turned their appointments into a weekly oasis.

The only apparent change by the time Anne was almost sixteen was Dr. Lewis didn't tower quite so much over her. The bigger change was the request Anne had planned, one she'd never made before.

Unwilling to break the routine too quickly, the safe routine, Anne waited for Dr. Lewis to ask all the typical questions first. Her time was running out, but no need to rush things. The last question was the opening she'd been waiting for, and dreading.

"Anything new going on this week, Anne?"

"I need an increase in my prescription."

As usual, Anne tried to figure out what he was thinking. She'd never managed so far. Not being able to when she knew how so many things were about to go wrong in her life made her feel a little bit more normal.

"What's going on?"

"I'm starting to feel anxious again," Anne said, staring at the floor. "A lot like I did before."

"You mean when you had such a bad break? When you were eleven?"

Anne nodded, still looking down. She'd been pretty honest with Dr. Lewis, certainly since the hospital. But she'd kept this particular vision to herself. She'd kept it from Evan, too, but not for much longer.

Her grandmother's death was going to upset everyone and everything around her, and Anne didn't want to make it worse. It was already going to be terrible.

"Are your dreams getting worse?"

"They're the same as always, just happening more often now. Right now I see a few people surviving most of the time, at the end."

"And are you having trouble seeing people's faces again?"

"Not everyone. Some people still look normal." Anne looked up, making sure. "You do."

"This hasn't happened for a long time, Anne," the doctor said, closing his notebook. "Do you have any idea what's different?"

Anne had rehearsed this over and over again in her mind and on paper, trying to get ready for this moment. She wasn't sure that had done her any good at all. She was more afraid of stumbling over her words and sounding like an idiot than ever.

And she was scared to death she was going to sound as crazy as some people already thought she was.

"A bunch of things are going to change over the next few months is all I can figure out. I've been thinking about that a lot lately."

"Are you worried about taking your driving test? That's in a couple of months, right?"

Anne smiled, relieved she could be honest again. She wasn't worried about the driving test at all. It wasn't gong to happen in a couple of months.

As far as she had ever remembered, that was never going to happen.

"I'm not worried about that. I'm more worried about getting a job this summer. And about graduation."

"That's right, you have a few friends getting ready to leave, don't you?" Dr. Lewis said, flipping the notebook open again. "Evan's graduating, isn't he?"

"Yeah. He'll be leaving for college in the fall. I'll hardly ever see him after that."

"That's not going to be easy for either of you. I'm sure you'll see him when he comes home for breaks and such."

Anne didn't say a word, afraid of giving too much away. Evan wouldn't come back to their neighborhood at all for breaks. Not even one time.

His father was going to sell their house before Thanksgiving and move into the city. She didn't think Ed had decided to do that yet, not consciously. He was gong to though, and no amount of protest from Gwen or Evan was going to make a damn bit of difference.

"Maybe," she finally said, knowing Dr. Lewis would sit there for ages waiting. "I'm getting a little worried about making it through the next few weeks of school myself. Finals especially. If I'm already having bad dreams, I won't be getting enough sleep. That always makes everything worse for me."

Dr. Lewis looked into her eyes again, and Anne was careful not to flinch or look away. She knew very well that the medication wasn't going to solve anything. It might even make things worse in the long run. But she had to do whatever she could to make the blow easier for herself and everyone else.

If she fell apart herself before her Gemaw died, she would escape the pain and upheaval. But everyone she cared about would have an even worse time.

Especially her father. She had to stop that if she possibly could.

"You remember as well as I do how you reacted to stronger medication before," Dr. Lewis said. "We won't try the same drugs, but I'm going to ask you to keep a journal just for this. Make a note of how you're feeling every morning and night. Every day, without exception. Don't try to make anyone feel better or keep them from worrying. Be honest. Can you promise me you'll do that?"

Anne looked down at her hands for a second, then back up into the doctor's eyes. She knew she would do that. She would dutifully write it down, at least what she promised to write. Every morning and every night.

Anyone reading what she wrote wouldn't have any reason to

suspect what was coming. Even people reading it afterward, including Dr. Lewis, wouldn't be able to find the clues they were looking for. The medication would help Anne get through the next few weeks a little more easily.

No medication on the planet would help her avoid another trip to the hospital for a much longer stay this time. But right now, she could look her doctor and anyone else in the eye and tell the truth.

"Yes. I promise I'll write it all down, Dr. Lewis."

Chapter 22

Spending time with her grandmother had been one of Anne's favorite things as long as she could remember. Now the visits left her perfectly balanced between sorrow and pleasure. Joy and dread.

Her Gemaw's time on earth was growing dreadfully short, and Anne felt that change in her own body. But she wanted to spend as much time as she possibly could with the only person who understood her odd experience of life so far.

Gemaw hadn't been back to the Fincastle's house for years, not even for a short visit. The last visit was not long after Anne returned from her stay in the hospital. Anne thought her mother was relieved by the end of the visits, when the nurses said the time away left Gemaw too agitated and confused.

Anne didn't have to ask her father how sad that change made him.

The two of them visited once a week, more often when they could. Even if they only stopped by for a few minutes, Anne and her father enjoyed the time as much as Gemaw did. The longer visits on the weekends and during summer were even better.

That window of peace, of not having to pretend at all any more, always helped Anne stay calm no matter what else was going on around her, or inside of her. If either of her parents dropped her off and went to run errands, she didn't even have to bother with Normal Face at all.

The spring before she turned sixteen, when she knew her grandmother was about to die, the visits only intensified Anne's problems. Before she got to the long, low brick building full of rooms and tiny apartments, noise and static started up.

Inside her head sounded like all the screams and crashes of all of Anne's nightmares at the same time.

When she walked into her grandmother's little apartment, the noise stopped, every time. Anne could sit on the blue loveseat with her Gemaw, chatting and laughing. She could pretend to be normal for however long the visit lasted.

As soon as she stepped back out into the world, the bedlam inside her head started up again. It wasn't loud all the time, thank goodness. But that low, disruptive background never went away outside of her grandmother's nursing home.

As on so many other visits, Anne sat with her grandmother on the overstuffed loveseat while her father sat in a matching chair close by. The beige walls had almost no empty space, and the shelves, coffee table, and chest of drawers were just as crowded.

Every painting, photo, and memento Anne had watched her grandmother pack over and over again had come with her to this smaller space. From that bedroom down the hall from Anne's room so many years ago to the four walls she shared with so many others, Mary Fincastle kept as much of her life and her memories around as she possibly could.

Anne understood that up to a point. She spent hours wishing she didn't remember all the horrible things that hadn't happened yet. If some kind of witch or scientist or even a priest offered her the chance to trade some of her real life memories to stop others crowding around her, Anne knew she'd likely jump at the chance.

Her Gemaw seemed perfectly healthy to Anne's eyes and ears, not much different than she always had. Her short wavy hair was almost completely white now, with barely a trace of brown left. She wore her thick pink-rimmed glasses all the time now instead of just when she read.

But her laughter was every bit as warm and strong as her grip on Anne's hand, the same as when she'd lived in the same house with them. Her face was firm and unlined enough that guessing her age would have been tough if she'd worn a wig or a hat.

Anne hoped she aged half that well, at least when the visions didn't have her convinced she'd never live half that long.

Anne's father leaned forward and smacked his thighs with both hands, a sure and predictable sign that he was getting ready to go somewhere. The memory slotted into place in her mind, strangely reassuring. Knowing the conversation a beat before it happened often let Anne relax.

"Mom, Anne wants to sit with you a while so I can get some errands done. Is that okay with you?"

"Of course she can sit with me!" the older woman exclaimed, her eyes sparkling. "There will never be a time when I don't want my beautiful granddaughter with me."

"Good. Walk me to the door, Anne?"

Anne waited by the door, watching her father hug his mother. Seeing her father as someone's little boy was disorienting and sweet at the same time. Even without the memory lining up in her awareness like a targeting scope, she would have known what he was going to say when he joined her.

"Are you sure you'll be okay here?"

"I'll be fine, Dad. I want to spend some time with Gemaw. You know how much it helped for her to sit with me in the hospital. I can't ever really pay her back for that, but I'm happy to try."

"I didn't mean to bring that up," he said, then he closed his eyes for a second. "Is an hour too long?"

"Two hours wouldn't be too long."

Mike Fincastle smiled, the worry leaving his eyes for a brief moment. He kissed Anne's cheek.

"All right. You already know this, but just use the nurse call button if you have any trouble."

"I will. And we won't."

Anne watched him walk down the hall, returning his wave

before he turned out of sight, before she went back to sit beside her grandmother.

She wondered if her Gemaw's different way of seeing the world kept her looking so young. Gemaw's skin was smooth, her eyes bright and clear. Her loose grasp on time and reality kept her living in a facility like this for years, but maybe there were benefits too.

Anne hoped the benefits were worth it in case she ended up in the same place.

"Where are we, Gemaw?"

Her grandmother laughed and took Anne's hands again. This was her favorite game, one Anne's mother hardly ever let her play. The answers ranged widely, with no way to predict the place, the company, or even the decade.

"We're holding a tiny little boy, one so laughing and happy I can't believe they've let me take him home."

"Who is he?" Anne said, though she thought she knew.

"Well, he's your son, my dear."

Cold washed over Anne, taking the fun out of the game and making her head pound. Familiar memory or not, she hadn't expected that answer.

One of the dreams that had tormented her during the last few weeks after the memories started getting worse was of a little boy dying, abandoned and lonely, starving to death in a small, dark room.

That little boy had had the exact same eyes Anne was looking into now, and the same ones she saw in the mirror.

"Do you think maybe that's my father instead of my son? Maybe that's your son."

Her grandmother looked at the floor and tilted her head, her mouth working just a little. She was talking it over, but Anne had never figured out who with.

Her brows drew down in concentration, and Anne wished she hadn't said anything. That had just been too close to her terrible visions. Her grandmother looked back at Anne then, and her eyes were happy.

"You're right, that is my son! The best little boy anyone could have ever wanted to meet."

"I like him too," Anne said, nodding and smiling. "I'm glad he's my Dad."

"I was a little confused, that's all. Your babies have the most beautiful blue eyes I've ever seen, blue like a robin's eggs."

Anne's jaw dropped, and everything inside of her ground to a halt. She'd had that exact thought when she first saw a shell from a robin egg on the ground, how Evan's eyes were the exact same color.

She hadn't thought of Evan or anyone else that way, like a boyfriend, for a long, long time. Knowing she was going to have to go away again, even though she was going to warn her friend before it happened, made thinking that way feel like an even worse idea.

"I don't have any babies, Gemaw," Anne whispered.

She dreaded seeing the confused look again, but it never happened. Instead her grandmother smiled and laughed, then she actually winked.

"Don't you worry, you will. They'll be safe and happy no matter how strange it seems to you. Trust me. I might not know much, but I know all about this."

Her enthusiasm was irresistible, and despite her fear, Anne smiled back. She knew it wasn't a good idea or even what she particularly wanted. But what could the harm be in letting her grandmother believe it? Her memories of the two of them talking were almost all in the past now.

"I'm glad they'll be happy then," she said. "How do they turn out?"

"They're both so smart and strong, and just beautiful," her grandmother said, her eyes unfocused but still happy. "And they're going to have so many babies, generations of them. You're going to live on forever, sweetheart."

Anne stared at her grandmother, at a complete loss for what to say. She knew better. The dreams and visions had been telling her differently for more than five years now. Too many other things had come true for her to be able to doubt it any longer.

The storm was coming, the terrible crash of almost one hundred percent of the human population. And that was the optimistic version of her nightmares.

Sometimes the storm took out everyone. Not a single human was left alive at the end of that one. Of course Anne wasn't going to live forever, but she could never say that. She couldn't say that any more than she could tell her grandmother she herself wasn't going to live out the rest of this spring.

"That sounds wonderful, Gemaw. I'm glad to have something to look forward to."

"You have more to look forward to than you know," she said, leaning forward to pat Anne's hand. "You have some rough times ahead, but you'll have sweetness in the end."

Anne's eyes filled with tears. That was exactly what she was trying to do. Give her Gemaw some sweetness in the end.

She hadn't been lying to her father about that. Her grandmother sitting with her through so many endless hours in that hospital had let Anne walk out of there with some part of her own mind still intact.

"Gemaw, can you tell me what happens to you? When you move through time? What is that like?"

"Why would you ask me such a thing? Is that what happens to you?"

She didn't sound angry or upset. Only confused and curious. For the first time in her life, Anne didn't mind the question.

"No, not really. I have a lot of dreams about the future, but I know I'm not really there. What I see is a long way off, nothing I'll be alive for."

"I'm really there," her grandmother said, nodding. "I know I'm sitting here with you, and I know I'm in every other time. All at the same time."

"Are you afraid?"

"Not at all. I've had so many wonderful lives and adventures, but I always get to go to sleep right here in my own bed. How could I be afraid of that?"

Anne smiled, unable to argue. She didn't seem to have any sense that her life was about to come to an end. Anne was relieved for her, but she wished she didn't know either.

"Are you afraid, Anne? Of what you see?"

She thought, wondering how much she should tell her grandmother. Any of her secrets were safe here, and they always had been. She'd never doubted that. But Anne didn't want to scare her grandmother or make her sad.

"I am sometimes, Gemaw. I don't want to see so many people get hurt. But I have wonderful memories too, things to really look forward too."

"I used to be afraid sometimes too, when I was younger. When it first started and I didn't know what was going on. Your father never seemed to have that part of it, or any of it really. Your aunts didn't either."

"I wonder why I do?"

Anne had asked that question more than she cared to count, and she knew everyone around her had done the same since the nightmares started.

Why had this horrible curse or sickness or mutation, whatever it was, skipped an entire generation and landed full force on her?

"Maybe you're the first one to come along who could handle it as well as I do." Her grandmother nodded, then burst out laughing.

Anne stared at her for a second before she was laughing too. She leaned over to hug her grandmother, and the two of them laughed until they were both wiping tears from their cheeks.

"See, that's all you have to do," Anne's grandmother said, sitting back. "Just figure out how to laugh at it and you'll be just fine."

"I'll remember that, Gemaw."

"How is Evan?"

Anne smiled, trying not to lose the lightness of such a lovely moment. Evan was just fine right now. He wasn't going to be in a few short weeks. Anne would have a lot to do with that. No matter how badly she wanted to, she wouldn't be able to stop it.

"He's doing great. He's leaving for college in a couple of months. I'm really going to miss him."

The older woman leaned over and patted Anne's hand.

"It's going to be fine, Anne, don't worry. He'll come back to you. He always will."

Anne's breath caught, and she was suddenly fighting back entirely different tears. She'd never seen a happy ending for herself or for Evan. She still didn't know how either of them were going to die, thank whatever gods had given her this terrible sight to begin with, but there was no happy ending.

She was afraid to hope her grandmother saw something she herself could not.

"I hope that's true, Gemaw," she whispered. "I really do."

Chapter 23

Anne sat in her bedroom, hands over her ears, eyes squeezed closed. Her head was buzzing, shrieking, echoing with every kind of noise she'd ever heard.

This was the static of her dreams turned up louder than she could possibly tolerate. And she couldn't do anything to make it stop.

The noise had been growing louder over the past several days whether she was awake or asleep. Her head had turned into some kind of organic alarm clock that got louder with every passing second. She was terrified of what would happen when that alarm finally went off.

Her journal and pens were on the desk beside her. She'd gotten everything ready a few days ago just in case. When it happened, she was going to be out of time, and she had to say something. She had to let her father know how sorry she was to be causing such a problem again.

Anne had tried everything she could think of to stop another break in her mind from happening. All she could do now was apologize while she had the chance.

Despite her covered ears and roaring head, Anne jumped when the phone rang downstairs.

That was it.

That was the alarm she'd been dreading for weeks now. She winced, wondering if her flesh and bone ears would bleed when the noise got even louder.

Every trace of sound stopped instead.

Anne held her breath, wondering if this was only some kind of calm before the storm, the eye of the hurricane raging inside her brain.

Silence. She slowly lowered her hands and opened her eyes. Her father stood in the doorway to her room, crying harder than she'd ever seen him cry before.

"Anne," he said, gasping for breath. "Your grandmother… your Gemaw…"

She walked over to him, not wanting him to force himself to say another word. For once, her wretched memories would help another person, even for a second.

"You don't have to say it, Dad. I'm sorry. I'm so sorry."

He cried harder, sobbing against her shoulder, and Anne stood calm and strong. This was the one chance she would have to comfort her dad, no matter how much she might want to again. She was barely going to make it through the next few days. Then she was going to make everything even harder for him.

"I'm so sorry," she whispered.

Anne listened to her father as he stepped back and started talking. Every word matched up with her memory, every pause and hitch in his chest.

Gemaw had died in her sleep, no signs of any suffering. He and Anne's mother were making the arrangements today, but he thought the funeral would be in a couple of days. People had to travel to get here.

So many people loved her.

Then he looked at her, his eyes still red and streaming, his heart broken from losing his own mother. But he had to be worried about his daughter.

"Are you okay, sweetheart? Are you going to be okay?"

Anne had to tell the best lie of her life.

"I think I'll be fine, Dad. Don't worry about me."

He nodded, hugged her again for a second, and left. Anne walked back to her desk and picked up her favorite pen. Gemaw had given her this pen a few years ago when she'd come home from the hospital in the city. It was the only one Anne owned that she could refill and keep using for a long time.

She hoped she never lost this one. She needed to keep her grandmother with her for the rest of her own life.

She wrote slowly, squinting through her tears, making the words as clearly as she could.

Dad.

I'm sorry to cause more trouble for you, especially right now. Please forgive me. I tried everything I could to keep it from happening again. There was nothing I could do.

I love you.

I'm sorry.

Anne tore the sheet out, then carefully folded it so the writing didn't show. She wrote Dad on the outside even though Evan would know who to give it to.

He was going to read it himself. She didn't mind that at all.

She did mind causing her friend more upset and stress when he was already anxious about leaving for college. She at least needed to warn him what was going to happen, especially since she was depending on him to give the note to her father.

She slipped the paper into her purse, then got up to get ready. They were going to the funeral home in a little while. Anne's mother would indeed be sad, but her relief would come through loud and clear too. Anne and her father would help each other get through the next few days and through the funeral.

He would be on his own after that, same as Evan would.

And so would Anne.

ANNE'S dry eyes and skin told her some kind of huge fan ran over her head, hidden by tasteful beige tiles, working hard to keep the funeral home air circulating. But even right by the glass front doors, the smells turned her stomach.

Mounds of dying flowers competed with too much perfume and cologne. The chemical stink of brand new carpeting fought with suits and shoes that normally stayed confined in a closet.

Anne was relieved she hadn't bothered with breakfast.

"Oh, honey, I haven't seen you since you were a tiny little thing!"

She turned toward the elderly man who had spoken, yet another person she had no memory of. Her whole morning had consisted of greeting people who knew far more about her than she did about them.

"Thank you for coming," she said, grasping his frail hands. "I'm sorry for your loss."

"Your grandmother was such a dear woman," he said, shaking her hands before he walked away.

Anne nodded, then looked back out to the full parking lot. Her father hadn't been exaggerating about the number of people coming into town for her grandmother's funeral. Every space she saw in the vast parking lot was full. She wondered how far away Evan's father would have to park.

She remembered Ed and Gwen would bicker all the way over here, and Evan would be more desperate than usual to get away. She spotted them at last, Evan and his sister walking fast to keep a few steps ahead of their father.

She made sure no strangers were swarming toward her, then darted outside to meet them. The cool spring air, fresh and lively after overnight rain, drove the musty funeral home smells away.

"Anne, I'm sorry about your grandmother," Gwen said, putting an arm around her before she walked inside.

Evan smiled at her, but he stood to the side. Anne smiled back, just for a second, then turned to his father.

"Thank you for coming, Mr. Griffith."

He surprised Anne by hugging her, a real hug. The first she ever remembered from him.

"Of course. You holding up?"

"We're all right, as much as we can be."

"Let me know if you need anything," Ed Griffith said, patting her on the shoulder before he followed Gwen.

Anne met Evan's wide blue eyes, and the two of them tried to keep a most inappropriate giggling fit under control. They walked off through the sea of cars before any of the adults smoking around the entry could notice.

"What was that all about?" she whispered.

"You got me," Evan said. "I've never seen him act like that either."

"Something about me and the Griffith men."

He smiled, pulling her into the one hug she'd been waiting for in a day filled with random physical contact.

Evan was still taller than her, that much hadn't changed. But at seventeen his shoulders and arms were warm and so much stronger around her, his voice deeper than her father's. He spoke softly, almost into her ear.

"How *are* you doing?"

"I'm okay right now, Evan, but I need to talk to you. I'm afraid I'm not going to be for long."

His answer unspooled backward in her head, far too long and slow to be his natural voice. Anne dreaded the fear in that voice when Evan's words caught up with her memory.

"What's going on?"

"I can't talk about it right now," she said, trying to fight the echoing mess in her head. "Take me for a walk tonight and I'll tell you."

Evan held her shoulders, and Anne couldn't look away from his pale blue eyes. No matter what else was going on around her, or inside her, she could always see her friend's eyes. He touched her hair.

"I'll hold you to that, Anne."

His words, and his smile, got her through the rest of the horrible afternoon.

Anne hoped she'd remember everything about him when her mind fell apart.

Chapter 24

Evan paced back and forth on the front porch at Anne's house, waiting for her to make her escape. He'd stayed inside as long as he could stand the noise and crowd, long enough to speak to both of her parents. He never had enjoyed huge crowds, certainly not for anything like a funeral.

He couldn't stand to see Mr. Fincastle looking so sad, either. His eyes were too much like Anne's.

Almost an hour later, Evan wasn't about to leave knowing she needed to talk to him. It seemed like everyone inside had decided to linger all night long. The wait was getting to him.

He could see Anne when he passed by the front windows, standing in a group of people he didn't recognize. Probably relatives from out of town. She didn't seem particularly happy, but she didn't have the desperate look he'd seen at the funeral that morning either.

He was at the far end, thinking about sitting on the porch swing, when he heard the door open.

"Thank you for waiting," she said, walking right past him and down the steps. "Let's go before someone else grabs me."

He followed her and they turned down the street, heading away from his house. No need to tempt his father or give him something else to ask about. Hurricane Ed had been more and more full of questions and advice as each day passed this semester.

Mostly about Evan *Leaving For College* in the fall.

College felt too far off and strange, like a daydream, to worry too much about for now. All Evan wanted to do was get through the next few months. If he could do that without too much struggle with his father, he'd be a happy young man.

The only thing interfering with his eagerness to get away was walking beside him right now.

Anne groaned, more annoyed than upset.

"If one more person tells me a story from when I was three years old, I'm going to scream."

"I remember that from when Mom died. I guess it makes them feel better, but I never knew what to say to them."

They continued on to the playground. After so many years, they'd never found a better place to escape. To talk. Evan was definitely too tall for the swings anymore, but the habit just felt safe.

A few kids were trying to stretch out the last few seconds of sunshine on the soccer field, but no one else was around. The two of them sat on their usual picnic table, feet on the splintery bench.

Evan noticed Anne had brought her purse out of her own house for some reason, but he didn't say anything.

"I need you do to something for me," Anne said, watching the kids playing. "Something you're not going to like."

Evan's heart beat too fast to be comfortable. She'd said just that morning that she wasn't going to be fine. He wanted to help her if he could, but he wasn't sure he wanted to know what that would mean.

"What's going on?"

She opened her purse and pulled out a folded piece of paper. It was blank on the outside except the word Dad in her neat handwriting. Evan took it, then looked back into her eyes.

"I need you to give that to Dad in a few days. Not until… You'll know when."

"Why can't you give this to him? What's wrong?"

She looked up at him, and even in the fading sunlight he could see how upset she was. She was scared to death.

"I'm going to have to go away again, Evan. Losing Gemaw, it's too much."

"Have you talked to Dr. Lewis about it?" Evan said, panic working through his heart and out into his body. "There has to be something we can do."

No, please. He couldn't stand this, not now. Not ever.

Not when he was already unhappy about leaving her to go to college. He had to at least know Anne was okay.

"All anyone can do is try to get through this," she said. "I did everything I could to make it easier, but nothing is going to stop it. The last thing I want is for my parents to be more upset. I was able to keep it together for an extra week, until today. After this though, I won't be able to stop it."

"Does your Dad know?"

Anne shook her head, finally looking away.

"I didn't want to make it worse for him right after she died. As long as I could manage, anyway."

"How long have you known about this? When did it start?"

Her dreams and visions scared him, but not as badly as the memories. Nightmares were bad enough, and he'd certainly had his share.

Remembering things before they happened sounded like the ultimate nightmare to him, especially if he couldn't do anything to change the outcome.

"I knew something was going to happen after New Year's," she said. "But not what. I started to see her dying in March. Right after that, I saw myself going away. Once I see something like this, it doesn't change. You know that, Evan. We just have to get ready."

"Well, I'm *not* ready, and I'm not going to be." He stepped back, took a deep breath, and squared his shoulders. "I'm not leaving."

"You can't think that way," she said, scowling at him. "Not because of me."

Anne jumped off the table and started walking. Evan grabbed her bag and followed. It was everything he could to keep a broad grin from taking over his face. Saying those words out loud - I'm not leaving - lifted a ten ton weight from his shoulders, one he hadn't realized he was carrying.

"Does it matter why, Anne? The world won't end if I hold off for a semester, or even a year."

She whirled to face him.

"Do you really expect me to explain why you have to go to college? Now? When I'm about to go back to the goddamn nuthouse?"

Evan drew breath, but her expression stopped him cold. Anne's eyes didn't match her voice. Neither did anything else about her. Angry as she sounded, she looked, somehow she felt, calmer than she had for a long time.

His friend was going through the motions for some other reason, reacting because she was supposed to. He recognized her carefully angry face as easily as her carefully normal one.

"You want me to go in the fall," he said. "No matter what I might want. Just like everybody else in my life."

Anne jammed her fists onto her hips and looked away from him. Chill loneliness Evan hadn't felt since she left him the first time settled into his heart.

"You're going, Evan. That's all. No point yelling or fighting about it. Maybe we're all saying the same thing because nothing else makes sense."

"It doesn't make sense when you're-"

She stepped forward and covered his mouth with one hand.

"This is exactly what I *don't* want. Shouting at each other when no matter what happens, we don't have much time left." She dropped her hand, but Evan still felt the heat of it. "Can you please give the letter to my father?"

"Yes."

"Thank you. Can we not talk about this any more?"

Evan listened to his own teeth grinding together. He hated being upset with her. If she was telling the truth, he wouldn't want to remember an argument as their goodbye.

"Okay."

They walked toward the edge of the soccer field, where only one boy and one girl kicked a black and white ball around. Evan wished he could take both of them back ten years. When getting home in time for supper was all they worried about.

Except he'd never known a time like that, not really. Neither had Anne, not since she turned eleven years old.

"How long?" he said. "Do you know when it's going to happen?"

She shook her head. When she looked up at him, Anne seemed older than her grandmother had been.

"I don't know. Not long."

Not long turned out to be the day after Evan's high school graduation.

Chapter 25

Evan paced around his bedroom, trying to work up the courage to talk to his father. His footsteps echoes around the nearly empty room. He was supposed to be excited. He was supposed to be leaving for college in two days, his first step into his own life. His first steps away from the constant rumble and clash of living with his father.

He'd been daydreaming about this as long as he could remember. Now all he could think about was how empty his life was going to be without Anne.

He sat on his bed, picking up a picture of the two of them at his graduation a few months ago. She'd told him just before she left that she'd already known things were going to fall apart then, but he couldn't tell from the photo. They were both grinning, he in his blue cap and gown, she in a dark green dress that had made him weak in the knees. He was going to pack this last so he wouldn't be without it. Now it was all he had left.

"Come on, Evan, grow the fuck up."

That's exactly what Gwen would say. That's what she *had* said when their father first started telling him where to go to college a year ago.

Don't waste your time, son, go on to the school that's best for you. Go now, start out in the right place.

His father hadn't listened to a word when Evan suggested staying closer by instead of going hours south to St. Louis. Hurricane Ed wouldn't hear a word about community college, either.

No, out of the question. I've worked and saved so you two wouldn't have to worry about this, and I'm not going to let your mother down by skimping now.

Evan stood, taking a deep breath and squaring his shoulders. His father hadn't listened to him about much of anything in eighteen years, not that Evan pushed all that hard. He'd done his best to keep his promise to Gwen, made right after their mother died, to not push Ed any harder than he had to without her around. Evan would have sworn she visited less and less often every year.

This was going to have to start changing sometime. He had to at least try. He walked slowly down the stairs. Dreading this all night and all day tomorrow wouldn't make it any easier. He would either manage to stand up to his father or he wouldn't.

"I need to talk to you, Dad."

Ed Griffith looked up from the television, eyebrows raised. Evan couldn't tell if it was curiosity or if he was already saying no. That didn't matter. He couldn't stop now. He might not ever get started again.

"What's going on?"

He did turn the baseball game off, though Evan half wished he'd be more distracted. He sat down and looked at his hands, then at his father.

"I need to delay going to college for a year."

"And why is that, son?"

"I'm just not ready, Dad. I know I'm too late to enroll anywhere else, but I want to get a job and go to community college in the spring. I'm just not ready to go so far away."

"You'll do fine, Evan. It will be tough at first, but you're going to meet people you'll know for the rest of your life. That's a hell of a lot more important than wasting time around here."

Evan shook his head, scowling at himself. He wasn't getting the words right, at least not in a way his father could hear.

"I know, and I can still do that. I will do that. I'm just not ready yet."

Ed leaned back and crossed his arms. Evan knew in that second how the rest of the conversation was going to go, or at least it always had. When his father crossed his arms that aggressively, he'd made up his mind.

Everything had to change for the first time though, and Evan couldn't give up.

"Evan, you talked about this all year and all summer like you were ready. You've made an awful lot of plans and arrangements for someone who's not ready. You've got your whole first year planned out. You have a job on campus. You've even met most of your professors."

"I know. I'm letting a bunch of people down, most of all you."

"No, son, most of all *you*. I'm not going to let you sit around and waste a year of your life over a case of cold feet. You're going."

"Dad, listen to me," Evan said, trying to keep his voice quiet. "It's not just cold feet. I'm afraid if I go now I'll be making a huge mistake. If my freshman year is a disaster, I might not ever recover."

"Oh come on!" Ed sat forward with his hands on his knees. "You've gotten what, two Bs the whole time you've been in school? The only way this could be a disaster is if you don't go at all."

"You're not listening to me."

"I'm listening, but you're not making any sense. You're not going to derail your life like this on some kind of crazy whim."

Evan closed his eyes, knowing it was no use. His father wouldn't have used that word, crazy, by accident. He confirmed it just a second later.

"What's this really about, Evan? Is it Anne?"

Evan wanted to say no, but he couldn't even manage to shake his head. He was exposed, frozen to the spot, unable to breathe. All he could do was nod.

"You're not leaving her, son. She's already left. She left reality."

"Her grandmother just died, Dad!"

"You've lost two grandparents, and I don't have to remind you you lost your mother when you were thirteen years old. You didn't have to go to a hospital to get over it, and neither did your sister. That's not what healthy people do."

"I can't just leave," Evan whispered, staring at the floor. He was too close to breaking that long ago promise, to getting angry and shouting. That never got anywhere, at least not when he did it.

He'd never been able to figure out why it worked for Gwen.

"You're not responsible for her, son. You're responsible for starting your own life. You're not going to sit around here waiting for someone who might not ever come back. There's no more discussing this. You're going."

Evan stood, trying his best to sound and act like his sister.

"I'm just not going to go then," he said, his voice rising. "You're not going to throw me in the trunk and drag me off to college!"

"Well, that's fine. You're eighteen now, and you can make your own decisions." The calm, hard tone in his father's voice sent a chill through Evan. "But I'm not going to support that either. If you don't go now, I'm not going to pay for college. Not one damn penny. And you'll have to find another place to live if you want to hang around here and get some kind of dead-end job."

"You'd just kick me out in the street? Way to be supportive, Dad."

"No, I wouldn't kick you out. I'd never do that. But I am going to sell this place, Evan. I should have years ago. I was only waiting for you to get finished with high school. You can come live with me in the city if you really want to. You have a home as long as I'm alive. But if you decide to live with me and you don't go to college, you'll be paying rent and your share of everything else. I'll support you any way I can, but I'm not going to support you in wasting your life."

"God dammit, I'm not a kid anymore!"

"No, you're not, son," Ed Griffith said, getting to his own feet. "But you're talking and acting like one right now. You can hate me if you need to, but I will not let you make a mistake this big. You need to get out of here and start your own life, and that's exactly what you're going to do."

He left the room without another word.

A few minutes later, Evan walked back up to his nearly-empty room.

He stared at the picture of himself and Anne until he fell asleep.

Chapter 26

"ANNE, you have a visitor. Feeling up to that?"

Anne didn't even turn away from the window. She didn't have to. The deafening static inside her mind had been getting quieter all day long. She had to take this chance while she had it.

"Yes."

She heard the low murmur of voices, and before the door closed she caught some of the words for a change. The nurse was saying Anne had been having a lot of trouble communicating and to be prepared for that. She said the one or two word answers were good signs over the last few days. Anne knew she'd finally be able to manage more than that, at least for a few minutes. Someone stood still, then slowly walked toward her.

"Evan," she whispered.

"I'm so glad to see you," he said, and his voice trembled. "I couldn't… I couldn't leave without…"

Anne turned around in the chair to look at her friend. He was as neatly dressed and put together as ever, with his clothes and hair perfectly arranged. The thing no one would have been able to miss was his eyes. He looked like he hadn't slept in days, and like he wasn't going to sleep for many more.

She knew that was probably true.

"Come sit with me," she said, putting her hand on the chair beside hers. "I want to see you, too."

He took her hand as he sat, and Anne let him. What she had to say wasn't easy. If this small contact made it even a little less painful for him, she wanted to do that.

"You don't have to talk," he said. "I just wanted to see you."

"It's okay. I need to talk to you. I don't think I'll be able to for long. And I want you to talk to me before you go."

"I didn't want to go at all," he said. "I *don't* want to. My father can't hear me no matter what I say."

Anne clenched her jaw. He had to go on with his life, he had to. She couldn't stand to see him get dragged into the mess inside of her.

"He might be right," she said, squeezing his hand. "What would you do around here anyway?"

"I know, I know," he said, wiping away a tear. "It's time to start my life and all that. He was pretty damned clear that he'd cut me off unless I stick to the plan."

"You're ready, Evan. You've been looking forward to this as long as I've known you."

"I'm not looking forward to leaving you here," he said, not bothering to wipe his tears anymore. "I feel like I'm abandoning you, Anne."

Here it was, the thing she'd been dreading for weeks. The memory was as strong as anything happening around her.

"You're not abandoning me. You're ready to go. I have to stay here, probably for a long while this time."

"You're doing better already," he started, but she shook her head.

"I'm doing worse, not better," she said, closing her eyes so she couldn't see his. "I have the nightmares every night, and I can hardly see anyone's faces now. They're not sure what to do with me anymore. The nurse wasn't lying. This is the first day I've really been able to hear anyone or talk since I got here. The noise is too bad."

Evan touched her cheek, and Anne forced herself to look at him. She wanted to remember the color of his eyes, the shape of his face. She didn't want to forget a single thing about him even after she sent him away.

"Can you see me? Can you see my face? Can you hear my voice?"

"You're the only one I can see and hear now, Evan. Now that my grandmother is gone, you're the only one left."

"I can't leave, I can't leave you," he said, pulling her forward into his arms.

Anne squeezed him hard for a minute, willing that moment to go on forever even though she knew it wouldn't. She sat back, taking both of his hands.

"Listen to me. You have to go. You can't stay here because of me. I'm not getting better, I'm getting worse. This is the second time this has happened to me and I'm not even sixteen years old yet."

"Don't say that-"

"I am saying it. They've found the right drugs for now, or at least they're starting to, but that didn't last before. Next time they might not find anything. I might end up in a place like this forever. They want to try shock treatments if I get worse again. I overheard them talking about it yesterday."

"Don't let them do that! If they don't know what's going on, that could make it worse, and you can't reverse it."

"I know, I think so too. And so does Dad. I don't think they're going to do that. I haven't seen it, anyway."

"You're not going to be her forever," Evan whispered, shaking his head, squeezing her hands. "No, that's not going to happen."

"It might already be happening. Look at me, Evan. I'm going to miss you, but I can't let you do this. You have to go. Don't think about me. You have to go find your own life."

"You sound like my goddamn father."

"Sometimes even he knows what he's talking about," she said, trying to find the courage to follow through with the memory. "I don't... I don't want you stay, Evan. I can't see past being in here, and I don't know when I'll ever get out. Knowing you're sitting around waiting will only make it harder."

"I don't think I can do this if I can't even talk to you."

"Listen to me. You can write to me, okay? I'll write back if I can. I can't promise much of anything right now, but I think hearing from you, how well you're doing, will help me a lot. I haven't even been able to talk this clearly to anyone else since I got here. Maybe if you write to me, that will help too."

Evan took a deep breath, looking steadily into her eyes. She knew when he made his decision. He didn't have to say a word. Another memory opened up to her then, and with it she felt a tiny spark of hope. She saw herself with his letters, so many hand-written letters, and those words were the only thing that made sense to her.

She knew the nurses would come in to help her, and she wouldn't be able to see their faces. The doctors would be no different. All she would see was the way they were going to die or some kind of waxen mask. Sometimes she wouldn't even hear their voices over the deafening noises inside her mind. Even her parents were going to look and sound that way for a long time.

But when she read Evan's letters, Anne would be able to see his face and hear his voice. She'd be able to imagine everything he wrote to her as if she were right by his side. She still couldn't see when she would leave this place, but she knew that line of sanity between her and her friend would give her a chance.

"Okay, Anne," he said, sitting up in his chair. "I'll write to you. I promise. I'll do the best I can if you promise me you'll do the same."

Now Anne was crying herself, tears of relief instead of fear. She hugged him again, nodding against his shoulder. This was the first thing she'd felt sure about in a long, long time.

Feeling sure about anything was the first good surprise she'd had all year.

"I will, I promise. I'll do the best I can."

PART V
DARKEST HOUR

Chapter 27

Evan backed out of the crowded common room, feeling like he'd been saying goodbye for at least an hour. The threadbare brown couches and chairs were covered with people in various states of intoxication and relief after the last finals of the fall semester.

Evan knew a little more than half of them. The other half, friends and a more solid support network than he'd ever had back home, made him surprisingly sad to think about leaving for good in a few more months.

The flat white walls had a few more dings and scrapes than when he'd moved in. The even flatter gray carpet would surely be replaced before another year passed. Some stains never washed out. Still, this dorm and the university and St. Louis itself made up the only real home Evan had now.

Hurricane Ed hadn't bothered waiting for Evan's first holiday break four years ago. He'd put their house on the market and moved into the city before the end of September. Gwen joked he hadn't even waited for Evan's bed to get cold.

Evan shook himself, then stepped from dingy carpet to shining green floor tiles. This end of term party was nice and all, but he really needed to get on the road. The drive was long even without holiday traffic and bad weather, and tonight he was afraid he was going to have both. He'd have more than enough time in the car to dwell on the past, and his future.

"Come on, Griffith, what's your hurry?" his roommate for the last two years shouted. "Got a hot date?"

Evan smiled, knowing his face was turning red. He certainly hoped that would be the case.

"Yeah, as a matter of fact I do. I've wasted more than enough time with you ugly fuckers."

Everyone in the room burst into laughter, including his roommate. Evan grinned, waved, and walked away before anyone else could try to stop him. He was going to miss these guys after graduation in the spring.

But he'd never miss anyone here as much as he'd been missing Anne.

The fierce wind drove the fog of nostalgia and the stink of beer and cigarettes from his head. Evan brushed a couple of inches of fresh snow off his car windows and headed north. Before he managed to get onto I-57, his huge, mostly ignored bag phone rang.

Only a handful of people had the number, and all of them knew how absurdly expensive every minute was. Evan could only think of one person who even knew he'd be in the car with the silly thing turned on.

"Hi Gwen."

"You're not driving tonight, are you?"

"Sure, clear as a bell down here. I'm fine, the interstate is wide open."

"You'll stop if you get tired, or if the snow gets worse?"

It wasn't really a question.

"Yes, Mama Gwen, of course I'll stop. I've made this drive a time or two, remember?"

"Right, I'm going to bed, smart ass," she said. "Let yourself in and be quiet about it. Love you, Ev."

"Love you too."

He ended the call, relieved he hadn't been lying about the roads. Snow was still blowing around, but the highway was clear. As long as it didn't come down harder, he'd be able to make good time. Everyone else must have gone early or delayed.

Nothing to do on the vast interstate but drive, listen to music, and think.

Expensive minutes or not, he wanted very much to call Anne, but he wasn't sure of her work schedule this time of year. Between his finals and her being busy, they hadn't talked or written much for a while. He'd see her tomorrow, certainly, and finally get to see her new apartment.

He closed his eyes for a second, no longer worried about hiding what he was looking forward to. Well, what he *hoped* to look forward to, maybe. Even his own thoughts were a jumbled mess.

Anne being nearly twenty was part of that. Evan could admit that to himself, at least inside his own mind. She'd had time to work out her own life a bit while he'd been away. Her having her own apartment certainly didn't hurt.

He was terrified enough of telling her how he felt about her without worrying about her father walking into the room. Mr. Fincastle had always seemed to like Evan, but that didn't change the fact that he was Anne's father.

Evan had seen his own father's reaction when Gwen brought her boyfriends home, how he'd had an eerie sense of who was dangerous to his little girl and who was not. Hurricane Ed had despised Mark on sight, and that never changed until Gwen's wedding day. All of them would deny it, but Evan thought their father's suspicion lingered until his first nephew was born.

Evan wasn't ready to set off those alarms in Anne's father, not just yet. He hoped graduating from college and doing so well would help with all of that.

It wasn't just nerves over Mr. Fincastle by any means. That would at least be typical. Evan knew his own father would never approve of Anne, no matter how much time passed, and even if she'd been perfectly fine that entire time. In the years since his Mom had died, Ed's opinion of Anne had only gotten worse.

Again, going by what he'd seen Gwen go through, it was going to be tough. The fact that Ed already distrusted the woman Evan wanted, assuming she wanted him, would make everything even harder.

Evan shifted in his seat, popping out one cassette and switching another, not quite so energetic. His normal driving music was keeping him too much on edge tonight.

Assuming Anne wanted him. Was anything else in the entire world worth worrying about? Gwen accused him of being a drama queen sometimes, and he supposed she was right. Evan knew he just needed to brood about things from time to time. He'd brooded about this one for a while.

He'd dated on and off, mainly to shut his father up and keep people out of his business, and plenty of his friends had gone through several relationships over the last four years. Just because he wanted Anne more than he'd ever wanted anything didn't mean she felt the same way.

What he would do if she didn't feel that way about him shut his normally active mind down cold.

"There's no hurry, Evan," he said, his voice rising and falling to match the song. "You have plenty of time."

He already had a summer job lined up closer to home, only an hour away instead of several, and he planned to go to grad school there too. He smiled, thinking how relieved his father would be that he already had an apartment arranged close to the university. No worries about asking Evan to move in with him and hoping the offer would be refused.

He had at least two years, more if he ended up with a job somewhere close by. He didn't want to rush Anne or himself, but he didn't want to wait any longer than he had to, either.

The snow was falling again, but the roads were still empty and fairly clear. In any case, he had two weeks on this break to see how things worked out, how he and Anne both felt now. Everyone had grown up, probably more than they should have, over the past four years.

Evan hoped they'd grown toward each other instead of away.

~

ANNE'S APARTMENT building didn't look all that different from some of the newer dorms Evan had driven past less than twenty-four hours ago. A three-story boring tan box jammed in with five or six just like it, nondescript holly bushes scattered around frost-burned winter grass. The biggest difference was the lack of bike racks instead of several jammed full of college commuter specials.

After a furious internal debate with himself, Evan decided to skip bringing flowers, candy, or anything else he hoped Anne might be happy enough to hug him for. No matter how vividly he'd imagined their reunion and hopeful happily ever after, that only existed inside his own head.

His confidence and excitement didn't quite insulate him from fear of a broken heart.

Evan was sure he'd been knocking for an unreasonably long time on the rusty steel door before it opened. He'd been starting to worry about disturbing the neighbors. The sight of Anne drove all thoughts of other people from his mind, but not in the way he'd expected.

"Evan," she said, closing her eyes and sighing. "Come in."

He stood for a second, watching her walk away, too stunned to move. He couldn't remember a time in well over ten years when she hadn't hugged him after they'd been apart, certainly not when it had been most of a year since they'd seen each other. That was the smallest thing in his mind right now.

The biggest was shock over how awful she looked. Her hair was dirty and uncombed, her faded t-shirt wrinkled and stained. She turned then, scowling at him as she sat down at what looked like a battered fold-up card table in the kitchen, probably older than either of them. He closed the door and walked slowly toward her.

The apartment was small but fairly neat, as similar on the inside to Evan's dorm as on the outside. Nothing was quite organized, but no distressing piles of garbage or rotting pizza boxes. What bothered him about the apartment was the smell.

The air was stale and heavily organic. Unwashed. A scent he recognized too well from all-night study sessions. No one here was in school, so unless there were crowds of teenagers playing too many video games, that didn't make sense.

Someone smoked far too many cigarettes, and the cloying sweetness of incense didn't quite cover up marijuana and alcohol sweat in the air.

He sat down at the scuffed table across from Anne, trying not to stare. She hardly looked like the same woman he'd said goodbye to in August. She covered her eyes with her hands, but he could see how pale and unhealthy her face was. She was thin, far beyond her normal slender build and into bony.

Something had gone terribly wrong in a short time. He had no idea what to say or do, alarm shorting out all of his reason. He couldn't just sit here silently.

"I'm glad to see you, Anne."

She never even uncovered her eyes.

"I didn't expect you so early."

Evan stopped himself from looking at his watch, but he knew it was almost two in the afternoon. Everything he could think of to say sounded terribly judgmental and condescending.

"How've you been?" The painful formality made him wince inside.

She grunted, then lowered her hands to cover her mouth. Her lovely green eyes were swollen and bloodshot, and she seemed to be having trouble focusing on him. As thin as the rest of her was, her face was puffy. This wasn't just a one-night drinking binge.

That much alcohol could not possibly be good with her medications, if she was still taking them. She finally took a deep breath, put her trembling hands on the rickety table, and answered the question he'd forgotten asking.

"Just great, Evan. Fantastic. Better than ever. You look like you're doing well."

"I'm good, long drive last night. Going to your parents' for Christmas?"

"Probably not, I have to work both days. Hazards of retail."

She looked away from him as she spoke, and her pale cheeks flushed. She was lying and not trying all that hard to cover it up. He wondered if she was still working at all.

She'd never looked so unhealthy or acted so strangely before she'd gone to the hospital before. He couldn't guess what, but she was on the edge of something.

Evan didn't want to be the one to push her over.

"They'll be disappointed," he said.

"Someone is always disappointed, no matter what I say or do. This way I don't have to listen to everyone harping on about it."

"Have you seen something, Anne? A memory or a vision?"

"Goddamnit, the biggest problem I have is everyone asking me if I have a problem! Maybe I'm just having a bad day, did that ever occur to you?"

"It occurred to me that you haven't hidden anything like this from me since you were eleven years old. Whatever's happening with you is more than a bad day."

"You need to go, Evan."

Reasonable or not, his temper finally caught up with hers.

"Come on, Anne, this is bullshit. I haven't seen you for months, and you're acting like you've never seen me before. What's going on?"

She glanced at him, then covered her eyes with her hands again. The reunion Evan had imagined all the way home had fallen apart before it ever got started.

"Nothing is going on. I'm just busy, that's all. I've got a lot on my mind right now. I don't have time to play hostess."

Gwen called him on being too nice all the time, and other people had too. This was definitely not the time for being nice.

"Hostess? Since when did you have to be my hostess? I offered to take you out to dinner, remember? That's why I'm here. You don't have to do a thing but get ready."

She lowered her hands and finally looked at him, really looked, and Evan was scared to death by what he saw. She was sick or badly hung over, and he wasn't sure it was only alcohol either. Whatever this was could not be a good thing.

"I'm worried about you," he said, reaching for her hand. "You look like you haven't slept in a week."

She jerked her hand away and drew back from him.

"Stop worrying about me, Evan, just stop it. I'm fine. You left to start your life a long time ago. Time for me to do the same. You need to get on with your own life and stop trying to fix mine."

Anne usually knew when things were going to get bad, actually, and she did everything she could to warn people and get ready. Had even that scant blessing failed her?

"I'm not trying to fix you or anyone else. I just wanted to see you, spend some time with you. I miss you when I'm gone, you know."

"I know," she whispered, holding her head again. "I'm sorry, I miss you too. I shouldn't be talking to you like this."

Evan rubbed his eyes, scrambling for what to say. Her mood swings were making his own head hurt. His ideas about having plenty of time seemed to make a lot of sense right now, but he didn't feeling comfortable walking away from her.

"Have you been sick?" he said.

She laughed, and the bitterness and anger in her voice broke his heart. Her laugh had always been light and free, even when it was rare.

"I've been sick since I was eleven years old. You know that. This is just more of the same."

"You look… I'm sorry to say this, but you look hung over. You look awful."

Anne stared at him. He heard his father's voice, his many lectures about thinking things through. This time he'd tried, choosing all of his words carefully, and that only made things worse.

"Are you going to tell me you never drink with all your college buddies?"

"Sometimes, sure. But I haven't drunk enough to get hungover since I was seventeen years old."

"Say it, just say it," she said, lifting her chin. "Go on. And you don't have the same kinds of *issues* I do, right?"

Evan winced. This was more than casual drinking. The Anne he knew would never have thrown that in his face. She knew he hated that part of his father, and that Evan would never repeat those words no matter what happened.

"I wasn't going to say that, Anne. I would never say that. Seems to be on your mind, though."

"Of course it is!" she shouted, leaning over the table toward him, then standing. "We're so relieved you graduated from high school, but maybe you shouldn't go to college just yet. Get a job, but maybe you should stay home. Don't get too stressful a job though, nothing that would possibly give you a way to advance or afford a place of your own. Maybe moving out isn't such a good idea, especially with your issues!"

Evan wanted to cover his ears, close his eyes, maybe find a closet to hide in. He had no idea what to do. He didn't want to upset her even more by leaving, but staying here didn't seem to be exactly keeping her calm.

"Anne?"

They both turned to see a guy standing in the hallway. He was as disheveled as Anne, with his hair standing up and ripped jeans on, but no shirt. His eyes were as red and his face as puffy as hers.

Evan watched as he stumbled across the kitchen and put his arm around Anne's shoulders. She didn't flinch away like she had from Evan, but her face was now bright red. She stared at the floor.

"What's going on in here?" the guy said, staring at Evan with narrowed eyes.

"Nothing, Joe, I'm fine. Just talking to an old friend."

Evan's chest was tight and hot, and his whole body felt like he was trapped in quicksand. He'd never wanted to get away from a place more in his entire life, but he couldn't move. He couldn't blink or look away from Anne's face, not even when she finally met his gaze.

An *old friend.*

Nameless and in the past, not even worth an introduction.

"Yeah, sorry to disturb you," Evan said, his throat aching. "I was just leaving. Have a good holiday."

He pushed himself up from the chair, wondering if his legs would support his weight or function well enough to get him out the door. After that it didn't matter anymore.

If he didn't escape this stinking room, he was afraid his heart would explode within him. He looked into Anne's eyes for a second longer, then he turned away and walked out the door.

He managed not to slam it before he leaned against the wall, his breath coming in sharp, painful gasps. He felt like he'd run up ten flights of stairs rather than walking fifteen feet. His head pounded hard enough that his body trembled in time with it.

Of everything he could ever have imagined, nothing came close to this. His heart had been so neatly ripped out that he wondered why it still beat at all.

He had no idea how long he stood there before his spinning brain finally settled on one idea, the only course of action he could take.

Get out of here. Get away. Don't let one of them open the door.

Don't let her see you like this.

Don't let him see you at all.

Go.

Evan walked down the hall, his head and his heart throbbing. What had happened to her? He didn't try to fool himself that seeing the guy, Joe, hadn't been horrible, but something far worse than a boyfriend had changed in Anne.

Just a few years before, he'd felt sure he could help her, stop the nightmares and the visions and keep her calm if he just stayed by her side.

Just a few hours before, he'd been sure he could love her enough to keep anything from hurting either one of them ever again.

Now he was wondering if anything could stop her from killing herself with drinking or whatever else she was doing.

He drew back from the brutal wind when he opened the door, lowering his head and walking to his car. By the time he shut the door, his face and hands were numb and his eyes were watering.

He wished his heart would go numb.

His heart was still sharp and aching, the scattered pieces cutting his insides to ribbons. Evan was far past the point of tears or anything else he could think of.

He had to get away from here.

Away from her.

Chapter 28

Before Evan turned toward Gwen's place, an idea finally floated to the surface of his jumbled mind. He'd asked about Anne seeing her family for a very good reason. The only other person she trusted was her father, and no one else seemed to understand her like he did.

Evan wasn't so sure he understood his friend anymore, but surely her father still did. He couldn't face his sister in this state anyway. Hurricane Ed would be even worse.

Not even 2:30 yet, that had all happened so quickly. Having the imagined course of his life altered so fundamentally should have taken longer than half an hour.

Anne's father would still be at work this early, and it wasn't far from here. A absurdly expensive call had never been more worth the cost than this one. When the phone on the other end started to ring, Even wondered if Anne's father answering or not answering would be worse.

He was out of time after three rings.

"Mike Fincastle here."

"Hey, Mr. Fincastle, Evan Griffith."

"Oh, Evan, great to hear from you. Are you home for break?"

"Yeah, just got here last night." Evan gripped the steering wheel hard enough to make his knuckles ache. Worry about his friend or not, he knew he'd be crossing a line with his next words. "Listen, have time for a cup of coffee? I'm about twenty minutes away, and I'm buying."

The silence only lasted a few seconds, not even a block at thirty miles an hour. Evan forced himself not to panic.

"Sure, I can meet you downstairs at three. It's called Jolt, but it's a pretty good place."

Evan laughed, hoping it didn't sound as artificial as it felt.

"Cute. Okay, I'll see you there at three."

By the time Evan finally found a parking spot a few blocks away, the lot split between dented and salt-covered cars like his own and gleaming new models, he was feeling a little bit calmer. He still had no idea what he was going to say to Anne's father.

He couldn't think about her being with some other guy, not right now. He was quite sure that would be on his mind more than he could stand for a long time after he wanted it to be.

Right now he had to think about Anne, not himself. He didn't have to be a doctor to know she was in real trouble. Even without what she'd gone through in the past, his friend needed help Evan couldn't provide.

Mike Fincastle sat at a table by the door, and he stood and hugged Evan hard. Evan had to squeeze his eyes closed for a second before he let go.

He'd been expecting Anne to hug him like that instead of standing with some other guy's arm around her.

Some half-naked guy who'd just crawled out of her bed.

"You look fantastic, Evan. How's school going?"

"It's going great, thank you for asking. I'll be graduating in the spring, then heading back up here for grad school."

"Oh, that's wonderful. We've all missed having you around. Are you staying with Gwen?"

"Yeah, crashing on her couch. I'm not sure the boys remember who I am yet, but they were very excited to wake me this morning."

Mr. Fincastle rolled his eyes and smiled.

"What are they, two and four? That's got to be an active household. Are they all doing well?"

"Everyone's great, thank you. How are all of you?"

Just as he'd feared, Mike Fincastle's warm smile faded. He didn't look as cold as his daughter had, but he looked as frightened as Evan felt.

"Have you talked to Anne?"

Evan took the excuse of asking the waiter for a double-espresso, hoping it would slow the pounding in his head. He hoped something resembling words would come out when he turned back.

"I saw her, just a little while ago. I stopped by her place."

Mr. Fincastle nodded, and his mouth compressed.

"Not exactly Shangri-La, is it?"

"No, not really," Evan said, looking out the window.

"Neither her mother nor I wanted her to move out, but short of…well, having her committed or something, we couldn't do much to stop her. How do *you* think she's doing, Evan?"

Evan looked into green eyes so much like Anne's that it made him want to cry all over again.

"Not very well."

The waiter brought his espresso then, giving both men a chance to regroup. Evan was thankful it wasn't boiling hot, or he would have burned the hell out of his mouth.

"I don't think she's doing well either," her father said. "I think she's been drinking."

"Yeah, me too. That can't be a good thing with her medication."

Evan felt like he was gossiping or breaking some kind of bond of secrecy, but neither he nor Anne were kids anymore. He cared too much about her to let her destroy herself without even trying to stop it, even if she didn't feel the same way about him.

Her father covered his eyes the same way she had.

"I don't think she's taking medication anymore. I think she's been drinking instead, using that to keep the nightmares away. I know I never dreamed the couple of times I drank myself blind back in college."

"Not the healthiest way to deal with it," Evan said. "I'm sorry, that was way out of line. That's none of my business."

"Of course it's your business! You're her oldest friend, her closest one, too. If anyone in the world truly understands her and cares about her, it's you. Did she talk to you?"

"No, not really. I wasn't there very long."

"I don't know what to do for her. She's twenty years old and paying for her own room and board somehow. I can't just drag her back home, and unless she has some kind of breakdown, I can't force her to get help. By then it might be too late."

His voice broke, and Evan closed his eyes, not wanting to see the older man's face. He couldn't save Anne, he couldn't comfort her father, and he couldn't calm his own reeling heart.

Maybe he should have just stayed in St. Louis. His life there at least had some kind of order. He accomplished things there, and he knew what was coming and how to handle it. Here it was all he could do to manage not to cry.

"Is she still seeing Dr. Lewis?" Evan said.

"Not for several months now, since a few weeks after she moved out. I don't think Anne wants to hear what he or anyone else would say." Mr. Fincastle sat back in his chair then, taking a deep breath. "Well, I'm sorry your holiday has gotten off to such a rotten start, but I really appreciate you calling me. It's long past time I did something, even if I have no idea what that might be. I can't just keep letting her get worse."

The silence between the two men went unnoticed in the noisy shop.

Dwight, a guy who lived two rooms down during Evan's freshman year had started drinking too much, or maybe he had been before he got there. No matter how much his roommate or the resident or his adviser or anyone else talked to him, he couldn't hear a word of it. Dwight made it through that year without getting suspended, but he didn't come back the next. His roommate said his parents forced him into rehab.

He returned subdued and quiet the next year. He'd told Evan he'd relapsed several times, but he was okay. Dwight backed it up by acing all of his classes, taking extra and steadily catching up on the lost time, but he'd never lost that quiet, restrained manner.

Evan was afraid if Anne didn't make some kind of change soon, she'd never have a chance to see what the other side would be like.

"Listen, I'm sorry to rush off," Anne's father said, startling Evan. "I need to make a couple of phone calls. Thank you again for calling and meeting me here. Can you stop by the house before you head back? I know Karen would love to see you."

"Sure, I'll do my best. I'd love to see her too. I don't know if I can do anything, but let me know, okay?"

"I will, Evan." Anne's father hugged him again. "I will. Speak to you soon."

Evan watched him walk out and duck into the bitter wind. He had an equally cold feeling in his gut that nothing was going to get better.

Not for a long time. Maybe not ever.

Chapter 29

Anne walked out of her parents' house, slamming the door behind her. She pounded on the heavy wood twice, knocking the gigantic wreath and a strand of glittering red and green garland off, trying to keep herself from screaming out loud.

Before one of them could open it, she ran down the stairs and across the street to Joe's filthy Datsun hatchback. He'd refused to go inside as always. This time she was glad he'd stayed out here. She closed the car door a little more quietly.

"Let's go," she said before he could ask any questions.

Anne tried to stop herself, but as Joe pulled away in a cloud of blue smoke, she looked back. Her father stood on the front porch. Even from this distance and moving through the oily haze, she could see him wiping at his cheeks.

Well, that's what he deserved for talking to her that way. She was nothing but glad.

"How'd it go, babe?" Joe said with his asshole smirk. "About like it does with my parents?"

Anne ignored him, turning toward the smeary window. She didn't want to deal with him any more than she'd wanted to deal with her father and his selfish demands.

She was not a little girl that he could order around. Not anymore.

Joe touched her hair.

"You all right?"

She turned back to him, suddenly quite sure who she did want to deal with.

Evan. His damn interfering had gotten all of this started, deciding he knew what was best for her yet again. Evan and her father thought they had everything worked out, typical fucking men.

It was usually her mother trying to force Anne to live her life to suit everyone else.

"I'm fine, Joe. Just fine. Can we stop one more place? It won't take long at all. I promise."

FASTER THAN HE would have thought possible, Evan adapted to the routines of Gwen's household. He didn't have much choice from his central sleeping location on the living room sofa. At the very least, doing everything he could to keep up with two whirlwind toddlers left him tired enough to sleep.

And busy enough to keep his mind off how badly his holiday, and his plans, had gone wrong.

The wakeup giggles had drifted back to quarter to seven that morning, as if the boys were gearing up for their pre-dawn raid on Christmas presents the next day. Evan sat cross-legged on the dark blue hearth rug so he could feed the fireplace, while his nephews created a noisy toy car war with rules only they could understand.

Gwen had the good grace and humor to bring him a huge mug of coffee before she retreated back to her bedroom. The promise of pancakes and maple syrup whenever she and Mark finally got up kept Evan and both boys relatively quiet.

Evan lurched to his feet when the apartment's intercom buzzed, not wanting the harsh noise to wake his sister. They weren't expecting Hurricane Ed yet, and he wouldn't bother with the intercom when he had a key. Evan crossed the room as quickly as he could with pins and needles climbing up both legs.

"Meet me downstairs."

"Who… Anne?"

"Of course it's Anne, you son of a bitch. Meet me downstairs or you'll wish you had."

Evan's jaw dropped at the vicious tone of her voice, but she cut the connection before he could say another word. He walked to the end of the hall and jerked the curtains back. Anne was out there, pacing beside an ancient tan car more rust than paint, glaring at the building every few seconds.

Her words finally sank in, and he dropped the curtain, squeezing his eyes and his fists closed.

Son of a bitch. If she was able and willing to say that to him, she was much further gone than he'd thought.

One of the boys squealed laughter just then, and Gwen's sleepy voice answered. They apparently hadn't heard those awful words, but Evan knew he had no choice but to go out there.

He didn't want anyone in that state of mind anywhere near his family. Especially not those kids.

"I'll be back in a minute," he said as he passed through the living room and grabbed his coat. "I won't be long."

Gwen stood in the living room in her robe, rubbing her eyes.

"Dad will be here soon."

"I know. This shouldn't take long."

Evan managed to close the door quietly, but he was more furious than he wanted to admit. After the way she had treated him two days ago, Anne thought she'd just show up at his sister's house making demands?

And he had *never* reacted well to that particular phrase. Call him a bastard, a jackass, an asshole, whatever seemed to fit. He knew he'd been all of those things at one time or another.

But he he'd never been able to tolerate *son of a bitch*, not from Anne or anyone else. He wasn't about to start tolerating it now.

He crossed the street and was nearly beside Anne before she

noticed him. Evan glanced at the smudged, yellowish car windows and saw Joe, to no surprise whatsoever.

Obviously he would be here too. Things might have had some chance of staying calm otherwise.

Anne turned and strode toward him. Her hair and clothes seemed to be clean, at least. Evan was too angry to hope that was any kind of good sign. From the look on her face, so was she. She stopped just a few inches away, and he tried not to draw back at the liquor on her breath.

"Did you talk to my father?"

"Good to see you too, Anne."

"I asked if you talked to my fucking father!" she shouted, jabbing her finger into his chest.

"Yeah, I did." Evan moved out of range of her hands and her breath. "You're showing me the reason why right now."

"Goddamn you! What fucking business is my life of yours, Evan?"

Evan saw her father's eyes, heard him saying of course Anne was his business. He tried to remember how badly he'd wanted to see her just a few days ago.

Now he just wanted her to go away before his sister heard her shouting like this. Or his nephews.

"It's my business because I care about you, and you're falling to pieces right in front of me. How are you possibly drunk at nine in the morning?"

She stepped forward again, cheeks flushed and eyes blazing.

"I am not fucking drunk, and it wouldn't be your concern if I was. You need to concern yourself with your perfect little life and stay the hell out of mine!"

He knew more curtains than his sister's were drawn back, but he didn't dare turn away. That was the second thing he never would have imagined her saying to him, not in a million years.

She knew better than anyone how *imperfect* Evan's life had been. She was one of the main reasons he'd gotten through it so far.

"Stop shouting or I'm going back inside. And I won't open the door or answer any calls while you're acting like this."

"If you don't like the way I'm acting, maybe you'll reconsider telling my father I need to go to goddamn rehab next time," she said, her voice quieter but no less furious. "You don't know the first fucking thing about my life."

"Who the hell do you think you're talking to, Anne? I know more about your life than anyone else possibly could. I know whatever you're doing isn't working."

"You knew me a long time ago. You ran off to college and left me to rot in that blasted hospital. If I did rot after all, you can fucking blame yourself. I know I do."

The blow would not have been harder if she'd punched him in the nose or kicked him in the balls. He had blamed himself, over and over again, through all the years since she'd started having so much trouble. And he'd nearly driven himself crazy with guilt for months after he'd left for college. Getting through that first semester had been the hardest thing he'd ever had to do, until just this moment.

"You can't… you don't know what you're saying."

"I know exactly what I'm saying, and I should have said it a long time ago. If our friendship meant so much to you, if I was so important to you, how could you walk away and leave me there? Do you have any idea how bad it got for me after that?"

Evan stepped back again, but she followed. His head was swimming, and not just from the horrible smell.

He did know. He knew she'd been there for months that time, much longer than before.

"I had to go, Anne, I didn't have any choice. I couldn't help you. I couldn't do anything."

"I'm sure that's what you told yourself. Just walk away, let someone else handle it, anyone else. Well, they handled it alright. They handled it by drugging me out of my mind for months, and they wanted to for the rest of my life. I wasn't able to think or feel anything again until I moved out of my parents house and got off… the fucking…drugs."

"You told me to go," Evan whispered, tears cutting a hot trail down his face. "You told me I had to go, that I had to."

"You know what? That's exactly what I'm going to tell you right now. Go. Get the hell out of my life and stay out. I don't need the drugs, I don't need rehab, and I don't need you!"

"Anne, please, listen to me…"

"No Evan, fuck off! Stay away from me and don't you ever, ever talk to my father again! Fuck off!"

She got in the car and slammed the door before he could say another word. Joe stared up at Evan for what felt like an unreasonably long time. Right before he finally drove away in a cloud that stank worse than Anne's breath, he smiled.

Evan couldn't move or think. He couldn't cry anymore, and the anger that had driven him down to the street had turned into ice in his belly.

Gone. She was gone. And she'd made it painfully clear she didn't want to hear from him anymore either. Not today. Not ever. There was nothing left for him to do but go back inside before he froze to death.

He had to get through the rest of this visit, Christmas and New Year's Eve and few days after. He had to do all of that without screaming until he sent the rest of his mind to wherever his heart had disappeared to.

He turned in time to see the curtain drop at his sister's window. Gwen. He couldn't imagine Mark or one of the kids wanting to watch this disaster unfold. His sister had seen the whole thing, and she'd probably heard quite a bit of it.

Well, unless he wanted to get in his car and head hours south to an empty campus, he didn't have anywhere else to go. Anne's parents' house and certainly his dad's were out of the question.

Evan had to speed up his pace to avoid a car, and by the time he got to the sidewalk the car slowed and turned into the driveway.

Of course. This couldn't have gone any other way.

Maybe he was just a little early, or maybe Evan's thoughts had conjured him out of thin, freezing cold air. Evan turned his head to wipe at his face, hoping the tear marks wouldn't show. That was the last thing he wanted to be explaining to Hurricane Ed.

"Hey, Dad."

"Evan! What the hell are you doing out here?"

His father got out and hugged Evan briefly, a typical grasp-and-pound guy hug. Anne's father had hugged him like a person, like someone he really cared about.

Evan couldn't be thinking about that.

"I had to bring something out to the car," Evan said, "and the boys were a little loud. Need help carrying anything?"

"The boys are always a little loud. Yeah, I could use some help. I brought a bunch more stuff for them to make noise with. Gwen loves it when I do that."

"You're right, Dad, she does. She told me so just this morning."

Evan ended up making three trips, wanting to give his father the chance to greet his grandsons. He also needed to clear his own mind before he could face everyone inside.

Gwen had seen, but he knew she'd never say a word until their father left. And even then, she'd give him the chance to talk to her instead of prying. That was one of the many things he loved about her.

He didn't know if he'd ever be able to talk to her or anyone else about this. All he could do was keep moving, putting one foot in front of the other. He had to just keep breathing until he could get out of here and go back to where things made sense.

Just before he walked back inside with the last armful, Evan stopped, wanting to duck right back out into the cold. He'd finally realized he might be able to escape in a few days, but he wouldn't be gone for long at all.

In less than six months, he'd be right back here, getting settled into his own apartment and a new job, getting ready for at least two years of graduate school.

He knew six months wasn't going to even let him get started pulling his own heart back into some kind of human shape again. He doubted six years would be able to do that. But once again, Evan couldn't think of anything else to do.

There was nothing else to do.

He just kept going.

Chapter 30

After the joyful furor and disruption of Christmas morning, Evan finally got time alone with his sister. Wrapping cleared away, huge brunch devoured, Hurricane Ed departed, Evan's brother-in-law and nephews crashed early, leaving the two of them stationed by the fireplace.

Both of them referred to this rare time as their annual bitch session, even though most of the time the catching up was positive. Evan hoped she wouldn't mind that this year he really did need to complain and commiserate.

Hot toddies in hand and sharing a plate full of ginger cookies, Gwen assured Evan that their father hadn't acted any worse than normal that morning. She was certain Evan's time away only made everything *seem* worse.

For his part, Evan knew he was arguing too much. Just as well as he knew he had no interest in stopping.

"I don't understand why Mom stayed with such a colossal prick."

Gwen smiled, but Evan didn't like the look in her eyes. The days since Anne had yelled at him then walked away were crawling slower than a snail. All he wanted was to get away from here, get back to school and try to make sense of his life again. Staying anywhere near his father wasn't going to help anyone.

"Mom wasn't such a saint herself, Ev."

Evan a deep breath. Did he want to know this? Did he want to hear anything his sister was so reluctant to tell him that she'd kept it to herself all these long years?

"I know she wasn't, of course not. But I don't think she could live up to such a jerk of a husband."

Gwen shook her head, looking away from his eyes.

"There's a lot you don't remember, kiddo."

Evan scowled, almost as annoyed with her as he was with their father. He'd lived away for almost four years, he was about to graduate from college, where he was doing extremely well. He wasn't a kid anymore.

"Yeah, well, why don't you enlighten me? Your advanced age should give you some kind of advantage. Maybe this is your lucky day."

She scowled back for a second, and he knew she'd risen to his bait. Assuming he couldn't take whatever she was talking about was exactly the kind of shit he was getting tired of from their father.

"All right, but remember you asked me. She had an affair, Evan. Not too long after you were born."

Evan couldn't stop his jaw from dropping, and he knew he was staring at her like an idiot.

"Horse shit. I don't believe it."

"Hey, you don't have to believe it, bro. I remember it, and I promise you Dad does too."

"You imagined it, Gwen. You were still a kid, too. There's no way they told you about something like that."

"No, they didn't tell me, not when it happened. I knew something was bad though, from the way they fought."

Evan sat back in his chair, clutching his borrowed pillow covered with cartoon characters he didn't recognize. Much as he'd wanted to vent earlier, now he only wanted to get away and not hear one more word.

No. She was making all of this up.

"They always fought. Up until the day Mom died."

She nodded, then pulled her legs up underneath her on the couch.

"Sure, of course they did. But not like this. Young as I was, I was scared to death they'd hurt each other."

Evan closed his eyes, his stomach twisting acid into his throat. That part he knew she wouldn't make up. Worse fights than he could remember had to be criminal.

"But you don't know…" he said, then he cleared his throat against the burning. "You don't know what they were fighting about. They fought all the time."

"I didn't know then, no. She told me herself. Not long after I left for college. She drove up to see me for the weekend."

Evan remembered his mother leaving like that, but it hadn't occurred to him to see if from her point of view until just now. He'd always felt like she was abandoning him, leaving him at the dubious mercies of his father.

Thinking about those weekends now, when he sat here desperate to escape his own shattered heart, he understood it differently.

"I remember her doing that. I hated it. I felt like she was dumping me."

"No, that wasn't it. She just needed to get away for a while. I understand that way better than I care to admit now. I'm sure Mark does too. Anyway, that weekend I was pissed at Dad, just like you are right now. And I was pissed at her for staying with him. Sound familiar?"

"And she just told you?"

"Nope, I asked her. I asked her what he'd been so nasty about back then, and why she didn't get the hell out."

Gwen looked out the window, and Evan wasn't surprised to see tears standing in her eyes. He'd regretted getting angry with his mom more than he cared to remember, especially about those visits to Chicago without him. He didn't want to imagine how much worse the extra years of adolescent temper made Gwen feel.

"I was pretty rude about it," she said, "but I don't think she would have told me if she hadn't had a few gin and tonics that night. She was always a lot more…honest after those."

Evan blinked, surprised yet again. By the time he'd gotten old enough to have cocktails with his mother, it was too late. He'd never realized how sad such a simple fact could be.

"She was quiet for a while," Gwen said, "then she said she stayed because you were so little. And that it hadn't all been Dad's fault. I of course argued with her, saying she couldn't have done anything to justify him being such a jackass."

Evan dreaded hearing the words, but the idea had taken root in his mind like a hideous burrowing insect. If he couldn't find a way to contain and control it, he was afraid all his memories of his mother would sour and rot.

"Then she just said it. Mrs. Megan Connor Griffith sat on that nasty old futon I used to have in her tidy little blue traveling dress and said, 'I had an affair.' I reacted about the same way you did, but I knew she was telling me the truth."

"What happened?"

"She probably had postpartum depression, that's what it sounds like to me now. Ed was working more hours than normal, trying to make partner, and she'd been home for a while. This is not about you, Evan. Don't you *dare* think that."

He realized he had been going down that exact road, his brain trying to make it all his fault. Such nonsense, as if he'd had anything to do with the timing or the fact of his birth. But his mind was trying to go there anyway.

"She started going out, taking you with her, finally finding a place she trusted to keep an eye on you. I remember that part," she said, smiling. "She assured me she was just as paranoid with me, and Dad did too. She acted like everyone in the world was going to steal you if she turned her back for a second.

"Anyway, she went to a book club, reading club, something like that, and she met a guy there. She wouldn't tell me anything about him except he paid more attention to her than Dad had for a while. At least she thought so. And all of it got out of hand."

The sympathy for his father was making Evan more sick than his anger had. He wasn't ready or willing to feel any sort of compassion for Ed.

"How did Dad find out?"

"It was stupid, really. I've wondered if she did it on purpose so it would all have to stop, but I never asked her. She told him she was going to visit Aunt Sandy in Pittsburgh. The hotel in Chicago showed up on the credit card bill. That could not have been an accident. She was way too smart for that."

"How long? How long did it go on?"

Gwen shrugged, shaking her head and sighing again.

"I never did get a straight answer on that, and I stopped asking. I think it was almost a year."

Evan felt like she'd punched him in the gut, or like his mother had. A year? An entire year? That wasn't just a betrayal of their father, not at all. She had to have been focused on this mystery guy when Evan himself had needed her most.

"For fuck's sake… A year?"

"I think so, that's the idea I got."

"Did you ever ask Dad about it?"

"You know, I did think about it. I thought about that a lot. By the time I thought it all over and tried to make some sense out of it, I was wondering why *he* stayed with *her*. A year is a hell of a lot different than some random one-night stand. But I never did ask him, and once she died I just couldn't."

Evan rubbed his eyes, trying to keep his tears from falling. Now he knew, he understood so many things.

Gwen coming home from college so rarely, seething and furious. His mother seeming to feel she deserved any amount of screaming Ed or Gwen cared to dish out.

And his father, the betrayed and horrified air he carried to this day whenever anyone mentioned their mother. Had he just been waiting, all those years, for his wife to finally abandon him forever?

A far worse thought than sympathy for his father burst through the mess in his head then, a thought that had been digging around in that muck most of his life.

"Hang on, Gwen. This is going to sound like some kind of adolescent pissed-off fantasy, and it probably is. If I don't ask, it's going to drive me crazy. Are you… Do you believe the affair started after I was born, not before?"

His sister pursed her lips, looking more like Ed than she ever would have admitted.

"I do believe that, Evan. I understand why you would have wished for a different father. I know I did. But I'm afraid you're stuck with Ed, just like I am."

"I don't look or act anything like him, and I don't think he ever did like me. That might be why."

"No, stop this. Even if there were any chance of that, and I'm sure there's not, he raised you. I don't think he likes much of anybody, but I know he loves you and me both. He's your father. There's no reason to dig into a mess like this. Sheesh, I'm sorry, Ev. I shouldn't have told you all of that. You were fine without it."

He shook his head, looking into his sister's brown eyes. Ed's eyes. He wondered then if his dad had always been so tough on him because he was looking into his lost wife's eyes in his son's face.

"Don't apologize," he said. "She wasn't a saint anymore than the rest of us are, but I'm not going to run down and get DNA tests or anything. If he ever even suspected…that, it explains a whole lot of things that have bothered me for years."

"Yeah, I eventually felt that way about all of it. But finding out what happened knocked me on my ass for a long time. Are you okay?"

"I think I'd rather know than not. I've spent a lot of time being angry about her dying, angry at her. And angry at you. You knew her as an adult. I never did."

"That could have been a blessing in disguise, brother."

"You don't really think that, Gwen. Good or bad, I never really got to know her. That's part of her I never had and I never will. Trust me. I'd rather know. Don't try to protect me, old lady."

She laughed a little, then stretched her arms above her head.

"Well, if you're going to sit at the grownups' table now, want to join me in one of Mom's beloved gin and tonics? I get the good stuff though. None of the cheap swill she had to put up with."

"Absolutely. Show me how to make one and we'll see who passes out first."

Evan hugged his sister tight.

"Thanks for telling me, Gwen. I'm glad to know more about who she really was, even if it sucks."

"That wasn't who she was," Gwen said, walking ahead of him into the kitchen. "It was just something that happened. I'm not saying it was justified, any more than Ed acting like such a prick was. She wasn't perfect. Neither was he. Once I got over being so pissed at both of them, I figured that took the pressure off of you and me."

Chapter 31

Anne woke slowly, painfully, her mind dragged up through the darkness and squeezed back inside her far too small skull. A vise, someone had a vise around her skull.

"Anne, come on, wake up!"

The vise shifted until it was driving into her skull through her ears, the points sharp and white hot. Someone shook her shoulder, someone who had been saying her name for a long time. She opened her eyes.

"What do you want?"

She tried to keep her voice from reaching her throbbing ears. The room was dark, thank goodness, but she could still see someone sitting on the edge of her bed. Someone who reeked of cheap cigarettes.

Joe.

"If you want to keep this shitty roof over your head, get up and let's go." He took a long, glowing drag. "You can get it filled again today."

Anne closed her eyes and turned away. The darkness had been good. It had been empty. It had been quiet. So far, the darkness was worth the hangover that came with it.

She'd hoped the hangover would get better with time. Lately it seemed to be getting worse.

"I'm not going to ask you again."

He'd only gotten really angry with her one time, a few months ago. She didn't want to go through that again. She pushed herself up to the edge of the mattress on the floor.

"I'm up. Get out of here so I can get dressed."

"Sure, whatever. Nothing I haven't seen before." He did leave her in peace.

Anne braced herself against the nausea when she stood up, but that part wasn't too bad. Her stomach twisted and clenched, but nothing threatened to eject itself out of her.

Today the headache was going to take center stage. That was easy enough to deal with. More booze took care of that, every single time.

When she turned on the light in the bathroom, Anne caught her reflection by accident. She tried not to look at herself in mirrors anymore.

Her eyes were the same, even bloodshot and swollen. Her face looked puffy and terrible though, as if it had been inflated somehow. And there was nothing in that mirror she could stand to see anymore. The woman staring back at her looked more like forty-four than twenty-four. Maybe fifty-four.

Anne looked away and turned on the water in the shower.

She couldn't go out looking this bad, not if they were going to score. She had enough trouble fooling people as it was. No need to take any more chances, not with Joe's temper stirring up.

More booze, that's all she needed, more booze. Anne stood under the hot water, trying to remember when she'd first had that thought. How long? Two years ago? Three?

Back then, it had only been a drink in the evenings, a new thing to her in her new apartment. A glass of wine, which she didn't love. A mixed drink, which she did.

Shampoo ran into her eyes, making her gasp, and she did remember the first time. It was before she'd met Joe, but only days before.

Five years ago.

She and her roommates had been celebrating something, lost to the fog of so many intoxicated days. Anne had had more to drink that night than she ever had before, and she'd passed out rather than falling asleep.

When she'd woken up the next morning, she'd had her first hangover. That one had been the puking kind. But as soon as she staggered away from the toilet, she realized she'd had her first dreamless night in almost ten years too. Not a single image lingered on her mind's eye, waiting to terrorize her daylight hours.

Anne turned off the water, stepping carefully onto the stained mat.

Stopping the medication had been easy after she'd repeated the experiment a week later. Drink too much, pass out, wake up with no dreams. She'd never even gotten the bottle out of her medicine cabinet after that.

A few days later, when Joe came back to her place the first time, he'd come out of the bathroom bouncing one of her pill bottles in one hand.

"What are these for, babe?"

"I have a lot of trouble with nightmares. I stopped taking them a few days ago. I'm not going to get the prescription refilled again."

"Hang on, let's talk about that," he said, putting the bottle in his pocket and sitting down beside her. "These are solid gold, babe. Do you pay for them?"

"No, I'm still on my Dad's policy. I will be for a few more years, then my doctor said I could get them through the state as long as they're prescribed."

Joe's eyes had widened, and Anne remembered now that his look made her uneasy. Why was he so excited about her prescription? She'd always been quietly ashamed of all the pills she'd used over the years trying to feel normal, trying to act normal.

"Well, listen, I have an idea. How about if you let me see what I can get for these. Don't cancel anything just yet. Then if it works out and you still don't need them, we'll be in business. Real business."

Anne winced trying to brush out her hair. It was too long again, that happened so quickly. She'd have to get it cut, even though Evan liked it better long.

"Where the hell did that come from?" she whispered.

She hadn't seen Evan for a long time now. Almost five years. She doubted she'd ever see him again after the way she'd talked to him the last time.

Well, he had been getting way too damned much into her business, and dragging her father into it too. She and her parents had been getting along just fine until Evan tried once again to fix everything.

He fixed things into a massive disaster. She was better off without him.

She walked into her bedroom to get dressed, wondering what day of the week it was. She could refill her prescriptions on the first, but she didn't know anything beyond that. The booze had taken the nightmares, but it had taken a lot of her short-term memory with it.

She pulled out a blue sundress, one that used to fit her well, and got out a cheap belt that almost matched. She had to have the belt to hide how loose the dress and all the rest of her clothes were now.

Joe was getting pretty good money for her pills, sure, but that didn't mean they had enough to waste on clothes. That's what he told her, anyway.

Anne walked over to her dresser and started opening drawers, looking for her paper prescriptions. That was when Joe had gotten so angry, the one time a new pharmacist asked to see the original prescription. She'd been afraid her parents had ratted her out and she wouldn't be able to get the pills anymore. All she wanted was the original paper scrip.

That short delay, time enough to go back to the apartment and dig until she found it, had been too long for Joe. He made sure Anne never forgot again.

She knew she'd need booze before they left. That trick had taken a while longer for her to learn, using the booze to stop her visions during the day too. At first she only drank at night, just enough to force herself into a deep sleep.

Enough turned into a moving target that never lasted very long, though.

Once she started drinking during the day, she realized the visions were getting weaker. She wasn't seeing the horrible death masks anymore, at least not clearly. All she saw was a shadow, then a hint as faint as Joe's cigarette smoke. And then they were gone.

She was having trouble focusing on their faces by then, but at least she could try. It had been years since she'd reliably seen anyone's face.

Anyone except Evan's.

"Goddamn it, get the hell out of my head."

She finally found the note behind a jumbled pile of socks with too many holes to wear, wondering as she always did why the doctor kept renewing it.

Anne hadn't been to a doctor since she'd started drinking so much. She wondered if her father put Dr. Lewis up to it, hoping Anne would take the pills someday if she still had them.

She wondered if either of them suspected the pills were paying the rent and the utilities and the food and gas for Joe's car.

And the pills payed for the booze. The booze that kept the bad dreams and visions away.

Anne walked into the cluttered living room, knowing Joe would be waiting for her. He would never let her walk by, not today. Not when she could get more of what he needed more and more, or at least the money to pay for it. And she could always tell where he was by the stink of his cheap cigarettes.

He was sitting on the beat up thrift store couch, clouds floating around his head after such a short time. If he was so desperate for money that he had to sell her pills, why did he waste so damn much money on those cigarettes?

Maybe she didn't care so much about his temper today.

"Where did you sleep last night, Joe?"

"I was right here, on this nasty couch."

She shook her head, heading into the kitchen for coffee. She hadn't caught anything from him for a few months, not that she knew of. But three trips to the health department in the last few years had taught her never to trust him again.

"Yeah, right. I'm sure you were on something. Somebody, more like."

"No, I was right here. I can't sleep with you anymore. Your crazy ass dreams keep me awake all night."

Anne froze, barely keeping a grip on her cup before she put it down.

"Dreams?" she whispered.

"Yeah, you toss and turn, kicking and thrashing, making all kinds of damn noise in the middle of the night."

She poured the coffee, having a terrible time keeping most of it in the cup. That was the whole point of the booze, that had been the *only* point of it.

The booze kept the nightmares away.

"When? When did I start doing that, Joe?"

"I don't know, a month ago? Two?"

She turned to get the sugar, her heart pounding in her ears. How could she not know about nightmares that bad? Drinking enough to knock herself out was the first thing that stopped them, the first thing since she was eleven years old.

Her dreams had always been worst right before something terrible was about to happen.

Always.

"I can't even trust my own mind…"

"What? Come on, get a move on. I got a score for these in a couple of hours, but she won't wait. We need to get that filled now."

Anne swallowed too much of the coffee, too hot, tears filling her eyes at the burning in her mouth and throat. She gripped the edge of the counter and drank the rest.

The damage was done now, why try to deny that? She had no idea if she meant her scorched mouth or the dreams.

She opened the freezer and got a bottle of vodka, only a few swallows left from the day before. They were down to only two bottles in there. They'd have to use the money from her pills for more today. She drained it, then dropped it on top of the others in the garbage.

The cold alcohol numbed her mouth and throat. She hoped it would do the same for her mind.

"You got the scrip?"

"Yeah, I got it. I got it."

That was one lesson she didn't have to learn twice. Getting between Joe and his scores for something as simple as needing her original prescription had turned into another kind of nightmare. She followed him out without another word.

While he drove, Anne studied the people on the sides of the road. She looked at their faces, trying to see their features. That was the other thing the booze had stopped, once she'd started drinking during the day. The visions of how everyone was going to die.

She'd had long stretches when she was a kid, months at a time, when she could hardly see anyone at all. She only saw a charred mess, a bloody mess, a blue and drowned mess.

There had been a few times when the only person she'd been able to see was Evan. Those had been right before her trips to the hospital, always. She jumped when Joe spoke.

"Wake up! Get in there in case there's a line. I don't want to miss this one. I think she'll be a repeat buyer."

Anne looked around, finally noticing they were parked outside of the drug store. Joe was still in the car, but he was watching her.

"All right, Joe. I'll be right back."

He never went in with her, not anymore. He'd gotten paranoid about being on the security camera or some such shit. He either didn't think Anne being on the camera was such a big deal, or he just didn't care. He told her it was her scrip and the doctor kept filling it, so why worry about that now?

Anne found she cared less and less about things like that. If she did get picked up, it would be what she deserved anyway, letting him sell her pills. She walked to the back of the store as fast as she could, to the pharmacy tucked away behind windows.

"Yeah, I need to get this filled?"

The pharmacist stared at her, and Anne looked away. She wasn't afraid of him seeing her. He saw her every month.

She was terrified of seeing him.

She hadn't seen his warm brown eyes behind his tiny glasses or the harsh lighting glaring off of his bald head. She hadn't seen him smiling or looking suspicious or even worried about her.

She'd seen a death mask, the first in more than four years. The man's face was wasted, way past the skin and bone she avoided in her own mirror every morning. Skeletal, with a huge discolored mass starting on top of his head and spreading down over one side of his face. Some kind of tumor, some kind of growth.

She didn't know if it would be inside his head, in his brain, or if it would start on that smooth, hairless scalp, but whatever it was would be the end of him. She stared at her feet.

"Ms. Fincastle? May I see your ID please?"

Anne fumbled in her purse. He'd never asked for it before.

Something *was* up. That didn't matter now. She just had to get out of here.

She pulled her state ID card out of her wallet and handed it to him, looking anywhere but at the corpse in front of her.

"Okay, this is fine. It'll be a few minutes."

He handed the card back and turned away. Anne let out her breath, and she dropped the card in her purse instead of struggling with her wallet. Her hands were shaking worse than before.

No, she couldn't trust her brain, her mind, her heart, any part of her. If this was going to start again after several swallows of booze, even that tiny bit of peace was failing her.

She knew it would only get worse. It always had, for most of her life it had.

First the nightmares, then the visions, then her memories would start up again.

She'd remember the terrible thing before it happened, and just like the visions, there wouldn't be a damn thing she could do about it.

She'd see it, over and over and over again.

Then she'd have to live it.

She paced around the store, staring at greeting cards, cosmetics, random junk, trying not to look at anyone. She didn't want to know if it was happening with other people or not.

She didn't want to know.

She had to know.

She was going to go crazy in the next five minutes if she didn't.

Anne almost crashed into a little girl, squatting down in front of a bunch of toys. The girl looked up, and Anne jerked away from her.

That little girl didn't have to worry about getting old enough to need reading glasses or adult diapers. That little girl wasn't even going to make it to needing tampons.

Anne saw a mass of blood and bruises, half of the girl's brown hair torn away. The little girl was going to get killed in a car wreck before five more years went by.

Tears stood in Anne's eyes and she turned away, right into another face. This man was going to get caught in a fire, some kind of horrible fire. His whole face was red and black. She hoped he would be asleep when it happened. She covered her eyes, not wanting to see one more thing.

How much more booze could she possibly drink in one day? She was already getting terrible heartburn at night, and her face and hands were always puffy even though she was so thin. She didn't know if she could take any more.

"Ms. Fincastle?"

Anne turned and walked back to the pharmacy, looking at her feet, wiping her eyes before he could see. Maybe she should just stop the booze, not have another drop. If it wasn't going to work anymore, she could try her pills again.

The dreams had never stopped with the pills, but they hadn't been quite as bad. And sometimes she could go a little longer before she had to go to the hospital. Maybe she could do that instead.

Or maybe Joe would blow his temper so badly that Anne wouldn't care about anything anymore.

"Here you go," the pharmacist said, handing her the little white bag with blue writing on the side. "Take care now."

"Thanks." She glanced up at his tie, making sure to avoid his face.

She turned to leave, opening her purse to drop the bag in. Something slipped out of her hand, and she caught it before it could hit the floor. A folded piece of paper, something she'd never gotten with her pills before.

She stopped just inside the door. Whatever it was, she needed to look at it before she got to Joe's car. Just as surely as she knew how everyone in the store was going to die, she knew she couldn't walk out the door first.

Mostly a blank page, with her father's familiar scrawl in the middle.

Anne, please get in touch with me, sweetheart. I have to talk to you, and I'm worried about you. Please give me a call or stop by my office as soon as you get this. I love you. Dad.

This time tears streamed down her face faster than she could stop them. She hadn't spoken to her dad in months, and she couldn't remember the last time she'd seen him. He was the only one left who understood how bad it could get for her when the nightmares started.

Only her dad or Evan had ever understood. She folded the note up and put it in a tiny pocket hidden in her purse, wiped at her face, and pushed the door open.

Joe was standing, chest against his car, hands behind him. He stared into her eyes and mouthed *You fucking bitch.*

Anne drew back, but not before the police officers standing behind Joe saw her. One of them walked toward her.

Anne knew he was going to die by his own hand, by his own gun, but she pushed that to the back of her mind. She couldn't even run, not with several others standing all around him.

All she could do was stare at Joe. For the first time since she'd met him, she could see what was going to become of him.

Joe was going to prison, and Joe was going to die there. He was going to be beaten to death. Skull was caved in, eyes swollen shut, the rest of his face a mass of bruises and blood.

Anne walked out the door to meet the officer.

Whatever was going to happen, she was going to walk away from Joe, and he was never, ever going to be able to follow her again. He was never going to *see* her again.

Even if her nightmares had started again, that one long nightmare was coming to an end.

Chapter 32

THE HARD PLASTIC chair hurt Anne's hips, her spine, the backs of her thighs. And the room was cold, so cold her bones were aching. The baggy cotton dress and sandals were fine out in the sun, but this place felt like a meat locker.

Anne shifted again, trying to find an unbruised place anywhere on her body. She didn't think there were any left. The officers had left the room again, but she knew someone would be watching her. There had to be cameras, and that huge mirror certainly had people on the other side.

She'd seen one of the cops glance at it way too many times when they were asking her endless questions.

The door opened slowly, and Anne cringed back against the awful chair, the bones she was sitting on crying out in protest. More questions, more accusations, more things she couldn't understand through the growing fog in her brain.

Her father walked through instead.

"Anne!"

She tried to stand to greet him, but she moved like an old, weak woman. He was around the metal table before she could get to her feet. He lifted her up, squeezing her tight. Anne was glad to see him, but she was more grateful for his warmth.

"Dad," she whispered.

"Are you okay? I've been here for over an hour, but they wouldn't let me back here to see you."

"I'm not having a great day, no." She sat as gently as she could. "I'm glad to see you."

"Listen to me, sweetheart. I can't say much, but have you told them anything? My lawyer can't handle this, but she found someone."

Anne closed her eyes, trying to remember. She walked out of the drug store, the police took Joe away forever, and then they brought her here. Her thoughts had been so hazy since then. She wasn't sure what she'd said or what she'd imagined.

All she could remember clearly was seeing how every single person in the police station was going to die. At least right now she couldn't see that with her father.

"I don't really remember, Dad. They have to know the pills were mine."

"They do. Joe sold to an undercover officer, or he was trying to. She saw the pill bottles, the empty ones he had with him. They've been after him for a while now, so that may help you."

That had to be the new score Joe was so excited about that morning, the reason he'd dragged Anne out the door so fast. She looked down at her hands on the freezing steel table. The shakes would start soon. She felt them long before she saw them.

Only one scorching cup of coffee explained her headache, and not a single bite to eat all day explained her weakness.

The biggest problem she was going to have was from only a few swallows of vodka more than three hours ago.

"What should I be saying, Dad?"

"Don't say anything else to them until the attorney gets here, okay? I talked to her just now on the phone, it shouldn't be more than half an hour. She did get them to let me see you. Do you need anything, sweetheart?"

The needs swirled through Anne's head, spinning into a mess she couldn't see the top or bottom of.

I need a soft chair. I need a warm coat. I need a gallon of coffee.

I need an entire pot of Mom's macaroni and cheese. I need a fifth of freezing cold vodka.

I need...

I need to see Evan.

The last one surprised her, but once that thought showed up it drowned out all of the others.

Years, so many years. How could she have passed so much of her life without seeing someone she'd been so close to for so long? So long without the closest friend she'd ever had?

She shook her head, trying to keep that howling empty pit where her heart should have been from taking over every other part of her.

"I could use something to eat," she finally said, looking into her father's green eyes. "And maybe a blanket?"

He leaned forward and hugged her hard again, and Anne couldn't think of how he must have been feeling. He'd always worried about her so much, always tried to do everything he could to keep her safe and warm and sane.

And now she was none of those things.

She hadn't been safe or warm or sane for so long.

"I'll see what I can do. Love you."

Anne squeezed his hand for as long as she could before he walked away.

"Love you too."

After he closed the door behind him, Anne sat forward, holding her head in her hands. Now the headache and even the cold were fading to the background.

The shaking was getting worse, so much worse, and faster than it ever had before. The trembling in her hands was spreading into her arms, her chest, every muscle and fiber in her whole body.

She hadn't gone more than three hours without a drink for... how long now? It had to be at least two years, maybe longer.

That was what usually got her out of bed in the middle of the night and again in the morning, the shivering and shaking that got so bad it woke her out of the dead sleep that had started the drinking to begin with.

After the first few times, that jittery stagger into the kitchen started to seem normal. That was the hell of it. She hadn't even thought about how fucked up that was for years now. Having to find a slug of whatever she could before she could even take a piss.

It was just how she got though the day.

The door opened again, but this time it was the police woman who'd taken Anne out of the car that morning. The full body and cavity search might have been a little bit harder if it had been a man, but she didn't think so. She didn't want to find out.

The woman put a sandwich on the table, a real sandwich from a restaurant, not one out of a vending machine. The smell of fresh bread and meat made Anne's mouth water. The officer also had a thick blanket and two pillows. Whoever this attorney was her father had found, she had some kind of pull around here.

"You getting the shakes?"

Anne looked up, trying her best to keep her eyes steady. The woman was maybe ten years older, and even in her dark, hard face, her eyes were as concerned as her voice was.

"I'm okay. The food will help, thank you."

The woman, Officer Murray according to her badge, looked Anne up and down. There was no way to hide the way her hands were trembling now.

"Want me to send someone in to help you with that?"

"No, I'll be all right."

"You realize you can't get a drink in here, don't you?" Officer Murray said, tilting her head and raising her eyebrows. "It's just going to keep getting worse. How long since you were sober, Anne?"

"I don't know," Anne whispered, staring at her jerking hands. "A long, long time."

"I'm sending someone in," the officer said, nodding once. "Just listen to her. She's not going to ask you about the pills or that guy or anything else that can get you in trouble. But she can help you with the DTs."

Anne looked back up, surprised and horrified by the word. DTs? She knew what that was, she knew what it meant. She had never thought of herself that way.

She'd been thinking a lot of bad things about herself for a while now, most of her life, but not that. That was for homeless men, bag ladies, bums she used to see hanging around digging through the dumpsters where she'd hidden the gun the day Evan's mother died.

Not her.

"Is it okay with my Dad?"

"I'll check first to make sure, I promise. I really think you need to talk to her."

"If Dad says it's okay, she can come in."

Once she got the pillows arranged on the chair and the comforter around her shoulders, Anne ate the sandwich as fast as she could. Officer Murray had left a bottle of water too, and she swallowed almost all of it in one go. That helped with her headache and with the gnawing in her belly, but if anything the shakes got worse.

The *DTs* got worse.

Anne wrapped the comforter over her head and rested her head on the table.

Was she an alcoholic? Had she crossed over that line just like she had so many others since she'd moved out of her father's house? Since she'd last seen Evan's beautiful blue eyes?

She was comfortable with lazy, worthless, whore, bitch, useless, any number of words Joe had called her over the past few months. And she'd called herself even worse words, taken those in and made them part of herself.

Crazy, loony, slut, nuts, psycho. A girl with real *issues*.

But this was a new word, and it chafed and hurt her with its sharp edges. All she'd wanted to do was make the dreams stop, give herself some kind of peace and calm for even a few hours at night. But it was those hours at night that were giving her the shakes, the fucking DTs, and Joe said the nightmares had come back already too.

If she was hooked on the booze on top of everything else, and the nightmares and visions were still coming back, what was the point of drawing another shaking, poisonous breath into her lungs?

"Ms. Fincastle?"

Anne jumped, jerking up from under the comforter. She hadn't been asleep, the shakes were way too bad for that. She hadn't heard anyone come into the room either.

"I'm Dr. Martinez."

The woman was tall, not nearly as dark as Officer Murray, and dressed in a black pantsuit instead of a blue police uniform. Even with her saying doctor, Anne thought she looked more like a lawyer than a doctor. Dr. Lewis had always worn casual clothes, slacks and a sweater, when Anne had talked to him.

But that was a long time ago.

"I'm Anne."

Anne shook her hand, embarrassed by how cold and damp her own was.

Dr. Martinez sat in the same place the police officers had when they asked her so many questions for so long.

"I just talked to your father, and I spoke to Dr. Lewis on the phone. Is it all right if I talk to you for a little while?"

Anne's eyes filled with tears. All she could do was nod.

"I can see your hands trembling, Anne. Are you coming off anything besides alcohol?"

Anne shook her head. She couldn't remember how long it had been since she'd tried anything else. Nothing Joe or anyone else had brought to her apartment had ever worked as well as the vodka had.

"Well, I hope you're telling me the truth, but it doesn't make that big of a difference today. Anything else will make you feel like shit. It's stopping the alcohol that can kill you. How long since you've had a drink?"

"Since eleven this morning."

"That's only about four hours. What about last night? Did you sleep?"

"Yeah, for a long time. But I had... I had a drink during the night."

The doctor took a deep breath, made some notes, then looked up at Anne.

"So for you to be shaking that badly you're in a pretty bad way, aren't you?"

"I'm in a bad way all around."

"I need you to listen to me, Anne. I've got some pills here that will calm the shaking down. You need to take them. If you don't, this is going to kill you."

Anne shivered again, this time from the cold settling into her stomach. The pills didn't sound like a good idea to her, not after what other pills had put her through.

She *did* want to quit the booze. She'd been wanting to quit that for a long time. Starting something else didn't seem like a good way to do that. Her very first experience with pills had put her into the hospital the first time, too.

"I just want to stop drinking. I want to stop all of this, not start something new. You said the drinking was going to kill me."

"No, not quite," the doctor said, reaching into her briefcase. "*Stopping* the alcohol could very well kill you in the shape you're in. You do need to stop drinking, but right now you've got to stop the DTs."

There was that word again. Anne hadn't heard it all that long ago, but it already fit into her inventory of herself. Dr. Martinez set a bottle of pills on the table.

"Wanting to stop drinking is great, I'm glad you said that. But letting the withdrawal take you out isn't the smartest way to do that. You have a decision to make, Anne, probably a lot of them. What you do in the next couple of hours will show me, and most of all yourself, whether you want to live or not."

Anne stared at the bottle, thinking of the day she'd gotten caught in the vision, caught up inside her own frozen body. She remembered screaming at Evan inside her head not to give up on her, but he'd walked away anyway.

Then she'd *pushed* him away, so hard her cheeks burned even now thinking about it.

For Joe. For fucking Joe.

She'd driven her best friend away for a worthless thug who only wanted her so he could sell her damn pills.

"Listen, you've got a little time yet," the doctor said. "I'm going to leave these with you. If your symptoms get much worse, it might be out of your hands before too long. You look thin and run down enough that seizures or a stroke are a real possibility. But I need you to pay attention to me now. Your best chance of turning your life around is to make the choice for yourself, Anne. Don't make us force it on you. You do it for yourself."

She put another bottle of water on the table and stood.

"If you need me, just let someone know. If I'm not here, Dr. Andrews will be. Take care."

Anne clenched her teeth, willing herself not to start humming as the doctor closed the door. That was one of the worst things that had been going on since she was eleven years old, the awful humming she had no control over.

The shakes seemed to be concentrating in her mind now, inside her fucking brain. She pushed against her eyes with the heels of her hands, bursts of purple and blue and black swirling against her eyelids.

That internal kaleidoscope faded and split into three fields, then glared into bright white. Anne kept her hands over her eyes, but she started rocking, humming and rocking even when the pillows slipped away from the terrible hard chair.

After so many years and so much drinking, she'd dared imagine this one thing would never come back, that this one bit of madness would leave her alone.

The screens exploded into life.

Anne sat on a bed on one screen, staring at the wall in front of her. Something about her eyes let her know it wasn't the same thing she'd had before, the catatonia.

Her eyes weren't frozen. They were empty.

Two nurses came in and picked Anne up, putting her in a plastic wheelchair. They moved her into a bathroom and started to undress her. They took off her diaper before they wheeled her into the shower.

At the same time, Anne walked down the stairs at her parents' house, taking each step slowly and deliberately. She listened to voices in the living room, her mother, her father, and one other, a man's voice she didn't recognize at first. Before she reached the bottom step, everyone laughed together.

Evan. Her parents were talking to Evan.

And in this memory, she was able to think and feel, and what she felt was elation. She was going to see her friend after so much time apart.

When she walked into the living room, he stood. Without a word, he had her in a huge hug, picking her up and squeezing her so tight it took her breath. In his arms, she found she could breathe again for the first time in years.

At the same time, Anne was in her stinking apartment, laying on the couch. Joe and his cigarettes were gone, but something else made her want to gag and retch. Something rotten. Something foul.

She had shit herself, but no matter how she tried she couldn't move to get away from the mess. She couldn't seem to move anything at all. Her heart pounded in her ears, making her head keep time with it.

Then her heart beat slower.

The beats were further and further apart until they gradually stopped. Anne heard her breath leave in a light gasp, almost like a sigh before falling asleep.

This was a sleep she would never wake up from.

She sat back in her police station chair and closed her eyes, her runaway muscles the least important problem she had to face. She didn't have to ask anyone what these visions meant, and she didn't need to learn a single new word.

Joe had brought a bunch of his buddies over to her apartment. From the beginning, he'd had people crashing on the couch, on the floor, anywhere they could fit.

One of the guys seemed like he was drunk every time Anne saw him, even though he never took a drink or smoked anything. He did buy her pills from Joe.

After he stopped coming around, she heard he'd poured a fifth of cheap whiskey on top of the pills. That guy would never show up anywhere on the outside of a nursing home again.

If she kept on going like this, that was how she would end up. Even if she did finally manage to stop, her mind would never recover.

Anne knew if she somehow got out of here and went back to her apartment, if that was even possible anymore, if she went back and never touched another drop, Dr. Martinez was right. Drinking was going to kill her, or at least kill her mind.

But not drinking could kill her just as dead.

She glanced down at the pills again. Her hands were probably shaking too badly to open the bottle now, but she was still afraid to touch them.

All that left was her parents' house. And Evan. Would he ever want to see her again? If she cleaned herself up and tried to make things right, would he let her?

Since that Christmas morning years ago, when she'd gotten Joe to drive her to Gwen's house to scream at him, drunk off her ass at nine in the morning, she hadn't heard a word from him.

She hadn't tried to find him either. She hadn't even really *thought* about finding him.

Up until Joe had shaken her awake that morning, she'd convinced herself Evan was nothing but a bad thing from her past, something she needed to put behind her. He'd been on her dad's side, trying to force her into rehab for a problem she didn't have in the first place.

That had been before the DTs though, before her body started trying to shake itself to pieces unless she poured more acid down her throat.

Seeing her father today, knowing he'd done everything he could to help her when it was probably already too late, had jarred her back into reality.

Of course her father didn't want to hurt her. He never had.

Had her mind gotten so twisted that she'd been thinking about Evan in the same screwed up way?

"Why would he ever want to see me?" she whispered, picking up the bottle. The pills inside rattled faintly.

Even if she did do all she could to get back to herself, to force herself back into some kind of normal life, whatever was left of it, she'd been so terrible to him. He'd turned away from her and never looked back. Why would years of no contact make him want to see her now?

The vision was so real, so deep within her. His strong arms around her, the heat of his body, the rich, safe smell of his skin, his much deeper voice whispering her name. Nothing she'd ever seen so clearly and moved toward had failed to happen.

She'd driven the visions away with the booze, but they had never been untrue.

Maybe this one was no different.

Anne had to try five times, but she finally managed to get the bottle open. The doctor said what, four of the pills?

She tried to get that many out, but a particularly vicious tremor spilled all of them onto the table.

She pushed four to the side, then went to work on the water bottle. She only spilled a little when she finally twisted the lid off.

All three of the visions were still strong inside her mind, each screen equally bright and vivid.

Anne with her brain destroyed by the vodka, people having to do every single thing for her. Anne lying dead in her own apartment, without nurses or anyone else to clean up her own shit before she died in it.

Anne walking into Evan's arms, stepping into his warm, safe embrace for the first time in so long.

She'd never known how to make one or the other of her visions come true. If she made the wrong choice now, the results could be much worse than getting picked up and going to jail.

Losing her own mind, such as it had become, would be even worse than Joe finally managing to beat her to death. But if she never made any choice at all, she wouldn't have any kind of chance.

Anne picked up four of the pills, watching them jitter in the palm of her hand. She hadn't made any kind of choice, good or bad, for longer than she could remember.

She had to make one now while she still had any mind left.

She swallowed the pills, closing her eyes as the cold water washed them down.

The only vision left found her in the arms of her friend.

PART VI
EVERYTHING TURNS

Chapter 33

ANNE FOLLOWED her mother into her childhood bedroom, caught in a waking dream that felt closer to a nightmare with every step. Back in her parents' house. Moving back home, at twenty-five years old.

Getting through the days in the hospital and weeks of rehab, gladly accepting probation instead of jail time, those certainly felt like some kind of success.

Her life was a different story, though. What kind of failure was she going to be if her life kept going like this?

"We can change anything you like, Annie. We want you to feel at home."

"I *am* at home, Mom," she said, walking over to look out the window. "Like I never even left."

She could see Evan's house from here, or at least where he used to live. His father didn't live there anymore. That was one of the things that had changed, and not in a good way. Not being able to walk into that house and even see pictures of her friend bothered her.

She wouldn't see his mother, with the same fair skin and pale blue eyes as Evan. She'd never see Evan's mom again. She wouldn't see his father, who had the same lanky body shape.

Evan's father, who'd never seemed to stop blaming Anne for the death of his wife.

Anne wasn't always sure whether knowing Mrs. Griffith was going to die had helped her, Anne, Mr. Griffith, Evan, or anyone else. The strain probably had sent Anne to the hospital just a little bit faster.

"It's going to be fine." Her mother walked in to sit on Anne's bed. "You can get your feet under you again. Take as long as you need."

"I've never had my feet under me. You know that as well as I do."

Anne regretted her words before she stopped speaking. Her mother was making an unusual effort to really talk to her, welcome her back and make her feel like she belonged here. Anne couldn't remember the last time her mother hadn't seemed afraid of her. She joined her on the bed.

"I'm sorry, Mom, thank you for coming up here. You're right. I need a safe place to stay for a while. This means a lot to me."

Her mother smiled, and Anne was surprised to see tears in her eyes. She squeezed Anne's hand.

"I mean it, Annie. Stay as long as you want. Do you need anything?"

Anne smiled herself, amazed at how her temper had adjusted in such a short time. When she'd been drinking so heavily, just a few months ago, she might have screamed that what she didn't need was her own mother not remembering how much she hated being called Annie.

Now she easily managed to keep from rolling her eyes.

"I need to get a list of local meetings together. I might need to borrow your computer."

Karen Fincastle's eyes lit up.

"You can borrow my computer anytime you want, and we can get you one soon. Let me get the list together for you, hon. I'd be happy to do that."

Anne had a nagging thought that she really needed to do that for herself, some kind of responsible step forward under her own steam. But her mother looked so happy, so excited to have a job.

It hadn't crossed her mind until just that moment how awful it must have been for her mother. When Anne's troubles started, when she was only eleven years old, her mother hadn't been able to do a thing to stop it or help. No one had, not even her father or Evan.

Her heart caught in her chest as it always did when she thought of how she'd screamed at Evan on Christmas morning years ago, how he'd walked away from her.

Anne wasn't sure anyone could help her with that or anything else now, but she did want to make her mother feel better if she could.

The clearest chance to make amends she'd had so far.

"Sure, Mom, that would be a huge help."

Her mother stood, nodding once.

"What kinds of meetings, just AA?"

"AA, NA, Al-Anon, whatever you can find close by. As many as you can find, at least for a while."

"You got it!"

Anne tried to remember when she'd last seen her mother so happy, so energized. She suspected the list would be a thing of beauty, organized by day, time, distance from the house, transit options, everything she or anyone else could ever need.

And her mother would feel better. Even if the list weren't going to be such a huge help to Anne, knowing her mother would feel better was well worth it.

She looked around her room, trying to connect herself to the things surrounding her. She hadn't been gone for decades or anything like that, but it was hard to remember being that nineteen-year-old, so full of hope and enthusiasm. Her grand experiment of living on her own hadn't been a roaring success. It had been more of a groaning failure.

"None of that, Anne F," she said under her breath.

She went to the closet, thinking the clothes might be a little big, but they should all fit eventually. She was still too thin, even after weeks of decent and regular meals in the hospital and in rehab.

Time was what she needed now. She'd heard it more than enough to finally start believing it, or at least wondering if it was true.

She hadn't gotten so low overnight. She wouldn't be fully recovered overnight either.

Nothing in the closet seemed to have been moved, but the overly fresh smell told her everything had been washed, and recently. Something else her mom had been able to do, and again, it really was a big help.

Anne hadn't kept any of her clothes from the apartment. Even if the stains or stink could be washed away, the awful memories couldn't. That was another thing her mother could do, take her shopping.

That might even be fun.

Her mother's constant patrols of her closet while Anne was growing up, digging out anything and everything that was worn or didn't fit, had gotten on her last nerve when she was a kid. For the first time, she looked forward to so much maternal attention dedicated to her appearance.

Anne sat at her desk, the same one she'd had since her very first day of school. All of her notebooks were still stacked up on the shelf, the records of her growing madness. She ran her fingertips along the metal spirals, afraid to touch them more than that.

For right now, her dreams and visions and memories were quiet and still. She wasn't sure if it was the medication, rehab, or simple exhaustion, but she was glad of the break. She worried reading the journals would bring all of them back.

Exhaustion.

That was exactly how she was feeling right now. Her mom had met her very early at the hospital, and getting everything arranged had taken longer than Anne had expected. Her dad had taken care of all of that in the past. He knew the routine of leaving a mental hospital better than any parent should have to.

Anne had been terribly nervous about him being stuck at a conference, even asking her counselor about staying an extra day so he could come get her. The woman had been right about letting her mother do this.

Anne still wished her father was home.

She sat on the bed again, then kicked her shoes off and stretched out. This wasn't the best mattress in the world, certainly not after she'd slept on it for years as a kid. But compared to the stinking pit of her apartment and the rock-like, vinyl-covered detox and rehab beds of the last six months, this felt like heaven.

Her eyes wanted to drift closed, and Anne tried to force herself to stay awake.

Keep busy, everyone had repeated that over and over again before she left.

Don't let yourself get caught up in boredom. That can lead right back into hell.

Sure, she understood that, but she remembered the other mantra that had drilled itself into her brain.

HALT. Don't get hungry, angry, lonely, or tired.

Well, right now she couldn't do a thing about being lonely, and it wasn't a good time to even think about that. But tired was starting to pull her into the void. The only thing she could do to stop being tired was to take a nap, rest for a while.

Anne didn't think she'd truly gotten any rest since she stopped sleeping in this house, this room, this bed.

She was long, long overdue.

Chapter 34

Evan jumped when his phone buzzed in his pocket, then grabbed for it before it could start ringing. He'd asked for a little time to himself so he could grade papers, and he was doing that. Anything to get some space, a break from Michelle's happy chatter about her work taking her to Seattle for a month.

The balance between how much he would miss her didn't fit well beside how much he was looking forward to having the tiny apartment to himself.

He didn't want Michelle thinking he was ready for company if he could take phone calls.

He flipped the phone open, wishing it had a caller ID box like the apartment phone did.

"Evan? Mike Fincastle here."

Before Evan's mind could quite put a person with the voice, his nerves already had. His heart pounded and a sweaty flush coved his whole body.

"Mr. Fincastle, great to hear from you," he said, walking out onto the small balcony. "How's it going?"

"Going great here. And you?"

Evan closed the sliding door behind himself. He wasn't sure why he did that, but he was sure he felt guilty about not wanting Michelle to overhear him.

"I'm good. Busy, but good."

"I don't mean to bother you, but I thought you should know Anne's coming back home. She finished up her rehab, and she's going to living with us for a while."

Evan let out his breath in a rush, closing his eyes and holding onto the railing. He shouldn't be feeling this way, not with his fiancé in the other room in a tiny apartment. His heart was ready to float the rest of him up off the balcony without asking his permission.

"I'm so glad to hear that, you have no idea. Well, you probably do. When will she get home?"

"This afternoon. I'm caught at work, Karen will pick her up."

"How is she?"

"She's good, Evan, she really is. She's been clean for six months now, and she looks so much better. Still tired and way too thin, but she's getting back to normal."

Evan closed his eyes, remembering the way Anne had looked the last time he'd seen her. Nearly skeletal but her face so awful and puffy, the furious look in her eyes and harsh sound of her voice.

He'd been so afraid that would be his last memory of her.

"Listen, are you busy tonight?" Anne's father said. "Or maybe tomorrow? I was thinking she could really use some company, a good friend she hasn't seen for a while."

"I…uh… I might be able to get away tonight. I'd love to see her."

"That's fantastic! What time should I tell her?"

Evan's mind raced, wondering what he could tell Michelle. They didn't have any particular plans for tonight, but he hadn't mentioned being out for several hours either.

He'd be going, no matter excuse he came up with. He didn't feel particularly good about that, but he knew when putting up a fight with himself would be a waste of time.

"I'll stop by around six."

"Great, I'll be home by 5:30 myself. Maybe you two can go out to dinner, somewhere where… You know…"

"I'll make sure no one's drinking, don't worry. Thank you for calling me, Mr. Fincastle."

"No problem at all, Evan. I'm glad I was able to reach you. Are you ever going to call me Mike?"

"I don't know, I'll work on it. Maybe when I turn forty."

"Okay, good enough. I'll hold you to that. See you tonight."

Evan put the phone in his pocket so he wouldn't drop it. What had he just arranged to do? Take his friend out to dinner, that's all. Nothing else.

But some deep part of him was groaning, turning over in anxiety and guilt, protesting in advance.

Anne had never seemed to return his feelings, not once since he'd fallen in love with her before he turned fourteen years old. That hadn't stopped him from feeling that way though, not even once.

He did care for Michelle, and he supposed he did love her. He surely wouldn't have asked her to marry him and been so relieved when she said yes otherwise.

He had no plans to tell her where he was going tonight, though.

He'd have to figure out what all of that meant later.

Chapter 35

Evan drove slowly through his old neighborhood, his face still burning and his heart pounding. Michelle hadn't questioned him. She was still operating under the assumption that he was trustworthy and loyal. He didn't think she suspected anything was going on but the last-minute faculty meeting Evan had plucked out of wherever lame excuses lived in his mind.

He would have felt a lot better if Michelle had grilled him under pain of deep suspicion for at least an hour before letting him go.

Whatever his own hopes or expectations might be, he wanted to get that under control before he got to Anne's house. He was too painfully aware of what happened the last time he drove through the night expecting to declare his love for her.

He kept seeing that guy's face, *Joe*, smirking at Evan with his arm around Anne. He couldn't imagine in a million years that such a weaselly asshole was still part of Anne's life. Evan snorted, glancing at his own eyes in the rear view mirror.

Who was a weasel?

He'd thought Anne was single then, unattached. Right this moment, Evan was leaving his fiancé behind to go see Anne. He knew himself well enough to know it couldn't be stopped. Not now.

He slowed as he passed the house he grew up in, the house his mother had died in. Sometimes that day didn't feel like almost fifteen years ago, not one bit. Ed had been as good as his word about selling the place. Evan had never set foot inside again after he left for college.

Seeing the house again now, he wanted to talk to his mother as badly as he ever had that awful summer when she died.

He wanted to ask Mrs. Megan Connor Griffith how she felt about that nameless guy so long ago.

He wanted to talk to her about what he was thinking and feeling about Anne, and about Michelle.

Had his Mom thought it was worth it, so many years of anger and resentment with Ed? Was Evan making the same terrible mistake right now? Was he no better than she had been, no more loyal?

Guilt warring with excitement in his belly let him know words like loyalty weren't up to this task.

All the lights were on downstairs at Anne's house, but none up where her room was. He didn't think her father would have called and then let her go out. Evan still needed to try to get a handle on his runaway hopes expectations.

Bringing Michelle's face up in his imagination helped, a little. But not enough.

"Manage your mind, Evan," he whispered as he got out of the car.

He didn't remember the walk from the sidewalk to the front door being several miles long. Evan had enough time to imagine Anne opening the door, and more than enough time to imagine Michelle opening it instead. He knocked rather than trying to aim a shaky finger at the impossibly tiny doorbell.

"Evan!"

Mike Fincastle caught him up in a huge hug, and Evan squeezed back, hoping his pounding heart didn't give him away. Anne's mother was right behind him, and even she gave him a quick hug and kiss on the cheek. Evan blinked, surprised and pleased.

～

"Anne, you have company!"

Anne opened her eyes, wondering who on earth even knew she was here. She hadn't called anybody. She didn't have any addresses or phone numbers. At least not any that weren't outdated, a bad idea, or for people who wouldn't likely want to talk to her.

"Be right there."

She had to look at the clock twice. Three hours? She felt like she'd only closed her eyes. That had been her dad's voice calling up the stairs though, so early evening did make sense.

A neat stack of paper on her desk told her just how hard she'd been sleeping. That was her list, and it was just as detailed as she'd expected. Her mother had had time to look it all up, get it all typed and printed, and bring it in without Anne noticing.

She'd needed the sleep even more than she'd thought. She hadn't even dreamed.

She took at look at herself in the mirror in the bathroom. Her hair was too long, the bangs covering half of her nose. It grew so fast, and she kept forgetting to get it cut. That was something else she could do with her mother, part of their grand shopping day.

She pushed the dark, heavy strands back, straightened out her clothes the best she could, then splashed water on her face. Even after sleeping so hard, Anne looked better than she had in a long, long time. Her face was too thin but not swollen, and her skin had a color besides death warmed over for a change.

Anne surprised herself by smiling at her reflection.

Years had passed when she couldn't stand to look at herself in the mirror at all, much less feel good about what she saw.

She took the time to rinse out her mouth to get rid of the nearly full-strength morning breath, but she didn't bother brushing her teeth. Whoever it was couldn't be expecting formal attire. Not without even a phone call.

When she was halfway down the stairs, Anne froze. She heard a man's voice, not her father, but one she knew just as well.

It wasn't the recognition that stopped her. It was the memory.

In her mind she saw Evan, sitting on the couch beside her mother. Her father had even turned off the television, a sign of how important this visit really was. She remembered going down the stairs, carefully avoiding the squeaky bottom one so no one would hear her coming.

She remembered Evan looking up, surprised to see her, his blue eyes brighter than the sun in the sky. He took three long strides to Anne and picked her up, squeezing her tight, saying her name over and over in her ear.

Anne remembered when she and Evan finally turned back to the living room, both of her parents were gone. They both laughed, and they couldn't stop looking at each other.

She knew something was going to change now, something that could never go back the way it was before. She stood still, terrified it would be another painful shift in her life that she wasn't ready for.

Was Evan married? He was twenty-seven, and unlike Anne, he was successful and out in the world. Was he moving, even further away than into Chicago or St. Louis?

She hadn't seen him for almost six years. Had he just stopped by to say goodbye?

Her heart and the memory told her it was something more joyful than that, something unexpected and true. Even the return of the memories didn't scare her the way it always had.

She couldn't recall any other strong memory that felt positive instead of terrifying.

Walking into Evan's arms, in a different way than she ever had, was going to filter out more of the noise of her in her mind than anything else ever had.

Anne knew she would find a space around herself, room to breathe and smile, room to be happy and content.

She and Evan would create that space together.

She didn't understand how yet, but she thought even her visions and nightmares were going to be calmer in that safe place with him.

Anne walked down the stairs and into her future.

~

EVAN SAT ON THE COUCH, making sure he had a clear view of the stairs. He was jittery enough. He passed what couldn't have been more than a few minutes but felt like the longest of his life, chatting with Anne's parents, trying not to watch the stairs like a stalker.

He had to accept whatever happened. He'd be overjoyed if she agreed to shake his hand after the way they'd last parted company.

Evan glanced over, not even trying to fool himself that it wasn't for at least the tenth time, and she was there. Her hair was too long, falling into her eyes. Jeans and a rumpled but clean t-shirt showed she wasn't nearly as skeletal as before.

Her cheeks were flushed, but her eyes were bright and happy.

After an endless second of being frozen into place, Evan was beside her. He never felt his feet touch the floor.

Now that it had started working again, his body wasn't consulting Evan at all. He picked Anne up and hugged her tight, all absurd ideas of a handshake long since abandoned.

How could he possibly keep himself distant when she was right here, in his arms, when he could smell her hair and her flesh again after so many years?

"Anne," he whispered, knowing he said it over and over again.

Evan finally managed to put her down and let go, and he was delighted that she held on just a second longer. He looked into her eyes, a little bloodshot with what looked like bruises under them.

She still looked a thousand times better than the last time.

"Evan. I'm so glad to see you."

They both turned to the living room, but Mike and Karen Fincastle had vanished. Their eyes met again and both were laughing, the tension of long separation dissolved in an instant.

She took his hand. "They're bored with us."

He managed not to squeeze too hard and followed her over to the couch. His arm twitched at his side, wanting so badly to be around her shoulders.

"Anne, you look great."

"Well, I look better. How did you know I was home?"

"Your Dad called me this afternoon."

She laughed again, and the sound withered a little more of the loneliness in his heart. Evan wondered, just for a second, what Michelle was doing.

"He thought you might want to go out to dinner with me."

"Of course, I'd love to," she said. "Do I need to change?"

"No, you're perfect."

Evan's face was burning, but he knew he'd told the truth. Hugging her changed the whole focus of his life. Right at that moment, he didn't give a damn what that would mean later on.

ANNE TRIED NOT to stare at Evan as he drove, forcing herself to look at her hands or out the window. He looked like a different person to her, far more than the few years could have accounted for.

He was so much more handsome than she remembered, that was part of it. All traces of his soft boyish face had faded away into high cheekbones and a strong jaw. Everything about him had gotten stronger, more solid somehow. His voice was deeper too.

Even with all of that, he felt just the same to her, just as comfortable and safe as he ever had. He kept up the conversation when she was quiet, a habit he'd picked up when she was just eleven years old.

The sound of the man's voice washed over her, reassuring as the little boy voice of her childhood friend.

"How's this look?"

She shook her head, realizing she'd been staring at his hands on the steering wheel this time. They were in front of an Italian place she'd never been with anyone but her parents before. She remembered it being nice.

"Sure, anywhere is fine."

Once they were seated across from each other, Anne no longer had to stop herself from watching him. He was so much more calm and confident than she remembered.

Her cheeks burned when she remembered why he'd looked so awful the last time she'd seen him.

"Evan, listen," she said, then she took a deep, shaky breath. "I owe you an apology."

He closed his eyes for a second.

"You don't owe me anything, but I'll listen to whatever you need to say."

She didn't want to cry in a restaurant, but she might not have any choice. No one was looking at them, no one at all. Everyone was involved in their own conversations. The room was dim enough that it didn't matter anyway.

"I'm so… I'm so sorry for the way I talked to you that day. You came over to see me and I was such a bitch. Then I was terrible to you at Gwen's house. I'm sure she hates me."

He smiled with one corner of his mouth and shook his head.

"The good thing about growing up with Gwen and my father is it takes a lot to shake me up. Upset as you were, you didn't hold a candle to her when she really gets going. She doesn't hate you at all."

Anne lowered her eyes, smiling a little herself.

"Good. I always liked her. I'm sorry I called you a son of a bitch, Evan. That was way out of line. I never should have done that."

He blinked a few times, and Anne's tears finally spilled over.

"Apology accepted. Maybe we can agree on asshole or jackass instead? Dipshit for a really bad day?"

She tried not to laugh, but that battle didn't last long. She took his hand and they giggled together, and she didn't even care when people did glance their way. They could have been in grade school again, the years between vanished in a second.

Anne could have never met Joe, gone to jail, gone to rehab. She might never have even gone to the hospital.

All she needed to do was hold Evan's hand and laugh with him.

"Listen," Evan said, wiping his eyes and squeezing her hand. "I'm not going to bug you about it, but you can tell me whatever you want to, or not a damn thing. I'm not going to judge you. I never have. If you need someone to talk to, I'm right here."

"I'll take you up on that, but you might regret it. I've gotten a lot better at talking over the past few months."

"Try me," he said, winking. "I've had a lot of practice in listening."

A strange look passed over his face, so fast she wondered if she'd imagined it. His eyebrows knotted together for the briefest second, then it was gone.

"You first. How's your job? You're teaching in the city, right?"

"Yeah, teaching history at the university, working on my doctorate. I'll probably finish up in the spring, just have to wrap up my dissertation."

"Your *doctorate*," she said, grinning. "I'm not surprised, of course it's history. What are you writing about?"

Evan rolled his eyes and shrugged.

"I'll bore you to tears if you get me started. I'm writing about the ways agriculture in the US, around the world, really, has changed with pesticides, how they've helped and hurt."

Anne stared at him again, painful chills covering her arms and legs. She couldn't even see Evan for a moment. She saw bees, piles and piles of dead bees. The images from her first nightmare flared into painful life inside of her.

Those dead bees had led to even more dead people.

Sometimes all the people.

"Bees," she whispered

"Yeah, that's a big part of it," he said, his eyebrows raised. "I'm not going to drag you through it right now, but I've been putting that data together over the past few months."

"I don't think I'd be the least bit bored if you explain all of it to me when you're finished."

Anne could remember that now, as clearly as she'd seen him picking her up in her parents' living room. Evan sitting cross-legged and barefoot on the gleaming wooden floor of his apartment, neat stacks all around him, going through every single thing with her. It made perfect, terrifying sense the way he explained it.

Despite that, knowing more about the exact problem was going to calm her fear of the future like nothing else ever had.

"Maybe I can help you practice, what is it, defending it?"

"You have no idea how much that would help," he said, running his fingers through his hair, leaving it standing on end. A flash of his younger self breaking through the confident man in front of her.

"I'm not even finished with the damn thing, and I'm already scared to death of everyone picking it apart."

"It's a deal. How are Gwen and your father? She has a kid now, doesn't she?"

"Two boys. Horrible brutes, they are," he said with a smile that made her heart melt. "They're great, so's she. Dad's the same as ever, I guess. Still a pain in the ass."

"Does he live close by you?"

"No, thank goodness. Neither one of us could stand that. We see each other at holidays, and that's plenty all around. All right, your turn. Tell me something I don't know."

Anne laughed under her breath. She wished the waiter would bring their appetizers, anything to distract him from that question. There was so much he didn't know. She was in the middle of a field of land mines.

"Anne," he said, so softly she barely heard him. "I'm not asking you to tell me gory details, though you could if you wanted. I just want to fill in some of the blanks. I've missed you."

A space inside of her opened then, like a muscle she'd forgotten clenching tight. Evan wasn't going to pressure her, and he wasn't going to leave her. He would never yell at her or hit her.

She didn't see the details of the memory, not yet. For the first time, she *felt* the memory all around her without seeing a thing.

And the memory felt like love.

Chapter 36

THE DREAMS WERE the worst of Anne's torments. Not all of her torments, to be sure, but the worst of them. The dreams told her, night after night, year after year, that life would end in disaster. Not just her own life, though that was bad enough.

Anne knew *all* life hung in that balance.

During the last few months, since she'd gotten sober, she'd learned to love the rare, precious minutes, when she hadn't quite woken up yet. Floating in warm darkness, not afraid of either a nightmare or the day to come. Drifting in the past, wandering through possible futures. Futures that weren't all scary, for the first time since she was eleven years old.

Futures full of hope. And of love.

"Time for your medication, sweetheart."

Anne did her best not to sigh or frown when she opened her eyes. Her mother had taken to her renewed role as parent like a champ. All the way to never remembering to knock on Anne's door anymore.

"Thanks, Mom."

"Any bad dreams?"

"No, none at all," Anne said, comfortable with the lie. She accepted the two orange pills. "I slept great."

"Good!" her mother said, beaming. "I'll see you downstairs."

Just as on the last many mornings, her mother was distracted enough by reports of a good night to skip watching her daughter swallow the pills.

Once the door was closed, Anne leaned over the edge of the bed. She unscrewed the lid and dumped the handful into the water jar already stained multiple colors.

Her fictional great sleep had gained her three weeks free of drugs so far. She just had to manage to keep her parents, especially her mother, from catching on.

Anne slowly got up, trying to stretch out the aches from another restless night. Every day off of the pills seemed to make her nightmares worse. What surprised her and made every terrible dream worth it was how her days were going.

For the first time in her life, Anne knew she was doing the right thing. She was doing the only thing she possibly could. For the first time in her life, her visions were calming her anxiety instead of making it worse.

She took extra care with her makeup, making sure the dark circles under her eyes were well-hidden. That would be the best way to bring this whole thing crashing down, for someone to notice how tired she looked.

Anne had studied carefully and practiced for hours before she'd ever stopped the pills. The whole thing just had to go on a little bit longer. Then she wouldn't have to worry about the medication anymore.

When her eyes looked awake and normal, Anne turned to the calendar. Wednesday, so she'd be seeing Evan today.

He was the key, she was certain of that. Everything depended on him. She'd always wondered why he'd stayed with her through so much hell, even as she was grateful for his support. The visions had given her the answer just a couple of weeks ago.

Finally satisfied with her appearance, her dark brown hair swept up into a knot that looked far more casual than it was, and her slender body as appealing as it could be with a tight skirt and fitted shirt, Anne went downstairs. She needed to have her cheerful facade firmly in place to get safely out the door.

Just a little chat with her parents, easiest thing in the world for a normal woman. Normal had always been particularly challenging for Anne, since long before she became a woman.

She managed to eat every bit of the food her mother put in front of her, and thankfully her father kept up the conversation.

Pleased with her performance, and giving her father an extra-long hug for his unwitting assistance, Anne turned to make her escape. Her mother followed her to the front door.

"What are you up to today, hon?"

"I'm working until six, then Evan's meeting me at the library. We're going to an old movie."

"That's so sweet," her mother said, handing Anne her coat. "I'm so glad you two have each other, even after… after so much time."

"I know, Mom. Me too. See you later."

Anne closed the door and leaned against it. Her mother tried, she really did. More than she ever had when Anne was younger. She'd been about to say since Anne had gone away for a while because of her problem. That's what her mother always called it, her *problem*. Like Evan's father talking about her *issues*.

That was understandable for someone who'd never had a nightmare about the end of the world, one so vivid she breathed the poisoned air and heard the dying screams all day long. All Anne's mother wanted for her was to calm down, settle down, get married, and have a family of her own, despite her *problem*. Anne had never even suspected such a thing was possible until very recently.

That was when her visions, her day visions, not her nightmares, had started to change.

Anne caught the commuter train and sat, closing her eyes. This was when she most often saw the memories now, on her hour-long ride to the university. Something about the noise and the motion lulled her and let her mind relax, even more than her stolen restful moments before she opened her eyes in the morning.

Today the vision was strong and peaceful. Anne didn't just see young boys and girls working in the fields, she was working with them. The fields were vast and well-tended, and they were full to bursting with short, leafy plants. Soybeans, that's what they were.

Anne recognized them from so many visions that she'd had to look them up to be certain. Row after row of healthy green stretched on as far as she could see in the rolling terrain. She knew it was nowhere near her home in the farmlands of Illinois. An ocean breeze was too sharp to be so far inland. That didn't matter though.

All that mattered was these people were alive, they were strong, and they were able to feed themselves.

Anne watched as the youngest children squatted beside each of the plants. Their small hands held smaller tools, and they were careful to touch each tiny purple flower. They moved from one plant to the next, making sure not to miss a single one. Anne knew the children were pollinating the beans.

Many of her nightmares gave her explanations for this, but they didn't always match up. All she knew was this work was crucial to the survival of everyone she could see. The kids were laughing and happy, seeming to enjoy such tedious and difficult work. No adults were even close enough to supervise. The children kept going of their own accord, moving in rhythm with the wind and the softly rustling leaves.

When the rumbling engine went still, Anne opened her eyes. The end of this route was her stop, a lucky coincidence she was happy to take advantage of. She followed a handful of people out.

Her job, the one Evan had helped her get, was as real as her dreamless sleep was a lie. She did work in the university library, the first job she'd ever had for longer than a couple of months.

The work was easy and repetitive, and the chance to be around so many reference books was a bonus. The Internet connection that her mother couldn't monitor was a lifesaver. She'd been free to research her medication and the risks involved in her plans over the next few days.

"I don't know how you do it, Anne."

She turned, afraid she'd been humming out loud again. Suzanne, her supervisor, smiling over what was probably her fourth cup of coffee at ten in the morning.

"What do you mean?"

"You can come in here to carts just overloaded with books, all out of order, first thing on a Monday morning, and still be happy about it."

Anne laughed, knowing she was blushing. If Suzanne or anyone else knew just how happy she was at the moment, a trip back to the psychiatric hospital might be her next step.

"I don't mind, I truly don't," she said, picking up another book. "It really does give me a chance to think."

"Well, you've taken to it like no one else I've ever seen. Keep up the great work."

Anne turned back to the shelf, effortlessly finding the spot for the book. The complicated numbering system had made sense to her from day one. Suzanne had told her that neither she nor anyone else minded the humming, but Anne was still a little embarrassed. She didn't like standing out any more than she had to, even when her days were going so well.

As clear as her visions had been lately, she wasn't sure if today or tomorrow would be her chance with Evan. She knew it was close, any time now. The increasing details in her imagination were only a part of her certainty.

She could feel the changes in her body, medication clearing out, the preparations too small for anyone else to notice. Too many negative things had come true for her to doubt something so positive. This was going to make the difficult early years of life worth living.

Anne was startled by a warm hand on her own, and she turned to look into Evan's pale blue eyes. Her whole body tingled with pleasure.

Complete surprises were rare for her, good or bad.

This one was certainly good.

"About quitting time, isn't it?"

"I hadn't even noticed," she said. "I probably would have worked all night if you hadn't shown up."

"I'll help you pack up and we'll get out of here."

Each of them grabbed an empty book cart and rolled them back toward the reference desk. Everyone else had already gone home, leaving them in warm, companionable silence.

"What did you do today, Evan?"

"Departmental meeting, I'm sorry to say, one even the lowly grad students couldn't escape. I've never understood how sitting in a room for hours on end is going to help us learn more about anything. Or teach anything."

"Was it about funding again?" Anne said, turning so he could hold her coat for her.

"Yeah, same old song. No one cares about the past when we're so busy running toward the future. The new millennium looms even over history departments, I suppose. I'm not even thirty years old, but I'm as antiquated as the books I collect."

"I wouldn't say that," Anne said. "I'm into antique books myself."

He smiled, leaning down for a quick hug. Anne felt the strange tickle of a memory about to come true, like an electric current through her nerve endings.

She kissed him on the corner of his mouth before she hugged him tight. That tickle disappeared in a blast of heat, deeper and hotter than in her most intense memories and daydreams. She felt Evan's heart pounding in that same warmth.

He drew back, looking into her eyes. Anne was pleased that her own face felt calm, especially once she saw how flushed his was. She never needed validation for something she'd seen so clearly, so many times, but she was swept up in his response all the same.

"Are you… ah, are you ready to go?" he said, taking a deep breath.

"I'm ready."

She walked beside Evan, listening to him chatter about his day. The random brush of his hand against hers didn't feel so accidental anymore. Much as she wanted to, Anne didn't grab his hand. Not yet.

She knew that time would come, maybe sooner than she thought. With so much pain and fear ahead for all of them, there was no need to rush through all of this pleasure.

They'd planned to have dinner and then see a movie, but the vision and the reality were lining up more quickly than she'd expected. A moment like this felt like a doubled photo slowly coming into focus, a lot like the truly antiquated stereo pictures he had in his apartment.

Every second brought them into alignment, an eclipse that would last for hundreds of years.

The way Evan kept looking at Anne during dinner, his eyes seeming to drink her in, left her no doubts. His knee against hers under the table intensified the heat between them.

"What time is the movie?" Anne said, knowing they were already ten minutes late.

As she'd known he would, Evan answered without looking down at his watch.

"I think we're going to miss this one."

As she knew she would, Anne laughed deep in her throat.

"Don't you have a copy of it at home? I'll bet you've seen it a dozen times."

Evan smiled and put his hand over hers.

"More than a dozen. I'd still like to watch it with you, Anne."

She looked into his eyes, the pupils wide enough to nearly obscure the lovely blue. She remembered looking into those same eyes when she told him she knew the world was going to end.

He hadn't panicked, not at first. He'd stayed with her even when he did panic later on. He'd stayed with her, remained her closest friend, through all of it, even after she did her best to push him away for years. He'd always been her way through the nightmare, even before she'd understood why.

"Let's go there now, Evan."

When they walked out of the restaurant, Evan did finally take Anne's hand. She looked up at him, trying to keep her relief and satisfaction to herself. After a lifetime of so many horrible visions, a beautiful vision was going to come true. She squeezed his hand and smiled.

His apartment was only a few blocks away, and neither of them spoke on the short walk. He didn't let go of her hand either. Anne tried to keep her memory of what was going to happen out of her mind.

She wanted to be surprised again. She wanted to have this moment for the very fist time.

Inside his apartment, Anne walked over to shelves full of books and music and movies. She knew he'd only lived here a couple of years, but so many well-loved things made it seem like he'd lived his whole life here. She ran her fingers along the row of old, leather-bound books, waiting for him.

Waiting for him to touch her.

Waiting for him to set the rest of their lives into motion. Lives filled with love from this night until the end.

She felt Evan's hands on her shoulders, and the reality obliterated all of her well-treasured and traveled memories. Her entire body was on fire, a spark lit by his flesh against her own. She turned to him.

"Anne, I've been so happy," he said, then he closed his eyes for a second. "I've been so happy to see you doing so well. I was afraid that would never happen for a long time."

Anne covered one of his hands with her own.

"So was I."

"Spending so much time with you these past two weeks has been like a dream. I keep expecting to wake up."

"This dream is real," Anne whispered, stepping into his arms. "No one knows more about dreams than I do."

She felt his heart pounding again, and this time his whole body was trembling. Anne was surprised to feel her own body doing the same, responding to Evan in a way she'd never remembered or imagined.

The joy of that, of something so simple as the natural reaction of her body to his, sent Anne's happiness spiraling around her. She was lightheaded as she turned her face up to his.

Her lips met his fully this time, and the touch turned Anne into nothing but heat. For the first time in her life, she was not terrified to be in exactly the right place at exactly the right time.

She opened her mouth and every part of her, wanting to let all of her past and her future perish in that raging heat.

Evan breathed deeply, then he pulled her against him, squeezing her body against his own. His hands were in her hair, against her back, on her face, always in motion, moving them closer together.

Anne knew this wasn't the first time for him, and she'd had plenty of her own sad attempts. Every time before, she'd been struggling, fighting against a memory she knew wasn't going to turn out well, but a memory she was unable to stop. This time she went willingly, gladly, bringing her life onto the course of her own destiny.

Evan drew back, breathing hard and holding the sides of her face. She held his hands, needing to hear what she knew he would say.

"I love you, Anne. I've never loved anyone but you."

She kissed him, trying to draw him inside of her. "I love you."

She took his hand and walked toward his bedroom, feeling and remembering the changes that would soon take place between them. Those changes would alter the courses of their own lives, and everyone around them would say it was about time.

Oh, how they'd *waited* for the two of them to get together forever, how they'd hoped. They never said once Anne got over her *problem*, and the fact that they surely thought that didn't bother her. Not anymore.

Anne knew her problem was going to be the salvation, not of all of them, but at least of enough of them.

Chapter 37

Anne turned over, stretching and groaning. She couldn't remember the last time she'd slept so deeply and woken so easily. Nothing hurt or ached. Every single part of her felt good. She opened her eyes, and for just an instant, she wasn't sure exactly where she was.

The space was small, barely the size of her own bedroom in her parents' house. But rather than staying trapped in the painfully outdated pastels and Day-Glo of a teenaged girl in the Eighties, this was an adult's room. Deep burgundy rugs covered parts of the smooth hardwood floor, beside the queen-sized bed, in front of a plain black chest of drawers. The bed itself felt like floating in a warm cotton cloud, with the softest sheets and pillows Anne had ever slept in.

Rather than being covered with tattered posters of Duran Duran, Prince, and Pat Benatar, the rich brown walls were mostly empty. Only one picture caught Anne's eye. A woman, maybe in her thirties, and a little boy. Both of them with black hair and vivid pale blue eyes.

Anne caught her breath, remembering everything. She was in Evan's bed, and she'd spent the night with him. She'd made love with him for the first time. Her memory had been detailed and strong, but it hadn't even come close to the reality of the way their bodies moved together.

Neither Joe nor any of the other random guys had ever made her feel this way. Sex had felt good, sure, at least some of the time. It had only been sex though. Joe was always close to the line of using her, not much more than a body-sized substitute for his hand.

A couple of the other guys hadn't bothered pretending she was anything else.

She sat up against the pillowy headboard, pulling the heavy comforter up around her shoulders. She realized being with Evan was her first time actually making love. She hadn't felt like an afterthought or some kind of convenient receptacle.

She knew everything about her, every single inch of her flesh and every way she felt, was the most important and beloved thing on the face of the earth for him. Anne couldn't remember ever feeling like that before.

When she looked over at Evan's nightstand to check the time, she saw a note nearly lost in the folds of the comforter.

Went out to get breakfast, nothing here at all! Be right back. Love you, E

Anne closed her eyes, surprised to feel hot tears in her eyelashes. That was another part of her memory that had fallen short.

Words, they were just words. Her parents, her grandmother, so many people had used that word. Love. It had never affected her like this, like it altered every cell in her body.

He'd left a robe on his side of the bed too, a thick goldenrod-colored robe far too big for her, but it was warm. She looked around the neat bedroom, making a bet with herself which door would be the bathroom.

She wanted to at least be presentable when he got back, not like she'd ratted up her hair on purpose. She wanted to look as good as she felt, though that might not be possible. Her first guess was wrong, but she held the hall door open long enough to be sure the apartment was still empty. She opened the door to the tiny bathroom next. Sink crowded close against tub and toilet, but again, everything from the spotless white tiles to the recessed medicine cabinet to the matching slate gray towels and shower curtain looked so cool and stylish and grownup.

Anne wasn't sure she felt comfortable borrowing Evan's toothbrush without asking, but she at least wanted to wash her face and rinse out her mouth. She laughed at her hair in the mirror, every bit as messy and tangled as she'd imagined. She could at least clean the loose strands out of his hairbrush when she was finished.

When she touched the flat metal handle on the mirror, meaning to open the medicine cabinet and look for a brush, Anne froze.

The sense of a memory was as strong as it had ever been, the feeling of tiny bolts of lightning all over her fingers. But Anne didn't see anything. She waited for the screen to appear in her mind, three scenes, or maybe only one, but nothing happened. She blinked, then looked back at her reflection.

She'd never felt the air around her, time itself, so thick and heavy with whatever she was about to see. Not even when Evan's mother had died.

Why wasn't she seeing it? Even the most horrifying memories hadn't hesitated, keeping her waiting like this. She let go of the handle.

That didn't lessen her certainty, not one bit. If anything, dread joined anticipation to make her anxiety even worse. There was something she had to know here, something she couldn't avoid. Even if she got dressed and walked away from here forever, she wouldn't be able to leave this behind.

And she didn't think she'd be able to walk away from Evan, now or anytime in the future, no matter what she saw. Anne opened the door before she could change her mind.

Nothing seemed odd or out of place at first. She saw vitamins, aspirin, the hairbrush she'd been looking for, nail clippers, an electric razor. She picked up the brush, feeling a little guilty at looking at such an intimate space when Evan wasn't home.

This was a different intimacy than sharing his bed. This felt a lot more like snooping.

A memory did surge forward then, but it was a normal memory out of the past. Joe had found her pills in the medicine cabinet the first time he'd been in her apartment. That was the start of the long nightmare with him.

Anne started to close the door, thinking the waiting memory must be about something else. Maybe thoughts of Joe made her uneasy enough to imagine her discomfort, and it would just fade away now.

She looked back at the shelves. It was true nothing was out of place, but a lot of things seemed to be missing. More than half the cabinet was empty. That didn't make sense.

Unless…

The memory exploded around her. Anne caught herself against the sink, the brush clattering to the tiled floor.

She was back the bedroom, sitting on Evan's bed, and he was sitting beside her, both of them fully dressed. A tiny black velvet box sat between them. It looked like a jewelry box, but this wasn't a happy occasion.

The ring in that box wasn't meant for Anne. That ring had been meant, had already been given, to another. To his fiancé. The box faded away, and she knew it wasn't still here, not right now. Evan was going to get it back though, sometime in the next week or two. She groaned, sitting carefully on the edge of the bathtub.

He hadn't given this ring to some nameless girl in college, a youthful relationship long forgotten.

Evan was engaged to another woman, *right now*.

The empty space in the medicine cabinet wasn't some odd kind of OCD on his part. His fiancé's things had been there, just a few days or maybe a couple of weeks before. Gods, had he hidden them away, on the off chance Anne would be in his bathroom?

Evan was *engaged*. He'd made plans and promises to be another woman's husband. Anne held her face in her shaking hands. She hadn't had a drop to drink in over six months now, but she recognized this sensation from more hangovers than she could possibly count. She was too certain she was going to throw up to get too far away from the toilet.

"Anne?"

Too late, she remembered she hadn't closed the door behind her.

Evan stood in the doorway. His brilliant smile faded and his eyes were frightened.

She wanted to feel sad that what should have been a perfect morning was going to be such a nightmare for both of them. She wanted to mourn that loss, but she couldn't quite manage. He was in front of her now, squatting to look into her eyes.

"Anne, what's wrong? Are you sick?"

She shook her head slowly, trying to figure out what to say to him. No words seemed possible until they floated out of her mouth.

"I'm not sick."

He reached up to push her tangled hair away from her face.

"Did you have a dream?" he said, stroking her cheek now. "Did you remember something?"

"Yeah, I remembered something. It's going to happen right now. I can't stop it."

"Come in the bedroom and tell me about it. Maybe that will help."

He stood, holding out his hands to her. She couldn't think of anything else to do but let him pull her to her feet.

"I need to get dressed," she said, pulling the robe tight at her throat, trying to ignore the gut-twisting certainty that it was *her* robe. "Can you… Can you give me a minute?"

Evan looked confused, then his face went white. He closed his eyes, his eyebrows drawing down. He turned and walked through the bedroom and back out into the hall. When Anne was dressed, her hair pulled back as neatly as possible, she sat on the bed. The jewelry box wasn't there, not physically, but that didn't matter. She called him back in.

"Anne, please tell me what's going on."

"You look like you already know."

He shook his head as he sat beside her. Anne couldn't stop herself from looking at the space between them, where the ring should have been. The space felt solid, physical, like the woman was lying there instead.

"I know something's wrong, and I'm terrified of what it might be."

"You tell me then." Anne drew her knees up against her chest. "Tell me what has you so afraid."

"Did someone call?"

"No, not that I heard."

"Did you find something? See something?"

"Nothing outside my memory. Evan, just tell me the truth. Just tell me. Lying can only make it worse."

The dread in his eyes made some part of her ache. Another part of her was ready to get furious, whether he managed to tell her or not.

"There's someone else," he whispered, not dropping his gaze.

"What's her name?"

"Her name is Michelle. I… We're engaged."

This was the second time in less than twenty-four hours that the memory turned out to be a pale imitation of the reality. Anne's vision of the ring had felt like a flood of icy cold water.

Evan's words felt like a kick in the guts.

"You're *still* engaged?"

"Yes. Right now we are."

"Does she live here, Evan? Did I sleep in her bed last night after I had sex with her fiancé?"

"She's in Seattle right now."

"I didn't ask you where she is *right now*," Anne said, clenching her fists. "Does she live here or not?"

He flinched at the sound of her voice, as if she'd taken a swing at him. Anne couldn't quite manage to feel sorry for him.

"She still has her own place, but yeah, she's been staying here a lot. She's going to… She was going to move in here in a couple of weeks, when she got back."

"She doesn't know a thing about me, does she?"

Evan just shook his head, his cheeks red and his eyes lowered.

"What did you think was going to happen, Evan? When were you going to tell her? When were you going to tell me? Were you hoping we could all just get along?"

"I was going to break it off with her, I *am* going to. I should have already. I didn't want to do that over the phone. And I wanted to be with you last night. I've wanted to be with you since before I even knew what that meant."

"That doesn't mean you can treat her this way. It doesn't mean you can treat *me* this way. I didn't expect you to be a virgin any more than I am, but you're fucking engaged! You lied to me, Evan, or at least you kept a hell of a lot from me. Did you hide her things before you met me last night?"

"No, I… I mean yes. Not last night, no, but I did after I saw you again. After we went to dinner that first time." He groaned, linking his hands together around the back of his neck. "I fucked everything up."

Anne buried her face against her knees, wanting to scream. Her memories of making love to Evan hadn't been the end of what she saw, what she knew would happen.

They were going to have more than one night together. The two of them were going to spend their lives together for as long as they lived. Unless some fundamental part of her was failing, a part that had never been wrong about a memory like this before, her future was going to be with this man.

That meant she would eventually recover from the spinning pit in her middle where her stomach and her heart used to be. And he would eventually manage to stop looking and sounding so terrified.

"I don't know what you've done," she said. "I know what I have to do though."

"I have to tell her."

"That's up to you. You have to tell her if you ever want to see or talk to me again."

Evan didn't move. He just watched her gathering her things from the nightstand and dropping it all into her purse.

"Please don't go," he finally whispered.

"I don't want to go, but you didn't give me much of a choice. I never would have chosen to sleep in her bed, Evan. I never, ever would have made love to you if you'd told me the truth. Joe cheated on me all the time, did you know that? I promised myself I'd never do that to another woman. And here I am."

"I'll listen to whatever you want to say. Please don't go."

"If I don't get the hell out of here right now my next stop is going to be the liquor store. I thought I'd gotten away from guys who drove me to fucking drink!" Tears spilling from his blue eyes only twisted the fury in Anne's guts higher. "The truth god damn well hurts, doesn't it? You keep on telling yourself you're better than that, that it's justified, that you're noble, whatever it takes. I've spent almost every day of my life staring the truth dead in the face!"

"Will you at least let me drive you home?"

"I'm a big girl. I know the train schedule. And you know where to reach me, but not one single word from you until this is finished. Not one word."

Anne wished she could see what she was walking into, or out of. She had no idea if she wanted him to try to stop her, to try to hold her and kiss her and make her stay.

She didn't know if that would be worse than him sitting on that bed, *Michelle's* bed, and not saying anything.

He didn't do either. He did something far worse than what she'd been trying to prepare herself for.

"I love you, Anne. No one but you."

She walked out of his apartment without saying another word. She managed to get out the door and down to the street before sobs kept her from walking or even breathing for a long while.

Chapter 38

Evan looked at the blocky white caller ID box beside his phone, dreading at least two of the numbers it could be. He was a little relieved to see it was neither, but he wasn't sure if this was going to be a reprieve or not.

"Hi Gwen."

"What the hell have you been getting into, little brother?"

Evan laughed, knowing it wouldn't fool his sister for one second.

"Not a thing. I've been bored to death up here, nothing but work. How's your life?"

"Not nearly as dramatic as yours. I had a long talk with Michelle a couple of days ago."

He rolled his eyes, glad no one could see him.

"I'm sure she was singing my praises."

"Not exactly. Listen, I'm on the way home from Milwaukee. I can be there in about half an hour."

"I don't want to bother you with all of this."

"You're not the one who bothered me. I just want to hear your side of it."

Evan looked around the empty apartment. Still too many books, too much antique stuff on not enough shelves. Still the same angular, overly masculine furniture, now without most of the fussy pillows and hand-knit blankets that kept the place from looking like a showroom at Guys-R-Us. A whole lot more than a few things in the medicine cabinet were gone now, back to Michelle's place.

Anne still refused to talk to him, only telling him it wasn't over, whatever that meant. He doubted he'd ever hear from Michelle again after telling her the engagement was off.

He did need to talk to someone.

"In a hurry to get back home, Gwen? You can stay here tonight if you really want to know what's going on."

"Are you kidding? This week was the first break I've had in ages. Mark will be fine with the boys. At least they'll all survive without too many bruises. Need me to bring the gin?"

"Yep. I'm fresh out."

By the time Gwen walked in with two small black bottles, Evan was fairly sure he was ready to talk. Trying to figure this all out for himself was not working. Within a few minutes, they were settled on the couch, upgraded gin and tonics in hand.

"I understand you're single again."

"Subtle as usual, Gwen. I don't know. Maybe. I hope not."

"That's not how your ex-fiancé sees it."

"I'm not with her anymore, no. I may not be with anyone."

"Has she talked to you?"

Evan took a long drink to avoid answering. Michelle was one of the calls he'd been dreading, even though whatever Anne was waiting for hadn't happened yet.

"No, not for a couple of days. I doubt she will."

Gwen raised her eyebrows, shaking her head a little.

"I'd be surprised if you didn't get another call, Ev. She has a lot of questions."

"I know. What I don't know is what to tell her."

"You better figure it out. I told her to make you tell her."

"You did what?"

"Don't glare at me like that, jerk. I'm not the one who dumped my fiancé out of the blue right before she was going to move in."

Evan was quite sure he'd misheard her, or at least misunderstood her. Her words weren't making any sense.

"You told her to do what?"

"I told her I didn't know what had gotten into you, that she needed to ask you. Well, to be honest, I told her she needed to drag it out of you if she had to."

"Way to have my back, sis. Whose side are you on?"

"I'm on your side, and I do have your back. But you pushed Michelle into my life, remember? And she pushed me into this. I don't know what to tell her even if I wanted to. What the hell happened?"

"It's just not working out," he said, knowing he was wasting his time trying to get her off track. "Nothing in particular."

"Horse shit. Your relationships are your business, unless your girlfriends force me into the middle. But don't you dare lie to me."

He looked into her eyes, wondering how much he could tolerate telling her or anyone else. He wasn't thrilled with Gwen for telling Michelle to drag the truth out of him, but he knew that was the right thing to do. He needed to try to do the right thing here too.

"It's Anne. I've been seeing Anne."

Gwen hummed under her breath, then took her own long drink.

"Why am I not surprised? When did this happen?"

"She got back about a month ago. Her Dad called me."

"I'm guessing he didn't know about Michelle."

Evan shook his head, sighing.

"Neither did Anne. I didn't handle any of this right."

"I don't know if there is a right way, but you definitely got your timing wrong. Where's Anne?"

"Once she realized… Once she knew about Michelle, she left. She keeps telling me there's something I haven't done, but she won't say what."

"Well, that might be the same thing I told Michelle. I'm guessing, since I haven't seen Anne in a long time, but they both need the truth, Ev. Michelle is going to drive herself crazy trying to figure out what she did wrong. You *know* that's not fair."

"No, it's not fair. She didn't do anything wrong except be the wrong person."

"So why does she think this is because of something she did or didn't do? She has the very strong idea it was her fault."

Evan swirled the ice around in his glass, knowing stalling was useless. This was the thing he felt worst about, even more than the lying.

"I'm sure she does believe it was her fault. I didn't exactly stop her from thinking that."

Gwen snorted, shaking her head.

"You mean you told her that, or you let her decide that for herself? Answer carefully. I know where you live."

"She got there on her own, but I let her do it. And I didn't tell her otherwise."

"Why the hell did you do that? How can you be such a fucking *guy?*"

"I don't know. Maybe because I am nothing more than a standard issue fucking guy after all. I just wanted her to go. I wanted it to be over. It all made sense at the time."

"Wrong answer on that one, brother. You're *not* just a guy, and you never have been. You'd have to do quite a bit more downgrading to get there, but this is a great start."

"I hate shit like that, Gwen. I always have."

"Yeah, so? Most people hate shit like that. But we do it anyway. You turn away from things you don't like too easily, Ev. You did with Michelle, you do with Ed, and you did with Anne here too. You might have turned away with Anne a long time ago. You have to start facing things like this, going through them instead of walking away."

"Easy enough for you to say. You've always been more of a bitch than I am."

"I had to learn it. Being an only child with our parents for six years wasn't easy. I do know what I'm talking about here. Stand up for what you want. Maybe that's what Anne's waiting for, you know? She needs to know you'll stand up for her, too."

"Maybe. I'll think about it."

"Listen, how is Anne? What's been going on with her?"

Evan finished his drink and ran his fingers through his hair. This wasn't his business to tell, but he knew Gwen wasn't interested in gossip. She was worried about him. That was one of her most annoying, and endearing, traits.

"She had a tough time for a while, then she was in rehab and a hospital for six months. This is the most calm I've seen her since we were kids. Before Mom died."

"Even after she knew about Michelle?"

"Yeah, especially then. She was furious. But she hasn't started drinking, despite my best efforts to drive her to it. And she's not backing down on whatever she does want."

Gwen smiled and nodded.

"If she's been in rehab and really made some changes, I was right. She does need the truth. I've dodged that addiction bullet myself somehow, despite inheriting a love for Mom's g and ts, but I know a few people who haven't. A big part of it seems to be just telling the damn truth, to themselves and everyone else. Why should she expect any less from you?"

"I don't think I told myself the truth for a long time, Gwen. It feels crazy now, but I thought everything I was doing was all okay. I had reasons for everything. I hope I haven't fucked it up for good between us."

"Well, I'll tell you the truth. I'm not happy about the way you treated Michelle. That was an asshole move, and I think you know that. You've been in love with Anne pretty much since birth. So if you can both be happy, I hope it does work out."

She got up, reaching for Evan's empty glass. He followed her into the kitchen and got the gin and ice out of the freezer. This wasn't a night for moderation.

"I do remember the way Anne screamed at you in front of my house," she said, measuring out the gin. "I saw the way you looked when you came back in. Are you sure you know what you're getting into here, Evan?"

He'd never known for certain if Gwen knew what happened that day or not. She'd never said a word about it until this moment. Evan was so grateful he didn't mind the question now.

"Of course I'm not sure. It took me years to get over that day. I don't think I really got over it until I saw her again. Were you sure with Mark?"

She laughed, nearly spilling the bubbling tonic she was pouring into Evan's glass.

"I'm still not sure about Mark! I love him, and he drives me crazy, and I don't think anyone else would put up with either one of us. I know neither of us could raise these hellion children alone. So I guess we're stuck with each other. That might be how it happens. Inertia."

"Inertia sounds like paradise to me. I can't even imagine what that would be like."

"I can't blame you for wondering." Gwen settled herself on the couch again. "We didn't exactly grow up with anything as calm as that, did we? Speaking of chaos, have you told Hurricane Ed yet?"

"Not a word. We don't generally speak unless we're forced to. I don't have to guess how he'll feel about all of this. He really likes Michelle."

"And he really doesn't like Anne."

"Nope, never has. I'm going to have to go tell him. Much as he gets on my damn nerves, I don't want to cut off all contact with him. At least I hope I don't have to."

"I'll go with you for that. Reinforcements are always better."

"No, I need to do this myself. It's past time I stood up to him, don't you think? You were just saying I walk away from him too easily. I'm not a kid anymore, Gwen."

"You're not. You've certainly fucked up this situation like a man. You don't want to be alone for this one, though. Trust me. Ed has more of a temper than you know. And he'll be edgy about this whole thing already."

Evan nodded, moving his hips lower on the chair so he could stretch out his legs.

"He already thinks I'm too much like Mom. This will prove it."

"Neither one of them handled that in a good way, far as I can tell. I don't think Ed ever got over it. Seriously, I don't want you going over there alone. I'll stay out of the way. I have no interest in spilling these particular beans. But he can be a bastard when he gets angry enough. He won't do that if I'm there."

"I'm not going to talk to him for a while anyway. Right now I wouldn't know what to tell him."

"Just promise me you'll let me know when you are ready. Okay?"

He looked into her brown eyes, Ed's eyes, and those eyes came with Ed's temper sometimes. Gwen wouldn't joke around with something like this. She avoided their father almost as much as Evan did. If she was volunteering, even insisting, on going with him, he did need to take that seriously.

"Did he… How bad did it get, Gwen?"

She examined her nearly empty glass for a long time before answering.

"If he ever did hit Mom, I never heard or saw that. But there were times he scared the shit out of me, Ev. Then and later on, after I left home. Something in him seems like it could break loose, you know? There were reasons I hardly ever came to visit. I worried about you, but you were better at staying under his radar than I was. I hate to admit this, and I'll kill you if you repeat it, but I think we were too much alike."

"Hurricane Gwen," Evan said, grinning. "How do you think I got so good at staying out of the way? I watched you two and took notes."

"Smart kid," she said, smiling back. "You still haven't promised me."

"Okay, okay, I'll let you know," he said, getting to his feet and taking her empty glass. "I promise. I don't know about you, but these aren't quite what I'm in the mood for tonight. Make you the best dirty martini you ever tasted?"

"You're on, brother. We'll toast the disaster of your love life, then I'll tell you how to make it as good as mine."

"Good thing you brought more than one bottle."

Chapter 39

EVAN HAD ALWAYS THOUGHT his apartment was two small for more than one person. Living room with barely enough space for a sofa and two chairs. Kitchen straining to hold the basics for feeding himself and a glorified TV tray that passed as a table. Bedroom that held his bed and stereotypically dull bachelor clothing storage, and the sad attempt at a second bedroom that had forced him to buy a new desk that could be assembled inside.

Michelle had made the place more homey and welcoming some- how, but only increased his sense of not having enough room to breathe. Anne was the only person who'd ever walked in and made Evan feel like his lungs, his heart, his mind, every part of him fit better because she was there.

He was terrified Anne would never set foot inside any room with him again.

And now some little boy part of him – the fevered part who believed the sore throat was going to last the rest of his life – was afraid Michelle would sit on the sofa she'd condemned as drab and boring until they both died of shouting or cold silence.

Gwen had told him he needed to talk to Michelle, but she'd told him over and over for years that he was too damn nice. Evan thought his sister had never been more right about that second part than this moment.

Michelle wasn't crying yet, but she was getting closer. She repeated the same question, the same sharp and jagged three letters, no matter what Evan said or did in response.

"Why?"

"I'm sorry, Michelle. I don't know how else to say it. I just couldn't."

"Then why the hell did you propose to me, Evan? What were you trying to accomplish? Did you just want to see how much you could get away with?"

Evan closed his eyes, trying to think of some other words, some other thing he could do to make her understand. After nearly an hour of this, he was starting to care a lot less about understanding or about telling the truth, even after he'd promised Gwen. He just wanted her to go.

"I knew it wasn't going to work, and I couldn't keep pretending. I thought it would be worse for all of us if we got married. Do you really think that would have been better?"

"It would have been better if you'd been man enough to tell me the truth a long time ago!" she shouted, the tears starting up at last. "I wouldn't have wasted so much time with you!"

Evan could only think of one way to get this to stop. He never wanted to hurt Michelle, not in a million years. He'd loved her as much as he could.

Letting this go on was cruel to everyone. He had to let her get it out, let her be right. Let her tear him to pieces if she needed to.

He deserved it.

"You're right. I should have been more of a man. I thought I could make it work, and I was wrong. Everything I did was wrong."

She stared at him so long he was fighting the need to fidget, to look away, to do anything. Finally her eyes narrowed, and Evan tried to brace himself. He remembered all the years of fighting between his parents, partly because of his mother's affair.

Evan had grown up in the middle of those consequences. He couldn't pretend it hadn't been a disaster.

"Is it because of her?"

A wave of heat flooded through him, then he was freezing cold. He might deserve whatever Michelle said, but he'd wanted to protect her from this. He wanted to protect himself, too. And most of all, he wanted to protect Anne.

"What do you mean?"

"I mean Anne, your insane bitch of a girlfriend. Your father told me all I needed to know about her. Is she out of the loony bin again?"

Evan held his breath, trying to get his pounding heart to slow down.

His father. His fucking father. Hurricane Ed had never even pretended to like Anne from the day Evan's mother had died, and the past few years he hadn't even tolerated hearing about her.

Dealing with Michelle, breaking off their engagement after two years, that was child's play compared to standing up to his father. Even after his sister's warning about Ed's temper, Evan knew more than ever that he had to face him.

"He never should have talked to you about that. It wasn't his place or any of his concern."

"He showed a hell of a lot more concern for me than you have. Your only concern is getting me out of the way fast enough!"

"He should have let me handle this my own way. I know I've been an asshole. All I've done is make all of this worse, but that's up to me to make a mess of."

"Is it her?" she whispered, and he wished she would start shouting again.

"It's not going to change anything."

"I don't care, Evan. I know it's over. I just want to know why. I need you to tell me why. You owe me that much."

"If you knew before you came over here, why didn't you just tell me? Why did you question me for an hour first? Did you just want to torture me?"

Evan knew he wasn't being fair. Even if Michelle did just want to torture him, who would have blamed her, or stopped her? Not even Anne would have.

"I wanted you to tell me the truth. That's all. I wanted to give you a chance to tell me the truth. I wasted my time and yours waiting for that."

"You're right," he said, shrugging. "I should have told you. I doubt it'll make anything better. I'm sure it won't, but I do owe you that much. It is Anne."

Michelle closed her eyes for a long time, and Evan was afraid she was going to start crying or shouting at him again. He was afraid they were going to be here all night. When she looked at him again, she was still calm.

"When?"

"A month ago. I first saw her a month ago." He forced himself not to look away.

"And you're only telling me now. Why, Evan? What changed? Has she been here? Was she here before you broke it off with me?"

He wished he had never even picked up the phone when she'd called, and he damned himself all over again for opening the door. He couldn't marry Michelle, but he never wanted to be awful to her.

At least he never wanted to have to tell her just how awful he'd already been.

"Yes. She was here. While you were in Seattle. She was here."

"God *damn* it. God damn *you*. You're the one who talked me into going, staying the whole time, you son of a bitch! Did you do all of that just to get me out of the way so you could fuck her?"

For the first time since his Mom died, Evan didn't lose all control of his temper at those words.

Son of a bitch.

He supposed in this case he was absolutely his mother's son. And this time, if no other, the words fit them both.

"I don't… I don't know how to answer you, Michelle. What I did was wrong. I handled everything the worst way I possibly could have. I never planned for any of this to happen."

"I don't give a damn about plans, though you were happy to sit by and let me plan a wedding you had no intention of attending. You had a choice to make, a hell of a lot of choices. Every time, every single time, you chose her instead of me."

He wanted to shake his head, to argue, to create some way to make this less his fault. He couldn't. He opened his mouth, but he couldn't find a single word. Michelle seemed to be having no problems finding her own words.

"When did this start? It wasn't just a few weeks ago, was it?" Evan shook his head, looking at the floor. "That wasn't a yes or no question!"

He didn't dare point out that the last one had been. Even he wouldn't be that big of a jackass.

"It started when we were in middle school. A long time ago."

"Jesus," Michelle said, her face going white. "Did you ever care about me at all?"

For the first time since she'd walked in the door, really the first time since he'd picked Anne up and held her in his arms, Evan wanted to hug Michelle. He wanted to take away all the pain he'd caused.

"Of course I did, Michelle. That's what's so hard about this. I do care about you. I'm not devoid of feelings here, I know this is awful for you. I didn't know it would be so awful for me."

Michelle's jaw dropped.

"Oh, *poor* Evan. Having a hard time with stabbing me in the fucking back? That must be just terrible. If you're suffering so deeply, why did you do it, why?"

Evan covered his face with his hands, wishing this would all go away. He'd created it, but he wasn't sure if he could live with the fallout. Even after Michelle left and went on with her life, and he knew she would, he would still have to live with what he'd put her through. He was afraid the damage to himself, and to his life with Anne, would be too big.

"I don't want to make it worse," he said, speaking from behind his hands. "Can't we just stop this now?"

"No, Evan, we can't stop this now. You got what you wanted. You got her, and you got me for a while too. You got to convince me you were worthy of being my husband for a long time. We're not going to stop until I say we stop. You tell me why."

He lowered his hands and took a deep breath, then looked into her eyes. She did need to tear him to pieces. He was sure he'd done the same to her, just like his mother had done to his father.

An ache twisted through his guts and his heart, the strongest need to talk to his mother he'd felt since he was thirteen. If she could answer that question, tell him *why*, maybe he could manage to tell Michelle now.

"Because… Because I fell in love with her when I was thirteen years old. I didn't think there was a chance, and I fell in love with you, too, Michelle, I did. I wasn't lying or trying to hurt you or trick you. I did want to marry you."

"You *did* want to. At least you're honest enough to use past tense." She wiped her eyes. "If you wanted to be with me, why did you go see her at all?"

"Her father called to let me know she was home. He thought she'd like to see an old friend. That's all. That's how it started, anyway."

"Before I went to Seattle," she said, her brow furrowing. "The day I was here with you, and out of the blue you told me you had a faculty meeting. A faculty meeting at night. That was it. That was when you went to see her."

Evan nodded, wishing he could send this whole day away.

"And none of them cared that you were engaged?"

"They didn't know. I wasn't trying to hide it. I just hadn't talked to any of them in years."

"Did you tell her when you saw her, Evan? Does she know I exist?"

"I don't want to do this, please."

"I don't care what you want anymore! I want you to tell me the truth. I want to know all of it, so I'll remember just what a nasty piece of work you turned out to be."

Evan took a deep breath, holding it until his head pounded. Maybe if he got it out, he'd be able to remember it too, and never, ever do something like this again. Not to Anne, not to anyone.

Most of all, not to himself.

"All right. You asked. I didn't tell her, no. Once I saw her, I decided not to tell her or her family. I was wrong from the second I picked up the phone and talked to her Dad, and that only got worse. She didn't figure it out until after, 'til we were together the first time."

"How? Did you tell her? Did she find something of mine?"

Evan shook his head, not wanting to say one more word. Everything got worse from here. He wasn't about to tell Michelle or anyone else how exactly Anne figured things out.

He was going to have to take the hit himself. Fair enough.

"She didn't find anything. I… I hid it all. I guess it was the way I acted the next morning."

"You hid my things," she whispered. "You got your inconvenient fiancé out of here then you hid the evidence. Were you protecting her or yourself? You sure as hell weren't protecting me."

"Myself. I didn't want… I didn't want what's going on right now, and what went on with her."

"What did she say, Evan? What did she say when she found out about me? That you'd lied to her too?"

"She wasn't happy with me. She was furious. She's not going to see me again until…unless I tell you everything."

"She was a lot more honorable than you are. That's why you agreed to talk to me, isn't it? For her."

Evan hadn't thought he could feel worse until that second, those words. Until he saw the heartbroken look in Michelle's eyes, all of it his doing. Even if what she said was the truth, he had to try to make this better.

"No, not just for her. It was making me sick to hide so many things from you. I knew it wasn't right. When you called, I wanted to make it a little easier if I could. I don't think I have, but I had to try."

"Does she know we were engaged now?"

All he could do was nod.

"Were you at least careful, Evan? Your father told me where she's been, what kind of life she's led. Do I need to go get tested?"

None of that had crossed his mind, not for one second, that first night with Anne. If he thought about it rationally at any point, he would have assumed she'd been treated for anything she had in the hospital. Once again, the truth was harder than he'd imagined.

"You can if you want, if it makes you feel better. You and I were never together after I was with Anne. You're safe."

Michelle smiled, and Evan thought it was the saddest smile he'd ever seen.

"I'm safe now, as long as I stay away from you. As long as I stay away from you as long as I live." She stood, picking up her coat and her purse. Evan stood but he didn't move toward her. "I hope she's worth it, I really do. Sounds to me like you're going to have your hands full with this one."

"Michelle, do you want…" He reached into his pocket and pulled out the ring box. "This is yours. I want you to keep it."

"Why the hell would I want that, Evan? You think I want to remember you or anything to do with you?"

"I'm sure you don't. Sell it, give it away, whatever you want to do. It's yours."

"Fuck you," she said, shaking her head. "Flush it down the toilet, shove it up your ass, give it to *her*. You did this. You decide what to do with the mess you left behind." She turned and walked toward the door. "I have to thank you for getting this over with before we did get married, I guess. The same thing would have happened if you'd seen her in ten years, wouldn't it?"

She looked back at him, her eyes overly bright. One more slice of her, one more shred of him.

"It probably would have. I'm sorry, Michelle. I truly am."

She laughed, a harsh grunt that broke Evan's heart at last.

"Yeah, so am I. Good luck to both of you. You're going to need it."

She closed the door quietly, and she was gone. Evan was tempted to slam it himself, to slam it over and over again until his ears were numb, or maybe to slam it on his own fingers.

Fair wasn't making him feel better, not anymore. All he had left was the guilt and shame he was nearly choking on.

He opened the box, turning it so the ring caught the light. He knew he'd never give this to Anne or anyone else. It didn't matter how much it had cost or if he did decide to flush it. The ring was pretty enough, but he'd never buy something so typical, so common, for Anne.

Just a big white diamond with smaller ones all around, nothing special at all. Michelle had loved everything about it, crying when he'd slipped it onto her finger.

She'd cried even harder when she threw it at him two weeks ago.

Evan put the box back in his pocket. He did the only thing he could think of, even if he didn't deserve comfort or support. He needed it too badly not to.

She picked up on the first ring.

"Evan."

"Anne. She just left. She knows everything."

"Are you okay?"

"No, not really."

"Come get me."

"I'll be right there."

Chapter 40

Evan sat in the passenger seat of Gwen's minivan, the smell of stale fries and little boy sweat rising all around him, staring up at an ivy-covered brick apartment building. Hurricane Ed's second floor windows stood open to catch the warm May breeze. Sensible tan curtains stirred in most, but three rippled with bright cartoon characters.

The small, tree-lined park across the street echoed with little kid yells and laughter, perfect for Ed's frequent weekends with his grand-sons. Evan sometimes wondered if his father had more adult company, but he'd never felt brave enough to find out. Gwen probably knew, with her willingness to ask questions no one else would even consider.

Right now she only sat quietly beside him.

They'd been parked for several minutes without saying a word.

"I don't know if I'm ready for this," he said, looking at his sister.

"I'm never ready to see him, not even when I have the boys with me. We can get out of there at any time, Ev. You don't live with him, and you don't have to. This isn't even the house you grew up in. You never lived here. He isn't in charge of your life anymore."

"He is until I stand up to him. Even if he never speaks to me again, I have to stand up to him now."

"Okay. Let's go."

They walked up the perfectly maintained wood and marble stair-case together, and Gwen squeezed his hand for just a second when they got to 2C. Evan smiled at her, glad she was with him after all. He couldn't remember ever being so nervous or afraid as he was at that moment. Anger at his father for talking to Michelle was the only thing that kept him moving forward.

He pressed the old-fashioned engraved brass doorbell, listening for the charming three-note tone. Neither Evan nor Gwen had ever listened when their father told them they could just walk in. Evan knew neither of them ever would.

After just a few seconds, Ed Griffith opened the door.

"Hey, two for the price of one!" he said, smiling and stepping back. "Come on in."

Evan and Gwen followed their father through a living room that seemed bigger than Evan's whole apartment, past a mix of heavy wood furniture from their childhood home and grandson-friendly beanbags and chairs. Shelves jammed full of games, toys, and video-cassettes, most of the kid variety, took up one brick wall.

The kitchen was just as spacious and comfortable, with room for the big oak dining room table from the house and a sleek granite island. Ed opened a glass-fronted cabinet and brought out a huge St. Louis souvenir coffee mug for Gwen. Ed's hair was still thick, but it was almost completely gray now. His shoulders were a bit rounded, his back not as strong. He looked so much smaller to Evan, so much less intimidating.

But some part of him was still scared to death of his father.

A steel carafe of strong coffee waited on the table. Gwen winked at Evan and reached into the fridge to get something for it. Evan was the only one who could tolerate Ed's coffee black.

"Well, this is a treat," their father said, sitting down across from his children. "What brings you both out here?"

"Evan's so damned cheap he conned me into driving," Gwen said, pouring milk into her mug. "No, I was hoping to borrow a few more books for the boys. They both read like fiends, thank goodness. You still have a few here, don't you?"

"Yeah, piles of them. You're not borrowing, hon, they belong to the boys here or at your house. The two of you will just have to work it out if your brother… Take as many as you want."

Evan didn't miss that hesitation, and neither did Gwen. She smiled at him before turning to Ed.

"They'll bring some back when they're here for Memorial Day weekend, if that's still on?"

"Absolutely it's still on. They're welcome here any time."

Evan watched the two of them, trying to hide his smile, and his confusion. He'd never imagined his father turning into such a stereotypical grandpa, unrecognizable from the father he'd once been. Even with Gwen's uneasiness about talking to Ed herself, she was perfectly comfortable with their father keeping her sons. Evan had seen Ed with his grandsons more than enough to know she was right about that.

"I'll just finish my coffee and go take a look," Gwen said.

"Is there any coffee in there?" their father said with a half smile. "Looks like mostly milk to me."

"A few drops of your coffee keeps me awake for days."

Gwen glanced at Evan then, her eyebrows raised just a little. He closed his eyes and nodded. He wasn't ready to face talking to his father, but sitting here drinking purified caffeine wasn't going to help.

"I'll be back," she said, walking toward the boys' bedrooms.

Evan turned back to his father, trying to gather all of his wits and his calm about him. He wouldn't be able to keep Anne and Ed from crossing paths forever, much as he might want to. He couldn't stay so angry about his father talking to Michelle, or angry at her either.

He owed it to her, to Anne, and to himself, to at least try to get through this. Before he was ready, his time ran out.

"What's been going on with you, son?"

"It's been an interesting few weeks."

"That's what I hear. Michelle called me a little while back."

"Yeah, she told me about that. You two had quite a talk."

Ed shook his head, then refilled both their cups.

"You don't have to tell me a thing, you know that. But she was pretty upset."

"I know. I didn't handle things very well. But I did what I had to."

"Want to tell me why?"

Evan stared at his hands for a few seconds, then closed his eyes.

No, he didn't want to. Not at all. But that was the whole point of coming over here in the first place.

"It was never going to work out between us, Dad. That's all."

"Did she know that?"

"No, she didn't know. Not before it was over."

Ed rubbed his face, a habit Evan hadn't noticed they shared until just then.

"You seemed happy with her, Evan. I know she was happy with you. What happened?"

"Michelle just wasn't the one for me. No matter how hard I tried, she never would have been. Going on that way didn't seem fair to anyone."

His father crossed his arms and sighed. Evan tried to brace himself. Too many conversations with Ed went downhill after that aggressive gesture.

"What made you suddenly realize she wasn't the one? Is there someone else?"

Evan forced himself not to sigh in return. His anger was trying to jump in and take over the whole conversation.

"You *know* this, Dad. You know this. You knew it well enough to tell Michelle what was going on."

"She called me, son, crying so hard I could barely understand a word she said. She'd just left your place, which she thought was her place until she got back from Seattle. What was I supposed to tell her? 'Easy come, easy go?'"

"You could have told her to talk to me about it. You could have said you were sorry, or tried to make her feel better. Anything else was up to me to tell her."

Ed narrowed his eyes and turned his head a little to the side.

"Is there someone else, Evan?"

The sharp tone in his father's voice tensed up all the muscles in Evan's neck and shoulders. That tone had almost always been the end of conversations that had already gone downhill. Either he got up and walked away, or the shouting started. He wasn't sure Gwen being in the next room was going to make any difference.

"It's Anne. It's always been Anne. No one else has ever come close. We're really happy, Dad."

For the first time, he honestly wished he had visions, like Anne did. Even if they weren't true, and Evan was starting to suspect they actually were, he might have some idea what to expect here. His father stared at him, and Evan could see him trying to keep his face neutral.

"That's nonsense. You were engaged for over two years, up until a few weeks ago. I know she wasn't pregnant, and you've never done much of anything on a whim, much less getting engaged or getting unengaged. You had to care about Michelle at some point."

"I did care about her, yes. Of course I do. But I didn't love her. No matter how hard I tried, I never could. That wasn't fair to her, or to me."

"I didn't even know Anne was back from the hospital. Again."

"She's been back for a few months now," Evan said, stretching the truth enough to be uncomfortable. Not quite eight weeks had passed. "She's doing really well."

"She always seems to, in the beginning." Ed at least had the grace to drop his gaze, and a few seconds later Evan understood why. "When did this happen, Evan? Exactly when did you realize you'd been waiting for Anne all these years?"

Evan chewed the insides of his cheeks, wanting desperately to avoid the question. Even such relative civility wouldn't last once they got into this.

"I've known that since I was thirteen years old. Time hasn't changed it at all."

"That's not what I asked you, and I know you heard me. When...did this...happen?"

Gwen somehow managed to use her anger and not let it get away from her, not let it take over. She'd used that anger to keep this man from controlling her the way he'd always managed to control Evan. Maybe that was the part he was missing now. His own anger.

"Two months ago. I first saw her two months ago."

"That was while you were still engaged, wasn't it?" Ed said, one of his eyebrows raised.

"Yeah, Dad, I was still engaged."

"So on top of everything else, Anne didn't give a shit that you already had a fiancé."

"She didn't know, not for a while."

"Hid that from her, did you?" Ed tapped his fingers against his biceps. "So you're starting this disaster on a good path already. Did she even care when she finally did find out?"

"She wasn't happy with me at all. She was furious. She refused to see me again until I ended things and told Michelle the truth."

"Well, good for Anne for having at least that much integrity. She wasn't unhappy enough to let you be though, to let you go back to your fiancé."

"I told you it's going really well, Dad, more than it ever could have with Michelle. Didn't you hear me?"

"You have to work at it, Evan, that's the whole point. It feels oh so exciting right now, sure. But time passes. The newness wears off."

Evan felt the mistake, the bad judgment, somewhere at the bottom of his brain. Somewhere in the old part. He knew how bad it was going to be, and it didn't matter. He couldn't stop the words once they started. They just kept moving, from his throat to his mouth out into the corrosive, dangerous air between himself and his father.

"The way you worked at it with Mom? Is that what you mean? The way you never, ever let her forget her mistakes until the day she died?"

Ed folded his hands on the table, and he kept his eyes focused on them.

"Son, be careful where you're going here. You don't have any idea what you're getting into with me."

"Maybe not, but I do know what you're getting into with me."

"Is that right?" his father said, glancing up.

"Yeah, that's right. I did everything wrong, and I'm not trying to deny that. But I'm not going to let you make this Anne's fault like you've done so many other things. I made the bad choices, not her."

"She didn't just have some kind of mental breakdown this time, Evan. She had to go to rehab to clean up before she could even go to the hospital. I'd say that counts as some pretty god damn bad choices. What makes you think she's going to stay clean now?"

Evan breathed deeply, trying to slow the pulse he could feel in his ears.

"That's not what I'm talking about, Dad, listen to me. Whatever she did in the past is her business. What I'm telling you is she wouldn't let me keep being such a jackass, not if I wanted to be with her. Doing the right things so I could be with her is the first good decision I've made for a long time."

"You broke a good woman's heart for a girl who'll probably end up back in the hospital before the end of the year. For a grade school crush."

Evan stood and shoved his chair forward. Everything on the heavy oak table rattled.

"That's enough, Dad, enough! This is not some kind of crush, no matter how much you want it to be. It's not a crush any more than Gwen and Mark are, or you and Mom were. I love her. I always have. If you can't deal with that, I won't bother you anymore."

"So you think if Gwen left Mark for some guy she knew twenty years ago, I'd be happy about that?"

Ed's voice had risen to full volume, his hands clenched into fists on the table. That voice had Evan wanting to shrink away and cover his ears forever. He managed to stop himself after only a few steps toward the door.

"I never loved Michelle or anyone else. Not like this. I never *want* to. This is the my life and my decision. If you're going to keep this up, I can't be around you anymore."

The two men stared at each other long enough for Evan to lose count of his own breaths. Ed finally leaned over and pulled the chair back out.

"Sit down, son. I might not like this, but I'm not going to turn my back on you. Sit."

Evan opened his mouth and breathed in until he couldn't anymore, then let it out in a sigh as he sat.

"I know Mom broke your heart, Dad. I understand now that it wasn't because she didn't love us or you. It was because she was human. She made mistakes just like all of us do. I know I have."

Evan wasn't sure if he should be heartbroken or frightened at fierce agitation he saw in his father's eyes. Ed had hardly spoken about his wife since the day she died. When he did, it was always "your mother," never my wife or even Megan.

Evan was afraid everything hidden away or forced inside his father would burst out in just a few seconds.

"Your mother's choices, and mine, were between us. That's just where they're going to stay. That was part of *our* life, not yours. It's not your or your sister's business."

"But it all affected us, Dad, you have to understand that. Knowing what she did, seeing how it changed both of you, I grew up with that. I can't pretend it wasn't part of my life too."

"Then why the hell did you treat Michelle that way?" Ed shouted, pounding his fists on the table, loud enough that Evan shrank back in his chair. "If you had even the slightest idea what that would do to her, how the hell *could* you?"

Evan felt the hand on his shoulder before he realized Gwen had walked into the room. His ears were still ringing, of course she would have heard it too. He was thankful she was there, and even more thankful that she didn't say anything.

"Because I made a terrible mistake, that's why. I got carried away with seeing Anne, with being so happy she was okay. Then when I realized she wanted me after so many years, I think I just lost my head. I didn't mean to be such an ass, but I know I was."

"If you know it was a mistake," his father said, "why did you keep making it? Why are you still making it?"

Evan winced at the entirely different sound of his father's voice. He was no longer threatening. He was heartbroken. Evan wasn't ready to feel sympathy, not after that shout and the awful things Ed had said about Anne. He wasn't ready, but he was feeling it deep in his guts.

"Because I didn't love Michelle, not the same way I love Anne. I was making the mistake by…by thinking…"

He watched his sister walk around to sit at the table. He wanted her to speak now as badly as he hadn't wanted her to just a few seconds before.

"It wasn't the same thing, Dad," she said. "I remember more about that time than you think I do. Evan was wrong, but he wasn't doing the same thing Mom did, not at all. For a while, Mom forgot the one she really loved was you. She stayed with you, didn't she?"

Their father blew out his breath, shaking his head.

"I think she regretted that more often than not."

"It doesn't matter though, she stayed," Gwen said. "Pain in the ass that you are, she stayed."

"Right back at you, kid." Ed turned back to Evan. "Are you just dating her, or what?"

Evan tried to keep his smile to himself. Of course there wouldn't be any happily ever after in this conversation, not with Hurricane Ed. Gwen winked at him again, flashing a crooked smile of her own too fast for their father to notice.

"We've been dating since right after she got back."

"Where's she living now, with her parents?"

"For now."

Ed scowled. "You want her to move in with you already?"

"Yeah, Dad, I really do. I hope she does soon. It's going beautifully, since you didn't ask."

"Does she even have a job, son? Or are you just supporting her?"

"Of course she has a job, but if I wanted to support her instead I would do just that. I just told you we're really happy, more than once. Why can't you hear me?"

Ed took a deep breath, looking at Gwen, then back at Evan.

"I heard you say you want to move in with a girl who's had issues since she was eleven years old, and I don't mean just bad moods sometimes. She's been in and out of hospitals her whole life, Evan. What makes you think she's going to get better? What can possibly have changed after all this time?"

"Maybe the change is she has someone who loves her. Maybe not having someone say she's crazy all the time is making a difference."

"I never said she was crazy," his dad said, his cheeks turning red. "I just think this is a lot for you to take on, son. Have you thought this through?"

Evan looked at the floor, gritting his teeth. He'd heard those words, have you thought it through, his whole life. Thinking it through had been related to jobs, school, renting an apartment, buying a car. Big decisions that made sense to take his time with.

What bugged the crap out of him was hearing it about going on vacation, going to a movie, ordering dinner, even buying a book. Evan couldn't remember if his father been like that before his mother died, or at least he hadn't noticed. Now everything in Ed's life seemed to be about thinking it through, whatever *it* happened to be.

And never, ever doing a damn thing about it.

"You know what, Dad? I didn't need to think it through. I've loved Anne since I was thirteen years old. Probably before that. That's never changed, not even for a minute. I've already thought through how much I missed her and how much every other woman I've ever dated isn't her. That wasn't Michelle's or anyone one else's fault. That's just the way it is. I've thought through how empty my life feels when Anne's not in it. No amount of thinking is ever going to change the way I feel about her."

His father shook her head, sighing again.

"What do you think about this, Gwen?" Ed said, turning to her. She shook her head, smiling a little.

"No way, I'm not getting in the middle of you two. You're both grownups. As long as you don't start throwing punches, you just have to work it out."

Ed narrowed his eyes, then turned back to Evan.

"What if she leaves you? What if she does have to go back to the hospital and leaves you alone?"

"I'll do my best to keep that from happening, but I know it could. That's the way life works, isn't it? None of us knows anything for sure. You didn't know when you met Mom, or when Gwen and I were born."

"Don't tell me you want to have kids with her." Ed scrubbed at his chin. "You never know with things like this."

"You're right," Evan said. "You never know with *anything*, Dad. That's just how it is. You had no way to know what would happen with Mom."

"Son, your mother had an aneurism. She never had to stay in a hospital because she was imagining things or because she tried to drink herself to death. You can't be telling me you want the mother of your children to be suicidal. And all the medication Anne must be on can't be good."

Evan hated feeling like this, his guts churning and cold sweat working down his back. Despite Gwen calming everything down, he was starting to hate this conversation even more.

If there was one thing his father did know, it was how hard raising two kids alone had been.

"We haven't really talked about kids, Dad. I don't know how she feels about it. I'm not the only one who'll make that decision."

"But how do *you* feel about it, Evan?"

He stared at his hands before looking into his father's eyes. That gentle tone was something he did remember from his childhood, from before his mother died. His father had hardly ever talked that way since.

"I honestly haven't thought about it," Evan said. "All I know is I want to be with Anne. The rest will work itself out. If she doesn't want kids, I don't want them. That's all."

Ed held Evan's gaze for a long time, longer than he had since Evan was a little boy. He was painfully aware his father probably didn't do that very often because Evan's eyes were exactly like his his mother's.

"Just tell me you're happy," Ed finally said. "I'm going to worry about you no matter what. Both of you. But I want you to be happy."

Evan smiled, surprised it was so natural and easy.

"I am, Dad. It has been a rough few weeks, but I don't think I've ever been this happy before."

PART VII

MENDING THE FUTURE

Chapter 41

Anne sat in the chilly white waiting room, staring at the ring finger on her left hand. Nothing was there, not yet. Even with a marriage so well-known and remembered to her, six months wasn't quite enough time for that. She knew exactly how her hand was going to look, though.

Evan was going to search his beloved antique shops for weeks, all the way into Chicago, until he found a ring with four matching stones the exact color of Anne's eyes. She didn't have to say a word to him about not wanting a diamond like he'd given Michelle, and she loved him all the more for that.

He would be trembling and nervous, and he would admit later that he'd been scared she wouldn't want a ring from him at all after what had happened. Anne would tell him the truth: that she'd been dreaming of a ring exactly like this.

The nurse sat behind her bullet-proof glass, calmly calling one name after another. Some women were here for an abortion, to end the life growing inside of them.

Anne wondered if any of them were like her. Did they know the dreadful fate awaiting the children they were never going to have? Years ago she'd wished she'd meet another person like her, just once. Now she didn't want to, not ever if she could help it.

If one other woman knew what was coming and decided to terminate her pregnancy, Anne was afraid she would lose her resolve. Her dreams and memories told her everything and everyone depended on what she was going to do tonight, but she still mourned the fate of their child. A child she would never know.

She looked at her hand again. Before another year passed, a thin white gold wedding ring would join the beautiful green stones. Evan would wear a thicker one to match, they would both wear them for the rest of their lives. Her engagement ring had already been worn and loved for well over one hundred years. Anne hoped to love it herself as long as she could, then send it further on into the future.

Her phone buzzed in her pocket, pulling her out of visions of her wedding day.

Her mother had managed to stop herself from calling Anne every day only this week. She might not ever be able to stop sending text messages. Anne didn't mind. After only a few months of living with her parents, such a short time of calm after so many years of screaming nightmares, Anne had abruptly moved into Evan's apartment three months ago.

She'd never been able to see such a joyful and incredible turn of events when she'd returned to her parents' house. Even remembering and reliving the visions after she started spending so many nights with Evan hadn't prepared Anne for the overwhelming reality of waking up beside him every morning.

Anne replied to her mother that she was doing fine, no nightmares, and she and Evan would be there for Sunday dinner. She'd lied about the nightmares, of course. She'd been lying to her mother about that for a long while now. Only Evan, the one who slept beside her, knew how often and how badly Anne had the dreams.

He was the one woken as often as she was, holding her close in the middle of the night as she trembled and cried. Anne tried not to let visions of Evan's death bring her to tears right now.

She felt terrible about interrupting his sleep in such an awful way. She dutifully took her medication out of the bottles, making sure he saw her do that much. She dissolved all of them in hot water and poured them into the toilet when he couldn't see her. Anne didn't like putting such strong medicine into the water supply, but that wouldn't matter for much longer.

The poison in the air was going to kill far more people than the poison in the water.

She'd be able to solve the problem of Evan's sleep and of the dissolved pills in just a few short hours. Once she was finished here, Anne would be taking her medication, at least some of it, once again.

"Anne F?"

Anne stood, nodding at the nurse. A sign beside the nurse's window announced the new experimental harvest procedure, the chance to share life with a couple who wanted to share love. Anne had dreamt about this for weeks now, but the sign announced the start date of only a couple of days ago.

The idea of even more people being born on a doomed planet nearly made Anne cry again. No matter how many desperate hours she'd spent thinking about that, hours that added up to years of her own life, she couldn't do a thing to stop it. She hoped her choices somehow made it better.

The only thing she could do was walk through the door and into her future.

The young woman was very kind and efficient as she took Anne's vital signs.

"Have you used a pregnancy test?"

"Yes," Anne lied. "I did last week."

"How far along do you think you are?"

Anne pretended to think back, to count the days since her last period. She knew the day and the hour she had conceived this baby, but she couldn't let this no-nonsense woman know that.

"About five weeks, I think."

"And you want the experimental harvest procedure?"

"Yes. That's exactly what I want."

The nurse made notes for a few seconds, then she looked up into Anne's eyes. Her brown eyes were warm and concerned.

"Have you talked to your partner about this?"

An unexpected tear rolled down Anne's cheek, and she knew the woman saw before she could hide it. Talking to Evan about this was one thing she had only imagined, never remembered. Her imagination had been painful enough, more than painful enough.

Anne had to tell a lie that hurt even worse.

"I don't have a partner. This was all a mistake. I don't want to carry a mistake inside my body anymore."

The nurse nodded, then she touched Anne's shoulder. Anne smiled, and she didn't try to fight her tears any longer.

She wanted to cry out that she wanted this baby, she wanted this baby more than she wanted to draw her next breath. She wanted to see what she and Evan had made together, what the most perfect joining of them would look like, smell like, sound like.

She wanted to see this baby, this new person inside of her, grow up and learn and explore and find out about the world.

Anne knew she couldn't do any of those things, no matter how badly she wanted to. The agony of this moment had come out of nowhere, stronger than the faint regret she remembered about this night. The memory was what she had to do though, even if she left her own heart in this lonely room along with Evan's baby.

The procedure was much easier than Anne expected. Less uncomfortable than the routine examinations she'd always hated. She wasn't sure if it was because she knew this one had a purpose, and she didn't care.

She was going to take the birth control the doctor offered. Evan would be sad about her not wanting to have children with him, but he would understand. Anne's parents would understand too. Of course she didn't want to pass her problem along to a child. Of course.

The secret that Anne would never tell anyone, not for the rest of her life, was that she was not going to pass her problem along.

Just as he had been in every other way, Evan was the key.

Something about him, maybe his own firm sanity, maybe his genes, maybe just the love between the two of them, was going to let their baby be almost normal. This child would have part of Anne's problem, the part that would somehow let life on Earth continue after so much disaster. But this child would not be driven crazy by her own mind.

Anne's breath caught at her first glimpse of the baby's gender, the first hint that she and Evan had made a little girl together.

"It's all right, we're all finished here," the doctor said, misunderstanding. "You can sit up and get comfortable."

Anne got dressed and watched the doctor working. She looked into a microscope, making notes with her left hand. She couldn't have been any older than Anne herself, maybe even younger.

"Do you have any requests for the donation?"

"I want the donation held for at least twenty years. Can you do that?"

The doctor looked at her, eyes wide, but Anne knew her request would be honored. She stood, ready to walk out of this room and away from this sad reality.

"That's an unusual request, but I will make a note of that," the doctor said, turning back to the microscope. "You were carrying twins."

Anne's jaw dropped and she sat down again, hard.

Twins? She'd never remembered that, not one time, not ever. Leaving them behind was more than twice as hard.

"Are you… Are you sure?"

"I'm certain. I see two perfectly healthy embryos here. You're giving an amazing gift, Anne."

Anne stood, this time on shaking legs. For the first time, she had no idea what was about to happen. She'd known she would be donating the child she carried, but finding out they were twins plunged her deep into the unknown. She'd longed for that ignorance, the ability to wonder what the future had in store, for most of her life. Now she wanted only to know what lay ahead for all of them.

"Thank you," she managed to whisper.

Anne turned and walked out of the room and into her unknown future.

Chapter 42

Evan lay still in the cozy darkness of his bedroom, his hand on Anne's waist. She was sleeping quietly, but he knew that wouldn't last much longer. He didn't need to look at the clock to be sure. His own body's clock woke him most nights just before she did.

The first couple of months had been rough, and Evan could admit that to himself now. He'd been red-eyed and bleary enough that people at work had asked him if he was sick. He'd just said he had a new girlfriend. Thankfully they'd just laughed and patted him on the back instead of asking any more questions.

He knew they assumed he was losing sleep because of all the sex, and that part had definitely been nice. Better than he'd imagined, actually, and he'd been imagining making love to Anne since he'd learned what that meant. What made him lose sleep was her nightmares.

She'd tried to warn him about that the first time she'd spent the night on purpose, that she might wake him. He'd been too dazed and happy that she'd come back to pay attention to what she was saying, but she'd been telling the truth. Just a few hours after they'd fallen asleep, Anne had started moaning, the most awful sound Evan had ever heard.

Her face, barely visible in the faint light from his clock that night and so many nights since, was what brought him to full awareness. Even with her eyes closed, she clearly saw the most dreadful thing anyone could imagine. Her face would look like she was crying, brow drawn down, eyes squeezed tight, sweet mouth pushed out and trembling.

Evan knew she saw visions about the end of the world, she had for years now. So maybe it *was* the very worst thing.

When she finally woke from her dreams, gasping and jerking, Evan was afraid to move at first. With her eyes open, the horrified look was a thousand times worse. She stared for a few seconds, then drew in a shuddering breath. Then she always moved against him, holding on tighter than he would have thought she could.

All he could do for a long time was stroke her hair and whisper that it was all going to be okay. Evan hadn't noticed the time that first night, but he knew now that she took almost ten minutes to calm down and get back to sleep. That first night, he'd fallen back asleep with her.

It wasn't until the third night that Evan really understood the worst part of Anne's nightmares. He hadn't asked her, but he had a pretty strong idea she'd slept alone almost all of her life. The hospitals she'd been in and out of certainly had single beds. She'd told him more about her time with Joe that he'd wanted to hear, and part of that had been drinking enough to stop the dreams. At least for a while.

So for most of her life, the woman he loved so dearly had woken up from those horrible nightmares all by herself. She hadn't had anyone to comfort her once she outgrew going into her parents' room. Joe certainly wouldn't have bothered, and he didn't have to ask about the others.

From that night on, Evan knew he would do whatever he had to to keep her from being so alone and afraid in the middle of the night.

He got into the habit of taking an hour long nap during the day to make up for the lost sleep, locking his office door and stretching out on the couch. That had turned into an unexpected pleasure he wasn't sure he'd give up if he had the chance to.

The two of them had started going to bed a little earlier to make up for the interruption. He'd tried to talk to her about the dreams, but she hadn't wanted to tell him. She told him her medicine helped sometimes, but she got into phases when it didn't. She thought this would pass before long.

The last two nights had been the worst he'd ever seen in her or anyone else. The first night she'd started thrashing around before she woke up, and she fought him when he tried to hold her.

Then last night, she'd woken screaming.

Evan decided then and there to find out what was making the dreams worse. He'd be heartbroken to have to stop sharing her bed, but if having him there was making it worse, that's what he would do. He was afraid he was disturbing her somehow, intruding on her space too much.

If she needed different medication, he would help with that. A noise machine, a different pillow, even a different apartment, anything at all within his power to make this better for her. Whatever it took would be worth it.

Evan focused on Anne again when she shifted, turning onto her back and moving closer to him. She wasn't dreaming, not yet.

Something about her, something he couldn't put words to even now, drew Evan to Anne like a moth to a flame. Even if he did burn up in that flame, like his father feared, Evan simply didn't care. Being in that fire with her, even for the briefest instant, would be worth everything.

Anne twitched against Evan's side, pulling him out of his thoughts and into his much more complicated reality. He watched her, determined to catch her before she started screaming this time.

Her memories sometimes were too accurate for him to doubt, but he'd never figured out where to put that inside of himself. He just knew to trust what she saw. He had to at least try to help her.

Her face crumpled up again, and she seemed to be shaking her head. She drew a sharp breath. Evan pulled her close.

"Anne, sweetie, you're dreaming," he whispered, bracing himself for whatever happened. "Wake up, you're dreaming. Everything is okay."

She pushed against him for a second, then all the tension drained away with her breath. When she breathed in, she squeezed him back.

"I'm sorry, Evan," she said against his chest. "I didn't meant to wake you."

He moved back enough to see her eyes. She still looked upset, but the horror had left her, at least for the moment. He wished she could be free of it forever.

"I want you to tell me about it," he said, brushing her hair back. "Tell me about the dream. You've never done that before. Maybe it'll help."

Anne looked at him without saying anything. He wondered if she was remembering that same day, that long ago day on the playground when she had first trusted him with her terrible secret.

He could only hope she knew he was as unable to turn away from her now as he'd been that incredible, awful day.

"The dreams change. I don't always have the same one."

"What about just now? Was that a new one?"

She nodded, rolling her eyes closed again.

"A new one. A bad one."

"Tell me about it. I'm not going anywhere."

She smiled at him, and Evan's heart knew that leaving him to stay with Anne all those years ago had been the right choice. The best choice. The only choice he ever could have made.

"You're not, are you?" she said, then she took a deep breath. "I got my medication adjusted a couple of days ago. That always makes them stop in a couple of weeks."

"But they start up again eventually, right? Maybe if you tell me, they won't come back."

"I'll try. I was dreaming about a volcano just now. A really big one. The sky turned black for a long, long time."

"What happened?"

"A whole lot of people starve to death. Most of the people do."

"Most of the people this time though, not all of them?"

She shrugged, then put her arm around his waist.

"That part changes too, it always has. It's been most of the people for a long while now."

"What do you think the difference is?" he said. "Is it random, or can you tell?"

She smiled a tiny bit, one he could barely see in the dim light. He was sure he saw her cheeks turning red.

"It's too sappy."

"Oh come on, you don't know anyone more sappy than I am. I do that part so you don't have to, remember? I'll tell you whether it's sappy or not, dear."

Anne smiled, then tried to hide a huge yawn.

"Okay, you asked for it. I've spent a lot of time thinking about this one, might be kinda nice to tell someone else. The dreams seem to shift depending on whether I'm with you or not."

"With me?" Evan was too pleased to be embarrassed. "Did that always happen?"

"Yeah, I think it always has. When we were apart for whatever reason, or when I was about to go into the hospital, dreams, visions, memories, everything I saw was *everybody* dying. When we were together, even as friends, at least a few people seem to make it."

"Do you know why?"

Evan had a wild theory about what the two of them could do together, a deeply held secret dream, but he wasn't about to tell her or anyone else that just yet.

"Who knows? I don't even know why I see these crazy things to begin with, much less what makes them change. Sometimes I see three things all at once, but I have no idea what to do about it. I do know they've always been easier to tolerate when I'm with you."

Evan spoke before his sleepy mind could stop him.

"Well, we'll have to make sure that never changes."

Anne laughed low in her throat, the same way she did when they were making love, and Evan felt his own face burning. He was hardly playing it cool about wanting to marry her, but he was nowhere near ready to ask her yet. He hadn't even found the ring despite searching high and low everywhere short of Chicago.

"I... I mean..."

"It's okay, Evan. It's all going to work out just fine."

"Have you seen something? Something about us?"

That was the second of the internal think-before-you-speak rules so carefully instilled by his father to fail Evan in just a few seconds. He wasn't sure he truly wanted to know about his own future, and he hated to bug her about something that tormented her so horribly. She raised up on one elbow and kissed him.

"Do you really want to know?"

"I do, I think. You said you love to be surprised, though, I remember that. Does it help to know what's coming?"

"Most of the time it's been awful." She held her cheek against his. "Most of the time what's coming has been something I would have stopped if I could have. Sometimes it's good to look forward to things. But I do love to be surprised."

"Then don't tell me," Evan said, relieved. "I'll be surprised enough for both of us. I'll just change the subject now so I don't keep putting my foot in my mouth if you don't mind. You said you have choices sometimes. Did you dream about choices just now?"

Anne lay with her head on his chest, her fingers playing with his curling hair.

"No, not this one. It went straight through. Not a thing I can do about this one. It might not happen, though. It didn't feel quite the same as the rest. It's hard to explain."

"Try me. I'm a good listener. At least you've told me that before. Maybe if you tell me, you'll be able to get back to sleep."

She shook her head against him. "I'm afraid you won't be able to, though."

"That's my problem, not yours. I'm tougher than I look. Tell me about your dream, sweetie. What makes it feel like it won't happen?"

"The other dreams feel heavier, more substantial, like something I could almost touch. They stay with me, some of them for years now. Decades. But this one feels like it'll be gone before morning."

"Tell me anyway. I want to know what you dream about, Anne."

By the time she finished talking, Evan understood why she'd woken up looking so upset and afraid. So many people suffering, fighting, dying, and all she could do was watch and wonder if only a few would live or none at all.

He could almost see the unsettling scenes playing out like a movie in his mind's eye. He was afraid he wouldn't be able to go to sleep after all, but he didn't dare tell her that. As long as she was calm enough to sleep, he was more than glad to let her. He only hoped he didn't wake her with a nightmare of his own.

"Are you okay, Evan? Tell me the truth."

"I will be. Do you feel any better at all for talking about it?"

"I do, actually. It's all faded. I don't know if I could remember well enough to tell you again."

"It's all worth it then," he said, "if telling me takes it away. I want you to tell me the others too, the ones that feel real." His heart ached almost as much as his stomach twisted at the thought of her having dreams worse than this one, but he'd just have to deal with that when the time came. "Will you do that?"

"Promise to tell me if you start getting too upset, or if you start having bad dreams too?"

"I promise. Think you can sleep now?"

This time her laugh, her deep sexy laugh, started heat in his belly that he couldn't ignore. That was the best way he could imagine to clear the terrible images out of his mind. Hopefully out of hers, too.

Her hand drifting lower, across his belly and into the thicker hair below, told him Anne was thinking the same thing.

"Maybe in a little while."

Chapter 43

Anne drew in a deep breath, closing her eyes so she could focus on the scent of Lake Michigan on the morning breeze. She caught a sharp, clean trace of last night's fog cutting through the sweet spring lilacs down in the courtyard .

All the windows in the apartment she'd shared with Evan for the last two years stayed open as soon as the two of them could stand the cold in spring until they couldn't stand the cold in autumn. Anne loved the faint rattle of the old-fashioned counterweights when she lifted the bottom panes or lowered the top ones. One of the many advantages of a building built before the Second World War.

Thick walls that shut out almost all the noise of neighbors and city alike were another. She'd been afraid of the sounds of so many people, that their presence jammed in around her would make the nightmares worse for her and for Evan. But the solidity of the stones around them, the broad hardwood beams under their feet, even the comfort of Evan loving his teaching position at the university so much, gave Anne the best sleep of her life.

Sleeping beside Evan, the man she'd happily vowed to sleep beside for the rest of her life, did more than a quiet bedroom ever could.

Evan shifted on the long couch beside her, tucking his bare, chilly feet under her leg. Anne opened one eye and caught his grin before he could hide it behind a book. He sometimes joked she was trying to freeze him to death with the open windows, but he never closed them when she wasn't home.

He wore a midnight blue terrycloth robe just like her own, the set an unusually thoughtful anniversary gift from Evan's father the year before. Hurricane Ed had surprised them both with the way he'd welcomed Anne into the family on their wedding day. Maybe he'd had a few dreams or memories of his own.

Anne's dreams over the past few weeks had turned as sweet as the lilac downstairs, as fresh and clean as the breeze off the lake.

"What's on your mind?" Evan said. "Did you have a bad dream last night?"

Anne shook her head. "I haven't had a bad dream without you waking up for a long time now. I hate to interrupt your sleep like that, but it's helped more than you know."

Evan got up and poured more coffee for both of them, but he kept staring at her, a strange, crooked smile on his face. She wondered if he knew he looked like his father in that moment if at no other time.

"You look like you want to say something," he said. "I'd swear I'm seeing the future for you right now. Want to just tell me?"

"I don't feel quite like I can do that, but maybe you can help. You told me once you didn't want to know what was coming. This time I think... I want to be sure about this one."

He shook his head, still smiling. "That's not quite what I said. I *do* want to know, sometimes I'm jealous of you for that. But I still want the surprises. Way too much to ask, isn't it?"

"Maybe not in this case. Tell me something, sweetie. Tell me how you feel about children."

Evan blinked and sat back, his pale blue eyes wide. Anne was afraid she'd misread him. That hadn't really happened in all the years she'd known him, all her life, but everything could always change.

"How I feel... You mean in general?"

Anne laughed, harder than she meant to, and she was relieved when Evan laughed with her. The memories of their baby, of their child they would raise together, grew ever stronger and more clear. But she'd never seen the slightest hint of this conversation.

"Well, yeah," she said. "In general, sure. If you hate all children on sight, this will go pretty quickly."

"No, I don't hate them on sight, not usually. You know as well as I do that our nephews are turning into surly beasts from the foul land of the teenager, but I still like them. I pretty much like most kids once I get to know them, if that makes any sense at all."

"That makes perfect sense. I feel the same way most of the time."

"Now that we've got that out of the way, I still don't know what you're asking me about."

Anne moved his feet into her lap, rubbing his cool skin between her hands.

"How do you feel about having children, Evan?"

"Is there something I need to know right now?"

"No, nothing like that. I know you like surprises, but that would be a big one."

He still looked confused, but he didn't seem upset at all.

"I haven't really thought about it much, not seriously. No more than daydreams. You told me a long time ago you never wanted any kids. You didn't want to…"

"It's okay, I remember what I said. I'm still worried about what would happen to them, what *will* happen to them, when everything falls apart. That's still true."

"Has something else changed, Anne? Do you feel differently now?"

Anne closed her eyes. Gathering her thoughts about all the things that had changed felt impossible, much less trying to find the words for any of it. That fear was still there, her dread about so many people dying. But somehow she felt stronger anyway.

The future felt less heavy inside of her, like Evan was carrying part of the burden.

And his strength was deeper and more steady than she'd ever imagined.

"I'm afraid," she said. "But I don't know if that's any different than anyone feels talking about this. If it's something you want, I don't want my fear to keep us from it. Just feeling so much better about it might mean things have shifted. You know?"

Evan moved until he was close beside her, arm around her shoulders. The solid comfort of his body reached every part of her.

"I do know," he said, kissing her cheek. "Have you seen something you need to tell me about?"

"Only that it's all going to work out just fine. Do you want to know more than that?"

Evan kissed her mouth hard then, hard and long enough that she forgot all about the dreams and visions and memories. All Anne could hold onto was how much she loved him, how much she wanted him. A lazy Sunday morning on this sofa in the sunny living room of their apartment felt like the perfect time and place to start bringing her memories into reality. He drew back, breathing as hard as she was.

"All I want to know is if we're going to be happy if we do this. That's all. If *you're* going to be happy. I know I am as long as I'm with you. I don't even have to ask about that."

"I won't tell you it's all going to be easy. I have a pretty good feeling a lot of it won't be. But I know this is the right thing, Evan. I don't have to see the future to know that."

"That's more than enough for me. Yes, Anne, I want to have children with you. I have for a long, long time. I'll tell you something else I've thought about for a while now, but I didn't think the time would ever be right to tell you. Maybe you feel better because this is what we're *supposed* to do. Maybe that's why you don't see everyone dying anymore."

"Maybe that's true," she said. "Maybe you make all the difference."

Anne was startled, amazed that he was saying what she'd so clearly seen. This was a gift she'd never expected to have when she donated her embryos, the first children they'd made together. Those babies, removed from her and from Evan forever, were going to be part of that chance of survival, but now she knew they could do the same thing right here.

She'd have the joy of seeing how Evan was with this child, how he took all the pain and struggle between himself and his father and turned it into love. And she knew if this baby, this sweet little boy, did turn out to have her issues, her gift, she'd make sure he understood what it was and how to deal with it.

What Anne didn't tell him, what she never planned to tell her husband or anyone else, was that she *did* know.

Parts of it were going to be hard, terribly hard. But most of their lives together, and the life of their son, were going to be good. Even after they were gone, and that felt further away than it ever had for her, their son would live on just like her grandmother had told her.

Back when Anne couldn't believe anything would ever be good again, her Gemaw had known. She'd seen this happening.

Her Gemaw had seen those beautiful blue eyes she was staring into, Evan's eyes, in her own baby's face. But what Anne saw now was a healthy boy, a strong and dependable man, with her own green eyes. The same as her father's and her grandmother's.

And even further away, so distant in time that she could only catch glimpses, a grandson who would help bring Anne's rare, sweet dreams of humanity surviving into reality. A grandson who would somehow have need of the four flashing hunter green stones of the engagement ring she wore alongside her wedding band.

Need, and necessity she couldn't quite understand.

And all of it out of love.

Chapter 44

The recovery room at the university hospital felt more like a modern apartment. Maybe one of the new lake view buildings, the location for so many expensive faculty parties and endless fundraisers. Warm beige and gold walls, thick rugs on the tile floor, soft lighting. A sitting area by wide floor to ceiling windows crowded with comfortable chairs.

The bed beside Evan's plush recliner had a discreet monitoring panel tucked into a gleaming wooden enclosure, but the sheets and comforters were rich shades of green and blue instead of blinding sick room white. And the much smaller bed in the sitting area looked more like a high-end bassinet than a standard infant hospital bed.

Neither he nor Anne had imagined being friends with faculty and staff because of all those parties would make such a difference on the day their lives changed forever.

Evan watched Anne sleeping in that comfortable bed, the pleasant buzz of low voices only adding to the awe-struck, dazed state of his mind.

Nothing he'd ever read or heard had prepared him for this day. Nothing ever could have.

"Come on over here, Dad."

He blinked and turned toward the other side of the room, where Gwen sat with Mark, Ed, Mike, and Karen. The most important people in his life had all been there to meet the newest member of their family. His father spoke again.

"Evan, you asleep with your eyes open?"

"I'm sorry, what did you say? Did you mean me?"

Everyone laughed, and Evan smiled, not quite sure what the joke was yet. His father shook his head, but he was smiling too.

"I mean you, Dad, come on over. I think you're about to be on duty."

All the air in Evan's lungs escaped, and he felt a little light-headed. Even though Ed had been speaking to him, Evan had just assumed that word, *Dad*, was meant for that corner of the room. After all, the three fathers he knew best were all right there.

Until that moment, Evan hadn't quite grasped that he was one of them now.

He glanced at Anne again, still sound asleep, her hands together under her face like the little girl he still remembered so well. The only thing as beautiful in the entire world was in that tiny bed. Evan walked over and stood beside his father.

"He's about to wake up," Ed said, his hand on Evan's shoulder. "He has the same look on his face you always did. I'd bet if you pick him up, he won't cry and wake Mom over there."

Evan looked up, right at his sister. She had a crooked, smartass grin on her face, but her eyes, so much like Ed's, were overly bright. Ed showed no signs of the weepiness both his children were caught up in, but Evan couldn't remember the last time he'd seen his father so calm. So happy.

Content, that was the word he was looking for. Ed might not be on the verge of sobbing, or even dignified blotting at the corners of his eyes, but he was content.

"Go on, he's about to let loose full blast," Ed whispered. "You'll get to be an expert at knowing every little thing that sound means eventually, so you might as well get to know the warning signs."

"I'm not sure…"

"Just pick him up, Ev," Gwen said, Mark nodding beside her.

"Mark was impossible the first few times too, but we didn't have any real disasters. You can handle it, little brother."

Evan leaned down, watching for those signs his father was talking about, wondering if their son would rise up out of sleep the same way Anne did when she had a nightmare. His head was full of all the advice and warnings about picking up a newborn. Support his neck, hand under his puffy diapered backside, hold him close to your body.

Evan doubted he'd ever be natural and easy picking his own son up, able to move without the litany of advice running through his head.

Connor's rosy little brow wrinkled, then smoothed, and he seemed to be pursing his mouth, like he disapproved of the situation all around him. Just as his eyes fluttered open, Evan snuggled Connor close against his chest.

So warm. So *small*.

"See, you're a natural," Mike Fincastle said, standing on Evan's other side. "He's already settling down."

"I'm here, Connor. Daddy's here."

At his whisper, Connor's dark blue eyes seemed to focus on Evan's. He was sure he'd read somewhere that a newborn wouldn't be able to do that for a long time yet, but Evan felt the contact, the connection.

No one else existed in the room, in the entire world, but the two of them in that moment.

Whatever beat out time in his chest after his heart had gone to Anne's so many years ago left him to join their son, but Evan had never felt more whole and full. Connor blinked a few times, pursed his lips again, then drifted back into sleep.

"What's he saying, Evan?" Anne's mother said. He smiled at his mother-in-law, at Connor's grandmother, trying not to laugh and wake his son.

"I'm in over my head with this guy. He has no idea what the hell he's doing."

Everyone laughed softly, and Gwen put her arm around Evan.

"Go sit down, relax. You look about as sleepy as my nephew there."

Evan started to hand Connor to Gwen, much as he didn't want to, but she shook her head.

"He's fine right where he is."

Evan walked with exaggerated care, wondering again if he'd ever be brave enough to just pick up the baby and go like he'd seen Gwen and Mark and so many other people do.

Gwen followed him, waiting until he sat in the recliner beside Anne's bed as carefully as he could. His sister grabbed an impossibly soft blanket from a chest of drawers and covered him with it.

"Here, let me put these pillows around you. I'm going to lean the chair back. No, you're fine. You're not going to drop him, Ev."

By the time she finished adjusting him and the chair, Evan felt like he was in his own warm cradle, Connor secure in his arms, tiny head on his shoulder.

Gwen kissed her nephew's forehead, then Evan's. He thought she'd last done that when he was thirteen, on one of those long, awful nights after their mother died.

"Mama Gwen."

"Well, you're Daddy Evan now, so we're even. Get some rest. You're going to need it."

"I wish…"

"I know, me too. Mrs. Megan Connor Griffith would have been over the moon right about now. We'll just have to make up the difference." She glanced at the rest of them, then spoke barely above a whisper. "We'll all be here for anything you need, okay? But you're going to do just fine."

She gave the blanket one final tuck under his shoulder, then rejoined the others. Evan watched them, trying to fight the sleepiness that seemed to flow from his wife and their son into his own mind and body.

All of them sitting together like that, like family.

Like *their* family, the strange and jumbled and fractured and pulled together bunch he and Anne had drawn around themselves. He didn't think any of them could have possibly imagined this quiet room, this completely unexpected turn in his life, even a few short years ago.

He couldn't wait until Anne woke up so he could tell her about it. He couldn't wait until the three of them were at home, really starting out on their new adventure.

"I'm here, sweetheart," he whispered, no longer sure if he was talking to Anne or to their little boy. Probably both. "I'm not going anywhere. You're safe. We're all safe."

Evan turned toward Connor, shifting until the baby was breathing into his face. That incredible sweet smell pushed away the tiny bit of consciousness Evan had left.

He hoped Anne's dreams were as sweet as their baby's breath against his cheek, as sweet as flowers after the rain.

Evan had a feeling his own dreams would be, too.

JOINING THE STORM

BOOK TWO OF THE STORMS OF FUTURE PAST SERIES

KARI KILGORE

AUTHOR OF IN THE PINES AND RESTRICTED SPECIES

For Jason

*Who knows what it's like to leave the mountains
and to come back home.*

Chapter 1

Alex Collins was never asleep when he was supposed to be. His parents gave up trying to hide holiday gifts or replace his lost teeth with money before he turned five. He was the kind of kid who didn't care for surprises anyway. He preferred to know what lay ahead of him. By the time his brother and sister were old enough to consider sneaking out of the house at night, they already knew it would be pointless.

Life on the outskirts Fond du Lac, Wisconsin, gave Alex the stability he craved. Giggling about the French translation of Fond du Lac as *Bottom of the Lake* before he even started school gave him the first taste of the humor that would always sustain him.

He saw patterns all around him. The orderly grids of streets, noises and bursts of activity with shift changes at factories, migrations of huge flocks of birds each spring and fall. All gave him the framework he needed to withstand the upheavals of childhood.

In the summer of his thirteenth year, the comfort of routine failed him. Patterns transformed into prison bars, hemming him in, dragging him inexorably onto a path no one around him thought to question. An approved set of classes in high school would lead to community college, then to the University of Wisconsin and a solid, respectable corporate job shuffling papers in Madison or Milwaukee.

He could detour into the factory, like his father. Or the farm, like his grandfather.

Either way, Alex knew he would sink into oblivion and disappear.

Around the same time, the fundamental honesty that kept him from pretending he didn't know about his parents' late night activities drove an impenetrable wedge through the middle of his family.

Alex wasn't quite old enough to know he should pretend he didn't notice when certain patterns changed.

Distance between him and his father grew first, and most painfully. Seeing the changes, less time spent together, avoiding Alex's activities, and more harsh words than kind, didn't help him understand what was going wrong. One conversation brought more clarity than anyone wanted.

Glen Collins had picked all of them up from school for the third time that week, a task he'd rarely done before the past several weeks. Alex sat at the desk in the den, while his brother and sister sat with his father on the sectional sofa lining three walls of the carpeted basement space.

The other kids had their mother's straight blond hair, and Alex had red like his father, just starting to curl enough to be horribly unruly.

Nearly as unruly as his mouth sometimes.

"Did Mom get a different job?" Alex said.

"No, son. She's had the same job for seven years now. You know that."

Alex looked up from his math homework, warning prickling along his spine. His father didn't sound annoyed as he had so often lately. He sounded afraid.

"I just thought..." he said, not sure how to make everything better but needing to. "So many things have changed over the past couple of months. That's all."

His father shut down his reader with an ominous sigh. He lowered his chin and looked at Alex.

"Is that so? Why don't you enlighten me about all these changes?"

Alex was scared he wouldn't be able to answer through a dry throat and mouth. His after school sandwich weighed heavily in his belly.

"That's okay, Dad."

"No, it's not." The other two kids were ignoring their own homework now, watching the exchange. "You're always so full of information, noticing every little thing, whether we want it or not. Well, I want it. Start talking. Now."

"You pick us up more," Alex said, forcing the words out. "So I thought she was working late more. She bought a bunch of new clothes. I wondered if they made her wear different stuff. And with her new haircut, I thought she seemed happier or something."

"New haircut," his father said. He sat back and crossed his arms. "That it?"

An alarm deep in Alex's brain, triggered by budding empathy or self-preservation, kept him silent.

"Know what I think, Alex? I think I've had just about enough of your vivid imagination and your little games. Next time you have a bunch of lies and nonsense you just have to tell someone, save it for school. Or for your mother."

"Dad, I didn't mean to upset you," Alex said. "I'm not imagining things. I'm not lying. I feel like something *good* is going to happen to Mom, not something bad."

This time the flash of fear and fury in his father's eyes made Alex cringe in the hard wooden chair.

"What are you doing, making notes of her movements? Spying on us? Do your damn homework! I don't want to hear another word. In fact, why don't you take yourself and your excess of attention up to your room?"

Alex gathered up his things, heart pounding in his throat, tears in his eyes. Worse than his father's shout was the fear he'd clearly seen in his brother and sister. They both drew away, faces pale and eyes wide.

When his mother got home two hours later, he heard more shouting that didn't stop until his mother talked to him a week later. She walked into his room looking sad and exhausted.

"Listen, Alex. I don't know what you told your father. But I'm not sick, losing my job, or having an affair. I've been going for a promotion, which I may not get after the last week of going to work asleep on my feet."

"I wasn't trying to cause trouble," Alex said, trying not to cry. "I just noticed something was different. I thought it was going to be something good."

"Well, it may still be if I can make up for the past few days." She rubbed her eyes, then looked at Alex again. Her brown eyes were red around the edges. "I know you think you see a lot of things, and sometimes you probably do. You're not old enough to know when to keep your mouth shut. Do me a favor, kiddo. Don't be on my side."

FROM THAT DAY ON, the patterns around Alex shifted. Instead of a safety net or a constricting trap, he saw a way forward. A way to move. His inner eye followed sidewalks, roads, even plants that leaned away from the lake he'd grown up at the bottom of.

Alex's mind, and his heart, were set on a path to the southeast.

He got into the habit of keeping quiet and keeping his head down at home. That routine left him lonely, but he was grateful for the calm. At school, though, he embraced the opposite and excelled beyond his own vague ambitions of living somewhere else. His love of math and the sure answers it provided refined into a passion, as did his perhaps less endearing habit of taking apart everything mechanical he could get his hands on.

People in Alex's life, even his parents, eventually stopped worrying about finding their belongings in pieces. He always managed to put things back together. And they often worked better than they had before.

His calculus teacher called him aside in the middle of his junior year. Ms. Powers was the best teacher Alex had had so far, challenging and pushing him beyond what even he thought he could do.

"So what are you planning to do once you get out of here, Alex?"

she said. She was perched on her desk, swinging her sneaker-clad feet like a kid.

"You mean today? Or after next year?"

"I mean next year," she said, smiling. "Today's all up to you, though I know you'll get your work done before Monday. What are your plans for college?"

Alex kicked at the tile floor, then tried to disappear into himself when his shoe made an obnoxious shriek.

"Community college for a couple of years, I guess. I don't know after that. Maybe the math department down in Madison."

"That's a perfectly sensible plan," she said. "And I know you can do better. Is any of that what you *want* to do? Do you want to teach?"

"I think it's what I *can* do. I don't love the idea of teaching, but we're not exactly rich."

Alex didn't say what he was really thinking. He hadn't had any big outbursts with his parents for the last couple of years. But he doubted sending their strange and overly observant son to a hugely expensive school right away was high on the list. Even with that big promotion his mother had earned after all.

"Well, I'd like to talk to a few people," Ms. Powers said, "but I wanted to talk to you first. You don't have to teach, Alex, though I think you'd be pretty good at it. I've seen you tutor more than one kid who was struggling. Do me a favor. Take some time over the weekend and look into engineering. With what I hear about the way you run circles around everyone else in your industrial shop class, you'd be a natural. The teachers are afraid you'll go through all their projects before the end of the semester."

"I am a little bored in there," Alex said before he stopped to think. He felt his face and ears blazing hot. "Please don't tell them I said that."

"No, that's what *they're* telling me." Ms. Powers was smiling, not scolding. "There are some fine schools here, but I have one in mind where a friend from my college days teaches."

Alex closed his eyes, waiting for the odd shockwave moving through him to subside. He saw all the decisions, small and large, leading to this moment. Doubling up on math for the past two years. Asking for extra work whenever he could.

Making sure he got into *this* class, correctly rumored to be tougher than the other two.

He didn't have to ask, but Alex knew he should. No one else knew about the patterns, the way motion and arrangement and confluence directed and shaped his life. That was best kept to himself.

"Where is it?"

"Chicago. Not too far from home, is it?"

Alex laughed, looking down at his feet to hide the quick tears in his eyes. The map resolved in his head, with his home at the bottom of a much bigger lake.

And himself in the middle of a much bigger life.

"Not too far at all, Ms. Powers. Not even close."

Chapter 2

Alex opened his apartment door to a blowing Chicago snowstorm, drifts he didn't want to deal with already building up on the concrete steps. Four people barely recognizable through heavy coats and scarves stared up at him. He'd seen two of them in considerably less clothing a few times over the past five years

"You're not honestly expecting me to go out in this?" he said, holding the door open.

A party had sounded like a good idea a few hours ago, before a blizzard settled in like a heavy blanket over his shoulders. They stomped enthusiastically before stepping inside.

"What exciting plans did you have instead?" said Kim, one of those friends he'd spent close personal time with. "Reading some journal, or working?"

"Neither, thank you very much," Alex said, kissing her cheek. "Just finished up work a few minutes ago. I had plans to watch a shitty movie and go to bed. That's what we do out here in the real world."

"For fuck's sake, Grampa Collins." That was another of Alex's more intimate friends, Thom. "You graduated college early. You didn't magically accelerate to fifty years old."

"Maybe not, but this isn't my crowd anymore. Seriously. Have a couple here if you want, but I'm going to sit this one out."

Kim and the other two, recent dates for his friends who Alex didn't know very well yet, shook their heads and headed back toward the kitchen to take him up on the offer. Thom crossed his arms and stared at Alex with his head tilted.

"I'm afraid I'm going to have to insist you get the hell out of here tonight," he said. "You have the rest of your life to work yourself into a rut like everyone else. And you need to act your age whether you want to or not."

"What am I supposed to talk to them about, Thom? Yeah, I'm still a kid, but I'm not drowning in finals anymore. I'm drowning in work. There's a major conversational disconnect there."

"How about you stop drowning, then, at least for one night?" Thom stepped forward and kissed Alex, hard and deep, cold hands slipping into his hair. He stepped back, grinning. "Just have some fun, man. You still remember how to do that, right? And unless there's someone I don't know about, it's been a while since you got laid. If we're both bored at this party, fine. We head back here and take care of that."

Alex looked around the space, a far cry from the cramped dorm he'd endured with three other guys for three years. This apartment wasn't huge, but it was all his. It did look like a guy in his thirties lived here.

An actual *adult*, one he didn't often feel like.

No evidence of secondhand furniture or dirty clothes, no trace of stale beer or piles of books. He was damn proud of accomplishing so much so young, of getting himself out of his hometown and his parents' house and into a great job.

And Alex wasn't quite ready to join his father's demographic before he turned twenty-three.

He'd been feeling strange and out of sorts all day, off track somehow. That kiss felt pretty fucking good, and it had been a while.

"All right, I'm in. We'll see about your generous offer depending on how the party goes. You and I are great at that part, not so much at the rest."

"Who said anything about the rest?" Thom said, walking toward the kitchen. "I'm planning to use you for your body."

"Works for me. I'll get my coat."

The first steps into the bitter cold nearly sent Alex right back inside. The wind was vicious, driving stinging snow into his face and eyes. Walking two blocks to a college party hoping for some kind of hookup felt like insanity at the moment, but not quite as pathetic as going to bed at nine on a Friday night.

The cars outside the building were already covered with snow. A thick trail of footprints showed the way through the tree-lined courtyard to the second apartment on the left. Alex again considered going back home despite the promise of time with Thom, or someone else. The drifts would surely be up past his knees in a few hours with the way this storm felt.

Alex blinked, sure his eyes were watering from the icy assault. He stopped on the sidewalk, looking back toward the street. That wind had died down inside the sheltered courtyard, leaving the snow to float rather than being driven through a howling tunnel.

Everything he saw, everything he felt, resolved into massive, interlocking patterns.

The streetlight caught the huge flakes and threw sparkling light across several inches on the ground, all lining up to point toward where he stood.

In a lifetime of sensing and feeling such things, he'd never imagined his entire life turning on one point, one moment he did not yet understand. As if a thousand train tracks from all over the world joined in this one spot, then continued on their way.

"Alex is in danger of abandoning us," Kim said from beside him. "He's staring wistfully toward his shitty movie and his bed."

"His *empty* bed," Thom said. "Get your fine ass in gear, old man. I'm freezing mine off out here." He squeezed Alex's backside and pushed, bringing them all in the door laughing.

The heat from an overachieving fireplace and way too many bodies hit Alex like a steaming hot shower while he was fully dressed. There wasn't enough room to stand, much less walk around. And still that movement forward, people shifting to give him a path when there shouldn't be space for one, Thom close behind him, no longer grabbing his ass but adding to the momentum.

Alex looked up, in the direction nothing less than what felt like orbital mechanics was pulling him. He saw one face out of dozens. One man with lovely green eyes, dark brown hair, and the sexiest smile he'd ever seen.

The crowd closed behind him, and Alex walked forward, pulling his coat off. Some part of him knew the years before and the years that would come after still existed. Other people, far too many of them, still lived and breathed all around him.

None of that mattered. This was the moment his whole life, all the choices and hard work and random events, would turn upon.

Alex stepped into his future.

Chapter 3

In an instant, in one flash of warm blue eyes, Etan's entire life made sense.

The party itself was depressingly typical. Far too many college students jammed into a Chicago courtyard apartment, music too loud, temperature too high despite heavy snow falling outside. Inexpertly rolled joints passed around as easily as fake phone numbers.

Second-hand clothing dragged back from the early decades of the twenty-first century, styles of their grandparents brought back from the dead. Every conversation competing to be the most important, the most revolutionary, and the loudest of all time.

Etan desperately needed a break from the toughest bunch of biology and math classes he'd been foolish enough to take in an indigestible lump, but he only went along to these nightmarish events out of a sense of obligation. If he'd wanted to sit in his own lonely shoebox apartment every night, why bother moving to such a huge city in the first place?

He could have easily taken most of his non-laboratory classes online for a lot less hard-earned money, even with the huge help of his grandfather's faculty tuition rate. And he could have stayed in Southwestern Virginia for all the rest, holed up in the mountains and living rent-free with his family.

And he would have long since dropped out, or dropped dead, from the never-ending routine and depression.

Etan forced himself to walk through the mob again, escaping the living room with its ear-splitting cheap stereo, broiling fireplace, and shocking chill every time the front door opened. Kitchen followed dining room on the way to bedrooms, all with too many people trying to get a warm body into the closest thing to a bed before they all disappeared into finals.

Several attractive guys and a couple of adventurous girls made it clear Etan was what they were looking for, or at least close enough for the night. Most of the time, he would have taken the chance, if nothing else to get the hell out of the crowd.

With the guys at least. Girls were an unknown territory, one he was more than a little bit afraid of.

He could have even stayed in Appalachia for the casual hookups. Just trade the pretentious wannabe artists for a bunch of grumpy high tech and tourism workers, most of the marijuana for tobacco, and self-conscious wine drinking for cases of nasty beer, and he'd be right back at home. Out in the open or furtive and sneaky, partners were around.

Going home alone, an option too many of the kids in either place seemed afraid of with so much pressure building up as the semester wound down, didn't bother Etan most of the time. The temptation to just say a quick goodbye and disappear was familiar and comfortable to him. He'd stayed a couple of hours longer than he'd planned to already.

Something was different tonight.

Since he was a little boy, Etan had felt a curious sense of dislocation. Hardly anything or anybody around him seemed to fit, and not a damn thing inside of him did. Only his grandparents and father made him feel at home and comfortable.

Part of the trick was they listened to him without trying to convince him he was imagining things. Being around them made him feel like all the sharp and jagged parts of himself at least kept still for a time instead of trying to slice him to ribbons.

As he'd grown up, once in a while he felt one of those parts slip into place. A tiny bit of the noise inside softened, quieted, fell into tune with a song he did not yet recognize. Minor changes like taking his first science class or kissing a guy for the first time, big changes like deciding to go to college so far away from home.

The relief of that smooth internal shift instead of relentless grinding gears let Etan know he was on the right track every time.

And every time, he had a feeling of oncoming alignment, an eclipse in slow motion in his chest. Perhaps a piece he never knew was missing completed several others. Maybe another that hadn't been meant for him in the first place slipped away.

Or simply a part of Etan that had always been used the wrong way, by himself or someone else, fell into perfect motion at last.

Walking around that overheated party in the middle of an early December Illinois snowstorm, he felt the adjustment long before he understood why. The rolling heat throughout his body told him this would be nothing less than fundamental. A change to last the rest of his life.

A burst of laughter from the living room brought a real smile to his face, easing muscles strained from faking for hours. He turned to see a crowd of men and women filtering into the few remaining open spaces.

Flowing into human eddies and currents.

The tides within Etan surged and roared.

One man looked back into his eyes instead of dodging forward to find the alcohol. Snow glittered in curly red hair that brushed his shoulders, with blue eyes framed by a neatly trimmed dark red beard. He smiled at Etan, a friendly, open smile, not the blatant come-ons he'd tried not to return all night long.

This man showed no signs of fear or arrogance, not even a trace of the desperation filling the room as people paired up and departed. Only a confidence too natural to be any kind of act.

And those gorgeous dark blue eyes that made Etan's knees weak. The man walked forward, slipping his heavy black wool jacket off.

"I'm roasting in this thing," he said, his deep voice setting off resonance waves in Etan's stomach. "Know where the standard coat pile is?"

"Not really. I left mine in the car."

"You're a braver man than me, driving tonight," he said, brushing the snow from his hair. "It's really coming down out there."

"I had a feeling it would be worth it." Etan's heart sped up, and he hoped his cheeks weren't turning red.

"Were you right?"

"Not til just now," he said, holding out his hand. "I'm Etan Griffith."

"Alex Collins."

Everything grew from that one warm touch.

Chapter 4

A STRONG GRIP on Alex's hand woke him from a light sleep, all he seemed to manage when he stayed with Etan. The room was still dark, with no sounds of traffic outside the windows. He thought for a second, trying to remember where they'd gone to bed.

Etan's place, that was it. He'd been looking forward to that breathtaking lake view early in the morning.

Not quite *this* early.

Etan's whole body jerked against Alex's back, and he let out a hard breath against his neck. Etan seemed to dream constantly, almost from the second he closed his eyes, but it hadn't been quite this noticeable before.

Alex thought about checking the time, but he didn't want to move far enough to pick up his watch. Etan's apartment was always cold, for one thing, and he had no desire to stir even an inch from their warm bed.

He had the strangest feeling Etan was supposed to have these dreams uninterrupted.

That didn't make a lot of sense, especially if they woke Alex, but that didn't change his certainty. He'd always been a light sleeper anyway, easily able to drop back off.

"Air," Etan said, his voice breathy and higher than normal. "It's in the air. The water. The earth."

He squeezed Alex's hand, curled against his stomach under Etan's, hard enough to hurt. Etan's breathing sped up, and his legs twitched like he was running.

"That doesn't sound like a good one," Alex said under his breath.

He turned over, shifting his grip until he was holding Etan's hand. Strange feeling about letting the dreams go on or not, Alex hated the thought of him being so upset.

"Etan. It's okay. You're just having a dream."

Etan groaned low in his throat, twitching all over now. Alex leaned over him and turned on the dim bedside light.

"Wake up, Etan. Everything's fine."

He could see his boyfriend's face in the light, and Alex drew back in surprise. Etan's eyes were wide open, but they didn't seem to be focusing on him or anything else.

"Everybody dies," he said in a voice that sounded younger, like a little boy's. "No matter what we do, how far we run, everybody dies."

Alex was covered in chills worse than the temperature in the room could explain. That may have sounded like a child's voice, but it didn't sound like a dream voice.

It sounded like the truth.

"Why do they die?" he whispered.

"Poison in the air. Poison in the water. Murder in their hearts. Everybody dies." Etan's voice trailed off on the last two words, and Alex's hair stood on end.

"What can we do about it, E?"

He touched Etan's sweaty cheek, not sure if he wanted to wake him or let the unnerving conversation continue.

"Have to go. Can't stay here." Etan's eyes were squinting but still open, and the edges of his mouth drew down.

"Where do we have to go?"

"Southeast. Our future lies southeast."

Alex closed his eyes, his own body clammy with sweat now. He'd seen that same direction leading him out of Fond du Lac five years before, into this city he loved, a job he loved almost as much. Most importantly into this warm bed with Etan, and a passion and connection he'd never even daydreamed about.

Etan's body went rigid, then he sighed in that same high voice. He turned over, moving back against Alex's chest. His breathing dropped to calm and regular right away, the same rhythm he kept until morning.

Alex knew Etan didn't dream again because he watched for the rest of the night.

His certainty about the solid permanence of their lives together, built into his internal foundation barely six months after they'd met, withstood a serious blow with that first speaking dream.

Alex's foundation wouldn't shatter and collapse until almost three years later.

He moved into Etan's nighttime routine as easily as he had his daytime one. Alex went to sleep a couple of hours before, claiming the early hours of an old working man forced him to. He really wanted to get as much sleep as he could before the dreams started.

He woke a few minutes before, keeping track of the time night after night. He started wearing his wristwatch to bed to make that easier without waking his lover. Three seventeen, three twenty, never later than three thirty. Over and over again.

If Etan slept for more than a few more minutes past that internal alarm, Alex knew he'd sleep right through the night. More than half the time, he opened his eyes and the eerie conversation started.

Etan dreamed of the problem with everyone dying most often, but other patterns emerged as the months and years passed.

Alex tried to ignore the first one that concerned him, tried to pretend it was just a normal dream that didn't mean anything. He was still unsurprised when he got laid off from his first job out of college. It hurt even with the warning, but the disappointment was tempered by awe.

Alex knew when his sister was going to call with news of her marriage, and very shortly thereafter, her pregnancy. Same with family members who died. Knowing he'd have a much better job with a great engineering firm with far better potential turned those two months of unemployment from uncertain to a delightful sabbatical.

He learned to accept what was coming, good or bad. Alex had no problem learning to love that secret knowledge he gained while everyone around him, including the source of that knowledge, slept.

Disturbances in his own sleep, even combined with the hair-raising descriptions of starvation and war, were worth it to Alex in return for those glimpses of their future.

He felt almost like he had a secret relationship, one only he knew about, with whatever part of Etan had the dreams. Etan never seemed to remember them, no matter how badly he was upset by them in the moment.

Alex's guilt at keeping that secret combined uneasily with not having a clue how he would explain it.

Hey, did you know you predict the future in your sleep? Night after night, for years now? Probably shouldn't have kept that from you, huh?

The adventure faded when the dreams shifted not long after Alex turned twenty-five, Etan twenty-two.

The routine of sleeping and waking stayed the same, as did the open-eyed interaction with a man sound asleep. But the intensity and the frequency grew. Uneasy dreams nearly every night, and always about the same thing for weeks on end.

They had to go. They couldn't stay in Chicago. They had to go home.

Southeast.

Alex didn't have to look at a map to know what that meant.

He'd visited Etan's family in Virginia several times. The mountains and deep valleys fascinated him after a lifetime spent in the wide open Midwest, and Etan's parents were lovely. He felt more at home on his first visit than he ever had with his own family, who they saw far less often.

But those mountains scared him, too.

Alex felt like they traveled back in time, and not because they had to drive miles along twisty roads to find groceries or alcohol or much of anything else. He felt fundamentally out of place, never losing his awareness that he had no idea how to survive in such a place without Etan. He hadn't driven much since leaving the open, predictable grid of Wisconsin roads at seventeen.

Even if he'd fought the city traffic every single day for those eight years, he'd still be anxious about taking the wheel on the beautiful, unpredictable, and amazingly narrow roads around Wolf Branch.

Every time he was there, though, Alex never escaped the sense of alignment, of every leaf and creek and path through the wilderness pulling him deeper into whatever waited for him there.

Magic Alex didn't know the name for, awareness that seeped into his bones in the Virginia Highlands, turned up his senses and imagination to almost painful levels.

Much as Alex loved being in those mountains, among family who felt like his own, he didn't want to give up their life together in Chicago. The terror in Etan's strangely flat sleeping voice, and even worse, the tears in his unseeing eyes, broke through his resolution and his fear at last.

Chapter 5

Alex transformed everything he touched. He and Etan
shared that same shoebox apartment overlooking Lake Michigan,
but the space no longer felt oppressive. Alex's photos on the walls,
his clothes in the wardrobe, his scent on the sheets turned the
temporary shelter into a home both of them loved.

A home they both knew they had to leave before three years
passed.

Alex walked into the living room with two glasses of bourbon
and ice, their traditional sign it was time to put away work or study
and spend the evening together after a challenging day. Etan closed
the book he was pretending to study, hiding the page he'd been
trying to read for the last half an hour. He normally managed to
spend the time he needed and get it over with, but more than a
strange lack of sleep kept him off balance lately.

His sense of things about to fly out of place had returned, more
strongly than since he'd met Alex. He was terrified of what that was
going to mean for both of them.

"Good stopping place?" Alex said.

He sat facing Etan on the dark grey couch, one of the upgrades
he'd brought when he moved in. It fit under the broad windows

overlooking the lake, by far the best feature in the cozy apartment, as if it had been custom built.

"As good as any. I'm not getting a damn thing done today."

"I'm not surprised, E. You're barely sleeping at all anymore."

"I'm sorry," Etan said, leaning over to kiss Alex on the cheek. "I didn't mean to keep you awake, too."

Alex stared out at the rough gray water of a storm coming in before speaking, leaving Etan's imagination to push him further into panic.

"No, that's not what's keeping me awake. It's what you say that does that. And the way I can't convince myself that every word isn't true."

Etan closed his eyes, not quite aware he was drawing his legs up against his belly. The goddamn dreams, the thing he'd been so scared of Alex or anyone else finding out about. Only his parents and grandparents had ever known about his nightmares.

Even he rarely remembered them besides waking up groggy and disoriented, suffering through the aftermath for the rest of the day.

"No, don't do that," Alex said. "Don't try to hide from me."

He moved the books and notebooks and gently pulled Etan toward him. Etan resisted for a second, then curled up with his head in his lover's lap.

"I never wanted you to know about the dreams. I feel crazy enough without you confirming it."

"Crazy isn't the question," Alex said, stroking Etan's hair. "Unless it's both of us. You missed me saying every word feels *true*."

"I don't even know what the dreams are, Alex. I know I have them, but I never remember a thing. That's not exactly stable."

"Well, have a drink and let me enlighten you."

Etan sat up, managing to keep himself from curling up into a knot of fear again. He drained the whiskey, watching Alex do the same.

"What you tell me in the middle of the night is all about how we can't stay here much longer. Something bad is going to happen, with the food supply I think, and none of the cities are going to be safe anymore. And we don't have much time to get ready before we're trapped along with everyone else who's not going to make it out."

Etan opened his mouth to argue, to protest, to at least keep Alex from saying another awful word. But the words had to be said, and he had to pay close attention. Every part of him knew understanding these dreams would be the difference between living and dying, for both of them and many others besides.

"Are you having the same dreams?" Etan said.

"Not at all. I normally sleep like a rock before and after you start talking. But this time, I'm too afraid to. They're not just words, E, not anymore. Don't you feel that?"

It was Etan's turn to stare out at the lake. The day had been cool and rainy, and the water was dark and choppy. He hadn't understood before Alex asked, but he felt exactly the same way and had for a few weeks now.

"Yeah. I've known something was wrong for a while. I didn't understand why."

"You said you never wanted me to know about the dreams," Alex said. He smiled and took Etan's hand. "I'm not sure why you thought I wouldn't notice, sleeping next to you every night, but it sounds like this isn't new. Does anyone else know about them?"

"My grandparents, Anne and Evan, the ones who grew up south of here. And my parents, a little. They tried to tell me I could talk to my cousins, but I never would let them tell me which ones. My grandmother had dreams that tended to come true, or at least they told me she did. A lot of them were nightmares when she was a kid."

"Maybe I don't understand, then. You keep saying we have to go home, over and over again. I don't think you mean Middle of Nowhere, Wisconsin, especially since you keep saying southeast. Does Virginia feel safer to you than Chicago even though your grandparents were from here?"

"Nowhere felt safe after they died, even after I moved up here," Etan said. "They were born a couple of hours south of the city, but my grandfather's family came from Virginia. That's why they moved back there in the end." He held his breath, then blurted out the rest before he could stop himself. "If we're going to talk about this like it could actually happen, the thing is anywhere out of a city seems like a better plan. Wisconsin is too open, at least where you're from. Nowhere good to hide."

Alex only nodded.

"Can't disagree with you there. I felt that way for seventeen years in Fond du Lac. Now tell me what we'll be hiding from, E. What's going to send us running southeast when both of us love it right here in Chicago? Can you remember?"

The dream opened in Etan's mind as if Alex's words, his attention, slowly turned on the lights on a darkened stage.

A stage the size of the whole world, the play too harrowing for anyone to sit through.

"You said I talk about the food supply, right?" Etan waited for Alex to nod. "I keep thinking about the way my family in Virginia kept food stored, especially for the winter, even with grocery stores in town. An old-school pantry and cellar aren't going to be enough for whatever this thing is. The air, the water, even the soil. It's all poison. Things won't grow properly anymore. Masses of people trapped in cities, and I know hardly any of them are going to make it."

Etan gasped, shocked and relieved that he'd said so much. He hadn't talked about anything he'd dreamed since his grandparents died when he was sixteen. Old enough to realize knowing he had nightmares but being unable to remember them was exactly the kind of strange he wanted to keep to himself.

"Did you remember any of that before I asked you?" Alex said. He was holding both of Etan's hands now, the contact like a lifeline in that choppy lake.

"Only the part about storing food. I don't really remember details of the rest. It's just… It feels true. Now you tell me something."

"You're wondering why I would believe you?"

Etan couldn't help returning Alex's smile. The tension pulling all of his nerves and muscles to the breaking point eased up enough for him to breathe.

"Most people wouldn't," Etan said. "Most people would have

already been on the phone to the psych ward. That's another thing about my grandmother. She spent time there more than once when she was young. She remembered all of her dreams, though."

"*Most people* don't know you as well as I do. From what you tell me, no one has slept beside you for more than a night, either. What I've been hiding from you is how the things you mutter in the night have a strong tendency to come true. If I could get you to dream about the stock market or sports, we'd never have to worry about money again."

"Bullshit," Etan said, unable to hide the flush spreading across his face. His whole body felt like he was trapped in the white hot spotlight on that vast stage. "You're making this up."

"I can't think of one damn reason why I'd make something like this up. Even I'm not enough of a jerk to think that would be funny. But let's see."

Alex took a deep breath and leaned closer, tilting his head and staring into Etan's eyes.

"Ever wonder why I'm never surprised by an odd phone call? How I knew exactly when I'd get laid off, and when I'd get this job? Why I already have my time off arranged anytime we have to go to a funeral or wedding or whatever else comes up? People probably think I'm the one who can predict the future."

"You can fucking have it, then, Alex!" Etan pulled his hands away and sat back. "I've hated this since it started, even more once I knew it drove my grandmother half crazy. If I could make it stop right this second I would!"

Alex smiled a tiny bit.

"You've always said you knew you'd meet me that night, at that stupid college hook up party in the middle of the biggest blizzard in twenty years. Wish you'd stayed home instead of going home with me that night?"

"Not usually," Etan said, trying to catch his breath. "Right now, maybe."

What an asshole he was, shouting like that. Alex had no way to know how desperately Etan needed to keep the damn nightmares a secret. How terrified he was of having as much trouble as his grand-mother did. Etan hadn't exactly been honest about any of it.

"Good thing you didn't know any better." Alex brushed the back of his fingers along Etan's cheek. "You've never told me how you knew. Did you dream about that night before it happened? About me?"

"I don't know. Maybe. Probably. I hate talking about this, Alex."

"Well, if even half of what I've been hearing and feeling is true, we're both going to have to be a hell of a lot more honest. It's way too late for me, sweetie. I'm not going anywhere. Is the way you know things more than dreams?"

Chapter 6

Etan forced his breathing to slow, hoping his heart would follow. He kept seeing his grandmother's green eyes, same as his and his father's. Near the end, he didn't think she knew who she was talking to, but she seemed driven, compelled to get the words out. Words that hadn't made sense to him then, but Etan, his father, and especially his grandfather listened to every one. That might be the key to everything now.

Maybe talking to the man he trusted more than anyone else would keep this thing from eating him alive like it tried to devour her.

"That night, lots of times, I can feel something moving toward me," Etan said, speaking slowly. "Once in a while I see an image, but usually I get the sense of a piece moving into place. I knew a big change was coming that night, and I knew it would be good. It has been."

Now Alex looked away and blushed, but not before Etan saw his smile. He wished they could continue along this path, warm and safe with the storm outside the window. Go back to that first night and discover each other's bodies, minds, and hearts all over again.

But what he felt shifting into alignment now, blasting everything else out of place, was too huge and moving too fast to ignore.

"What I feel now is just as big, maybe bigger," he said. "And nothing will ever be the same again. When you asked me about it, my mind focused, I think. Or cleared. Whatever's coming is going to break everything."

Alex groaned, soft and low, but Etan heard it. He nodded, his blue eyes terrified.

"That's what I've been feeling, Etan. Everything's going to break. Your dreams are part of it, but this comes from inside me, too."

Alex looked down, at the fist he'd made so tightly the tendons stood out along his wrist.

"What comes from you, Alex? What's got you that upset?"

"You said you had your grandmother to talk to about all of this. I haven't had anyone. I've never mentioned a word of this to a single person. And I'm the one who said we had to be more honest with each other."

He opened his fist, staring at the red half circles in his palm. Etan rubbed his hand.

"I didn't know I was going to meet you that night," he said, looking at Etan. "But I did know something was going to happen. I don't have dreams like you do, or visions or anything like that. It's not that easy to explain."

"You think this is easy?" Etan struggled not to laugh with Alex so anxious. "You missed your chance to turn me in to the shadowy authorities for having dreams that predict the future. You're stuck with me now."

"I see…" Alex stared at the lake again, opening and closing his mouth. "Patterns is the clearest way to put it. Movement and alignment all around me when something's going to happen. Before I left Fond du Lac, everything I saw for months lined up and pointed toward Chicago. Clouds, leaves blowing down the street, ripples in water. All I had to do was follow whatever was pulling me. The rest was effortless."

"What about the night you met me?"

"Nothing until I was outside the apartment, not really. Then the light and the snow and the people inside pointed me to you. I couldn't even see anyone else's face in the room, E. Only yours."

His own internal world whirled and adjusted, lining up with the forces inside and around Alex. Completing the synchronization that started the second he'd seen Alex walk through the door and into his life.

"You did walk right toward me."

"Thank the gods," Alex said, his tense face relaxing into a small smile. He brought Etan's hand to his lips, then held both of his hands again. "I never thought I would admit this, not even to you, but whatever these dreams are feels even bigger to me, too. I see the same patterns I did before, pointing in the same direction. Southeast."

"But it doesn't make any sense," Etan said, pulling one hand away to rub his eyes. "It's probably stress over these damn classes and worrying about whether I should keep going or give it up and get a job. I *am* studying fucking environmental policy right now, everything that can go wrong."

"That's something else you forget. I've already been out in the world for a few years instead of neck deep in academia. Some strange things are starting to happen. I might not have thought much about it besides typical gloom and doom bullshit, but it's close enough to make me uncomfortable."

"What things?" Etan whispered.

He would have sworn the surface of his brain was swelling, bubbling up, trying to change shape. Alex's words, and his belief in these crazy dreams, set off a change neither of them would be able to stop.

"Remember the bees and other pollinators having trouble a while back? When a bunch of them died off, before we were born? Stories about that happening again are springing up all over the world. Faster than back then when it started, too, and no one knows why. Everyone just figured we had it beat, so all these years later we're as dependent on them for our food as ever."

Etan rubbed his arms, trying to stop the crawling sensation before it could spread to his whole body. He'd refused to visit his grandfather Evan's bee hives with all the other kids, no matter how much they picked on him about being scared. Yet another thing he had in common with his grandmother.

She'd told him she never liked bees, either. In fact…

"Alex. My grandmother told me she dreamed about bees, all the time when she was a teenager. Awful dreams. Gods, she told me she saw all of the bees dying, then almost all the people dying not long after."

Etan realized he was shivering when Alex moved closer and put both arms around him. He grasped his lover's strong forearms and tried to keep his teeth from chattering.

"She told you that? How old were you?"

"This was not long before she passed, so I was fourteen, fifteen. Their house wasn't far from us, so I was over there all the time. I guess I was old enough, but by then she was getting a lot more honest than she should have been."

"You were just a *baby*." The harsh edge in his voice surprised Etan. "If it upsets you like this now, she definitely shouldn't have told you when you were so young."

"No, listen. Dad told me she wanted to make sure we were all ready just in case we had the dreams too. It was the right thing, Alex. Gemaw said that was what made it so bad for her, when no one believed her and she had to hide what was going on."

"Gemaw?" Alex said. "That's a new one on me, sweetie."

The laughter, always sweeter when they shared it, stopped most of the trembling.

"Welcome to the Griffith family, sugar pie. Just wait till we figure out what to call you when the time comes."

"That's something else we haven't talked about as much as we should have if any of this is going to happen," Alex said. "Maybe we should go ahead and get the DNA merge now instead of when we're ready to have kids. Hang on, hear me out."

Etan hadn't realized he was shaking his head.

"If everything's going to go to hell, this is the last thing we should be worrying about. If things get bad enough, we'll barely be able to keep ourselves alive, much less kids."

"No, listen, you stubborn jackass," Alex said. "We get it done while we can, then all we're worried about is keeping the cells frozen."

"What, in a cooler? And we're still talking about raising children at the end of the world."

Alex sighed, rolling his eyes at the same time. Etan knew that combination well, but he knew he was right no matter how upset Alex was.

"Tell me all of it, then," Alex said. "You feel like food supply is going to be a problem. That feels right to me. Stores barely have a few days' worth at the best of times with the way distribution works. What about technology? What about the power grid? All the solar panels and windmills in the world, all over the Midwest and Southwest—and in your Blue Ridge Mountains, I might add—won't do a damn bit of good if transmission fails, will they?"

"I don't feel like much of anything is going to do a damn bit of good. What if this is what my grandmother dreamed about, Alex? She told me hardly anyone survives anywhere in the world."

Alex scowled, his pale eyebrows drawing together. His ability to hold on to his natural optimism no matter how gloomy Etan got was normally one of the best things about the two of them. Right now it was pissing Etan off.

"But she didn't say *no one* survived. Maybe your dreams and hers mean someone will."

"We can't argue about this right now," Etan said, closing his eyes and tilting his head from side to side. His neck muscles felt like over-coiled springs. "If you're telling me you believe this, that the whole fucking world is going to fall apart, we have bigger things to deal with. Right?"

Alex stared at Etan for a few seconds, then shrugged and shook his head at the same time. Yes, he was letting the discussion about having children go for now. And yes, it would come back up again.

"Just promise me you'll tell me if you feel differently? About the food thing, I mean. I don't want to leave here any more than you do, but my gut is telling me we don't have a hell of a lot of choice. Or we won't before long."

"I promise," Etan said. "You'll be the first to know, since I don't even remember the blasted dreams. But I promise."

Alex smiled, but it barely touched his eyes. He gazed out at the lake again for a long time. His breathing slowed, and his grip on Etan's hand slowly tightened. When he finally turned back, tears stood in his eyelashes.

"What are we going to do, E?" Alex whispered. His optimism and confidence vanished in the slightest downward movement of his head, the slump of his shoulders. "How are we going to get through this?"

Chapter 7

THE BUSY OFFICE hummed around Alex, his co-workers going about their days, and their lives, as if everything were perfectly normal. Floor to ceiling windows dimmed strategically with the sun to maximize heat gain or loss as well as showcase the stunning views of downtown Chicago along the corridor wall. Everyone buzzed with excitement over news of the major renewable energy contract their small firm had just been awarded.

Alex's door was usually open, the blinds on his window raised, when he was there. He enjoyed the white noise and talking with other engineers and managers about their various projects.

Today he had the door closed and the shade drawn. The only light in his office came from his monitor.

The email was one he'd been struggling for, hoping for, daydreaming about for months. Long hours of work and planning, and the most careful and well thought out proposal he'd ever put together, were a huge part of the success the whole firm was celebrating today.

That approval notice arrived with an offer of Alex serving as the project manager. Success at such a huge role would bring promotion not far behind, and eventually a partnership.

For once, he wished he'd at least had the chance to be surprised. He'd known what was coming for the last several nights.

Instead of joining in the elation all around him, Alex was barely managing not to puke all over himself.

None of that was going to happen. Not only because of Etan's strange and insistent dreams about the end of the world, though that was a factor.

Alex was about to quit the perfect job for him, better than he'd imagined for himself or anyone else, on the day of his biggest success.

He rubbed at his mouth, the scratchy noise of his short beard clear in the silence. Etan's idea of just not showing up for work any more had its appeal, especially now that he was faced with walking into his manager's office and going through with this. The temptation to simply disappear threatened to take over Alex's mind and body, more and more the longer he sat there staring at the email.

He knew he'd never do such a thing. Not only because it was the coward's way out, a choice he'd never made in his life and didn't intend to start now. The real reason was hard to admit to himself. He doubted he'd ever admit it to Etan.

Deep in his mind, so deep he could barely hear the nervous whisper, Alex wasn't completely sure the dreams meant anything. Not on this scale, so much bigger than predicting a phone call or wedding or funeral.

Alex was willing to go with his lover on this terrifying journey into a new life. He wasn't willing to burn any more bridges than he had to on the way out of town.

If this turned out to be a tremendous mistake, some kind of misunderstanding or flat out nonsense, begging to get his job back would be distasteful to him in the extreme. Even hard core groveling likely wouldn't work after Alex let everyone down in such a spectacular fashion on the biggest day in the firm's history, one he'd played a huge role in bringing to reality.

But disappearing without a word would make his return here or to any other firm in Chicago impossible.

If only the damn dreams had started sooner. Then he could

have…what, exactly? Quit sooner, with even less to go on and less money to go with? Slack off at the job he loved so much instead of working harder than he ever had in his life? Manage to fuck something else up badly enough that he'd get fired before he had to quit?

No matter how difficult the next half hour turned out to be, Alex didn't have any of those options in him. At least walking in there and facing this like a man—a terribly reluctant and anxious man who was still determined to do the right thing—would be true to who he was in his heart.

His phone buzzed in his pocket, and he didn't have to look to know who was calling. Turning his life on end was about to get a hell of a lot more difficult. Alex saw exactly the name he expected to when he glanced at the screen.

May as well get all the suck over with for one day and move on.

"Hi Mom."

"Hi Alex. Do you have a minute?"

"Sure. I've got all the time in the world."

She laughed, and Alex wished he could laugh with her.

"You're every bit as much a workaholic as I am, son. You might have surpassed me over the past few months."

"You're right about that," Alex said, leaning back in his chair and closing his eyes. "What's up?"

"I'm getting the plans together for your father's birthday party next month. Will you be able to get that Friday off, or do we need to wait until Saturday?"

Alex was usually grateful for his mother's obsessive planning for his father's birthday, for some reason far more important to her than any other national holiday. Including her own birthday, or any of her children's. That gave him the out of keeping visits down to a once a year minimum most of the time.

This time, he doubted he'd make it up to Fond du Lac at all this year. And if Etan's dreams held true like they had for the last three years, like his grandmother Anne's had, Alex had already made his last visit.

"I doubt we're going to be able to make it." He tapped the back of the phone, disgusted with his own weak language. "No, I meant to say we're not going to make it. I'm sorry."

The silence stretched out long enough for Alex to slowly count to ten.

"I'm sure you can explain to your manager that you need at least one day off," she finally said. "You can fly up on Saturday morning and fly back that night. Even I don't work the *whole* weekend. Not that often, anyway."

"It's not for work, Mom. That's not going to be a problem much longer."

"Not a problem? I don't like the way your voice sounds, Alex. Maybe you better tell me what's going on."

The pause was on Alex's side this time. He didn't like the way her voice sounded, either. And there wasn't a damn thing he could do about that. He couldn't disappear from his parents' lives with no explanation any more than he could from his job.

He couldn't even manage the lie they were going to tell Etan's family about his getting laid off again. His mother would quite possibly investigate that story. He knew she'd done that with his first job. Looking for investment opportunities, so she'd said.

Alex knew better.

"I'm resigning today." He took a deep breath. "And we're moving."

"Resigning. You're obviously moving for a better position, then. Why don't you tell me about that?"

"There's nothing to tell. We're moving to Virginia where Etan's family is. We'll worry about jobs when we get down there."

"*Jobs?* You have worked long and hard to have a career, young man, and a damn good one, not so you can settle for whatever manual labor you scratch up out of the dirt. Unless there's some secret enclave of engineering hidden away in the backwoods, I have to be missing something. What the hell is going on, Alex?"

He rubbed his mouth again, blowing through his fingers. This conversation was going about as well as he expected.

"You're not missing anything, except understanding that I've been out here making decisions for myself for almost ten years now. We both need a change, and we're making one. That's all."

"So first you support him so he can keep going to school, and now he's got you leaving your whole life behind to disappear into the middle of nowhere. I know you love him, son, but don't you think this has gone far enough? Etan might not understand what you've been working so hard for."

"Just stop, Mom. That's enough." Alex dug the heel of his hand into his thigh, over and over again. "Etan understands more than you know, and he knows exactly how hard this is for me. He's giving up a lot, too.

"Giving up what? A free ride on your coattails, except now that's a free ride into poverty. Right back where he came from."

"Well, it's been great talking to you," Alex said through his teeth. "I'll let you know when we get settled. Take care."

"Don't you dare-"

Alex ended the call, then turned the phone off. He glanced back at the email, snorting at how upset he'd been before his mother called. At least talking to his manager would be a hell of a lot easier now.

Talking to his father once his mother shared her big news would be far worse, if he even bothered after that disaster.

He gasped when he stood, the long muscles of his right thigh cramping. He'd at least have a bruise to deal with, if not spend the next few days limping while they got most of their belongings ready to sell and packed up what was left.

Something to remember his family by.

Chapter 8

When they left Chicago for what they both knew to be the last time, Etan didn't miss how Alex grew more quiet as the terrain changed. Farmland and orderly rows and divisions fell to wild, disorganized trees, rocks, and streams. The flat, uncurving highway they'd followed for hundreds of miles—along with ruler-straight roads jutting off at regular intervals—flowed into curving roads with the mountains of eastern Kentucky soaring high alongside.

After hours of Illinois and then Indiana, Etan had to admit not being able to see more than a few hundred yards ahead was shocking. The green even changed, from the pale cultivated version of hundreds of acres of corn and soybeans dotted with bright wind turbines to the wild hues of fir, oaks, maples, and more other trees and brush than he knew the names for.

The pace slowed a bit as well, with some cars flying through on the way further south, especially when they exited the main artery of I-64 for Mountain Parkway. The smaller road that followed cut through deep valleys alongside a massive lake for this part of the country, with equally massive antiquated coal power plants scarring the land.

Even the arrangements of those towering white wind turbines

that helped replace those power plants changed as they continued southeast. The orderly grids of Illinois and Indiana, massive curving blades all spinning at the same height, gave way to undulating waves that followed the ridgelines. Alex never failed to comment on how they seemed to rise up out of the earth, showing contours of the land they couldn't see any other way.

Instead of sharing one of what seemed like a thousand stories of a summer spent helping build several turbines in Indiana, he didn't say a word about that or anything else.

Alex watched the traffic, sometimes pretending to pay attention to the navigation computer Etan didn't need. They weren't in his sleek autonav sedan, the one Alex had been so thrilled to buy for Etan when he'd gotten his second job out of college.

The job he'd fought for, the one he'd worked so hard to get qualified for and excelled in.

The one he'd quit a few days before.

Etan now drove an antique, a hybrid van with options for gas, electric, and manual navigation. He'd forced himself to shut down the primitive autonav at their last stop, reasoning he should have at least a little bit of practice with handling the car himself. He hadn't done such a thing since his driver training years ago. Many of these cars were still on the road for stubborn drivers, those who were convinced they could do better than any computer no matter how qualified and tested.

Etan didn't feel that way, not even a little bit. Having to watch the other cars, his speed, and the steep curves all at the same time left him anxious and exhausted. He had plenty of relatives who did feel they were superior to even the newest network-controlled vehicles.

He'd refused to ride with them once he was old enough to understand what they were standing up for. The right to be as erratic and unpredictable as they wanted. And he understood as he got older that he'd been getting a sense of how some of them would end up.

He'd missed being in more than one wreck not long before it happened.

This van, reasonably well-maintained and easy enough to drive, just made more sense with the disaster both of them sensed growing closer every day. Once the grid failed, and the technology that controlled so many of the cars around them with it, being able to move around under their own power would be a tremendous advantage.

At least until the gas ran out. And he was afraid depending on the grid to charge an electric vehicle would quickly turn the most modern cars into junk.

As Etan navigated the long, sweeping curve off the parkway, trying not to get too nervous maneuvering through the choked streets of a tiny historic town, he knew he had to get Alex talking. Confirming his suspicions about what the problem was, or at least having Alex admit it, wouldn't be pleasant no matter what.

Going through that with Etan's very close and very curious family right there would make everything a thousand times worse. He didn't need any kind of prescience or dreams to know that.

"Need to stop for anything?" he said, glancing at Alex.

"I'm fine. We're not even an hour away, right?"

"Just over an hour, sweetie."

Alex had made the trip several times over the past three years, but usually for some kind of happy occasion. A couple of funerals, of course, but generally it was for a wedding or a holiday. He seemed to enjoy the mountains once he got used to being in such a different landscape.

"I know this is hard for you," Etan said, trying to feel his way forward. The only sense he got was Alex had to say something. "Can I do anything to help?"

"I doubt it. I'm not exactly coming to my new life in triumph, am I?"

"I don't know what else we could have done. We can still change our story if we need to, but we couldn't stay in the city."

Alex breathed deeply, then let it out in a harsh rush.

"Yeah, I know. I understand. I'm not arguing about that. We have to move, I get it. I'm not thrilled about telling everyone I lost my job. Again."

"It was your idea to-"

"I know it was my idea!" Alex winced, looking at Etan. "I'm sorry. I loved that job, you know? It was exactly what all those years of busting my ass in school were for. I feel like such a fucking bum, moving down here to sponge off your family."

"You know this is only for a little while, right? I doubt we have a year left."

"Probably not even a year from the way I feel. And the way you've been dreaming. I just don't love having to look your parents in the eye when they think I couldn't keep a damn job for more than a couple of years. I was supposed to be the one keeping us going while you finished up school, remember?"

Etan concentrated on the road, letting his lover get through his frustration. This was all a horrible game, a series of lies neither one of them wanted to tell. A game they were both sure they had to play well to give anyone a chance to survive.

"You *would* have kept us going, Alex, and a hell of a lot more. We both know that. I don't want to imagine how hard it is to give up your career. I never even got there. I'll be lying to them too. I have no intention of working on a thesis about environmental risk management. It wouldn't do any good if I did. The environment is pretty much screwed already, and no one will be alive to review the damn thing."

Alex snorted, turning to Etan and taking his hand. The tension was slowly leaving the car.

"At least your lie is one you could have been proud of if it were true. You would have been trying to accomplish something. Pathetic as it sounds, my pride is taking a beating even though I know this will all be over before another year passes."

"You'll be in the pressure cooker, I'm afraid. People I went to high school with have been waiting for me to fail and run back here with my tail between my legs since the day I left. Well, some of them have. My parents will be fine, Alex. They both love you. But the others, just ignore their hillbilly asses. They're not worth worrying about even if you wanted to."

The narrow streets full of pedestrians slowly opened up to a clearer road, nowhere near as easy to navigate as the interstate. Etan loved the way the road seemed to sink down into the mountains, as if he were being welcomed home by the land around them.

No matter how much he loved Chicago and everything the city had to offer him, a deep part of him relaxed and uncoiled the further he moved into the land of his birth.

"Want to drive for a while?" he said. He knew the answer very well.

"Are you crazy? I'd somehow manage to run us into the side of a mountain even with the autonav. If I try driving this thing, we won't make it a hundred feet."

"You may have to get used to it, you know. What if we both have to drive? Or what if I can't for some reason? You can't hide behind being a spoiled non-driving city boy forever down here."

Etan tried to keep a straight face until Alex caught up with him. The lingering upset and stress showed when it took Alex several seconds longer than his normal instantaneous understanding of Etan's humor.

"Well, I guess we'll have to walk, then. Or find donkeys or mules or something. You still have those down here, right?"

"Absolutely. Along with the outhouses and swimming holes down in the creek. That's how I got ready for school every morning."

The van chugged a bit going up a long hill, forcing Etan into a far less humorous mood.

"Alex, have you thought about that? What if we do end up using goddamn holes in the ground? I'm lying through my teeth about a thesis, but I know enough about water chemistry to know we don't have any good way to keep the water clean. Not that they do in the cities."

"We'll be a hell of a lot better off here than there from what you've been seeing lately," Alex said, the lightness missing from his own voice as well. "Whatever we can do here will be safer than all the water that can be poisoned at once in a city reservoir. Listen, this is going to sound like a joke but it isn't. Are there still survivalists down here? I think there still are in Missouri, in the Ozarks."

"What, like the militia types?" Etan took his eyes off the road at a stoplight before their last turn. Alex looked completely serious. "I guess there probably are. I'm sure I'm related to some of them. I don't know a whole lot about it. I was in too big a hurry to get out of here."

"We may want to see what we can learn," Alex said. "I read a bunch of books about that stuff, back when I wanted to get away from Wisconsin and everywhere else in the world sounded like a better option. These people were determined the old government was coming to take away their food or their guns or something. They stockpiled canned goods, water, weapons, all of it. They had to have some way to purify water and deal with waste and such."

"I'm sure I have a cousin or two with those same books. Maybe the original copies. We'll probably have great luck with my Grandpa Evan's books. He was a fiend for that kind of stuff. He was collecting them back when those people were still everywhere. He has a private library in the house we're going to be living in."

"Didn't your grandmother say something about a library?" Alex smiled. "Your Gemaw?"

"Yeah, smart ass, she did." Etan was silent for a few seconds, following a steep curve and trying to think of how to put it. "She told me she dreamed about a giant library, the really awful dreams. She was trapped in there watching a bunch of giant screens. The floors, the walls, the ceilings, everything was a screen showing how people were going to die in great detail. She couldn't make it stop and she couldn't get away."

"How old was she then?"

"She was eleven or twelve, same as when I started having the dreams. But she remembered all of them most of the time. That drove her kind of crazy, I think. Before she figured out some way to keep them under control."

"That's horrible. No wonder she wanted to warn you. I know you hate to talk about it, but I've been wondering if your dreams are going to get worse as this thing gets closer. They have been over the past year or so."

"Worried you'll have to get me put away after all?" Etan said. He wasn't quite joking.

"Not a bit. I've been feeling it more lately. Seeing it all around us. I was hoping I could do something to help. Keep you calmer or whatever. Don't be such an asshole."

"I'm sorry. It still makes me nervous to talk about the dreams. I always thought I was going crazy, unless I was with my grandparents. Or with you. What she told me was she talked to my grandfather about the dreams. Once she did that, she started to feel calmer."

"Did hers ever stop?"

"No, I don't think they stopped until she died. But talking to him made all the difference. That and she said something about other things moving into place. That I do understand. I felt that way when I met you."

"Do you feel that way about moving here, E? About making such a big change?"

Etan wished he could say yes, that he felt everything in its right place. A bit of the tension did seem to be shifting, changing, but it wasn't going away. Different direction or not, the velocity, the sense of calamity heading toward them, was stronger with every mile he drove.

"I feel like I can stop worrying so much about getting us out of the city," he said. "Now I can worry a little bit more about getting us through the next couple of years. I'm not sure if that's better or worse. What does it feel like to you?"

Alex looked around at the narrowing road twisting through a deep green and blue valley, following the path of a river like so many of the roads here did. They were in shadow hours before the sun set.

"Right now I feel the same way I always do when we first get here. I can't see far enough. I have no idea what's coming around the next corner. Anything in the world could be waiting for us, and I can't do a thing to stop it. I'm scared to death I'm going to let us both down."

Etan closed his eyes for a second, his heart turning into a ball of hot water in his throat. That aspect of being the younger one, still a kid in school, of feeling like Alex was sometimes the mature adult between the two of them, was usually more annoying than anything.

Right now he felt like he was failing the person he cared more about than anyone else.

"I don't know if this helps or not," he said. "But I'm the one who should be figuring this kind of stuff out now that we're down here. I'm supposed to know my way around, or at least I should. I'm the native, right? Trust me, Alex. I don't like this role reversal thing any more than you do."

Etan slowed, remembering to put his turn signal on at the last second. One left turn, a quick drive of a few miles past this very small town, and they'd be face to face with the dramatic, sudden change in their lives.

Nowhere left to hide.

Barely a month ago, they'd been happy in Chicago, moving forward with their lives. Looking forward to Etan finishing school, Alex getting promoted again. Buying their own place, putting down roots. Starting the family that was now eternally delayed.

Today they were both jobless and homeless, everything they'd worked for and planned and dreamed of derailed. Their lives on permanent hold. And they had to make believe all of this was according to a bigger plan, one they'd had any part in creating.

Alex either read Etan's mind, or his own mind was putting him through worse. He spoke as they took the last turn, his voice weak and airy.

"I think I'm going to be sick."

Etan glanced over, and Alex was indeed pale and sweaty. A sprinkling of freckles across his cheeks and nose stood out more than they usually did unless he was ill. He'd gotten carsick on their first couple of trips a few years ago. Etan didn't believe the change in elevation and terrain were creating the trouble now.

"Let me pull over. We'll walk around for a little while. Get you something to drink."

"If we stop now, I'm never going to make it," Alex said. "Maybe your family and everyone else will have mercy on me if they remember I'm the new kid."

"Don't worry. They won't forget that anytime soon. Won't be

long until none of that matters anymore. Sure you don't need to stop?"

"It's just hitting me all at once. We're never going to leave here, are we? This is it, live or die. This is it."

Chapter 9

Etan was in for his own surprise when he parked in front of his grandparents' house. His heart pounded, his gut twisted. As was often the case, Alex recovered by having someone to help. He leaned over and touched the back of Etan's neck

"You okay?"

"I haven't been here since they died." Etan rubbed his face, not surprised by the clammy sweat there.

He and Alex were only half a mile past his parents' house, but they seemed to be miles from another human being. From this small valley set back from the road, the only thing anyone could see was mountains covered in thick trees. The house was brick, one-story, with a few steps leading to the broad screened-in porch. A dark brown steel roof helped the house blend into the tree line.

Everything looked exactly the same, and that somehow made it a thousand times worse. His grandparents' blue sedan was still sitting in the driveway, the same gas-powered model they'd driven south from Illinois decades ago. All the same trees, the brightly painted wooden lawn furniture, the flowers his grandmother planted and cared for so carefully.

It wouldn't have surprised Etan to see both of them opening the door, arms around each other's waists, smiling and so happy to see him.

Instead of the huge group of people Etan and certainly Alex had been afraid of, the place was deserted. He couldn't hear anything but their footsteps through the grass and the breeze blowing through the swaying oaks and pines.

"Do you have a key?" Alex said. He looked much better now that he was out of the car and moving around.

"No. I expected someone to be here."

They walked toward the porch, Etan hoping no one had moved the hiding place in the last several years. He found the stone sculpture of two stylized adults with a child: a gift from Etan's grandparents who'd lived their whole lives in Illinois. He tilted it back to reveal two keys on a small metal ring.

"See," he said, grinning at Alex, trying to reassure himself. "Nothing ever changes here."

Inside the house was just as disorienting. All the low, comfortable furniture covered in dark greens and browns was unchanged, as were the pictures of family and locations from all over the world on the tan walls. The arched passage, so like the ones in their apartment back in Chicago, revealed the next small room where his grandfather's books still lined every inch of space.

Alex picked up a small blue envelope from the table beside the door. *Welcome Home* was written in Etan's mother's looping script.

"Go ahead," Etan said. "This place is way too small for us to have secrets."

"The house or the town?"

Alex winked as he opened the envelope. He smiled as he read, and a couple of tears spilled over before he could catch them. He handed the note to Etan, then stood close with his hand on his lower back.

So glad our beautiful young men are home! Get some rest, get settled in. Stocked up a little, wasn't sure what you wanted. Tried to get your favorites, but don't know Alex's yet! Give us a call when you're ready for company.

Love, Mom and Dad.

"My favorites?" Alex said.

"Unless my mother has changed drastically, there'll be more food in the kitchen than we ever had our apartment. Come on. You hungry?"

"More curious than hungry," Alex said. He followed Etan through the library toward the kitchen. "Looks like we have all the research materials we'll ever need."

All four walls were covered floor-to-ceiling with bookshelves stuffed full of every sort of book Etan could imagine. He flinched again when he saw the two old fashioned burgundy wingback chairs sitting by the window, a huge matching ottoman positioned for both of them. His grandmother's fluffy pink blanket was still folded up on hers.

He'd spent many happy evenings curled up under that blanket with her until he got too big to fit in the chair.

"Wait till you see their computers," he said. "They may be a little bit outdated, but we'll never get to the end of everything stored there. No cellular to speak of in this little valley, and only satellite TV for as long as that lasts. All the peace and quiet either of us can stand."

The kitchen was small, only a few paces across, but with everything painted a bright, cheery yellow, it was more welcoming than the dark, modern space they'd left behind.

True to her word, Etan's mother had filled the refrigerator and all the cabinets. A plate full of chocolate chip cookies sat beside a bottle of their favorite bourbon on the counter, everything wrapped in red ribbon. Two shot glasses engraved with the same roses as the bottle stood in front.

"She did pretty well with my favorites," Alex said. "Maybe I *am* gonna like it here."

Chapter 10

A couple of shots of their welcome gift, combined with relief of being off the road, led to Alex and Etan's best lovemaking in a long while. That feeling of being in the eye of the storm, in a calm they both knew they'd miss when it was over, heightened every touch, taste, smell, even with bodies long familiar.

Difficult times were ahead, neither of them doubted that. But they'd gotten through a huge part of their journey with hard-earned time for recovery.

As often happened after they had sex, Etan's plans for unloading everything right away dissolved when he fell deeply asleep. Alex didn't hesitate to take advantage of time on his own, wide awake, to prowl around their new home.

Just as predictably, he went straight to the library at the heart of the small house.

The space wasn't large, only a few of Alex's long strides across in any direction. Anne and Evan had managed to pack a remarkable number of books into every available inch, with dark stained wooden shelves reaching almost to the low ceiling and across the doorways and windows. They ranged from tall and deep at the bottom, with room enough for textbooks and large format photo books, to two rows perfectly fitted for small paperbacks all around the top.

Alex walked slowly around the shelves, his eyes drinking in the remarkable variety, his fingers brushing smooth or slick or scratchy spines.

He'd never seen so many physical books in one house. All of his textbooks in high school and most in college had been electronic, and Alex himself only owned a few printed reference books.

After his first circuit, Alex stood in the middle of the room, turning as he examined the photographs on the top shelf. In three years of hearing about Etan's grandparents, he only had a vague idea of what they looked like. Now that he could see pictures of her, he suspected he would have recognized Anne in a crowd of strangers.

Etan was an eerily perfect male version of her, from his green eyes to his light brown hair to his fine, almost delicate features.

Etan's grandfather Evan had the most striking blue eyes Alex had ever seen, pale but not cold at all. His smile was far too gentle and warm for that. The photos of the three of them, so clearly delighted to be together, lifted a bit of the discomfort and sadness from Alex's heart.

The books ignited his curiosity, and not just because he'd never had the chance to get his hands on so much paper. The arrangements of the shapes and colors of those hundreds of spines shaped an unmistakable pattern, one that cried out to his restless mind.

Logic and reason told him that spark, that need to dig into everything laid out before him like a road map, was only a coincidence. But he knew better, from Etan's stories of his grandparents, and from his dreams.

Evan surely grew up every bit as ignorant of dreams and their potential as Alex had. Yet Evan had been the witness to Anne's dreams, the one who listened and understood and did his best to give comfort in the middle of the night.

Alex wouldn't have been surprised if Evan knew exactly what he was doing when he arranged these shelves. He'd be more surprised if Etan's grandfather had *not* left a vital secret message somewhere in all these shelves.

A message especially, and only, for Alex's eyes.

He glanced around the room again, eyes unfocused, mind at last calm and ready. The colors and shapes resolved to a point. A beginning.

Alex pulled a book off the highest shelf, settled himself in the larger of the two chairs, and started to read.

Chapter 11

A FEW HOURS LATER, Etan and Alex walked down to the house Etan grew up in. Dinner with only the four of them felt like the perfect way for Alex to get comfortable without getting overwhelmed. A bit of Alex's unusual gloom seemed to have lifted with a solid bit of sleep. But Etan suspected Alex wouldn't quite be back to his normal, cheerful self just yet.

The younger Griffith's house was almost as private as Etan's grandparents' retirement home, two stories and white wooden siding hidden from the main road by trees and a curving gravel driveway. More yard hid behind the house rather than stretching out in front like at Evan and Anne's house. And unlike what seemed like a museum down the road, this one changed constantly.

Furniture shifted inside and out, along with paint colors, carpet, and an endless variety of projects. Etan rarely needed his decorating and repair skills once he'd taken up apartment living, but he had a feeling he'd soon be thankful to have them.

They smelled steaks on the grill before they could even see the house.

"Ready for this?" Etan said, taking Alex's hand.

"I have been here before. I don't think I've grown a third arm or anything since last time."

"You've never been guest of honor at a welcome home sympathy dinner before. My parents and all my other relatives are of the firm opinion that just about anything can be made better with a good enough meal. I'll have to roll you back up the mountain tonight."

They rounded the last curve to see the main feature of the small front yard had been upgraded yet again. The massive brick grill, complete with three cooking areas, including one for old-fashioned charcoal to complement the gas, had gained an miniature roof against hot sun or rainy weather. The stone and brick patio a few feet away now held low lounge chairs with thick cushions beside a long picnic table.

Etan's father stood with his back to them, moving with athletic grace between the three surfaces. Connor Griffith alternated whistling and singing to himself, and Etan didn't need to see his dad's face to know he was smiling.

Etan's mother stepped out onto the screened-in porch, even larger than the one at the other house. Laura Griffith wore blue jeans and a green t-shirt, her curly blonde ponytail making her look about thirty years old. She carried a plate with six huge ears of corn, cleaned and ready for the grill.

"Hey, you made it!" she said, grinning.

"We wouldn't miss it," Alex said before Etan could respond. Alex grabbed the plate, managing to give her a huge hug at the same time without any of the ears rolling off. "Thank you for shopping for us. That's a huge help."

"Well, I hate to come home to an empty kitchen after even a few days away," she said. She caught Etan in a hug that nearly squeezed the breath out of him. "I hope you have everything you need."

Etan shared a wink and a smile with Alex. Everything he'd needed after such a long, difficult drive had meant a couple of shots of the bourbon, the best sex they'd had in ages, and a long nap.

"We settled in just fine, thank you," Etan said. "This smells fantastic, Dad."

A little more silver than Etan remembered glinted in his father's brown hair when he turned away from the grill, but his smile flashed as youthful and joyful as his wife's had.

"Everything will be ready in an hour or so. Go grab yourselves something to drink, make yourselves at home." He hugged Alex, then Etan. "You *are* at home."

"I'm starting to feel that way," Alex said.

After they managed to carry huge plates of food, enough for at least a few more people, to the table on the patio, no one spoke for a long while. Etan was sure he'd grown up eating steak and potatoes and corn and tomatoes and butter this good, that he'd had it every time he'd returned for a visit over the last four years. But his nose and his mouth and his ravenous belly were certain nothing had ever tasted so good in all his twenty-two years.

"Can I ask you a strange question?" Etan said when he was finally able to slow down. "It's about the house, Gemaw and Grandpa's house."

"That's your house now," his mother said. "That's what they both wanted."

"Did they say anything about that?" Alex said.

"To tell you the truth, my mother did," Etan's father said. "She talked about keeping it up in case you needed it. Same thing with the car, Dad asked us to take good care of it. They didn't want things changed or updated unless they had to be. So that's why everything is a bit behind the times."

"Don't apologize," Alex said. He glanced at Etan before going on. "It's going to be just what we need, and the timing is perfect."

"Did she tell you why she wanted to leave it that way?" Etan said. He was sure he knew.

"Yeah, she told me she dreamed about it," his father said. "She wouldn't say much more, just that if you needed a place to stay, they wanted you to have the house. We've been using it as a guest house, but not very often. The place is yours for as long as you need it."

Etan tried to smile, but he couldn't quite manage. Alex put a hand on his leg under the table.

Alex had been right. This was it, where they would stay until the end. After that, even Etan couldn't yet guess.

"We appreciate that," Alex said. "We'll do whatever we can to keep up the place if you'll show me how. I'm afraid I don't have a lot of experience with house maintenance after years in apartments, but I'm happy to learn."

"I could use a refresher course myself," Etan said, gripping Alex's hand.

"I know this is hardly polite conversation," Etan's father said. "But I figure you're family, Alex, so you have to put up with me being as subtle as an ox just like Etan and Laura do. How are you two set for money?"

"We sold quite a few things before we left," Etan said. He didn't want Alex to have to answer this, not when he was already feeling bad about the lies he had to tell. Thanks to both of them being almost maniacal about savings, they had more than enough to last until money didn't matter anymore. "We'll be fine for a good long while."

"There are a bunch of other things I'd like to learn, speaking of money," Alex said. "Do you know anyone who still does a lot of gardening? Maybe preserving food?"

"Well, I haven't done anything like that for years," Etan's father said. "Mom and Dad insisted I learn how, but it does take up a lot of time."

"Time I have," Alex said. His cheeks were a little red, but he sounded okay. "I grew up in farm country, but neither of my parents gardened. I've always been curious."

"It really is too bad you didn't get to meet my father," Connor said. "He loved studying about self-sufficiency and growing things. His doctoral thesis was about pesticides and other advances in agriculture. How they helped, but the troubles around the turn of the century, too, how the bees were all dying off."

Etan met Alex's gaze, not even trying to hide his surprise. If he'd ever known that, he'd forgotten. He watched his father reach for another ear of the corn.

"Dad had a thing about certain crops, too, you'll find that in his writing. Things that were better or worse to grow out here." He waved the corn, now properly coated with fresh butter. "He loved fresh corn, but said we should enjoy it while we could. I never could work out why, but people around here hardly grow it anymore."

"There used to be a cannery in town," Etan's mother said, leaning back in her chair. "They shut down right after Anne passed. She and Evan really kept the place running. I know you remember, Etan, you were down there with them all the time. Everyone bragged about how good you were, even when you were little."

"Yeah, huge noisy place, but I loved it," Etan said, smiling a little. "I was afraid of all the equipment at first, then afraid they wouldn't let me go back if I acted up."

"If it's still in decent shape, maybe we can get something started," Alex said, staring into the thick trees beside the house. "Not a bad skill to learn or help other people learn."

His words left Etan dying to ask if Alex had dreamed for a change, if their late afternoon nap and lovemaking weren't the only things that led to such a change of heart.

"You remember Mom used to have a huge garden at your house and one up at the school," Etan's father said. "That's why we were always canning and putting stuff back. We couldn't eat it all, even after we gave a bunch of it away. I'm sure the soil is in good shape still. Dad had a ton of gardening books he bought, too."

"Yeah, I had a look at some of his books this afternoon while Etan was asleep," Alex said with a half-smile. "Seemed fair since he did all the driving. Might be a good way to get to know people, too."

Etan stared, trying not to laugh. He would have sworn Alex slept beside him the whole time, from right after they both collapsed in a sweaty, satisfied heap until Alex whispered him awake in time to get ready for this dinner. Instead Alex had used hours to himself to transform from scared to death in a strange place to eager to get out into the community, while Etan slept harder than he'd thought.

Alex's switch from anxiety to curiosity lightened Etan's guilt about dragging them into the unknown considerably.

"I know I'll feel a lot better once I'm busy again." Alex put his arm around Etan's waist, leaning against him for a second. "And I'll feel less like an outsider, you know?"

"Don't worry, you won't feel that way for long," Etan's mother said. "Anne always talked about how fast she felt at home here. I know you'll feel the same, Alex, as soon as people get to know you. We'll do everything we can to help, but you're going to do just fine."

Chapter 12

Etan jumped when he heard the front door open. He'd gotten so deeply into his grandfather's book about threats to pollinators, his grandmother's pink blanket tucked in around his knees, that he hadn't realized how much time had passed.

"Hey handsome," Alex said, walking through toward the kitchen with his arms full of paper bags. "Let me put these down."

"What have you got so much of?" Etan pushed the footstool aside and stood, stretching his arms over his head. The ceiling was low enough that Alex could easily reach it, but it was a few inches above Etan's fingertips.

"All the lettuce and spinach we'll ever need. My reward for asking around about food preservation. You'd be amazed how many people here have small greenhouses and gardens already. Now if we can just figure out how the hell to preserve it."

He put both arms around Etan's waist and buried his face against his neck. Alex's red hair smelled like rich, warm soil and fresh air.

"Freeze it, I suppose," Etan said. "Not very practical once the grid goes down."

"You have an excellent point there. I've found plenty of people who have gardens to go with those greenhouses I see everywhere, just hardly anyone doing much with them long term."

"Still no luck on the cannery?"

Alex leaned back with a crooked half-smile that warned Etan a second too late.

"I didn't say that. Your mother had the most amazing suggestion. She was a bit surprised you hadn't thought of it yet."

Etan shook his head and moved back toward the chair.

"Why do I get the feeling I've just been volunteered for something I'm going to regret?"

"Because you haven't heard me out," Alex said. He sat on the footstool and rubbed Etan's thigh. "She thinks we may be able to convince the high school to start classes out there again. Then it would be a legitimate school resource, so we'd have access to the funding to get it open and running."

"Sounds great. Now tell me the part I'm not going to like."

"That's the beauty of it, you *will* like it," Alex said. He was grinning, but Etan was somehow not reassured. "I'll do whatever I can to help get the equipment repaired and working. Might be my last chance to use my Engineer Alex skills before they get too rusty, assuming local folks will let the city boy mess with anything. As far as the rest, they just need someone to help get things set up, someone familiar with how it was run in the past. Keep up with paperwork and maybe write a couple of grants. Someone local folks will trust. You know, like Anne and Evan's grandson, recently come to his senses and moved back from the big city."

"Write grants? Paperwork?" Etan tried to get up, but Alex squeezed both of his thighs, pushing him back. "What makes either you or my mother think I could pull that off? Or that I want to?"

"Well, let's see. Your lovely mother—who's quite sure I'll be comfortable calling her Laura if she asks me often enough—was talking about how much you remind her of dear Anne. How you so loved going down there with your Gemaw when you were a kid. That's when the idea hit her. Since we're wanting to learn more, and Anne kept everything organized and enjoyed being out at the cannery so much, you're sure to be the best one for the job."

"I can't imagine anything I'd rather not do more than this!"

"So now that we're agreed on that first part, I'll tell you why I *know* you're the man for the job." Alex leaned forward, running his hands further along Etan's thighs. "You've been talking, asleep and awake, about how we're going to have to make a community here. How we'll never make it unless we help each other. What better way than creating a place where we can learn to take care of each other while we get to know each other better?"

"Fine, that makes all kinds of sense." Etan was trying not to want Alex to move his hands another little bit further without much success. "I'm losing the thread on the part where it has to be me."

"There's got to be a reason we came down here so early, E. Other people are going to show up, hopefully not too late. Now that I'm getting over the culture shock, I can see this will be a great place to do our best to make it through. But people even newer to this than us will have a hell of a lot of questions. We'll need a true community to survive. You're sitting in the middle of the best collection of the information we'll need within a hundred miles. This is a perfect way to start creating that community."

"No," Etan said. Much as he hated to, he grabbed both of Alex's hands and pushed them away. "That's not me. I'll learn as much as I can and help whoever I can, but I'm no social director. I hate that kind of shit, Alex. You know that."

"Don't worry, I'm not going to try to talk you into it. That never does any damn good anyway. You always kept our little household organized and on track a thousand times better than I could. I saw you do the same with a bunch of projects for school, too, and you never let anything slip. Whether you want to believe it or not, you're really *good* at that shit."

Etan stood up, stepped around Alex, and walked into the living room. He hated the suggestion almost as much as he hated the echo, the resonance in his belly. He rubbed his forearms, trying to ignore the hair standing on end. He knew Alex was watching him from the archway without having to look.

If he was going to live with this broadcast inside his head, one he hardly ever remembered when he was awake, he had to have the free will to disagree with it from time to time.

And if this community depended on *him* to create it, to bring it together, they didn't have a fucking chance.

He knew it was a mistake, but Etan turned to look at his lover. Alex was indeed watching him, leaning against the side of the archway with that same half smile. Nearly a thousand miles away from his home and in many ways even further from his career and life in Chicago, but trying his best to figure out their weird situation. Adjusting faster and more easily than Etan, even though Etan's dreams brought them here.

Alex was out in their new world like a grownup, meeting people and working out how to move them forward, while Etan still holed up at home and studied like a kid in school.

Was it really that much to ask, helping get this cannery set up? Especially when they both felt how important it would be to their survival?

Yep, looking into Alex's eyes was definitely a mistake. But Etan did it anyway. And he couldn't help returning Alex's smile.

Etan walked back and took his hand.

"I'll think about it, Alex," he said. "I'll help out, and I need to learn as much as I can. But I don't want to be in charge. I can't do that."

"You're going to like this suggestion even less, but just sleep on it. See what the middle of the night brings. Then maybe we can go talk to them in a couple of days."

Chapter 13

Alex paced outside the white cinderblock building, shaking his head over being so early. He was half-annoyed at Etan for giving in to his agitation that morning and dropping him off more than half an hour before the time everyone had agreed upon. He'd also smiled, kissed Alex soundly, and refused to stay and keep him company.

Despite the key in his pocket, Alex felt strange about barging into an unknown space without anyone from town there. That left him wandering around the parking lot between the bulk of the red brick high school and the abandoned cannery at half past seven on a Saturday, like a demented stalker who'd lost track of the days.

Several windows interrupted the uniform white on the front of the building beneath blocky, faded purple letters declaring this the Wolf Branch Cannery. Alex hoped the windows were frosted, not just that horribly dirty. The steep, dark gray roof looked sound as far as he could tell. Double brown brick chimneys that seemed too large for the space rose on either end.

Steep mountains crowded close behind the high school buildings. The close-cropped grass of the football field and several baseball fields behind the cannery was still brown, the trees surrounding them barely flushed with pink buds. Plumes of pale smoke rose from many smaller chimneys throughout the town spreading out below Alex, matching the mist of his breath. He didn't think he'd ever get tired of the sharp wood smoke, welcome and strange to his city boy senses.

Even with the lingering chill, they'd have to work fast to get everything ready for early spring harvests, especially if the equipment inside was a mess.

He wore his own wide leather tool belt with a few of Etan's father's tools added to the jangling load. Alex hadn't had much use for big things like hammers or large crescent wrenches over the past few years, but Connor had insisted. He'd also insisted on the faded but well cared for clothes Alex wore.

Nothing Connor or Etan had would fit Alex's much larger frame, and his mostly business casual wardrobe was worse than useless now. So they'd dug into Evan Griffith's storage. The heavy blue jeans and long-sleeved dark blue denim shirt were almost a perfect fit. Both Conner and Etan had been happy enough about that to make Alex even more self-conscious.

Not only was he a stranger in this town, more out of his element than he wanted to admit in the privacy of his own mind, but he had to borrow another man's clothes to even pretend to fit in.

A dead man's clothes.

"Hey there," a cheerful voice with the slow local cadence called from the parking lot. "You must be Alex."

Alex turned to see a man taller than he was, but quite a bit thinner. He was probably in his sixties, gray hair mostly covered by a green baseball cap, body as lanky as his smile was friendly.

"Yeah, that's me."

"I'm right glad to meet you," he said, holding out a huge hand that swallowed Alex's. "Name's Walt Colley. I hated when this place closed down after Etan's folks did so much hard work to keep it going. Proud to help get everything working again."

"Alex Collins. Good to meet you, Walt. I'm hoping to help out a little bit, if you and the others don't mind."

Walt smiled, the effect like warm sunlight on an overcast day.

"Why on earth would we mind? We're needing to get more folks out here to work, not less. I'm sure you'll do just fine, Alex."

They walked over to the metal double doors. Conner had given him the key the night before, along with the same reassurances that he'd do just fine.

"Let's see what we've got to work with," Alex said, turning the key and pushing. The door didn't move.

"Naaah, you got to give it a good shove. Been locked up for years now, and never did quite work right." Alex stepped back, and the older man pushed into the door with his shoulder. The metal broke loose with a screech. "You and me can take care of that once we see how bad the rest has got."

Alex brought out one of Etan's many flashlights, borrowed with great reassurance that he'd bring it back home. Musty air assaulted his nose and sinuses. The light switch was to his right inside the door.

"There we go," Walt said when the lights flickered and sputtered.

Alex wanted to turn them back off and lock the door again. Only about half of the outdated long fluorescent fixtures were working, and the ones that were buzzed and burned at half strength.

They showed enough, though.

The big room, easily forty feet wide and sixty feet long, was dominated by two rows of huge stainless steel tables, all of them covered in what looked like equal parts dust and grease. Half a dozen gigantic cauldrons with a purpose he could only guess sat at the far end of the tables. Several silvery, square-bottomed cylinders with huge lids standing open, each large enough for Alex to bathe in, lined the opposite wall under more windows.

Deep square sinks were scattered throughout the space, along with various devices Alex couldn't even guess about. The only things he recognized were a few commercial ranges and ovens along the wall behind them, and at least those looked like they were in decent shape under all the filth. Massive steel storage shelves stood between two doors to the left, covered with enough pots and piles of utensils to supply a dozen houses.

"What a mess," he whispered.

"Yeah, take us a day or two to get this straightened up, I guess. We'll have more help directly, but we may as well take a look."

"I don't even know where to start."

Thick black metal pipes ran the length of the room under the peaked ceiling, with smaller pipes dropping down to most of the cauldrons and contraptions. A long metal grate down the middle of the gray concrete floor mirrored the overhead structures.

"I'm guessing there's a boiler or something," Alex said. "Do you know if it runs on gas or something else?"

"Gas far as I know, two boilers down in the basement. Just about everything in here runs on steam. We'll need to clear out those lines after so much time, make sure they're not gobbed up."

They walked around the vast room, Alex making mental notes of everything that had to be done. The problem was they really wouldn't know until they got the place cleaned up and tested the strange machinery. It was anyone's guess what was hidden under all the grime.

"Looks to me like all the equipment is sound," Walt said. He rapped his knuckle on one of the giant pots and grinned at the ringing bong.

"We can probably get it working if we don't run into too many big problems." Alex leaned down to get a closer look at six burners on one of the cooktops. "Might be a bigger problem finding people who know how to use all of this."

"That part's easy," a woman's voice said from the door. She was dressed as casually as Alex and Walt, in blue jeans and a stained old gray sweatshirt. Her hair matched the shirt, and it seemed desperate to escape the bun she'd wrangled it into. "Linda Burns. I was in charge of this whole operation, or the high school's part of it at least. Anne and Evan Griffith kept the whole thing running, really."

"Good to see you, Linda," Walt said, enclosing her small hand in his. "This here's Alex Collins. Just down from Chicago with Etan, Anne and Evan's grandson."

"Oh, I'm so glad to meet you," she said, taking Alex's hand in both of hers. "Etan knows a lot more than you think about how this all works. He was here with Anne all the time when he was a kid. Connor tells me you're a mechanical engineer?"

"I was before we left Chicago," Alex said. He hoped saying that in the past tense would stop hurting eventually. "I worked more with renewables than anything like this. Wind turbines, solar panels, that kind of thing."

"Hey, you're just the man we need, then," Walt said, grinning. "Most folks around here can rig something up like we have done all our lives, or manage to keep it limping along. Seems like we're going to need to do a whole lot better than that over the next few years."

A chill ran up Alex's spine. He was used to hearing such talk from Etan, awake or in the middle of the night. Walt seemed about as far from fanciful as a human being could get. Far from lying about something like that, too.

"What makes you say that?" Alex said.

"Nothing I can put my finger on," Walt said, but his cheeks were bright pink now. "One of them things you feel. Once you get to my age, you learn to trust that feeling."

"I know just what you mean, Walt," Linda said. She looked more pale than flushed. "After years of me begging for funds to make repairs to the classrooms I use every day and not getting one thin dime, suddenly the school board agrees to help us pay to fix this place up. I'm glad to have the money, sure. But I won't lie and say I don't wonder what changed."

"That's good enough for me," Alex said. "Sounds like we're about to have company."

Three men and a woman walked in, looking around in equal parts horror and anticipation. All of them were dressed and ready to work.

"This here's Alex Collins," Walt said before Alex could say a word. "Just down from Chicago, came with Etan Griffith. He's a mechanical engineer. Gonna show us how to get this place back on its feet."

Alex never got the chance to protest and declare his lack of fitness for the job at hand. His fears were swept away in the welcome and enthusiasm all around him.

He knew he had an intimidating, and exciting, amount to learn, and fantastic teachers eager to get started. By the time everyone made their introductions and they all took a closer look around the cannery, Alex was finally starting to believe he had more than a little bit to teach.

Chapter 14

Even though he helped nearly every day for three weeks, Etan was amazed at how quickly the cannery was ready to open. Six years of neglect created an intimidating layer of dust, but not nearly as much damage as Alex and everyone else feared.

A few days of hard scrubbing had the stainless steel tables, cauldrons for cooking down huge batches of fruit or vegetables, ranges, and pressure canners spotless and gleaming. Alex and several local folks, most easily old enough to be his parents, enjoyed every second of talking and bullshitting while they worked.

Just as he had since the first night they'd met, Alex still transformed everything he touched. But Etan was determined he wasn't going to fall neatly into line with at least a few of Alex's plans.

Every morning, he explained to Alex he was only going along to help out, always including something along the lines of not wanting to be in charge. Every morning, Alex grinned and said yeah, he knew that.

And every day, Etan's high school vocational teacher Linda Burns, Alex, and Etan's own mother asked him for advice over and over again. Before long, the men and women helping with the cleanup started to do the same.

The rhythm of the work, of the cannery itself, found its old place firmly under Etan's skin, inside his mind and heart.

Help Alex open the cool, dark building and start everything up for the day. Lights, boiler, steam lines that now worked better than they ever had in the past.

Welcome the ones who'd helped clean up and get the cannery as they arrived, carrying baskets and bags full of fruit and vegetables, often still dusty and warm from the garden. Breathe in the air as it slowly transformed from morning cool to afternoon warmth, humid and rich with the scent of cooking, then early evening muggy, with earthy but not quite unpleasant smells of human bodies.

Watch people walk out proud, with spotlessly clean and bright jars full of food, knowing at least that group understood how important their weeks of hard work getting the facility up and running had been.

Etan understood what was happening. He just couldn't quite manage to stop it. After a couple of weeks, even he admitted he didn't want to.

On the afternoon before the cannery officially opened, he caught Alex watching him. Etan stood surrounded by everyone who'd helped so far and several high school and middle school teachers, explaining his grandfather's planting schedule for optimum food preservation, crops they should focus on and some to avoid.

Alex's face was sweaty and smudged from his own work, but he wasn't even trying to hide his pride in Etan. Or his amusement.

Etan turned his back, flipped Alex off, and kept talking.

The truth was Etan was bursting with pride at what Alex had accomplished. His time here with his grandparents had been filled with clanking equipment, leaky pipes, boilers that required constant adjustment. Every bit of that and more faded into Etan's fond memories. More people than either of them imagined—or dreamed—wanted to do more than use the new cannery for more projects than he could easily keep up with.

Students and adults alike wanted to learn as much as they could, about updating their homes, putting in their own gardens, even filling out the grant applications Etan disliked almost as much as he enjoyed getting the award letters.

By the time early May crops of asparagus, beets, peas, and strawberries flooded into the cannery, both Etan and Alex were every bit as involved with the sprawling community garden next door as with paperwork and classes. After years trapped in the ongoing routine of college and studying, Etan enjoyed the labor more than he would have believed possible.

Maybe it was the deep, often dreamless sleep brought on by digging and weeding or hours spent in the steaming hot cannery. Maybe seeing what they'd accomplished only a few months after leaving Chicago with almost nothing built up his confidence.

Either way, Etan felt the smallest trembling optimism deep in his heart.

The catastrophe would strike, no doubt or way around that. But perhaps they had a chance of getting themselves and the others through to whatever awaited on the other side.

Another piece of their lives slipped gracefully into place.

Chapter 15

Mary Shadrin walked into their lives in July.

Etan caught motion out of the corner of his eye, looking up from a batch of strawberry preserves in an old-fashioned steam canner on one of the cooktops. He and a group of ten surprisingly attentive teenagers were watching the water boiling in the dark blue metal pot and listening to the finished jars cooling on the counter, waiting for the telltale pop of the cooling lids sealing themselves.

The scent of the remains of fragrant berries on the table behind him floated through the humid air, matching the perfectly ripe sweet flavor on his tongue.

He'd gotten used to the constant level of noise and humidity in the cannery faster than he'd expected. Clattering knives on other tables, churning or whirring machines, fragrant steam thick with early spring herbs. Etan's senses welcomed the comfort even though his grandparents weren't physically with him anymore. This place brought them close enough.

Movement that didn't match the general chaos distracted him. A small, slender woman with long, black hair stood in the open doorway, wearing a flowing blue gauze dress with open-toed sandals. Her features were delicate and severe, and he thought she was several years older than he was. Maybe closer to his parents' age.

Etan stared, trying to remember why he was sure he knew her, why she seized all of his attention. Something about her, besides those sandals that she couldn't wear with all the boiling and steaming in here, put his mind on edge.

"Was that it, Mr. Griffith?"

He turned back, searching through his memory of the last few seconds. Before he had to admit he hadn't been paying attention enough to hear anything, two more of the lids on the cooling jars compressed with a soft metallic *tink*.

"That's it. Anyone have your checklist?" Three of the kids raised their hands. "That's fine, I never had things like that with me when I was in school. Divide into three groups and go through your list. Make sure everything's set up. When they're all ready, start pulling them out. What are you watching for?"

"Anything that can burn the shit out of us?" one of the boys said, grinning. Despite his flippant attitude or maybe because of it, fifteen-year-old Jimmy Adams was one of Etan's best students. "Mr. Griffith, sir."

"Close enough, Jimmy. I'll be right over here."

The strange woman walked toward him when he turned back, and Etan held up his hands.

"I'm sorry, we can't let people wear shoes like that in here," he said. "Too many things at the boiling point. Can I help you?"

She stopped and crossed her arms

"I just wanted to see how things are going over here. We were all so disappointed when they closed down before. The previous managers died."

Etan did his best to smile. He noticed she was tapping one of her feet on the concrete floor, toe ring and painted red nails glinting. She followed him into the small office beside the double doors. With a fan in the only window on the street side of the building, it was a bit less humid.

"Everything's going really well, thank you. Pretty busy, but we have lots of help. I'm Etan Griffith."

She shook his hand with a satisfied smile. Etan was certain she'd known exactly who he was before she walked in.

"Mary Shadrin. Are you related to Evan Griffith? Or Anne?"

Etan didn't bother smiling this time. "The last managers. I'm their grandson."

"So sorry for your loss." Her expression didn't change.

"That was six years ago. I'm pretty much recovered. What can I help you with, Ms. Shadrin?"

"I just stopped by to introduce myself, Etan, and see if we can help you. My friends and I believe in being well prepared. Having this facility open again is a vital service to the community. A time of great need may be in our future, for us and for our neighbors."

"Well, I appreciate that," Etan said. He saw Alex waiting outside the office, dusty and hot from the garden. "We're happy to be here. Please tell your friends we're up and running, and they're welcome to come by."

"I'll be sure and do that."

Mary looked Etan up and down, glanced around the office, then turned on her heel and strode away. She made a show of scrutinizing Alex and his grubby, sweaty state on her way out. He wrinkled his nose and smiled as Etan reached him.

"Who the hell was that?"

"Mary Shadrin," Etan said. He looked out the doors, but the unsettling woman had disappeared around the corner toward the road. "Ever seen her before?"

"Don't think so. I think I'd remember someone that grouchy looking. I'm heading home to scrub my nasty ass. How long will you be?"

Etan glanced at his group. All of the remaining jars were out of the water, and the kids were milling around, looking his way.

"I'll be right behind you as soon as we finish up this batch," he said. "I'm reeky as a goat after sweating in here all day. If you can stand yourself long enough, I'll join you in the bath."

One of the few and welcome updates in their house was a huge soaking tub, one Etan's father had helped his grandfather install. There was more than enough room for himself and Alex, assuming they wanted any space to themselves.

"That's a date," Alex said, winking before he walked out. Etan rejoined his students.

"Three of them never popped, Mr. Griffith," one of the girls said. "The rest are cooling."

He'd given up trying to get them to call him Etan.

"Anyone know what to do with the ones that never seal?"

"Keep 'em in the fridge and eat 'em up fast," Jimmy said. The same one who'd suggested not burning the shit out of themselves.

"You got it. We'll let them cool down a bit, then do just that with the bread the last class baked. Help me clean up while we're waiting, and we're finished for today."

Etan meant to ask his parents about Mary. His attention got wrapped up with the kids and helping a few adults, then turned decidedly to Alex for the rest of the evening as soon as he got home.

By the time he remembered his plan to ask his parents about the disquieting woman, he didn't need to any more.

Chapter 16

Alex woke with a start, certain he'd barely put his head on the pillow. One of those weird falling sensations he hadn't had for years must have jerked him awake. He was weary enough for that, between working at the cannery, helping build out a couple of gardens, and setting up a handful of small wind turbines over the past week.

An odd hissing noise in the darkness cleared the sleep from his brain in an instant. No, not quite like the snakes they'd disturbed in old garden boxes. That was Etan, shifting his legs under the sheets. Alex didn't remember any nightmares for a few days, but he didn't need to check the time. It would be just after three. The nearly six hours since they'd gone to bed had passed in a flash.

He jumped again at Etan's shout.

"Not you! No! Let me do it, *not* you!"

Alex turned on a dim bedside light, then reached into a tangle of sweaty, shifting limbs, twisted up in the sheets and blanket. Etan pulled away, groaning before his voice wound up into a scream.

"No one can save them!"

"Etan!" Alex caught Etan's hands and pulled, moving until he held Etan immobile with his own arms and legs. "Hey, I'm right here. It's okay."

Etan strained, his chest rising. Alex braced for another scream.

"Shhhh, calm down, sweetie," he whispered. "It's over now. I got you. You're safe. I got you."

Etan froze, then he shook his head.

"Not you," he said, his voice rough. "Let me, please."

"I'll let you, Etan, but you have to calm down first. You've screamed yourself hoarse."

Alex watched Etan's staring eyes, relief welling up in his belly when Etan finally focused on him in the faint light.

"There you are," he said, leaning down to kiss Etan's cheek. "You were starting to scare me."

"What's wrong?" Etan's voice sounded like he'd been to a concert or was just getting over a terrible cold.

"I don't have the slightest idea, E. You haven't told me yet."

Alex let out his breath, then moved onto his back. Etan followed him, curling up with his head on his chest. Shudders moved through him one after another, each one making Alex's heart ache.

He wished for at least the thousandth time that he could take the dreams away. Or at least take turns having them, give Etan a break from whatever demons he fought with in the night.

"Tell me your dream," Alex said. He pulled the covers over both of them. Etan was drenched in sweat despite the shivering.

"I don't remember. All I know is no one is safe. That keeps circling in my mind. No one."

Alex brushed back Etan's damp hair. "Safe from what? I'm not going anywhere, and no one else is here. We're both safe. Tell me about it so I can keep it that way."

"What did I say?"

"You were shouting. Not you, not you, let me do it. Then you screamed no one can save them. You've never had one that bad before."

"I can't remember what… No, that's not right. Almost everyone is dead." Etan squeezed tight, and Alex could almost see the dream ripping through his mind. "We can't stop them. A bunch more people going up there to die. In the higher mountains. They drink the water and turn into cartoons, stick figures. They bleed real blood, from everywhere."

"Do you know when?"

"How would I know when in a dream?"

This wasn't making sense. Alex couldn't tell if Etan was dreaming or awake. Etan rarely remembered his own dreams, not clearly. This sounded like one Alex would rather not know more about.

"Etan, are you awake? Do you understand what I'm asking you?"

Etan drew back, and his grip on Alex's arms loosened a little.

"Why wouldn't I understand? Of course I'm awake. I'm answering you."

Alex shook his head. "You answer me all the time after one of these. You hardly ever wake up all the way. You remember the dream, too?"

Etan shuddered one last time, then his body stilled and calmed.

"I still see them, crumpling away into dust. I don't know who I was shouting at. I can't remember, but I know I should."

"Listen, it's okay. If it's important, you'll dream it again. You do that all the time. If you don't wake up next time, maybe you'll be able to tell me more."

"I don't want another dream like that," Etan said. "The stick figures are worse than flesh and bone. I know how that sounds, but it's true."

Etan's heartbeat and breathing were almost back to normal, but now the images caught and invaded Alex's mind. What was coming toward them? Would he possibly be able to keep himself or Etan safe, much less anyone else?

"I wish I could make it stop forever, sweetie," Alex said. "Maybe I can for tonight."

Alex did stop the dream for both of them, with his mouth and his hands and his body.

But only for the night.

Chapter 17

The first rumors of food shortages drifted into town gossip late that October, right around the time everyone realized Wolf Branch had brought in a record harvest.

Etan's least favorite part of helping manage the cannery was the meetings, and this one felt a thousand times worse. Partly because it seemed like a thousand people were jammed into the high school auditorium, red and blue and green work clothes clashing with the purple and gold school colors around them. They'd hurriedly relocated from the cannery half an hour ago when it was obvious most of the town was showing up.

Five or six of them could usually stand around the gleaming steel tables, talk for a few minutes, maybe half an hour, then be done with it. Hardly anyone who didn't work with them seemed to care much about how everything stayed open, as long as it did.

The news—and rumors that grew from it—changed everything. Crop failures all around the country, from California to the Midwest to Florida, threatened to bring a nation long used to surplus uncomfortably close to rationing. The slowdown, some feared a new collapse, of the pollinators was impacting almost every staple food.

The weaknesses of a short, fast food supply chain only amplified the rest. Shelves didn't take a month to empty, or even a week. Shortages barely took days to get too big to ignore.

The same problems in different parts of the world kept food imports at their lowest levels in half a century.

In reassuring and sharp contrast, everyone's hard work had led to a huge surplus of food in Wolf Branch, fresh and put by. Reviving the food bank Anne and Evan were so proud of was the next logical step, but this harvest overran even those long ago plans and visions of helping people who were hurting for whatever reason.

Especially with the holidays and cold weather coming up, deciding what to do with shelves of canned fruit and vegetables along with refrigerators and freezers full of produce, meat, and dairy turned a quick conversation into a logistical challenge.

Etan sat in the back row of the auditorium with Alex, hoping no one would ask them to walk down the purple carpeted aisles to the stage in front. He still wondered if they should have kept this meeting secret instead of letting people know like they usually did. Folks were still wandering in out of the early time change darkness at ten past seven.

"What the hell are they all doing here?" Alex said, his arm around Etan. "We don't have that much food even if they did need it."

"It's more than that. They're hearing what's going on out there, finally starting to pay attention." He rubbed his tight shoulder muscles, relieved when Alex took the hint and took over. "Something worse tonight, though, not just the food. The first part of whatever we're going to face is about to land right in our laps."

"You've been restless enough lately," Alex said. He leaned close enough that his warm breath sent chills down Etan's legs. "I hope this lets both of us relax a little. We're overdue for some down time."

"Do you really think it will?"

Alex looked into Etan's eyes for several seconds. Etan saw the emotions chase across his lover's face, so much more out in the open than his own were. Alex was trying to hold on to his confidence, his assurance that they'd handle whatever came their way as long as they stayed close and worked hard enough.

And he was failing.

"I don't feel good about this either," he finally said, shaking his head. "We have to handle this right, all of us, or we'll have even more trouble down the road."

Linda Burns finally stood up at fifteen past, when all of the space behind Etan and Alex was filled with shuffling bodies. She constantly pushed the gray hair straggling out of her bun behind her ears and tugged at her green sweater. Linda was clearly used to speaking to a classroom full of teenagers, not hundreds of people in this packed auditorium.

"Thank you all for coming out tonight," she said. "We're a bit surprised, but we appreciate the interest. I guess you're here to help us decide what to do about the food bank and the surplus we have put by."

A rustle of whispered conversation passed through the room, but no one spoke out loud.

"When we did this in the past, we picked out a few families who were having troubles. That was just the easiest thing to do when we had extra. This year, we're going to have a lot left over after that. We were thinking of passing it along to other communities, other folks near us who might not have so much put by."

An older man near the front stood, pulling his faded green base-ball cap off. Etan would be forever grateful to Walt Colley for working so hard with Alex, getting the mechanical parts of the cannery up and running. Even more for doing so much to help Alex finally feel welcome in their new home.

"I sure am sorry to interrupt you, Linda, but I imagine you been watching the news same as the rest of us. We might not be set up to pass anything along to another town. A lot of people are going to have trouble finding enough to eat this winter."

He paused, looking around, his face and ears bright red.

"I don't mean to sound so selfish, and it's not hardly Christian of me I guess. But we need to keep what food we can right here. We worked hard to end up with so much. We might need it before this winter's up."

Etan focused on breathing deeply, trying not to let himself get upset enough for anyone but Alex to notice. They were going to need a hell of a lot more food, and for a hell of a lot longer than this one winter. The way they made it through the next six months might set the course they followed into far worse trouble.

He still didn't feel like that was all that was happening around him, though. Something deeper, darker, moved through the huge crowd, keeping everyone as on edge as he was.

"We can sure talk about that," Linda said, raising her hands to try to quiet the crowd a bit. "I've been watching the news too. We're lucky we had such a good harvest here. A lot of the bigger farms and such struggled this year. I hate to hoard it all when most of us have plenty put back in our own houses."

"Most of us do, sure," said a small, dark-haired woman Etan didn't recognize, off to his left. "That doesn't mean we have to provide for people who didn't bother. Maybe they'll learn their lesson this winter and do better next year."

"Hang on now," Carla Phipps said from one of the chairs on the stage. She was one of the most tireless workers in the community garden. "I don't mean to be hateful, but I didn't see you doing a whole lot of work to build up the food bank, Crystal. None of us were before this year, to tell you the truth. If it weren't for Etan and Alex getting everything back on track and getting such a big community garden put in, we'd be hurting just as bad as all the towns around us."

Etan tried to shrink down in his seat, but Alex put an arm behind him. People were turning, looking for them, trying to put faces to the names if they hadn't already. Alex smiled, his cheeks flushed but unafraid. Etan thanked him mentally for not forcing them to stand up.

"Sure, we owe them a great debt," Crystal said, her face now red as the beets lining the shelves of the cannery. "We appreciate it, and I know Etan's grandparents would have been proud. But that doesn't change the fact that we *are* prepared. We worked hard to get that way. I still say that food needs to stay right here where we can get to it if the Food Lion ends up with even more empty shelves in January."

A smattering of applause floated through. Etan was relieved it wasn't louder, but he wondered if it should have been. He hated the idea of hoarding the food, especially if people only ten miles away were lacking. But he knew they had to get into this mindset, of understanding how important it was to plan ahead. Sooner might be better, even if it did feel like a horrible response to a worse problem.

"Well then, if you think we have to keep it, how do you propose we deal with that?" Carla said. She stepped up beside Linda, crossing her arms. "We're still busy putting this year's harvest away, and we'll run out of room before too long. Who's going to decide what to do with it when the time comes?"

"We might have to keep it back longer than we think," a woman said, standing near the middle of the crowd.

Etan couldn't see her face, and he hadn't heard her voice for months now. But he knew exactly who it was before she turned, making sure everyone in the room could see her.

Mary Shadrin.

Chapter 18

"We know you've been studying on such things for a long time now, Mary," Linda said. Her voice sounded calm, but even from the back row Etan saw the frustration on her face. He remembered it well from classes with her years ago. "One crop failure isn't the end of the world."

"It may not look like it from where you stand," Mary said, "with the key to months worth of food safe in your pocket. But we've been preparing for a long time now, getting ready for what's coming. If we decide this isn't that big a deal, that everything will recover in time, who are you going to for help when the whole thing crashes all around us?"

"What are you proposing, Mary?" said Joey Price, the preacher from the Episcopal church in town. He'd started a clothing drive to go along with the food pantry over the summer, so he sat on the stage behind Linda. "Are we supposed to ration food or something, when our neighbors are in need?"

"We're going to have to do exactly that," Mary said, her voice rising. She gazed more slowly at the crowd, and Etan would have sworn she picked him out without any effort at all. "You know we've been here for a long time, getting ready, watching the signs from all around us. This isn't just an isolated problem, Father Price. The food is starting to drop off all around the world."

"I think we can vote to keep this year's surplus," Linda said, trying to speak over the rumbling crowd. "But I'm not ready to say we're facing a worldwide crisis just yet. I know we can all work together to do more next year, especially with Etan and Alex learning and teaching us better ways to grow and preserve things every day."

The crowd again looked their way, but this time Alex wasn't so calm. He shrank back too, and Etan knew he was feeling that riptide current. The air was thicker, heavier. Things could turn against them, against all of them, before another heartbeat.

"I think they'd be just the ones to be in charge of the whole thing myself," Walt Colley said from the front row, still twisting his cap in his rawboned hands. "You're right, not a bit of this would be here if it wasn't for the two of them. They done a right fine job getting us ready for this winter. I say they should be the very folks to make sure we stay ready for the next one."

"This isn't right," Alex whispered, leaning into Etan's arm. "This isn't where we need to be."

"I say that's a fine idea," Linda said. She did what Etan dreaded, waving to them to walk up front. "If they'll join us and maybe say a few words, we can put it to a vote. We don't technically have to hold a vote of the whole town for something like this, but maybe we should hear what everyone else has to say."

"We can't do this," Etan said. "They'll rip us to shreds."

Etan's legs were made of lead, holding him to the seat. He knew if he tried to walk up to the front of the auditorium in front of what felt like an increasingly threatening crowd, he wouldn't make it more than a few steps.

Mary stepped in and saved him, at least from that much.

"Well, I propose they're *not* the ones who should be in charge," she said, her eyes flashing. "They've not even been back here a year, and one of them isn't *from* here at all."

Etan felt Alex go rigid against him. He gripped Alex's thigh, hoping he would be still. Etan had a terrible feeling they'd be lost if they spoke out now, especially if Alex let his temper get the best of him. He knew in his gut that this was not the right time for them to step forward.

"I don't see how that's relevant, Mary," Linda said, hands on her hips. "Sure, Etan was born in the hospital right here in town. But you need to remember his grandparents and his father weren't, and they did more for the community than most ever have. Alex is Etan's partner, and he's worked himself half to death helping everyone else out with the cannery and solar panels and windmills and everything else since the day he got here. That's all we need to know."

"I was born here, raised here, never have lived a day anywhere else," Mary said, her voice rising. "My friends can say the same, most of them. All of them have been here at least twenty years, getting ready. No one knows more about what's coming and what we'll have to do to survive it than we do."

Father Price stood, holding out his hands. "Mary, I just can't stand by and let you get everyone all riled up with this talk of some kind end times disaster coming." Etan felt Alex laugh under his breath, his tense muscles relaxing a little bit. "We can certainly listen to what you have to say, and we're glad to learn from you and your friends. But we're not going to turn everything we've worked so hard for over to you just because you want us to."

The crowd rustled again, and Etan felt the shift toward himself and Alex as clearly as if he'd seen flags moving in the wind. But that still wasn't right.

Having everyone, especially Mary, paying too much attention to them was the last thing they needed. Not now.

He hoped not ever.

"I suggest we have a voice vote," Linda said, holding up her arms. "We can get an idea how people feel, then we'll have something more formal later on. I probably should stay out of these things, but I've worked with Etan and Alex for the last several months, almost every day. I know they're good men, and I know I trust them. I say they should be the ones we're looking to at least until we know more about what's ahead of us."

A few people applauded, then more joined in a wave. Etan's flesh crawled with wanting to run, to get them out of there before the situation flew out of control. Mary whirled around, her eyes wide and staring.

Before the noise died down, she raised her voice to a shout.

"*I* am the one who can lead us into the future! *I* have seen where we're headed! If we don't correct our course now, we'll all end up in disaster!"

The silence hit hard enough to make Etan's head ache. No one moved, and he would have sworn no one was breathing either. It wasn't only Mary's words, shocking and strange as they were.

The air felt coarse, full of transparent gritty sand. It would be painful to try to move against the resistance.

Harry Mullins, a businessman who'd been in town his entire life, stood a few rows in front of Etan and Alex. His dark blue suit was terribly out of place among the flannel shirts and denim jackets, but Etan had never seen him wear anything else.

"Care to elaborate on that, Mary? You having visions now?"

"I have *always* had visions," she said, her voice harsh. "That's why I have the group of people around me, the ones who understand what we're going to be up against. I've seen more things come true over the last two years than I did in the twenty before. We are coming to the crossroads, and the wrong choice will be deadly to all of us!"

"Are you saying you hear from God?" Father Price said. He stood beside Linda, his hands now folded the same way they surely were on Sunday mornings.

"I don't need to hear from God. I see the future. I *dream* the future. And our future will be a nightmare if we do not make the right choices now."

A group of about twenty people stood around Mary, all of them nodding. No one else in the room spoke or moved. When she turned, her eyes fierce with triumph, Etan gasped.

"What's wrong?" Alex whispered, grabbing his hand.

Etan shook his head, too terrified to speak.

He didn't see the same woman, not even one as scary and possibly unhinged as Mary was right now. He saw eyes wild and lost, features gaunt, black hair streaked with gray. She stood with a different stance, not one of triumph, but one of bitter defiance.

No one made a sound, but Etan heard Mary's voice, hoarse with talking and shouting and screaming. He saw her raise a skeletal hand, pointing right at him.

"False prophet!" she said, the words booming and repeating through his head. The same crowd stood behind her, all of them equally unhinged and aged, echoing her in a terrifying chant. "Follow him to your death, to the death of all of us. We must remove the false prophet, cleanse him from our midst, if we're to survive. There is no other way forward!"

Time finally moved again, with Harry speaking to jar Etan out of whatever dream he'd been caught in. The horrifying vision of Mary was gone, replaced with her bright red face. Unlike most of his dreams, he saw and heard and remembered every detail of whatever had just happened to him.

"I don't want to be dragged into this kind of thing," Harry said, and now his own face was blazing. Etan saw he was sweating, even from so far away. "But this can't go on. Mary, I don't doubt that you have dreams. I don't doubt that they come true. The same thing has been happening to me for years now. And I'm not the only one."

The room erupted into noise then, and the temperature seemed to soar in an instant. More people stood, most of them shouting. Alex turned to Etan, eyes wide and terrified.

"What the fuck is going on here?"

"We must have some kind of order!" Linda shouted. "We can't turn into a mob, no matter what else is going on!"

After a minute of what sounded to Etan like pandemonium, but he was later sure was merely disorder amplified by his ragged nerves, people calmed down enough for Linda to speak again. Her voice was nearly as hoarse as Mary's had been in his hallucination.

"I don't know what to say, but we can't keep shouting at each other. Harry, do you have something else? Do you want to speak?"

Mary stomped toward the stage, fists clenched. She looked frightening, but back to being herself in Etan's eyes.

"I would like to speak! I am *not* finished!"

"For tonight you are, Mary," Harry said. He walked slowly up onto the stage, pulling out an absurdly old-fashioned white handkerchief and wiping at his face. "I don't know what the hell is in the air here tonight. But I do know you've said enough for now."

He stood in the middle of the stage. Despite towering over Linda at well over six feet, with barrel chest and broad shoulders to match, he looked for all the world like a nervous kid forced to give a speech for a class.

"I meant what I said. I've been dreaming about something happening, more and more all the time. I'm not going to call names, but I know I'm not alone. I'd sure appreciate it greatly if at least one of you would stand by my side."

Alex squeezed Etan's hand.

"No," Etan whispered. "Don't move. Don't make a sound. Please."

A few seconds passed, with Harry nervously mopping at his brow again. Finally several people got to their feet. Etan had seen all of them out at the cannery and working in the garden. Every single one of them had donated to the food bank or the clothing drive without being asked. Father Price joined them as well.

More people stood, and within a couple of minutes, twenty people stood beside Harry on the stage. At least that many more stood in the rows of seats. Etan could see Harry was still breathing hard, but the relief was a physical force in the whole auditorium.

"I don't know what all this is going to mean," Harry said. His voice trembled as if he was going to cry. "But it means the world to me for you to be here with me right now."

Mary stood again, but Linda stepped to the front of the stage, her hand on Harry's arm.

"I think we've all had just about enough for one night. We'll leave the food bank as it is for now. The same way it's been since Evan and Anne Griffith, who both grew up a long way from here, got it started for all of us."

"We got to bring the mayor and the town council in on this," Walt said. He stood not far from Harry on the stage, his hat now invisible in his red-knuckled hands. "I sure don't know what's happening, but we got to try to make sense of it."

"We'll do just that, Walt," Linda said. "I know a lot of you have a lot more to say, and we'll make sure that happens sooner rather than later. But for tonight, let's all go home and be thankful that we're arguing about having too *much* food to go around. A lot of folks in the United States of America might be in a different mess long before the spring comes around again."

Chapter 19

THE TENSION in the room broken, everyone stood at once, turning toward the exits. Right toward Alex and Etan. After a few stunned seconds and increasing pressure on his hand, Alex realized Etan was trying to drag him to his feet.

"We've got to get out of here," Etan said. "Now, before it's too late."

They pushed through the crowd and out into the still empty lobby, moving at almost a run toward Evan Griffith's blue sedan they'd been driving lately. It started on the first try, just as the door to the auditorium opened.

"What's going on, E?" Alex said as Etan hit the gas a bit too hard going out of the parking lot. Gravel spun beneath the usually easy to handle car before he let off a bit.

"We can't get involved in this now," Etan said, shaking his head. "It's too dangerous. Everyone's too upset, and I don't want them upset with us."

"I think we're already involved, sweetie." Alex tried to take his hand, but Etan refused.

"No, I'm not just being stubborn or shy or whatever. This is not a joke. Something is wrong here."

Alex fought back a laugh that would have only made things worse. Mary Shadrin and everyone with her stopped just short of insisting she be put in charge, half the town outed themselves as dreamers, and all Etan could say was *something is wrong?*

"Explain it to me, then," Alex said. "I don't want to be in charge of some kind of sinister food rationing center either, but we *have* put a lot of this together. I doubt they'd have food to argue over if it weren't for us."

"I'm sure you're right, but you didn't see her face, Alex. She wasn't sane, not even a little bit."

"Mary? Aren't you overreacting? She seems a bit out there, but not dangerous. I did see her face. She looked like some kind of religious nut to me. What Harry said-"

"No, you didn't *see* her! She had… I could see something else there, something that hasn't happened yet. She's nowhere near as crazy as she's going to be."

Alex remembered to breathe when Etan slowed down, but not before the back wheels skidded sideways on the long curve at the edge of town. Running them over the cliff and onto the railroad tracks far below would at least bring everything to a quick end.

"You saw what? I don't understand what you're saying."

"I saw another version of her." Etan took a deep breath. "Her and everyone with her. They were all older, thinner. Her eyes were horrible. She was trying to get us put out or killed or something."

Alex scowled, pushing his hands flat against his thighs.

"Wait, are you telling me you saw that just now? Not when you were asleep?"

"That's exactly what I'm telling you. Please, let me get it out, I know it doesn't make any sense. I *saw* her, and I know it was her. Screaming, calling me a false prophet, saying I'd lead to the end of everything. Then it was gone."

"As clear as the dreams are?" Alex reached for his hand again, and this time Etan grasped his.

"More clear than the dreams are to me. I've only had a handful that I could remember at all. This was just like looking at her, like being in the same room with them just then. She's going to cause some kind of problem, one we might not live through."

"Don't you think we need to talk to someone about that, then?" Alex said. "Make sure she doesn't argue her way into getting put in charge of something?"

"No, we can't do that. I don't know what it is, but I know if we speak up right now, we won't survive it. She might turn directly against us instead of biding her time. I don't understand why, but I wasn't kidding about feeling like this will tear us to shreds. We have to let this work itself out. Please, please don't say anything, Alex."

After a few minutes of silence, Alex knew he'd stalled long enough. But he still couldn't work out what to say. What *could* he say about Etan having some kind of waking visions now, much less finding out they'd moved into a town half full of fortune tellers?

"I won't say anything," he said. "Not that anyone would listen. I'm the evil outsider. Not even from here, remember?"

"*Fuck* her and her fucking small town bigotry!"

Alex held his breath for a few seconds, trying to fight it, then he burst into laughter. The two of them laughed until they were both wiping their eyes.

"Tempting as that might sound to some," Alex said, "I'm going to pass. Do you understand what happened, Etan? A bunch of people have the dreams. Looked like half the town to me. I don't think she can hurt you with that many people having the same thing happen to them."

"I don't care, I can't be out there as a target. *We* can't be. That feels like a cliff under my feet, and one wrong step will pull you down with me. We have to wait it out and see what happens. What we're doing at the cannery is too important to risk. I can't let them know about my dreams. We have to keep our heads down. I got that loud and clear with the way she looked at me."

"I won't say anything, I promise," Alex said. He leaned against Etan's shoulder and whispered in his ear. "You're not the only one, E. Not anymore. You're not alone with this."

Etan shook his head, but when he glanced at Alex, he was smiling.

"That may take me a while to get used to," he said as he turned up the long road heading out of town. "Listen, we need to stop and talk to my parents. What happened tonight isn't going to stay a secret, probably already made it back to just about everyone here. We need to make sure they know not to say anything. They're not safe either."

Chapter 20

Etan's mother looked startled when she opened the door and saw them. Her hair was pulled back and she clutched a blue robe with pink flowers embroidered all over at her throat.

"What's wrong with you two? Did something happen in town tonight?"

Etan glanced at Alex, and both of them snorted out laughter before they could stop themselves.

"Yeah, you could say that, Mom," he said, fighting to keep the mad giggles from taking over. "Have you and Dad got a few minutes?"

"Of course we do. Did you two have dinner yet? I've got leftovers I can heat up in a couple of minutes."

Etan locked the door without thinking about it. When he met Alex's wide gaze, he realized what he'd done. He just took Alex's hand and kept walking.

"That sounds great, Laura," Alex said. "All this talk about food definitely hit me that way."

"We have company," she called into the living room. "He'll be out in a minute. Some kind of game on, but it's not baseball so I don't give a shit."

Alex laughed again, a normal laugh that didn't sound like it might take his breath. By the time they got settled at the table, Etan's father walked in. He wore sweatpants and a t-shirt so faded Etan wasn't sure what color it had been. Neither of them expected company so late.

"What brings you two out here?" he said. "Did you eat?"

"Mom's getting it right now," Etan said. "We just wanted to talk to you two about the meeting tonight. It won't take long."

"Something go wrong?" Etan's father said, sitting across from Alex.

"Something went strange," Alex said.

"What went strange?" Etan's mother said. She set two plates full of baked chicken, mashed potatoes, and green beans in front of them. Every bit of it from within a few miles of where they sat. "Husband, go fetch your sons something to drink. What do you want?"

"Beer would be perfect," Alex said.

"A glass of Mom's red wine might take the edge off."

A few seconds later, when his father returned with two of each, Etan was out of time. He was starving, and the food smelled amazing. But he knew if he tried to eat before he got this out, he'd end up sick.

"So what happened over there that got you so spooked?" his mother said. She sipped at her own glass of wine. "You looked awful when I opened the door, pale as a sheet."

"Mary Shadrin happened," Etan said. "What do you two know about her?"

"She's been holed up with a bunch of survivalists for the last fifteen years or so," his father said. "She was always an odd duck, worked as a psychic down in Asheville for a few years. That's gotten a lot worse since she brought a bunch of people back here to reinforce her crazy ideas. What did she do now?"

Etan tried to swallow a mouthful of potatoes without much success. Even his own parents thought someone else with the dreams was crazy. He'd been right to keep his mouth shut at the meeting.

"She tried to take over the food bank," Alex said. "Partly because she's seen a vision of the End Times Disaster to come. And partly because she couldn't tolerate a foreigner like me being involved."

"Oh come on!" Etan's mother said. Her light alcohol flush deepened into an angry one. "What the hell business of hers is it where you or anyone else came from? She was happy enough to cozy up to your grandparents when they were still alive, and neither of them were born here."

"Yeah, she mentioned them to me a few months ago," Etan said. "Said she was *so* sorry for my loss, wanted to see if she could help me down at the cannery. I told her to keep moving."

"You were right," his father said. "I've never trusted her, and Mom and Dad didn't either."

"Did they say why not?" Alex said.

"I got the feeling Mom dreamed about her, to be honest," Etan's father said. "And Dad always took that seriously. All of us did. She was always right about things like that."

"Well, apparently Gemaw wasn't the only one dreaming," Etan said, trying to smile. "Mary says she does, too."

"Bullshit," his mother said. "I'm sure she wished she could tell the future, or at least that people would believe she did. But she never said a word about anything like that."

"She's not the only one, Mom," Etan said.

"I know you always did," she said. "That doesn't mean…I don't want you to think we think you're…"

"It's okay. I felt that way myself for a long time," Etan said. "Until I met Alex, really. Harry Mullins stood up and said he has the dreams too."

Both his parents stared at him without saying a word, their eyes so large he had to once again force himself not to laugh. He finished his wine instead and poured more for himself and his mother.

"A bunch of other people too," Alex said. "I think it was about forty. They backed Harry up and made Mary shut up. I get the feeling she's not finished, though."

"They all said that, in front of everyone?" Etan's mother said. "I never even heard Anne say that in public. She never hid it from your father, or from you, of course. But she kept it to herself otherwise."

"That's what we're going to have to do now," Etan said. "I saw something else strange tonight, first time that's happened to me. Am I remembering right that Gemaw saw things while she was awake sometimes?"

His father nodded, a sad smile on his face.

"She didn't talk as much about that as the dreams, but she told me that, yeah. She said she saw how people were going to die, over their faces like a mask. She had times when the only face she could see clearly was Dad's."

"Jesus," Alex said under his breath. "Her whole life?"

"Started the same time as her dreams did," Etan's father said. "I think that was the hardest thing for her. That's probably what led to a lot of her trouble, even more than the dreams. Is that what you saw tonight, Etan?"

Etan's heart twisted at the worried sound of his father's voice, surely remembering stories about how badly his own mother suffered.

"Not how Mary's going to die, no. I think I saw how she's going to end up. What she's going to try to do. Whatever problem she has is going to get worse."

"Etan said she would try to get us killed," Alex said. "If anyone finds out about his dreams right now, that's where we're headed."

"Trying to get you killed?" his mother said, her eyes flashing. "That's enough. Time to tell Sheriff Grant about this."

"No. Please, don't do that," Etan said, leaning forward. "You said there were times when Gemaw saw things you ended up believing, right? Was it ever anything like this? When she asked you to keep quiet when you didn't want to?"

"There were a lot of times like that," his father said. "Times when Dad told me something she dreamed about, but she didn't want any of us to do anything about it. Some things I've never yet told anyone about. She was right. Every time."

"Well, I believe Etan is right, too," Alex said.

Etan loved him more than his own life in that second.

In every second.

Even in the house he'd grown up in, the resistance was as thick and painful as it had been in the auditorium. Etan had never requested belief in his visions, much less demanded it. Alex had simply offered that belief, with no idea what he was doing, to save Etan's sanity months ago. And both of their lives in the months ahead.

Right now, he knew he had to expect the same from his parents, demand if he had to. That was the only possible to way to keep all of them safe. He was terrified he'd demand the same belief from everyone around him before another five years passed. But not now.

"I can't explain this any more than I can explain why we had to come back here when we did," Etan said, grasping Alex's hand. "But I know we have to keep our heads down. Things are going to change in the future, but if we get pushed in the middle of this right now, everything is going to fall apart. We won't be able to stop Mary or anyone else."

"I've never trusted Mary or anyone who's with her," his father said. "You two still have a gun up there?"

"We have a gun," Alex said. "I haven't handled one since I was about ten years old, and that wasn't for long. I'm afraid I'd shoot my foot off."

"I don't like this business of Mary or anyone else making threats against you two," his father said. "But I'll let it go for now, if you let us make sure you both know how to defend yourselves. I doubt she or anybody else with so goddamn much bluster will be brave enough to come up here. If they do, though, make sure they understand exactly why they need to get the hell out."

"I haven't shot in years," Etan said. "Not since I moved to Chicago. I was pretty good at it back in the day. We might be able to train Alex up enough to be at least passable."

"Good luck with that," Alex said. He didn't sound afraid, though. He sounded excited.

"Your grandmother always dreamed about the world coming to some kind of hellish end," Etan's mother said. She'd finished her second glass of wine as well, but Etan knew the flush in her cheeks didn't mean she was the least bit drunk. "Is this why you started up the cannery and the food pantry, Etan?"

"Yeah, that's part of it," he said. "Same with all the power systems Alex is setting up. That's not gonna be enough. Not nearly enough. But we had to start somewhere. I'm sorry we haven't told you more of this before now."

"Well, you're telling us now," his father said. "You and Alex have done wonders for this community in such a short time. If Mary or anyone else can't see that, or if they resent it, they're even crazier than we thought."

THE FOOD SUPPLY held out through that winter, at least in the developed world. Many parts of the planet were not so lucky.

People who did have enough understood it was a near thing, nearer than it had ever been before. They worried things would get worse in the future.

Before another year passed, every person on the planet understood how far off their most dire predictions had been.

How mild their deepest fears.

Humanity would never again have so lofty a goal to fail as enough food for a modern world.

Chapter 21

THE BASEMENT of the cannery seemed like the worst place in town for storing anything the first time Etan saw it. Less than an hour of poking around the musty and dank space, an ominous boiler at either end, the middle filled with broken equipment that had probably been down there since before he was born, sent him rushing home for a hot shower that day.

Another huge spring harvest, along with whispering fears of nearby towns finding out about their growing food surplus, sent Alex and his dedicated crew of amateur engineers down to clean the place up.

By the time they finished in mid-August, the basement was as bright and clean as the grocery store in town. Alex even managed to add another class to what he was already teaching high school kids and adults. Along with working with solar panels, wind and water turbines, and batteries, people learned how to install a generator to run the lights and ventilation fans, one that ran on gasoline or fuel alcohol. They finally had a use for the piles of sugar beets everyone was able to grow, and a reason to set up legal distilleries out in the open for everyone to see.

Walt Colley looked up from where he was helping Etan count the latest batch of donations, several cases of canned goods.

"Hey there Alex," he said with a slow smile.

Etan turned to see Alex looking over his shoulder as he hurried down the new wooden steps, buckling his brown leather holster around his waist. Etan couldn't remember when he'd last seen Alex carrying his gun when they weren't practicing shooting. His normally open and happy face was tense and grim.

"Hey Walt," Alex said. "Everyone needs to get upstairs. I don't want them seeing how we get down here."

"Who?" Etan said. "What's wrong?"

Alex pulled his green work shirt out of his jeans to cover up the holster, but not before everyone in the room saw it.

But Etan was more alarmed by his father's face than his lover's words. Connor Griffith steadied himself with one hand against the white cinderblock wall, his face nearly as pale.

"I don't know where they're from," Alex said looking up the stairs again. "Hope I'm just being paranoid, but let's go. Come on."

Alex starting turning off the lights before everyone made it up the stairs. Etan touched his father's shoulder as he passed by, but he just shook his head. Alex's back felt like vibrating wires under Etan's hand.

"What the hell's going on, Alex?"

"Several big pickup trucks drove into town a little while ago," he said. "Gun racks fully loaded and on display. We should have help in a few minutes."

Etan followed Alex up the stairs, watching him lock the door behind them. No one ever did that until they locked up the entire cannery at night.

Everyone was gathered around the frosted windows overlooking the parking lot by the time Etan got upstairs, peering through the open edges. Linda kicked the rubber stop away from one of the double doors.

"No," Alex said. "We're not going to lock it with all of us standing here in plain sight. We need to hear what they want and not let them know we're afraid. Everybody stay calm."

Three men and a woman, their own firearms clearly visible, walked toward the door of the cannery. Etan had never seen any of them before. Several others stood beside their huge antique pickups in the parking lot.

"Don't just stand here staring," Etan said, taking a few steps back himself. "If they didn't come looking for trouble, this is the best way to make sure it starts anyway."

Everyone managed to be busy by the time the three strangers got to the door. Etan walked back over, hoping his shaking hands didn't give them away. The four of them looked normal enough, all wearing work clothes just like anyone else in town. He had to bite back a laugh at the faded blue and red kerchiefs they all had pulled up over their faces, like redneck caricatures of an Old West museum exhibit.

Etan had the strongest feeling this was beginning of trouble that would not be over that day.

"Good afternoon," he said, trying not to cringe at his own nervous formality. "Can I help you?

"Afternoon," one of the men said in a slow drawl. He was taller than Alex or even lanky Walt Colley, with wavy gray hair that fell to his collar. The woman beside him, her graying blond hair pulled back in a ponytail, was nearly as tall.

"We hear you been doing good things over here," he said. "So we figured we'd stop by and say hello."

The other three didn't say anything, but their eyes never stopped moving, looking over all the people and equipment in the steaming hot room.

"We just got opened back up last year," Alex said, stepping up beside Etan. "Figuring out how everything works, teaching a few classes at the high school."

"Quite a garden you have put in out there," the man said, waving his hand toward the door. "Making good use of the harvest?"

"Same as with the cannery," Etan said. "The main thing is making sure the high school kids know how to grow things and take care of themselves. Having a problem with dust where you came from?"

"Just trying to keep healthy. Never can be too careful these days with all the trouble out in the world."

"We'd be glad to help you set up a program for your own kids," Linda said. "Did you come from close by?"

"Close enough," the man said. "I get the idea you had quite the surplus last winter. How's that looking for this year?"

"Not as much as we'd like." Alex leaned against a metal table and crossed his arms. "We're all doing the best we can to get ready for another rough winter."

A huge clatter made everyone jump, and Etan turned with his heart pounding. His father crouched beside a huge pile of pots and utensils, red-faced instead of pale, trying to disappear into the concrete floor.

When he turned back, the other men and the woman had taken several steps toward the middle of the room. Alex moved forward.

"We're only in for short hours today," he said. "We'd be happy to talk to you about setting something up where you came from. Right now we're about ready to lock up and go home."

"We'll head out here a little while," the woman said, walking toward Connor and the pile he was still cleaning up. Uncomfortably close to the door down into the basement. "We'd sure like to hear more about that surplus you had last year. How that's holding up?"

"Just like anywhere else I suppose," Alex said. He shifted his hand to the gun hidden under his shirt. Etan would have sworn he heard Alex's muscles thrumming. "Working hard to make sure we have enough to feed our families."

"Where you finding to keep your stores?" the woman said.

She continued her slow walk around the room, taking notice of everyone pretending not to notice her. Alex watched her more closely than the others.

"I'm starting to think the Sheriff's office might be the best place," Etan's father said. He looked horrified at the words that had just come out of his own mouth.

"Is that right?" the first man said. He walked up beside Connor, standing easily six inches taller. "Pretty goddamn easy to be cocky when you're sitting on enough food to feed your families and a bunch more besides."

"I think we're just about done here," Walt Colley said in the loudest voice Etan had ever heard from him. "Hiding your faces, strutting around like you own the place. Unless you all have something useful to say, about time you head outta here and quit bothering us."

Sheriff Grant and two of his deputies walked in before anyone else could speak. None of them looked the least bit tense or upset. Just out for an afternoon drive, decided to stop by for a visit. Alex caught Etan's attention and winked.

"Looks like you got quite a crowd in here for a short day," Sheriff Grant said. He stood with his arms relaxed at his sides, nowhere near the handgun on his belt. But Etan couldn't stop himself from realizing they now had as many guns as the strangers, and three officers well-trained to use them.

"I believe our visitors were just about to head out," Alex said, standing by the doors. "We sure wish you all the best of luck with your own harvest."

The strangers turned slowly, looking at each of them in turn. The tall man met Etan's eyes for several uncomfortable seconds. The woman's gaze, emotionless and flat, chilled him to the bone. She jerked her chin toward the door, and the others fell in line behind her.

"We certainly did have an informative visit," the tall man said as he walked toward the door. "I'm sure looking forward to when we cross paths again."

When they passed through, Alex closed both doors and turned the deadbolt.

"Thank you for getting over here so fast," Alex said, shaking hands with the sheriff. "That settled them down, at least for now."

"We did a little checking on the way over here," the sheriff said. He shook Etan's hand, too, and clapped him on the back. "This wasn't the first place they dropped in to, hokey handkerchiefs and all. They haven't caused any real trouble yet, but they're making it clear they'd like to."

"Where the hell are they from?" Etan said. Now that the strangers were gone, he was shaking and covered in sweat.

"Well, they've got fake plates on their trucks," Sheriff Grant said.

"Antique gas models, no tracking sensors. Can't see enough of their faces to recognize even if we did know them, which is just what they wanted. They haven't done anything we can arrest them for or even make them admit who they are without causing a lot more trouble. Everyone I talked to has their hands too damn full to follow them home right now, same as we do."

"You got any security set up over here?" Deputy Wiggins said. Etan thought her first name was Melissa. "Alarms or anything like that?"

"Nothing besides the basement and locks on all the doors," Etan said. He walked over to Alex, thankful for the warmth of his arms. "Those days might be over."

"We'd be happy to keep an eye on the place for you," the sheriff said. "But if they're out looking for an easy target, best thing may be to make sure you don't give 'em one."

Etan's stomach sank at the thought of arming themselves against their neighbors, though his heart and what Alex told him about the dreams let him know that was the next step. Modern security systems would be useless before much more time passed, but they couldn't ignore the threat. Alex squeezed him and rubbed his shoulder.

"We'll talk to the school administration about it," Alex said. "It's probably time to move everything out of the food pantry in town as well. I'm afraid this winter's going to be a rough one."

When the sheriff left, Etan helped his father with the last of the cleanup.

"What's going on, Dad? You look like you're about to pass out, then you just about dared those goons to start shooting."

"I know, I'm sorry. I couldn't stand by and let them threaten you and Alex. You're too important to risk."

"So are you, old man," Alex said, smiling and helping both of them to their feet. "You grew up here, Etan. Is there a basement under the high school we could use instead of the food pantry? That would be a hell of a lot easier to secure than the old building in the middle of town with those huge windows."

"Yeah," Etan said, still watching his father. He seemed fully recovered if a bit shaky. "The basement's at least as big as the whole building. They had classrooms down there when I was in school. We could turn it into a ton of storage space."

"Mary and her cronies aren't going to like that idea," Linda said, leaning on the storage shelf. "They're still saying we all have to work together, that we need to share all our food and ration it so we can help everyone."

"Sounds like a great way for all of us to starve," Connor said. "They've been talking to a lot of people in town, though."

"We're going to have to do the same," Linda said. "And we may just have to get our stores moved without Mary and her followers finding out about it."

Alex looked at Etan, his brow creased, his blue eyes worried. Etan knew they were thinking the same thing that neither of them were willing to say.

All the hiding in the world wouldn't stop dreamers from knowing the truth.

～

SMALL GROUPS STARTED STRAGGLING in as the weather turned cooler. Several were returning home much like Etan had. A growing number followed dreams to a small mountain town they'd never heard of before.

They settled into houses long empty, breathing a bit of life into Wolf Branch after years of quiet decline. Almost everyone showed a quick interest in growing and preserving food, drawn to the cannery and community garden as if by magic.

Even as the outside power grid supplying Wolf Branch weakened and grew more erratic, the new arrivals adjusted with enthusiasm and relief. Too many to be a coincidence brought equipment they didn't know how to use with them. Precious space and resources taken up with glossy solar panels, small water and wind turbines, boxy storage batteries.

Neither they nor Alex and his growing crew of installers were surprised to find themselves in the same small town.

The influx continued as news from around the world worsened over the fall. The harvest was better worldwide, but stores depleted by previous winters in both hemispheres were still terribly low. Shipments were more erratic, leading to many things disappearing, then reappearing sporadically.

Fear of worsening riots joined fear of starvation, and those fears became reality far too often.

One of the last large groups to arrive in Wolf Branch captured all of Etan and Alex's attention. A doctor bringing years of emergency room experience along with years worth of medical supplies replaced their worries about people getting hurt or sick in the future with worries about how to keep the priceless medicine and equipment safe in the growing uneasy climate all around them.

Mary and her followers found out about the community's growing supplies, and where they were stored, through their own magic.

Chapter 22

THE SPACE under the high school was larger and more useful than Alex expected, and much cleaner than he'd feared. Unlike the neglected mess under the cannery, the maze of rooms, hallways, and closets was mostly empty. Everyone who'd been there for the disturbing masked strangers' visit to the cannery pitched in, and the whole space was clean in a few hours.

Shrinking class sizes left this part of the school abandoned a few years ago, but Alex couldn't help imagining Etan trudging through the purple and gold tiled hallways. Maybe when they got home from this late night supply run, he'd ask his lover about that.

He walked up the narrow concrete steps, playing the scenes and questions out in his mind. Was your first kiss with a boy or a girl? Where was it? Alex stepped out into the quiet November night, grinning to himself.

Did you ever have sex down in that basement?

Whether Etan ever had or not, Alex definitely thought the two of them should.

"Working late, Mr. Collins?" a woman said. He couldn't see her face where she stood in the shadow of the building, but he knew her voice.

"Not working at all, Ms. Shadrin. Just cleaning up for new classes. What brings you out this time of night?"

She stepped toward him, the security light Alex had installed a few days ago showing her narrowed eyes and pursed lips. She was wearing dark pants and a dark jacket, and her hair was pulled back. He'd never seen her dressed in a way to avoid attention rather than her normal flowing pastel wardrobe.

"Even with all these newcomers, there aren't enough students to open up that basement again," she said. She glanced toward the big enclosed truck they'd been using for these nighttime runs, rescued from a previous life as part of a delivery fleet. "Looks like a lot of cleaning supplies for one building. Strange that you feel the need to lock up a bunch of mops and brooms."

"Like you said, we've had a lot of new arrivals over the past few weeks, and their kids need school as much as anyone else. Strange that you're so worried about the high school basement."

"Is this where you're hiding the food, Mr. Collins?" She crossed her arms. "The food our town and our neighbors need so badly?"

"I'm not in charge of the food or the cleanup. You'll have to talk to Linda Burns about that. She's pretty damn busy with teaching and helping run the cannery. And if you're going to accuse me of hiding anything, drop the mister nonsense. My name is Alex."

"I fully intend to speak to Linda, once she shows some courage and stops avoiding me. I have a voice as part of the town council. Linda and a few others need to remember that."

"We're all well aware of who's on the council," Alex said. "That has nothing to do with what we do here at the school or at the cannery. You're on the wrong track here."

"If you're not hiding food down there, I'm guessing that's where you keep the guns. Robert Phillips dreams about them, night after night. The dreams are coming to me, too. These weapons you cling to will lead to a slaughter, one neither we nor our neighbors can afford as the end draws near."

Mary walked toward him, stopping a few inches away. She smelled flowery but a little too much, like she'd been rolling in an overripe flower bed.

"I know you're a reasonable man, Alex."

"No, Mary. You don't." Alex shrugged and leaned against the cool bricks, arms crossed. "You don't know anything about me at all. Let me give you a hint. If you continue to interfere with our work here, I'll get downright *un*reasonable."

"Maybe Mr. Griffith will listen to me then," she said. "Connor, I mean. He might not have graduated from this school like his son and I did, but he's lived here for thirty years."

"Like I *haven't*, right? Something else you should know about me, since you're so fond of saying I'm not from around here to anyone who will listen. I'm happy to play the perfect big city hothead you seem to expect when the situation calls for it. Damn good at it, too. If you or anyone around you bothers my family, I won't just be unreasonable. I'll be pure hell to deal with. Got it?"

"You have not yet seen the hell we'll all have to live through because of such arrogance! We'll be lucky if anyone lives through it at all."

"I suppose we'll all find out when the time comes," Alex said. He and Mary both turned at the sound of voices in the stairwell. "Right now all you're accomplishing is keeping us from doing everything we can to make sure we survive."

"We *will* find out, Alex." She walked toward the curving asphalt road heading into town. "I hope none of you does anything you live to regret. If you live at all."

Chapter 23

Sandy Hughes, another returning native of Wolf Branch, brought the truck full of medical supplies south from Chicago. She made no attempt to hide the dreams that brought her back to her birthplace. A hectic week spent storing and arranging everything Sandy brought ended with dinner with Etan's parents.

"How did you get all the supplies out of there?" Etan said.

"No one's really paying attention anymore," Sandy said. Her dark blond hair was caught back in a thick braid from the workday, and she still wore her faded and patched coveralls. "They're too busy trying to keep up to watch things like medical supplies walking on their own."

"We figured the government is keeping a lot of things quiet," Alex said. "And most people would rather not know anyway."

"I wish I didn't know about most of it," Sandy said. "Bigger sections of the city than you'd believe are empty, but I just about waited too late to get out. Some of my friends who got out a lot earlier barely made it."

"What's happening?" Etan said. "Is it still safe to travel?"

"I wouldn't go back up there," Sandy said, shaking her head and sitting back. "Takeovers of links in the food chain started a while back. State and federal government so far, but that's not going to last. The police are so busy with trying to protect supply trucks that they're not able to stop raids and attacks on grocery stores and warehouses. Every time something disappears, then shows back up, the whole cycle gets worse. Traffic around cities is getting worse, too, and roads are falling apart."

"What about north of Chicago?" Alex said, his voice quiet. "Around Wisconsin."

Alex had never been particularly close to his family, but Etan had heard several phone calls trying to convince his parents and brother and sister to join them. They seemed determined that the trouble wasn't going to be as bad as most people said.

Etan and Alex both knew it was going to be worse than most people imagined.

"I'm afraid it's bad where it's colder, Alex," Sandy said. "Most of the roads didn't get repaired after last winter. A lot of supplies never made it up there, either. Illinois was bad enough. I can't imagine how bad it's going to be in Wisconsin."

Alex grunted, then rubbed his eyes.

"How's the hospital in town looking?" Etan said.

He wanted to get Alex focused on something else. Something he could actually make better.

"It's outdated, certainly compared to the teaching hospital I left behind," Sandy said with a lopsided smile. "We'll be able to handle the basics here. The much smaller building will be a lot easier to manage, really. As long as the power holds out."

"Alex is your man, then," Etan's father said. Whether from his own sense of future events or from simply paying attention, he hadn't missed Alex's mood shift any more than Etan had. "He got the cannery and a bunch of other places set up with their own power."

"Using gasoline?" Sandy said.

"Some of the generators can, yeah," Alex said. "They're all capable of running fuel alcohol when that dries up. Good bit of solar wherever we can fit the panels, small wind and water turbines. I keep hearing there are a lot more big turbines up on Maple Ridge that should be keeping the power more consistent than it is, but I haven't had a chance to go up there yet. Batteries for storage here in town, but never enough of those."

"Alex set up good old-fashioned stills to take care of the fuel," Etan's mother said. "Not a thing goes to waste, and we'll be able to grow what we need."

"Interested in helping me out with power at the hospital, Alex?" Sandy said. She pulled a tiny spiral notebook out of her back pocket. "I've been wondering how we're going to handle everything once the grid goes down."

"For a building that size, we need to look at the river," Alex said, rubbing his chin through his beard. "It's just a few blocks away. We have bigger water turbines I haven't set up yet. We could keep running water, too, at least for a few buildings. What kind of power are you going to need?"

"As much as you can get me. Mind if I steal your husband for a couple of months, Etan? I promise to send him back as good as I found him."

Etan looked into Alex's blue eyes, now sparkling with the prospect of a huge new project to dig into. And at least for the moment, no longer sad and worried about the family he'd left behind.

"Keeps him out of my hair, so that's fine with me."

"Etan hasn't made an honest man of me yet, anyway," Alex said. He winked at Etan. "I'm still a free agent."

"I've been meaning to ask you about that, boys," Etan's mother said. "People are starting to talk, and I'd love to help plan a wedding while we still have the chance. I think early December would be the perfect time for a party."

Etan lowered his head, looking at Alex out of the corner of his eye. He remembered silvery wedding rings from a few dreams. From the first night they'd spent together, the first moment they'd met, he'd always assumed it would happen.

He'd never considered the timing.

"What do you think, Alex? Might be your last chance to trade up before the end of the world."

"Twenty-six is too old to ask me to change my ways," Alex said. He was smiling, but Etan was surprised at how bright his eyes were. "You'll have to do."

Chapter 24

Alex paced around the basement of the Episcopal church, his gleaming black shoes silent on the tan carpet. He could hear people walking around up in the sanctuary. Too many people. Far more than he and Etan planned for.

The borrowed black suit fit him surprisingly well once Linda asked the crafts teacher at the high school to alter it for him. He wondered how Etan's had turned out. He'd find out in a half hour or so, if his nervousness didn't stop his heart before then.

What the hell had he been thinking, agreeing to antiquated notions of not seeing each other before the service? Alex doubted those superstitions ever applied to two grooms in the first place.

They were already racing to beat the end of the world. Bad luck coming up seemed to be a given.

He grinned and shook his head, then glanced down at his watch. A beautiful gold model with a black leather band, something else borrowed for the occasion with supplies of such luxury items or fabric for new suits almost impossible to get now.

Twenty-one minutes to go.

Plenty of time to get himself good and freaked out when all he was doing was marrying the only person on earth who could have suited him so perfectly. That outran a hell of a lot of bad luck.

Alex kept pacing.

The long tables throughout the huge basement, the space of the whole church above and then some, were set with more places than he wanted to pay attention to. People had brought their own plates, bowls, and silverware, but the unintended patterns of colors, shapes and sizes appealed more to his eye than bland sameness ever could have.

Plans for a quiet service at the town hall evaporated before they ever got started. Between his soon to be mother-in-law and just about everyone else he'd met in Wolf Branch, Alex was sure the entire county would be in attendance.

No one from his own family would.

There was only so much he could do. Even if he and Etan had made the increasingly dangerous trip back up north and attempted to physically put them in the van and head south, none of them were going to leave Fond du Lac. That terribly risky effort with bad weather underway would certainly have ended in tears and a heart-broken journey back to Wolf Branch without them. Alex shook his head, trying to dislodge the thoughts before they could dig in and spoil his pleasant, nervous anticipation.

A door behind him creaked, and Alex jumped. He was more anxious than he thought.

Walt Colley walked toward him, for once not gripping his faded green baseball cap in his massive hands. Walt was as nicely dressed as Alex himself. He wore a lovely dark gray suit, a few tiny flowers from the greenhouse they'd built not that long ago pinned to the lapel. Unruly gray hair tamed, the old guy looked downright handsome.

"Hey Alex," he said with his slow smile. "How you holdin' up?"

"Hey Walt. Sounds like the whole world is up there. I'm okay other than that."

"Yeah, they sure are packing in. Been a long time since we had something as happy as a wedding. Everyone wants to pay their respects and wish the two of you best of luck."

"I'm going to need it to remember what I'm supposed to say."

Walt laughed, a huge, booming guffaw that brought a smile to Alex's face. That movement of his tense muscles felt fantastic.

"If I recall how these things generally work, Father Price will help you get through that part just fine."

He joined Alex in the next loop. Down one side of the row of gray steel support posts, up to the table against the far wall already bulging with an alarming amount of food. Then back down the other side toward the stairs Alex hoped he wouldn't be too nervous to climb when the time came.

"I sure would like to meet your folks, Alex," Walt said. "Be sure to introduce me if you get a chance."

"Well, you've met the ones you're going to. That would be Connor and Laura. No one else is going to be here."

"I'm real sorry to hear that."

"Eh, thank you. I'm not surprised. This is sort of how these things go, you know?"

Walt put a big hand on Alex's shoulder to stop him from turning and heading back toward the food table.

"That's too bad," he said, nodding. "They're missing their fine son marrying another fine young man, two of the best I've ever known. I'll tell you something I'm glad you don't remember for yourself. When I was your age, a long damn time ago, some people got themselves tied up in knots about two men or two women marrying. Thank God that time passed."

Alex nodded, glad he'd missed that time as well.

"What I'm wanting to say to you is a lot of people back then had to find their own families. The ones they was born to fell away, lots of times for the better. I hope there's nothing that hard in your past with your folks, Alex. But all you got to do is go upstairs and see how many people showed up to wish you and Etan well. That's the best kind of family. The one you make for yourself."

The heat in Alex's stomach shifted up to his throat, threatening to spill over into tears. He grabbed Walt in a quick, back pounding hug.

"Thank you, Walt. That's exactly what I needed to hear just now. I couldn't imagine a better family myself."

Walt nodded once before he turned to head up the steps toward the sanctuary.

"It's all gonna work out for you two," he said. "I feel it. See you up there."

Alex heard the door upstairs open, then Walt talking to someone before polished black shoes descended toward him. Connor Griffith leaned his head down, pretending to sneak.

"Everything all right down here?"

"Everyone's worried about me, huh?" Alex said with a laugh. "I'm not about to make a run for it, Connor. Not without your son."

"I'm awful glad to hear that." He carried two tiny green velvet boxes in his hand. "Just got these back, sorry they're so late."

"I don't know what you have there, so no need to apologize."

Etan's father flipped both boxes open before holding them out for Alex to see. Each held a silvery band with matching angular patterns.

"I know you two weren't planning on having rings," he said. "But I get the feeling you would have if we could get things like that anymore. Old Charlie Kennedy used to be the jeweler in town up until about ten years ago. He still does work on the side if you ask him nicely."

"Where did these come from?" Alex reached for the larger ring, but Connor moved that box aside.

"No, not yet. You take Etan's." He handed the box with the smaller ring to Alex. "These were my Mom and Dad's. Charlie melted them down together, then made these for you. You might remember Laura getting your ring size a couple of weeks ago?"

Alex grinned, not even trying to stop the tears now. Laura had brought out an ancient rattling key ring full of bunches of smaller rings while Alex was mostly distracted with the fitting for his suit. He'd accepted her tales of wanting to imagine what it would be like if only they could find something in time without a second thought.

Alex slipped the ring onto his pinky and turned it toward the overhead lights. The white gold gleamed, facets reflecting the light in patterns he'd been waiting his whole life to see.

"These are beautiful, Connor. I don't know what to say."

"Hope you'll forgive me for the biggest cliché on the face of the earth," Etan's father said, already heading up the steps. "But the words you're looking for are *I do*. See you in a couple of minutes."

Alex replaced the ring and dropped the box into his jacket pocket, wiping his eyes. He'd made a foolish promise to himself to keep it together until after the ceremony, one he was clearly going to break. That was by far the least important promise the day would bring.

Three minutes.

He adjusted the suit and ran his hands over his hair and beard, wishing he had a mirror down here for a last check. One more deep breath, and Alex walked up to join his true family.

Chapter 25

Etan sat with his eyes closed, listening to his heart beating. This meditation room beside the sanctuary was lined with acoustic pads that looked like giant gray egg cartons and a thick carpet that matched. All of that lead to near silence, broken only by that slow, regular beat.

He knew people were gathering just on the other side of the heavy oak door. More people than he'd expected despite his mother's warnings.

He and Alex had given up early on when it came to most of the plans for the day. His mother, her friends, even his father focused on their wedding to the exclusion of just about everything else in the world.

He certainly couldn't blame them for that. Even with what Alex had been telling him of his dreams, none of the news was good. This winter promised to bring the hunger everyone feared a year ago, with more crop failures from already weakened pollinators.

Trade was down to nearly non-existent, with fears of starvation along with fear of the various diseases. Not that anywhere on earth seemed to have surplus, not on a large scale. Wolf Branch still did.

Neither Etan, Alex, nor anyone else had forgotten their visitors from Maple Ridge.

He opened his eyes and got to his feet. An odd mirror arrangement that reflected itself endlessly, one on each opposite wall, worked well enough for him to make sure he looked as calm as he felt. Everything, from his suit to his shoes to the cufflinks he'd borrowed from his father, matched what he'd seen in his waking and sleeping dreams of this day.

The only thing missing was the ring.

The huge door opened, and his mother walked in with a burst of murmuring crowd noise. She was happier than Etan had seen her in a long time, glowing and gorgeous in her dark purple dress. He was relieved all over again that she'd taken on so much of the planning. For her sake, and for Alex's and his.

"Almost time," she said, hugging him. "Quite a crowd out there."

"You got your big wedding after all, Mom."

"I surely did, and I deserve it every bit as much as you do." She held out a small green box. "Your father and I wanted to give you these together, but Charlie just got here with them. Alex already has yours."

"Charlie? The jeweler?"

Etan opened the box and saw the one thing missing from the images in his mind. A white gold ring, too large for his own finger. He didn't have to ask Alex how much he'd love the geometric, angular patterns that caught the light almost like a gemstone.

"These came from your grandparents, Etan. Charlie melted them down together and made them for you."

He slipped the ring over his thumb.

"This is gorgeous, Mom. Thank you so much. I know Gemaw and Grampa would have been pleased."

"Of course they would have. They left it in their wills and final wishes, hon. Just like the house. One of those odd little paragraphs, make sure Etan has this if he needs it."

Etan smiled as the last piece of his wedding day slipped into place. Anne and Evan were with him after all.

"Did they leave me any other surprises?"

Laura Griffith shook her head, then reached up to adjust his tie.

"Nothing I'm going to tell you about until the time comes. I'm sure you won't be surprised Anne was clear about that, too."

"Not the least bit surprised. Almost time, isn't it?"

"Only a couple of minutes left. Father Price is already out there. Ready for all of this, son? You nervous?"

"I thought I would be, but I'm not. Not even a little bit. This just feels like the next step on the path we started years ago." Etan chuckled, shaking his head. "At a college party in the middle of a damn blizzard."

"Wherever it started, I'm so glad that path brought you both back home to us," she said, squeezing his hand. "See you at the reception."

Etan stood with his hand on the door, giving her time to get settled. His body felt like those mirrors, with a thousand reflections of himself slowly lining up. Focusing in on the next steps of his life, with Alex by his side.

When all the parts inside of Etan moved into the right place, he opened the door to see his love opening the one opposite the low stage.

True to his word, Father Price had removed all of the religious symbols. He stood in the middle in a black suit much like the ones the grooms wore. More candles than Etan had ever seen brought a perfect glow to the flowers, dried and fresh from the greenhouse, surrounding the spot left for the two of them.

He walked forward, unaware of the crowd, the music playing, the scent of all those flowers and candles. Etan only saw Alex, even more handsome in his wedding suit than he'd been walking out of the snow in Chicago.

And he saw him with traces of gray in his beard, the same silvery highlights gradually taking over his gorgeous red curls. Alex with metal-framed reading glasses, lines from countless smiles around his eyes.

They met in front of Father Price, Alex holding out his hand.

Young and strong and firm, old and worn and thin, with the ring he didn't yet have still on his third finger. Etan took his hand, and he saw his own many years from now, the veins and tendons visible just as they had been in his grandfather's right before he passed.

His fingers linked through his husband's, always.

Etan's composure held true almost until the end. Neither of them had expected it to mean much, not after several years together. Not with most of that time being consumed by planning for the end of everything rather than for new beginnings.

It was the simplest words that did it. Words that sounded so meaningless and unimportant when Father Price showed them his revised version.

What love has joined together, let nothing tear asunder.

Saying the same things to each other, with their whole worlds watching, granted their lives together a permanence they'd never had. A solidity, a foundation they could build from and depend on. They and everyone around them would come to depend on that bedrock in the months and years to come.

That was the last happy day anyone in Wolf Branch had for a long time.

Chapter 26

THE WHISPERS DRAGGED Alex out of an exhausted sleep, far deeper than usual after the stress and excitement of his wedding day. He blinked until he could see his watch. Three twenty-one.

Etan was curled up against his chest, an arm around his waist. He squeezed hard enough to force Alex's breath out.

"It's in the house *in the house!*"

Alex jolted wide awake, heart pounding, ears humming with the strain of listening for the slightest sound. All he could hear was Etan's ragged breathing.

"What's in the house?"

"The record. The ledger of days to come. Find it, Alex. Time is so very short."

"You mean the computers? We've looked at those."

Etan shook his head against Alex's chest.

"A journal in his own hand, hidden in the house. Meant for your eye. No other."

"In whose hand? I don't know where to look, Etan."

"In *Evan's* hand. Etan must never see."

Even after so many years, countless dreams, knowing he often wasn't really talking to Etan in the middle of the night, the words made Alex uneasy as he said them.

"Tell me where it is. I promise I won't let Etan see."

Etan whispered again, too soft and fast for Alex to hear. He leaned closer, struggling to understand.

"Okay, shhhhh. Go back to sleep, sweetie," he finally said. He kissed his husband, trying to stop the disturbing sound. "I'll find the journal. I'll go right now."

The frantic hissing slowed to even, regular breathing. Etan squeezed Alex tight, then turned over. The storm was over, at least inside his mind.

Alex was afraid it was only beginning for him.

He sat up, groping with his toes until he found his slippers, then grabbing his thick robe off the chair beside the door. The bedroom was cold enough with winter well underway. The rest of the house would be frigid with the fire long out. Grid power was too unreliable and expensive to run the furnace, and Alex hated to draw from their batteries for heat unless they had to.

He repeated what he'd caught of the whispers, feeling his way along the hall.

"In the library. Too high to see."

He flipped on the light, squinting in the glare. The room was almost exactly as it was the first day they'd stepped inside. According to Etan, it was just like his grandparents had left it. They'd created their own stacks of books on the end tables beside Anne and Evan's chairs, shifting and rearranging as they both searched for the clues that would help them survive the collapse.

Alex suspected it wouldn't be one huge secret revelation. Each small thing they learned and passed along to the community, to their family, would add up and give them the slim chance.

He scanned the top row of books, a collection of fiction that varied widely enough to seem like ten people had put them together. All were older than he, many older than his in-laws, all marked with wrinkles and creases of repeated reading.

Framed photos lined the highest shelf, many of them tucked right against the low ceiling. Anne and Evan, their parents, Connor and Laura. Etan at every possible awkward stage. Despite Alex's growing sense of urgency, his need to find this thing Etan so badly wanted him to have, he smiled at Anne's brown hair and green eyes. So much like his new husband.

Too high to see.

He grabbed the flashlight on the table between the two reading chairs. Etan had always insisted on having one in every room, by every door. The unreliable electricity had turned his desire into nearly an obsession.

Alex carried Anne's step ladder from the kitchen and held the wall as he slowly climbed up, not sure the delicate thing would hold him. Once he had both feet in place, it felt sturdy enough. He moved the light along the wall behind the photos. Nothing but an appalling layer of dust he wished he hadn't seen.

Except…

A glint of metal in the corner. Two hinges and a latch. A thick frame just above, the same as the door frames in the rest of the house.

He frowned, thinking what was on the other side of that wall. More books and photos in a recessed shelf built into the hallway. Evan Griffith had found an unused doorway to hide his journal. A man after Alex's own tinkering heart.

He moved the ladder and climbed up again. The photo in front of the rectangular opening was of Etan and his grandparents, their heads on either side of his, all of them smiling. Etan looking gawky and shy and adorable to Alex's eyes. Anne and Evan silver-haired and wrinkled, easily in their seventies or eighties. That must have been taken not long before they'd passed away.

Alex moved the frame aside, leaving tracks in the thick dust. He doubted anyone had opened this since the two of them had died, or not long after. The latch was a little stiff under his fingers, and the hinges protested movement after so much time.

He paused, listening. The house was still silent.

A small spiral-bound notebook with what looked like a faded red vinyl cover waited inside. The kind he'd seen in a few of his professor's offices in college, but he'd never used himself. Alex thought they'd stopped making them before he was born.

He stood on his tiptoes and pulled it out. The cover felt brittle, the wire around the left side rusty.

Dust floated through the flashlight beam as Alex climbed back down, shaking his head at this odd time capsule. If he'd needed more proof that Etan's dreams carried real weight and authority, this was too clear and strange to ignore.

Three yellowed envelopes slipped out of the notebook before he sat in Evan's chair. *Connor* and *Etan* were written in Evan's neat script on the front of two of them.

Alex's heart skipped when he saw his own name on the third. His fingers shook when he opened it.

Alex. We so wish we'd had a chance to meet you and get to know the wonderful man who will make our grandson so happy. It breaks my heart to introduce myself in such a way, and with such dreadful words inside this journal. We've only passed along what we had to. Please know Anne's seen you many times in her dreams. You and Etan have a chance to be as happy as we've been. We truly hope you take it. Much love, Evan Griffith.

Goosebumps raced over his already chilled flesh. That was exactly the same handwriting he'd seen on so many academic papers and books all over this room. Alex couldn't imagine anyone going to such lengths to create an elaborate hoax, complete with antique props and heavy gray dust.

Evan had to have written this at least three years before Alex met Etan.

And Etan dreamed of this, just as Anne had apparently dreamed of Alex.

He sat back in Evan's chair and pulled Anne's fluffy pink blanket up to his chest. He put Connor's envelope and his own back in the pocket inside the journal, leaving Etan's aside to give to him later. Easy enough to say it was tucked into one of the other books after he hid the journal again, before Etan woke.

Alex started to read.

THREE HOURS LATER, he stood on stiff and aching legs to start the wood stove before Etan woke up. Alex knew his shivering wasn't entirely from the cold, but he had to move. Do something. He hid the journal and put the step ladder away first.

The clouds were pink and red, the sun still hidden behind the mountain, when he stepped outside to get wood from the massive pile under the eaves. He glanced toward Connor and Laura's house several times before he went back inside.

The sacrifice will be terrible, but it will not be in vain. The sacrifice is necessary for any of you to survive.

"I should just burn the damn thing right now," he said under his breath as the kindling caught. "Forget about every fucking word."

Alex stared into the fire, wishing it would burn the words out of his mind. Out of his perfect little memory that he'd wished would fail him more than once in the middle of the night with Etan's dreams.

This was the first time he'd seen something so awful fully awake, and with his own eyes.

He added three heavy oak logs across the smaller ones and closed the door with its squeak he'd already come to love.

Maybe the whole journal was outdated now, fallen away into other choices and decisions. Etan said his grandmother often saw choices in her dreams and visions, though he never seemed to. Alex hoped something they'd already done, some action they'd unknowingly put into motion, would cancel out the horrible loss the journal warned him about.

Etan removed all of Alex's room for doubt when he started dreaming about Connor's sacrifice that night.

Chapter 27

A LEX LET his breath out slowly through his chilled lips, the stillness in his body steadying the gun. His feet were shoulder-width on the frosty ground behind their house, arms straight in front of him. He and Etan's father were much further back from the target on a bale of hay against the hillside than a couple of months ago, easily fifty feet instead of ten.

He squeezed the trigger, letting the revolver's momentum carry it upward, then sighting the target again. Sharp, metallic gunpowder smoke filled his nose with every deep breath.

Four shots rang out. Five. Six.

Even at this distance, Alex saw every bullet strike within an inch of the bright red bull's-eye. His new father-in-law clapped him on the back, and he heard Connor's laughter through the earmuffs.

"Damn, son. I believe you're a better shot than I am now!"

"Hardly," Alex said, the frigid air digging into his ears when he pulled the earmuffs off. "I'm a hell of a lot better than I used to be."

Alex holstered the revolver as they walked toward the target to verify the accuracy they'd both seen. His right wrist and palm ached from the repeated recoil. He wanted to practice a bit more with the semi-automatic pistol on his left hip before his hands got too cold, but he couldn't pretend that was the only reason they were out here.

"You handle a gun as well as Etan does," Connor said. "Once you put your mind to it, you're a natural."

"He'd never admit it. At least not where I can hear him."

Every bullet hole was within the smallest ring. Connor pulled it down and handed it to Alex, beaming. He pushed another one over the sharp sticks driven into the hay.

"Keep this in case he gives you trouble about being a better shot than you."

"Will do."

Connor picked up his dark green metal Thermos on the picnic table near the house, taking away Alex's chance to distract both of them with the next practice round. He poured steaming light brown coffee into two metal coffee cups. Alex sipped his, staring at the narrow valley beyond the small back yard. He was prepared for Connor's overly sweet concoction after nearly two years.

He wasn't prepared for his father-in-law's next words.

"You're up awfully early for just a couple days after your wedding. What's on your mind, Alex?"

Connor was watching him, one eyebrow raised, but he was smiling. That expression was so much like Etan's that Alex laughed.

"Etan had to go into town to help out at the cannery. Not much time for a honeymoon these days. What gives you the idea I've got something on my mind?"

"Just a feeling, I guess. You're way too good at shooting to need an old man's help any more. I figure you have something you want to talk about without your husband along. Or my wife."

"You got me," Alex said. He was out of time. He pulled his black gloves on and sat beside Connor on the picnic table, feet up on the bench. "I've been reading Evan's journal, the one hidden behind the bookcase. Ever flip through it?"

Connor held the cup in both hands, breathing in the steam before he took another drink.

"I have. I think it was meant for you a lot more than me, but I read through the whole thing. I imagine you found a few things he wrote about me that you don't like."

"That's an understatement." Alex chewed his bottom lip, part of his mind still trying to find a way to avoid this conversation. Even more, he was desperate to stop the things Evan wrote about. "How the hell did you find it? I didn't have a clue that door was there until Etan dreamed about it."

"Dad left me a note for after he passed. You should have found it, right there in the front."

"I didn't read it," Alex said. "It was meant for you."

"Well, you're the one other person on earth who needs to read it. I want you to. He just said that notebook was for me and my future son-in-law." He grinned at Alex. "Dad grew up in a different time. Guess he thought I needed a warning that Etan was going to be so happy. He did leave me a real warning, though, that Etan should never read that journal. Or anyone else in the family. It was meant for me, and for you."

"Does Laura know what he wrote?"

"No. And I don't want her to. Does Etan?"

"If he does, he hasn't said anything to me. I'm damn sure he would have if he knew you were supposed to be some kind of sacrifice."

Connor nodded.

"I'm sure he would, too. Laura would string me up if she saw it." He turned to Alex, his green eyes clear and steady. "You know the end game, son. Etan dreams about it. Dad wrote it, and Mom dreamed it over and over again. Neither one of them ever said a word to me, but they made sure to write it all down. Every single thing in that journal was sent to us for a good reason."

"I need to know if there's any way to avoid this, Connor. Please just tell me the truth."

The older man refilled both their cups, blowing on his own before taking a sip. Alex was afraid he wasn't going to answer. He knew he wouldn't have the courage to ask again.

"You read the same thing I did," Connor finally said. "I don't know what it's going to be any more than you do, or when."

"Did Evan talk to you about it? Or Anne? They talked to Etan about a lot of things they never wrote down."

"And there's a lot more they wrote down and didn't tell him

about," Connor said, his hand on Alex's shoulder. "This is a hard thing for you to know about on your own, but Etan carries so much in his mind already. Dad talked to me about Mom's dreams. How talking to him helped her get back to sleep, but *he* sometimes couldn't. They both knew Etan would find you, Alex. I hope you get back to sleep eventually."

"Not lately I don't. Listen, I get the feeling Sandy knows where a group of scientists are hiding, close to Chicago. If we explain what's going on, we can get you up there and away from this."

Connor shook his head again. He rubbed his bare hands together, then blew into them.

"Is Etan dreaming about it? What's going to happen to me?"

Alex leaned forward with his elbows on his knees, rubbing his hair. The black fabric gloves rasped in his ears.

"He started dreaming about it night before last, right after he told me exactly where to find Evan's journal. He's not seeing when or how either. He doesn't remember it when he wakes up, but he's sobbing in his sleep, every time. I *can't* pretend I don't know."

"Is he saying we need to stop this, Alex? Whatever's coming? Or does he just see it, like Mom did?"

"I don't care about that!" Alex slammed his fists into his own thighs, his tired right wrist protesting.

Distant shots cut through the cold air a few minutes later, breaking the long silence between the two men. Someone else out practicing. Probably for the same reasons.

Getting ready for the end of the world.

"He only ever sees something is going to happen to you," Alex said. "He's never said a word about stopping it."

"Same as Mom did, then. Did you know she remembered her dreams? Pretty much every one of them, even before she started telling them to Dad?"

"Yeah, Etan told me about that. He thinks that's why she had so much trouble, that he stays sane as he is because he rarely remembers. After hearing what he sees, I believe it."

"Well, think about that," Connor said. "She knew this was going to happen to me. So did Dad. She either never saw what the sacrifice will be, or she and Dad decided not to write it down for some reason. But they both knew I was going to die. I know you want to have a family someday, son. Raise your own children. Do you really think they would have made this choice if they didn't have a damn good reason?"

"It is a fucking curse," Alex whispered.

"Mom never thought so, at least not that she admitted to me. She understood it was part of what led to being with Dad, and having me, and later Laura and me having Etan. Think you would have met him if it weren't for his curse?"

Alex glanced at Connor, then shook his head. He didn't say what he was thinking for a change. If it weren't for his own curse, none of this would have been part of his life.

Not Chicago. Not Etan. Not this morning in the early Virginia winter, talking to the father he'd wished he had his whole life.

The father he was about to lose.

"This is going to break Etan's heart. Mine, too."

"I don't have to ask if you read to the end of the journal. You're not the type who can stand not knowing something. That's part of what makes this so tough. Whatever's going to happen to me will let Etan's heart keep beating, and yours. Everything else depends on that."

Alex crossed his arms across his stomach, trying to stop the shivering deep inside from spreading to his whole body. Every word Connor said was in Evan's journal, and in Etan's dreams, night after night. For the first time in his life, Alex wished he didn't know what was coming toward them.

"How am I supposed to live with this?" he said. "I can never tell Etan I knew. Not as long as I live."

"Same way I live with not telling Laura. Or Etan. Same way my parents lived with not telling me. I put it out of my mind as much as I possibly can and enjoy the time I have with my family. They'll both make it through to the other side of whatever this thing is. So will you. That has to be enough for both of us."

"You're a stronger man than I am."

"No, I'm not. You witness these terrible dreams and remember them when Etan can't. I never have. You're the man who's strong enough to make it through and help him make it through. And you're the man who's going to help raise my grandbabies, Alex. You'll be a fantastic father."

Alex squeezed his eyes closed, but hot tears ran down his cheeks anyway. Not because of his father-in-law's words, though they were bad enough.

He'd felt and seen the motion, in the wispy clouds in the dark blue sky, the bare trees swaying in the wind. His condemnation flowed from the direction of frost-killed grass on the ground all around them.

Even when he had no choices, Alex was certain he was making the wrong ones.

"If I'm half the father you are, Connor, our kids will be just fine."

Chapter 28

ALEX SAT in Evan's chair, pretending to read one of his fiction books while Etan read one of Anne's. He couldn't tell if his husband was making progress on the story or not. Alex hadn't turned a page in at least half an hour. He kept glancing toward that hidden compartment behind the bookcase.

He was equally tempted to either take the notebook to the wood stove after all or to hand it to Etan and watch him read every word.

The phone rang in the living room, a harsh, churning old-fashioned ring. Alex usually found that a charming feature of the heavy old black phone they'd found in the basement, one that worked during the more frequent power outages. Mobile phones had never gotten much signal at their house even before so many things started to erode.

Tonight the sound of that ring drilled deep into his skull, twisting and echoing and building on itself.

His teeth seemed to vibrate with it. His bones.

Whatever was coming toward them would get well and truly underway with whatever Etan heard on the other side of that phone.

Alex closed his eyes, trying to hear half of the conversation he dreaded knowing more about. He couldn't make out a word, not until Etan stepped back into the library. He was pale and his hand shook when he reached for Alex's.

"We need to go down to Mom and Dad's."

"Connor?" Alex said before he had a chance to think.

"No, they're both fine. Everything out in the world just got worse. One hell of a lot worse. They're still getting a couple of news channels."

"Anything they can't tell us about?" he said.

Please. Just let us stay here, safe and warm and ignorant for one more night.

I don't want to know any more.

I *can't*.

"Dad said we need to see it," Etan said. "Some kind of disease in the corn, way more serious than what we've seen before. This may be what makes it all crash."

"The corn everyone here has been planting less and less of, without either of us having to say a word about what Evan wrote." Alex stood beside Etan with his arm around him. "We can go whenever you're ready."

"I'm not. I don't even want to be. But if we wait five minutes, I might not ever go out the door again."

CONNOR AND LAURA were as pale as Etan, and Alex knew he probably looked worse. On their television, the headline screamed white against a blood-red background.

WORLDWIDE PANDEMIC AND STARVATION: FATALITIES MOUNT.

"They're saying it's in feed corn, and all the animals that eat it." Laura held out her hand, and Alex sat beside her on the couch. Etan sat beside his father. "Everything they make out of corn, too. Soda, syrup, plastic. All kinds of food. Even baby formula. Some kind of fungus, getting shipped all around the world for a long time. They're saying that awful stomach flu that's been killing so many people and animals was really this thing called aflatoxin."

"They test for everything now," Etan said, his voice shaky. "How could they miss something that kills people?"

"They *did* test for this," Connor said. "Big farmers have for decades. They used to catch the fungus before corn or anything else got into the food supply. But it mutated or changed, or someone changed it on purpose. Weaponized it. Now the toxin doesn't show up until it's way too late. Mom dreamed about poison in the air and water. Dad wrote about the risks of disease in giant fields full of the same crop."

Alex spoke out loud without meaning to, his reeling mind losing control over his mouth.

"Etan dreams about the same thing."

He tried not to, but he finally turned toward his father-in-law. Connor didn't seem angry or afraid, things Alex felt more than anything else right now. He looked curious. Wondering if Alex was going to keep their secret.

In that second, Alex had no idea whether he'd manage or not.

"There were riots all over the world last winter," Etan said. "With so many people knowing they'll get sick and it could have been prevented, this year is going to be worse."

"No one in the mountains has gotten much food in from outside for months now," Alex said, trying to shake fear for Connor from his mind and heart. "Turns out that's a good thing, but shortages are already bad in other towns. Too many people know Wolf Branch has more than we need."

"We have several people armed and well-trained," Connor said. "You and Alex are two of the best. We may need to set up guards at the food bank and cannery."

"That's not going to be enough," Laura said, squeezing Alex's hand in her chilly fingers. "So many people have stores at their houses. We all do. Protecting all of that's going to be impossible."

"Etan dreamed of everyone living in town," Alex said. He was surprised his voice still worked. "Neither of us could figure out why, since that makes water and sewer and everything else harder to maintain. This could be the reason."

The phone rang, another noisy old model that made everyone

jump. The scene on the TV screen shifted as Connor answered. Now a giant white LIVE took up the left corner, and no one needed the banner running underneath.

That word Laura used, *aflatoxin*. And video of a riot. Not in a poor country on the other side of the planet this time.

Philadelphia.

The screen split, adding horrible, violent scenes from San Diego.

"That was Harry Mullins," Etan's father said, standing in the doorway. "They've already got a few people staying at the cannery tonight. We'll get together in the morning and work out a schedule."

He stared into Alex's eyes again. Alex wondered, not for the first time, how much of Anne's talent Connor had inherited after all.

"Feels like we have to get this next part right," Etan said. "What we do here is going to put a bunch more things into motion. I can't even imagine where all that will end up."

"Let's try to get all the main people involved as soon as we can," Alex said. "Make sure we aren't working against each other."

He didn't say what he was feeling.

If all of them were together, maybe whatever was supposed to hit Connor would hit someone else. He struggled to block the other families out of his mind.

He wasn't proud, or trying to be stubborn.

Alex simply couldn't stand his own family being torn apart so soon after he'd finally found them.

Chapter 29

THE EXHAUSTION of his own fear, and of not being able to sleep every time Etan spoke of Connor's death in the darkness, caught up with Alex when they got back home that night. His sleep was deep and dreamless.

Etan's words, clear as if he were wide awake, yanked Alex into consciousness a few hours later.

"The time has come. What we do now decides the future."

Etan was facing away from him, close up against his body. He fought a nearly overpowering urge to shake Etan, turn on the bright overhead light, scream at him to stop. He touched his shoulder instead.

"The time for what, sweetie?"

"So many sacrifices, so much loss. All to prepare for this moment. Greater sacrifices will see us through or see us extinct."

Evan's words, and Etan's, of Anne seeing choices surged into Alex's mind. After her long life of options and free will, were they reduced to only one way forward?

"Do you see anything else we can do, Etan? Do we have choices? Decisions we can make?"

"Each choice has consequences. None easy to live with. Most impossible to live through."

"Tell me what our choices are," Alex said. Every cell in his body screamed this was foolhardy, the best way to make difficult nights intolerable, but he couldn't stop himself. "Maybe I can find another way."

Etan breathed deeply several times. Alex had time to wonder if it would be harder to never know what his lover would have said or to hear the words.

"Connor's sacrifice is the way forward," Etan said, tears obvious in his voice. "Every other way is disaster."

"This whole thing is disaster. Just tell me, please. I won't do the wrong thing. I promise."

"Mary's wish will see us overrun. Starvation and torture. Those who destroy us will die in their own turn. All the lights of humanity will go out."

"I understand," Alex said. "I won't let that happen."

"The task is far harder than you believe. Her words are strong, her followers many. Without the sacrifice, she will triumph. All will be lost."

"There must be another way. Another sacrifice." Alex gritted his teeth against the nausea working from his stomach through his whole body. If he couldn't say this, how could he possibly let it happen? "Someone besides…besides Connor."

Etan shook his head.

"Only one other would drag us away from Mary's madness. The loss too great. The end merely postponed. The darkness unavoidable."

Alex pulled Etan's shoulder, gently turning him onto his back. He needed to see his face, even in the faint light. All the nerves and blood in his body thrummed in time, anticipating the horrible words his husband would speak.

"One or the other," Etan said, his head turning his sightless eyes toward Alex's face. "A beloved man cut down for all to see and bring everyone into alignment. Toward a broken future."

Alex put his hand over Etan's mouth, shaking his own head.

Too much.

Etan was right, as Evan and Connor had been before him. Alex wouldn't be able to live with any of these choices.

Etan's lips moved under his fingers. The shape of the names was enough even without the sound.

Etan, or Alex himself.

"Why?" Alex whispered, removing his hand. "Will no one else do?"

"No one else can end the madness. Mary brings us all to quick ruin. The loss of Alex or Etan prolongs the suffering to no end. The loss of Connor gives all a chance to survive."

"I can't. I can't do this."

"The paths are clear before you now. The choice yours alone to make."

Alex turned away from Etan and curled up as tight as he could. No matter what he did, even if he left Wolf Branch right now and never looked back, he would never be free of this decision. He was afraid he'd never be able to smile, sleep, breathe again.

Etan sighed, his mind and body released from the dream. He curled against Alex's back and legs.

The warmth never made it through to Alex's heart.

Chapter 30

Etan brushed eraser debris from his spreadsheet yet again, keeping his eyes focused on the increasingly messy schedule. Starting with everyone marking up their own printed copy, same as they'd always done, seemed to make sense an hour ago rather than worrying about getting copies made afterward.

That was before Alex got himself into some kind of fucking auto-dispute mode neither Etan, Alex himself, nor anyone else could break him out of.

Six others gathered around Linda's conference table in her office at the high school, trying to agree on a work schedule for the next few weeks. These get-togethers never had been long enough or formal enough to call them meetings.

Just like the disastrous mess at the auditorium, a friendly few minutes had somehow stretched into a grueling marathon. The afternoon sun faded perilously close to early evening through the high windows along one wall, glinting through Alex's red hair and beard.

His odd resistance to adding the patrol schedule for guarding their supplies had them all tense enough that Etan wasn't the only one glaring at his husband. He felt less and less like protecting Alex from everyone else's frustration with every passing second, every objection.

These two people shouldn't patrol together. This area needed three guards instead of two. One instead of three. Alex pushed the tiniest details into endless discussion.

Etan's gaze was drawn to the huge map of the world behind Linda's ancient, scarred wooden desk. His mind filled in the growing problems in cities and countries in a blink of his eyes. Riots now in every wealthy nation to go along with all-out war in most of the poor ones.

Cities all over the US falling into chaos one after another, seemingly a new one every hour. The closest so far was Cincinnati, only a few hours away.

His imagination, or maybe his waking nightmare, saw each of those cities as a glowing dot. The centers of human population all over the world.

The death count from riots and violence was estimated to be well into the millions in the US alone. The oncoming winter was expected to kill far more with starvation and the horrible foodborne disease, if people didn't manage the trick themselves first.

The lights on the map of the world winked out in Etan's mind, one after the other. He looked away, too afraid to see how many would be left in the end.

Wolf Branch's good luck couldn't possibly hold out much longer, not with the way he and everyone else were feeling. That surely explained some of Alex's attack of peevishness, but Etan hadn't had any dreams for days.

Those two things, Alex's distress and Etan's sound sleep, didn't match up.

"I'm not sure what else we can do to make this work out," Linda said, rubbing her eyes. Her right pinky was smudged gray from the pencil she'd been writing with. "No one seems to be happy no matter what we do."

"I think we need to take a little bit of a break," Etan's father said. He glanced at Etan, then met Alex's gaze across the table. "We're getting all bent out of shape over this and chasing our tails."

"Sure," Etan said, shoving his chair back with a grinding noise he immediately regretted. "Walk with me, Alex?"

Alex stared at him, and the hot anger in Etan's chest cooled in an instant. Alex didn't look mad or stubborn, nothing like the way he was acting. He looked nervous and scared half to death.

"I think I'm going to head over to the cannery, get something for all of us to drink," Etan's father said. "You have the key, Alex?"

Now Etan was watching his father, more confused than annoyed by his strange behavior. That sounded more like an invitation than a simple request for a key.

"Sure, Connor," Alex said. He slid the key across the table, avoiding meeting the older man's eyes. "I'll be back in a few."

Alex walked out of the room alone without looking back.

Father Price scowled at the open door. Etan couldn't remember ever seeing him so frustrated.

"Any idea what's got him so ornery, Etan? I've never known Alex to argue every little thing like this."

Etan shook his head, then stood, not sure whether he should follow Alex or give him that time to himself. He hated to even think such a thing, but he hoped Alex decided to skip the rest of this meeting altogether.

"I have an idea," Etan's father said. He was scooting the key around on the table, making an irritating scratching noise, but he made no move to leave the room. "Let's go with the work schedule from last month. Whoever's not on at the food bank or the cannery can fill in on patrol where the new volunteers can't. I think that will leave one of us on just about every shift, won't it?"

"It would," Linda said, flipping through her folder to the older schedule. "What makes you think he won't argue about that, too? Sorry, Etan."

"No, don't apologize," Etan said. "I don't know what's going on with him either. Maybe he'll see a pattern that worked several times before, and he'll feel better about the whole thing."

Etan rubbed at his temples, trying to stop an alarm blaring through his head.

Patterns. Alex saw patterns better than any of them, and his behavior had been following an ever growing pattern of upset and distress for several days now. Ever since, well, a few days after their wedding.

Frustrated as he was, Etan couldn't get himself worked up over imagined regrets on his new husband's part. He'd stood beside Alex that day. There was no mistaking the look in his eyes, the sound of his voice. The heat of their lovemaking that night.

Something else was going on here, and not just with Alex.

"Yeah, let's go with that old schedule," he said. "I'd love some of the cherry cider, Dad. Alex could definitely use a beer."

"What? Sure, of course. I'll be back in a minute."

Etan's internal dislocation increased as his father walked out, shaking his head. Without asking what anyone else wanted. He hadn't remembered offering to get drinks at all. That had all been a ploy to get Alex to go with him.

Now Etan had to get the truth out of both of them, unless what they were hiding matched up. He had an unsettling feeling it did.

"Does everyone have a copy of this old schedule?" Linda said, pushing hers toward the middle of the table. "We can use these blank ones to do the patrol schedule and hopefully be done with it."

"We're done with it now," Alex said. No one had noticed him standing in the doorway. "That's fine, Linda. We can use that this month and see what happens. We'll adjust to whatever comes, like we always have."

He put his hand on Etan's shoulder as he walked by. Etan grabbed it and looked up. Alex started to turn away, then closed his eyes. When he met Etan's gaze, his blue eyes were red around the edges.

"You okay?" Etan whispered. He kissed Alex's hand where his ring finger joined his palm.

"I'm as okay as I'm going to be for a while," he said. He sat, linking his fingers through Etan's. "This isn't going to be easy, Etan. Whether anyone comes here causing trouble or not, we're about to witness the end of the world."

"Yeah, we are," Etan's father said as he walked in. "Nothing's ever going to be the same again. We'll get through it the best we can as long as we watch out for each other."

Alex watched his father-in-law arrange several bottles of their cider and beer, sweat already beading on the pale brown glass. He stared up at Connor with an intensity that only made Etan more uncomfortable.

"Thanks, Connor," Alex said, taking a beer and a cherry cider. "You too, Linda. I'm sorry for being such an asshole. Let's get this wrapped up and get out of here."

Linda put a chipped white coffee mug in front of each of them. Not the most appropriate glassware in the world, perhaps, but more than adequate for such a tough day.

"No one's happy about this, Alex," she said. She added a few threadbare white towels to the middle of the table. "You're doing the best you can, just like the rest of us."

Etan's father must have carried the bottles as carefully as any bartender in an elegant restaurant back in the city. Not one overflowed when they flipped the tops back.

"To doing the best we can," Etan said, holding up his mug. The bubbles in the light red liquid landed on his wrist.

"And living through the end of the world," Alex said.

Etan couldn't help but notice how much those words sounded like a threat rather than a promise. He was afraid that was exactly what they'd turn out to be.

Chapter 31

Alex was thankful for the silence on the drive home after they picked Laura up from the food pantry in town. He knew his mother-in-law was perfectly capable of handling her own handgun, probably a bit better than any of the men in her family as it turned out.

He was still relieved an armed guard was always there any time the food pantry was open. That wouldn't likely protect Connor when the time came, but at least Etan wouldn't lose both parents.

Laura didn't even try to lighten the mood in the vehicle after greeting the three of them. She picked up on the tension as fast as she usually did.

That made Alex as guilty as anything else about the future intruding so horribly on their present. She couldn't have that many more conversations left with her husband, and his own pissy little temper tantrum had stolen at least one of them.

None of them spoke until Connor parked in front of Alex and Etan's house.

"Any reason we should bother getting together for dinner tonight?" Laura said, turning around to look at them.

"I don't know if any of us are fit for company," Connor said. He rubbed her shoulder.

"Well, you're certainly not," she said. Alex was relieved she touched her husband's hand. "Maybe the three of you can take a nap or something. Or tell me what the hell the problem is."

"We'll see what we can do," Etan said. "Talk to you later."

Alex walked toward the house, glancing back over his shoulder even though every nerve in his body told him not to. Connor watched him, nodded once, then turned the car around and left.

"What's it going to be, Alex?" Etan stood with one foot on the porch steps, staring after the car. "You going to tell me what's up or make me ask my father?"

Alex crossed the yard, detouring around the flower and vegetable beds casting long shadows in the twilight, wondering how long his mind could possibly stay so utterly jumbled and useless. Hundreds of words flashed through his brain, every one too fast to make it all the way to his mouth. He put his hand over Etan's on the wooden rail.

"I'm just tired, sweetie," he said. That much was the truth. "Maybe I do need that nap."

Etan shook his head, the movement small but impossible to ignore. The compression of his lips made Alex's heart plummet.

"Perfect, that's where we'll start. I'll brew us a pot of coffee, and we're going to sit down and have a talk we probably should have had a few days ago."

He went inside, letting the screen door slam behind him.

Alex wanted nothing more than to sink down on the concrete steps and stay right there. Pretend he was in front of their apartment in Chicago, or even in his parents' back yard in Wisconsin. Worried about things he couldn't even bring to mind now that the whole world had changed. Either place felt a hundred years ago and a million miles away.

And Etan was in neither one of them, and never would be again.

He pulled himself up the steps and went inside.

What he and Etan had read about the disease spreading all over the world—started by someone intentionally infecting huge corn crops—had them both avoiding their library. The fungus that spread the horrific toxin wasn't only in corn and things made from it anymore. Peanuts, walnuts, wheat, even cotton crops had been infected and spread the toxin to humans and animals.

Even if the world could afford to destroy so much food when millions were starving, it was too late for that in more places than Alex wanted to think about. The genetically altered fungus lingered in the soil itself. Liver failure, immune-system failure, cancer, and a dozen other problems awaited exposed people and animals who managed not to starve to death.

Alex couldn't think of a hell in any mythology or imagination deep and damned enough for whoever spread this poison.

Instead of the library, he waited on the couch in the living room. The same gray couch they'd brought with them, the first piece of decent furniture he'd bought for himself before he ever met Etan. He hoped they'd stored up enough good memories in the sturdy canvas to withstand this bad one.

Etan brought two steaming mugs in, the rich, sharp smell alone making Alex feel more alert. He handed one to Alex and sat at the opposite end of the couch. After a few minutes, Alex knew he needed to say something. He couldn't imagine what his husband was imagining for himself, and he didn't want to leave Etan in the kind of pit he could work himself down into.

But he had no way to bring this up, and no idea how he'd respond once Etan did.

"Great, so you're tired," Etan finally said. "That doesn't make a whole lot of sense to me, Alex. I haven't had any dreams for at least a week now, at least not that you've told me about. That's never happened before in all these years. Why would you be getting more and more tired, and acting more like a jerk, when you've been sleeping through the night beside me?"

Alex was afraid to drop his gaze and confirm Etan's suspicions that he'd been hiding something, and the pain and worry in his husband's eyes was tearing his heart out. It was probably way too late, but he at least had to try to protect Connor's secret.

"You've been dreaming the same thing for a while now," he said, glancing away when he took a sip of the strong coffee. "More about crops failing, especially the corn everyone's so dependent on. Nothing new to tell you about."

Etan nodded again, his lips disappearing into a thin, pale line.

"Did you know I can feel the click when you tell me about one of my dreams? A shift inside me, your words matching up with whatever happens inside my head?"

"No," Alex whispered. "You never told me that."

"I never had to before. You never lied to me about a dream. I didn't know how that would hit me until just this minute. That one felt like splinters inside my mind. You'll have to do better."

"That's the best I *can* do, Etan."

"Is my father going to lie to me, too, Alex? Does he know what this huge secret is that I've been dreaming about?"

Alex pressed the heels of his hands into his eyes, willing Etan not to make the leap to how many dreams he'd kept to himself before they left Chicago three years ago. Admitting to that, back before he'd had any idea the conversations in the middle of the night could affect more than the two of them, had been a hell of a lot easier than trying to dodge this particular bullet.

"The only thing I can tell you is this dream wasn't about you or me," he said, folding his hands in his lap. "It doesn't feel right to tell you."

"You act like you don't understand a fucking thing about me. Anything that upsets you and my father this much absolutely affects me. If you're not being honest with me about a dream this important, how can I believe what you've told me about all the others? We could have thrown our lives in Chicago away over some bit of bullshit you made up to see how far you could push me."

"You can't really believe that," Alex said, forcing the words out through a tight throat. "You *have* to know I'd never do that to you. You just said you feel it when I'm telling you the truth about the dreams."

"Yeah, I did say that," Etan said. "I didn't say anything about when you decide to hide them from me altogether. If I can't trust you, I can't ever know what's coming. If I can't trust you, there's no point in surviving."

Alex pulled his feet up on the couch and wrapped his arms around his knees. He still felt exposed in a million agonizing ways.

"There's no way I can do the right thing."

Etan moved beside Alex and put both arms around him

"You told me not to hide from you that same way, remember? When we first talked about these fucking dreams. If we can't trust each other, especially when it comes to this, we're lost, Alex. We're lost."

"I know that. I believe that. The thing is *you* keep saying you must never know," Alex said, his voice breaking along with his heart. "'Etan must never see.' Every time you have that dream, you make me promise. What the hell am I supposed to do?"

"You know it's too late for that, don't you? I can't live with not knowing, and you can't live with telling me. I've wondered before if this whole mess is something evil using us without having the grace to tell us why. Nothing else makes any sense."

"The only thing that makes any sense to me right now is you," Alex said. He kissed Etan, relieved when he responded to his touch instead of drawing away. Alex needed the contact more than he needed to breathe. "Hurting you like this doesn't. I'm trapped no matter which way I turn."

"We both are." Etan held his forehead against Alex's, then stroked his cheek and sat back. "This probably isn't fair to ask, but none of this is fair. You said I'm not supposed to see whatever the dreams are about. Is there something I *am* supposed to see?"

Alex groaned, covering his face with his hands. He should leave lying to people who were better at it.

"Yeah, there is," he said. He walked into the library and pulled the old envelope from the top shelf where he'd left it. "I forgot about this, but yeah. You're supposed to see it."

Etan flinched when he saw his name on the envelope.

"My grandfather's handwriting." He slipped his thumb under the seal. "You didn't read it?"

"No, E. It wasn't mine to read."

Alex sat beside Etan, watching his face. His lovely green eyes, wide and unbelieving at first, slowly filled with tears and closed. He held the note out for Alex to read.

My dearest Etan. We're terribly sorry such difficult times will be part of your life, but we're overjoyed you have Alex to help you through. What happens won't seem fair, now and in your future. You'll both deal with heartache and sorrow no one should have to, separately and together. The love you share and the lives you build out of the struggle will all be worth it in the end. Take care of each other, and never forget how much we love you. Grampa and Gemaw.

"Where did you find this?" Etan said, his voice soft. "They died three years before I met you."

"It was… You told me where to find it in your dreams."

"And there was something for you, too," Etan said. "Something I'm not supposed to see."

"Mine said they only passed along what they had to, and that we have a chance to be as happy as they were." He turned away, shaking his head. "A lot of the same things about difficult times ahead of us, too."

Etan drummed his fingers on Alex's knee, staring into space.

"I need to talk to my father. I won't tell him you said anything. You don't have to go if you don't want to. But I have to talk to him."

Relief so strong it hit like a marijuana buzz from his college years flooded through Alex. He'd done the best he could, now it was between Etan and Connor. That was the first thing he felt like he could live with for several days.

"I'll go, sweetie. I'll talk to your Mom so you can have time with your Dad. He doesn't want her to know, either."

"I'm glad it's not just me."

The phone rang, the awful, grinding buzz setting Alex's teeth and nerves and bones on edge again.

Just like the night the riots started.

"Etan, don't…"

But Etan answered, turning to stare at Alex after a few seconds.

His face was dead white.

Chapter 32

Etan's mind reeled, threatening to take his body down with it. He didn't need Alex to speak the words to know the dream was moving into place all around him. That familiar deep alignment pulled all rational thought into the black abyss with his heart.

"Now. We have to go now, Alex."

Alex started to speak, then his face turned hard and cold.

"Those raiders. The ones from from the cannery."

"Maybe," Etan said, grabbing his holster from the table beside the door. "Probably. Whoever it is already hit the food pantry, soon as it got dark. Threw a firebomb in when they didn't find what they wanted. Only the one building burned before they got it out, but that distracted everyone. There's a damn blackout in town, of course, one they may have caused. No lights to see where they are."

"We have to stop Connor from going down there."

Alex slipped his own holster low over his hips, then added two leather bags with extra ammunition from hooks beside the door.

"That was Mom," Etan said, the spinning in his mind making him dizzy. "He left a few minutes ago, as soon as he got the first call."

Alex's face twisted, his lips drawing back from his teeth.

"Let me get the rifles. I don't know how to shoot the damn things yet, but someone else will."

Etan ran down the steps and out to his grandfather's car, dropping the keys twice when he tried to start it.

"Why the hell didn't you tell me, Evan?" he whispered. "We could have done something to stop this!"

Alex opened the back door, dropping three rifles and another ammunition bag. He slammed the door hard enough to rock the car on its springs.

"I think we need to stop and get your mother."

"I'm not dragging her into this mess. She's better off right where she is."

"Hang on, listen," Alex said. "She's the one who mentioned everyone having stores of food at home, remember? If this is a big raid, especially if they're local, they'll know that. We can take her to the sheriff's office or something, but I don't want to leave her out here alone."

"You don't know her as well as you think you do," Etan said. "If we take her into the middle of this, we'd have to lock her in the jail to keep her out of whatever's going on."

He drove as fast as he dared, watching the woods beside the gravel road. The idea of gangs roaming the mountains made too much sense to ignore. The sky still glowed with a faint purplish light, but the trees were in full darkness. He smelled Alex's sweat, and his own.

"I know you can't say any more than you have to," Etan said. "But could we have stopped this? Whatever's happening?"

"This may not be what you dreamed about. You never say exactly what happens, and Evan didn't either."

"I can feel it, Alex! The dream is all around us! Please, just answer me."

"All either of you said was there were choices, Etan. All of them are bad. Bad enough that stopping the dream isn't one of them."

"Bad for who? For my father? Are all of them bad for him?"

They turned onto the paved road, unlined and pure black. Only a minute or so until they were at his mother's house. Every second Alex waited drove the terror deeper into Etan's heart.

"They're all bad for him," Alex said. "And for us. The other choices… They end up with all the lights of humanity going out."

The sweat turned to ice on Etan's skin. He didn't try to stop himself from shouting.

"Did I say that to you before? About the lights? Alex? Did I?"

"No, not while you were awake," Alex said, frightened, nearly shouting himself. "Not until last night."

"Christ," Etan whispered. He turned up the driveway to his mother's house. "That's what my grandmother dreamed about when she was a kid. I told you about the library she was trapped in? She saw lights going out on a map of the world in there. Whole cities dying. One after another until only a few were left. Or if things were bad for her, before she was with my grandfather, all the lights went out. I saw the same thing at that meeting this afternoon on Linda's map."

"That's our other choice, E. Some survive, or everyone dies. That's what we're faced with."

The motion light in front of his parents' house was still on from his father leaving.

Everything, from the thick air in his lungs to the frost sparkling on the grass to the bruised light fading from the sky told Etan they were running out of time.

Chapter 33

Laura met them at the door, wearing her cold weather gear and handguns. She was about to follow Connor in her own car, whether he wanted her to or not. Alex was equal parts impressed with her determination and heartbroken that she was going into the middle of whatever storm awaited them.

His body felt overloaded, muscles and nerves twitching with excess energy. Only massive electrical storms coming in across the lake in his childhood or touring a huge power plant had ever hit Alex that way. He was half convinced blue sparks would fly off his fingers if he got close to metal.

"Do you know any more about what's happening?" Etan said when she got into the front seat.

"Only what Father Price said when he called," Laura said. "Whoever this is has at least a little bit of training, and they know where to look. They're scattered all over town, but no one doubts they'll head to the cannery."

"And the high school," Alex said. He remembered Mary Shadrin stepping out from the darkness, asking him why they needed such a big truck for cleaning up an empty basement. "They probably know we've got food stored there now. Medical supplies, too."

"Connor told me about those assholes who barged into the cannery," Laura said. "I'd bet that's who this is."

"Any chance you'll stay out of this?" Etan said, glancing at his mother. "Maybe at the sheriff's office or somewhere else safe?"

"Etan, son, are you forgetting who first taught *you* how to shoot? If my husband and my sons are going into this mess, I'm not sitting on the sidelines fretting and wringing my hands."

"Maybe you can teach me how to use these rifles when this is over with," Alex said. "At least stay off the front line if you can?"

"We'll see. Go to the cannery first. Someone will tell us where they need help."

Etan had to slow the car as he drove over the steep hill down into Wolf Branch. People were walking everywhere, not nearly enough of them with flashlights so he could avoid them. More than one stepped into the dark street nearly too late.

Alex thought he recognized everyone, but he didn't want to depend on that. Anyone who hadn't been in one of his classes, at the community garden, or at the cannery could be his next door neighbor and he'd have no idea.

The crowd grew thicker the closer they got to the high school. Several cars and pickup trucks were scattered all over the parking lot, and Alex did recognize the people standing around the cannery's locked door. Walt Colley, Linda, Father Price, even Harry Mullins. Alex had never seen him wearing jeans instead of his suit.

He didn't see Connor anywhere.

"We're not ready for something like this," Etan said as he parked. "Everyone's just running scared."

"We'll have to do better," his mother said. "But we don't have time for that right now."

An endless stream of traffic flowed along the road by the high school. Cars, trucks, a few motorcycles. The gap between the headlights wide enough to plunge their eyes back into near-blindness.

The whole town was in a dull roar, everybody within earshot talking or shouting at each other. Alex heard screams and yells from other parts of Wolf Branch, but he couldn't tell where they were coming from in the near darkness. Only a few motion lights scattered among the buildings and the parade of headlights gave off any light.

"Have you seen Connor?" Laura said, walking up to Harry Mullins.

"He got here a few minutes ago, yeah," Harry said. His eyes moved constantly, watching every vehicle and every person prowling around. "He said something about going to check the high school."

"I'll go get him," Alex said, loud enough for only Etan to hear.

"I'm right here." Connor walked across the parking lot from the high school, his hand on the gun at his right hip. He hugged Laura, then stood with his arm around her. "Didn't see anything strange at the school. A couple of people are watching the door now."

"Want to tell me what's going on here, Dad?" Etan said. "Why you came running down here without letting either one of us know?"

Connor looked at Alex, eyebrows raised. Alex shook his head.

"This isn't the time, at least not for that. We'll talk about it when this all settles down. If we can."

A crunching explosion on the other side of town, not far from the hospital, had everyone looking that way. Alex didn't see much light, just a whole lot of noise.

"That's a distraction," he said under his breath, then spoke louder. "They're just trying to distract us."

"Everyone pay attention now!" Harry shouted. Several of the people milling around the cannery were already heading toward the hospital. "Don't follow every god damn false lead they throw us."

The group remaining drew closer, backing toward the cannery. The flow of traffic going by didn't slow in response to the explosion, a disjointed pattern that put Alex even more on edge. Etan grabbed his arm, squeezing hard enough to hurt.

"Something's wrong," he whispered. "Right here, all around us."

Alex saw Connor freeze, staring at the road. He turned and looked at the two of them. He kissed Laura's cheek before he stepped away. He frowned, shook his head, and walked toward the road.

"Get them all behind the building," he said to Etan and Alex. "Take care of her."

"Connor, wait!" Alex said, his voice an intense whisper.

"It's something there, the road," Etan said right into Alex's ear. "I can't see what, but I know it's that way."

"Then we have to stop it," Alex said.

"We don't know what we're trying to stop." Etan's fingers sank into Alex's bicep as he pulled him backward. "I can't see, Alex! Maybe he can!"

"Behind the building!" Connor shouted. "Now!"

Alex saw his silhouette against the headlights turning the corner toward the school.

Then he was gone.

"Connor!" Laura tried to run toward the road.

Etan grabbed her around the waist.

"Everybody back!" he shouted, dragging his mother backward. "Get away from the road!"

"Behind the building!" Alex couldn't see his father-in-law any more. Only that slow line of headlights against the darkness. "Laura, get back!"

He helped Etan with his mother, lifting her off her feet as she screamed into their ears.

"Stop it! Connor! Let me go!"

The others followed, looking around with wide eyes.

One of the big trucks slowed, veering toward the parking lot, the double cab full of people. A man crouched in the back.

The lights shifted. He was gone.

They pushed Laura behind the building.

Alex saw a shadow dart forward. Connor ran alongside the truck.

He reached into the open window of the huge double cab truck.

Shouts from within and from the bed.

The truck jerked away from the cannery, too sharp.

It overturned on the steep road. Metal barrels and what looked like sticks spilled out of the bed.

Alex had one last glimpse of his father-in-law dropping away from the window.

Chapter 34

T HE MASSIVE BLAST knocked everyone to the ground.

Etan saw the others in the orange glow, felt heat on his skin. He crawled forward, shaking his head. His ears weren't working.

His mother was still, slumped against the wall, Harry Mullins trying to get to his feet beside her. Linda sat against the building, hands over her ears.

A twisting black hole in the middle of Etan's gut threatened to drag his awareness into the void with his mother.

Someone touched his shoulder.

Alex was on his knees beside him. His mouth moved in the dead silence. Etan staggered to his feet, but Alex blocked his way.

He thought his husband was saying *too hot*. The air felt more brutal than late August in Chicago, but with no humidity to slow the effect. An oily, chemical stench permeated his nose, mouth, and throat.

Etan tried to push forward around the edge of the building again. Alex wrapped both arms around him and pulled him against the cinderblock wall.

Etan watched Alex move his hand around the edge, toward that orange light.

The light his father had died in.

Alex shook his head, then pointed the opposite direction.

His mother was straining against Harry Mullins and Walt Colley, trying to get to the same corner. Her mouth was open wide, her throat bulging, arms outstretched. Etan slipped his own arms around Alex's waist, holding tight before he was ready to help his mother. Both were crying when he finally let go.

Etan and Alex caught Laura Griffith's hands, trying to get her to focus, to pay attention. She twisted and writhed, shaking her head. Etan finally held her face, staring into her eyes from a few inches away.

Her wild gaze softened as she finally saw him. His mother said no, over and over again. Etan caught her before she could hit the asphalt.

Father Price staggered forward and put his arms around Etan, helping support his mother's sagging weight. He bowed his head, his lips moving.

Etan turned away. What god would let a good man like his father die in such a way? And what good did praying do now that it was all over?

Whoever Father Price was trying to reach was as deaf as Etan. Or simply didn't care.

He helped Walt and the priest settle his mother against the side of the building, then turned to look for Alex. He stood at the edge of the building with Harry and Linda, the three of them trying to communicate in broad gestures.

When Alex pointed toward the still-raging fire, a vision ripped through Etan's mind. He grabbed Linda and Alex.

"No!" he shouted, sure they still wouldn't hear him. "More bombs! They haven't exploded yet!"

For the first time in his life, Etan understood why the death masks tormented his grandmother so horribly.

Harry and Linda stared at him, trying to understand.

Both of them screaming, tearing at their flesh burning and torn by shrapnel.

Alex nodded, pulling the other two back.

Alex rolling in agony, unable to stop the chemical fire that devoured the flesh from his bones.

Etan moved behind the three of them and pushed them toward his mother and Father Price, still huddled on the ground.

This time he didn't hear the blasts, five in rapid succession. The ground rumbled under his feet, the orange shadows blazed into daylight. His already tender skin protested at painful levels of heat.

He kept his eyes squeezed closed, not wanting to see the sickening visions again. Gritty fingers on his cheek forced him to look.

Alex's tense features fell into relief, and he pulled Etan into a tight hug. Alex's face smudged and dirty, but no longer melting into slag. Harry and Linda leaned against the wall, covering their mouths against the increasingly noxious air.

Etan dug in his pocket. Even with several of the windows shattered from the first blast, they'd be better off inside the cannery. The basement didn't have any windows at all.

When he moved toward the corner, Alex resisted. Etan held the key up, shaking his head. If there were any more bombs, he didn't feel them coming yet. At least for a few minutes, he thought they were safe.

Stepping around the corner drove that word out of his mind for a long, long time.

Chapter 35

Alex followed Etan, stopping as soon as he cleared the edge of
the cannery. His brain rejected the input of his watering eyes, threatening to shut down all activities until he provided something more
sensible.

The burning truck was invisible under a thick plume of black
smoke, sunken into a crater across the two lane road. Another truck
and a car were on fire, one in each lane. Several bodies were scattered
along the road and in the parking lot.

Alex didn't have to look closer to know Connor wasn't one of
them. He was thankful for that much.

A crowd grew as people followed the light and stench, far worse
than the diversion over toward the hospital. A few knelt over more
bodies, probably caught in those last explosions.

Etan's hot hand pulled him into the cannery, into blessedly
cooler and less polluted air. The window on the other side of the
double doors held crazed glass still intact. Alex's engineer mind
seized on the chance to assess the damage.

Damage he might actually be able to repair.

The two windows in the small office, closest to the road, were
gone. Alex felt glass crunching under his shoes as he closed the door,

then looked for some way to block more smoke from getting inside. He wedged several towels under the office door.

Pots and utensils were scattered all over the floor, nearly as grimy as when he'd first set foot inside nearly two years ago. He turned to tell Etan everything looked okay before he remembered his husband wouldn't be able to hear him.

His panic at not seeing Etan died when he walked in, supporting his mother with Linda on the other side. The way his mother-in-law hid her face against her son's chest tore Alex's heart out all over again.

Alex unlocked the basement door, hoping the ventilation system hadn't drawn the foul smoke down there. The emergency lights showed them a dim but clean path. Walt grabbed several bottles of cider from the cooler as he passed by.

The ice-cold liquid made it clear how badly Alex's throat hurt. He wished for something stronger for Laura. He'd settle for not being able to hear her crying, though he hoped that damage wasn't permanent.

His legs gave out and he slowly slid to the floor beside Laura, still leaning against Etan. She gripped Alex's hand without looking up.

Linda started to give Alex a note written on the back of an inventory sheet, then hesitated. He took it with his free hand.

Sandy's outside. At least twenty dead, maybe more later. Trouble seems to have stopped. Still, plenty who live in town offering for folks who live out a ways to stay here tonight or longer.

So sorry. Brave thing he did.

Alex glanced at Laura to make sure she wouldn't see, then handed the note to Etan. His carefully neutral expression didn't change as he read, then nodded.

Linda handed Alex one more note, this one on a tiny sheet torn out of a spiral notebook. He didn't have to ask who this one came from.

Have to head back to the hospital. Like to check all of you over first. S.

Alex nodded, and Linda headed back up the stairs. He showed the note to Etan, then passed it along to Walt and Harry.

Sandy was hardly formal in her medical practice, and tonight she was wearing pink sweatpants and a matching hooded sweatshirt, both as sooty and stained as her hands and face. She pointed to her ear, then to Alex.

When he shook his head, she knelt and shined a bright light with a tiny magnifying glass into his ears. She sat back with a grim smile, scribbled for a few seconds, and showed him the notebook.

No rupture. If not hearing in 24 hrs, will reexamine. Should be fine, tho. Hurt elsewhere? Dizzy? Lose consciousness?

He shook his head again, then got to his feet when she took Laura's hand.

The exams were all the same, except asking all of them to help keep an eye on Laura for concussion. And depression.

Alex stood beside Walt and Harry, all of them glancing at Etan, then each other. Harry finally held out his hand for the notepad.

Sandy showed her answering note to all three of them.

Could certainly use help if you feel up to it. Will take Etan and Laura to my house. You too, Alex. Long as you need to stay.

The fire was out when they got upstairs, and people were covering up the bodies. The whole ones, at least. Alex forced himself to ignore the smaller parts, the bloody ones. Twisted bits of metal and tiny glittering pieces of glass were all over the road and parking lot.

The endless line of traffic was gone with no way to get past, but several vehicles ringed the parking lot with their lights on. The town beyond remained mostly dark.

Sheriff Grant and the deputies helping near the still hot crater stopped when Etan walked by with his mother. She never raised her face, letting him lead her to a waiting van. Etan looked each of them in the eye and nodded.

Walt, Harry, and Linda joined the cleanup. When Alex tried to get into the van, Etan shook his head. He slowly mouthed "You want to stay."

"Your Mom," Alex said, strangely aware of the silent rumble in his own throat and chest.

Etan held up a small pill bottle. He folded both hands under his cheek and closed his eyes. Alex hadn't seen Sandy give it to him.

"Sure?" he said, reaching for Etan's hand. "You okay?"

"Sure. Okay for now." He pointed to himself, then mimed being asleep again. He kissed the back of Alex's hand. "Love you."

Alex held his hand over his heart, watching the van drive away. He felt more relieved than guilty at leaving Etan alone with his mother and with his own grief.

That relief made Alex's guilt worse.

Unbearable pain lurked hot and heavy in his chest. That would probably hit him when he finally could talk to Etan. And Laura. But right now, he held on to knowing the thing he'd been dreading was over. The brief delay in dealing with their loss might help him get through the next few days.

Nothing would make the weeks and months ahead any easier.

By the time he crawled into bed with a deeply sleeping Etan several hours later, Alex was exhausted enough that he didn't need any of the pills on the bedside table.

Chapter 36

Etan gazed around the strange bedroom for several seconds, trying to figure out where he was. Walls covered in pastel flowers, comforter on the bed frilly and pink. Neither their house nor his parents' house was so elaborately decorated. Alex was snoring softly beside him in the narrow bed, though.

His parents.

Etan looked at the bedside table, where a clock covered with plastic flowers and balloons told him it was nearly ten in the morning. A small prescription bottle told him why he'd slept so hard, enough that his left arm was numb.

He saw orange light, felt painful heat. His ears still felt muffled, but he heard his own breathing along with those faint, sweet snores.

His father had died in that explosion.

Etan groaned, turning back toward Alex and his warmth. Connor Griffith had saved all of them, and who knows how many others besides. More than firecrackers or even a simple explosive caused a blast that huge.

And Alex had told him the alternative was all the lights of humanity going out. If his grandmother's dreams, and his own, were true, far more than the population of Wolf Branch owed their lives to Etan's father.

That might make sense someday. Right now the loss was too huge and terrible to contemplate, much less accept.

"Etan?" Alex sounded barely awake. "Can you hear me?"

"Yeah, sweetie. I hear you."

"Thank the gods," he said, turning over and kissing Etan's cheek. "Mine's not quite back to normal, but a hell of a lot better."

"I need to go check on Mom. Get some more sleep."

"No, I'm awake," Alex said. "I left you alone last night. I'm not going to today."

Etan stood up and picked up his clothes from the floor. They really did need to get home just to find something less filthy to wear.

"Mom and I were both asleep a few minutes after we got here. I think today's going to be a lot worse."

Alex moved across the bed and caught Etan's hand.

"I'm so sorry about this. I wish I could have stopped it."

Etan shook his head, not ready to deal with Alex knowing what was coming. A small corner of his broken heart, perhaps still controlled by a shy eleven-year-old with horrible nightmares, wanted to be angry at Alex because he let it happen.

That wasn't fair, not if he was telling the truth about Etan's own dreams and his grandfather's journal.

Alex *did* tell the truth, always, certainly about something so serious. Yet he'd kept this to himself for the last several days of his father's life. That was something else that might make sense later.

"He made his own choice," Etan said. "And he did save a lot of people. Maybe all of us."

The murmur of conversation in the dining room had too many deep voices with Sandy's husband the only other man. Sheriff Grant was there, along with one of his deputies, all around the huge round table with Sandy's two children. Etan's heart sank toward his empty stomach at the way his mother sat, leaning forward with one hand holding her forehead.

His chance to avoid facing this particular reality was already over.

"I normally wouldn't say this, but I hope you're awake because you heard us in here," Sandy said.

She'd changed out of the battered pink sweats into plain green scrubs, but her weariness showed in her voice and the dark circles under her eyes. She poured two cups of coffee from a stainless steel carafe.

"You didn't wake us, but I can hear you just fine," Alex said. He put an arm around his mother-in-law's shoulders, and she hugged him.

"Oh sweetheart, you smell awful," she said with a ghostly smile.

"I can help with that." Sandy's husband stood, herding a little boy and a slightly older little girl in front of him. "Probably not the best fit in the world, but they'll do while I throw what you're wearing in the wash. I'll be back in a minute"

Etan sat beside his mother, settling for a kiss on the cheek. "You okay, Mom?"

"No, hon, I'm not. But I'll keep breathing. Sheriff Grant wants to talk to all of us for a minute."

"I won't take up too much of your time," the sheriff said. "Sandy had a long night and you all have a hard day ahead. There haven't been any more problems, so we think the ringleaders were driving that big truck."

"Same ones who came to the cannery before?" Etan said.

"That's how it's sounding from everyone we've spoken to. Everyone who can talk says they're from Maple Ridge. They didn't even have a grocery store up there in good times, and the road was in pretty bad shape from last winter. They've had trouble finding enough to eat for a long while."

He ran his fingers through his short brown hair, looking everywhere but at Etan or Laura for a few seconds.

"A few people pretty much set up a prison camp over the last couple of months, real nasty business. Told everyone we were stopping food deliveries to that convenience store they had, said that was why it shut down back in the fall. Said we were keeping all their food for ourselves. That's why they were shutting down the power from the wind turbines up there, too. Trying to shake us up while they terrorized their own people. Set up barricades to stop people from leaving, made the roads worse themselves. Once the satellite

TV got taken over for the emergency services, they couldn't get hardly any communication from the outside world that far up in the mountains."

"The ones that came with them last night didn't have much of a choice," Deputy Wiggins said, her face cold and pale. "They were rounded up, promised the first food for their families for a few weeks."

"Most of them are half-starved or worked to the bone," Sandy said. "Desperate to check on their families still left up there more than anything else. I don't think they knew about the bombs."

"No, neither do I," Sheriff Grant said. "Not the big ones. Everyone I've talked to is sick over what happened, they truly are. They had a few noise and smoke bombs to scare people, but it looks like the bed of that truck was full of dynamite and steel cans. Hard to say for sure, but it stinks like diesel fuel and fertilizer. That dynamite had to be ancient. Crazy as the leaders may have been, they never would have driven over those bad roads with such an unstable mess unless they planned to use it. I'm sorry, Mrs. Griffith."

Etan's mother shook her head and sighed.

"I'd rather know Connor died for a reason," she said. "Sounds like he saved a lot more than the few of us standing there."

Etan grabbed Alex's thigh under the table, squeezing hard. The dizziness threatening to pull him out of the chair had nothing to do with the explosion.

A thousand massive gears roared and moved around and inside him, joining up the past and the future.

Alex gripped Etan's hand, returning the squeeze. His own disorientation showed in his blue eyes.

"Thing is, we have to figure out what to do with them," Sandy said. "We kept almost thirty at the hospital overnight, but they can't stay there forever."

"All involved in the raid?" Etan's mother said.

"Yeah, at least all from Maple Ridge," Deputy Wiggins said. "Like Dr. Hughes said, they're all in bad shape, but worried about their folks still up on the mountain."

"Maybe we should take them right back where they came from,"

Alex said under his breath, but everyone around the table heard him. Sheriff Grant broke the long silence.

"A bunch of them told me there are people still left up there. Women and children. Rumors of some men too sick to make it. I feel sick myself that we didn't know what was going on so close by."

"I don't know how bad off they'd have to be to get left behind," Sandy said. "One boy they dragged along has a shattered kneecap, one he got within the last couple of days. Anyone on Maple Ridge won't last long in this cold with worse on the way. Smells like snow outside, and they'll get it worse than we do. The raiders brought all the working vehicles and locked up all the food."

"I figure we have tough choices to make here," the sheriff said. He refilled everyone's coffee cups, not really paying attention to what his hands were doing. "Now and going forward as things get worse out in the world. Do we take folks like this in, or do we try to lock the place up tight?"

Etan swallowed the coffee just as absently, inhaling air across his scorched tongue.

He'd always wondered what Anne's map with the glowing lights looked like. Right now he saw one zoomed in so close that it looked like the view from a helicopter hovering low over Wolf Branch. The contours of mountains and valleys surrounding the town sharp with trees bare for winter.

The small grid of downtown, only a few blocks in either direction, held a few hundred red lights. Some moved down the streets too smoothly to be walking, others clustered together inside the buildings. A larger cluster huddled inside the hospital. A few of those were as pale as the little girl's comforter he and Alex had slept under the night before.

The view shifted, pulled back, and followed the wider two lane heading out of Wolf Branch. The gentle right turn toward Maple Ridge led to a narrow road, twisting as it climbed the steep mountain. A few dozen lights were scattered through the tiny community near the top, almost all of them faded to barely visible.

A few, though, blazed so brightly that his inner eye squinted from the brilliance.

"We've lost how many in the US alone?" he said, focusing on the room again. "Close to fifty million already? And easily three billion worldwide? We all know that's just the beginning. Probably twice that will be gone by the end of this winter, even if we stop hearing about it."

Everyone watched him silently. Only Alex responded with a tiny nod and by squeezing Etan's hand.

"Can we afford to take people back up there to die? Or leave the ones trapped up there to starve to death? We *will* have to protect ourselves from something else like last night. I doubt they'll be the last. But if we forget what we're fighting for, why we're even trying to survive, none of this will be worth it."

Chapter 37

Barely a week later, the Griffiths' house felt like it had been abandoned for years. The floors and walls were clean, and everything was in perfect repair inside and out, just the way Connor had left it. All the large furniture was already moved out, with several people helping out over the last few days.

But even before Alex helped Etan and Laura empty and pack up the last few things, the heart that made it a home was gone.

A pile of boxes waited for them on the broad front porch. Neither he nor Etan had the strength to protest when Laura insisted they take many of Connor's things. Her smaller apartment in town simply wouldn't have room for so much. That sounded like a reasonable argument, until Alex saw the place.

Laura was going to have more room than they did in their house. But again, it was easier to go along.

They were taking a break for one last lunch at the picnic table where they'd shared dinner with Etan's parents, after the awful drive from Chicago. Connor and Evan had built this one around the same time they built the one at Etan and Alex's house. The sun high overhead had melted the last of the snow that fell the day after Connor died, and the fire pit nearby kept them warm enough.

"Is anyone going to move in here, Mom?" Etan said.

"I don't know," Laura said. She looked around, then smiled at Etan. "I hope one of the families from Maple Ridge will, until they get themselves settled. Maybe you two will when you start a family."

Alex met Etan's gaze, expecting the sadness he saw there. He knew children would be in their future, just as well as he knew Etan would take a while to get there while he was awake.

He hadn't yet told Etan about the strong recognition he'd been caught up in during the first rescue trip to Maple Ridge, for one thing. Snow fell up on that mountain as hard as the blizzard the night he'd met Etan back in Chicago. Patterns in that snow led Alex right to two women he knew would be part of their future as surely as he'd known Etan would be part of his.

"I don't know about moving," Etan said. "We love our house. This may not be the best time to be raising kids."

She snorted and rolled her eyes.

"There's never a *best* time for that, not really. Just easier and harder times. Whether you want to think about it this way or not, now is an important time, though. There won't be enough of us left at this rate unless your generation joins in."

"We'll see," Etan said.

"I have to ask one more time, Laura," Alex said. "Are you sure about moving into town? This is really soon to make such a big decision."

"I know, hon. I love the house, and it just feels empty. Like a tomb. Ghosts around every corner. Getting through a winter out here with the power out half the time by myself sounds like a nightmare. I'm not so sure you two should try it this year."

"The power will be a lot more stable now that we can keep an eye on things at Maple Ridge," Alex said. "I've already got electricity set up at our place. The water turbine will keep the basics going even if the wind turbines have trouble, and I'm going to add solar over the next couple of weeks. I could easily do that down here if you want to stay."

She shook her head and patted his arm.

"I appreciate it, Alex, I really do. If someone does move in here, that would be a fine welcome gift. But I'm ready to go."

"Fair enough," Etan said. "The cannery is as good as new, so we'll be helping Sandy with the hospital. Or Alex will. I'm just a hired mule for this kind of thing. If the weather holds, maybe we can get started on your apartment building next."

The three of them finished their sandwiches in silence. Alex was sure he wasn't the only one remembering the first night after they'd arrived from Chicago. Connor and Laura stuffing them full of enough food for at least four people.

He watched the smoke from the fire pit drifting in the cool wind, the changing directions lighting up a warning in the pattern recognition machine in his mind.

"I need to ask you two something," Laura finally said. "It's taken me a couple of days to work up the courage, so just let me get this out." She drummed her fingers on the table, so much like Etan often did. "Did you know what was going to happen to Connor? I'm not asking whether you could have stopped it. I know both of you too well to think you wouldn't have. But did you know?"

Alex looked into his mother-in-law's eyes, wishing he could call a time out and talk to Etan for just a few seconds. He hadn't stopped asking himself whether he could have prevented Connor's death since Etan's first dream about his grandfather's journal.

That question would likely haunt him for the rest of his life.

"We didn't know exactly what would happen," Etan said. He took his mother's hand across the table. Alex held her other one. "I dreamed something was coming, some kind of big change, but I didn't know what it would be."

"That could have been about the raid, too," Alex said, thankful for his husband's lead. "But not clear enough to stop it. I don't know if we could have stopped something that big even if we'd known when it would happen."

"Probably not," Laura said. "Not before we knew what to watch for."

"Exactly," Alex said. "Deputy Wiggins, Melissa, I mean, being able to sense who will cause trouble is going to be a huge help. I'm starting to suspect everyone from Maple Ridge can do the same."

The efforts to welcome everyone had started the night after the raid and hadn't yet slowed. From a huge dinner in the basement of the same church where he and Etan had gotten married, to offers of clothing and shelter, to the new arrivals increasingly asking what they could do to help in their new home.

The country and the world continued to tear themselves apart all around them, but after the one horrible night, Wolf Branch remained calm.

Etan's mother and everyone from both Wolf Branch and Maple Ridge seemed to be channeling their grief and fear into building a new community together.

"There's more talk of organizing the town council again," Laura said, watching Etan instead of Alex. "Harry Mullins, Linda Burns, Father Price. A few people from Maple Ridge. Your new friends Iris and Gena. The two of you would be a welcome addition."

Alex tried to hide his smile. Laura might not be able to see anything unusual about the future, but she retained her full abilities to read her family. She'd recognized Iris and Gena as surely as he had. Etan shook his head, then turned to stare into the fire pit.

"That's not…"

"Safe?" Alex said, remembering the night of the last big meeting. When they'd fled from the riptides and furious energy in the auditorium. And from Mary Shadrin and her followers.

"I hate to admit this, especially to both of you," Etan said, turning back with a faint smile. "It doesn't exactly feel dangerous anymore, no. I'm not ready to jump into anything like that yet. I need to…catch my breath."

When Etan's voice broke, Alex bit back the arguments, persuasion, even the encouragement he had ready. He had his doubts about his mother-in-law making such a huge change so soon after Connor's death. And he'd spent every night since the explosions with Etan held tight, both of them caught in mourning that felt endless and impossible.

He had no doubts that Etan *wasn't* ready for the council or anything else.

Not yet.

"We could all use a little time to catch up," Alex said, rubbing

Etan's back. "Mary isn't in much of a position to cause trouble anymore, but the more people we have who can see what's coming, the better."

"What gets me about Mary is she *does* see what's coming," Etan said. "A form of it, anyway. It's like she gets a warped version, or the people around her twist it. They all stayed away from town that night."

"Sure, because they thought *we* were going to attack *them*," Alex said. He trusted Etan's perception, but he didn't think he'd ever trust Mary. "That wasn't particularly helpful."

"But there was an attack," Laura said. "They had that part right, and by staying away, they stayed safe. To tell you the truth, I don't see how any of you can stand it. Knowing what's coming, even a little bit. I never understood how Anne could, either. Hard as this has been, I'd rather not know."

"Gemaw didn't stand it very well," Etan said. He moved closer to Alex and put an arm around his waist. "Not until she was with Grampa. That makes all the difference."

"Well, I have something I've been wanting to ask you two," Alex said. "That night, that last night, Connor looked toward the road before that truck could have been in sight. He was there before they were, before any of us could have seen anything. Do you think he saw things? Not as often as Etan or Anne, but sometimes?"

"I think he did," Laura said. She rubbed her wedding ring with her thumb. "He was pretty damn confident when we met. And when you two met."

"That much is hereditary," Alex said, smiling at Etan. "We both knew as soon as we met."

"Connor knew I was pregnant with Etan before I did. Same thing when I went into labor. He wasn't the least bit surprised when Etan called to say you two were moving back home."

Alex knew he had to keep his own thoughts about Connor's abilities—and Etan's—to himself for now. Etan wasn't ready to know how much they'd have to be involved in the struggle to keep Wolf Branch safe and strong over the next few years. Not when he was awake, anyway.

The community wasn't as stable as they'd need to be, especially as more survivors straggled in with their own terrors and challenges. Etan's dreams suggested many more would join them over time.

Alex also knew his husband could take a while to adjust to new situations, especially after the terrible shock of losing Connor. But Alex had no doubts that their time on the council, their future children, all of it would come more easily if he let Etan get there on his own.

He didn't need Etan's dreams or anyone else's to know difficult and dangerous times lay ahead.

For his family, for Wolf Branch, and for the world.

But for the first time since Etan's dreams of the end back in Chicago, Alex's own thoughts of the future were touched with hope.

INTO THE STORM

BOOK THREE OF THE STORMS OF FUTURE PAST SERIES

KARI KILGORE

AUTHOR OF IN THE PINES AND RESTRICTED SPECIES

For my uncle, Frank Kilgore

For helping raise awareness of our region as worthy of so much more than extraction and exploitation.

For highlighting the beauty and untapped potential that will carry us and future generations forward, strong and proud.

Chapter 1

Most people were a little bit afraid of Iris Rutherford's paintings. The strange ones, at least. And so many of them were strange.

Her home town of Maple Ridge, Virginia, was a former mining camp that hung on when most of the old company coal and timber towns in Appalachia dried up and blew away. Part of it was the stunning beauty of the mountaintop community. Once clearcut and barren, the steep mountains and deep, blue valleys now held mature oaks, pines, poplars, and of course, several stands of huge old sugar maples.

A few people complained bitterly not long after the turn of the century when soaring white windmills appeared to sprout out of the forest, following the curves of the highest ridge lines. Decades later, agreements with a university to test new designs led to free electricity for the residents.

Broad, three-blade models still dominated, joined by single blade turbines and several with more than a dozen blades contained in an outer circle. But many looked more like sculpture, artwork that happened to supply power. Graceful upright blades in endless curves and variations, whirling in a dizzying ballet, bulky control units hidden among the trees.

Most natives and visitors alike now found the additions to the landscape charming, if not beautiful.

The main road into town twisted and curved, giving attentive drivers breathtaking views of the Blue Ridge Mountains, with the sparkling Grasspe River cutting through the valley far below. Enough people pulled off of the narrow two lane road to take a look that muddy wide spots were a permanent fixture.

The town, and the region, were too remote and isolated for anything as official as a scenic overlook. The few tourists who found Maple Ridge were always enchanted, and their business at the restaurant, craft shop, and convenience store was much appreciated.

Visitors savored and treasured their maple syrup and candy, wishing for just one more taste when it was gone.

The other reason Maple Ridge survived was the fiercely independent - some said stubborn - nature of the few hundred hardy souls who clung to their ancestral homes. The elementary and middle school teachers and administration prided themselves as much on their efforts to get less than one hundred students ready for high school and life down off the mountain as on their traditional old school house. The brick walls had been built to last, over one hundred and fifty years ago.

More of those children returned after their educations than folks from other parts of the state would believe. They returned well-qualified from good colleges and universities, frequently after turning down or taking and later leaving excellent jobs elsewhere.

Many took advantage of the lightning speed Internet brought through town fifty years ago on the way to a bigger town and worked from home. A few took on the challenging but beautiful commute into nearby Wolf Branch or an hour further on to Hidden Springs.

More than the peace and quiet, the slower pace of life, and the deep fondness for the Grasspe River brought so many people back to Maple Ridge. The natives, and after a while the partners they often brought back with them, found they could not do without the peculiar magic and eccentricity of their home.

Iris Rutherford loved her home town as much as anyone else.

But her own peculiar magic made her an outsider in a town full of them.

Everything changed for Iris when she started to draw and paint at age eleven. Seemingly overnight, the shy, quiet child who happily let her older brother and sisters take all the attention found her passion. The art teacher, delighted to see such unusual drive and raw talent, offered to let Iris practice before and after school.

She did both.

She understood the technical aspects of composition, color, and balance immediately. Iris surpassed most of what her young teacher had to offer within a few months. She moved on from typical bowls of fruit, faces, and landscapes to startling, surreal visions that even she didn't quite understand.

Shapes often vaguely human, colors that should have clashed but flowed smoothly under her brush, and wild, thick strokes that followed a pattern no one could define poured forth. The art teacher spoke to Iris's parents, and later to the high school art teacher in Wolf Branch. A student with so much promise must be handled carefully, guided in appropriate and controlled paths.

The high school counselor was the first to realize that whatever drove Iris to spend so many hours practicing would never be controlled.

After enough stern conversations about disturbing the other students, and the teachers, Iris learned to keep her special paintings - the *true* ones - private. She developed great skill with more accept-able work, and the talk died down. She never stopped painting the wild visions and images, the ones she saw burning in her mind as soon as she opened her eyes many mornings.

Her bedroom walls were lined with those distressing sketches and paintings, the ones she had no choice but to get out of herself. Iris learned of abstract and impressionist art from many decades before. She had high hopes of finding acceptance for her true work in art school.

The first person to understand what Iris painted, to see the meaning and significance even she never did, was Gena Wallace.

Chapter 2

THE *EYES of the Future* art exhibit was meant to introduce incoming Appalachian Art Institute students to the community, and let the art-loving residents of Hidden Springs discover up-and-coming talent before anyone else.

The most exciting aspect for Iris was choosing three of her true paintings to go along with the six her teachers suggested.

Other students and even the faculty warned Iris she'd likely be bored to tears and not sell a thing. She was pleasantly surprised to sell everything except the true paintings. She wasn't surprised people barely glanced at those. Not one person asked about them until a soft, rich voice spoke from behind her.

"It's a real shame these aren't for sale."

A small woman stood in front of a large canvas, one Iris had only painted a few days before. She wore typical student garb. Faded blue jeans, brown hiking boots, and a hunter green sweatshirt from the law school in Bountyfield, a couple of hours away. Dark blonde hair hung in a thick braid down her back.

"They *are* for sale," Iris said, standing. She was a few inches taller than the mysterious woman, and at once self-conscious about how much her own black hair provided an unruly contrast. "No one's interested in them, though. They're not as good."

When the woman turned, Iris smiled despite her desire to play the cool, unconcerned artist. She was beautiful, with light brown eyes and full lips curved in a mischievous smile of her own.

"You're mistaken there. The others are nice enough," she said, then a delightful blush spread across her cheeks. "I don't mean that the way it sounds. They're technically just fine. But these are *amazing*. Is this one your family?"

Iris frowned, examining the painting. The background was broad strokes of various shades of green, the swirling patterns overlapping and contrasting. Four distinct oval areas in the middle were black, red, brown, and yellow. Several smaller splashes of the same colors ranged throughout the canvas.

She hadn't named that one. She hardly ever named the true paintings.

Family settled into place in her belly, warm and comforting like hot soup on a cold day.

"I hadn't thought of it that way," Iris said. "Why did you say that? What do you see?"

"Well, I think it's obvious." She pointed to the larger colors. "These are the parents, or adults who go together somehow. The smaller ones are the children. Is that not right?"

Iris shrugged, shaking her head. That was a lie, though. She had no idea where the colors might come from, but every single brush stroke finally made sense. She'd never imagined such a huge group of people all around her, but Iris felt that desire in every part of her now.

"Almost everyone in my family has black or gray hair, so I don't think it's them. Feels right somehow, though."

"Your future family, then. I'm Gena Wallace." Gena turned back to the paintings. "The more I think about it, buying these doesn't seem right. They're pretty personal, aren't they?"

"Iris Rutherford, but I guess you see that on the name card." Iris fussed with the white tag pinned to her shirt, not used to feeling so flustered and awkward talking about her art. In that area if nowhere else, she was normally confident. "I don't know if they're personal, but hardly anyone ever wants to talk about them."

"I think they're the only ones in this whole place worth talking about. What about this one?"

The smaller canvas, only two feet square, disturbed Iris more than she cared to admit. The background ranged from dark red to bright orange. The effect was close enough to flames and blood that even Iris thought it should be warm to the touch. Dozens of gray slashes, many dug deeply into the thick colors underneath, seemed to spill from the middle of the top of the painting all the way to the edges.

"No idea," Iris said, rubbing her upper arms. "Makes me a little anxious even though I painted it."

"Of course it does," Gena said, turning back to the painting and nodding. "If it were bigger, there'd be thousands of dead bodies. Maybe millions. All coming right toward you."

Iris gasped and stepped closer. Her fingers brushed against Gena's arm, but neither of them moved away. That word, *dead*, dropped like a ball of ice through her middle. It was no less true than *family*. She wanted to avoid the unknown slaughter more than she wanted to be part of that family.

Iris knew in her gut the slaughter was coming anyway.

"How are you doing that?" she said, looking into Gena's lovely brown eyes. "I don't even know what they mean. I just wake up with them in my head and I have to get them out."

"I don't know, seems obvious to me. Listen, why don't you mark them as sold. We can work out the price over dinner if you want."

Iris knew, in a flash of understanding as clear as any of the visions she woke up with, that Gena would understand a lot more than her paintings.

Chapter 3

Dinner with Gena led to a date, then another. Before autumn turned into winter, they were spending weekends together at one apartment or the other. None of the boys or girls Iris had dated in high school were worth the trouble after a couple of months. Now hours spent driving didn't frustrate Iris nearly as much as time spent apart.

That frustration led to her first painting that passed into reality.

Iris woke early on the Sunday morning of the first heavy snow in December. Getting out of her bed, away from Gena's warmth and sweet-smelling hair spreading across the pillows, was the last thing Iris wanted.

But the visions never let her sleep in.

She kissed Gena's cheek, then got dressed as quietly as she could. Iris had gotten into the habit of keeping her cleanest painting clothes by the door for days like this. If she finished quickly enough, she might be able to sneak back into bed before Gena was awake.

The apartment's second bedroom, with hardly any space and far too much morning light to be a good place to sleep, was perfect for a miniature studio. Iris kept as much as she could ready in advance, so she could start the coffee then pick up a brush. A sketchpad and colored pencils were a workable substitute at Gena's place.

Several inches of snow turned up the light in the already bright room, shifting it far toward cool blue. That suited the image nearly blinding Iris's mind. Her thoughts wandered as she worked. Her early morning painting was as automatic as the coffee maker.

Even with the tiny electric car on hands-free for the drive between Hidden Springs and Bountyfield, letting Iris read or study or even sleep, the time away from Gena was driving her crazy. And the loneliness she'd felt around her edges for most of her life was far deeper and stronger now that she had someone she missed so badly. Gena had two and a half more years of law school, Iris three and a half of art school.

Something had to change.

Before she'd finished her second cup of coffee and just as she finished the painting, Gena slipped her arms around Iris's waist.

"That's lovely," she whispered. "Perfect for our first house together. You dreamed about that last night, too."

Iris turned in Gena's arms.

"I don't remember any dreams. I hardly ever do."

"You dream all the time," Gena said. She kissed Iris's cheek, then poured herself a cup of coffee. "It's the ones you talk about that show up in your paintings, though."

"You never told me I talk in my sleep."

"I only noticed it a couple of weeks ago." Gena sat on the worn and faded red loveseat, curling her legs beneath her. "We're not sleeping together nearly enough, or I might have caught it sooner."

"What did I say?" Iris said, sitting beside Gena. "We need to find a house?"

"No, nothing that concrete. It didn't make sense until I saw the painting. You said things like 'It's blue,' 'Three of them,' and 'Thirty-seven miles.'" Gena leaned forward with a coffee-scented kiss. "I say there's no reason to get out in this lovely snow anyway. If we're lucky, we won't be able to get out tomorrow. Let's get online and find that house."

～

THEY MOVED IN TOGETHER before the holidays. The house was indeed blue, with three bedrooms, and thirty-seven miles from Bountyfield. Almost perfectly in the middle of their two schools. Thick trees and seclusion, hidden at the end of the road in a narrow valley, reminded Iris of the best parts of living in Maple Ridge.

Iris did well in her classes, gaining skill in conventional subjects and techniques. The far more important work never left that cozy little house. Sleeping beside Gena turned up the frequency on the visions Iris often worked with, or perhaps cleared out the channel. Either way, her true paintings increased in depth and frequency.

Not all of the paintings, or the dreams, were so positive.

Joyful and happy images continued to appear, but as time passed, the tone turned darker. Gena understood more of each distressing image, and Iris felt the unease of the dreams even though she rarely remembered them.

The world around them reflected the images within.

Food shortages unheard of since the pollinator crisis of the Twenties threatened, then materialized the next winter. Their corner of far southwestern Virginia escaped the riots and starvation, but no one escaped the worry.

Before another year passed, disease joined hunger in Iris's nightmares, on canvas and in her sleep. Turmoil increased in the outside world as well. Death tolls rose to the millions in the US, billions worldwide, as much from violence as hunger and illness. By the time both the law school and the art institute suspended operations in the fall, with the hopes of resuming when things calmed down, neither Iris nor Gena expected they'd ever be graduating.

Along with most people on a planet with a fatally broken food chain, their only hope for the future was surviving.

Chapter 4

Iris paced in front of a huge canvas covered with what looked like several inverted tornados, black and gray and bruised purple. The perspective was strange, with the largest one also the closest, just to the left of center. She not only couldn't remember the dream, this time she barely remembered picking up her brush.

"Did I say which this happens in?" Iris said, shivering as she stared at the painting. "Maple Ridge or Wolf Branch?"

"No, honey, you didn't. Same with the one with the prison a couple of days ago. I couldn't tell which. But I think you're right. It's one or the other."

That prison painting had clusters of dots ranging from a dozen in palest white, more in shades of pink, and a handful in a vivid crimson. Those seemed to glow against the brooding background.

"I don't know what to do," Iris said. She paced back and forth, looking at all of the true images, growing stranger and more upsetting as the months passed. "If we go up there with food riots just a few hours away, we might not ever get back. I don't know what the hell the two of us could do about this anyway."

"How long since you've heard from your parents?" Gena caught Iris's hand, then pulled her into a hug.

"The phones have been out for the last couple of weeks," Iris said. She let out her breath in a rush, trying not to cry. "They had it pretty bad over the winter. Trees probably took out the phone lines. Maybe the power lines too."

"That's not what you're dreaming. Nothing as simple as trees. Something's wrong. Those three paintings go together."

"We just have to figure out why," Iris said. "Sounds simple enough."

She stood in front of the first one she'd done just over a week ago. Most of the canvas was dark orange, with streaks and spots of red and yellow cutting through it. The motion of the brush and the way the colors mixed created a feeling of velocity, of movement. Iris didn't need Gena's remarkable insight to know time was running out on whatever was heading toward them.

"What do you see here now?" she said. "Any different after the one from this morning?"

Gena stood beside Iris with her arm around her waist. They might have been enjoying an art exhibit in some exotic city if the air in her lungs wasn't thick with dread.

"It *is* different. This is a change, a huge transition. Whatever happens here, or doesn't happen, is going to affect everything else. You've heard the gloom and doom news reports about all of us dying out before someone figures out how to stop that disease from the corn?"

"I have," Iris whispered. "They say the tipping point may have already passed."

"This convergence or explosion or whatever it is feels like *it* will be the tipping point. For everyone."

Iris groaned, trying to turn away, but Gena locked her fingers together around her waist. This was too much, for her or anyone else to handle.

"No, don't run away. Tell me what you see here, Iris. What you *feel*."

"I feel like we can't do a damn thing about that one," she said, jerking her chin at the orange painting. "We will all live or die according to what happens there, but we can't make it better or worse. What the hell was the point, then?"

"No, hang on," Gena said. "Look at them together. That and the one from this morning. Look at the colors."

Iris closed her eyes, resisting the urge to slip out of Gena's grasp and walk away. Her unwillingness to deal with her own dreams and visions certainly didn't give her any right to be so rude to her lover. Especially not when Gena was usually right. She opened her eyes, deliberately not focusing on either.

Iris blinked and drew back.

"The red spots," she said, stepping closer. Iris was glad Gena moved with her. "They're the same. Aren't they?"

She moved forward and picked up the orange canvas at the same time Gena picked up the purple and black one. They put them on a double easel they'd made months ago, back when art shows were still possible there or anywhere else in the world.

The dark red spots in both paintings matched perfectly.

"You're right, Gena. They do go together."

"This is something we have to do," Gena said. "Don't you feel that? I don't know what or where, but we can't just ignore this."

Iris's dreams brought the answer that night.

Chapter 5

The room and the window across from the bed were still dark when Iris woke. The clock was dark, too, yet another power outage. She sat up, trying her best not to wake Gena, but she felt a hand on her shoulder.

"You know, don't you?"

"Did I say something?" Iris said, snuggling with Gena again.

"Yeah. 'We have to go,' over and over again. I still don't know which town, but I feel it in my gut. We can't stay here any longer."

"I'm sorry, Gena. About waking you, dragging you into this craziness, not making any sense half the time. You don't have to go up on that damned mountain with me, you know. Your brother's place in Hidden Springs has plenty of room, and he'd be glad to have you with him."

Gena laughed, the low, throaty sound of it stirring up heat through Iris's body despite her nervousness.

"I'm not going anywhere you're not," Gena said. She kissed Iris, hard and deep. Her warm mouth was almost enough to keep Iris in bed instead of stumbling through the darkness into a cold studio. Almost.

"You do know where we're going. You just haven't caught it yet."

"I know where…" Iris said, her mind fogged with sleep and lust.

"Up on that mountain. Come on, gorgeous. Look at something with me."

Each of them grabbed a flashlight, and Iris headed into the studio. The sky was brightening from indigo to pale pink, but it wasn't nearly bright enough to see by yet.

"Can you get the orange one, please?" Iris said as she picked up the purple and black painting. "This will be easier than taking the other one down."

"You mean *Family*, don't you?"

One of the few paintings they'd framed properly hung over the sofa. The shades of green coordinated with the burgundy fabric as if they were made for each other. Iris put her smaller canvas on the cushions, and Gena did the same.

"Just like you said yesterday," Iris said, aiming her flashlight. "Look at the colors."

Gena moved her own beam between the three paintings, not saying anything for several seconds. Iris knew she'd seen it when she grabbed her hand, squeezing tight.

"They match," Gena whispered. "They all match."

Iris stepped forward and picked up the orange painting. She rotated it clockwise until the placement of the red spots matched the red in the larger one. Another turn, and those matched the black spots in *Family*. The same worked for the brown and the yellow markings. She'd never noticed her repetitive pattern in that original painting.

"I don't suppose it's any more strange than you painting this house before we ever saw it," Gena said. "But what the hell is going on here?"

"Whatever we have to do in Maple Ridge goes along with the rest. One leads to the other, I think."

"Or one makes the other possible," Gena said.

As always, her words caught the chaos in Iris's mind, transforming it into harmony.

"For us and everyone else. I don't have a clue what we're supposed to do, though."

"Well, you did say you haven't heard from your family up there,"

Gena said. "We pack up all this food we've been stockpiling, and whatever else will fit in your big art show van. Then we go up there and see what else falls into place."

"I hope you're right. We could be driving right into a waking nightmare."

Chapter 6

Iris wasn't quite sure if her suggestion was based on a real feeling from her dreams, or from a need to put off the drive up the mountain. Gena either agreed or she was just as nervous. They set the van to drive through Wolf Branch on the way to Maple Ridge, telling themselves it was to make sure that wasn't their destination.

The four lane road through rolling farm country crested a ridge, then followed a wide, gentle curve down toward the Grasspe River. As the van came out of the shadow of a deep road cut, Wolf Branch opened up all around them. The town was as beautiful as ever, even with trees barren for winter.

Tucked into the bend of the river, the small grid of streets followed the gradual rise away from the banks. More buildings and houses followed the contour of the mountains that surrounded downtown, with Iris's high school at one end and the small hospital at the other. No one seemed to be on the streets today.

Several mountains rose up all around, creating a sheltered bowl for the community that felt almost as much like home as Maple Ridge did.

"You should see it in the spring and fall," Iris said as the van slowed, turning right and heading into town. "I'm sorry I never brought you over here for that."

"I'm not so sure we won't be back here, Iris. Don't you feel that?"

Iris glanced at Gena. She had one hand on her chest, gazing out at the neat rows of brick buildings. The pull in Iris's mind, and in her body, was strong to stay right there and not continue on to Maple Ridge. It didn't feel like fear, not really.

This felt like comfort. Like home.

"I do feel it," Iris said. "A pressure in my chest. A good one, like right before I met you."

Gena snorted, but she was smiling.

"That's your high school?"

The three story dark red brick building sat at the highest point on the east end of town, with two matching smaller buildings on either side. A huge flat area off to the side held the football, baseball, and softball fields, with everything painted the same purple and gold Iris remembered so fondly.

A low, white building with *Wolf Branch Cannery* freshly painted in matching purple sat across the high school parking lot. The whole area was much cleaner and more inviting than Iris remembered, with a huge garden area and a greenhouse beside it. Rows of greens, hardy long past frost and snow, still waited for harvest.

"That's it," Iris said. "Everything looks the same, but I don't remember that garden by the cannery."

"A cannery? You mean like canning food?"

"Yeah, they used to be everywhere. This one was open before I went to school here. I remember my grandmother driving down here to can deer meat years ago. Looks like someone is smart enough to have it running again."

Gena wrinkled her nose. "Did you say deer meat?"

"I sure did, smart ass. You wouldn't be a snob about it if you tasted the stew she made in the middle of the winter. There were more deer up there than people, anyway."

"That's probably true most places now, about the deer," Gena said. "No one can be a food snob anymore."

Iris hated to hear that gloomy edge in her voice. Movement caught her eye a few streets away. People were streaming out of the

Episcopal church by the time they passed by, the women's dresses and everyone's smiles too bright for a funeral.

"I think we may have crashed a wedding," Iris said.

"Wow. People in Wolf Branch are more optimistic about the future than I am lately."

"Maybe we can do something about that." She took Gena's hand, glancing in the rearview mirror. She never spotted a typical huge white wedding dress, but that many happy people in the middle of the week couldn't be anything else. "Then maybe it will be our turn."

"If we get off of your mountain alive, I'll hold you to that."

Chapter 7

THE VIEWS on the drive up to Maple Ridge were as stunning as ever, maybe even more so. But the feeling couldn't have been more different to Iris. The pressure in her body shifted lower, from warm and comforting to hot and threatening, more so with every twist in the narrow road.

Iris had to disable the autonav so she could drive around many of the potholes, and increasing elevation had her slowing to maneuver through cracks all the way across the faded asphalt.

"Has the road ever been this bad before?" Gena said, holding on to the door as the van rocked over another massive rut. "Looks like it's about to fall off the mountain."

"I've never seen it like this," Iris said. She kept forcing her hands to relax on the wheel, but her shoulders and jaw wouldn't obey her. "Winter's barely started. This has to be from last year and never repaired."

"I'm sorry we didn't get up here more often. We might have seen some of this coming."

"That's not your doing, Gena, don't apologize." She tried her best to keep disgust with herself for not visiting since the previous holidays out of her voice. "We've both been pretty damn busy over the last couple of years. No one besides my parents has made the effort to visit us, either."

The last switchback should have brought only the straight road heading into town into view, with the ever changing models of wind turbines snaking through the ridges. Or at least they had been changing, when people had time and resources enough for testing new designs.

Iris slowed the van to a near stop when she saw a man and a woman standing on either side of the road. Both wore brown scarves that covered most of their faces and carried what looked like old assault rifles.

"What the hell is going up here?" Gena said, gripping Iris's arm.

"Try to look calm. They've already seen us."

The woman spoke into some kind of radio, then walked toward the van. Iris tried to keep her own breath under control as she drove forward. She stopped and rolled her window down an inch when the woman held up her hand. The fierce wind that always blew across the ridge carried the strong odor of menthol cigarettes into Iris's face.

"Some kind of trouble?" Iris said.

"Up to you," the woman said. The rifle was slung over her chest, but she kept her fingers loosely over the trigger guard. "What business you got up here?"

"I grew up here. Haven't been able to reach my family for a couple of weeks. Figured it was time to come check on them."

"Phones down just about everywhere, I guess." She leaned forward and stared at Gena, then looked back at Iris. "Who you up here to see?"

"My parents. I'm not sure why I have to announce myself to get back to my own house."

"Things change here like everywhere when the world goes to hell. Doing what we can to keep Maple Ridge safe. Who'd you say your folks are?"

Iris glanced at Gena, horrified that she'd brought her into whatever this mess turned out to be. Gena should be safe and warm at her brother's house in Hidden Springs. Not facing down fucking assault rifles on a ridge in the middle of nowhere.

"I *didn't* say. Listen, we can head right back down the mountain, no trouble at all. We didn't come up here to cause problems."

The man walked slowly toward them, scarf pulled down to his neck, hand on his own rifle. Iris recognized him from high school when she saw his spiky brown hair and smug asshole grin. Matt… something. A few years older than her, constantly in trouble here, down in Wolf Branch, even as far away as Hidden Springs. Fighting, drinking, assault, even stealing. The dread in her gut sank deeper, threatening to drag her down through the seat.

The woman shook her head. "Well, won't be a problem unless you try to turn this thing around. Tell me who you're here to see. I'll let 'em know you're coming. You two don't much look like thieves. Never can tell these days."

The man, Matt, stopped outside the passenger window. He didn't move, but he didn't take his eyes off Gena, either. His grin deepened into a leer. That was enough.

"I'm here to see Carol and Sid Rutherford," Iris said. "They've lived here their whole lives, just like the rest of my family going back a couple hundred years."

"Thought you might be Iris," the woman said, nodding. Iris still couldn't recognize her face behind that scarf. "Ain't seen you around much since you graduated high school."

"Yeah, I've been real busy. Sure would like to know your name since I can't see your face."

The woman stared at Iris for several seconds, then nodded at Matt. He walked back toward town.

"Suppose you can find out easy enough. Name's Haga. Couple of years behind you in school. We'll make sure your folks know you're on the way."

"I'd appreciate that," Iris said. "We'll see you on the way back out."

"Sure you will."

She stepped back and gestured toward town with the gun. Iris managed not to stomp the accelerator pedal with her shaking legs.

"What the hell," Gena said, her voice just as shaky. "Did she say her name was Haga?"

Iris watched the rear view mirror for several seconds, until she couldn't see those damned rifles anymore. Where did they even get those things?

"Yeah, she always was an odd duck. Her name is Hanna Garrett, but I remember that Haga stuff from years ago. I'd like to know who thought it was a good idea to give her a gun. That guy Matt is a thousand times worse, staring at you like that. I should have left you at your brother's house whether you wanted me to or not."

"What, so you could disappear up here and I'd never hear from you again? I'm harder to get rid of than that."

The road curved to the right, passing through a stand of huge sugar maple trees. Several rows of brick or white clapboard houses lay just beyond. Maple Ridge was every bit as deserted as Wolf Branch, but Iris didn't think for a second people were gathered out of sight for something as positive as a wedding.

"Something's wrong here," she said under her breath.

The street wasn't as damaged as the road into town, but leaves and debris were piled up along the gutters and drifting across. The usually neat yards in front of the small houses didn't look any better, with branches on the tall grass and several windows boarded up. Iris would have thought it was just another dead logging town.

If there were any reason to have armed guards in front of one.

"What do you feel here, hon?" Gena said. "I can't say I'm feeling a warm welcome."

"I'm feeling like we should keep driving straight through and get out of here. I doubt they left the back road open after all that nonsense."

She turned off a Main Street with rows of shops that looked every bit as abandoned as the houses. Just behind the shops, the two-story Craftsman homes built for long-ago timber barons still stood. The broad lawns and deep porches were in a little better shape, but Iris had never seen her street looking so shabby and abandoned.

She'd also never seen a man carrying another of the old military rifles walking out of her parents' house.

"Stay in the van," Iris said, shutting down the engine.

"Like hell I will. You forget I'm a grown-ass woman, Iris, four years older than you. You go out there, I'm going with you."

Much as she wanted to argue, that tone told Iris it was useless. She got out and activated the security system as the man drew even with her.

No, not a man. Dale Hileman had been a couple of years behind Iris in school, so he was barely seventeen. He smirked as he walked by.

"Come on," she whispered, grabbing Gena's hand. "It's not safe out here."

Dale whistled as he strolled down the street, as if he were walking in a park in the middle of July with a picnic basket. The door opened as soon as Iris stepped onto the porch.

"Get inside," her father said in a low voice. He locked the door, then hugged Iris hard enough to make her spine crackle, then did the same to Gena. His black hair had gone mostly gray in the months since Iris had seen him. "I'm glad to know you're safe, but I wish you hadn't come here."

"What's going on out there, Dad?" Iris said. "People everywhere with guns?"

"Come on through, your mother will want to see you. I wish we could offer you something to eat."

"We brought a bunch of food with us," Gena said.

Iris's father stopped in his tracks, then slowly turned. Lines ran deep into his face, and his shirt was too loose on his frame.

"In your van? We can't leave it out there. It won't last ten minutes. Bring it around to the back yard. At least we can lock the gate and get everything inside."

Iris grabbed his arm as he headed back toward the front door.

"No, wait! Please tell me what's happening. Where's Mom?"

"Nothing that's not going on all over the world, Iris," he said, his voice shaking. "A few assholes have managed to put their own special redneck twist on it up here. With the way people are talking, no women are out on the streets unless they're part of the Asshole Squad. Your mother went down to the den in the basement when that kid knocked on the door."

"Then let's load you and Mom up and get the hell out of here," Iris said. She knew it was already too late for that, and had been from the second Haga saw the van. But she had to try. "Can we get out the back road?"

He shook his head, looking down. In that moment, he looked a hundred years old instead of in his fifties.

"They have a couple of their guards back there. I'm not sure why, though. They blew part of the road off the mountain a couple of weeks ago." He started toward the door again. "I'll tell you everything, what I know at least. But we have to get your van off the street."

Iris followed, tears blurring her vision. How could no one know about this? How could she not have known? She *had* brought Gena into the middle of hell.

"Where did they get explosives that strong?" Gena said as he stopped long enough to check the street before they went outside.

"Word is someone found a stash hidden in a cave not far from here," he said, walking out onto the porch. "Some lunatic must have raided all the mines as they closed down, roadwork jobs, even the armory over in Walton's Gap. They're smart enough to know how to use that old stuff and crazy enough to do it."

"But why force everyone to stay up here?" Iris used her touchkey to open the doors, not trusting her fingers to work the code. Her father's nervousness was seeping into her. "It won't last forever, but there's more food around here than most places in the US. Just not in Maple Ridge."

"They're not after food, not yet. Pull around the block, then go down the alley. They're trying to set up some kind of prison camp here, take charge and scare everyone. I get the feeling they'll steal food before they try to grow it. Steal people, too."

Iris gripped the steering wheel, her already aching hands protesting. She'd heard the family legends just like everyone else, about how the Rutherfords knew more than they should. Other people in Maple Ridge supposedly did, but not as much as her folks.

Asking her father so bluntly, so openly, still made her anxious.

"You get the *feeling* about all of this, Dad?" Iris said. "Or you've been dreaming about it?"

He didn't say anything until after he got out and opened the gate in the chain link fence behind the house. Gena gripped Iris's knee as she drove through.

"It's okay, hon," she said in a low voice. "I think you're on the right track."

Her father looked both sad and proud when he joined them by the back door.

"I always wondered if you'd inherited that," he said. He put his arm around her shoulders for a few seconds, then unlocked the back door of the house. "None of your cousins seemed to. Seemed strange that it would skip a whole generation."

"I didn't know until Gena told me about it," Iris said. Her head swam with both relief and curiosity. "That's what I've been painting all these years. The dreams."

"That's what brought you up here?" he said. "A painting?"

"A few of them," Iris said. "I didn't understand what they were, but Gena helped me figure it out. We brought them with us."

He looked from one to the other of them. He smiled, but his eyes were sad.

"Better get them inside too, then. Come on, let's see your Mom first. She'll take me out herself if we keep her waiting much longer."

Chapter 8

Iris's mother opened the basement door before any of them could knock. The den beyond was comfortable enough, with a couple of old couches, a big TV, and previous generations of gaming systems. It was also pitch dark and cold with the electricity out for the first time Iris could remember. The lantern her father carried didn't reach far.

"Carol, you need to keep this door locked unless you know it's me," he said, shaking his head.

She was thinner than usual, too, and the gray roots in her hair made the aging just as unsettling to Iris. She grabbed both young women at the same time in a breathless hug.

"I heard Iris on the stairs," she said when she stepped back. "Y'all kept me waiting long enough. What are you two *doing* here?"

"Iris has been dreaming about Maple Ridge," Gena said. "Or Wolf Branch. Probably both. We brought her paintings, and food."

"Come on back upstairs," Iris's father said. "We'll bring everything in, then you need to look at the paintings. See what they tell you."

The curtains were closed in the huge windows in the front of the house, something else Iris had hardly ever seen. A few oil lamps and flashlights made it bright enough to see the paintings.

"How can the power be out? Gena and I saw the turbines turning like usual on the way here."

"That's a fine question, isn't it?" Iris's mother said, scowling. "From what we can tell, the whole town is out. Except for the houses where the people with machine guns live, and their asshole fearless leaders."

"We're not sure about that yet, Carol." Iris's father hunched and relaxed his shoulders, so much smaller than Iris remembered. "But rumor is they're cutting power to Wolf Branch, too, but not all the time like here. Not sure why."

Gena and Iris sat close together on a beige loveseat near the roaring fireplace, trying to stay warm. Iris's mother paced back and forth in front of the paintings, very much like Iris herself often did.

"Something about this one," she said, stopping in front of the orange painting. "It's terrifying. But I'm not afraid of it."

"I was scared," Iris said. "Until we got up here. Something about being here, no matter what's going on, makes that one look a lot less threatening."

"I still don't care for the gray one," Gena said. "They all go together, though."

Iris's mother picked up the gray painting and rotated it, making the colorful spots match like Gena had.

"What did you say this first one was called, Iris?"

"We call if *Family*, but I don't know whose it will be yet."

"The two of you, I'd imagine," her father said. He didn't sound happy. "I think that would be wonderful if things were better. But we'll have to be careful with you here now."

"They're not actually saying that." Gena's face was pale.

"They're paying real close attention to the young women," Iris's mother said. "All the ones that are old enough, or not too old."

"There's not enough food here now," Iris said. She was too sick at her stomach at the thought to imagine eating anything. "What makes them think they'll need breeding stock?"

"I know," her mother said. "You remember Bill Hicks, used to run the convenience store here? And the sugar barn?"

"I remember he was a damn thief," Iris said, taking Gena's hand.

"Charged what he wanted when people had no other choice. Anytime there was a blizzard, his prices jumped up until the snow melted."

"Well, he's put himself in charge of everything up here," her father said. "Even rounded up everyone's hunting dogs, says he'll make sure they're fed and trained up *properly*. A lot like what he's trying to do to the humans. Most of us think Rita Hicks is helping run the show, but he's the one running his mouth."

"They're planning to raid somewhere close by for food," her mother said. "Probably Wolf Branch, but we're not sure. Between that and hunting with all those dogs, he figures he'll have enough to need the young women before much longer."

"He's just proclaiming this?" Gena said. "Not even trying to hide it?"

"Not in so many words, no," Iris's father said. He added another log to the fire, then sat on the couch beside the paintings, hands dangling between his knees. "Mostly a lot of talk about getting us all through this crisis that the outside world can't handle without a bunch of riots and killing."

"He hasn't killed anyone yet," her mother said. "Not that we know of. But no one doubts that he will."

They all jumped when someone knocked at the door. The pounding was hard enough to rattle the windows.

"Downstairs," Iris's father said, jumping to his feet. "All of you, go."

"I'm sorry we're causing so much trouble," Iris said, "but they know we're here. Won't hiding make it worse for you?"

"Come on, Sid." Her mother held out her hand. "She's right. I'm sick of hiding anyway."

He scowled, but he didn't argue. He did hold his arm out to keep everyone else behind him when he opened the door.

Haga stood on the porch, still carrying her rifle slung across her back. She'd pulled the brown scarf around her neck. The awkward school girl with acne and limp hair was long gone, a beautiful young woman taking her place. Haga's dark brown hair gleamed, and her skin was pale and flawless. The slight smile curving her full lips said she was fully aware of her transformation and how it affected others.

She showed no sign of the hungry gaunt look overtaking Iris's parents.

"Glad to see you're settling in," Haga said, nodding. "Want you to feel right at home."

"We were planning to take Mom and Dad down to Hidden Springs for the holidays," Iris said, stepping in front of her father. "We can bring supplies up to you when we come back. Just let us know what you need."

"Well, that sure is a generous offer, Iris. Not sure we'll be able to accommodate you there, but you never know about such things."

Iris's father put both hands on her shoulders, pulling back a tiny bit.

"What do you want, then?" he said. "Come inside out of the cold."

"Mr. Hicks and Mrs. Hicks want to welcome you both personally," Haga said. She made no move to step in and stop the slight heat from escaping. "They remember you fondly, Iris, and they'd like to meet your friend here."

"Maybe another time," Iris's mother said. "These two need a rest from the drive up."

"They've been awful busy, better all around if they come on in now." Haga shifted her arms enough to reveal a handgun in a holster around her waist. "Won't keep you long. We all need our rest for the hard times coming up."

Iris closed her eyes for a second, then looked back at Haga. Orange and red flames rose in a halo behind her shoulders and head, Iris's painting brought to moving, disturbing life. And the motion was pulling inward, not pushing Haga back out into the cold. The same feeling pulled like an anchor attached to Iris's spine.

"That's fine, send them in," she said. Her mother drew breath to speak and her father squeezed her shoulders, but she went on. "If we're going to be here a while, we should get to know folks."

"Just give us a minute?" Iris's mother said. "We can't offer you much, but I'll get something to drink."

"So kind of you." Haga's smile was full and confident this time. "I know they'll appreciate that as much as I do."

She stepped back and let Iris's father close the door. He turned to Iris, his brow drawn down.

"What the hell are you thinking?"

"Wait, just listen," Iris said. "If they're after breeding stock, they're not going to hurt us. Gena, can you please grab that bottle of rum we brought? We'll be as hospitable as we possibly can."

"No, this is ridiculous," Iris's mother said. She peeked out the living room window. "Bill in his damned SUV, uses up what little gas we can get anymore. What good can this possibly do?"

"I saw something," Iris said, trying to find the words. She took the bottle and glasses from Gena and arranged them on the coffee table. "Just now, flames raging all around her head. This has something to do with that orange painting. You saw as clear as we did that that one is important."

"You saw it, like a vision?" her father said.

"Right behind her, clear as I see you right now." Iris said. "That never happened to me before."

Her father stared into her eyes for several seconds, apparently finding what he needed to see. He gathered up all the paintings and hid them behind the couch.

"Sit with me," he said stepping over to the door. "Don't let them get between us."

Chapter 9

Bill Hicks had lost all of the dark brown in his thick, spiky hair since Iris had last seen him, but he was still every bit as intimidating. He'd grown a thick gray mustache to match, and he towered over her father.

Rita Hicks could easily be mistaken for someone's kindly youngish grandmother, with her blond-streaked-with-gray hair pulled back in a sensible ponytail. She was almost six feet tall herself, and her figure was soft and matronly. That softness did not extend to her pale gray eyes.

"You remember Iris," Haga said, closing the door behind her. "I didn't catch her friend's name."

"I didn't give it," Iris said. She sat on the couch between her mother and Gena, with her father sitting on the arm.

"I'm Gena Wallace."

"I'm certainly glad to see you again, Iris, and to meet you, Gena," Mr. Hicks said. He and his wife sat on the loveseat close to the fire. Neither of them removed their heavy denim coats. "What a pleasant surprise in the middle of difficult times to see both of you up here."

Haga stood by the door, her guns too visible to forget. Iris didn't want her parents any more involved than they already were.

"I'll be honest," Iris said. "We came up here to bring my parents back to our place. Looks like they're not getting enough to eat."

"Well, that's been a problem, with such trouble out in the world," Mrs. Hicks said. Neither she nor her husband looked like they'd missed a meal. "That won't be a problem much longer."

"Then you don't mind if we make it a little bit easier," Iris said. "Give you four less mouths to feed."

Mrs. Hicks leaned forward and picked up the bottle of rum. She filled the seven small glasses with a half-smile.

"Seems like you're pretty direct, just like when you were in school," she said, pushing a glass toward Iris. "So I'll do the same. We'll have plenty to eat and a safe place to raise new little mouths. You two are perfect for that."

Iris tossed the tall shot back. The rum was cold and burning, but she managed to keep a straight face. Everyone else picked up their glasses. Both of her parents' hands were shaking.

"You might be missing an important point here," Gena said. She took Iris's hand in her clammy one. "Iris and I are engaged. The battle over telling people who they could and couldn't marry ended forty years ago."

"I don't give a damn about who you marry," Mr. Hicks said. He leaned back and crossed his long legs at the ankles. "No one else does, either."

"See, this isn't a question of anyone's battles." Mrs. Hicks poured herself another full shot. "Some people still carry on about religion and the law, but none of that matters anymore. All that fuss and nonsense is in the past. I'm afraid all you got left now is biology. And that's exactly what you're going to fulfill."

"I think we've heard just about enough," Iris's father said. He leaned forward, but he didn't stand. "No one in this house is interested in your little project, Bill."

"Interested or not doesn't matter anymore, either," Mrs. Hicks said. "In case you haven't noticed, the world is in the process of tearing itself to pieces all around us. I'd wager we'll see more people dead than alive by the end of this winter."

"I dreamed of you coming back home, Iris," Mr. Hicks said.

Cold sweat covered Iris, but she tried her best not to show it. She wondered if these two were among the dead bodies in her paintings.

"Did you now?" she said in a reasonably calm voice.

"You and your friend here," he said. "I didn't know who she was, but the dream was clear as day. I saw the two of you with many healthy children. Those babies will be the salvation of all of us."

Iris clenched her fist until her hand ached. She wished for more of the rum, but she didn't want everyone to see how badly she was shaking.

Those words sounded true to her. They felt true, in her whole body and mind. Gena's trembling against her said she felt the same.

"Well, all this talk and we lost sight of why we dropped by in the first place," Mrs. Hicks said. She had the same broad, perfect smile she used to welcome tourists to their overpriced shops in town. "You must be worn out from that long drive with so much going bad out in the world. Hadn't seen your folks in a while, Iris, been so busy. I think you're right. I'm sorry to say they're looking a bit unwell."

"We brought you all a good supply of food." Mr. Hicks nodded at Haga, then tossed his shot of rum back. "Should be enough for several fine meals for all of you. Wouldn't want anyone to get too thin and unhealthy now that you're safe and sound back home."

Haga lowered her head and smiled at Iris, her eyes sharp as any predator's. She stepped outside for a few seconds, then came back in with Dale Hileman, smug Matt from the guard post on the main road, and one other man Iris didn't recognize. All of them carried boxes filled with food into the kitchen.

And they all had the old machine guns slung over their backs.

"We brought plenty of food for the four of us," Gena said, her voice strong. "Maybe the neighbors could use this instead."

"That's a generous offer," Mrs. Hicks said, standing. "Gena, isn't it? We want to make sure everyone here is safe and healthy."

Her husband stood beside her.

"In fact, we'll leave two of our finest guards here to make sure of it," he said. "Iris, you already know Haga, and I believe you know Dale, too. They'll take the first shift. If you need anything at all, you just let one of them know. They'll take care of it."

"Glad to be of service," Dale said. His smile slipped past leering into predatory. Matt stood shoulder to shoulder with him, grinning before he actually winked at Iris.

"You two get settled in and don't worry about a single thing," Mrs. Hicks said. "We're taking care of everything to make sure Maple Ridge is the safest place in the world for you and all of your children."

Chapter 10

IRIS WALKED from one side of her childhood bedroom to the other, doing her best to avoid the wooden floorboards that squeaked. Nine steps, from the shelf-covered wall that still held many of the books and toys she'd outgrown a decade before to the nearly floor to ceiling windows at the back of the house. She was thankful she'd replaced the frilly little girl purple curtains with sensible blue panels before she moved out.

"Iris, honey, you got to come to bed."

Dim light from an oil lamp on the nightstand showed Gena, already burrowed down in the heavy blankets that matched the curtains. The full-sized mattress was a close but cozy fit for both of them, and her lover's warmth in the frigid house was tempting.

The sharp aftermath of the coffee she'd had too much of with dinner didn't feel like quite enough to keep her awake if she got too comfortable.

Iris switched directions instead, her bare feet numb with the cold. Twelve steps this way, from the bathroom door to the hall door, both still full of tiny holes where she'd hung countless of her smaller paintings over the years. For the first time in her life, Iris wasn't curious about the next thing her mind would create. She was too horrified by what she could already feel coming.

"It's after midnight and I'm freezing to death," Gena said. "There's nothing more either of us can do tonight."

"I know that, Gena. I know. We never should have come up here in the first place."

That was a lie, one Iris wasn't comfortable telling herself anymore. Every part of her knew she was exactly where she was supposed to be, and that Gena was too. That didn't make the danger for everybody in Maple Ridge any easier to take. Or the idea of going to sleep any less terrifying.

"Maybe not, but we *are* here." Gena sat up, clutching the blankets under her chin. "Neither of us will be any damn good tomorrow if we don't get some rest. What's wrong with you?"

Iris stopped beside one of the windows, wishing it weren't too cold to open it. She'd stared out at the trees behind the house for hours as a kid, watching the way they moved together, listening to them whisper to each other. Anything to quiet her whirling mind before she'd known picking up a paint brush would do that. Now bringing the looming vision into reality was the last thing she wanted.

"I'm afraid to go to sleep," she whispered.

"Come here and talk to me about it, then," Gena said. She held out one hand. "You're driving me crazing pacing like that."

"I'm driving *me* crazy too." Iris sat on the bed and took Gena's warm hand. "I don't know what else to do."

"Listen to me. At least come here and keep me warm for a little while. Why are you afraid, sweetheart?"

Gena put both arms around Iris's shoulders. The heat of her body was too much to resist.

"I know what you're trying to do," Iris said.

She slipped under the covers anyway. They both wore thick flannel pajamas scavenged from her father's old clothes.

"Don't you touch me with those ice feet," Gena said, and Iris could hear her smile from the long-standing joke between them. "I'm trying to keep from freezing to death. Now tell me what's going on."

Iris let Gena pull her back against the cushioned purple headboard, a remnant of her middle school decorating scheme that hadn't yet been replaced. Her legs and lower back ached with cold and tension.

"I'm not sure how to say it," she said. "I feel like I'm dreaming already. Like part of my brain is taken over even when my eyes are still open. This is not going to be a good dream."

"Maybe it's just stress." Gena kissed the top of her head. "The last few weeks have been a nightmare. Today certainly was."

"I don't think so. It's more than that." Iris tried to wipe her tears before Gena saw them. "I don't *want* to see what's coming. Not anymore."

The truth was agony had settled into Iris's chest, the worst broken-hearted longing she'd ever experienced. She didn't want to dream of the horrible loss heading toward them, even if she didn't remember when she woke. She wasn't certain she'd survive pain so deep once she knew what was going to cause it.

"Shhhhh, I got you," Gena whispered into her ear. "I'm not going anywhere, no matter what happens."

"You don't know that," Iris said, not bothering to stop her tears now. "No one feels safe to me. We're in the middle of something terrible here."

"And yet we have to be here, right? We both knew that before we left."

"Yeah, we have to be here. I still feel that. But I don't want to know why anymore."

"I have an idea," Gena said. She scooted down under the covers. "Keep me warm for a little while. See how you feel if you stay still and listen to my heartbeat. I know I'll feel a hell of a lot better than shivering under here by myself."

"For a little while," Iris whispered.

She had every intention of getting back up as soon as Gena fell asleep, maybe even going back downstairs for more of the cheap, bitter coffee the guards brought with them. A few minutes curled up around Gena, face against her breasts, the soothing rhythm of a heartbeat in her ear, left Iris barely able to keep her eyes open. The long, difficult, frightening day and rich, heavy meal settled into her limbs, pulling her under despite her fear. Her sleep was sound and deep.

The dream threatened without coming to life in her mind, or under her brush, that night or the next few.

Iris didn't truly see what was coming until only minutes before the nightmare burst into reality.

Chapter 11

The routine was the worst part. Every day exactly the same, with no promise or even a threat of change. Bill and Rita Hicks didn't return, but the rotating pair of guards never left, each shift bringing fresh supplies. Iris's mother seethed at the repeated deliveries of food they hadn't seen in town for months, but none of them refused the meals.

Worry about what the cost would turn out to be never left any of them.

Iris's father walked along Main Street at least once every day, usually at dawn, hoping for news from the outside. None of the other local men outside the makeshift militia had heard anything. The fear in his eyes when he begged the three of them to stay inside worked, but Iris wasn't the only one losing patience with virtual imprisonment.

Books, games, even painting failed to distract any of them for more than a few minutes.

Even with her odd senses, and Gena's, telling her they had to stay, Iris's mind twisted and writhed, desperate for a way out. By the end of the week, she was ready to beg for something, anything different.

The long-anticipated and dreaded dream left her wanting to beg for dull routine to return.

Iris opened her eyes in the frigid pre-dawn light, looking right into Gena's. Her lover sat against that absurd headboard, arms wrapped around her knees.

"You know," Gena whispered.

"I don't remember anything. What did I say?"

Gena shook her head.

"What do you see, Iris? A new painting?"

Cold worse than the chilly room moved from Iris's heart out through her body, raising gooseflesh all over.

"No, not a new one." She shivered, but Gena didn't move closer. "I see the one with the gray tornadoes."

"Same one I see," Gena whispered. "But they're moving now."

Both women jumped at a sharp rap on the door.

"Wake up," Iris's mother said, her voice sharp. "Come on now."

Iris opened the door before she could knock again. Carol Rutherford's hair stood on end and her cheek still held pillow creases. She held a flashlight in one hand and clutched her heavy blue robe tight against her chest with the other.

"Something's going on in town," she said, glancing over her shoulder. Iris could hear her father moving around downstairs. "They're rounding women and children up. Your Dad heard they're taking us to the sugar barn."

"What for?" Gena said. Her grip on Iris's hand was painfully tight.

"Dad heard where they're taking us?" Iris said. "Where are they taking *him*?"

Her mother's face clenched tight for a second, then she shook her head.

"No one knows, or at least they're not saying. He thinks we don't have long, so gather up what you can before the guards come charging in here."

She walked down the hall toward their bedroom, her feet silent in thick wool socks.

"The sugar barn?" Gena said, her teeth chattering. "Where they sell the maple syrup?"

"Yeah, sell it, make it, store it, the works." Iris pushed the door shut. She nearly ran into the bathroom, stepped up onto the toilet, and reached on top of the medicine cabinet. "I used to work weekends helping cook it down, out in the store selling it. Painted a few advertisements for them once I started college."

After a few panicked seconds of fumbling, her fingers brushed against ridged metal. Iris pulled the ring into her hand and stepped down, blowing dust away from two keys.

"I pretended I lost these my last year working in the back," she said. The keys jangled when she dropped them onto her dresser. "I had no idea why at the time. Not sure why I'm getting them now, either."

"Any advantage can't hurt," Gena said. Both women pulled on jeans, t-shirts, and flannel shirts, and Iris tucked the keys into the tiny watch pocket at her hip. "Has your Dad heard what they're planning to do?"

"Not that he's told me." Iris sat on the bed and pulled Gena down beside her. "Listen, you were upset when I woke up. What did I say, Gena? Come on, I need to know what we're walking into here while we can still warn him."

Gena hesitated, staring at the floor before she met Iris's gaze.

"You said something about a grandfather," she said. "Their grandfather."

Iris felt a hollow space in her middle, an odd fit to her lover's words. That was the truth, but maybe not all of it. Before she could say anything, a heavier knock startled her.

"Time to go," her father said.

He wore heavy work pants and a lined winter jacket, and he held leather work gloves. The gauntness was leaving his face after several days of steady meals, but the bruised hollows under his eyes had only gotten worse.

"Same place you're going?" Iris said, watching him closely.

"I don't know. I don't think so. Just dress warm."

Haga and Dale Hileman stood in the living room, both holding their rifles for the first time since Iris and Gena arrived. A sullen glare had replaced Dale's smug grin. Iris saw the swirling flames behind both of them, even stronger than before. She was honestly surprised she couldn't feel the heat in the freezing cold room.

"Move it now," Dale said. "Don't want to keep 'em waiting."

"Who would we be keeping, Dale?" Iris's mother said, coming down the stairs behind them. "I'd like to know where my family is being dragged at the ass crack of dawn. And why the hell we should go with you in the first place."

"You go where I say and when I say," Dale said, his voice rising. "Unless you want to see your daughter and her pretty little friend living up to their biology right here and now!"

Dale lunged forward.

Sid Rutherford pushed Iris and Gena back and stepped in front of his wife.

"That's enough," Haga said. She never moved, and her voice wasn't loud, but Dale froze. "Every one of you settle down."

The younger man stood inches from Iris's father, face red and fists clenched. Iris smelled strong coffee on his breath, and stronger whiskey.

"I said settle down, Dale." Haga's voice was calm, but Dale stepped back, shaking his head. "These two won't go to the likes of you, and you know it."

"Then what's the damn point?" Dale shoved the front door open hard enough that it slammed against the wall.

"The point is for each and every one of us to do our part so we all have a future," Haga said. She jerked her chin toward the door. "Do your job, and you'll get your reward. We all will. Keep causing trouble, and you'll pay the price."

Iris knew her words were meant for Dale, but Haga stared at her and her family. Dale's rifle was now slung over his back. Haga carried hers over one shoulder. Much easier and faster to reach.

Especially with Haga's calm demeanor, Iris had no doubt which of the two was in charge.

And who would make sure that price was paid.

Chapter 12

They walked in silence, the two guards behind them. The feeble winter sun still hadn't risen at nearly seven. Iris recognized other families heading toward the middle of town, each with their own armed escorts. Everyone moving in the same direction, at least for now.

Iris forced her free hand to her side, away from the small bulge in her pocket.

When they turned onto Main Street, Iris saw two groups forming in the distance. Women and children in front of the log-fronted sugar barn, and men beside the brick school building on the other side of a graveled parking lot. Guards surrounded both, but the ones around the men held their rifles in their hands rather than slung over their shoulders.

"Taking volunteers, are you?" her mother said. She held her husband's hand, her knuckles white.

"Call it whatever you want to," Haga said from behind them. "Won't make a damn bit of difference in the end."

A low moan ahead of them caught all of Iris's attention. A vaguely familiar woman pushed against the guards by the barn, trying to get to two men walking toward the school. The older man put his arm around the younger, keeping him from turning back.

"Sam Williams," Iris's father said under his breath. "And his youngest boy, Ben."

The woman ahead of them, Sam's mother, wailed again. Bill Hicks broke away from the crowd of men, Matt with his grin close behind. Bill held one arm low, out of sight behind his body. Rita Hicks moved from the middle of the women, closer to Mrs. Williams.

"Ben was in school with me." Iris tried to will Ben's mother to be still, be quiet. She didn't want to see how the disruption would be dealt with.

When Ben's mother cried out again, Rita Hicks put her arm around the much smaller woman's shoulders. Iris was close enough to see Mrs. Williams try to pull away.

Bill Hicks reached the two men, speaking too softly for anyone else to hear. Both turned back toward the women. Matt stepped sideways between their little group and the other men. Before anyone else could move, Bill swung a short iron pipe.

Iris did hear the sickening thump as it connected with the side of the young man's knee.

Mrs. Williams' scream drowned out her son's, but Rita Hicks held her firm, not letting her move forward or look away. Both crowds shuffled, but no one broke out of the loose circles.

"Why aren't they fighting back?" Gena whispered. Her hand was a vise on Iris's arm.

"They're half-starved," Iris's father said. His plodding march never slowed. "More than half terrified. We've had it a lot better than most of them."

Mr. Williams tried to help his son stand, but Ben screamed again as his leg buckled under him. Matt tried to hide his face, but his laugh rang out in the cold air. Mrs. Williams fell to her knees in the dusty parking lot, hands over her mouth.

Rita Hicks crossed her arms and returned her own husband's smile.

"Shame to waste a good man like that," Haga said. Iris could hear the smile in her voice, too. "Might open up the way for Dale here."

"Fuck off, Haga." Dale kept his eyes forward. "You'll end up on your back before all's said and done."

"We'll see about that, I suppose. If I do, won't have a damned thing to do with you."

The violence may not have been specifically for Iris and her family, but it worked. Iris's mother hugged her father tight, fast enough that neither of them stopped walking. She grabbed Iris's hand as she and Gena continued toward the women's side.

"There you go," Haga said, nodding. "Just do what you ought to and this will all go better than you think."

Iris opened her mouth, but sharp pressure on both her hands kept her from speaking.

"Now's not the time," Gena whispered. "Can't you feel it?"

Iris closed her eyes, wishing she could deny the clammy chill in her gut. Right now, they were caught.

Right now, the wrong move could get everyone she loved killed. Or worse.

Right now, all she could do was watch. And wait.

A few more people followed, splitting silently to the men's or women's sides, then the streets were empty along with all the storefronts opposite the school and the sugar barn. Haga and the other women with guns stood in an arc around the women and children. Iris wished Dale didn't stand so close to her father.

Bill Hicks walked away from Ben Williams without a backward glance. Neither Ben, his mother, or his father made a sound now. Rita Hicks joined her husband on the street between the two groups. Matt stood behind them, arms crossed, rifle clearly visible.

"Now listen up," Bill said, his voice sharp and clear. "We're real sorry to drag you out in the cold at such an hour. But we got things we need to take care of. The kind of dangerous work that means we have to split families up for the time being."

Rita stepped forward. Iris wondered if they'd rehearsed this whole speech.

"I know some of you don't like the way things are changing, here and out in the world. You're gonna have to understand that things *have* changed, though. And me and Bill are doing everything we can to make sure we get through these hard times. Each and every one of us has a role to play. Roles as old as time itself."

The men gathered in front of Ben Williams, almost too slowly to see. Iris was torn between fear and pride as her father stepped right in front of him.

Bill Hicks didn't notice, or he pretended not to.

"The safest place we have to keep you women and children is in the sugar barn. We can't protect you out in all your houses, and you're going to need protection. Some of the guards will stay with you, but we can't spare many when we go."

Iris felt her mother start forward. She made it a few steps before Iris and Gena managed to grab her. Carol Rutherford's whole body vibrated.

"Where the hell do they think they're going?" she nearly growled, still pulling forward. "What kind of madness is this?"

"Madness we're not going to survive if we do this now," Iris said into her mother's ear. "They're all armed. Haga's looking right at you, Mom. Dale hasn't looked away from Dad. We have to wait!"

Rita Hicks took her turn, staring at Iris and Gena.

"Many of you share the same gift of the sight that me and Bill do. Most of us knew hard times were coming. What you might not know is we've been holding off, waiting for the right time to do what we have to do. The last pieces of that vision are in place. We got to act now to protect our future."

Iris was one of the few who didn't jump at the squeal of wood and cold metal behind her. Two men pushed the broad red-painted doors to the sugar barn open, wheeling them back along their tracks. What looked like old traditional wood slats on both sides was actually solid metal with tight weatherproof seals.

Despite the frigid temperatures, the men didn't bother with the smaller single door set off to the side for cold weather days. Dust and stale air cut through the crisp morning.

"Don't worry now," Bill Hicks said. He smiled and held up one hand as if he were comforting a fussy child. "We'll get the heat turned on right quick, and we have plenty to feed you. Your men will be right over at the schoolhouse until it's time."

The two semi-circles of guards didn't say anything. They just started walking forward. Iris willed herself to resist, to stand right where she was. To at least make sure they knew she wasn't going without a nasty fight.

Her father met her gaze across the parking lot. He shook his head, almost too fast to see, then turned and followed the rest of the men and boys.

Iris didn't have to hear him to understand. She wasn't there to fight. Not yet. She had to keep Gena and her mother safe until they could all get away.

She walked into the sugar barn, still holding her mother and her lover's hands.

Chapter 13

THE ONLY THING that had changed in the store right inside the barn doors since Iris last saw it was a thick layer of dust. Shelves made of pine stained brown covered the walls, still piled high with tourist junk. Wooden whistles and flimsy knives, cheap harmonicas, rough-edged cap guns with rolls of red tape for bullets.

Iris's parents told her this stuff was antiquated garbage when her grandparents were alive, already mass produced overseas. But strangers who found their way to Maple Ridge bought handfuls of it. Rotating stands full of postcards, books, and download cards for screechy mountain music dotted the center of the rough-hewn hardwood floor. The gummy filth over everything looked like no one had found their way up here for a long, long time.

The only spaces cleared of dust and everything else were supposed to hold food. Bins for chips and crackers, shelves for bottles of maple syrup and boxes of candy, even the huge wall coolers for soda and water stood empty.

Iris suspected Bill and Rita Hicks had hidden everything edible away rather than selling it to tourists or anyone else. Maybe in the locked production and storage area at the back of this sprawling building. She forced herself not to check her watch pocket for the keys.

At least fifty women and young children had room to move around in the store, but hardly anywhere to sit down. Sunken eyes and bony faces made it clear most hadn't had regular meals for a while, especially the pale, quiet children. Only a few were dressed for winter weather instead of wearing night clothes.

Two women Iris remembered from grade school helped Mrs. Williams sit on the chair behind the long checkout counter, behind the antique cash register no one knew how to use.

Mrs. Williams was silent now, but tears ran down her crumpled, red face.

Haga strolled through the crowd, rifle still over her back, a sneer curving her lips. She nodded to one of the guards still outside. He stepped away for a second, then the long lights overhead popped and buzzed into life. Seemed the power did work where the people in charge wanted it to.

Steam rose from Haga's mouth when she spoke into the clammy air. Iris was sure it was near freezing inside even without the broad doors standing open.

"Don't be shy, now, move whatever you need to out of the way. Not likely we'll need any of this crap for suckers to buy anytime soon. Get yourself comfortable however you need to."

Iris grabbed piles of dark green t-shirts from hangers beside her, wadding them up to hide the image of the sugar barn printed on the front. Her mother and Gena passed them along. That would do fine for sitting on the floor, but not much to keep warm. The pile of blue and red sweatshirts under the shirts wasn't nearly enough for everyone.

"Can we please get the heaters on?" Iris said, handing out the last of the sweatshirts. She raised her voice over the noise of women dragging displays across the floor. "It's freezing in here."

Haga turned slowly, sneer deepening into a smile. She wasn't going to miss one damn chance to show her power to a group she was certain didn't have any.

"Mr. Hicks said he'd get that done, and he will. I'd imagine he's too busy next door to worry about that right now."

"I know how to start them." Iris crossed her arms and met Haga's gaze. "I worked here for years."

"Yeah, a bunch of us did, Iris." Haga shook her head, still smiling. "And like I told you, Mr. Hicks will take care of it."

"Iris…" Gena whispered. Her cold fingers slipped along Iris's wrist to her hand.

The crackling orange flames danced behind Haga again, so clear and bright Iris was surprised no one else saw them. The flames drew Iris forward rather than pushing her away.

"Then at least get us something to eat," Iris said. "None of us had breakfast, and I know the kids are hungry. Have been for a long time, by the looks of them."

"That's awful sweet talk for someone who hasn't much been up here for the past couple of years." Everyone moved aside as Haga walked forward, stopping inches in front of Iris. "Seems to me you got better things to worry about than running your mouth."

Flame blocked everything behind Haga now, turning the whole room into a raging inferno that even *felt* hot to Iris. She smelled the burning, heard fierce crackling and roaring wind.

But she knew without needing to see that all the women behind the guard were moving, too, standing shoulder to shoulder in front of their children and the oldest among them.

Iris didn't understand the shape of it yet, but she knew Haga, Matt, Bill and Rita Hicks, and everyone else who assumed they were in control of Maple Ridge had badly misunderstood how these desperate people would behave.

After staring up into Iris's eyes for a long moment, Haga stepped back and turned toward the room.

"Now listen here. Best way to get food for your children is to keep yourselves calm. Best way to keep the power for the lights on, too. Best way to sit here cold and hungry in the dark is to think about causing trouble."

Haga grinned at Iris this time before she strode out of the building. Two of the male guards rolled the barn doors closed. Iris was sure they purposely made as much noise as they could chaining and locking them.

A low whisper moved like waves through the store, no one daring to raise their voices. The wall of fire departed with Haga, leaving Iris with a clear view of everyone's eyes. Only a few were avoiding hers. Most met her gaze and nodded.

"What were you playing at, Iris?" Gena said into her ear. "She's got a fucking rifle!"

"I know she does. Everyone else knows, too. That's the whole point."

Iris held up her hands for a few seconds, until every woman looked her way. She whispered into Gena's ear, then her mother's.

"Tell them to keep talking, but not too loud. Move around a little. I'm going to check the security systems."

Gena tried to keep Iris from walking away, grabbing her hands. Iris squeezed them, smiled, and jerked her head toward her mother. Carol Rutherford was whispering to the women nearest her, who then turned to whisper to someone else. The noise level was rising again. Gena scowled and turned away.

Iris moved toward the checkout counter, stopping every few steps to help someone. She wasn't surprised to find the smaller entry door beside the big rolling doors locked tight, the keys in her pocket useless for that.

Her message moved so quickly that Mrs. Williams rolled the chair to the side before Iris got there.

"Let me get out of your way, honey," she said. "You can sit down right here and do whatever you need to do."

"You're fine right where you are." Iris pulled the smaller woman into a quick hug. "I'm so sorry."

"We have got to get out of here, Iris, and make sure they don't get away with what they're trying. Now, what do you need me to do?"

Iris glanced out at the store, a perspective she knew well from summer and winter shifts behind this counter. More than a few times, she'd been resetting or updating the payment systems.

Or the security systems.

If the cameras had started back up after the power was off, the casual but constant movement should be distraction enough for anyone who happened to be watching.

"Just sit tight. The security cameras won't work without the town's internet connection. That's on a different circuit. I'm betting no one thought to start that up or link them together."

Mrs. Williams nodded, dabbing the corners of her eyes with the corner of her scarf.

"They've had the internet shut down for months now, just like the power. Last thing them assholes want is for us to get word to the outside world."

Iris pulled a black metal drawer from under the counter, then raised a flat glassy display barely the size of both of her hands up. She didn't raise the screen waist high, like anyone standing here helping dozens of customers would. That would be too easy for anyone on the other side of the security cameras to catch.

The screen was dark, definitely a good sign. She pressed her fingertips into a nearly invisible bar on the bottom edge. While she waited for the store's system to start up, Iris thought through all the cameras she knew about.

Not quite as big as her pinky fingernail, the networked devices were scattered anywhere small things might be slipped into a pocket. Above the racks of music download cards, hidden in the shelves that used to hold maple candy.

Iris knew at least a couple were behind her with a good view of the screen that flashed into grey and blue life. Bill Hicks might not understand a whole lot about how the store systems worked, but he was always eager to find someone to yell at.

System Check Failure: Establishing Connection…

Iris puffed air out through her cold lips. That connection wasn't going to get anywhere until - unless - someone outside started up the town's server.

"The whole thing is still offline," she said. "Cameras and everything. That will make the rest a lot easier."

Mrs. Williams touched Iris's arm before she could walk away.

"Make what a lot easier? What if Bill remembers to turn everything else on? I hear he's taking a lot more care with all our poor dogs than he is with any of us. Saw that for myself a little while ago, too."

Iris didn't have to hear her unspoken question.

What if they hit you like they did my boy?

Or your mother?

Or Gena?

"Bill won't, not likely, anyway. He's plenty good at running things in the back and yelling at everyone out here. Not so much at this part. We'll have to watch out for Rita, though."

Iris walked toward the back of the store, waving for Gena and her mother to join her. The heavy steel double doors were painted to match the rustic plank siding everywhere else. If Bill hadn't changed the locks or chained this door like the one at the front, they might still have a chance of fighting back.

"What did you find?" Gena said, grabbing Iris's hand.

"Cutting the power cut the internet," Iris said. "For the store and most of the town. I'm sure Bill and Rita had no such problems at their house. But for now, no one's remembered to restart the security cameras."

The three women stood shoulder to shoulder, with Iris in the middle. She fit the key into the doorknob, holding her breath until it slipped into place.

"But one of them could remember to turn the damn thing on," her mother said. "Any second now. Lift up and shove it with your knee."

Iris snorted, somehow not surprised the door had the same quirks as when her mother was young enough to work here. She lifted the handle, turning the key until it rotated. Her knee to the rough spot between the doors did the trick.

Several of the women closest to her glanced at the noise of cold metal shifting, then went right back to their conversational cover.

Iris reached far enough to depress the switches on the wall, bringing long rows of overhead lights to life. The three women stepped inside the echoing warehouse and pulled the doors shut behind them.

Chapter 14

JUST AS IRIS EXPECTED, the broad cinderblock and concrete space hadn't changed since she worked her last shift a couple of years ago. Long silvery pipes ran from the edges of the room to a central collection area, all of it driven by a vast boiler built halfway through the back wall. Raw maple sap took the long journey through those pipes, picking up heat and shedding water as steam, coming out the other side as the prized driver of Maple Ridge's tourist economy.

Pallets of several sizes of containers stood against the wall to the left, near a tall door that rolled up toward the ceiling. Supplies waiting for a late winter harvest Iris doubted would be coming this year. She'd spent plenty of February and March hours after school learning how the whole contraption worked.

The right wall held all the tools for working in the rows of huge old maple trees on the outskirts of town. Short, tubular metal spiles to tap through the bark, metal buckets with curved lids to collect the sap. Axes, handsaws, and chainsaws to work on the trees themselves.

After more early morning shifts than she cared to count, Iris could have started up the boiler to warm the women and kids inside the store in about two minutes. She wouldn't even have to go outside to add wood as long as the power held out. And Haga, Dale, Matt, or Bill and Rita Hicks would spot the steam venting in about two seconds.

To no one's surprise, all the food and useful supplies from the store - supplies a starving town desperately needed - were piled up in front of the empty bottles and jars.

No matter what the consequences, Iris wasn't about to let everyone stay hungry and thirsty on top of being cold.

"Grab as much water as you can carry," she said, picking up a case of cheese and crackers. "Won't be the most nutritious breakfast, but we'll do our best."

"This is where they make the maple syrup?" Gena said.

"Most of it," Iris's mother said. "They have a little hand driven demonstration area around back, all kinds of fire and steam, but that's just for education. And for the tourists. They can run gallons a day through here."

When the three of them stepped back into the store with their gifts of food and water, everyone else gave up pretending not to notice.

"Did you get the heat started?" one of the women called.

"We can't do that," Iris said. "At least not while it's light out. I'm sorry. That boiler vents to the outside, and we'd have to feed it out there after a couple of hours. They'd know we can get in the back. Drink and eat fast as you can, and we'll hide what's left."

"A full belly won't mean much if they take it out on our kids and our men."

Iris didn't recognize the woman who'd spoken, not with a pink scarf covering most of her face. Her mother did.

"I don't know about you, Nancy," Carol Rutherford said, her voice sharp. "But I don't intend to sit quietly by and let them push all of us around. I doubt they're taking our men and boys out for some kind of charity run."

Nancy crossed her arms, refusing the water Gena held out.

"There *is* a back door in case you forgot. I doubt *they* forgot about the food and water stashed in there for a hot second."

"We saw the door, ma'am," Gena said. Iris knew that smile was full of venom. "Thank you for the reminder. Please do let us know if you have a better idea than what we're doing."

Iris watched several women and a few children step toward Gena, each of them making a point of thanking her. She couldn't tell if Nancy scowled before she walked away.

Iris did recognize one of her middle school teachers. Ms. Blevins nodded her thanks at the cheese and crackers. Her round, cheery face looked strange without a smile.

"Probably taking our men down to Wolf Branch. Rumor is they got plenty of food put by. My nephew Zach heard they went down there a couple of times already, scouting the place out."

Iris shivered, meeting Gena's worried gaze. The idea of an attack on Wolf Branch brought the flames surging in her mind again. This time tinted with black and red. Flames her father and the other men might be dragged into, along with a whole community that didn't deserve the violence.

"Whatever they're doing," Iris said, "we need to figure out some way to fight when we can. No matter what that Nancy says."

Ms. Blevins laughed, a low, throaty sound Iris remembered well.

"Nancy Nelson is pissed she's not out there with a rifle bossing everyone around like her rotten boy Matt, not that he seems to be treating her any better than the rest of us. Rita Hicks doesn't like Nancy any more than I do, or she would be. I'd watch that one."

Food and water shared out, the three women ducked back into the warehouse.

"Hate to say it," Iris's mother said, "but Nancy's got a point about the door. I saw your key, but I'd bet they've got it locked from the outside. Wonder if we could cut the power? Raising it by hand would take a lot longer. Probably be a lot louder, too."

"Looks like we could jam it." Gena stepped forward, toward the boxy metal housing for the door's motor. Chains looped out and up to the top of the massive door.

A cold deeper than the air around her twisted up through Iris, from her feet to her heart.

"Wait," she said. "Not now. Not yet."

"They can just walk right..." Gena's forehead wrinkled when her eyes met Iris's. "What did you see?"

"I didn't see anything, not really. But this isn't the right time. We need to get back out there, get everything hidden."

Her mother nodded. "You're probably right. They won't set out on their grand men-only mission without making sure we all know about it."

All three women pocketed a makeshift weapon when they passed by the maintenance bench on the way out. A long screwdriver, a chisel, a thin steel icepick.

Iris had no doubt all three of them would use them the second they got the chance.

Chapter 15

By the time the barn doors jerked, squealed, and rolled open
several hours later, all evidence of their thin breakfast was hidden
under the checkout counter along with the system monitor panel.
Bill and Rita Hicks strolled in as the small bit of heat generated by
so many bodies floated out.

"Glad to see you settling in," Bill said, his gaze moving slowly
over the group. "Happy to say most of your men are doing the same.
I understand you'd like the heat turned on in here."

Haga walked up behind him, staring at Iris with a half smile.
Dale stayed a few paces behind her, face red and stony. Iris knew she
wasn't the only one who noticed three guards outside, Matt's smug
face among them, making sure their rifles were visible.

"Heat would help, sure," Mrs. Williams said. "So would letting
us out of here."

"Well, we can't do that just yet." Bill spoke as if he were
comforting a small child. "But I'll see what I can do about that
boiler. Dale."

Dale glared at everyone close by as he followed Mr. Hicks
through the same door Iris had carefully locked.

"Everyone doing all right in here?" Rita Hicks said. She walked
through the store, eyes constantly moving. Haga stayed by the open

door. "We'll get you all something to eat and drink here in a little bit. Coffee if you want it."

"We're going to need restrooms before long," Ms. Blevins said. "The kids especially."

Rita shrugged. "There's the public restroom around the side of the building, but I'm afraid those pipes are busted. Cold weather and no power most days, you know. Might be able to take you in shifts back to the warehouse toilets. Assuming those are working, of course."

Everyone jumped at a rumble from the overhead vents. Barely warmed air flowed after a few seconds, along with the singed smell of dust in the pipes.

"There now," Rita said. "That will get warmer before long. You just sit tight and I'll check on those toilets."

She glanced at Haga, then joined her husband in the warehouse. Haga walked into the middle of the store. She didn't have her rifle, but her hand rested on a handgun in a holster around her waist. She brought the orange flames with her, and at least to Iris, the stink of gunpowder, burning flesh, and death.

"How long are we going to be in here, Haga?" Iris said. "It's almost one o'clock and these kids haven't had anything to eat. We'll need more than food and toilets."

"Don't know why you think I'm going to tell you any such thing, Iris. You know as well as I do you're asking the wrong person. We all got more important things to worry about right now."

Ignoring her racing heart - and her rational mind screaming at her to stop - Iris stepped forward. A stronger force drove her on. She spoke quietly enough that no one else could hear.

"Like what's going to happen to you when the little raiding party is over, maybe? Do you really believe you won't get used up just like the rest of us?"

Haga's eyes narrowed for a second, then a slow smile broke across her face.

"If I didn't know better, I'd think you were trying to distract me for some reason. Trying to start something you might not be willing to finish. I know you're smarter than that. Least you think you are."

Iris shrugged, much like Rita had, frowning a little.

"I guess we'll see who's smart in the end. Or thinks she is."

Haga raised one eyebrow. She looked away from Iris, but directly at her mother and Gena.

"Everybody takes big chances in times like these. Might want to make sure you can live with the results."

The double doors to the warehouse swung open with a metallic squeak, breaking the silence all over the room.

"All right," Rita Hicks called, standing in the doorway with her arms crossed. "Both toilets back there are working. Can't say they're clean, but they work. Figure out who needs to go and get moving."

Haga locked gazes with Iris again, ignoring everyone else moving around them. She only turned when Rita Hicks stood beside the two of them.

"If you'd be so kind as to keep an eye on everyone, Haga, I'll make sure breakfast is on the way."

"Will do, Mrs. Hicks. Wouldn't want any unfortunate accidents over here."

Everyone started moving at once when the front doors finally rolled closed behind Mrs. Hicks and the two guards outside. Iris hung back with Gena and her mother, watching Haga station herself by the doors to the warehouse. Dale and Bill Hicks were still back there.

"Can you explain to me why you're trying to piss her off?" Gena said. "I didn't have to grow up here to see she's not exactly stable."

"I don't know what to tell you." Iris held out her arms. Gena resisted for several seconds before she stepped into a hug. "You know how we both felt like we had to come up here? Something like that."

"So far they haven't noticed we can get back there," Iris's mother said. "At least we have that one advantage. I'm more worried about that Dale than Haga."

"You should be," Iris said. "And his buddy Matt Nelson. Dale made me uncomfortable every time I saw him back in school, and every police and sheriff's department in the region is well acquainted with Matt. Giving those two rifles is about the dumbest move I ever heard of."

The restrooms were awful, but functional enough. Grubby toilets still flushed. Cracked, stained sinks still drained. After making a grand show of leaving fresh boxes of rough toilet paper and coarse brown paper towels, Mr. Hicks busied himself and Dale with inspecting the boiler instead of keeping too close an eye on the quiet parade of women and children relieving themselves.

Mr. Hicks sauntered out of the warehouse when everyone was finished, locking the door behind him. Haga smirked as she left, and Dale continued to scowl as he walked close on her heels. Nothing had gone as badly as Iris feared.

The "breakfast" Rita Hicks returned with was another story.

Chapter 16

Boys not old enough to be out of high school wheeled cafeteria carts into the store under Matt Nelson's scornful gaze nearly an hour later. The way the boys picked up the tall pots and wide pans without oven mitts or even gloves, along with the way they refused to meet anyone's eyes, confirmed her worst fears.

They dropped everything unceremoniously on the checkout counter, along with bags of paper plates, plastic bowls, spoons, cups, and cafeteria napkins. They hurried out without a word or backward glance. Matt grinned and bowed low, sweeping one arm toward the food before he walked out

"Best we could do on short notice," Rita said with a broad smile. "Things are moving fast now that they finally got started. We'll have better for everyone before many days have passed."

Rita walked out, leaving the guards to roll the doors shut behind her. Before they did, Haga leaned in long enough to catch Iris's gaze. She raised a huge mug of something that steamed in the cold air.

"What was that all about?" Iris's mother said when the doors finally closed.

"Somehow I doubt anything they brought us will steam like that."

The first women to carefully lift the lids confirmed her suspicions. What Rita had finally delivered at two in the afternoon consisted of a solid mass of congealed oatmeal, a yellowish mess of what resembled rubbery scrambled eggs, and black coffee. Every bit of it as cold as the air outside.

"What the hell did they do?" Ms. Blevins said, her cheeks flushed. "Leave it sitting out on the street all day?"

"Probably did just that." Nancy Nelson had removed her pink scarf but still clutched it in one hand. Now nothing hid the permanent frown etched into her flesh when she glared at Iris. "That's what comes of giving them trouble."

"I'll invite you to skip it then," Iris's mother said. She opened the other containers, revealing more of the same. "Can't do much about these eggs, but a little hot water from the boiler and a touch of maple syrup will do the rest a world of good."

Everyone moved at once, getting the children settled and eating first thing. The oatmeal and coffee were better than expected after a few modifications. Hardly anyone touched the whatever was supposed to pass for eggs.

Full bellies and the room shifting from frigid to comfortable to hot left heads nodding despite the coffee and fear. Gena and Iris leaned against the counter, away from everyone but Mrs. Williams still perched on her chair. Like the women and many of the kids, they'd taken off their winter coats.

Gena spoke Iris's thoughts before she could.

"We're a lot easier to manage if we're all sound asleep. They may as well have drugged the food."

"No point in that if they can just heat us half to death," Iris said. "I hate to say it, but it's probably better if everyone is calm until we figure something out."

"Wouldn't hurt you to take a nap." Gena kissed Iris's cheek. "I'm going to go stretch my legs, look around a little bit. Maybe check out our tool supply back there. I think I spotted a machete."

She held out her hand, waiting for Iris to drop the keys into it.

"Watch that back door. And don't hurt yourself, city girl."

Gena winked, then walked as quietly as she could through the rows of dozing and sleeping bodies.

Iris tilted her head from side to side, trying to loosen her painfully tight shoulders. She closed her eyes against the glare of the overhead lights.

Just for a second…

Mrs. Williams's voice and hand on her shoulder startled Iris out of an unexpected sleep.

"There's some kind of noise under here." She pointed to the security terminal Iris had checked earlier.

Iris rubbed her grainy eyes, trying to focus on her watch. She hadn't noticed what time Gena went back there, but her body felt stiff enough to have slept for an hour rather than a few seconds. Almost four o'clock.

She heard the low beeping then.

Iris pulled the screen out, blinking at the blue words against the gray background.

Connection Established. System Normal.

A clammy knot clenched her gut, making her regret the late meal.

"Did anything else change? Any other noises?"

"No, honey," Mrs. Williams said, now sounding worried herself. "Did someone get that security system started back up?"

Iris shook her head, trying to think around a nagging headache. The room was hot enough now that sweat ran down her back and between her breasts.

"Maybe. This could be automated, but I can't risk it."

Everyone Iris could see either had their eyes closed or might as well have. Only her mother stared back at her, tense and alert. She got to her feet and met Iris at the double doors leading to the warehouse.

"What's wrong?"

"The security system is back on. Or it might be. Right now we have to get Gena."

Her mother's eyes widened. "I didn't see her go back there!"

"Stand behind me, block that camera in the corner." Iris knew no one watching any of the cameras would miss the two of them leaving the room, but none of that mattered. "She said she was going to look for a machete."

Iris pushed one of the doors slowly, keeping the noise to a whispering scrape. The room beyond was dark and quiet except for the low rumble of the boiler working overtime.

Gena didn't have a flashlight.

"Wait by the door," Iris said, grabbing her mother's hand. "If someone comes in the front, I'll need to know."

Her mother stepped forward, peering into the darkness.

"If Gena's back there, they've already got her. She'd have to see the door open. Why would she have the lights turned out?"

Painfully brittle fear froze all of Iris's muscles, and she bit her lip to keep from throwing up a mass of overly sweet maple syrup, coffee, and oatmeal.

Why? Why had she brought Gena up here?

"I have to try, Mom. There may still be time."

A scream rang out in the darkness, piercing through the terror in Iris's heart and mind.

Gena.

Chapter 17

Before Iris could move, her mother flipped all the warehouse lights on.

The dusty concrete floor was covered with too many footprints to show which way Gena had gone, but Iris caught movement against the right wall. Near all those axes and saws.

"You *bitch*!"

Dale staggered toward the middle of the warehouse, clutching his bloody right hand to his chest. His rifle bounced uselessly on his back.

"Gena!"

Iris sprinted forward, aiming toward the flash of blonde hair darting behind the row of supplies.

Dale turned toward Iris, face red and furious, trying to grab his rifle with his left hand. More blood poured from the fist still held against his body.

Everything around Iris slowed, too bright and loud, bringing every detail into hard reality around her.

Dale's mouth opening, chest rising.

Neck muscles straining as he fought to grab the rifle with his dumb hand.

Dust motes floating in the endless space between her and Gena.

Her mother's pounding footsteps.

Gena's fierce and raging eyes as she walked up behind Dale.

The sharp blade of the axe flashing over her shoulder.

The furious scream through her blood-ringed mouth as she swung.

The meaty thunk of steel sinking into flesh where Dale's neck met his shoulder.

Dale's gurgling cry, the only sound he made before his dead body hit the concrete.

Iris didn't realize she'd skidded to a stop until her mother crashed into her. She landed hard enough to jar the world back into normal time.

"Gena!" her mother shouted, sprawled out beside Iris.

Gena didn't look at either of them. She knelt beside Dale, shoving him until she could yank the rifle away. She picked up the axe when she stood and turned.

She didn't seem to notice the blood she streaked over her hands and shoulder when she slipped the rifle's strap across her own back.

"What happened?" Iris said, gasping for breath. On top of her fear, she'd knocked her wind out when she fell.

Gena wiped her hands absently on her jeans, then reached down to help Iris and her mother stand.

"Must have been back here waiting. After I walked across, he turned the lights out. Blinded me with a huge flashlight. Wait, I need to get it."

She turned away, and Iris glanced at her mother. Iris could feel where she'd scraped her own chin and cheek, but her mother's face was unmarked. And her eyes were as wide and shocked as Iris's had to be.

Gena kicked Dale over again, reaching toward something that clattered against the floor. She grabbed a heavy black flashlight almost as long as her forearm. Iris hadn't seen an old one like that since she was a little girl exploring in her grandfather's basement.

"Did he hurt you?" Iris said, trying not to look at the spreading pool under Dale's body.

"I don't think so." Gena stared at her palms, then wiped them on her jeans again. "I saw you open the door and I just...I lost my head."

Iris let all her breath out again, the closest thing she could manage to a laugh.

Dale was the one...the one who nearly lost...

Gena wiped at her mouth, frowning at the blood there.

"He grabbed me, had his hand over my mouth. Dragged me toward that back corner, pushed me down." She rubbed the back of her head. "Knocked my skull pretty good. Smacked him a few times, kept him from getting what he wanted. I was afraid others were with him, so I didn't scream until I saw you."

Iris reached out and touched Gena's trembling hand, then slipped hers around the axe handle. Gena let go and went back to rubbing her crimson-stained leg.

"I bit him," she said. "Right through his hand. Had to spit it out back there."

She grabbed her stomach and covered her mouth.

"Still taste... I can still taste it."

Iris caught Gena before she could fall, easing her to her knees just as the retching started. Iris's mother knelt beside them, holding Gena's hair back and away from the chunky brown vomit.

When Gena sat back, still spitting and breathing hard, Iris's mother got up and walked over to the food stash. She brought back an armful of bottles of water and Coke.

"Here hon, this will help," she said, holding the water out.

Gena filled her mouth and spit into the mess a few times. When she reached for the Coke, her hand shook worse than before.

"They'll notice. That he's gone. What... What are we going to do?"

"Get you out of here," Iris said. She hugged Gena close. "We're armed now, thanks to you."

Chapter 18

When they started toward the bathroom to let Gena wash up, the flames raged hot and bright inside Iris's mind.

"We can't do this right now," she said, shaking her head. "We may be running out of time."

Iris's mother looked at the axe over Iris's shoulder, the rifle over Gena's.

"Wait here just one minute. We're gonna need more than this."

She set out at a fast pace back toward the tree trimming supplies, detouring wide around Dale's messy remains.

"You're bleeding," Gena said. She touched Iris's undamaged cheek, turning her face to the side.

"That might help us. If everyone out there sees what went on, they'll be willing to fight."

Gena and Iris walked forward to help with the load of weapons Carol Rutherford carried. Three more axes, several loops of loose chainsaw blade, and four of the stout machetes Gena had been after in the first place.

"That's about all I could manage. Might want to send a couple of the others out to grab more."

Iris didn't bother trying to be as quiet walking back through to the front of the store as she had been going out back. If someone *was* watching the cameras, they were taking their sweet damn time responding.

Gasps floated through the women, followed by children's moans and cries. Before the shouted questions could really get started, Iris's mother stepped forward, drawing attention away from the bloodied younger women.

"Now listen. One of those guards was waiting back there in the dark. If we hadn't gone out when we did, he would have done his best to act out Rita's almighty biology whether Gena wanted him to or not." Fists on her hips, she turned her head to look at everyone. "And if Gena hadn't gone out there, how long do you think he would have waited before he came in here after us? After our little ones?"

"What did you *do*?" Nancy shouted, clutching her pink scarf to her throat.

"I killed him," Gena said. Her voice was calm and steady now, just like the hand that gripped Iris's. "Right before he would have used this to kill Carol and Iris so he could get back to trying to rape me."

She lifted the rifle, bloody strap and all, above her head before dropping it back into place.

Iris spoke into the silence.

"I think the security system is back on, but no one seems to be watching it. If they were, they'd be here by now. So they probably don't know Dale was even back there. We might have a little time to get ready, but not much."

Iris's old teacher, Ms. Blevins, stepped forward. The tight set of her mouth was grim, but her eyes were bright. She nodded at the weapons.

"Are some of those things for us?"

"These and plenty more in the back," Iris said. She couldn't stop her own grim smile as Ms. Blevins pulled on thick winter gloves and took one of the loops of chainsaw blade, looking deceptively like a thick bicycle chain rather than a vicious cutting tool. "I think we need to get the kids close against the wall in the warehouse, right inside this door. Then we'll set up by the doors."

"And then what?" Nancy's voice rose to nearly a shriek. "Sit here and wait until they shoot us all to death? One assault rifle against a dozen, with all of us caught in the crossfire?"

Nancy glared at Iris's mother, not seeming to notice the whispers and sobs of children all around them. Iris forced herself not to say anything. She couldn't explain it to anyone besides Gena or her mother, but she knew, she *knew* there were nowhere near that many guards left outside.

Her sense of calamity, of whirling orange and gray catastrophe, had shifted away from Maple Ridge and down the mountain toward Wolf Branch.

Whatever disaster she'd been dreaming about was well underway.

"You do whatever the hell you want to, Nancy," Iris's mother said. "Maybe your boy will finally remember to sneak in at the last minute and rescue you, right? Until then, you keep out of the way and let us do whatever we can. If you don't, I'll tie you up and lock you in the bathroom myself."

All the other women moved then, either herding their kids toward the warehouse or walking through themselves to help gather what weapons they could.

Mrs. Williams left her perch beside the checkout counter. She stepped up beside Iris, face pale with high spots of color in her cheeks.

"Can I have one of those?" she said quietly, pointing to a machete.

Iris didn't have to ask if she was remembering the iron bar swung at her son's leg, or his scream as he collapsed.

She gave the blade to Mrs. Williams without a word.

Chapter 19

By the time Ms. Blevins thought to distribute boxes of maple candy to keep the children quiet and distracted, they were as ready as they could get.

The tree maintenance wall was nearly empty, with even the palm-sized spiles that normally drained sap out of the maple trees rounded up and shared around. Not nearly as sharp as the cutting tools, but Iris had nicked her winter-chilled fingers on the spouts and hooks more than enough to know they'd do some kind of damage.

Someone, Iris wasn't sure who, had taken the time to find an old gray tarp and used it to keep the kids from seeing what had really happened in the warehouse earlier. Someone else had jammed a long screwdriver through the chains that raised the warehouse door, keeping it from moving more than a few inches no matter who triggered the switch.

Several women arranged themselves out of sight on either side of the rolling front doors of the store. The others surrounded the group of kids gathered on the warehouse side of the passage between the two spaces.

Only Nancy Nelson had refused any kind of weapon. She hadn't resisted when Carol Rutherford told her to sit outside the bathroom door, then, and stay the hell out of the way. Iris wasn't the only one to keep an eye on the disagreeable woman on top of everything else she was trying to pay attention to.

Not nearly the preparations Iris or anyone else would have liked. But nowhere near as helpless as they'd felt - and been - only an hour before.

"How many do you think are out there?" Gena said in a low voice. She sat close beside Iris behind the checkout counter, where they could both watch the unchanging screen for the security system.

"One less, and a nasty one at that." Iris kissed Gena's cheek, finally scrubbed clean of the remains of Dale. "I get the feeling a lot of them are gone already."

"Down to Wolf Branch," Gena said, nodding. "That's what I feel like, too."

"So probably Haga, Rita Hicks. Maybe a few of the younger men."

"Do you really think they're arrogant enough to leave us here with so few watching us?"

Iris shrugged, wishing she had some way to honestly answer. To *know*.

"They've left us in here for a long time already. I'm sure if they suspected we could get into the warehouse, they would have left a guard back there. They're assuming we're weaker and more afraid than we are."

"And we may be assuming they're better prepared and organized than they are. But we have to be ready."

Those words, *they've left us in here for a long time*, echoed and rebounded in Iris's mind, getting louder and more angry with each repetition. How long had she left Gena out there while taking a nap?

How long had Gena had to fight off Dale and his filthy hands and mouth and everything else?

"I'm sorry, Gena. I shouldn't have left you out there alone for so long."

Gena turned her head and shoulders toward Iris, shaking her head.

"What? You mean when I… When he was back there?"

Iris closed her eyes, wishing she could banish the horrible images from her mind.

"Not only did I drag you up here into mountaintop hell, but I sat up here, right here, sound asleep while you were back there by yourself with that worthless pile of shit."

Gena blinked, but she smiled instead of drawing away.

"I was only out there for a few minutes, Iris. Pretty much long enough to walk across the floor and look at the tools. Wish I'd grabbed one before he turned the lights out, but he ended up the same either way."

"A few minutes?" Iris rubbed her stiff neck with one hand. "Really? I feel like I was asleep sitting up for ages."

"There might be a lot more to that than a quick nap we could all use." Gena pulled Iris forward, digging her strong fingers into the knots around Iris's neck and shoulders. "You didn't abandon me, no more than I would have abandoned you to drive up here all by yourself. I'm exactly where I want to be. Today and every day."

Iris closed her eyes for a second, wanting more than anything to let Gena soothe her to sleep. But the weariness that surged through her mind and body were much too heavy and deep to give in to.

"Listen, are you… Did it bother you, what you had to do?"

Gena half-smiled, but her eyes didn't look happy this time.

"You mean did I mind nearly chopping that asshole's head off? I won't say I'm perfectly fine, no. When we finally get out of here, I expect I'll have enough sleepless nights to make up for your dreams and then some."

Iris leaned back and put her arm around Gena's shoulders, wishing she could make the whole thing go away and never bother Gena or anyone else trapped in this nightmare again.

"But for now?"

"For now, I'm not thinking about it. I might have to do a lot worse before this is over. I can't fall apart until then, and neither can you."

Iris nodded, then glanced back at the monitor.

Her breathing, heart, and all her thoughts jerked to a halt.

The gray screen and blue words had vanished. Instead she saw several tiny windows, like miniature television screens. Most of the scenes seemed as frozen as her body, showing the boiler out back, the chained doors in front of the store, the empty parking lot between the sugar barn and the middle school. Other locations around and inside other buildings in town, places Iris had never noticed cameras before.

Or where Bill and Rita had recently added them.

But she also saw women shifting around inside the warehouse.

And she saw herself and Gena, the tops of their heads obviously in range of a camera designed to watch whoever ran the cash register.

"The screen," she croaked, her throat tight and dry. "The whole thing is on now."

Gena caught her breath and tensed against Iris.

"That's the whole town, isn't it? Where is that coming from?"

Iris shook her head, trying to get her numb feet and legs to move.

"I never saw that before, only the inside of the store and the warehouse. It could be some kind of default view. I promise you someone else can see it all, too."

Just as Iris dragged herself up with Gena's help, one of the tiny scenes finally changed. People walking in front of the middle school. Haga and Rita Hicks clear even at barely an inch high.

Their guns every bit as visible before the screen went black.

"Get ready!" Iris shouted. "They're coming!"

"Remember they don't know we're armed," Gena said, her voice lower but no less urgent. "All they can see is we moved around. We can still surprise them if we're careful."

Besides shouts to warn the women by the warehouse doors, everyone was surprisingly quiet. Iris held the assault rifle, leaving Gena to carry the same axe. Sally Lee, a neighbor not far from Iris's parents, crouched behind Gena with a handsaw.

They stood just inside the rolling doors, with other women across from them, armed and ready. Mrs. Williams watched Iris, machete gripped low against her legs.

"I'll turn the lights out as soon as they move the chain," Iris said, low enough for only the women around the door to hear. "The sun went down a while ago, so they'll be as blind as we are. Hopefully more."

At a metallic rattle outside, Iris took a deep breath and squeezed Gena's hand.

She reached forward and flipped the row of switches. Out in the warehouse, her mother did the same before she closed the double doors.

They waited in darkness.

Chapter 20

ONE OF THE doors creaked and rolled a few inches to the right.

Frigid dry air invaded the silent room, and brilliant white light cut through the black in front of Iris's eyes.

The beam aimed straight back to the far wall, over the closed doors to the warehouse. Down along the floor, left and right across the empty store shelves pushed back out of the way.

"Not sure what you think you can do here," Haga said, still outside the door. "Take all of us out and walk yourself down that mountain, I suppose."

Silence, even from the warehouse and the group of children.

"The warehouse door is still closed," Rita Hicks said, anger and frustration clear in her voice. "Unless Dale's dumb ass managed to kill them all, they're in there."

Iris forced her finger to stay loose, flat against the loop of the trigger guard, no matter how badly she wanted to open fire. Despite her strong feeling almost all the men were gone, she had no idea what waited outside.

Haga spoke quietly, but with the same irritated edge.

"Go on, then. You were full of piss and bluster about how you'd keep all us *females* safe when Bill rolled out. Now's your chance."

The light bobbled for a second, then the door squealed and

moved sideways again. The blunt end of a short, modern flashlight slipped into sight. Propped on top of the hand holding the light was a hand holding a gun.

Iris forced herself to breathe, tried to will everyone around her to do the same.

After a few shuffling steps forward, skinny arms clad in faded blue corduroy came into view. Iris was certain they belonged to Bob Kaiser, one of the men she'd seen gathered around Bill Hicks that morning. Bob's local claim to fame might normally be hauling tourists around the vast ring of maple trees in a creaky wagon full of hay, for an absurdly expensive fee.

But right now, he was armed, wanting to impress Bill and everyone else, and walking right into the middle of their little group of women and children.

"Don't be stupid, now," Bob called out, his voice booming in the nearly empty store. "Hiding out like a bunch of cowards won't help."

He moved one hand away from the gun and waved the light around, never quite reaching the sides where Iris and the other women stood. More of those shuffling steps took him away from Iris.

Toward the light switches.

Bob swung the hand with the flashlight to his right, but before the beam touched the small group, Iris heard a faint metallic shift.

Right before Bob's scream drowned out everything else.

The light jerked along with his body to the right.

Iris barely had time to register blood surging under the chainsaw blade around Bob's wrist before he brought the gun around.

Mrs. Williams stepped forward and swung the machete.

A bright flash and bang.

Bob fell to his knees, dropping both the flashlight and the gun.

Another light from outside flared toward the back of this store just in time to show Bob's kicking legs as he was dragged out of sight.

"That's enough!" Haga shouted, with Rita's bellow close behind.

"Every last *one* of you will pay for this!"

The light focused on the handgun, about five feet away from Iris on the floor. None of them could reach it without stepping into range of Haga's assault rifle, and probably more than that.

But no one outside could walk in without ending up like Bob. Moaning mixed with screaming himself hoarse even when something - or someone - was obviously pressing on his throat.

Iris wasn't sure whether she hoped more for the machete or the chainsaw blade.

Whoever held the light outside stepped closer, the bright circle covering most of the room now. And no doubt that the next person to walk in would shoot to either side of the doors before setting one foot inside.

Shouts rang out from the warehouse, loud enough that even Bob shut up. Gena pressed up tight against Iris's back, trembling, and she didn't have to say a word.

Iris's mother was back there. And the children.

The flashlight beam lit the double doors as they shuddered, then metal squealed when one opened barely an inch.

"Gun! They have a *gun*!"

The door slammed hard enough to rattle in its frame, and Nancy Nelson's shrieking voice stopped.

Bob's moaning started up again.

"Dale's dumb ass got inside after all." Rita still sounded like she was well away from the barn doors. She also sounded strangely calm. "Managed to lose his gun, maybe his worthless life. Not much of a surprise there. Guess we'll have to deal with him when this is all over. Unless you already took care of him for us. Then we'll just have to say thank you."

Iris barely had time to wonder why Rita was suddenly so damn chatty before she heard a grunt and a metallic clatter from behind her. Gena's body twisted, then disappeared.

She turned in time to see Gena step over Sally's dropped handsaw and dart out the open side door, axe still in her hands.

Chapter 21

IRIS WALKED AWAY from the middle of the store - from the handgun on the floor and Bob's moans and the other three women - without a backward glance. Gena's insistence that she'd only been in the warehouse alone for a few minutes hadn't entirely left her mind.

She wasn't about to leave Gena on her own again. Iris raised the assault rifle and stepped through the door.

Cold starlight outside helped her see a little better, but not much.

Rita Hicks off to the side, well away from the barn doors.

Two young boys and a girl, surely still in high school down in Wolf Branch during less insane times. One of the boys held a huge flashlight toward the inside of the store.

All of them turning toward where Iris stood.

In between, Haga with one arm around Sally Lee's neck, dragging her backward, the other hand over her mouth.

Gena with the axe raised over her shoulder, moving to get behind Haga.

Iris saw Rita realize Haga had brought more than a hostage along with her, and at a gesture from her, the boy swung the light around.

Iris yelled as loud as she could, breath she felt like she'd been holding for weeks exploding out.

"Get down!"

All she saw before she opened fire, all that mattered, was Gena lunging forward toward the frozen ground.

Iris didn't stop until the stinking hot gun was empty and the bolt locked open.

The boy's light bounced and rolled, ending up pointing toward the partly open door of the store. Iris crouched beside the building, trying to hide and see into the darkness.

"Gena!"

"I'm here." Gena's harsh whisper cut through more moans than Bob Kaiser could have managed in his prime. "We have to get their guns."

A light from inside the store traced a jagged path along the floor and outside. A few seconds later, all the overhead lights went on, along with several big floodlights above Iris's head.

Before she managed to turn away, Iris saw what was left of two of the young guards who'd been standing beside Rita. One of the boys huddled on the ground, hands over the back of his head. He'd thrown his gun far out of reach.

Rita herself was still breathing, but she wouldn't be much longer. From the looks of her chest and stomach, she didn't have enough left to be bleeding for much longer, either.

For one horrible second, Iris thought the blood covering Gena's arms and hands was her own. That she'd miscalculated how fast Gena moved and had managed to hit the last person on earth she wanted to hurt.

But her eyes finally focused enough to realize Gena was trying to cover the wound in Sally's shoulder. Sally herself sprawled across Haga's chest and stomach.

"Get the gun, Iris." Gena moved Sally forward as gently as she could, stopping at each sharp intake of air. "Under her."

Iris shook her head, trying to force her brain to re-engage so it could slow her furious heartbeat. Could this possibly be over? She didn't see anyone else or hear movement she couldn't explain.

But part of her remained convinced that danger waited just outside the bright circle of light.

Iris pulled herself up, bracing against the building. The women who'd been waiting inside the store stood around Rita Hicks.

No one's face or eyes showed the slightest trace of pity or compassion.

Haga watched Iris, her own eyes bright. Her face deathly pale and splattered with blood. The pattern of bullet holes across her chest and the dark stain spreading underneath her said all Iris needed to know. And more than she ever wanted to remember.

She leaned over to help get Sally to her feet, hot tears surging up at Sally's whimpering cries.

"I'm sorry," Iris whispered. "I didn't mean to hit you, Sally."

Sally tried to smile. "You really think I'd prefer Rita's tender mercies? Or the one who dragged me out here?"

"She tried to get down," Gena said, walking Sally over and helping her sit against the wall. "Haga tried to use her as a shield. She's not going anywhere, but get her gun. We don't know who's still out there or when the others will come back."

Iris forced herself to focus on the low conversation of the other women, Bob's moans and complaints, the noise of her own footsteps on the gravel. Anything to avoid hearing the gurgling noise from Haga's chest when she tried to breathe.

"You want me to turn you over?" Iris said, finally looking into Haga's reddened eyes. "Or you want to do that yourself?"

Haga's voice came out weak and breathless.

"Whatever the hell you think you need to do, Iris. You'll be glad to know I can't feel a damn thing past my shoulders anyway."

"I'm not glad about any of this." Iris squatted, trying not to inhale the meaty, metallic scent mixed with the sharp fumes of Haga's bladder letting go. "Except getting away from here and from you."

She gripped Haga's shoulder, raising her up enough to pull the rifle loose. Iris nearly dropped it when she realized the length of cold metal was coated in everything that was leaking out of the dying woman. She gritted her teeth, ignoring Haga's grunts, and yanked the gun and strap free.

Haga stared up at Iris, her words even harder to hear when she spoke again.

"Kill me then. Bullet in my head, knife at my throat. Whatever you got."

Iris stood, picking up Gena's axe along with the rifle. After a long look around - Sally's face twisted in pain, the other women walking slowly out from the warehouse, her mother's furious eyes - she leaned both weapons against the wall beside Sally and Gena. She returned to Haga's side and met her gaze.

A single handgun shot rang out, and Iris knew Rita Hicks had breathed her last. Someone in that circle of women had more compassion than she did at that moment. Iris didn't move or break eye contact with Haga.

"I don't have anything for you, Haga. You can bleed to death or freeze to death. Either one is kinder than what you were going to help them do to the rest of us."

Chapter 22

THE BOY CROUCHED on the ground turned out to be Jessie Estep, an unwilling participant, or at least that's what he claimed to be. The other women and a few kids verified that he'd been visiting from Laurel Pass a couple of hours away and got caught up in the whole mess.

The only thing Jessie wanted to know was how soon he could get to a phone and call his parents. No one knew when the phones had been cut, or whether it was done in Maple Ridge or somewhere else. The only thing they knew for certain was none of the digital lines or even the old copper lines worked. And mobile phones only gave fast busy signals.

What Iris and the other adults knew in their hearts was Jessie's parents would have long-since come to get him if they'd been able. But no one was willing to say that while looking into his worried blue eyes.

Jessie did help them get Rita's keys so all the women and children could take shelter in the middle school for the long, long night. Cots, mats from the gym, and sleeping bags let the kids get some real sleep, and most of the adults pretend to. After settling the children down in the echoing, warm gymnasium, they locked Bob Kaiser into one of the music rooms to muffle his noisy complaints.

No one argued with Iris about leaving Haga right where she was.

Or with Iris's mother about locking Nancy Nelson in a classroom not too far from Bob.

Jessie thought all the other men and older boys had gone on the raid down to Wolf Branch, but he was hardly part of Bill and Rita Hicks' inner circle. He had seen Mrs. Williams's boy Ben loaded into one of the pickup trucks, horribly swollen and useless knee or not.

The cold, bluish light visible through the windows around the top of the gym had warmed to pink and the pale yellow of a winter morning, but hadn't yet woken the others. Assuming any of them had actually gone to sleep. Iris guessed they were all enjoying the relative safety and comfort after walking away from a nightmare.

She and Gena had refused one of the gym mats. But after the last few days, being warm in a big sleeping bag, together, and safe as they could get felt like paradise.

"They probably took Ben to make sure he didn't try to help us," Iris said, snuggled as close to Gena as she could manage.

"That or using him as bait. I don't mean to sound that way, but I didn't see a whole lot of kindness out of anyone who was with Bill and Rita Hicks. How are we going to get out of here?"

Iris shook her head. Even though the huge room had been dark all night, she hadn't wanted to close her eyes. The images that flashed up as soon as she tried had her terrified she'd never sleep again.

"When the others are awake, or admitting they are, we'll go see if our van is still there. They might not have thought to take it with them on their grand raid. We can get Sally down the mountain at least. There's a hospital in Wolf Branch. Not exactly a major medical center, but better than what we can dig up out of the school nurse's office."

"Assuming Wolf Branch isn't a disaster by now," Gena said, her voice low and harsh. "Your father said those assholes had enough explosives to destroy the back road, didn't he? Or we could meet Bill and his glorious raiding party coming back up."

Gena didn't seem to realize how tightly she was gripping Iris's hand. Iris stroked her hair, kissing her forehead and both cheeks.

"We'll face whatever comes. They don't expect us to be out of the sugar barn, much less armed."

The sense of something horrible happening in Wolf Branch, whirling gray and orange heartbreak, hadn't entirely left Iris. But part of her - the same part that drove her to bring the paintings out of her mind and into reality - was certain Wolf Branch and the people who lived there survived. And that they would thrive.

Both jumped at a voice out of the gloomy darkness.

"I hate to disturb you," Ms. Blevins said. "I thought I heard you talking."

Iris sat up, not liking the worried tone in her former teacher's voice.

"We're awake. What's wrong? Something on the road?"

One of the women who lived closest to the main road into town had volunteered her house for the closest they could get to a guard outpost overnight. She and two others had spent the night with walkie-talkies liberated from Rita Hicks and Haga.

After several seconds of quiet shifting and brief flashes with a soft handheld light, Ms. Blevins sat beside Iris.

"Not the road. No word from there. It's Sally Lee. Her shoulder, it's still soaking through every kind of bandage we put on it, no matter how tight. She's cold but she's pouring sweat, doesn't seem to know where she is. And her poor little heart is just pounding."

Iris rubbed her eyes, wishing she'd at least tried to sleep. Their few hours of quiet and calm were over before anyone was ready.

"Okay, we can't wait. We'll walk down to the house, see if the van is still there. If it is, we'll get her and as many of the kids as we can out of here. Can you try to keep everyone quiet until we get back, Ms. Blevins?"

Ms. Blevins snorted. "I'll do what I can, at least until Bob Kaiser wakes up and starts his moaning again. But only if you drop the Ms. Blevins nonsense. My name is Lucy."

Iris was surprised by the smile on her own face.

"I'll do my best, Lucy."

Chapter 23

The quiet, nerve-straining walk through Maple Ridge chilled Iris more than the frigid wind driving stray bits of snow. The same streets, shops, houses, even the trees she knew so well had taken on threatening new life in the last twenty-four hours. Every leaf skittering down the sidewalk, creaking branch against heavy clouds overhead, and especially a few open doors rattling and slamming in the wind sent her heart pounding.

The deserted town left Gena and Iris's mother every bit as jumpy. Iris carrying an assault rifle while her mother carried a handgun and Gena carried the axe only made things worse. A quick dash inside to get the van keys and too-fast drive back to the middle school was all any of them could manage.

Iris didn't think she had enough space in her mind and heart for more fear. Not until she saw a group huddled together against the wind and more snow in the parking lot between the school and the sugar barn. All women except Jessie Estep, the boy who'd managed to escape Rita Hicks with his life when hers ended. He stood close Ms. Blevins - Lucy - and both turned and watched Iris drive up.

Her mother was out the door before Iris could get the van parked.

"What's going on?"

Mrs. Williams walked away from the group, one of the walkie-talkies clutched in her hand.

"They're hearing some kind of vehicle outside of town, probably more than one. No one can see them yet, so they're not sure who. But someone's on the way."

A bone-deep shudder unrelated to the cold tore through Iris. Gena's wind-reddened face paled, and she grabbed Iris's arm.

"Can *you* see anything, Iris? Like you you saw flames behind Haga when all this started?"

Instead of the swarm of black, gray, and flaming red tornadoes focusing behind Haga or Bill and Rita Hicks, Iris saw and felt them all around her. Whirling noise and fury threatened to consume all of Maple Ridge, then spread devastation out across the mountains, Virginia, and all the rest of the country.

"I see…" Iris gritted her teeth, trying to stop the chattering. "The nightmare. All around us."

"From the road?" Gena pulled Iris close and whispered into her ear. "Is it Bill and the rest?"

Iris forced cold air into her lungs and squeezed her eyes closed.

The horrible cyclones didn't fade or weaken, but light broke through the angry sky over their heads. Light that felt warmer than the December day, warmer than anything besides Gena had for many long months.

Light breaking through from the southeast. From Wolf Branch.

Yes.

From the road.

"I think…help. Trying to reach us. But danger all around."

Iris felt someone lean in close.

"They just said Nancy Nelson got loose while it was dark," her mother said. "Bob Kaiser, too. Not sure if they had help from outside or not. Is that what you're seeing, hon?"

The light concentrated, drawing to a blinding point so bright that Iris drew away and reached up to cover her eyes.

And opened her eyes facing the road out of Maple Ridge.

The rumble of engines reached her ears at the same time.

"Something's wrong, but I can't tell where. We can't stay out here."

Movement flashed at the last rise, some kind of vehicle, hard to make out in the thickening snow. Too far to tell if it was one of the trucks that had carried so many of their men and boys away.

Mrs. Williams jerked the radio to her ear.

"That's not them! It's not the trucks from Maple Ridge!"

Iris gripped her mother's hand.

"We're not safe out here, Mom. No matter who it is."

Gena started toward the group, Iris's mother close behind her. Iris herself stayed frozen, helpless, locked into dread of what her next few breaths would bring.

The vehicles rumbled closer, moving at a fast clip down the empty road. With the whole of Maple Ridge only a few blocks long, they'd be there in less than a minute.

Along with whatever held the terrible storms in Iris's mind.

"Let's get everyone inside," Iris's mother said, holding up both hands. "Just to be safe."

"Go," Iris whispered, unable to force her voice any louder.

The women took a few steps toward the middle school, then Mrs. Williams shouted.

"They brought an ambulance! We need to get Sally out here!"

Everyone turned, and Iris managed to move her head along with them. A bright white van, with the clear bulge of red lights on top, drove right behind a brown Wolf Branch police car. An old van not much different than hers followed, then several trucks.

A shot rang out, the bullet ricocheting off the bricks of the school building.

Three women whipped their rifles around, taking aim at the road.

"No!" Lucy Blevins cried. "They're from Wolf Branch!"

The next shot caught her in the chest.

Iris moaned as the police car, the ambulance, then the rest of the vehicles slammed on their brakes hard enough to squeal on the cold pavement.

She ducked behind her van, jerking the passenger door open.

She grabbed her own rifle, making sure she stayed out of sight of the police car. And out of sight of the line of shops across the street.

Gena and her mother shouted, telling everyone to take cover. The next shot broke a window in the school, sending them running toward the sugar barn.

Iris expected the twisters to point the way, or the increasing light in her mind to let her know where the shooters were. They'd come from at least one of those shops, she was sure of that.

She saw the muzzle flash of the next one instead.

Iris raised the rifle, sighted the open door of the bakery, and fired once.

Bob Kaiser fell through the door, screaming.

Now the whirling maelstroms did shift, moving toward a clothing store on the opposite side of the street. Before Iris could adjust her aim, she heard a rifle burst from beside the school.

Glass shattered all along the storefront.

Two police officers jumped out of their car, crouching behind the open doors. An amplified voice roared through the snow.

"Do not fire! Lower your weapons! We're here to help you!"

Only the fierce wind broke the silence for several seconds. Then a wavering cry rose from the clothing store.

The voice from the police car boomed again.

"Please, lower your weapons. We know what you've been going through up here. We came to help."

Iris let the rifle slip from her shaking hands, back into the van's floorboard. She raised both arms and stepped forward, making sure Gena and her mother could see her.

The gray sky seemed close enough to touch, and the snow was settling in and getting serious. But all traces of the twisting storms had vanished. Iris only saw and felt the warm light all around her.

"It's over," she said, not bothering to wipe the tears from her cold cheeks. "It's finally over."

Chapter 24

An eternity passed while the officers from Wolf Branch searched and cleared the rest of the stores across from the middle school and the sugar barn. Iris stood hand in hand with her mother and Gena, struggling to hold on to what little reserves she had left.

Mrs. Williams waited close by, gripping an openly sobbing Jessie Estep in her arms. When Lucy Blevins's lifeblood splattered his chest and face, Jessie had grabbed one of the rifles and fired back. He'd stood by pale and silent while the police dragged Matt Nelson's lifeless body from the store.

When they'd carried Nancy Nelson out, wounded and wailing for Matt, Jessie didn't know how to stay strong anymore.

Bob Kaiser only managed to cry for help a few times before it was too late. Iris's former teacher and new friend Lucy hadn't had the chance to say a word.

The first person from Wolf Branch to cross the street was a compact, serious deputy named Melissa Wiggins. Her dark features somehow managed to be sympathetic and angry at the same time.

"Did any of you hear shots from somewhere else? Or just from these stores?"

"Only those two locations that I heard," Iris said. "We haven't seen or heard anything since that stopped."

Deputy Wiggins nodded. "We're not seeing signs of anyone else. I think we should search the houses to be sure, but it would be best to get all of you down off the mountain before this snow really starts to pile up."

"One person inside needs to go now in that ambulance," Gena said. "She has a gunshot wound to her shoulder that won't stop bleeding."

"Now that we've got the area cleared, we'll get Dr. Hughes in there to have a look. A whole bunch of other folks came along to help as much as they could." She glanced at Nancy Nelson, now crouched on the steps up to the elementary school. No one besides the other officer was anywhere near her. "Unless someone else is hurt, there's plenty of room for two in the ambulance."

Iris's mother stepped forward, her smile chilly and terrifying.

"We'll just see how Nancy's doing and let you know."

Either missing or ignoring what Iris understood from her mother's tone, Deputy Wiggins turned toward the waiting vehicles and waved her arm. Under almost any other circumstances, Iris would have laughed at the way all the doors opened at once.

A woman wearing purple hospital scrubs under a heavy winter coat jumped out of the ambulance and ran toward them, thick dark blonde ponytail bouncing on her shoulders. She detoured toward Nancy, but Iris's mother moved faster. Iris and Gena followed as fast as they could, getting there at the same time as a young man dressed in the same scrubs.

"I'm Sandy Hughes," the woman said, grasping each of their hands. "This is my nurse Jeff."

"I'm glad to meet you, Sandy," Iris's mother said. "I suspect Nancy here was a big part of the violence we just had on top of every damn thing else. We have a good woman inside who's in much worse shape."

Sandy didn't even glance down.

"Understood. Take me to her."

"Let me ask you something before we go anywhere. Did you treat a man named Sid Rutherford down there in Wolf Branch? He was with that bunch from up here, but he wasn't one of them."

"I don't remember that name," Sandy said. "A whole bunch of men insisted on making the trip, though. He might be one of them."

Gena raised her head, looking at something behind Iris. She closed her eyes and smiled. When she opened them, she winked at Iris.

"I'll take you inside, Sandy."

Iris turned at the same time her mother did.

"Sid!"

Both women caught Sid Rutherford in a tight hug, nearly knocking him off his feet.

"It's okay now," he whispered. "It's all okay."

Similar quiet, joyful reunions filled the street, with women and children pouring out of the middle school into the street. After a few minutes, Iris stepped back, leaving her parents to a more intimate reconnection.

Her breath stopped when a man she'd never met before fell to his knees beside Lucy Blevins.

Iris turned away, nearly stepping right into another man, one she'd never even seen. He was nearly as tall as her father but not as lanky, with a thick red beard and curly red hair that caught the blowing snow.

In Iris's mind, the vivid shade danced in tiny shapes behind him, joined by matching bits of black, brown, and yellow.

"I'm sorry, I just about knocked you down," he said. He spoke with a flat Midwestern accent, and his smile was warm and friendly. "I probably need to stay the hell out of the way until someone tells me where to go."

Iris laughed, grinning back at him. Something inside her shifted, thawed, even as a fresh gust of wind seemed to drive the temperature down another ten degrees.

"What are you up here to do?" she said. "I'm Iris Rutherford."

He grasped her cold hand in both of his warm ones.

"Alex Collins. I need to get a look at the wind turbines, see if I can figure out why Wolf Branch isn't getting power from them anymore. But that can wait. The men we brought back up here said there are food stores? We should be able to get that loaded up today."

He scowled and shook his head. "I mean, we'll leave enough for anyone who stays, of course. But we're glad to take in everyone for as long as you want."

"I think pretty much all of us will be ready to go as long as you have room for a pack of hunting dogs. There's food in the school, but the sugar barn is a little less crowded right now."

Too late, Iris remembered the remains of Haga and Rita Hicks. Both were in the same place, frozen solid from the looks of them. Alex didn't say a word as they approached the sugar barn's doors, but Iris knew she had to.

"We had a hard time up here last night. It went on a lot longer for some, but last night was the worst."

She'd thought he was in his mid-twenties, a few years older than Gena, but in that moment, tension and sadness around his blue eyes left Alex looking older than her parents.

"Last night was a rough one all around," he said in a soft voice. "Maybe we can tell each other about it someday."

They both turned at crunching footsteps on the gravel to see Gena walking toward them.

"Alex Collins," Iris said, "meet my girlfriend, Gena Wallace. My fiancé. Alex is going to help us get loaded up and get out of here."

A silvery flash caught Iris's eye when Alex reached for Gena's hand. A wedding ring with geometric shapes and ridges, sharp and bright and new.

"I'm glad to meet you, Gena. You'll meet my husband Etan tonight." He looked away and grinned, and his cold-flushed cheeks blushed a little deeper. "We've only been married a couple of weeks, still sounds strange to my ears."

Iris caught Gena's gaze, and she knew they were thinking of the same thing. The wedding party in Wolf Branch, back when they'd driven to Maple Ridge.

The deep, strong feeling they'd both had of their future being there, in that beautiful town by the Grasspe River.

The weave and pattern of colors in Iris's painting *Family*.

"Congratulations, Alex," Gena said, slipping her arm around Iris's waist. "I can't wait to meet him."

Another piece of their lives slipped gracefully into place.

FIGHTING THE STORM

BOOK FOUR OF THE STORMS OF FUTURE PAST SERIES

KARI KILGORE

AUTHOR OF IN THE PINES AND RESTRICTED SPECIES

To Kelly

For helping bring these babies into the world.

PART I

COMING BACK TO LIFE

Late March in Wolf Branch, Virginia, was beautiful and pleasantly unpredictable.

A soft, warm breeze drifting across the forested mountains surrounding the town felt like spring. The faint pink blush washing across the trees promised flowers, leaves, and fruit to come. Children begged to go out without coats or even long sleeves, and adults often followed, eager to work the soil for early planting.

The simple promise of sun against skin brought people, animals, and the earth back to full life after winter's long hibernation.

One short day later, heavy gray clouds blocked the mountaintops and the sky before delivering a late blizzard with a couple of feet of snow to bring everything to a temporary halt.

An all-powerful reminder that winter still held sway.

Temperatures plunged to well below freezing, eager to take out much of that early planting with a good hard frost. Kids delighted with one last snowball fight and chance to build their own tiny towns full of blinding white buildings and creatures. Adults smiled and shook their heads, knowing they'd take the chance again next year for the potential reward of fresh vegetables.

In days past, snowplows and salt trucks would have rolled out, ready to keep the neat grid of streets cleared before the first flakes fell. Driving and walking to the businesses and shops might have been slow going, but entirely possible.

Residents of the close-knit Appalachian town tucked into a bend of the winding Grasspe River would have grumbled, bundled up, and made their cautious last-minute runs for bread, milk, and beer just ahead of the storm. Back home, they would have enjoyed the chance to relax, warm and full, confident in the knowledge that empty store shelves would be full once the snow melted.

Folks who lived farther out along the twisting, narrow roads might have fared a little bit worse with a sudden change in the weather. Valley roads that rarely saw the sun sometimes stayed dangerous or impassable for days. But as long as firewood and pantry supplies held out, people in the deep hollows around Wolf Branch had no real problems.

Worries of keeping enough gas on hand for generators and frequent power outages had dwindled nearly half a century before, with a modern power grid driven by an experimental windmill farm near the mountaintop community of Maple Ridge. The majority of vehicles that navigated the tricky snowed-in roads were electric and guided by automatic navigation systems.

Even in such a remote and pristine area, surrounded by hundreds of acres of re-grown wilderness, all the convenience and security of the passing of the fossil fuel era eased modern lives.

Even in the middle of an unexpected March blizzard.

Until the end of the world changed everything.

Chapter 1

ALEX COLLINS STEPPED outside the white cinderblock walls of the Wolf Branch cannery, wiping a couple of hours' worth of maintenance gunk from his hands. His breath rose in a white plume, a lot like the wood smoke rising from houses and buildings all around him. Aside from those plumes, the town spread out silent and still below where he stood.

His curly red hair was longer than it had been for a while, brushing his shoulders. His full winter beard would be ready for a springtime trim once warm weather finally arrived.

He breathed deep, taking in the warm, homey scent of burning wood. What he affectionately called the original means of heating with stored solar energy. That comforting smell and the quiet would have been unimaginable to him only a few short years ago, when he still lived in Chicago.

The community garden and greenhouse that Alex and nearly everyone in Wolf Branch had worked so hard to get going still held the remains of an unusually late snow. The curved roof of the greenhouse shed just like it was supposed to, leaving a nearly waist-deep drift all around its edges. The garden waited for planting, flat except for a few leftover stands of kale standing defiant and tall.

The greenhouse already held seedlings started a few weeks ago and a few rows of spring greens. Alex could see bright yellow, pink, and other shades from flowers they managed to grow all year long through the transparent sides. Those traces of color always made him smile.

Some were for practical purposes, like the edible nasturtium and medicinal herbs. But the flowers grown just because they were pretty were Alex's favorites.

The red brick school towering three stories to his right was as empty as the parking lot, waiting for safer conditions to start regular classes. Most of the school-aged kids in Wolf Branch lived in town, close enough to walk to school. Several of them would be descending on the cannery shortly with their parents in tow, most on foot.

Carpool lanes and school buses were in the past.

The solid thunk of a door closing behind him, followed by footsteps on the concrete floor of the cannery made Alex smile again. A warm hand grabbed his.

"And you accuse *me* of liking the cold."

Alex turned into the embrace of his husband Etan. Four months and more than the usual amount of troubled hours passing hadn't dulled his pleasure in those two words.

My husband.

"Cold outside is one thing," Alex said. "You're the one who wants to see your breath in the bedroom."

"Easier to warm up in there. When will everyone get here?"

"Any time now. I think everything inside is ready for spring. Shouldn't be any more surprises."

Etan leaned back and smiled, but his green eyes were sad. That sorrow lifted more and more often now, sometimes for days at a time. Finding bits of shattered glass and grime behind a storage cabinet earlier that morning - remnants of the attack that had taken the life of Etan's father - had brought the sorrow back full force for both of them.

"I can deal with the things I expect to see every day, you know?" Etan said. "It's the things I don't expect that get me."

Alex couldn't stop himself from glancing at the steep, curving road going past the cannery. A darker patch of pavement, rougher and not quite level, marked the spot where his father-in-law had lost his life. And quite likely saved everyone else's.

Both men turned at the unusual sound of an engine, the faint electric hum clear in the quiet. A small brown truck that used to be part of the town's fleet headed up toward the cannery.

A group of adults and older teenagers had been out hunting that morning, taking advantage of the growing population of deer around Wolf Branch. Humans who could no longer go to a grocery store provided the balance wolves had two hundred years before.

"There's our distraction for the day," Etan said. "Better get ready."

Chapter 2

Etan Griffith grumbled about the early mornings, having to be up and in town before the sun came up. Snow plows never had made it all the way up to the house where he grew up outside of Wolf Branch, or the house just down the road he now shared with Alex.

The frequent snow days had been a treat when he was a kid. Having to go to school nearly into summer never outweighed the pleasure of sleeping in and playing in the snow all day long.

He'd never imagined being the one who had to drive at a crawl over snowy roads to get to town to open the classroom on time, no matter how badly he wanted just a few more minutes of sleep.

Even on those mornings, the comfort and familiarity settled over Etan like a well-loved blanket as soon as he stepped through the cannery's double doors. That was the only time the huge building was silent and still.

Two rows of wide stainless steel tables ran the length of the room, with connections to the black pipes overhead dropping down every few feet. The cauldron-sized pressure canners they'd need today took up one whole wall, as did storage shelves crowded with every kitchen tool imaginable.

Deep square prep sinks and a row of commercial ranges and

ovens rounded out the space, along with more specialty machines and devices than even Etan's grandparents had known how to use.

The cannery finally started to warm up around him with a crowd of kids and adults, bringing three big deer and ten chickens from local flocks stowed in the old town truck. Despite many happy hours spent in the heat and noise of the cannery with his grandparents, Etan had never learned how to process meat.

Processing the animals down into manageable chunks was hardly his favorite thing in the world. But he certainly appreciated the quick and easy meals later on.

He and Alex both stayed out of the way when the huge band saws in the corner fired up to handle the venison. The high-pitched whir and drop was familiar from hours of helping his father and grandfather build or repair things. Watching this saw used for breaking down a deer once - knowing what that drop in the sound of the saw meant - had been enough for both Etan and Alex.

So today they busied themselves starting up the silvery barrels of the pressure canners and bringing out out heavy skillets and stock pots. All of the massive industrial strength ranges would be busy getting the meat browned and chicken stock ready.

The long, echoing space, all concrete and cinderblocks and steel surfaces, filled with chatter and the unmistakable ring of the big saw. But none of the squeaks and bangs of equipment trouble Etan remembered from his childhood. Alex and an enthusiastic group of locals had gone to work almost as soon as they'd arrived in Wolf Branch two years ago, cleaning up the abandoned building, updating every pipe and gear and nozzle.

Fresh from Chicago and leaving his engineering career behind, Alex had led the way in turning a hulking old empty building into the thriving focus and heart of their new community.

Crashing glass from the front of the building had Etan jerking his head up and around. The remains of a couple of quart jars were scattered on the floor, light from the overhead windows highlighting the jagged, sparkling bits. Jessie Estep, one of the young teenage boys from Maple Ridge, his face blazing red, ran toward the office for a broom.

Etan snorted and turned back to the pot he was filling with water.

"The only thing Alex can't replace or repair," a woman said from his other side. "I wouldn't be surprised if he figures it out, though."

"Hey Gena. He frets about that more than you've believe. Iris and her hunting party brought in a good haul."

Gena laughed, looking back toward the noisy back room. She'd been part of the group rescued from Maple Ridge back in December, the day after the nightmare raid on Wolf Branch. Her dark blonde hair shifted over her shoulders, and she was a bit shorter than Etan. He could see Gena's partner Iris, her black hair caught back in a braid that made sense with what she was demonstrating.

"She's happy as a pig in shit, as my great-grandmother would have said. The hound dogs are, too. I'm happy to sit that part out, but Iris says even city girls have to know how to cook venison to make it out here."

"The cooking part I can handle," Etan said. "I'm glad someone else wants to do the hunting."

Jessie ran back out, stopping himself so abruptly beside the broken glass than his shoes gave a harsh shriek against the concrete floor. His cheeks and ears deepened to ripe tomato red, but he shrugged and grinned at Etan and Gena before sweeping up the glass.

"How's Jessie doing?" Etan said, arranging meat forks and tongs beside the cooktop.

"Still worried about his parents, but he's not talking about them coming to get him anymore. I think seeing how many of the rest of us have tried to adjust helped a little. It's so tough not knowing."

Jessie's family had been far away when disaster struck in Maple Ridge, Wolf Branch, and the rest of the country and the world. Along with Gena's family, Alex's, and so many others. Iris was one of the few who had both parents with her.

"Classes starting up soon will help get him settled," Etan said. "Did Linda talk to you about maybe helping teach a few?"

Gena paused in sorting out tiny jars filled with the surprising number of herbs and spices they'd been able to grow in Alex's greenhouse. She rolled her eyes at Etan.

"Linda talked to me, yeah. I'm no poet or source of artistic prose after a few years of law school, but I can handle basic English. Same with math that isn't Alex-level. Iris beat Linda to it, though, by a few days. She painted the loveliest impressionist vision of me in a classroom surrounded by my eager pupils. I promptly suggested I'd be happy to teach, as long as she handles the art classes."

Etan grinned, wondering if he could get a look at that painting. That was how Iris's dreaming talent came out, in wild and often frightening paintings as soon as she woke. Gena knew better than Iris or anyone else what the images actually meant.

Alex often got a strong idea about the paintings, probably because he'd spent years listening to Etan's dreams in the middle of the night. Those dreams had led the two of them to give up the lives they'd loved in Chicago and venture back to these mountains.

And Etan could no longer deny how that choice had *saved* their lives, just as it had many others who'd arrived in Wolf Branch before and after them. Worldwide, chronic food shortages had weakened the distribution systems and the societies that depended on them. A genetically engineered fungus, purposely released into the corn crops so many staple foods and industries were built upon, destroyed modern food chains and populations and so much that went with them.

News sources like radio, television, and the Internet were years gone. But best guesses and dreams suggested hundreds of millions dead in North America, billions more worldwide.

"Hey Gena." Alex had returned from the meat processing room, face paler than usual under the scattering of freckles. "I think that's enough deer dismemberment for me for today. What can I help with out here?"

She grinned and handed him a thicker than normal pair of kitchen scissors.

"As soon as they finish up in there, we'll be ready for breaking the chickens down. Sounds like you're our man."

Chapter 3

Deer and chickens safely broken down, cooked up, and canned, Alex and Etan escaped the warm air of the cannery for the empty football and baseball fields next door. Idle talk over the long, difficult winter had given way to an eagerness to get started, to turn the huge expanse of cleared land over to food production.

A few Wolf Branch natives grumbled about the change, around town and at the organized - and closed - council meetings. But none of them in any meaningful or serious way.

The fields were more scenic than most, with the steep hills covered with trees rising up all around them. But the value of flat, cleared land in a mountain town was too high to ignore.

Just another growing pain for their new community, and a reluctant admission of how much things had changed. No one in the new world would honestly argue that they'd ever have need of the carefully groomed and maintained spaces once set aside for large-scale sports.

Everyone left, including the kids, worked way too hard to have need of such a diversion anyway.

After the flood of tools they'd gotten when the community garden started up, Alex knew what they'd get for much more land would outgrow their tiny shed beside the cannery. That left him and

Etan sorting through the drafty old equipment shed sitting between the baseball and football fields.

One dusty window opposite the door gave just enough light to show how carelessly everything had been thrown inside.

Alex tried to envision uses for the odd workout equipment stacked on shelves and on the concrete floor with more success than he'd expected. A bundle of flags could work for keeping seeded crops straight, along with various sizes of traffic cones and the square plots for agility training.

A slightly modified tackling sled would make short work of taking up the grass sod, with one of their alcohol-burning ATVs pulling it along.

But much as he might want to, Alex couldn't work out how they could convert the charging dummies nearly as tall as he was into anything useful.

Etan turned with his arms full of discarded practice shoes and laughed so hard he almost dropped all of them.

"The way you're standing and staring at it. Like you expect it to head butt you or something."

Alex snorted and pushed the vaguely human-shaped thing backward. It slowly rolled back, then up and toward him.

"I guess we could turn it into a scarecrow," he said. "I think we have enough uniform rags out here to outfit every one of them."

Etan dropped the shoes in a pile on the snowy grass outside, then knelt to gather up knee and elbow pads.

"I never realized how much of this stuff translated to gardening when I was wearing it."

Alex smiled, running his hands along Etan's shoulders.

"I didn't know you played football. My father wanted me to, of course. By the time I was old enough, he was used to me not living up to his expectations. Tell me about your playing days."

"Not that much to tell. I was small and fast enough to always make the team, and I had fun with it. I was better at baseball, but not good enough at either to worry about it by the time I got to college."

"Wish I'd seen you play," Alex said. He took the armful of

smelly padding, some of it rotten and crumbling, and dumped it outside beside the shoes. "I probably would have enjoyed the games a lot more. Maybe you can try on your old uniforms for me sometime."

Etan laughed and shook his head. He'd never begrudged Alex his recurring fantasies since they'd moved here, made all the more vivid by the collection of photos Etan's grandparents left in the house they now shared. He played along more often than not, to Alex's ongoing delight.

"I'd be happy to," Etan said with a wink. "If you can stand the lingering stench of adolescent boy."

By the time they finished, there was more than enough room inside to store anything short of a full-sized tractor.

"I'll let Linda know to get the word out for equipment people don't need," Alex said, leaning back with his fists pressed against his lower back. "Hopefully Walt and the rest will take pity and tell me what it's all for. My Wisconsin childhood didn't prepare me for life as a farmer as well as you'd think."

"The Council will be thrilled. More to debate and argue about."

Alex considered, but only for a few seconds. He had the strongest hunch that Etan's reluctance to join the Council was finally starting to crack.

But he still needed to go carefully.

"Iris tells me a few people on the Council are starting to have dreams about this place," he said, watching Etan's face. "The ones you had back in January about clearing all the grass out, planting the fields. Not that I'm supposed to know about that."

"Yeah? Well, good. They can thank us for emptying this shed out and help us with the rest."

Etan pulled the door closed and leaned against the shed with his arms crossed, looking up under his eyebrows at Alex.

Yep. He knew what was coming.

"They have every dream you do, E. But they have them a long time *after* you do. You're out ahead, almost every time."

Etan shrugged, but he stared down at his feet now.

"Just say it, Alex. I've been hearing it from Mom, Iris, Gena.

Half the people in Wolf Branch are afraid to bring it up to me, the other half won't shut up about it. Let's see where you stand."

Alex leaned against the wall beside him, their shoulders touching.

"You don't have to wonder about that. I'm always going to stand with you. But in this case, I'll say it. You *need* to be on the Council. *We* need to be, both of us. You're the strongest dreamer we have. We might not be finished with threats we need to see coming."

"I can't even remember the damn dreams. How pathetic is that? I'm not sure how much good I'd do them."

Alex looked away to hide his smile. They'd gone from a firm "No" to "Not right now" to "I don't belong."

Almost there.

"Most of the dreamers don't seem to remember," he said. "Iris doesn't, sometimes not even after she finishes the paintings. Not until Gena sees what they mean. You told me last year you know when I'm telling you the truth about the dreams. I think most of us are set up to work in pairs. Did you miss the part where I said we *both* need to do this?"

He reached over and took Etan's hand, the warmth reassuring against the increasingly chilly air.

"You don't realize how people trust you," Alex said. "How they *want* to follow you. They all did when we first got here, with getting the cannery up and running. That was before anyone else talked about the dreams. Whether you want to be or not, you're a leader. We need all the real leaders we can get."

Etan sighed and squeezed Alex's hand.

"Are you ever going to stop asking?"

"Yes. When you agree to go." Alex stopped and reconsidered at Etan's raised eyebrows. "Never mind, I'm not leaving you an opening that big. I'll stop asking when you actually *do* go."

Etan surprised Alex by laughing under his breath and leaning over to kiss his cheek.

"Okay, okay. I don't like it, but I'll do it for you. Can you do something for me? Wait a couple of months, for one thing. I promise I'll go, but give me some time to get ready."

"Done. They're not meeting all that often anyway. I promise I won't bug you about it again until at least June."

"Thank you. And maybe see if they can have a subcommittee or informal meeting or whatever they want to call it? If I have to walk in there in front of a huge crowd like I'm auditioning or defending a thesis, I'll never make it. I think I can handle talking to a smaller group first."

Tension he hadn't quite been aware of left Alex's shoulders and neck. He hadn't wanted to admit it with Etan so jumpy, but this wasn't a simple matter of keeping their hard-won place in their new community.

Alex had a feeling, far more deep and resonant than a hunch, that he and Etan and everyone else in Wolf Branch weren't finished fighting to survive the end of the world.

Some part of him knew more struggles waited, and wanted every possible advantage they could get.

"I'll see what I can do, sweetie," he said, pulling Etan after him and away from the shed. "If you'll take me home and figure out how to warm both of us up."

Chapter 4

Alex was as good as his word, biding his time before arranging for Etan to meet with six people instead of the full council. And none of those six would be Mary Shadrin or any of her followers.

The disturbing woman hadn't been as openly disdainful of Alex - or as obvious in her desire to be in charge of more than her own group - since the disastrous raid from Maple Ridge. But she hadn't been exactly friendly and warm, either.

Etan was still nervous when he and Alex parked outside the town hall. Etan stared at the one-story red brick building, the same one he'd seen his entire life. Concrete steps up to the white front door. Windows at even intervals around the whole thing. Cheery blue curtains hanging in each one.

The only thing that seemed to change over time was the color of those curtains and the contents of the row of stone planters out front. Etan remembered helping build them one summer when he was twelve or thirteen, and helping his grandmother plant flowers in them. This time of year, vivid purple irises shared space with cheery yellow black-eyed Susans and bunches of mums and daisies.

Etan was touched that someone cared enough to carry on that little tradition when so much had changed around them.

This wouldn't be an unruly gathering like they'd had at the high school what felt like years ago, when half the town outed themselves as dreamers in front of the packed-full auditorium. Not even the typical meeting Etan imagined and dreaded, with a dozen or more people arguing around the big oval table in the main room inside.

Even with a group well-known to him and no set agenda, he couldn't help feeling like he was walking into a lion's den.

The only thing that gave him even the hope of going in there was knowing he hadn't been the only one to dream of this. Everyone else in there waiting had the dream, or slept beside someone who had.

"You're sure it was tonight?" he said, knowing how silly it sounded before he finished speaking.

"I'm sure, E."

Alex made no move to get out of the car or tease Etan into it. He simply sat and waited.

Maddening.

And more than enough reason to marry Alex all over again.

"All right. I guess it's just as well I never got the chance to defend a doctoral thesis or anything else remotely public, huh? I never would have made it. Let's get this nightmare over with."

The room itself was a pleasant surprise, one Alex had surely helped arrange. They weren't scattered across the big conference room, or even crowded into one of the smaller rooms with a table. This was more like a break room than anything else, as in a *real* break from work rather than a refrigerator jammed into two cabinets with a constantly dingy microwave and unreliable coffee maker in the middle.

Several comfortable chair were tucked into a carpeted room, with non-glaring lighting and even a television on the wall. Someone - Etan again suspected Alex - had supplied their own bottled beer and cider to go along with fresh fruit and a cheese plate that could have come from a fancy grocery store in Chicago rather than entirely from Wolf Branch.

A blonde woman who looked strange wearing something besides hospital scrubs stood to shake his hand. Doctor Sandy Hughes, another Wolf Branch native who'd returned back home from Chicago before the end.

"Glad to see you, Etan, Alex. I'm here for you more than the Council. Moral support and all."

Right behind Sandy was Linda Burns, the high school teacher who'd helped so much in getting the cannery up and running. Her gray hair was caught up in its usual unruly bun.

"I'm not officially on the Council, Etan. Just here to back you up."

"I'm relieved to have at least two people on my side." Etan winked at the two women, waiting for Alex to elbow him. Right on cue, he did. "Three I suppose, even though Alex did drag me here."

"I love how he accuses me," Alex said, "without mentioning that he drove us here. Should I go get the others?"

"We're all here," a deep, rich voice said from behind them.

Etan turned to see George Light, a former preacher from eastern Virginia who'd arrived with many of his congregation not long after Sandy had. He towered over Etan and even Alex, and his dark brown face held a broad, welcoming smile.

Harry Mullins, a local businessman who'd finally given up his blue or black or gray suits for jeans and flannel shirts, followed behind George. He'd even grown a bit of a neatly trimmed beard, streaked with gray like his thick brown hair.

Harry had pushed for the Council in the first place, and Etan's more cynical side might have suspected a profit or power motivation in the past. But Harry had also admitted his dreams in public that night in the high school auditorium, making it safe for dozens of others to do the same.

Etan wanted to cry with relief when Iris and Gena walked in and closed the door behind them. Ever since he'd met the two of them - the night his mother had organized a massive church feed to welcome everyone who'd survived imprisonment up on Maple Ridge - Etan had felt at home and comfortable with Iris and Gena.

He didn't quite feel relaxed, but a good bit of his fear of walking into some kind of interrogation room had eased by the time the greetings were over and everyone finally found a seat.

Alex spoke before Etan had a chance to worry about what to say himself.

"We all know Wolf Branch doesn't run on anything like parliamentary procedure. Our community is doing as well as it is because so many of us are running on dreams. Our dreams, our partner's dreams. That's how Etan and I got here, why we left Chicago. We're here in this room because Etan's dreams seem to run ahead of everyone else's. Months ahead."

He turned to Etan, eyebrows raised. *Ready to talk?*

Etan was surprised to find he was.

"I was afraid of getting into all of this, and I still am. But I think Alex is right that these dreams work in pairs. For most of us, anyway. If whatever happens inside my head can help get all of us ready, maybe we won't have…as many surprises."

He'd thought he could just say it.

Another attack like last year.

But…

Seeing Iris and Gena, knowing the hell they'd gone through. Remembering Linda and especially Sandy taking care of him and his family after that awful explosion.

The way his mother hid her face against his chest that night, the next morning, and more than once in the long days that followed.

Simple words weren't always so simple.

Linda rescued him before he could catch his breath.

"We wouldn't have been nearly as ready if it weren't for you and Alex and all your hard work. The cannery and the garden and everything you've both taught us, that made all the difference when the outside world tore itself apart."

Sandy nodded. "We're sitting here in a room with lights and food and even this fine beer because of you. We have a hospital with lights and fresh water that we wouldn't have otherwise. You're already leaders in Wolf Branch, Etan. If you're willing to do more, we'd only be lucky. And grateful."

Etan stared at his feet, fighting his desire to argue with everything both women had said, but only for a second. He looked up at everyone's nods and smiles, and he couldn't ignore his sense of being in the right place. On the right path.

On the same path as the love of his life, who pretty much *had* dragged him into this room, but with damn good reason.

"Okay," Etan said. "I'm not sure what I can offer, what we both can. But I want to try. What's next?"

Harry leaned forward, fingers knitted together between his knees. Etan managed not to smile when he noticed mud around the cuffs of his jeans, a far cry from those spotless suits.

"I don't mean to sound like I'm doubting you, Etan. Just trying to understand what might be happening. What kinds of things are you dreaming about before the rest of us do?"

Etan was afraid he was going to freeze up again, trying to drag words out of himself to explain what he still didn't understand. He suspected Alex had known something was going to happen before the raiders attacked.

But he'd never yet worked up the nerve to ask more about what, and how.

And why Alex hadn't told him.

"Etan doesn't usually remember his dreams," Alex said, his words getting out just ahead of Gena's.

"Iris hardly ever knows what her dreams are until she finishes the paintings. Sometimes not even then."

Etan caught the flash of humor and recognition between Alex and Gena, and he was nothing but grateful. And he remembered the hint Alex had already given him.

"They're right," he said. "None of this works without Alex as my witness. One thing I remember is everyone seemed to decide all at once to get those fields planted around the high school. Alex told me I dreamed of that for a few months before anyone else mentioned it."

Harry nodded, lips pressed together in a tight smile. "My wife Cindy said the same thing, but only a few days before we started."

"*Witness* is a lovely way to put it, Etan," Iris said, smiling at Gena. "I felt like that the first time Gena saw one of my paintings.

That I finally had a witness to whatever makes that come through my fingers. What are you dreaming now? Anything new?"

"I'll be more honest than I want to," Etan said. "This is one big reason I hesitated so long. I don't know how to answer that even though I *have* the dreams. Maybe if Alex explains what he hears, I'll remember more."

Alex grinned. "This one's easy, then. Over the past couple of weeks you talk about gathering more supplies, while we still have vehicles that work well enough to get us outside where we've already looked. Going out to get things like eyeglasses, old solid-state computer drives, things we can't make that will last a long time. But the newest thing is paper."

Sandy pulled out her tiny spiral notebook that she was never without.

"You mean like this?" she said. "Or printer paper?"

"Everything and anything you can find," Etan said. "Talking did make it clear in my mind. Journals, notebooks, all of it. Pens and pencils too, for as long as they'll last. We need to start writing the dreams down, recording them. I don't know why, but it's going to be vital. We can figure out how to make paper and even pencils someday, but for now we have to get all we can find."

"That makes sense," George Light said, staring up at the ceiling. "We've been keeping the dreams secret outside the Council, as best we could at least. We'd be able to verify things then, more like a prophecy than a prediction."

"You sound like you want to start a religion," Etan said. "That's the last thing we need. How many of the problems that made everything worse at the end were because of religion?"

Etan tried to keep himself from groaning out loud. What had he just said, to a former preacher of all people?

"I'm sorry, George. I shouldn't have said that."

George laughed, deep and loud, holding his huge hands up toward Etan. "No, the whole point of this is we *want* to hear what you have to say. Both of you. We need to hear it, and not the polite version. If you're dreaming so far out ahead of us, things like this could be crucial."

Iris shrugged. "Most of us agree with you, that's the hard part. What happened on Maple Ridge started out with a kind of twisted religion. Going by what little we know of how things fell apart, different beliefs about the end times killed as many people as sickness and starvation did. But we need some kind of motivation for people to listen. To follow us. What we have to say won't always be as easy as gathering paper."

"We've had more arguments about the food stores already," Linda said, fussing with loose ends of her gray hair. "Some of it from within the Council from what I've heard, and not just Mary Shadrin. We'll have to find a better way to work together to have a chance."

Etan didn't have to look at Alex to know he was biting his tongue, dying to say something. He could feel how tense Alex's leg was against his own, could just about *hear* his agitation.

"What are you wanting to say, Alex?"

"I don't want to be an asshole, but if we have to set you up as a prophet, that's what we need to do. I hated what happened in Maple Ridge and everywhere else. But we can't have gone through so much hell to get here and let everything fall apart again. If people will follow the Great Prophet Etan and that lets us survive, then that's who you need to be."

Etan did groan then, closing his eyes for a second. Not only because this was what he'd been afraid of. Because the words and the ideas sounded true.

They *felt* true, no matter how much he might dislike them.

"I don't know if I can agree to that, not right now. I have no idea how to do *any* of this, much less create a new religion. I'm scared to death of making a hard situation worse."

This time Alex didn't hesitate.

"How could you make it worse? You don't even remember the dreams, E. If anyone should be nervous, it's me. I'm the one who has to figure out what's got you so stirred up in the middle of the night and try to remember it all."

"You always do, Alex."

"Exactly," he said with a grin. "What are you so worried about then? Especially if I start writing them down on all this paper we need to find."

Etan realized he'd finally learned to recognize when it was time to stop resisting, even if he still wanted to. Another of those scratchy, dissonant pieces inside of him moved the tiniest bit at Alex's words.

Shifting into harmony.

"I won't make any promises," he said, smiling to soften the words. "But I'll do my best. Let's figure out what comes next."

Chapter 5

One thing Alex hadn't counted on when they joined the Council was Etan deciding to move a few months later.

Everyone on the Council lived in town, either in a few scattered houses or in brick apartment buildings built well over a hundred years ago. All of them within walking distance of each other, the cannery, and the town hall.

That all made perfect sense to Alex, and he couldn't think of a real reason for arguing about it. The apartment was lovely, for one thing.

One floor up from Iris and Gena, a few blocks from Etan's mother Laura. A bright, sprawling space, with gleaming original wood floors and window seats, and a big, well-designed kitchen.

Four bedrooms seemed like far more space than they'd ever need, but Alex wasn't bothered by that. He knew in his heart, as strongly as he ever had, that their future would include children to fill up all that space in the beat of a sweet little heart.

This building had a modern boiler in the basement like the others did, one Alex and his dedicated crew had updated to run on what they could grow. No more shivering in an old, under-insulated house while they waited for a creaky wood stove to get going every morning.

After the heartbreaking departure from their shoebox apartment in Chicago overlooking Lake Michigan, he'd never imagined a move of a few miles would bother him.

But Alex had come to love their little house hidden away in the woods more than he'd realized.

He couldn't explain it to himself, much less to Etan. Maybe because it wasn't just one thing.

It was the memory of their first day in Wolf Branch, when Etan's mother had welcomed them with chocolate chip cookies, a fully stocked kitchen, and a bottle of bourbon. Many walks just down the road to Laura and Connor's house for spectacular meals in Connor's outdoor kitchen.

He and Etan learning they did have a place here, that they'd actually be needed and happy. Settling in where Etan's grandparents Anne and Evan had spent so many wonderful years, surrounded by all their books and photographs.

Alex had even come to love that creaky wood stove, the routine and satisfaction of heating the house with his own labor rather than touching a screen. He would miss the way he could adjust the scent of the fire depending on how he selected and arranged the wood almost as much as the aroma and taste of apple cider heated on top.

He leaned against the curved archway in the heart of the house, the now-empty library where first Evan and Anne, then he and Etan had spent so many hours reading and studying and learning.

Seeing shelves Etan's grandfather and father had carefully built left without a single book or photo broke Alex's heart. But the hundreds of volumes had been too valuable in helping all of Wolf Branch get ready and have a chance at survival to leave them here.

Neither he nor Etan could abandon the pictures for far more sentimental reasons.

All the books and photos, the burgundy wingback chairs, and the matching ottoman waited in a jumble in the apartment, along with the antiquated but still functional computers. Even Anne's fuzzy pink blanket had made the trip.

Alex had agonized over the contents of Connor's secret hiding place, the tiny door above one top shelf. He'd finally taken the journals written in Evan's hand and built a secret place for them in the apartment, in the bedroom that would be their new library.

The message sent from a man who'd died before they could have met would stay safe as long as Alex lived.

He heard Etan's steps echoing in the empty living room behind him. Alex held out his arm, smiling at the way Etan still fit perfectly against him after five years.

How well must Etan's grandparents have fit after knowing each other for nearly eighty years?

Alex hoped to find out.

"This is hitting you almost as hard as leaving Chicago, isn't it?" Etan said, slipping his arms around Alex.

"Almost. I thought we'd be in this house the rest of our lives, you know?"

"I know. I'm sorry, Alex. I didn't realize-"

Alex turned to face Etan, brushing his hair back from his forehead.

"No, it all makes sense, moving into town. We might have plenty of power from Maple Ridge now, but we can't do a whole lot for these old roads. It was bad enough trying to get around this past winter. I'll love it there, too, once I get settled in. As long as you're there, it's home."

"Leaving Wisconsin and your family didn't bother you like this, did it?"

Alex laughed and pulled Etan close.

"Not even a little. I hope they're as okay as anyone can be out there now. But my life didn't start until I left. My family is right here."

Etan leaned up for a kiss Alex was happy to provide. A kiss that quickly made Alex wish the bed was still here, or at least some of the furniture. Hell, a blanket, or maybe a beach towel would do.

They were both laughing when they stopped to catch their breath.

"Too bad we can't take the tub," Etan said. "We've had some damn good times there."

"I can't imagine how we'd move a stone soaking tub built into the wall and the floor, much less get it up four flights of stairs. I doubt even the apartment's service elevator would manage. We'll have to make do without it."

"That rickety old hand crank thing you keep telling everyone is safe? I wasn't thrilled with putting our furniture on it."

"Worked just fine," Alex said with a grin. "And saved us lugging a couch up four flights."

They laughed together, ending up in another kiss. Etan grabbed Alex's hand and pulled him unresisting toward the bathroom.

"That last load of books will be fine out in the yard for a while. Time enough for one more memory."

PART II
WITH NEW LIFE

Chapter 6

Even after a year, Etan's favorite thing about the apartment was the first thing he'd noticed. All the morning light. Not in their bedroom, thank goodness. That was tucked away on the north side of the building.

But the kitchen and the living room and the tiny little dining nook were all on the east side, set under lovely tall windows. Neither their apartment in Chicago or the house here had much light at all, and definitely not in the morning.

Here the early daylight streamed in from the time the sun cleared the mountains circling Wolf Branch until it set on the other side, gleaming off the aged hardwood floors. The natural light was a lovely change of pace.

The high ceilings kept the rooms from overheating even when summer was in full swing. And the winter sun had supplemented the ornate antique radiators and sleek modern baseboards quite nicely.

His mother worked her magic in this new place just like she had when they first arrived in Wolf Branch more than four years ago. She didn't have nearly the resources, with the grocery store getting its last delivery years earlier, and the liquor store longer ago than that.

But she'd still managed to stock up their kitchen with spring produce fresh from the community garden that now thrived on the old football and baseball fields, Iris's venison, and fresh baked bread. She'd helped figure out how to arrange their furniture in the larger space, and even where to hang several of the photos from the old house.

A quiet conversation about how much the images mattered now that printed photographs had slipped into history added more ritual than routine to what seemed like a simple task.

She'd helped Etan and Alex transform one of the bedrooms on the same bright side of the apartment into a wonderful library, larger than what they'd had in his grandparents' house. Anne and Evan still lingered, in their chairs and photos and even their ancient computers.

Still providing the guidance that had already proven so essential in getting Wolf Branch through the first pains of the end of the world.

Etan smiled at the sight of Alex curled up on the same charcoal gray couch he'd brought with him when he moved into Etan's apartment years ago. The sturdy canvas had held up beautifully after so many hours and miles. He leaned over the back and put his arms around Alex's shoulders.

"Good morning, handsome."

"Good morning to you."

Etan drew back, surprised at the odd sound in his husband's voice. His expression didn't help. Alex was smiling, but he had one eyebrow raised.

"What's wrong?"

"Not a thing. Sit down, I'll get you breakfast. The tea's still hot."

Alex put eggs, toast, and greenhouse strawberries in front of him before he sat down. The spring mornings were still chilly enough that Etan curled his fingers around the warm mug full of dark holly tea.

A few dedicated caffeine addicts had finally managed to get yaupon hollies to grow in the greenhouse the year before, and the resulting brew was more treasured than moonshine. Dreamers and their witnesses especially appreciated the energy boost after a long night, even though their honeybee colonies were too few and precious to gather honey from just yet.

Alex sipped at his own mug with that strange little smile until Etan rolled his eyes and sighed.

"What is going on with you this morning?"

Alex shook his head. "Just wondering how you slept last night."

Etan chewed the last bit of toast, trying to remember. He didn't feel tired as if he'd had a nightmare. He couldn't have been too restless for Alex to be up so much earlier.

Etan felt great, in fact, better than he had for a long time.

"Did we… You didn't violate me in my sleep, did you?"

"Not exactly," Alex said with a soft laugh. "Someone did, but not me."

Etan grunted, pushing his plate away.

"What the hell are you talking about? Just tell me, I'm not in the mood for a guessing game."

"Okay," Alex said, still with that odd smile. "You were dreaming about sex, all right. Sex with Iris and Gena."

"Oh come on. That's a load of shit."

Alex tilted his head to the side.

"Okay, then. Tell me I just lied to you. Tell me what I just said didn't feel true."

"No," Etan said, wishing he *could* argue for some reason. But he did feel that little click of truth, along with a distant, echoing excitement. "You don't lie about much of anything, even when you should."

"You were noisy enough that I had an idea what was going on. You sound pretty much the same making love asleep as when you're awake, by the way. When you finally woke up, you told me you were with the two of them. So you could have children."

Etan stared up at the speckled white ceiling, trying not to let his upset show. That was one of the losses Alex felt the most keenly, enough that it had broken Etan's heart. One of their *someday* plans had been to go to the university in Chicago, to have their genes combined so they could father children that would belong to both of them.

The world had ended before *someday* ever came. Even if that were still possible, if anyone was left alive who knew how, Chicago was several days dangerous journey to the northwest.

"You know I don't want kids if they're not yours too, Alex."

"I do know, I understand. We might have missed our chance at that, sweetie."

"So that's done then," Etan said, pouring more tea for both of them. "We're not having kids."

"Look around you, E, pay attention. There aren't enough of us, not by a long shot. We can't afford to be sentimental about this."

"Well, I don't want to, not without you."

"Sometimes I wonder if your brain only works when you're asleep. What makes you think you'd be raising them without me? Do you really think I wouldn't love a kid that came from you?"

"I'm sure you would, Alex, but I wanted them with you. That was the whole point. You matter more to me than propagating the species."

Alex leaned back in his chair and crossed his arms.

"You're gonna have to reconsider that point of view. We all have to step up on that one. None of this is going to matter if we die out after a couple of generations. We've been on the Council long enough, heard enough stories, to know we have to have the dreamers if we're going to survive. You *know* that. Whatever causes this has to be passed on."

Somewhere deep in his heart, and in the warm trembling in his belly, Etan knew arguing was useless. Alex hadn't just brought this up out of the blue. So far, Etan's dreams had never been wrong.

Having children now, whatever the means, scared him to his bones.

"But I don't have to pass it on, Alex. I'm not going to."

"Yeah, *you* do. Especially you. Listen to what I'm saying, and remember you *dreamed* about this. No one else here has the same kinds of dreams you do. Maybe no one else on this empty planet. You're months or more ahead of everyone else, sometimes a year. You usually see more than anyone else, too. Whatever gift or curse you have is too important to not try and preserve it."

Etan got up and walked over to the window, his precious tea forgotten. The cherry, plum, and apricot trees in the sheltered square between four of the apartments would be full of flowers in a few weeks, with rows of greens planted in between. Several stacks of honeybee boxes - the winter homes to several of their precious surviving colonies - clustered together in the middle.

For a brief, disorienting second, Etan saw it full of children, heard their laughter.

His children. Alex's.

Their children.

He shook his head.

"I'm not the only one who's not thinking, jackass," he said. "If it weren't for you, no one would ever know about these crazy dreams. They might happen inside my own skull, but I can't remember them. How pathetic is that, Alex? Such a supposedly great resource, and I'm the only one who can't use it. It doesn't mean a damn thing without you. Nothing does."

Etan heard Alex get up. He was torn between wanting him to leave the room, leave him alone to fume and get more agitated, and wanting Alex to put his arms around his waist and comfort him somehow.

He sighed and leaned back into his husband's warmth. As usual, Alex made the right choice when Etan couldn't even begin to think.

"Well, that's the other part of the dream, E, the really interesting part," he said in a low voice, his lips against Etan's ear. "You told me we're both going to make love to Iris, and we're both going to make love to Gena. Both of us. Apparently when you're asleep, you do appreciate me, or at least you appreciate that I have something worth passing along too."

Etan turned, putting his arms around Alex's shoulders. That touch fractured some kind of mental wall, revealing a glint from deep down inside his mind. He rarely remembered anything about his dreams at all, at least not the prophecy dreams.

Right now he saw, he *felt*, everything that was going to happen.

"Both of us, at the same time," Etan whispered. "We'll be with them together."

"That's what I've been trying to tell you, but you won't close your runaway mouth long enough to listen to me. I can't think of a better way to solve this problem for all four of us, can you?"

Alex stopped Etan's mouth, and his thoughts, with a kiss.

"We'll both be with both of them, together," Alex said against Etan's lips. "You said we'd do that so we wouldn't know who the father was. So the father would be *both* of us. You said we'd do that so neither of us would be alone."

"I've never even been with a woman," Etan said, pulling Alex against him. "Much less two."

"I have." Alex laughed under his breath. "Well, one at a time, at least. It's not all that complicated. I'll be right there with you."

Alex kissed him again, then moved to Etan's ear, his throat.

"Will they even agree to all of this?" Etan said.

"I think Iris will have the same dream, don't you? She seems to be the one closest behind you. Gena will know as soon as Iris does."

"They'll probably be the ones to bring it up." Etan gasped when Alex bit the sensitive flesh where his neck joined his shoulder. "Neither of them strikes me as the shy type."

"You wouldn't be so damn shy if you'd just listen to me a little more often. Come back to bed."

Etan followed gladly, amazed at how clearly everything was coming back to him. He remembered all of it - the first time he'd ever recalled a dream like this.

The four of them would be awkward at first, himself more than the others. His touch would be hesitant, so uncertain, but having Alex with him would push that away. The four of them would find a rhythm, a comfort and a passion he never could have imagined.

As he was in everything else, Alex was the key.

He unbuttoned Etan's shirt, following the lines of his fingers with his mouth. He sat on the bed, pushing Etan's jeans down over his hips.

"It's not just that you haven't been with a woman, is it?" he said, so close that Etan strained toward the heat of his breath. "You've never been inside someone else, not like that."

Alex took him into his mouth then, and Etan groaned.

"Just your mouth," Etan whispered. "Just your sweet fucking mouth."

Alex stood and moved Etan's hands to his own shirt. He kissed him while Etan fumbled with the buttons. Naked, Alex moved onto the bed, pulling them both down together.

"I want you to, Etan. I want to be your first."

Etan drew back.

"You don't... Have you ever?"

Alex smiled, nodding.

"A few times when I was a kid, yeah. Around the same time I was with women. That was all before I met you."

"I don't want you to be uncomfortable," Etan said.

What Etan wanted was to be done with talking. He wanted to be done with thinking and everything else besides the two of them in this warm bed, at least for a while.

Alex laughed. "Just hush and listen to me, stop arguing with me. I *want* to, with you. Right now. I don't want your first time to be with someone else."

Alex moved Etan's hand down along his body, into the heat between them.

"Let me be your first," he whispered, moving against Etan's hand.

"I don't want to hurt you, Alex."

"Have I ever hurt you?"

"No, you never have. It's always good with you."

"Remember your first time then. Your first *good* time."

Etan closed his eyes, letting that deep, hot memory move through his body. Until that night, sex had felt like something he should do, a requirement. A chore on a list, or a way to relax enough to get to sleep.

Alex changed the chore into a necessity. Making love turned into a craving as deep as the need for food, for air, and that hadn't lessened over the years.

"You were my first good time, Alex."

Alex shifted, moving until Etan's hips were between his legs.

"Do what I did, then. Take your time, go slow. We don't have anywhere else to be today. You're not going to hurt me. Don't you want me?"

For the first time, the first time since he'd started being honest with himself about such things many years ago, Etan did want to be inside of another person.

He wanted to move inside of Alex, to push toward him.

He wanted to try to be part of him.

"Yes," he whispered, his breath speeding up along with his heartbeat. "I want you. I want every part of you."

"Then take me. Take me the same way I took you. I want to feel you inside me."

Etan laughed, the intensity of his body's demands making him dizzy. He took Alex's mouth first, exploring every wet, warm fold like they'd never kissed before.

Their first time together surged into his mind like a vision, like the strongest dream he'd ever had.

His mouth, Alex's mouth, that's what they always started with. No one else had ever turned Etan on so much, like Alex was starving to death for every inch of him. He understood where that fierce appetite came from now.

Etan drew back and looked at Alex's flushed face, nearly lost in his memory. Their roles reversed, both of their bodies unknown and so much younger. Every motion and taste a revelation.

So many years, so much passion between them only made this sweeter.

Like his dreams of the two of them with Iris and Gena, his movements were hesitant at first. Unsure.

But Etan caught the pace of his lover, and he knew that rhythm was a part of him, a song he'd known since the first day he'd looked into Alex's eyes.

The same song that would sing new life into the empty world.

Chapter 7

ALEX HAPPILY REACQUIRED his lifelong habit of walking every-where he needed to go. He'd thought that simple activity was lost to him once they'd left Chicago. Distance from their first house in Wolf Branch made it impractical, and often impossible in bad weather.

But their apartment changed the rhythm of their lives in more good ways than bad.

And just like in Chicago, walking in early summer after a long winter was pure joy. The sun wasn't yet fierce enough to force him into long sleeves and a hat, with commercial sunscreen long expired. The early harvests coming into the cannery had eased enough to give him and Etan short days. They'd be glad for the break once the hectic late summer and autumn harvests rolled in.

The two of them turned the corner into the courtyard behind their building to see a bigger crowd enjoying the late afternoon weather there than at the closed-in cannery.

Alex spotted Etan's mother Laura, Linda Burns, and Iris and Gena, all working around the new grape vines. Walt Colley beside the beehives towered over all of them, standing out even more with his white beekeeper's hat covering his face.

Neither Alex nor Etan had mentioned the dreams of Iris and

Gena, not least of all because neither of them had any idea how they possibly could. The dreams continued, though, almost every night.

Neither of them minded the pleasurable waking results of so much sleeping time focused on lovemaking.

Walt bent over one of the hives for a few seconds, and Alex was glad to see him slide the thin wooden cover back into place. He didn't mind the bees at all himself. In fact, he was predictably fascinated by the way they constructed and maintained their homes. Natural structural engineers.

But Etan's grip on his hand loosened when Walt pulled his hat off and turned around. Etan had never been comfortable around the honeybees or carpenter bees or bumblebees that helped keep their food supply healthy.

"Hey Walt," Alex called. "How's it going in there?"

"Hey there Alex. Etan. Just got the girls all settled in after a good checkup. Queens setting plenty of new brood, all through every one of the hives. We should have enough for the new colonies out by the cannery before it gets too hot."

Walt slipped the hat and face net under one arm so he could swallow up Alex's and then Etan's hands in his huge paw.

"I'm glad to hear that," Etan said. "We might have honey for our tea before too much longer."

Walt nodded, a grin on his long, friendly face.

"Why sure, I don't see why not. Once we have a bunch of colonies in good shape, they'll make more than enough to share with us."

Etan's mother joined them, trying to wrangle her blonde and silver curls back under her hat. Laura didn't seem quite as young as before Etan's father died, but she still looked closer to forty than nearly sixty.

"I'm just hoping for mead to go along with the wine we'll have before long," she said. "The vines are training up just fine. Did you two know Gena worked a couple of summers in the vineyards over near Hidden Springs?"

Gena stood a few steps away, Iris close beside her. They had their heads close together, clearly watching Etan and Alex. Iris's cheeks were flushed; Gena only seemed curious.

He would have bet a large sum of now-useless money that Iris had caught up with Etan's dreams. And that they were just as unsure of how to approach the whole thing as he and Etan were.

"I didn't know we had any vintners among us," Alex said, smiling at Gena. "We just need someone to crack the code on bourbon."

Gena took the hint and joined them.

"I wouldn't say I'm a vintner," she said, rolling her eyes. "I mainly helped out with the vines and carried things around. I *will* volunteer for tasting whatever we come up with. Laura might need a little help."

Iris walked up, still flushed but looking Alex, then Etan in the eye.

"I don't know if it's up to your bourbon standard, Alex," she said. "But a few folks from Maple Ridge do amazing things with maple syrup and a little bit of mash."

Alex didn't need Etan's dreams or the pre-memories Etan's grandmother had. Iris had just led Gena to the next step between the four of them.

The patterns of the bees in the air, the play of the breeze across his skin, even the shape of the wispy clouds overhead let him know his life was about to change.

All of their lives were.

Gena smiled at Iris, then at Alex.

"I'm not making any promises, but we still had a bottle or two left last time I checked. We're about ready to head upstairs if you'd like to give us your expert opinion."

Etan spoke before Alex had a chance to.

"We're in. Our beer and cider isn't half bad, but I'd guess any whiskey will be good after a couple of years without."

As they followed Iris and Gena, Alex caught Etan's mother watching. Her proud and somehow mischievous smile told him all he needed to know about Laura's opinion of the whole situation.

And for whatever strange reason, his mother-in-law's smile finally brought Alex's nervousness front and center. He reached for Etan's hand, and the answering tight grip let him know he wasn't alone in that.

Iris and Gena's apartment on the third floor had the same layout as theirs. Kitchen by the door, dining room and living room by the windows. If anything, their furniture was more eclectic and colorful.

Alex was too caught up in the paintings hung on all the walls to pay much attention to anything else. He'd seen them before on brief visits, but today the shapes, the movement, captured nearly all of his attention. One in particular, full of inverted gray tornadoes, seemed to twist and shift even though he knew it couldn't be.

He was surprised when Iris handed him a clear shot glass full of amber liquid.

"Not much left that they made from corn," she said, holding her own glass up to the sunlight. "They're working on a wheat version now."

Etan and Gena held glasses, and they were clearly waiting on Alex. He turned away from the extraordinary paintings.

"To friends," Gena said. "And to the future."

The whiskey was as smooth as any bourbon, with the taste of maple but barely any sweetness.

"If we can keep making this," Alex said, "we might just survive."

Iris glanced at Gena, and Alex heard his own words echoing in his mind. Whatever caused this, the dreamers and the witnesses, had to be passed along. They'd just have to get past feeling shy and awkward and nervous.

"I'm going to guess you've had the same dreams I have," Iris said. Her cheeks were red, but her voice was clear and steady. "About the four of us."

"For a few weeks now, yeah," Etan said. "We didn't… It didn't make sense to try to explain it until you had them, too."

"Well, no." Gena smiled, holding up the bottle with the whiskey, then refilling everyone's glasses. "It's not exactly an easy thing to put into words. Even when it makes this much sense."

Alex chewed his lip, trying to figure out how to put his thoughts into words until the second he opened his mouth. Unfortunately, speaking got harder instead of easier as he went

"This sounds strange coming from me, I know. I did move here with Etan, we both turned our lives upside down because of what he dreamed. But is this... Are we all just following along because we feel like we have to? Or is this something you want to do? With us, I mean."

Iris stepped closer to him, laughing under her breath. She touched his lips with her fingertips. One thing Alex didn't have to doubt was the tingle that lit up his entire body at her touch.

"We invited you, remember? Having kids was always for *someday* for me, I'll admit. Mainly because I had no idea how it would happen short of a doctor's office, you know? Now, though, meeting you two, getting to know you. We can't get away from all the talk of population crash and having babies. But even without that, you and Etan are the ones I'd *want* to do this with. Okay?"

"Iris and I heard all about the *inescapable biological imperative* on Maple Ridge," Gena said. "We know perfectly well how that can be abused. Better than most, I hope. That's not what this is. I can't think of anyone better than my two best guy friends. You'll both be wonderful dads."

The last one to speak was the one Alex most needed to hear from.

Etan smiled at Alex, tears standing in his eyes. "You know I've wanted kids with you since we first met. I never imagined finding other people I'd want to share that with. I'm glad we're all here."

Alex held up his glass this time, waiting for the others to do the same.

"To family, then," he said. "In every form that might take."

"I need to show you something," Iris said, grabbing Alex's hand. "A painting I've been waiting years to understand."

The bedroom was night and day to Etan and Alex's. Rather than a queen bed with comfortable but ordinary dark sheets and blankets, this king-sized bed looked soft and inviting. A purple padded headboard backed up pillows in several shades, and a matching comforter looked thick enough to sleep on by itself.

On the wall opposite the bed, Alex saw the painting.

He would have sworn it was a digital frame if he'd seen it a few years before, not a flat painting. The sensation of motion was strong in the thick brushstrokes of green in the background, the carefully arranged patterns of red, yellow, black, and brown.

Those colorful markings ranged from the four ovals in the middle, not much bigger than his palm, out to smaller ones that matched, surrounding and completing the circle they created together.

"That's us," he said without thinking. The same way he understood Etan's dreams. "And our children."

"I *knew* you'd see it, Alex," Gena said, her eyes bright. "Iris painted this years ago. Before we met you two."

Alex's heart knew before his mind understood.

This was the family they would bring into this strange, broken world.

"It's beautiful," Etan said. "Did you know what it was, Iris?"

"Not until Gena saw it," Iris said. "Just as fast as Alex did. I didn't even know I was painting my dreams before then."

"Did you know it was us?" Alex said. "When we met up on Maple Ridge?"

Gena tilted her head to the side, looking at the painting, then at him.

"I knew you'd be important, that we'd know you for a long time. I wasn't sure until the dreams started. Did you know that day?"

Alex laughed, relieved he finally felt more excited than nervous.

"Sounds about like how I felt. I knew you'd be important, but I didn't know why."

"I'd say this is pretty damn important," Etan said. "Assuming we get through whatever comes next."

He and Alex had talked, probably way too much, about how this moment might go.

Would they invite the women upstairs to their place? Cook dinner, give them gifts, all in some kind of effort to prove they were good enough providers?

Or would the women invite them down here, all flirtation and seduction, both meeting them at the door wearing some sexy slip of a dress?

Neither one held a candle to the reality he felt surrounding him now.

And none of those dating rituals made sense, not here. None of them were looking for partners, or even lovers. Nothing as cold and clinical as sperm donors, either.

Something different, then.

Their own kind of family.

"If we're both having the dreams," Iris said, reaching for Alex's hand, "I think that means the time is right. Would waiting and trying to plan something dramatic make any difference?"

"I think we'd all be a hell of a lot more nervous," Alex said.

In the laughter, the reminder of the friendship they already shared, Gena stepped into his arms, Iris into Etan's.

Gena felt so small and fragile to him, like he might break her if he squeezed too hard. But her arms were strong around his waist, and he found she fit him in a way no one besides Etan ever had.

Alex looked into his husband's eyes and saw the same surprise and relief there.

Then Alex focused on Gena, on the way she seemed to dance with him to music he couldn't hear, but felt in every part of himself.

The music of their shared future.

Chapter 8

ALL THE DREAMS and wondering and talking in the world couldn't have prepared Etan for Iris, then Gena, announcing they were pregnant. Alex's laughter and hugs all around didn't quite cover up the tears of joy in his blue eyes.

Etan's tears didn't come until hours later, until he and Alex were at home alone. In their home that was about to change forever.

While they wouldn't be husbands to the mothers of their children, or even boyfriends, both men were more than happy to take on the roles of expectant fathers. Helping around the apartment, bringing in the craved food they could still get. Attending appointments with Doctor Sandy, who was delighted to report that all seemed well.

Etan's sweetest fatherly duty so far was having his mother Laura and Iris's parents over for dinner at Iris and Gena's apartment to share the news. The excitement of three grandparents-to-be helped make up the five who were missing, and missed.

Laura even managed to bring Etan's own grandparents in on the celebration. She stated quite pointedly (and more than once) that his and Alex's wedding rings were looking dreadfully scuffed and dirty. That old Charlie Kennedy had made her promise to bring them in from time to time to get cleaned up and polished back into presentable shape.

When she returned them a few days later, each white gold band held a deep green stone set within the facets and angles. Two of the four Anne had worn on her engagement ring for so many years.

Charlie had set each of the other two stones into thin bands perfectly fitted for Iris and Gena. The last request in Anne and Evan's will, and Anne's last vision brought into reality at last.

Whether it was a real shift in the lives of everyone in Wolf Branch, or simply the four of them focusing inward, the whole community seemed calm, waiting. These babies would be the first born to Dreamers and Witnesses since they understood what those roles were.

And the first in Wolf Branch since the end of the old world.

The Council meetings and even everyone's dreams slowed to background noise. Nothing but static compared to the stirring of new life.

Both babies quickened and moved as summer gave way to autumn.

Etan's mood cooled along with the weather, though he tried to keep the change to himself. He wasn't afraid or starting to regret the oncoming change in their lives. He wasn't even worried about not knowing what to do with a newborn, not yet. He and Alex planned to stay with Iris and Gena for the first few weeks, with frequent grandparent attendance, so they could make mistakes and learn and finally figure it out together.

Yet something dragged at him, a fear he couldn't define.

His dreams didn't give him any insight, at least not that Alex could catch. Nothing more than restless nights that kept both of them from sleeping. Etan knew Alex was worried too, even when he joked it was just practice for pacing the floor with an infant.

But with all of Sandy's tools and experience still saying everything was normal, all they could do was sleep when they could.

And wait.

One afternoon halfway through October Etan jumped at the knock on the door, not sure where he was for several seconds. He'd been dreaming, a normal dream of their shoebox apartment in Chicago. The only remarkable part of that dream was how much he still missed those simple, silly days he and Alex had together before everything fell apart.

Another knock, this one more urgent. He sat up slowly, pulling his mind and body bit by bit away from that far-off life. This was the gray sofa Alex had brought with him, but the view out of the windows was mountains rather than an endless lake.

He was in Wolf Branch. He and Alex both were. This was their much larger apartment right in the middle of a much smaller town.

"Hang on," he called, finally getting to his feet. He'd been sleeping far more deeply than he usually did in the afternoon.

He opened the door to see Gena with her hand raised to knock again. Her face was pale, but she had bright spots on her cheeks.

"Hey Gena. Come on in."

"I'm sorry, I didn't mean to wake you," she said. Most of the grogginess left Etan at the anxious tone of her voice. "I think I need help."

"What's wrong? Come sit down."

"I think I need to go to the hospital." Tears stood in her eyes. "I wouldn't bother you, but Iris is at the high school. I'm bleeding, Etan. Pretty bad."

Cold flooded his whole body, and a gut level panic. He reached for her slightly rounded belly. She covered his hand with hers and shook her head.

"Of course you're not bothering me," he said. "Let me get my shoes and we'll go right now. Alex is at the hospital working with Sandy, so she's already there. Do you feel okay?"

Gena carefully walked inside and sat at the kitchen table. Her movements were stiff and awkward.

"I feel like I'm having cramps. Like they're about to get worse. My back is killing me." She held her breath, then let it out in a rush. "I'm losing the baby."

Etan tried to do the math, to remember what he'd read about miscarriages, but his brain refused to cooperate.

"Hold on, we don't know what's happening yet. We're too far along for that, aren't we? You were fine at your last checkup."

He stepped into his shoes and helped her stand. Her hand was now hot and trembling.

"I know, it's usually fine after five months, but the baby hasn't moved all day long. I don't think… I can't remember for sure, but I haven't felt anything for maybe a couple of days."

"Sandy will know better than both of us," Etan said, closing the door behind them. "Definitely better than me. Can you manage the stairs? We can use Alex's elevator, or I can go get Sandy."

"No, I can walk. I just didn't want to be alone."

Gena's breath caught, and she covered her face with both hands. Etan put his arms around her, desperately trying not to press on her belly. She squeezed him tight, sobbing against his chest. Her face was burning hot through his shirt.

"I thought I was doing everything right. Eating right, resting, I've never taken better care of myself in my whole *life*."

"You *are* doing everything right, Gena. Listen, we don't even know what's going on yet. I'm right here with you."

She made it down the four flights of stairs, but she grabbed his hand before they'd taken two steps down Main Street. No one was out in the cool, early afternoon. Probably at the high school or at the big garden, still unaware of this private, painful drama.

Her grip was strong enough to make his knuckles ache.

"I'm sure that's a contraction," she whispered, then gasped. "I'm so sorry."

Etan put his arm around Gena's waist, supporting as much of her weight as he could.

"Hang on, maybe not. Will you be okay here if I go get Sandy?"

She squeezed her eyes closed, shaking her head. After a few deep breaths, she looked up at Etan. Her brown eyes were rimmed with red.

"We should get to the hospital just in case Sandy can do something, but I think it's too late. My water just broke."

After the third time she had to stop and breathe through the waves of pain, Etan knew. His mind tried to convince him otherwise, but his heart had no doubts.

They were losing one of their babies, saying goodbye to a child before it was ever born.

Before *any* of their children were born.

And neither he nor Iris had seen this coming.

Chapter 9

The delivery room at the hospital in Wolf Branch felt too quiet, too still, for such a joyful occasion. One mother-to-be paced the floor, each of the fathers and her own partner taking turns walking with her, holding her hand, rubbing her back.

Her partner - a woman who wouldn't be having her own baby today - did everything she could to stay happy and cheerful and honestly excited, but Alex caught Gena's unguarded expression more than he wanted to.

Thankfully the room wasn't the same cold, bright operating room where they'd lost the baby and left that part of their dream behind a few months before. This could have been a living room if you ignored the especially fancy adjustable bed with monitors built in.

Warm and comforting gold walls, soft rugs on the floor. Couches and chairs for all the hovering in-laws rather than a distant waiting room with uncomfortable plastic backside torture devices. And more than enough space for Alex, Etan, and Gena to fret and worry, wishing they could do more to help Iris.

Etan's mother Laura was proud to tell everyone how Anne and Evan – her own former in-laws and Etan's grandparents – had gotten this homelike birthing room set up. When they'd moved to Wolf

Branch decades ago, such things were unheard of in small town hospitals.

Sandy and her nurse Jeff checked in from time to time, but both of them said the same thing so far. Nothing they could do with labor progressing so well. They didn't expect to do much at all, really, besides calm folks down and stand by just in case.

Alex knew those words and the reassuring smiles rang hollow to everyone else as much as they did to him.

Yes, of course everything was fine.

Just like it had been for Gena's baby.

Until it wasn't.

And thinking that way would only make a wonderful thing sad and a bad thing worse.

He took his turn walking with Iris, leaving Etan and Gena to concentrate on the soon-to-be grandparents. They'd all agreed earlier that the flood of advice, even when offered with love and the best of intentions, was best channeled away from the laboring woman.

"Did you paint anything about today?" he said, taking her hand in his. It felt cool and small, but her grip was fierce. "Besides the one about family."

"They've all been jagged and strange lately. Like this baby dancing on my spine at the moment. She could have at least worn ballet slippers instead of stiletto heels."

"She, huh. Is that you or Sandy talking?"

Iris laughed, but it ended in a groan.

"Gena absolutely forbade Sandy from telling us one way or the other. She doesn't want me to tell her either. I've seen this little one's face in my dreams for weeks now. I hope I haven't let it slip before I wake up."

"Etan's been seeing a girl in his dreams, too," Alex said, smiling. "He threatened my life if I told him, so it's our secret for a little while longer."

They made another circuit of the big room, with Iris leaning against Alex twice to stretch her back. Neither of them said it, but Alex knew they were thinking of the little boy Gena had been carrying.

Sandy made it clear none of them had done anything wrong, and there was no reason they shouldn't try again. None of the four of them wanted to, not for a while.

"I'm sorry to ask this now," Alex said when they were on the far side from everyone else, "but are you sure you want us to raise this one? We're more than happy to, but not if it makes anything worse for you or Gena."

Iris shook her head, then pushed her black hair back over her ear.

"I think Gena's right. Us raising this one alone would be harder on her. Seeing her every day, thinking about what could have been. This way you two can focus on the baby, and I'll focus more on Gena. We'll see you plenty for nursing anyway."

"Fair enough. And I can't *thank* you enough."

"She's a lucky girl, getting to grow up with you." She stopped, hands on her knees while Alex rubbed her lower back. "I don't want to walk anymore. I think I'm ready. Walk me back to the bed and go get Sandy?"

Alex looked up and caught Etan's gaze. At his nod, Etan smiled and walked out.

The second Iris sat on the bed that had been lowered to make movement easier for her, Sandy, Jeff, Gena, and Etan seemed to materialize beside Alex.

His focus, his awareness and ability to know what was going on around him had shifted.

Narrowed and changed to a tunnel-like vision.

He knew everyone else was still there, including Etan's mother and Gena's parents. But the pattern recognition engine inside his head only saw, only understood one connection right now.

The tiny strand of light and life between him and the little girl who was about to enter their world.

His eyes saw Sandy adjust a monitor of some kind, attaching a cable to a transparent patch on Iris's hip. His ears heard low conversation between the two of them, but not a word registered with his brain. Sandy nodded and tapped again, and Iris's vise-like grip on Alex's hand eased.

His skin felt the cool air in the room. He tasted the tea they'll all shared earlier, the sweet, herbal blend Sandy swore would help all of them relax. Excitement mixed liberally with fear had Alex about as far from relaxed as he'd ever been in his life.

And still, the experience of his physical body felt muted, distant compared to the way this little girl would surely be transforming his heart.

He did mange to look into Etan's eyes, calling back all the conversations and hopes and dreams they'd shared about this moment. Always assuming they'd be in a Chicago hospital, with the great, teeming city waiting to welcome their children into a world that no longer existed.

The world that would greet this child might be utterly changed and empty, but she couldn't come into a room more full of love.

"Okay, Dads," Sandy said, looking up from her perch between Iris's thighs. "Everything is about to change. Better get ready."

She'd raised and adjusted the end of the bed into a nearly upright position, with Iris sitting against it and staring into Gena's eyes while she counted. Etan and Alex stood on either side, ready to brace Iris when she was ready to push.

Etan winked at Alex, clearly aware of his shell-shocked state. He mouthed *Ready?*

Alex shook his head and reached for his husband's hand. They leaned forward when Iris did, shoulders behind hers like Sandy had shown them. He felt her muscles tense, heat rolling off her flesh. Gena gripped Iris's hands, sitting on the bed beside her, never looking away from her face.

Alex couldn't have said when it was all over whether the delivery took ten minutes or ten hours. All he knew was the growing pull of that new life force, their daughter charging into the world, demanding every bit of attention from his mind and his heart.

Sandy handed the screaming bundle to Gena, who kissed the tiny, red, wrinkled forehead before turning to Iris's waiting arms.

Alex knew before he looked that the little girl had a thick fuzz of red hair.

Several of their endless discussions had been about names, and having to come up with names for a boy or girl had only made it harder. But Alex was thankful a thousand times over for all that talk now.

When Iris turned to him, smiling with tears in her eyes, he knew exactly what to do and what to say. He took the delicate creature with the healthiest lungs in all the world into his arms, only then noticing Etan stood beside him.

Alex put his free arm around his husband and kissed his cheek.

"Welcome to the world, Caela."

Chapter 10

Alex sat across from Gena in her apartment, watching her nurse their newest baby. She and Iris had both made it clear when Caela was born three years ago that they preferred him and Etan to just be honest about it instead of pretending not to look, then sneaking glances. Neither of them saw any reason on earth why they shouldn't watch such a lovely thing as feeding their babies.

Alex and Etan couldn't possibly have agreed more.

Gena held Connor to her left breast, eyes closed, rocking slightly. The sun caught her blonde hair as she shifted. Their tiny boy, only five weeks old, had understood from his first moments of life exactly what he was supposed to do. He latched onto her dark red nipple and stayed there whenever he had the chance.

"Do you ever resent it?" Alex said. "Having to do this over and over again?"

"You mean being pregnant? Or nursing?"

"Either one. They do go together."

"They do. This wasn't exactly what I planned, you know? When I worked my ass off for a law degree." She shifted, adjusting Connor along with her legs. "But everything changed all around us. If we don't do this, *especially* us, we'll all be gone in less than fifty years."

"That's almost exactly what I told Etan a long time ago," Alex said, smiling. "I hope you know how much we appreciate both of you."

"I know. You too, hon." She touched Connor's face and her breast, pulling her nipple away until he let go with a pop. "Plenty on the other side, hungry boy. Hey, have you had a chance to read through Iris's journal? The one from a year ago?"

"Not yet, but I did look at Etan's from two years ago. I think you're right about the dreams matching up now," he said, shifting his hips lower on the chair and crossing his legs. "I'm sorry I didn't look those over yet. We need to find a better way to manage things like this. We're spinning our wheels. Just because we don't have databases in our pockets anymore doesn't mean we have to be so disorganized."

"Well, maybe we need to talk about that," Gena said. Connor settled again, just as enthusiastically. "The Witnesses, all of us. You and I keep similar records, so we can cross-reference when we need to. We have no idea what everyone else is doing. We have to remember someone may be reading these long after we're not around to explain what we *meant* to say."

"Witness each other, you mean."

"That would be a nice change of pace, wouldn't it?" Gena said with a wicked smile. "Being the center of attention, at least among ourselves."

"I do sometimes feel like the town crier, repeat what I've heard and shut up. Especially since I can hardly ever get Etan to speak up in the Council. If we can at least get our records standardized some-how, have an idea what everybody is concentrating on, we'll have a much easier time verifying the dreams."

"Leave it to a lawyer and an engineer to recreate standards and practices," Gena said. "Some things never change, even after the end of the world. Let me interject a bit of *best* practices, then. We'd have to do this without the Dreamers."

"Otherwise we'll never know if the dreams come from them or from someone else. They shouldn't even read each other's journals, really. Listen, Gena, have you ever heard something bad enough in one of Iris's dreams that you didn't tell her or anyone else?"

She pursed her lips and looked away from him.

"Yeah. I kept what I saw in her paintings to myself in the beginning, a couple of times. Again before I had the miscarriage, before Caela was born. I knew something was wrong, but I pretended I didn't, even to myself. I thought if I admitted it, I'd let it come true. It did anyway. A few other times back in the world, too."

Alex nodded, but he couldn't speak. Not about the loss of their first child, or Etan's dreams about his father dying. He'd still never spoken to another person besides his husband about his father-in-law's sacrifice, and he didn't plan to. If anything so awful came up in the future, he'd love to at least have the option.

"Same here," he finally said. "It would be great to have someone else to talk to. Someone to just listen to some of this who didn't dream it."

"We can make sure these little ones get trained properly, too, so maybe they won't be bumbling along with no idea what they're doing. Like we are. He's just about finished."

Connor was finally getting full and sleepy. His mouth moved more slowly against Gena's nipple with every passing minute. Alex draped a thick towel over his shoulder and stood.

This was one of the many reasons he'd volunteered to bring their babies down while they were nursing so often. The scents, the warmth of their bodies. The heady sensation of holding such a tiny creature safe in his arms. All the rituals of feeding delighted him.

The babies might seem defenseless, but Alex never doubted he was the one disarmed.

"We'll have to do some of the training at home," Gena said. She lifted a drowsy Connor into Alex's arms. "They'll be up in the middle of the night like their parents are."

Alex breathed in their son's sweet milk breath before shifting Connor to his shoulder. He gently patted and rubbed his back, walking back and forth on the dark, flowery rug.

"I can't imagine trying to keep up with a bunch of them all at once," he said. "We won't know if they'll be Dreamers or Witnesses, or neither, until it starts. Maybe we can give them the basics, teach them the routines when they're younger. At least let them know what to expect whichever way it goes for them."

Gena walked quietly into the kitchen, returning with a huge glass of water, an apple, and a wedge of cheese.

"I never stop eating at this stage. Don't let me forget to give you the bottles for overnight. I'd be willing to bet the Council will want to keep focusing on work training for now, at least for the kids born before. The general consensus is we need farmers more than we need Dreamers."

"We'll have to have both," Alex said. He smiled when Connor's chest rumbled. "Etan's at the cannery right now."

"This is going to sound awful, but we have to train the ones who won't be on the Council or Dreamers or Witnesses just as carefully. We need them to all be on the same side."

"*Our* side." Alex glanced out the window toward the cannery, as if his husband would be able to hear him. He sat beside Gena, half caught up in the milk-drunk sleepiness and warmth radiating from the baby. "We'll have to merge the government and the religion together, much as Etan despises the idea. Otherwise we won't make it. Do you miss this part? With the ones Etan and I raise?"

She rubbed Connor's back, then touched his wispy brown hair.

"Sure, a little. It helps to have our own running around. I know they couldn't be in better hands than with you two. Honestly, I'm glad Iris has ours at her parents' place right now, and every time Etan's mom stays with them or keeps them. The quiet time does me a world of good. It's more exhausting than you can imagine nursing and being up with the babies or with Iris all night, too."

"Being up with Etan was exhausting enough." Alex kissed Connor's warm forehead. "Add these precious little screamers in and I don't *want* to imagine how tired you two get."

"You know we're more than halfway to a religion already, Alex, or something close enough. We can set that in stone as Witnesses."

"And we can try to live with the consequences. For us and our children."

Chapter 11

MEETINGS in the conference room at the Wolf Branch Town Hall weren't the nightmare Etan had convinced himself they'd be years ago. But he never stopped wishing he were back in the cozy little break room next door with Alex and a few of their friends.

This room was several times as large, with room for four typical long conference tables making a square. In theory, almost as egalitarian as a round table where they could all see each other, if not nearly as poetic. The current Council of fifteen fit easily, with room for at least twice that many in the future.

Etan didn't want to imagine that many sitting under the lights too bright for his taste, even with the usual slight dimming to save electricity. The old rectangular ceiling tiles full of tiny little holes made him feel like he was a kid at the dentist's office, bored and trying to count how many holes in each one.

The meeting's endless droning wasn't quite as bad as the whine of the dentist's drill, but some days he thought it came close. Once a month of these meetings was more than enough for him.

He had to admit the navy blue chairs were almost adjustable enough to lean that flat, with arms and lumbar support and head-rests able to fit pretty much every variety of human. He kept meaning to ask his mother how the town had managed to pay for so many expensive chairs.

The pleasant, fruity aroma of their yaupon tea and Walt's honey covered the stuffiness of having the doors closed. Etan was thankful for the caffeine to keep himself awake, and a bit worried about how long everyone else would be able to keep talking.

Not entirely because of the tea half-finished in front of him, Etan's leg shook, an anxious movement he couldn't seem to control. He barely managed not to tap his heel against the flat gray carpet loud enough to disturb everyone else.

Even more than the usual routine meetings, nothing about this afternoon was going to be easy. Having the same awful dream several nights in a row convinced him he had to act, but the dread was only getting worse.

"It's going to be okay," Alex whispered.

He moved his hand along Etan's thigh, squeezing just above the knee until his nervous motion stopped.

"You're not alone, E," he said, only loud enough for Etan to hear. "I know the dream's been the same every night. I'm right here."

Etan managed a quick smile, and he covered Alex's hand with his own. The sense of responsibility was so strange, almost detached, but still deep within him.

He didn't remember this dream, not a shred of it. He'd read every word Alex had written down though. The words matched, almost perfectly night after night, on every precious sheet of paper.

And the words felt true.

The meeting washed over him even more slowly than usual, taking forever and going too fast at the same time. He surprised himself with how much he loved working at the cannery and teaching. But he was still bored with the day to day business of building their little group of survivors.

He knew it was crucial work, the only thing giving even a small number of humans a chance. But Etan could never quite manage to pay attention until it was his turn to speak.

He hadn't quite worked out how people having the same dreams could argue so much.

For once, he wished this dull part would just go on for the rest of the day, for the rest of all the days.

All too soon, George Light stood, his huge, dark brown hands held out as if in prayer.

"Let us now turn to the Dreamers."

Etan looked up, squeezing Alex's hand. George had used his own dreams to build a following before everything had gone to hell, a large and powerful church if his stories were to be believed. As much as that idea bothered Etan, George had brought many of those followers though to safety.

He'd also proven invaluable in helping the Council move forward. He knew how to turn prediction into prophecy, and leaders into prophets.

"Have any of you a Dream to share with us?" George said.

His former life as a preacher was on full display in his booming voice, capital letters clear enough to hear, and grand gestures taking in everyone in the room.

Etan held his breath, hoping someone, anyone would speak first. This Dream was too important to ignore, and he would have given his right hand to avoid having to do just that.

Iris looked at him then. She sat pushed back from the table, hands on her hugely swollen belly. Her pregnancy was going as well as her others had, with Gena beside her every bit as glowing and healthy at the same stage.

Right now though, Iris looked anything but maternal. She probably hadn't had this Dream yet, but she knew *he* had.

If Etan didn't speak, she was going to speak for him, and not kindly.

"I have… I've had a Dream I need to share," Etan said, then he turned to Alex. "We need to share."

"Please share with us, brothers," George said as he sat down.

Etan didn't dare try to stand on his shaking legs, but he did raise his voice. He'd never equal George, and he didn't bother trying.

He simply didn't want to have to repeat himself.

"We're going to have to start turning people away," he said, then he shook his head. "Not *away*, exactly, but we can't have unlimited people living here. We're going to need other settlements."

Etan's breath caught, and the whole long conversation opened up in his mind. He knew who was going to speak, who was going to argue, who was going to support him.

He didn't have these pre-memories as often as some of the others did, not nearly as much as Iris. Nowhere hear as much as his grandmother Anne had. This one was exceptionally clear. Seeing it didn't make going through it seem any easier.

He heard a deep sigh to his left, just as he expected.

"Don't you think that's a little premature, son?" Harry Mullins said. "There are barely a thousand of us here now. This town had almost five thousand with no problems, more during boom times."

Before Etan could speak, Alex was shaking his head. Alex was suspicious of Harry as much as Etan was of George. Harry's use of his own Dreams to make obscene sums of money might be unquestioned evidence of leadership ability in some circles, and that had been true in the past.

That was not true in this room filled with Dreamers and Witnesses.

Much of Harry's money had gone toward getting Wolf Branch ready. Buying up solar panels, wind turbines, and water turbines before the prices soared and supplies dried up at the end. Almost all the equipment Alex had installed and taught everyone how to maintain.

Still, Alex had his doubts.

And Alex had always especially hated being called *son* by anyone besides his own father, and Etan's.

"There were that many here, Harry, certainly," Alex said. "But there was also grid electricity, sewage treatment, modern medicine, grocery stores. We can't build back up to the same levels we had then, not all in one place."

"I believe you're underestimating what we can accomplish," Harry said, nodding to himself. "We've done very well for ourselves in such a short time, and that's only going to continue."

"Harry, you're forgetting we've called the Dreamers to speak," Iris said, her voice not inviting argument. "We don't even know what this was about yet. Please, Alex, tell us of the Dream."

Etan caught Iris' wink, and he smiled in return. He'd known she would speak, and he was no less grateful when she did. Alex held up his current journal, this one a thick spiral-bound notebook with a blue vinyl cover.

"The Dream was the same six nights in a row, with no variation. We have choices here, but they come with consequences. If we continue to let everyone who shows up settle here, we'll run out of resources. We won't have the food long before we run out of shelter. And worst of all, we won't be able to handle the waste. Disease will take hold, and we won't get through it this time."

He stopped, looking around the room. Etan was sure he wasn't the only one who noticed Alex looked at everyone but Harry Mullins. Harry crossed his arms, obviously wanting to speak but not willing to tangle with Iris, eight months pregnant or not.

"If we start now, we'll be ready before we have to deal with turning people away," Alex went on. "What we do now is crucial."

Etan tried to force himself not to look across the squared tables, even though he knew Mary Shadrin was going to speak. She was one of the few remaining Dreamers without a Witness, something he and others were starting to distrust.

She was also the source of most of the dissent in these meetings and in the community, as she had been from the beginning. She stood, her slender frame and delicate features vibrating with indignation.

Or at least that's what Etan let himself imagine to keep himself calm, knowing what she was going to say. Her gray-streaked hair and gaunt face too nearly matched the first vision he'd seen of her so many years ago.

"What exactly are you suggesting?" Mary said, scowling at Etan and Alex. "We can either turn people away to die or we can outright kill them? We've already suffered one slaughter over keeping our bounty to ourselves at gunpoint. What was the point of all this if we're going to start making the same stupid mistakes?"

"Don't even start with that, Mary," Alex said, his overly calm voice a warning. He took a slow, deep breath, then let it out in a rush through his lips. "They were going to steal everything we had, not join together in some kind of big happy commune. You know as well as I do they would have used those explosives to kill a lot more of us if they'd had the chance. Any other choice we made ended up with *all* of us dead."

A few people murmured, and Etan couldn't tell if they were agreeing or not. This time, Gena spoke.

"Iris and I know the raiders from Maple Ridge were capable of far worse, Mary. They *planned* far worse. Until we understand what Etan's Dream actually was, what it will become, we can't know how to move forward. In the years we've been listening to his Dreams, have any of them not come to the rest of us in time?"

The soft voices stopped, but Mary still stood. Neither Gena nor anyone else had to say Mary's Dreams rarely came to any of the rest of them. Whatever brought on the Dreams seemed to be erratic in her.

Mary tossed her long hair and straightened her shoulders.

"I have Dreamed of creating a security force, of turning people away," she said in a ringing voice. "And that was a nightmare. If we arm ourselves, if we create some kind of militia, we'll go down the very same road that got us here in the first place."

"Etan has not had that Dream yet, Ms. Shadrin," Alex said, his voice hard, but calmer. "But security may well be another choice we eventually face. You raise a crucial point. If we do nothing, if we don't protect what we've worked so hard for, we may be overrun like we would have been the day Connor Griffith died. That would *just* as surely end with many of us dead and humanity scattered into dust."

Alex stood, bringing everyone's attention to him and Etan. And away from Mary

"If we make sure to keep ourselves safe, that's the only thing that can prevent the violence. We're not saying we must slaughter every person who staggers into town, or even that we need armed guards just yet. All we were suggesting is we take new people in, make sure they're healthy, then get them ready to settle someplace else."

Etan closed his eyes, wishing this would come to an end. Mary was never going to agree, no matter what he or Alex said. Her suggestion of a security force sent a chill through him that he felt pass through many others in the room.

If they'd set up some kind of patrols before the final collapse years before, his father might still be alive.

They couldn't forget what Mary said, even when so many of her Dreams were broken.

But Mary was going to stand alone today. Everyone else might not be happy with turning survivors away, but they wouldn't be willing to ignore such a strong Dream.

Logic mattered less and less. Not as much as belief.

The religion had taken shape all around Etan. Even worse, largely *because* of him.

"So you choose to ignore my Dream of ruin?" Mary said, her voice breaking. "We'll just send them out into the wilderness and wish them luck?"

"We'll help them until enough are gathered to start a new community," Alex said. "And when they're ready, one of our families will go with them. People who've been part of rebuilding, who know what needs to be done and what to avoid. That's one reason we've been studying how to grow things we can't grow here. We have to find new ways to feed ourselves, and part of that is settling in other areas."

"Of course, of course," Harry Mullins said, not quite able to hide his smile. "Trade. We have to reestablish trade, get ourselves back on a paying basis."

"No, not like that," Etan said, surprised at the confident sound of his own voice. "We'll have surplus and so will they. The other communities will be able to find more supplies of medicine, eyeglasses, clothing, things we're going to run out of here. We'll have to learn to share the supplies in a fair way. And we will *not* be using food for leverage or for profit. We can't afford to do that."

Alex sat, then ducked his head toward Etan and grinned, keeping himself out of everyone else's sight. Etan rolled his eyes and smiled back.

Alex had been trying to get him to speak up more in meetings for years.

"Listen," Alex said, "just because we can see *what* needs to be done, what we have to do to survive, doesn't mean we see all the details of *how*. Etan said this Dream felt like an opening, like something all of us would participate in. Everyone may get a different part, and each part is going to make a difference. I don't like the idea of turning people away either, or Mary's Dream of arming ourselves. But if we don't take steps now, before it becomes a problem, we're not going to make it. We won't. Our children won't. Our grandchildren won't."

The room was silent for a long while, and even Mary finally sat. Iris looked around the room, then got slowly to her feet with Gena's support.

Etan knew no one missed the significance of Alex's words and the shape of Iris' body, and Gena's. They might have been the first such arrangement four years ago, but they were only one of many now.

Iris standing proudly before them, carrying Alex and Etan's baby, spoke louder than anyone's words possibly could.

"We've worked too long and too hard to let everything die out in a couple of generations," she said, looking at Etan and Alex in turn. "We've all had to adjust, and some things have been much harder than others. I believe this will be the next step we need to take. I believe this Dream is true."

At her words, the ceremonial invitation to accept or reject a Dream, the tension finally left Etan's body. None of this was going to be easy, but at least they were going to move forward.

Harry Mullins stood as Iris carefully sat down.

"I believe this Dream is true."

Even without his memory guiding him, Etan knew no one was going to move to validate Mary's Dream.

Hardly anyone did anymore.

One after another, the people around the table stood and spoke, adding support to what they all had to do together. Dreamers and

Witnesses, often paired as couples but some as companions, raised their voices and judged Etan's Dream true.

Finally only Mary Shadrin and George Light were left.

Mary looked around the room, meeting everyone's gaze. She looked into Etan's eyes last, and he knew no words or gesture would change her mind. She shook her head and looked down at her hands.

Etan had seen it coming, but some part of him was surprised, and hurt. She wasn't saying this wasn't a good idea, that they shouldn't take this action.

She was denying the truth of what he'd seen. That denial was far more serious than an opposing vote.

Etan knew it seemed to call his Dreams into question, his Dreams or Alex's ability to remember them. The lowered eyes all around the table and his own churning gut told him Mary had called her own ability to be part of this Council into doubt.

Her judgment could no longer be trusted, any more than her own Dreams could.

George compressed his lips, but he got to his feet, going last as was his tradition.

"I also believe this Dream is true, and I *declare* that it is so," he said, his voice filling the room and somehow filling their bodies. "Dreamers and Witnesses, all of us must be watchful for the parts we will all play. Let us all go forward together, today and well into the future."

PART III

A REMNANT OF THE OLD WORLD

Chapter 12

Tiny hands grasping along Etan's back and ribs, trying their best to tickle, dragged him from a dead sleep. He wanted nothing more than to ignore the giggling efforts to wake him after the night he'd passed. A particularly rough pinch jerked him into awareness.

"Over to this side of the bed, hellions," Alex said, trying to keep his voice low. "Daddy E isn't ready to wake up yet."

"Why not?" Gwen said, her high voice much louder. "*We* gotta be up!"

"Cause he works all night long while you lazy sods lay in bed and snooze. Over here or you can't go with me today."

Etan opened his eyes and stretched just as Gwen and Connor thundered around to Alex. The bedroom was still dark, a sliver of early dawn pink visible through the window. He was constantly amazed at how much noise four-year-old and three-year-old feet could make.

"Daddy E don't sleep?" Gwen said.

"*Doesn't.*" The bed shifted as Alex sat up. "Daddy E doesn't sleep much lately."

"I don't sleep at all with you two rumbling around here." Etan turned to see both kids staring at him with comical surprise in the faint light, Gwen's blonde head several inches taller than Connor's brown curls.

"Morning Daddy E!" Connor cried, running right back around to Etan.

"Daddy A said you don't sleep," Gwen said. She stood with her hands on her hips, clearly disapproving of her little brother's giggles when Etan picked him up.

"Sometimes I do, sweetheart. I just didn't last night. Where are you all off to so early?"

"Well, it's not that early," Alex said with a half smile. "Not by farmer standards, anyway. Linda asked me to help out today, with a bunch of teenagers ready to learn how to harvest soybeans. I might take these two pests with me, put them to work."

"Wanna work!" Connor shrieked into Etan's face. Alex picked him up, slung low under one arm like a sack, then lifted Gwen to his other hip.

"You *will* work, especially if you keep squalling like that." Alex looked at Etan and frowned. "I think Daddy E needs to stay right here and get more sleep, don't you?"

"I'll be fine, just let me get some tea. Linda asked me to help, too."

"Forget it, young man," Alex said. "We'll be fine. Seriously, get some rest. You're exhausted."

Etan couldn't manage to argue. He'd spent a terrible night in and out of Dreams, never quite waking up enough to understand what was going on around him.

The same thing had been happening for the last few weeks, but Alex couldn't make sense of what the Dreams were about either.

Sometimes they were just static.

Etan had just about fallen back asleep when a warm body snuggled up against his chest, another against his back. Alex kissed his cheek, then whispered close to his ear.

"These two will be out for another couple of hours. Caela's off with me. Sleep if you can. Maybe you can meet us for lunch."

Etan nodded without opening his eyes. More stomping moved

through the apartment, Alex's deep voice mixed with their children's higher tones. Finally all he heard was Eddie and Meghan's regular breathing.

He joined them before three more of his own breaths.

The Dream shattered their lives barely an hour later.

Chapter 13

Linda was already out in the soybean fields beyond the cannery when Alex got there, her grey head standing out among all the teenagers around her. None of the kids had clear memories of football or baseball fields instead of neat rows of fading green plants stretching nearly out to the mountains surrounding them.

Caela, Gwen, and Connor ran to the group of older kids, each sending wisps of steam into the mid-October air with their chatter. The light and the last few days let Alex know it would be warm enough for the short sleeves they all wore under their jackets by the afternoon.

"Where do you need us?" Alex said as he joined Linda and several of her former students.

"Help me keep an eye on these troublemakers," she said, slapping Jimmy Adams on the back. He'd been one of Alex's and Etan's most challenging, and most talented, students right before everything fell apart. In his twenties now, Jimmy stood nearly as tall as Alex. "They're going to keep the new ones in line so us old folks don't have to."

"Mr. Griffith, Etan I mean, just threatened to throw me in one of those giant pots if I got too far out of line," Jimmy said with a grin. "I figure that's all there is to it."

"More or less," Alex said. "I'll keep the little ones out of your way."

"No, they're right where they need to be." Linda shielded her eyes with one hand, watching the kids playing with the rangy red hound dogs. "I've been thinking about ways we could get children involved since we finally have a bunch of them again."

"You mean with farming?" Alex said. He watched Jimmy, another young man, and two young women getting the teenagers organized. His children listened to every word they said with wide eyes. "Connor was shouting his fool head off this morning about wanting to *work*."

"That's what I had in mind," Linda said. "Pollination isn't a game for people my age."

"We could make it into a game for them," Alex said. "Anne saw it years ago, the little ones doing the hand pollination. It's as good a way to help them start learning as any."

"They *are* a lot lower to the ground," Linda said.

The teenagers spread out into the rows, recycled cloth bags slung over their shoulders. The plants closest to them were in full sunlight, so they worked from there toward the still-dark section close to the mountainside.

Caela, Gwen, and Connor had small bags of their own hanging past their knees. The dogs ambled from one person to the next, tails high and wagging, sniffing for treats.

"Where's Etan this morning?" Linda said.

"He hasn't been sleeping well," Alex said. "Worse than usual. He did want to help, but I told him to get some more rest."

"We'll do fine. Dreaming all night has to keep him exhausted."

One of the dogs lowered her head to the ground, her tail wagging faster. She darted forward, turning left, then right.

"He normally…" Alex trailed off, distracted by the abrupt change in the dog's motion. He shook his head, trying to keep his words straight. "This doesn't seem like a Dream, not a real one. Nothing I can follow, anyway."

Several of the other dogs joined the first one, all of them with their noses down.

The pattern took shape between one beat of Alex's heart and the next.

"Anything different out in that old equipment shed?" he said without looking away from the dogs. "They seem to be headed that way."

"Don't think so." Linda shaded her eyes again, the corners of her mouth turned down. "We hardly ever keep anything but tools in there. It was great for sports equipment, too drafty for food."

Alex took a few steps forward, his eyes on the small building still hidden in deep shadow. The rows, the motion of the hounds, even his children's breath rising into the air pointed toward that shed he and Etan had cleaned out together years ago.

The first dog to catch the scent raised her nose, her bay shocking in the quiet morning air. When she ran toward the thick trees beyond the fields, the others joined in her musical and somehow unsettling chorus.

Alex had seen the hunters training these dogs, heard them out in the woods on the trail of deer or elk. The barking was faster now, too quick to count, and far more furious than when they were chasing game.

"They're onto something," Alex said. For the first time since not long after Etan's father died, he wished he had his gun at his hip. "I'll be right back."

The dogs resumed their zigzag search, moving from the woods to surround the shed. Alex glanced toward the group of children, making sure his three were still occupied. A few of the older ones were watching, and Jimmy Adams was walking toward the shadows himself.

Alex started to wave him back, then reconsidered.

If the dogs *had* scented something, he might not want to face it alone.

Chapter 14

Etan woke, eyes wide, heart pounding, Meghan's sleepy protests in his ears.

"Too tight, Addy E. Too tight."

He forced his arms to relax even though his entire body was screaming for movement, for action.

Gods, how could they have been so stupid?

"I'm sorry, Meghan, but we have to get up. Right now. Eddie, wake up. I need to go find Daddy A."

Etan put Meghan on her feet then got to his own, shaking his head. He didn't have time for tea or anything else.

Alex didn't have time.

"Eddie, we can't go back to sleep now. We have to go."

The dark-haired boy, barely a year and a half old, gripped the covers and squeezed his eyes closed. Etan scooped him up blanket and all.

"Meghan, I need you to be a big girl right now. Can you do that? I need you to get dressed as fast as you can. Right now."

He forced himself to focus over the screams crashing through his mind.

Kids, teachers.

A snarling face he barely recognized as human but would remember for the rest of his days.

Alex's screams.

"Big girl shirt?" Meghan said, rubbing her eyes. "Caela's shirt?"

"Whatever you want, baby. We have to go."

Etan stepped into his shoes and followed into her room, untangling Eddie's fingers and dropping the blanket as he went. Meghan pulled her drawer open as he did the same on the other side of the room.

"Fast as you can," he said, pulling out pants he hoped were Eddie's size. "You can finish up at Mama G's place, okay?"

"Go to Mama G's?" Eddie said, his voice still soft with sleep.

"You both are. I have to go see Daddy A for grown up stuff, so you have to stay here."

"Go see Daddy A!" Meghan wailed.

No, he couldn't deal with this. Meghan stood with one of Caela's old shirts hanging down to her knees, her green eyes wide and full of tears.

"Now listen. We're not going to argue, understand me?" Etan hated the sharp tone in his voice, but he couldn't wait any longer. "You're staying downstairs with your brothers and sisters. Let's go, right now."

Meghan started crying when he picked her up. Rather than suffer hearing loss, Etan let her slip down into sack position the way Alex often carried them.

Alex.

"More blood," he whispered, tears welling in his own eyes. "He's not bleeding enough."

By the time he made it down the flight of stairs, both kids were howling. At least Gena and Iris would hear them coming.

Iris opened the door before he knocked.

"What's going on? Where's Alex? Neither one of us can see. Did you Dream?"

"Something at the fields," he said, handing Meghan to Iris, Eddie to Gena. Both women looked as terrified as he felt. "I'm sorry to-"

"Go, you're running out of time," Gena said, her voice tight. "He doesn't have long."

Etan moved as fast as he dared, taking three flights of stairs two at a time. As soon as he stepped out into the cool morning air, the Dream exploded back into his mind.

Someone in the woods, so thin and dirty he couldn't tell if it was a man or a woman. Hiding close by for so long, finally desperate enough to try stealing their food or tools or weapons.

The dogs, lean and rangy and coats nearly as red as Alex's beard. Noses to the ground, zigzagging across the field.

Tracking into the woods, then back to the storage shed. Swarming around it, noses high, throats baying.

Alex watching, then glancing at the crowd of kids scattered through the rows of beans. Caela and Gwen and Connor not far away, focused on the fuzzy green pods that fit so perfectly into their small hands.

Etan ran through the middle of town, screaming at everyone he saw to bring help.

Alex walking slowly around and into the shed. Never noticing Connor following with dramatic sneaking steps. The dogs running into the small building behind him, barking furiously at the open window on the far side.

Alex stepping back outside to see the scrawny creature grab the little boy.

Their son's scream bringing every head up and turning their way.

George Light stepped into the the doorway of the food pantry, Walt Colley beside him.

"Find Sandy!" Etan shouted. "Bring one of the rescue trucks out to the fields. Now!"

Gwen running toward her brother. Six-year-old Caela grabbing her little sister, screaming so hard she almost fell herself.

Alex holding both shaking hands up, walking forward. Calling the dogs back. Trying to reason with a person a decade past reason.

Connor nearly disappearing into filthy rags as the creature backed toward the woods.

Alex never saw the rusty knife.

Chapter 15

ALEX TRIED to grab the dog closest to him. She twisted out of his grasp, her bark fast as a machine gun. His body was burning hot, freezing cold.

If the filthy thing ran off into the woods, they might never find Connor.

"No," he said, stepping forward. "Let him go. I'm not going to hurt you."

The bundle of filth and rags was small, barely past Alex's chest. It had more than enough strength to hold his shrieking child just out of his reach.

"Please don't hurt him. Can't you hear how scared he is?"

The dogs circled, nipping at the creature grasping Connor, howling and barking. Alex smelled the stench of long-unwashed human, his own stinking sweat. He held up shaking hands.

"Get back! I'll call them off if you let him go!"

The vaguely human shape took another step back. Fierce brown eyes, almost hidden in matted hair, watched Alex. Glanced at the shelter of the trees.

"We can help you," Alex said. "Just let my son go."

He saw the others out of the corner of his eye, moving closer. If they could just get between the creature and the woods, he might have a chance.

Caela and Gwen's cries cut through the noise, driving shards of glass into Alex's heart.

He would have sworn he heard Etan, shouting in the distance.

"I will *not* let you do this. Let him go!"

Alex moved and the thing stumbled and fell backward into the dust. Alex jumped forward into the middle of snarling dogs, grunting savage, and his screaming baby boy.

He grabbed at Connor's shirt, dragging him out of dirt-caked fingers and pushing him back. Trusting someone would catch his son, Alex closed his hands around the painfully thin throat.

His own throat was shouting, bellowing, but he could barely hear himself over the roaring inside his head.

Connor was safe.

No more compassion. No more mercy.

Alex held only fury in his hands and in his heart.

A shift, motion beneath him.

Etan's voice cutting through the howling in his mind.

A blow that passed through his whole body, deep and hard enough to take his breath.

The desperate need for air cooled Alex's fury in an instant.

Chapter 16

Etan's eyesight and his vision clashed, stuttered. Moving into real time.

Alex running out of time.

He heard people shouting behind him. The piercing shriek of his little boy was still impossibly far off.

The community garden he and Alex had labored over was full of autumn herbs and flowers, the scent heady in the rising heat. Around the bulk of the greenhouse Alex worked so hard to build.

Etan finally saw the class across the fields.

So far away. Yet he could hear his husband's shout as he took another step toward their son.

Every step brought Etan closer to too late.

"Alex, stop!"

Alex moved again, the dogs barking and circling. Only a few steps separated his body from the filthy, dull blade.

Linda grabbed up Caela and Gwen, shouting to the older kids to move back.

A hundred feet now. Fifty.

Alex stepped forward. The pathetic figure stumbled, falling backward with Connor still clutched to its chest. Alex darted forward, tangling with cries of inhuman fury and sobbing boy.

Twenty feet away.

Connor staggered out of the mess, through the howling dogs. One of the older boys snatched him up and ran toward the staring group. Another young man ran toward the bodies twisting in the dusty soil.

"The *knife*, Alex! The knife!"

Alex shifted on top of the thing, his fingers around its neck. He howled louder than the dogs, terrible in his fury.

Etan saw the reddish blade sink into his lover's body from ten feet away.

Alex's voice cut off. He twisted away and grabbed at his side.

Etan had no voice left for his own cry.

Etan and Jimmy Adams, his long-ago smart ass student, grabbed Alex's shoulders and dragged him away.

"Get down!" a man shouted from behind them.

A hail of fist-sized rocks struck the creature before it could stand. These same teenagers had piled them up, helping clear the field when they were toddlers.

All was still except for his husband's labored breathing. Etan gasped for his own breath, heart pounding in his ears, sweat running down his face and back.

"Alex," Etan said, falling to his knees, his voice a harsh whisper. "Don't move. Sandy will be right here."

"Where's Connor? The girls?"

"They're fine, now be *still*."

Alex's face was pale and tight, his mouth twisted. His chest hitched with his struggles to draw air into his body. Etan tried to lift his fingers away from his side.

"Get the kids away, Etan. Just need to catch my breath. Don't know what the hell that thing punched me with, but I'm okay."

"The kids *are* away, let me see."

Etan lifted Alex's hands and pulled up his shirt. A jagged wound at least three inches long stood out just under his ribs. Blood welled up to mark his pale skin, spilling down his side.

Not enough blood.

"See?" Alex tried to raise up, then groaned and coughed. "Hardly a scratch."

A moan built from low inside Etan's chest, near where Alex's life was spilling away in his own.

"Alex, listen to me. You're bleeding inside. You have to be still. I hear the truck coming now."

Shouts and footsteps approached with agonizing slowness. Etan wanted to see how close they were, but he was too terrified Alex would be gone when he looked back.

"Just help me stand up," Alex said, his voice weaker. "Don't waste fuel for a truck."

"Gods, *listen* to me, you stubborn jackass," Etan said. Tears dropped onto the dusty ground, onto Alex's skin. "Something is wrong inside. You have to let them help you."

"Let me see, Etan," Sandy said from right behind him.

"It stabbed him," Etan said, shifting out of the way but not letting go of Alex's hand. "He should be bleeding more. I Dreamed all the blood stayed inside."

"Hey, Alex," she said, kneeling beside Etan. "Your neck or head hurting? Anything numb?"

"Wish I was numb. Can't breathe right. Damn boulder…in my chest when I try."

"Okay. I'm going to feel your stomach now. I'm sorry, it might hurt."

She pressed in a line away from the wound, barely enough to move the flesh. Alex grimaced at first, then relaxed as she moved lower.

When she reached his abdomen, she shook her head.

"Hard as a rock," she said. "Probably got his spleen. How you feeling, Alex?"

"Like shit," he said, trying to smile. "Didn't hurt until just now. Don't think I can walk."

His hand was sweaty in Etan's despite the cool morning, his forehead clammy under Etan's lips.

Sandy shouted at the crowd milling around behind them.

"There's a stretcher in the truck! Bring it and enough people to lift him, now!"

"Someone get it?" Alex said. "Whatever attacked me?"

"Don't worry, sweetie," Etan said. He glanced at the bundle of rags on the ground, several men and women surrounding it. Harry Mullins walked toward them with a thick rope coiled over his shoulder. "I'll take care of that."

George Light grasped Etan's shoulder when he tried to climb into the bed of the huge farm truck with Alex.

"Hang on, you need to see to your children."

"Linda has them, George. I need to go with him."

"Etan, listen, listen to me," he said, his rich voice soothing Etan through his panic. "I know you're scared, but Alex is in the best hands he can be. He'll be all right for now. Don't you feel that?"

"He might not make it through the surgery! I can't let him go in there alone."

"George is right," Sandy said, taking Etan's hand. "We have him stable. The hospital is barely five minutes away. We'll send the truck right back for you. I promise."

"He's got to be terrified," Etan whispered, trying not to fall apart.

"I'm sure he is," George said, "but he knows Sandy will do her best for him." He put his arm around Etan and turned him back toward the field. "Your babies just saw one of their fathers get stabbed. Go see to them. He'd want you to."

Etan closed his eyes, gritting his teeth against the agonizing heat tearing through his chest. Alex got stabbed trying to protect Connor, and he would have done the same for any child.

He climbed up to the back of the truck where Alex lay on the stretcher. He was terribly pale, but he squeezed Etan's hand.

"The kids?" he said, confusion in his eyes. "Are they safe?"

"*You* kept them safe," Etan said. "I'll meet you at the hospital in a few minutes, okay? Sandy's going to take good care of you."

Alex squeezed his eyes closed when the truck started.

"Don't let them see me like this, E. Love you."

"I won't. I love you, Alex. Hang on. I'll be there as soon as I can."

Chapter 17

THE PAIN ARRIVED loud and clear when hands lifted Alex onto the stretcher. He knew they didn't mean to hurt him, not like that maniac who was trying to steal their little boy. But the shift and motion woke up a dark heat inside his chest. Trying to force air into his lungs had been hard enough before fire settled under his ribs.

His head swam when they lifted him, making the blue sky and Etan's green eyes fade to gray. Alex gritted his teeth, trying to stay in the world.

"Still with us, Alex?"

That was Sandy, at least he thought so. She sounded a thousand miles away, her words distorting with the impossibly fast beat of his heart.

"Not quite." His voice sounded tinny in his ears. "About to pass out."

"That's blood loss and shock," she said. "Hang in there if you can."

Alex couldn't focus on who was holding the stretcher, but he felt it when his back hit the bed of the truck a little too hard. He couldn't spare enough breath to cry out, even when pain forced a silent scream.

The pressure on his chest was worse than the buzzing in his ears.

The truck jounced on its springs, waking up the inferno in his ribs a little more.

Someone grabbed his hand.

Etan.

Alex would have given anything to be able to hear what his husband said, but the noise in his ears was too loud. Etan disappeared, and the truck lurched into motion.

Gray took over the world for several beats of his racing heart.

Chapter 18

THE SKY MOVED, shifting smoothly over Alex's head. He was having a terrible time focusing, but he could see the motion. He could feel it.

Was he in the back of a truck? That made no sense. People squeezed in around him, containers he couldn't see well enough to recognize lined the sides.

Something was wrong with him, something about his chest.

A fire burned deep inside of him.

A *fire*.

Connor was lost in a fire.

"Get him away from here," Alex said.

A woman leaned close to him, her fingertips on his throat just under his jaw.

"Get who away? We're almost there."

"Don't let Connor near this fucking truck!"

The shout, or as close as he could get to it, left Alex coughing, gasping for enough air to stay conscious through the flaring pain.

"Connor's with Etan, Alex," she said. "You protected him. We're going to do the same for you."

"He *won't* run. Full of bombs. Taking it right to him!"

"No, hon, no." She brushed his hair back, then touched his forehead. "We don't have any bombs. Not one. I promise. Your Connor is safe."

Alex shook his head, tears squeezing out of his eyes, hot against the cold sweat covering his shivering body. He caught glimpses of the red brick buildings behind her, foggy but unmistakable.

They were driving right through the middle of Wolf Branch in a truck full of explosives, every bit of it unstable.

Connor – Etan's father and the closest thing Alex ever had to one – was at the end of that road.

At the end of his life.

"Can't watch him die again. Get me away."

"Alex, this will all make sense once we get you stabilized." The woman's voice sounded full of tears. "That was years ago. Etan's father died saving all of us. I'm telling you your son is safe. Connor *is* safe, thanks to you."

Before he could catch enough breath to speak again, to beg this woman to warn Connor away before it was too late, Alex recognized the faded blue awning in front of the emergency room.

"We've got to lift you again," she said. "Stay with us if you can."

He couldn't.

Chapter 19

Etan climbed down and stood beside Walt Colley, watching the truck drive slowly away. He held up a hand to Sandy in the back, hoping she'd tell Alex.

He lowered his hand to his eyes, the terror and sorrow getting the best of him. Walt put strong arms around Etan, humming low and soft.

"We'll get you back to him," Walt said, leaning back and holding Etan's shoulders in his huge hands. "Let's get you to your babies first, then I'll take them home to their mammas."

Etan finally got a good look at Walt, the first thing that got through to his whirling mind besides Alex's blood where it wasn't supposed to be. Walt's eyes were red and wet, and he'd lost his constant green baseball cap somewhere. Wild gray hair stood up all over his head.

Etan had heard Alex talk countless times about how Walt welcomed him to Wolf Branch all those years ago. How Walt helped him feel at home when he needed it most.

Now Alex's good friend was trying to talk sense into Etan through his own worry and fear. Etan knew he'd left any kind of sense or calm behind when he'd left their apartment.

The least he could do was listen.

He let Walt walk with him over to where Linda sat on the ground, Connor curled up in her lap, Gwen tucked under her arm. Caela ran over to Etan, hitting so hard she knocked him back a couple of steps.

She was a perfect miniature version of Alex, from curly red hair to blue eyes now full of tears to sometimes furious temper. Etan knelt on one knee beside her.

"Is Daddy Alex going to die?" Caela said.

"Doctor Sandy is taking care of him."

"But that monster hurt him with a knife!"

Etan pulled her close, and her arms went around his neck squeezing tight. Her horrible sobs ripped Etan apart.

"I know. He got Connor away from the monster. Doctor Sandy will do the same for him. I'm so sorry you saw that, baby."

"I wish it never, ever happened," she said. Her voice trembled, and she hiccuped trying to catch her breath. "I don't want it to happen anymore."

"I wish it never happened too. Sweetheart, can you help Walt and Linda with the little ones? I know you're upset, but they could use someone to keep the babies calm. Can you do that?"

"Where are you going, Daddy?" She sat on his knee, gripping his arm so tight it hurt. "I'm scared."

"I'm going to help with Daddy Alex, that's all. I'll be home to you as soon as I can. You can stay with Iris and Gena. They'll make sure you're not scared."

"Is Daddy Alex scared?"

Etan squeezed his eyes closed, trying to turn his head so their daughter wouldn't see him cry. She caught his face with both hands, not even big enough to cover his cheeks. He opened his eyes.

Caela stared at him. She didn't say a word, but his heart knew she was begging him to tell her the truth.

"Yes, hon. He's scared."

She nodded, her features solemn.

"Tell him not to be. Tell him to come home where it's safe, as soon as he can."

Etan nodded, unable to speak. He was relieved when Caela

turned to take Walt's big rawboned hand. And just as relieved when Walt held out the other to help him get to his feet.

By the time he reached Linda, Gwen and Connor were staring at him. Connor was dirty and had his thumb firmly in his mouth, but he looked unhurt.

They both held out their arms to Etan. He didn't try to hide his relief this time.

"Are they okay?" he said, standing with four little arms wrapped tight around his neck.

"They're upset, but I don't think they're hurt," Linda said. Her gray hair had mostly escaped its bun, and she was streaked with dust and sweat.

"Are you?"

"Pretty shook up," she said, tears cutting fresh tracks through the dirt on her face. "I'm so *sorry*, Etan. It happened so fast, I couldn't get them away. I should have been watching Connor."

"No, Linda, no. Connor's going to be all right. And if…" Etan breathed deep a couple of times before he could go on. "If one of the kids had gone in there instead, it would have been worse."

"Still, I'm sorry. Do you need me to take them home?"

"Walt is going to, but he may need help if you want."

"Where's Daddy A?" Gwen said, her face pressed against Etan's ear.

"He had to go see Doctor Sandy. She's going to make him all better."

"Bad thing," Connor whispered around his thumb. "Bad thing hurt Daddy A."

"Yeah, that was a bad thing, baby," Etan said. He glanced toward town, where he'd seen Harry and the others dragging the heavily bound figure. "The bad thing is gone. Can't hurt you or Gwen or me or Daddy A anymore. Never, ever."

Etan heart sped up at the rumble of the truck, the rare sound of an engine unmistakable in the silence, just as it crested the hill by the cannery.

Was it already too late?

Walt saw Etan's face and stepped to his side, Caela still holding his hand.

"I still feel like he's doing okay," he said, nodding. "Sandy did too, remember? You best get to him, though."

"Listen, Gwen, Connor," Etan said. "I have to go help Daddy A. Mama Gena and Mama Iris are going to take care of you for a little while."

They both moaned, saying no over and over again in his ears. Etan squeezed them tight.

"I'm so sorry. I have to go. I'll be there as soon as I can. I'm sorry."

Their moans escalated when Walt and Linda pulled them away. Etan separated their fingers as gently as he could, kissing their tiny hands.

"I'll be home as soon as I can," he said. "We both will."

Gwen and Connor both cried and reached out for him as Walt and Linda walked away. Caela held both of the adult's hands, but she kept looking back over her shoulder.

Etan was thankful the truck stopped right beside him. Every bit of strength and courage had been wrung out of him.

He had a terrible feeling he was going to need more than he'd ever had.

He and his family weren't even half an hour into a long, long nightmare.

Chapter 20

Icy wetness slipped over Alex's chest and stomach, dragging him back to some pale imitation of consciousness. A sharp scent burned his nose, and the pressure still weighed on his chest.

He felt painfully bright lights against his face before he managed to open his eyes. Huge round spotlights hung above him. He narrowed his eyes against the brightest glare he'd seen in years.

Had lights always been so harsh in the old world?

The wetness withdrew, but an irritating, ticklish buzzing replaced the chill. He flinched away, then groaned at the tearing sensation in his ribs.

"Hey Alex," a deep voice said. Not Etan. "Jeff here, Sandy's nurse. Try to hold still. I don't want this to hurt."

"What to hurt? What the hell are you doing?"

"I just finished cleaning up the blood so I can see a little bit better. Now I'm going to get the hair off where we need to work. You're feeling the clippers."

Alex tried to raise up from the table enough to see his chest, but the pain only dug deeper. The man wearing purple scrubs and matching hat touched his shoulder. Alex realized his own worn out blue work shirt was gone.

"No, don't try to move like that," Sandy said. She appeared

beside Jeff, dressed in a matching shirt and hat. "Feel a little bit better?"

"A little. Not so damn cold, at least. What did you do?"

"We haven't done anything yet besides give you a couple of units of blood and fluids." Sandy leaned down to look at whatever Jeff was doing, then moved back. "We needed to get you stable before surgery."

"Surgery," he said, trying to force his groggy brain to work. "I don't understand."

"Do you remember the shed out in the fields, Alex?" Sandy said. "The person trying to get Connor?"

He smelled filthy human flesh, heard their little boy screaming.

"Etan was right," he said. "It stabbed me."

"Yeah, got you pretty good. Your spleen is bleeding, so we'll have to take at least part of that. We're going to get a look and do our best to repair whatever we find."

"You're taking out my spleen? I don't even know what that means, Sandy. Don't I need it?"

She nodded at Jeff, then leaned closer to Alex.

"It means if we don't get in there quick, you'll bleed to death, hon. We'll save part of your spleen if we can, but you'll be fine. We'll have to watch you for infections, and you will have to take it easy."

"Is that why I can't breathe? My spleen?"

Sandy pursed her lips, watching Alex for several seconds before she answered.

"I hope that's your diaphragm. The muscle that helps move your lungs."

"But it might not be."

She tilted her head to the side and shook her head.

"We don't know yet. Don't worry until we see what's going on."

Alex wished he could sit up and look her in the eye. He settled for the scowl Etan knew so well.

"Come on, Sandy. You know me better than that. You can't exactly wake me up in the middle to discuss what's going on. Just *tell* me."

"You're right," she said with a shrug. "Your lung isn't collapsed, at least not that I can tell without an x-ray. I don't want to take that long since I have to go in anyway. We're pushing it right now. I'll just say it's a hell of a lot easier to repair your diaphragm if it didn't nick your lung."

Alex closed his eyes, turning his face away from the bright lights.

"Am I going to wake up?"

He didn't say what he was thinking.

Will I leave all of them alone and lonely?

Will I ever see my children, or sleep beside my husband again?

"Look at me, Alex." When he did, her eyes were bright. "You want me to be honest, so I will. This is a serious injury. Assuming we get your spleen in time, we'll still have to do our best to clean the wound out and put you back together. *Nothing* about this is going to be easy. I'm going to do everything I can to get you home to your family. Understand?"

"So will I and everyone else," Jeff said. "I think most of the town is in the waiting room donating blood."

Alex nodded, trying not to cry. His shallow breath caught with the effort, and he groaned before he could stop it.

"Let's get the sedation started, Jeff."

"Not until Etan gets here," Alex said. "Please. I need to see him in case-"

"In case nothing." Sandy waved Jeff forward. "We're not putting you under yet. I'm not going to let you lie there in pain, either. This will let your muscles relax a little, that's all."

The nurse adjusted a tiny valve on a plastic tube running from a plastic bag filled with clear liquid into Alex's arm. He hadn't even noticed it. Another tube was attached to a different bag, the nearly black shade of the blood shocking in the harsh light.

Sandy focused on a silvery box on a small table near Alex's feet. Instead of a tube feeding into his bloodstream, the box trailed blue and green wires. They merged into a black cord that ended in a thick translucent patch the size of his palm. Full of tiny cables and colors, the patch lay flat against the opposite side of his ribs.

He had a vague, impossible-to-grasp memory of seeing the machine and the patch when their children were born.

"What is that?" he said, trying to look closer without hurting himself again. "Looks like some kind of circuitry."

"That's exactly what it is," Sandy said. "You'll know what it *does* in just a second."

She touched the box a few times, and Alex heard a soft click. The pain deep in his chest stopped in an instant. He let out what little breath he had in a humming sigh.

"Magic. What you have there is magic."

Sandy smiled and took Alex's hand.

"I can't disagree with you. That's got the pain blocked. When we're ready, I'll use a higher setting to put you under for surgery. Safer and easier than anesthesia, and the supply will never run out since you set us up with steady electricity. Smuggling this little beauty out of the hospital back in Chicago was a trick, but damn well worth it."

Alex nodded, closing his eyes.

"I'll say. Make sure I'm awake when Etan gets here."

Chapter 21

Etan drew back when he saw several people through the rows of floor to ceiling windows, waiting in the emergency lobby of the hospital. The gray and pale green space was normally empty, and usually closed unless there was an accident. Sandy usually worked out of a normal office on the other side of the three-story brick building for appointments.

The lights were on low, ticking and humming along with the generator. This one was set up in line with the massive water wheel in the Grasspe River a few blocks away. The generators that worked with the windmills up on Maple Ridge to supply the operating rooms were fueled by alcohol from the massive sugar beet crop they brought in every year.

All Alex's work, results of a months-long project helping Sandy get the hospital onto a sustainable footing.

Work that would hopefully help her save his life now.

"I'm so sorry, Etan."

"We'll do whatever we can."

"They said they may need more blood."

"Such a brave thing he did."

Etan nodded, unable to follow their words or do more than shake their hands as he walked through. His legs felt a hundred feet long, his feet wooden boxes he'd never seen before and couldn't understand.

Carmen, one of Sandy's nurses from Chicago, met him in the middle of the crowd. Her round, normally smiling face was tense and worried, her long wavy black hair caught back in a messy bun. She put an arm around Etan's waist.

"Thank you all," she said, raising her voice. "I'll be back with you for the next round in a few minutes. I've got to get Etan back. They're ready to start."

Etan let Carmen lead him through the double doors into a dim corridor.

"Is Alex still all right?" he said. His spinning brain shifted under him. "Why are you out here?"

"He's holding his own, but they need to get started. I'm handling the blood donations."

"Blood donations?"

"For Alex, honey," she said, opening another set of double doors with huge windows in them. "He's lost a lot already."

Before Etan could answer, he saw his husband on the surgical table. Everyone moving around him wore faded purple scrubs and hats, but Alex only had a white paper sheet pulled nearly up to his waist. The lights in here were steady and painfully bright. Carmen squeezed Etan's arm before she left.

Sandy spoke from beside him before Etan could get his mind or legs moving again.

"There you are. He's here, Alex." She took over for Carmen, taking his arm to lead Etan toward the table. "We're ready, great timing. Everything points toward his spleen, with luck not his lung. That's what I'm feeling in my gut, too."

"Carmen said they were giving blood for him," Etan said. "I want to donate."

"I'd be glad to let you," she said, "but in this one case you're not his type. He's O positive, you're A positive. We've got plenty on the way. You're going to need your strength. You can help next time."

"Etan," Alex whispered.

He was nearly as pale as the sheet, but vivid dark bruises stood out against the swollen skin of his abdomen. He lifted his fingers. Etan took his hand, forcing his eyes away from the cleaned wound, startled at how cold Alex's hand was.

"I'm here, sweetie. The kids are with Iris and Gena. Everything's going to be fine."

"Do they know? What's happening?"

"They know Doctor Sandy is taking great care of you. And they know you kept the monster from hurting Connor."

"Some savior, laying here flat on my back. Can you feel anything, E? Do you know if I'm going to make it?"

Etan bit the insides of his cheeks, hot, metallic blood flooding his mouth. Blood that couldn't help Alex.

If he'd seen the fucking Dream more clearly before it was too late, he wouldn't be standing here at all. His husband wouldn't be waiting for emergency surgery with people lined up in the lobby to try to help him through it.

"I don't see anything right now except our babies' hero." He kissed Alex's cool, bluish lips. "And mine. I'm waiting to see you back home in our bed."

"It's a date."

Sandy stood on Alex's other side, over the gash below his ribs. All the dark red hair was gone from that side, and she held a blue drape with a hole in the middle in her gloved hands. Etan forced himself to ignore the tubes and cables attached to Alex's body.

"We're ready," Sandy said. "We'll take good care of him, Etan. Hang in there. See you on the other side."

Chapter 22

Etan tried walking up and down the length of the pale blue tiled hall, but after Carmen took the fourth bag of blood into the operating room, he couldn't stand to know any more. He walked to the exit door and part of the way back, stopping before he could accidentally see where all that blood was going.

He wished for one of Alex's beloved watches, though he wasn't sure if keeping track of the time would make this better or worse. Even with a stopwatch or his long-dead smartphone, he had no idea how long a splenectomy was supposed to take. He hadn't thought to ask.

Squeaking shoes in the hallway got his attention, and he looked up before he could stop himself. Carmen was carrying two more bags of blood, her round face worried until she saw Etan. Her features shifted into a calm smile before she backed into the operating room.

Etan leaned against the white wall and sank to the floor.

He couldn't watch. He couldn't think. He couldn't do anything but wrap his arms around his knees and hide his face.

He fell into a half-Dream, not quite deep enough to shut out the cold hard tile under his backside or the wall against his spine.

Nowhere near deep enough to block out the twisting in his heart.

He saw himself and Alex, both of them barely Caela's age, holding hands and running through a rolling field of wheat. He felt the sun on his face, felt the grain tickling against his arms and legs. Etan felt Alex's hand, warm and firm in his own.

He saw them on an airplane, side by side peering out the tiny oval window, an adventure they'd only taken a few times before everything ended. A vast blue ocean stretched beneath them as far as he could see. Etan knew it was the Atlantic. That was a trip they'd talked and dreamed about, but never managed before it was too late.

He walked with his arm around Alex's waist, both of them with white hair and wrinkles on their faces. His husband's only held lines from smiling around his mouth and his gorgeous blue eyes. Their grown children, grandchildren, and great-grandchildren circled around them, laughing and playing.

"Please," he whispered. "Please give him back to me."

A hand on his shoulder jerked Etan back into hard reality.

Sandy stood beside him. She'd pulled off her gloves and her gown, but he saw spots of blood on the blue cloth booties covering her shoes. He stood as fast as he could to get away from it. Stiff muscles in his legs and back protested the sudden motion.

"Is it over?"

"He's hanging in there, Etan," she said, her voice weary. "Long road ahead, but we're past the crisis."

"Can I see him?"

"You can look in if you want, but he's still out. It takes a while to wake up after something like this."

"Do whatever you can to keep him from hurting," Etan said. "I can wait."

"It's not just that, hon. He had a rough time of it. So did we."

Etan's brow wrinkled and he rubbed the bridge of his nose. He wasn't sure he'd be able to hear the rest of what Sandy needed to tell him. And he knew Alex would never admit how badly he'd been hurt.

"Tell me."

Sandy leaned against the wall with a long sigh.

"The incision will be bigger than you expect. I couldn't have done this much smaller eleven years ago in a fully stocked hospital, not with how fast he was bleeding. But we had to take extra care in cleaning this wound out."

"He had one of the last tetanus shots," Etan said. "A couple of years ago."

"Right, that's a good thing. We have to watch for infections from how filthy the knife was, too. I repaired his diaphragm, but we had to take his entire spleen. He's going to have to watch for infections for the rest of his life, Etan."

"We still have some antibiotics, right?"

"We do, but what we have left won't last much longer. I'll give him a round for the next couple of weeks, and I'll give him the few immunizations we have left, too. What kind of patient will he be?"

Etan let out a laugh that sounded more like a groan.

"He's *terrible*," he said, leaning against the wall beside Sandy. "Worse than the kids. I've always been thankful he doesn't get sick much."

"Well, that may change. His immune system just took a big hit that takes a while to recover from. It would have been a lot more serious for Connor, but this is bad enough. We'll do everything we can to keep it to a minimum. The good news is he worked his ass off to give us a lot of other options when the drugs are gone, in the greenhouse and in the gardens. Will he eat garlic?"

"He hates it. All the rest of us love it."

"He's going to have to get over that," she said. She pulled out her usual small notebook that had to be one of the few left. "I'll make sure you get a supply of the larger bulbs, much milder flavor. We'll set some aside for you this autumn."

"I have to tell you he's going to hate *all* of this, Sandy. He didn't even want us to use fuel for the truck to bring him over here."

She scribbled a few lines, then stood upright and looked Etan in the eye.

"Again, he's going to have to get over it. He has to let us help him, and I'll need *you* to make sure that happens. If it weren't for the two of you, we wouldn't be standing here in a hospital room with lights and running water, worrying about which variety of garlic he'll choke down. Every last one of us would be dead or wishing we were. Alex has to let us take care of *him* for a change. Got it?"

"Got it. I can be more stubborn than Alex if it keeps him with us."

"Good." She wrote a few more lines before she closed the book. "With no infections or other problems, he's got at least a month, maybe closer to two before he starts to feel normal again. I'll get all of this written up and tell him myself so you won't be on your own. No picking up the kids or anything else, and they'll have to be careful of his incision."

"I'll definitely need help with that," Etan said. He saw Alex slinging Connor under his arm, lifting Meghan with no effort. The joy all of them took in the game and the affection. "None of them will be happy."

"I know, I've seen him with them. With any other kid, too. He'll have to let his body heal. *All* of you will need time to heal. We've got a few herbs that will help keep everyone calm, but it's going to take time and probably a lot of talking. Everyone will help if you'll let us. Understand?"

Etan looked down the hall toward the room where Alex waited, probably still too out of it to know what had happened. Getting himself and his husband through would pale beside trying to help their children believe their world was safe.

Especially since that was a lie Etan himself could never afford to believe again.

"I understand. We're going to have to take security more seriously once we deal with whoever that was."

"Mary's armed militia," Sandy said. She rubbed her upper arms. "I doubt anyone will argue now. I know I won't."

"How long do you think he'll sleep?" Etan said.

His heart had seized upon the next thing he had to do with the force of a Dream. He didn't want to give his reeling mind a chance to talk him out of it.

"Jeff is just about finished checking all his vitals, but with the e-sedation we can safely give you an hour before he's really aware. Whatever an hour means anymore. The rest will do him good if he's as bad as you say. He'll be staying here for at least a few days. Go out that back exit if you want privacy. I'll let everyone out front know Alex is okay."

"You'll get to see just what a rotten patient he is, then. Does someone have his things?"

"Yeah, they're in the OR," Sandy said. She touched his arm. "Do you want to go in? I can bring everything to you if you're not ready."

"I need to see him. At least for a second."

She linked her arm through his and they walked through the door together. Etan took a deep breath before he looked up.

A clean white sheet was pulled up to his husband's chin, thankfully covering his belly. His face was nearly as pale as the sheet, a horrible contrast to the red in his beard. Alex was still except for the slow rise and fall of his chest. Jeff looked up from the machine he was watching, nodding and smiling at Etan.

Sandy squeezed his arm for a second, then stepped away. Etan couldn't move. He wanted to get closer, to touch his lover's body, prove to himself that Alex was still alive. His own body wouldn't respond.

What if he passed along a head cold, some silly thing that would barely make him sneeze but proved fatal to Alex? How would he ever be sure enough that their kids' hands were clean enough to touch their father?

A simple sweet kiss could lead to an infection none of them would ever recover from.

He jumped when Sandy spoke.

"Here you go." She handed him one of the same fabric bags they used in the fields, this one made from threadbare blue jeans. "Everything's in there except his shirt. I can give it back if you want, or if Alex might."

"No, thank you for thinking of that," Etan said. "Hold on to it in case he wants it, but I don't."

He'd never get the spreading crimson stain on that faded blue t-shirt, Alex's fingers pressing into the bleeding gash in his side, out of his mind. He didn't ever want to see it again.

"I just need a couple of things."

Sandy watched him for a second, then took his arm again.

"He's good right now, Etan. Jeff and I will stay here until you get back, then we'll move him to a room. Go do what you need to."

Far from being reassured by Sandy's voice, Etan was chilled. Her eyes were worse, colder and harder than he'd ever seen them. He'd always thought her Dreams and visions focused on her patients, the general health of the community.

But right now he knew she saw exactly the same thing he did.

This was not a day for mercy or compassion.

Not anymore.

"I may need..." he said, hot sweat covering his body at the near confession of his plans. "In case someone's there."

Sandy crossed to the other side of the room and opened a wide metal drawer. He heard several taps against plastic. She returned and pressed an old brown prescription bottle and a shrink-wrapped syringe into his hand, angling her body so Jeff couldn't see.

"Crush these, then dissolve them in water. Ingestion or injection, there's no stopping it. And *no one* in this hospital would try."

He gazed into her blazing eyes, then nodded once. He dropped everything into his pocket.

Etan watched Alex long enough to see the steady rise and fall. He dug into the bag, leaving the dusty pants and shoes. He handed the rest back to Sandy.

He pulled off his wedding ring, then slipped it back on above Alex's larger version. He carefully lined up Anne's green stone set into each. Both of them together pinched his finger a little, but they wouldn't fall off. Etan fastened Alex's current black digital watch with a worn black leather band onto his wrist. It was loose, but not enough to fall off over his hand.

"An hour?"

"A bit longer if you need it. We'll tell him you're taking care of your children."

"I will be. Thank you, Sandy. For everything."

Chapter 23

Cool air against his face. A horrible taste in his mouth. And nothing hurt, not even a whisper.

Too vivid to be real, his sluggish mind whispered. *Better enjoy it while it lasts.*

Alex heard a soft click near his right ear, the same noise Sandy had somehow used to block his pain and send him into oblivion.

The sedation withdrew as quickly as it had come, the fog clearing in seconds. His senses shifted into clarity.

The hard table under his shoulders, the lingering sting of antiseptic in the room, all too mundane to be part of some kind of hallucination. Alex knew Sandy was worried about whatever she needed to do to him, but he couldn't remember why just yet.

Though he couldn't feel the painfully bright lights against his eyelids, Alex still squinted as he opened his eyes.

"Hey, Alex," a man said. Not Etan. "Don't worry, the lights are back to normal."

Alex blinked what felt like grit away, not much different than when he'd fallen asleep too hard after one of Etan's Dreams. Jeff sat beside him, still wearing the purple shirt, but without the hat or mask.

"How… how did it go?"

"Everything went fine," Jeff said, smiling. "You gave us a bit of a challenge, but we all feel good about it. Anything hurting?"

Alex closed his eyes for a second, trying to locate the various disconnected parts of his body. Back cool and stiff from the table. Head still a bit swimmy from Sandy's magic machine. Legs achy from being still so long. He frowned at the numbness, the lack of feeling from his armpits to below his waist.

"I still can't feel my chest. My stomach."

"But everything else is good?"

"Yeah, more or less."

"Well, that's by design," Jeff said. He held a straw to Alex's lips. The cold water was the best thing he'd ever tasted in his life. "We'll use the pain block until you're ready to go back home, maybe after that depending on how you're feeling."

"Are my lungs okay? Feels easier to breathe."

"That was a lucky break. The knife got your diaphragm, just like we thought. Didn't even scratch your lung, though. Getting your spleen out of the way made it a lot easier to repair the damage."

"There's the silver lining," Alex said. "Does Etan know?"

Jeff blinked and his lips compressed, so fast Alex wasn't sure he'd actually seen it.

Something didn't feel right. Not threatening, just strange.

"He does, Sandy talked to him. He had to go take care of your kids for a little while. He should be back any time now."

"Any chance you'll tell me what Etan's really up to?"

Jeff grinned, shaking his head.

"Yeah, you're pretty damn awake. Not a chance that I will. Mainly because I don't know. You'll need to ask him yourself."

Chapter 24

Etan kept to the alley behind the cinderblock hospital, walking between it and a bunch of red and brown brick buildings. Sandy's advice was accurate and welcome. The late afternoon was usually a fairly busy time. Today no one was out, at least not that he could see.

The town jail had seen surprisingly little use since the end of the old world. The brick building Etan remembered from his childhood had been replaced with a modern blue vinyl-sided version years before, jarring against the rest of the original structures on the edge of town.

Etan had only been inside the new building a couple of times, back at the beginning of the end. Random drunken brawls as news filtered in of how bad things were going to get died down within a few months.

After the raiders from Maple Ridge, everyone understood there were too few people left to spend all that time and energy trying to destroy each other.

Etan had tried to convince everyone, including Alex, that ending a human life when almost all of them were gone was the closest thing they had to a sin. Up until that morning, he'd still felt that way.

He hoped he'd recover that belief in everything they were struggling for.

Maybe around the time the scars on his husband's belly faded.

The glass front door of the jail was unlocked, and Etan saw a faint yellow light inside. He hadn't even thought to ask where they'd brought the monster that attacked Connor and then Alex. Nowhere else made sense.

Harry Mullins stood up from behind a cluttered wooden desk.

"Etan. How's Alex? Come through the surgery okay?"

"He's hanging in there, Harry. He's going to have a long recovery, but that may be harder on the rest of us than on him."

"Glad to hear it. Listen, I'm real sorry about what happened today. Guess all of us need to take Mary's crazy militia idea a little more seriously."

Etan leaned against the chest-high counter opposite the desk, hoping the pills didn't rattle in his pocket.

"I'm not even sure she ever Dreamed that, you know?" he said. "She wasn't exactly thrilled with the little bit we did talk about it. But we'll have to talk about it now. At least when we have people out in the fields."

"I know a woman who'd be perfect to take charge of all that." Harry rubbed his chin. "Got a good feeling about how she'd work out. Don't mean to be rude, but what the hell you doing down here?"

"I need to see whoever did this, Harry. I need to know why."

"Whoever that used to be can't tell you much, son. She's skin and bones, half wild and more than half starved to death."

"She, huh?" Etan said. That made no difference to him at all, not after what she'd tried to do to Connor and Alex. But he knew it made a lot of difference to some people. "She tried to take our son, and she nearly killed Alex. All I'm asking for is to see her."

Harry took a deep breath, tilting his head as he studied Etan.

"You know there may be a lot more of them out there," he said slowly. "This one may be the key to learning more about that."

"I don't doubt there are more out there. This one doesn't know enough about them to help us. She's by herself. No one to report back to."

"Dreamed about it, did you? I'm real sorry to sound so harsh, but when was that?"

Etan forced his mind to be still, to not turn and bite and claw itself with guilt. That wouldn't make all of this go away, no matter how badly he tore himself up.

"I didn't see it until this morning. I wish to hell it had been sooner, but I saw it just a few minutes before it happened."

"I thought so," Harry said. He walked out from behind the desk and stood beside Etan. "That's what bothers me most. We got a town full of goddamn fortune tellers, and not a one of us saw this thing coming. We can't let that happen again."

"You're right. We can't. *I* can't."

Harry put one arm around Etan.

"You sure about this?"

"I'm sure as I can be after the worst day of my life."

"Well, all I'll say is make sure you're not about to make it worse, Etan. Make *real* sure of that."

Harry left a key ring and a small black handgun on the high counter before he went out the door.

Another piece of Etan's vision slipped into place.

Harry didn't look back when Etan turned the deadbolt.

None of these buildings on the edge of town had running water. Pretty much only the hospital, the greenhouse and cannery, and the Council apartments did. Alex and a few others hoped to get that expanded, but who knew how long that would take now?

Almost every building had a few containers of water inside, though, filtered from rain or the river and stored away. Behind the high counter, Etan found a broad, white ceramic jar that must have been the base for a water bottle when such things were still delivered. Luxury none of them had known to think twice about.

He pulled the lid off and picked up two of the navy blue coffee mugs still lined up around the cooler. He filled one for himself, drained it, then filled and drained it again. He hadn't realized until that moment that he'd never gotten anything to eat or drink since the nightmare drove him out into the morning hours ago.

Etan poured all seven of the pills into the other mug, using a spoon out of the sugar container to crush them. A crust of sparking white lined the jar, so he scraped all of it out and dumped it in before he poured water in and stirred.

Shame to waste any kind of sweetness here, but he'd take any shortcut he could get.

After one more long drink of the cool water, almost the last in the jar, he replaced the lid and picked up Harry's lantern.

The syringe was still in his pocket, but he hoped he wouldn't need it.

Etan stared at the handgun, trying to remember the last time he'd held one. Probably when he and his father took Alex target shooting when they first moved back. Again, the luxury of using up bullets for fun was hard to imagine.

He popped the magazine into his hand, made sure it was loaded, and clicked it back into place. Etan flipped the safety off, then back on before he slipped it into his back pocket.

Badly as he needed to go through with this, he had no intention of risking his own life on the day they'd almost lost Alex.

The cell row was just inside a thick wooden door. Six bleak concrete rooms with doors made of metal bars on the front, and only the first one locked closed. Etan stood for a long time watching the woman inside lying on the bed. He wouldn't have been able to tell by looking that she was female.

He could hardly tell she was human.

Her hair was long and matted, her clothes barely qualified as rags. Her hands, face, and feet were so filthy she seemed to have shoes, gloves, and a mask on.

When Etan unlocked the cell, she sat straight up, staring at him.

"Relax," he said, leaving the lantern on the floor outside the cell. "I just want to talk to you."

She drew her feet up onto the bed, but she never took her eyes off Etan. He didn't know if Harry and the others had pushed her hair back or if he'd been too upset to notice, but up close her features were obviously feminine. Small jaw and nose, high cheekbones. The snarling rage he'd seen directed at Connor and Alex overrode everything else.

He stepped inside the shadowy cell.

"Are you thirsty?"

Her eyes darted to the mug he carried, then back to his face.

"Just tell me why you were there today. I need to know what happened."

She only watched him.

"Are there others like you? Out in the woods? Someone you're trying to take care of?"

Her eyes narrowed, but she was silent.

"Here, just drink the water. Maybe you'll feel more like talking."

She looked down at his hands again, and he wondered if she noticed the rings he wore, the facets of white gold flickering in the lantern light.

He wondered if she understood why he was wearing two of them.

Etan's voice dropped to a menacing whisper.

"What were you going to do with the little boy?"

She drew back, blinking. Etan stepped closer, keeping his body between her and the door.

"If you can still talk, you'll be a lot better off answering my questions. See, I'm all for keeping things as civil as we possibly can. That's what I've spent the last eleven years of my life trying to do."

He leaned forward and put the mug on a steel table built into the cinderblock wall. Her eyes followed his hand.

"What you did today is exactly what I'm trying to keep from happening. I need to understand how we can do that."

She looked back at Etan, but she leaned forward slowly, reaching for the water.

"What's your name?"

She scowled as she picked up the mug, sniffing at the water. Etan held his breath.

He hadn't noticed a smell from the pills, but he hadn't been looking for one.

She settled back onto the bed, holding the mug in both hands.

"My name is Etan Griffith."

The woman sipped the water. She jerked her head back and glared at Etan.

"It's sugar. Probably the last refined sugar in this part of the world."

She drank slowly, then more deeply.

"My husband's name is Alex Collins," he said, his heart beating faster with every movement of her throat. "Our son's name is Connor. He was named after my father, who never got to meet him. Thieves killed my father. Strangers who wanted to steal from us and hurt us instead of working with us, letting us help them."

She held the empty mug in both hands, watching him.

"I wish you *would* talk, to tell you the truth. I think you understand me though, so that will have to do."

Etan squatted, noticing the woman moved more slowly when she drew back. If she'd taken Sandy's pills on a long-empty stomach, this whole thing could be over in minutes.

"I truly am sorry you're in such a state. I wish you'd come to us a long time ago, or gone to someone else. We took in as many people as we could, even from Maple Ridge, and we still help everyone we can."

He shifted and drew the gun behind his back, flipping the safety off. Her eyes tracked his movements a split-second behind.

"There's no way I can help you now, though. I don't know what you were trying to do with Connor, and I don't care. We should put you on trial and try to figure that out. But we're not going to."

The woman blinked several times, then looked down at the mug she still held.

"You gave up your chance for help when you tried to take my son. And you earned this when you almost killed my husband."

Etan brought the gun around, holding it pointed at the floor. The woman blinked again, looking from the gun back into his eyes.

"I want to shoot you through the heart and be finished with it. But that's not what I saw. I saw myself giving you the choice between the gun and just lying down and going to sleep. I couldn't see past that. You're not going to see another day, but I won't dishonor my own vision no matter how much I want to. The choice is yours."

Chapter 25

The lights were still on in the emergency lobby of the hospital when Etan returned, but no one was inside.

Except one man, once again sitting behind a desk.

"Harry."

"Etan. Everything's fine here."

"Everything's fine with me, then."

Harry stood, his broad shoulders more stooped than Etan remembered from less than an hour ago. Forty-two minutes according to Alex's watch.

"Anything I need to know before I head back?"

"Starvation is a terrible thing. So is dying alone."

Etan dropped the keys into Harry's hand as the older man walked past.

"Let me know if I can do anything to help with Alex or the kids," Harry said as he stepped outside. "Or you."

"Thank you. I will."

Harry never asked about the gun in Etan's pocket, still fully loaded.

Sandy and Jeff sat on a gurney close by the operating table. Alex was still far too pale, but he looked up as soon as Etan walked in.

His smile was all the absolution Etan needed.

Chapter 26

Alex couldn't remember being more grateful for a soft bed in his entire life. Softer than the operating table, at least, and that was more than enough.

The lights in the room weren't nearly as blinding, either. They were dim enough that he wasn't quite sure if the walls were the same soothing blue as the rest of the hospital.

Another bed sat on the other side of the room. Etan slumped in the middle of it, face nearly as pale as the walls but definitely not soothing.

"Etan, you're about to fall over," Alex said. "Just lie down and close your eyes."

"I'm fine," Etan said, shaking his head. "I'll rest when I know you're settled for the night. Do you need anything?"

"Besides not worrying about you? I'm freezing."

"That's the hangover from the full block," Sandy said from the doorway. She opened a closet by the window. "Pretty much the only side effect. Unfortunately the pain block we're still using can make that worse."

She covered the thin white sheet pulled up to his chin with a thick brown blanket, then glanced at the silvery box hanging on the wall above the bed.

The magic box.

"We can start reducing the block over the next day or so, but I'd rather have you a bit chilly than in pain. Need me to turn the mattress heat on?"

Alex frowned, once again checking past the odd numb sensation of his chest. His legs ached terribly, and he felt like he should be shivering. The sensation of an involuntary movement that couldn't happen was strangely disorienting.

"Yeah, crank it up." He caught Etan's head drooping out of the corner of his eye. "Sleepyhead over there is the one who likes to be cold."

"You got it." She touched the screen over Alex's head, just out of his sight. "Etan, you're asleep sitting up."

"So Alex tells me," he said with a half smile. "I can sleep here if that's okay."

"That's not my call," Sandy said, her own smile was mischievous. "Someone else has strong opinions on the subject, and I'm not about to cross her."

She stepped out into the hall for a few seconds. Laura Griffith peeked around the doorway.

"Mind if I come in?"

"Of course not," Etan said. He stood and caught his mother in a hug. "I'm so glad you're here."

She turned to Alex, her eyes bright and sad. Laura looked ready for bed, long silver and blonde hair pulled into a braid, wearing the same soft pajamas covered with songbirds that she wore for frequent sleepovers with her grandchildren.

"Does anything hurt, hon?" she said, kissing Alex on the forehead.

Tears made Alex's eyes ache nearly as much as his legs. His own mother had rarely shown so much affection, not even when he was Caela's age.

"Not with Sandy's magic box," he said. "She's even got my ass warming up so I'll stop complaining."

"Good. You just tell me if anything bothers you at all. Etan, go home."

Etan snorted and shook his head. He winked at Alex. Alex found the tiniest of lighthearted gestures from his husband helped more than all the pain medication in the world.

"You wouldn't think I was thirty-three years old with kids of my own, would you?" Etan said. "I'd swear my mother just told me to go home."

"That's *exactly* what I just told you." Laura sat beside Etan. "Alex is in the best place he could possibly be, and you're about done in. You look the same as when you played out in the snow too long as little boy. I'll watch over him, sweetheart. You go home to my grandbabies."

Alex watched the two of them, wondering how Etan could believe it was worth arguing with his mother with that tone in her voice.

"Maybe you could stay with them, Mom," Etan said. His own soft voice made it clear he knew it was no use. "They're always happy to see you."

"I *did* just see them, son. They're fine, but they're scared to death. They need Daddy E while they're so worried about Daddy A."

"That does make sense," Alex said. He noticed Sandy in the doorway this time. "Sandy said I'm going to be asleep soon anyway. I'll be home getting on your nerves soon enough."

"That you will," she said. "I'll be right next door. I pretty much have an apartment set up, almost as comfortable as my house."

Etan groaned, but he let Laura pull him to his feet. He brushed Alex's hair back. Alex caught his hand and kissed it.

"What do you want me to do, sweetie?" Etan said.

"I must still be knocked out," Alex said, grinning at his mother-in-law. "I'd swear Etan just asked me what I want him to do. First time in fourteen years."

"Jackass," Etan said under his breath. "How's he doing, Sandy? Physically, I mean."

"Everything looks good. He needs rest more than anything else right now. Laura's right. You're run ragged. Seeing your kids will do you and them a world of good. We'll both be right here with Alex."

Etan crossed his arms, drumming his fingers against his biceps. He looked at each of them in turn, then last at Alex.

"It's fine, E," Alex said. "I'll be sound asleep in a minute anyway. You'll *all* feel better at home, and I will too knowing you're with our kids."

Chapter 27

Etan knocked on the door to Iris and Gena's apartment barely ten minutes later, hoping all their children were asleep. He was too early for their normal bedtime, but this had not been a normal day. Gena opened the door a crack, her blonde hair and one eye barely visible past the chain Etan had never seen her use.

His heart ached at such an antiquated notion, as if locked doors would keep the monsters away ever again.

"Etan, hon, come on in. Laura just left, she said Alex came through the surgery."

She pushed the door closed, then opened it wide. He had time to relax into her hug, her warmth, for a few seconds before he took in the room behind her.

Iris sat on the floor, surrounded by nine children. All of them awake. All of them staring at him with their eyes wide and afraid. Caela jumped to her feet and ran over to him.

"Where's Daddy Alex?"

Before Etan could answer, all of their children thundered toward him. Iris picked Eddie up when the youngest of them started crying as his brothers and sisters left him behind. Etan knelt, holding his arms out to gather all of them as close as he could.

"Daddy Alex is staying at Dr. Sandy's for a little while," he said.

"She's going to help him get all better. He misses you, and he asked me to tell every one of you how much he loves you."

All of them started talking at once, and Iris and Gena tried their best to keep everyone calm. Their children who lived down here with their mothers adored Alex just as much as the five he and Etan were raising.

Caela stood beside Etan, her hand on his shoulder as the younger ones clamored for his attention. He turned to her.

"How long does he have to stay there?" she said, her tiny brow wrinkled.

"We're not sure, baby. For a few days at least."

"Will someone watch out for him and make sure he's safe?"

"Dr. Sandy will be right there," Etan said. "She's taking really good care of him. Your Gramma is with him, too."

"Do Dr. Sandy and Gramma know to watch out for the bad thing so it won't hurt Daddy Alex again?"

Etan knew, in the clearest flash of intuition he or any of the other Dreamers would have for months, that Caela would need to know the truth about what he'd done someday. He'd have to tell Alex as well, and a hell of a lot sooner.

He couldn't see why, but he knew their daughter would need that knowledge for a deeper reason than satisfying her curiosity. And he knew that day was safely distant, years in the future.

"The bad thing is gone," he said. The distressed voices of their children fell silent at his words. "The bad thing is gone, and it can't ever hurt anyone again."

"Go see Daddy A?" Connor said. He was leaning on Etan's thighs and against his chest, his fine brown hair sweet from a recent bath.

"Not yet," Gena said. She knelt beside Etan, her hand on his other shoulder. "Maybe in a few days."

"Dr. Sandy will tell us when we can go see him," Iris said. She swayed back and forth with Eddie droopy-eyed in her arms. Etan wished he could join their son in that safe embrace.

"We'll all have to be extra careful when we do," he said, looking at each of them in turn. "He's getting better, but we don't want to hurt him or make him sick. We'll talk more about that when it's time."

"Are you hungry, Etan?" Gena said. "We have plenty here. People have been bringing food all day."

"I'm starving, but I'm about to fall asleep on my feet. I'll get our bunch rounded up and head upstairs."

Iris kissed Eddie's head and smiled.

"Don't be ridiculous, Daddy E. You'll eat while we get the kids settled in together. Then you'll stay here with us for as long as you need to. No arguments. You know it's the only thing that makes sense."

Etan's breath caught, and he hid his face against Connor's soft hair. It hadn't occurred to him yet how awful it was going to be, sleeping in their bed without Alex. Trying to pretend everything was all right for their children's sake while trying to keep his mind from flaying his heart to bits.

"I'd love that," he said, looking up. "We all would."

The younger kids followed their mothers without too much complaining, but Caela hung back. Etan nodded at Iris, then held out his arms to their oldest, catching her in a strong hug.

"Want to stay in here with me while I eat?" he said. "Are you hungry?"

"I'm not hungry, Daddy E. We ate a whole bunch. Can I ask you something?"

Etan stood with her, surprised at how heavy she was when he was so weary. That was something else that had never occurred to him. In a few short years, he wouldn't be able to pick Caela up anymore.

He hoped Alex would be able to lift her again before she got too big.

"You can ask me anything, baby."

She sat at the long wood plank table where they often shared meals while he roamed around the kitchen, piling two plates with enough food to make up for his three missed meals and a little bit more.

Caela held her chin in her hands and stared at him when he sat beside her.

"What did Dr. Sandy do? About the cut in Daddy A's belly?"

"She fixed it up," Etan said, glad he hadn't started eating yet. "It will take a little while, but he's going to be fine."

"Did she sew it? Like our clothes?"

Etan nodded, smiling at her quickness even as his empty stomach protested.

"She did. Pretty cool, huh?"

"I guess. Is that why we have to be so careful?"

"That's why. We don't want to hurt his belly. We'll have to wash our hands even more than usual, too, so we don't make him sick."

Caela watched him eat, her mouth pursed and her fingers drumming on the table. Etan wondered how often Alex's parents sat with their nearly identical little boy doing exactly the same thing.

"If he gets sick, he'll have to stay at Dr. Sandy's longer, won't he?" she finally said.

"You're right. We want him home as soon as possible, so we'll have to do everything we can to help him get better."

"Even if that means no playtime."

"For a while, yeah, sweetheart. No playtime with Daddy A. You can have playtime with me, though. I know I'm not as much fun, but I'll do my best."

Caela stared at him, her pale eyebrows raised. Etan had never felt so thoroughly examined and evaluated.

"Okay. I'll teach you. Night, Daddy E. Love you."

She kissed his cheek and walked away.

"Night, Caela. Love you," he said, then continued under his breath. "Alex loves you, too."

Iris and Gena came in just as he finished the absurd amount of food. Etan didn't feel overly full, but the gnawing in his belly was gone for the first time all day.

"Come on, Etan," Gena said, holding out her hand. Etan stood and held on tight. "We'll get this tomorrow. Time to go to bed."

"Anything change with Alex while you were there?" Iris said.

"He's stable right now. Mom's staying in the room with him,

Sandy next door. The next couple of weeks will be the hardest. If he…" Etan stumbled – the words and the reality of how much ground his husband still had to cover robbing the tiny bit of strength he had left. "Once he gets through that, things will be easier."

Etan didn't protest when Iris and Gena pulled off his shoes and clothes. His breath hitched in his throat twice before they finished. When they settled in on either side of him, each with an arm across his chest, he gave in to the tears he'd been fighting since the Dream ripped through his mind.

He'd never slept with Iris and Gena without Alex, the four of them spent and satisfied, hoping another life would join their family. Another chance at eternity, at a future for humanity.

Their warmth and comfort that night kept him from flying apart, helped him sleep when he thought he'd never be able to again.

Chapter 28

ALEX HELD Etan's hand tight as they walked toward the storage shed at the edge of the old football field. Months of rain and weather, harvest and replanting had long since washed away the footprints, and the blood. All of the plants out there had young, early summer vigor rather than the near slumber of October.

Yet he knew he'd always be able to spot exactly where he'd nearly lost his life.

Two of the red hound dogs ranged ahead of them, noses to the ground, but without the urgency they'd shown that terrible day. Their warning may have led Alex to that encounter with a knife in his belly, but they'd prevented what could only have been far worse if one of the students walked in there instead.

Or one of their children.

He couldn't see Dana Chen, their new head of security, or any of her armed guards. Alex knew they were there, especially with him wandering around out here at dusk. He was already growing weary of so much attention coming his way.

He couldn't sigh or twitch or cough without someone asking if he was okay.

And still, the shadows deepening in the woods beyond the field seemed to crawl up his legs, making his balls draw up tight and try to disappear. Alex was as uneasy as he'd been the first few weeks after they'd moved from Chicago to Virginia. He couldn't see anything specific, but everything that creaked or groaned or shifted felt like a threat to him.

The structures and paths and patterns Alex had depended on for most of his life had deserted him, with the students and his children as Witnesses.

His sense of the shape and boundaries of his life had shattered, leaving him more vulnerable and afraid than he'd ever been.

As he so often did, Etan voiced his thoughts before Alex could find the words.

"Maybe we shouldn't be out here yet, sweetie."

Alex looked around one more time, turning in a slow circle. He wished for the coarse comfort of his gun on his hip, though it would have dragged too much on his weak muscles. He glanced down yet again to make sure Etan carried his.

"Probably not, but I'm sick of being scared. I need to see it."

He was grateful when Etan put his arms around him, carefully, so carefully. Alex's face twisted when he realized Etan was turning them, angling their bodies so *he* could still see out into the woods with the shed at his back. Neither of them had been so fearful and timid less than a year ago. He was afraid neither of them would ever recover.

"What did you see, Etan? Not in your Dream. I mean what did you see here? I know you've told me more than once, but I need to hear you where I can see it all for myself."

He felt Etan's chest rise and fall slowly. He leaned back and touched Alex's cheek with his fingertips. Checking for fever, of course. A stubborn infection in Alex's wound had led to more surgeries, then a dreadful struggle with pneumonia that knocked his recovery back even more. He understood how it all made Etan's overly protective impulse worse, but the effect was no less frustrating.

Alex worried that Etan would never stop, and that both of them would only grow more resentful with the constant attention over time.

Partly because he was so deeply afraid himself.

"Let me get a lantern, then sit down with me," Etan said. "I'll tell you what I remember as many times as you need me to."

Alex watched Etan unlock the heavy padlock on the door, unable to breathe until he stepped back outside with a lantern from their stores, then re-locked the door. He didn't want to ask and confirm it, but he was certain Etan wanted to make sure the shed was empty more than he wanted the light.

Alex would have done the same, and he probably always would.

His knees were weak enough between fear and the walk out here that he sat on the low porch rather than argue about it. The dogs settled down on the ground at their feet with exaggerated sighs.

Etan took Alex's hand in both of his. "Honestly, the line between the Dream and what I really saw has only gotten more blurry. I woke up with the whole thing screaming through my mind, took the kids to Iris and Gena, and ran. I guess it was all memory until I made it over the hill back there by the cannery."

Both of them looked at a rustle off to their right. The dogs didn't move. A yellow light that had to be another lantern grew brighter around the contour of the hill, but Alex's flesh crawled until he recognized the woman carrying it.

Dana, personally overseeing his security after all. She raised a hand and kept walking.

"I saw you going toward it right before it fell and you grabbed Connor," Etan said, then he shook his head. "*She*, not *it*. I couldn't tell that day, not then. I saw Connor get away. And I saw her stab you."

Alex's stomach twisted and heaved. He squeezed his eyes closed, desperate to keep his dinner where it belonged. Throwing up would be pure agony. And yet another sign of his weakness.

"All of you saw her stab me," he said, his jaw tight. "Our *children* saw that. Caela still wakes up screaming and I can't even pick her up to make it stop."

"Yes they did, sweetie. They saw you doing everything you could to keep Connor safe. They see you back home with us now, getting stronger every single day. Caela's nightmares are getting better over time, just like we thought they would."

The forest was nearly black now, and the early summer noises were louder. Alex remembered feeling this way thirteen years ago looking out at the trees and brush around their house in the middle of the woods. Nothing was ever so unknown, so mysterious and dark, in the suburbs of his Wisconsin childhood or in Chicago where he'd met Etan.

He'd known then as clearly as he knew now that humans were at the mercy of whatever moved in that darkness. Even more so now, as the defenses of bright lights, terrifying noise, and machines to chew through the wilderness fell away from the earth.

They once again huddled around campfires and inside their shelters, hoping the wild things weren't bold enough to break through that fragile circle of safety.

Alex had always hated lies, but he hated the unknown even more.

"What happened after that?" he said. "After the surgery? I know you went to the jail, Etan."

"That doesn't matter," Etan said. He shifted away long enough to light the lantern, then put his arm around Alex's shoulders. "She's gone. She'll never hurt you or our family again."

"It *does* matter, how can you say that? All of us are having nightmares. I don't know when you or I or our children will ever feel safe again. She's still hurting us, right this second."

"Let's go back home," Etan said. Alex heard the strain in his husband's voice, felt it in the tighter muscles in his arm. "Maybe we can talk more somewhere else."

"No, Etan, no! Tell me now. She'll keep slicing both of us up as long as we let her. Every time I imagine it for myself the cut gets deeper."

Alex pressed his fingers into the flesh under his ribs, trying to ease the pain. Shouting when his diaphragm was barely knitted back together and his lungs were still weak from pneumonia wasn't the smartest thing he'd ever done, not even compared to walking into this goddamn shed that morning.

But just like the stubborn infection he'd struggled so hard to fight through, the poison had to get out somehow.

Etan watched him, his face tight and worried.

"I did what I had to do to keep walking around when I didn't know if you ever would again. That's all."

"Then tell me what happened, E. No one else will. I think I deserve to know. At least tell me if another bunch of them is going to come out of those woods after her. Don't make me check over my shoulder for the rest of my life."

"She's dead, Alex. Probably starvation. I didn't see any others in my Dream that showed up too fucking late. She was alone. Dana's patrols will take care of any others out there."

"We don't know that. No one else had a Dream in time, either." Alex ran his hand along Etan's thigh, his old distraction trick that he knew wouldn't work at the moment. He did it for his own comfort rather than his husband's arousal. "I need to know. I'm not used to having nightmares. I don't know how you stand it almost every night. If I know what happened to her, they might stop."

"Mine never have. No one's Dreaming at all anymore, not the Dreams we need. Maybe we will again now that you're getting better. I can stand my nightmares because you're beside me every night."

Etan closed his eyes for several seconds. "I'm afraid of what you'll think of me."

"Then *listen* to me," Alex said. "The only thing I have any right to say is thank you if you were involved. I would have taken care of the problem if I'd been able to get up off that hospital bed. You know that. And you know I'll just keep asking until you get sick of hearing it."

"Okay, Alex. Okay. I did go back and talk to her, yes. And she did pass away while I was there."

"Natural causes, right?" Alex said, his eyes following another one of those patrol lanterns, the person carrying it hidden in the darkness. "Please don't lie to me."

The silence dragged out long enough that Alex thought he'd have to truly start begging. He didn't want to try to sleep again, to go willingly into the horror movies playing over and over in his mind until he dragged himself back to consciousness.

Not without knowing the truth.

Etan shifted until he sat cross-legged facing Alex. He moved the lantern between them, and Alex turned so he could watch his husband's face.

Whatever horrors waited for them beyond this faint circle of light would have to find satisfaction elsewhere.

"Right after Sandy came out and told me you made it through the surgery, I had a vision. I saw myself standing over the creature that attacked you, holding a gun in one hand and poison in the other. I knew I was meant to give her a choice. She could take the poison or I could shoot her."

"What did you do?" Alex whispered.

"I didn't quite give her that much of a choice." Etan's attempt to smile hurt Alex's heart. "I gave her poison, then told her I'd shoot her or she could lie down and go to sleep. I don't know if she decided, or if the poison kicked in. She was starved enough that it could have been that fast. Either way, I stood there until I knew she was dead. I'm not proud, but I was satisfied when she drew her last breath. Then I got back to you as fast as I could."

Etan stared into Alex's eyes, not flinching or drawing away. He was simply waiting.

"I wish you hadn't gone through that," Alex said. He didn't bother trying to hide his tears. "I never wanted you or our children to go through anything like that. *I'm* supposed to be the one keeping the monsters away."

Etan smiled. Not much, but it was real.

"Why's that, Alex? Because you're older, or more of a butch man than me, or some other such bullshit?"

"No, not even a little bit. Because you're the better of us. No one in this whole town would be here if it weren't for you. You've shown us the way more times than any of us can count."

"You know I still can't remember the Dreams, right? And no one puts these things together better than you do. Without that record-keeping and making connections and paying attention, all the

Dreams in the world wouldn't matter. Without you, I would have been too lonely, or too crazy, to have the damn Dreams a long time ago."

Alex didn't have the heart, or the energy, to argue. He *had* felt protective of Etan since the night they'd met, and that would never change. Not even when his own body was still too weak to even pick up their children.

He'd never wanted Etan to do something so hard, so cruel. An act that would change his gentle nature.

Etan reached up and touched Alex's cheek, but the caress was different now. Not only for comfort or reassurance, not anymore. The balance between them - gentle and strong, protective and perceptive - was altered forever. Alex didn't yet know what that shift would mean for them or the shape of their lives.

He took his own comfort in seeing that pattern again, sensing connection and motion all around them, for the first time since he'd last been in this field. The clouds of fireflies in the trees and on the ground aligned with the billions of stars above them, so many more than they'd imagined less than twenty years ago.

All of them turned and sang together with the rhythm of Alex's heart.

"Thank you for telling me, E," he said, leaning forward for a kiss. Much to his surprise, the catch under his ribs was a bit lighter. So was his heart. "And thank you for what you did. I know that wasn't easy. I probably wouldn't have been so kind."

Chapter 29

THE APARTMENT WAS QUIET, their bedroom dark, with all the children and probably everyone else in the building asleep. Alex held Etan's head, trying to keep him from drawing away. They'd never gone as long as a couple of weeks without making love before the attack.

Healing belly and weak muscles or not, he was climbing the walls with wanting his husband.

And with needing to feel normal again.

"Are you sure?" Etan whispered, his breathing as fast as Alex's.

"I'm sure. Sandy's sure. Nothing hurts anymore, E. I want you. It's been way too damn long."

Etan ran his fingers down Alex's chest, across the ticklish hair and over to the still-growing stubble on the other side. His light touch along the thick scars felt hot, like the nerves hadn't quite healed yet. The muscles hadn't yet either, still aching deep inside when he moved a certain way or coughed too hard.

Alex was determined to keep that much to himself.

"I don't want to hurt you," Etan said, pressing his hand flat over the scars. "We almost lost you."

Alex forced himself to breathe slowly, deliberately. It was one thing to be frustrated and moving into angry at how gingerly everyone was treating him, as if he were made of glass. Another thing entirely, and far worse, to let his own upset push away the person he needed most.

"No one knows that better than I do," he said, covering Etan's hand with his own. "I can't imagine anything worse than leaving our babies while they still need me so much, leaving you alone. Unless it's having all of you act like I'm not alive, not me, when I *am*."

He moved Etan's hand higher, over his pounding heart.

"I'm right here, Etan. I feel like a ghost everyone's afraid to touch or look at. Even our kids are afraid to hug me. I barely feel like I exist anymore. I need to feel like myself, not some pathetic invalid. I need you to *touch* me, and not like you're nursing me back to health."

Alex pulled Etan's head down and whispered, his lips against his ear.

"Touch me the way you used to. The way I used to touch you. Take me. Take every part of me. Like you're starving to death for me. Like your life depends on it."

"It does," Etan said. He groaned when Alex moved his hand from his heart to his straining cock. Alex nearly came with the heat and pressure of his lover's fingers after too much time. "I *am* starving to death for you."

"Then prove it. Make me feel it. You're not going to hurt me. Not unless you stop."

Etan kissed him again, softly at first, then hard enough to bruise Alex's lips. Alex didn't dare draw away, and he didn't want to. He squeezed Etan's body against his own, the aching heat in his chest only driving him on.

Etan wasn't the only one who needed to get over being afraid of infection, of scars. Of tearing open wounds no one could see anymore, and those no one could ever see.

Alex was choking to death, not on healing flesh but a half-lived life, too careful and rigid and cool.

Using his body the way it was meant to be used, even if that catch in his ribs lingered longer because of it, was the only way either of them could get close to normal life again.

Etan took both of them a long way toward normal that night.

Chapter 30

Alex charged up the concrete steps to their apartment, not fast enough to be called running. Not just yet. He'd started this little game with himself a few weeks after he and Etan had visited the fields where he'd been attacked, every time he managed to get to the ground floor unattended. Determined to rebuild his strength on his own terms.

He hadn't even pretended to argue about needing the old hand-crank elevator at first. His family would have had to move down to the first floor otherwise, especially once the pneumonia set in. Alex had despaired for a long time of even having the energy to turn the damn crank, much less climb the stairs under his own steam.

The first several attempts had him running out of breath at a slow walk, stopping several times on the way up, grasping his loose jeans to keep them on his hips. After weeks of having to slow down after one flight, then two, he was finally making it to the fourth floor without breathing too heavily. And his clothes weren't two sizes too big anymore.

His triumph was no less sweet for being private. Neither Etan nor Sandy would have approved. That alone, taking charge of his own body, did as much good for Alex's attitude as for his legs and heart.

The return of Etan's Dreams after nearly a year gave Alex even more reason for his solitary exercise. Gena's suggested weekly meetings among the Witnesses three years ago, right after Connor was born, helped Alex keep a hold on his sanity. Back then, comparing their journals let them see similarities developing, or other Dreamers sharing one of Etan's Dreams months later.

The strict rule preventing any of the Dreamers from attending, or reading each other's journals, assured them all that the Dreams were pure.

During the long time of no one Dreaming, they'd focused on standardizing their records, making sure they'd be useful for years into the future. When their children, grandchildren, and hopefully more might need to study their first tentative steps and stumbles.

Those long months of feeling blind tested more than Alex's patience, certainly. But he was equally certain he was the only one who felt he'd somehow caused the temporary blindness. And so his relief – as not only the Dreams themselves but all of Wolf Branch's *faith* in those Dreams recovered – buoyed Alex like floating in warm water.

He walked slowly down the hall toward their apartment, breathing deeply to hide any signs of his exertion. He hadn't even broken a sweat this time. His smile when he opened the door was genuine, as much for his own accomplishment as for the news he was excited to share.

"Daddy A," Gwen cried, jumping up from what looked like a terribly serious game of marbles. "Caela lost another tooth!"

Alex knelt, groaning at the deep stretch in his long thigh muscles, as everyone but their oldest daughter ran to greet him.

"Did she?" Alex said from the middle of the scrum. "We'll have to borrow money from the tooth fairy at this rate."

He saw Caela roll her eyes as he stood to hug Etan.

"How long before they figure out they can't spend their money anywhere?" Etan said before Alex stopped his words with a kiss.

"Such an embarrassment of riches," Alex said. "Looks like Caela's caught on already."

Caela didn't move from her chair beside the window as Alex walked over, a book open on her lap.

"Let me see, sweetheart."

She pursed her mouth for a second, then flashed her three missing teeth.

"No such fing as a toof fairy," she said, her temporary sweet lisp forcing Alex to hide his grin.

"I didn't believe in that stuff either," he said. "But we won't tell the little ones just yet."

Alex leaned down to pick her up without thinking, and her arms went around his neck in a flash. When he stood, he sucked air through his teeth at the first twinge he'd felt for several weeks.

"Alex?" Etan said. "Be *careful*, Caela!"

She twisted in his arms, and Alex's efforts to keep from dropping her drove the pain deeper beneath his ribs.

"No, no!" she cried, tears filling her blue eyes. "Didn't mean to hurt you!"

The rumble of voices and activity behind Alex stopped, and he knew what he'd see before he turned. Etan and the younger children were all watching him, their eyes equally wide and frightened.

Alex turned his head away from Caela, trying to hide his face. The pattern of fear and avoidance was clear and painful all around him. Making love with Etan a few times softened the edges between them, but not nearly enough. And not at all with their children.

Now was the time to break it.

"Listen to me, Caela," he said. "All of you. I'm not hurt anymore, and I'm not sick. It's time you all stopped treating me like I am."

Everyone but Etan and Caela stared for several seconds, then seemed to understand what he was saying. Or they were more easily distracted by the marbles.

Alex was more worried about the two of them.

"I'm not going to bite you, either," he said. He sat on the couch with Caela, pleased that moving more carefully kept the pain at bay. "I've got news for you two anyway."

Etan sat beside them, his face too carefully neutral.

"That's the first time anything has hurt for a while, E. If it does sometimes, but less often, that means I'm getting stronger. Not weaker. I'm strong enough to pick you up now, Caela. Understand?"

"I guess," she said. "I'm the oldest, so I guess you can pick all of us up."

"Maybe not all at once, but that's good enough for me. Etan?"

"That was my fault," he said, squeezing Caela's arm. "You didn't do anything wrong. We can both do better if we help each other remember, okay?"

She glanced at Alex, her face serious, then she grinned at Etan. All of their kids turned to Etan more than before. That made Alex a tiny bit more happy than sad.

"Okay, Daddy E. We'll remember together."

"What's your big news, sweetie?" Etan said. He moved closer to Alex, head on his shoulder. Caela scooted until her legs were across both their laps.

"Everyone's Dreaming of training now. In general like we've been doing when they turn nine, but especially for the Dreamers and Witnesses. It feels like we can cover the basics while they're young, like this hellion. Then as they sort themselves out, we'll work out the specialized classes."

"I get to go to *Dreamer* school?" Caela said.

"Maybe," Etan said. "Depends on what happens when you grow up. You might be a Witness just like Alex and Gena."

"You get to go to school either way," Alex said. "No one feels like we should be delaying until they're older, not anymore. You'll be going with the older kids every morning instead of with your brothers and sisters. That okay with you?"

"Yeah! Will you be teaching us?"

"We both probably will, and Iris and Gena," Alex said. "A lot more when you get older. We'll all figure it out together. You're the oldest born here, and Daddy E didn't start Dreaming until he was eleven. Same with Mom Iris. So we've got at least five years before we have to worry about you starting."

Barely two years later, they all understood how quickly things were changing.

Chapter 31

ETAN GOT out of bed slowly, doing his best not to wake Alex. All of the Witnesses seemed to sleep lightly, but he had to try. The fear of his husband getting too run down and getting sick again never quite left him.

He was rarely awake first, and the children seemed aware of that fact. Testing his ability to keep up with them and keep them quiet left him wondering if they did the same to Alex.

Caela answered him before he asked.

"They're *always* like that, Daddy E," she said, shaking her head.

At eight, Caela was fully aware of being the oldest of all of them. She didn't take *too* much advantage of her status, but she didn't feel like one of the babies, either.

"Are you feeling okay, Caela?" Etan said. She was pale and more quiet than usual. He touched her forehead like he still sometimes did Alex's. She reacted in exactly the same way, drawing back and scowling.

"I'm *not* sick and I *don't* have a fever. I had a bad dream again, I think."

Etan stared at her, his stomach a mass of swirling knots. She was too young for the Dreams, wasn't she? She had to be. Nightmares were one thing. He'd thought hers had finally stopped two years after she'd seen what happened to Connor and Alex.

"You think? Do you remember your dreams, Caela?"

She shrugged and shook her head. Such a perfect imitation of Alex that Etan couldn't help but smile.

"Sometimes. I think Daddy A remembers them for me."

"Has he been talking to you about your dreams?"

"I think he does at night, when I have the bad ones. The ones I can't remember."

"Okay. Maybe we can both talk to him about it when he wakes up."

Alex still wasn't up by the time Etan got everyone settled down and out to their morning playtime outside and sent Caela off to school. The courtyard behind the apartment building was a perfect setting to keep so many young children occupied and keep parents still concerned about another attack from worrying too much. The new security patrols helped even more. The group playtime was also a perfect way to keep teenagers involved and out of trouble.

Etan sat on the bed beside Alex, watching him breathe. Everything sounded normal, not the rattling strain of when he'd fought off pneumonia. Still, he slept too hard for so late in the morning.

Helping Caela with her bad dreams could explain it.

So could getting sick again.

Etan leaned down and kissed his cheek. Cool, not feverish. And not scowling. Alex smiled, stretching before he pulled Etan down into a hug.

"What's got you up so early?"

"I'm not up early, sweetie. You slept in."

"How much?" Alex said, sitting up on the edge of the bed. "I don't hear stampeding feet."

"They already stampeded downstairs. Caela reassured me they do their best to overrun your authority every morning, too."

Alex blinked. Etan knew he didn't mind getting up with their kids most mornings. Watching the way they all rumbled and laughed together made it clear Alex loved every second.

"I slept through the morning rampage? I'm sorry, E. They're a handful at the best of times."

"No, don't worry. You must have needed it. Come on, breakfast is ready."

"I could get used to this."

Etan waited until Alex ate a reassuring amount before bringing up the Dreams. He usually lost his appetite early on when he wasn't feeling well.

"Caela informs me you've been remembering her Dreams for her."

Alex sighed and closed his eyes for a second.

"For a few weeks now, yeah. I hoped it was normal bad dreams for a while, but I think it's more."

"She's only eight," Etan said. The thought of their daughter having the Dreams at all was bad enough after what'd he'd gone through as an early teenager. And the much worse his grandmother had suffered. "She's still a *baby*."

"I know. She Dreams too early, and they're so damn strong. The strangest thing is she seems to be on the same cycle you are. About the time you start to fall back asleep, she's right in the middle of it."

"The same Dreams?"

"A lot of the time they seem to be. She's not good at describing them yet, but they sound the same. That part *does* worry me. The other adults don't have the same Dreams when you do, E. Not for a while after yours start."

Etan took Alex's hand, the worry forming a harder knot in his belly.

"I don't want her to go through this," he said. "Not so early at the very least. It was hard enough on me at eleven, and I had my father and grandmother to explain what was going on."

"She has us. She's never known a world where the Dreams weren't normal, Etan. Where the Dreams weren't good. She's been learning about it in school for almost two years now. She wants to be just like you, anyway. That's all she ever talks about."

"Like me?" Etan said with a broad smile. "Oh come on. She's your clone, Alex."

"That's probably *why* she wants to be like you. Defying the natural order or something like that. I think she's doing fine. We'll just have to help her as much as we can."

"What if this is too strong in her?" Etan said. "We've never seen the children of Dreamers and Witnesses. I'm afraid it will be like it was for my grandmother, even if we help her."

Alex pushed his chair back, stretching his legs under the table.

"All we can do is pay attention and talk to her. That's what I've been trying to do, make sure she's not so scared in the middle of the night."

"That's not making me feel better. You have to sleep some time. If you get too tired–"

"I'm *fine*, Etan," Alex said, the scowl making an appearance. "I can't just sit by and let her be that afraid and ignore it. I won't. Like you said, she's just a baby."

Etan looked out the window, breathing out hard through pursed lips. The three years since the attack hadn't altered his opinion that Alex was a far worse patient than their children. He knew it for a fact now.

Just as well as he knew his own escalating fears could easily push him into a black hole he was afraid he'd never climb out of.

"Well, I'm not going to sit by and pretend I'm not worried about the two of you. If we're both Dreaming now, we'll have to make some changes. There are four more not far behind Caela who'll probably need just as much attention when *you* need to sleep. If nothing else, staying awake half the night at almost forty isn't the same as when you were twenty-two."

Alex laughed under his breath.

"I was feeling that difference before Sandy relieved me of my spleen. Very much so, and that was only with you. I've already thought about the rest of them coming along. Even I'll admit trying to calm down six Dreamers in one family would be too much for me. Think we'll get lucky and half will be Witnesses?"

"That's a damn good question," Etan said. "We're right in the middle of a giant experiment with no way to figure too many of these things out. Maybe we can talk to Sandy about that, see what she thinks of how the inheritance will go. We probably need to understand more about that going forward no matter what. That doesn't solve the problem of you not getting enough sleep, Alex."

"Well, I have an idea about that, too. I don't much like it, and you won't either. But I'm not sure what else to do with the living arrangements we have here."

Etan looked around their apartment. The big living room beyond the kitchen, cluttered with books and toys and every other evidence of life with kids. The space that felt so huge and decadent when they moved in, especially compared to their cozy shoebox in Chicago, had gotten crowded in a hurry as children joined their family.

"I think joining up two apartments when more houses are ready makes a hell of a lot of sense," Etan said. "Much as I love my grandparents' place, I think we should stay here."

"Yeah, I do too. I'm talking about here. What if we set up a bed in our bedroom, a small one for whichever kid is starting to Dream?"

"We're already jammed into the smallest room in the place. I'm not quite ready to give up all my privacy with you."

"Neither am I."

Alex smiled with the same warmth in his eyes that made Etan weak in the knees the first time they met. Even with all the changes and trouble and struggle, not to mention five children, that response hadn't faded a bit in all those years.

"We don't have to stay in the smallest bedroom, especially if we do this," Alex said. "And I don't mean they sleep in there all the time, either. From talking to you and other Dreamers, it seems to hit really hard for the first several months. Maybe a year. Then it settles down a bit. Sound right to you?"

"Yeah, I think so. I didn't remember mine back then, either. And I didn't have you to notice things like that."

"How things worked for you and Iris and the others doesn't matter that much, not anymore. We're on the front lines with Caela. She's the first I know of to start Dreaming so young. Maybe she'll settle down sooner. Or at least be able to come wake me when she needs me instead of getting so scared. I need to figure out some way to teach her to know when she's Dreaming, to find me and ask for help. If you're on the same cycle like it seems, I'll be awake anyway."

"The best thing would be a small room close to ours," Etan said. "That might work when we have more space. You're right, we should talk to Sandy. She'll know a lot more about how inheritance works, or at least which of her books to look in. Everything we learn with Caela will make it easier for the younger ones."

"And the ones on the way. It means a lot more sleepless nights, but I'm looking forward to meeting the new babies."

Etan took Alex's outstretched hand. The break from newborns made a lot of sense while Alex was recovering, and for all the rest of them to catch their breath. Iris and Gena were raising four of their children as well. With their youngest just turning three, everyone was excited about new little brothers and sisters.

"Everything we learn about all of them will make it easier going forward," Etan said. "We'll have grandchildren to spoil before we know what hit us."

Alex groaned. He stood and pulled Etan into a hug.

"I am *not* ready to think about that. I'm not ready to even imagine letting our kids go."

"Will you ever be, Daddy A?"

"No. Not even a little bit."

PART IV

OLD WAYS PASS AWAY

Chapter 32

NNEARLY TWENTY YEARS passing hadn't dulled Etan's love of the bright sunlight in the living room of their apartment. Especially now that he'd finally admitted he needed reading glasses, even for studying Alex's neat handwriting. The warm breeze drifting in through the open window, perfumed with lilacs even four stories up, managed to lift Etan's gloomy mood a little bit.

He took off the metal-framed glasses and rubbed the ache between his eyebrows, trying to get it to ease up enough for him to be able to think. He could feel the ridge there, the muscles underneath his skin taking on a permanent crease that sometimes looked like a chasm to him in the mirror.

He wasn't a kid anymore at forty-two, but surely he was too young to have such sharp evidence of his own anxiety right there on his face.

He opened his eyes and looked at Alex sitting at the ancient and scarred wooden desk against the opposite wall. All the kids used it for study and homework, resulting in a permanent drift of books, paper, and the wood and charcoal pencils they all knew how to make.

Alex had long ago stopped putting away what the teenagers left there when he needed the space, or asking them to keep the desk neat. He unceremoniously shoved it all into one of the boxes he kept beside the desk just for that purpose and let them sort it out.

Alex wasn't quite as ruthless with the drifts and clutter the younger kids managed to produce in their wake. As long as they confined it all in the corners – and out of the path where adult feet might step on a painful edge – the ongoing games continued. Etan agreed that keeping the toys out in the main living area rather than scattered in the bedrooms made life in general and cleaning in particular much easier.

Etan wasn't sure if he was proud or annoyed that Alex looked so much younger than he did. Alex's hair was still red, though not as dark as when they met. He'd found his own reading glasses in the supply they'd hoarded back when they scouted nearby towns for paper, though he didn't need them as often as Etan did.

If the sunlight caught Alex just right, Etan could see smile lines around his eyes and mouth. Right now, with the light behind him, he looked closer to twenty-five than forty-five.

The biggest sign of his age was the gray in his beard, matching the silver highlights Etan remembered from his vision on their wedding day. Etan thought that only made him more handsome.

He wasn't sure the gray taking over the brown in his own thinning hair did the same at all.

"You okay?" Alex said.

"I'm okay. I'm afraid we're going to have a tough time tonight. I can feel it coming."

Alex raised one eyebrow and sighed, then stood up and stretched. He'd grown a little thicker around the middle, but Etan thought he and Alex were the only ones who knew that. It only showed when Alex was naked, along with the pale, twisting scars below his ribs.

"What Dreams do you think I've been looking at just now?" Alex said, stretching out on the battered but still beloved gray couch with his head in Etan's lap.

"Let's see," Etan said, running his fingers through the red curls. "Couldn't be Mary stirring up trouble here, could it? Taking all of us down with her?"

Alex laughed, shaking his head, then put his hand on the back of Etan's neck. Etan leaned down to meet him in a kiss.

"Of course it is. Do you remember what's going to happen yet? Or when?"

"No, not yet. I can never decide if I envy Iris that or not. Just dreading something doesn't help a damn thing, but I'm not sure remembering it sooner would either."

"Have you asked her about it? Or Gena?"

Etan shook his head, rotating his neck to try to loosen his shoulders.

"They're too wrapped up with the baby coming. If either of them felt something really strong, they would have told us."

"Think this will be the last one?" Alex said, rubbing the back of Etan's neck.

Etan smiled, thrilled all over again at meeting one of their children for the first time. Gena was carrying this one, and with her blond hair and fair skin, they might not have any idea who the father was. Not that it mattered.

Caela, their first child with Iris, was now a fiery-haired teenager with a temper to match. But Etan loved her every bit as much as the brown-haired, studious little boy who'd come next, and all the others. Every one, whether they lived with them or one floor down with Iris and Gena, belonged to all of them.

"Maybe," Etan said. "Iris is thirty-eight this year, Gena's what, forty-one? I kind of hope not, but we're already more lucky than most. They might be getting tired of being pregnant."

"We do have the easy part," Alex said. "At least for the first nine months."

He sat up and moved to the end of the couch.

"Come here. You feel like a bunch of steel cables."

Etan leaned against him, groaning when Alex dug his fingers into his shoulders.

"You keep all your stress right here, don't you?"

Etan tried not to scowl and failed miserably. "Everything I don't keep on my face."

"I love your face, you jackass."

Etan turned toward him, and Alex's lips unerringly found the spot just above his nose, the exact place Etan was most self-conscious about.

"Listen, Alex, I know you Witness-types like to keep your records to yourselves, but has anyone else had this Dream? About Mary?"

"No. I keep hoping someone else will. We haven't had to do anything like this yet."

"You mean stopping her from causing trouble?" Etan said. "We already got her off the Council."

Alex sighed. "That wasn't so bad, just a lot of arguing. It might have made the whole situation worse though. She brings more and more of her followers to every open meeting we have. It's like a fungus. I'm afraid it's all going to play out just like your Dream. I don't think we'll be able to stop them."

Neither of them spoke for a few minutes. Etan was happy to let him work out the knots in his muscles. He hoped Alex wouldn't bring the Dream up again, but he knew his husband too well to expect that.

"I don't see any way around this," Alex finally said. "She *is* going to cause some kind of trouble. And cause a lot of damage for the rest of us while she's at it."

"Unless we're willing to lock them up or get rid of them some-how, yeah. Trouble we might not be able to recover from."

Alex ran both hands down Etan's chest, pulling him closer. He kissed Etan's neck just below his ear.

"No wonder you're so tense. I'm sorry, sweetie. I'm glad you can't remember the Dream."

"Living it's going to be bad enough."

Chapter 33

Etan watched Caela walking ahead of them toward the Town Hall, her long red curls shifting across her back as she talked to her friends. They walked so naturally in the middle of the street, without even a trace of the need to look both ways. These days a moving vehicle in Wolf Branch or probably anywhere else in North America was rare enough that everyone stopped to watch.

The roads in town were in remarkably good shape over two decades after the last repaving crew passed by. Sort of faded, a bit cracked. Threatening to form a pothole or two in the lowest spots. Etan tried not to think too much about how the roads far to the north where Alex grew up must look.

No one Caela's age or younger would ever have seen an airplane overhead, much less the crisscrossing lines of vapor trails against a blue sky.

She and several of the oldest children had been going with them to Council meetings for months now. Learning the routines and rituals made sense for the next generation of Witnesses and Dreamers. So did letting them learn patience by sitting quietly and listening no matter how much the adults droned on and on.

He had to at least try to stop their daughter from being in the middle of whatever was going to happen now.

"I don't think Caela should be there tonight."

"I tried stopping her earlier," Alex said. "She made it clear if I wouldn't tell her *why* not, she'd bloody well go whether I *want* her to or not."

"That's pretty much what she told me. I guess she has a point. She's been going for almost a year now. I just don't want her in the middle of this mess."

Alex had been helping Caela with the same kinds of Dreams as Etan's since she was eight, and all of her training and education had been geared toward developing that, and dealing with it. At fifteen, she was nearly ready to be on the Council herself.

The time when either of them could say "because I said so" about this or much of anything else was far in the past.

"I was afraid she'd Dream about it, or remember it," Alex said, then he smiled. "She's too damn much like her mother."

"If she Dreamed or remembered, she hasn't told me. That doesn't mean anything though."

"Are you sure it's going to be tonight, E?"

Etan stepped off to the side and stopped, and Alex stopped with him. They were within sight of the red brick town hall, but no one else on the street was paying any attention to them.

"I *feel* it. Don't you? This hasn't lightened up all day."

Alex gave a half-hearted shrug, then he looked out at the people walking past them. Everyone older than Caela was walking slowly, quietly, most of them looking at the ground.

All of them clearly caught up in the dread he could almost see floating in the air, between the brick buildings and through the garden and orchard spaces scattered throughout town.

"I think everyone feels it," Etan said "Everyone who remembers the end, anyway."

"No one her age could know what it means. Not really. Not in their bones the way we do."

"What are we walking into?" a low voice said from right behind Alex.

Iris, Gena beside her. The four of them stood together and watched the nearly silent procession.

"I thought you were staying in," Etan said, his hand on Gena's shoulder.

"I wanted her to, but she never listens to me when I'm awake," Iris said, trying her best to look angry. Gena was rosy and healthy, and well into her ninth month of pregnancy.

"Look around you," she said. "I'm as worried about whatever's happening as everyone else is." She turned to Etan, and he dreaded her question. "Do you know what's going to happen?"

"I haven't had any Memories. Have you, Iris?"

"You don't need to have the Memory," she said, her eyes narrowed. "You had the Dream."

"Is it Mary?" Gena said, looking at Alex. "The trouble she's going to cause?"

That was something many of the Witnesses seemed to share, the ability to hone in on what was coming, even if they didn't foresee it themselves. Etan had seen it happen too many times to doubt it.

"That's the one I've been drawn to," Alex said, taking Etan's hand again.

A few people stood outside the doors of the town hall, but other than that the street was empty. Everyone would be waiting for the four of them.

Between Etan's Dreams and Iris's Memories, they were always in the middle of difficult choices for their community whether they wanted to be or not.

"Can we do anything to stop them?" Iris said.

"I don't think so," Etan said. "We couldn't even stop Caela from being here."

"Where was she going to learn respect for authority?" Gena said, smiling at the three of them. "Not from any of her parents."

He and Alex followed the two women into the conference room. Everyone was already gathered around the long tables set up in a square, Caela with several young people sitting in chairs behind them. Even with such a large crowd – nearly thirty on the Council now – four chairs together remained empty. No one wanted to try to take over leadership on such a difficult night.

As soon as they sat, George Light got to his feet. His curly hair was nearly all white now, but his dark face was nearly unlined. His rich voice hadn't aged one day.

"Welcome brothers and sisters, I hope this day finds you healthy and well. We only have a few things to take care of before we get to new business and new Dreams."

Etan tried to let his mind wander, to let the meeting wash over him as he'd done for so many years. That wasn't working this time. The dread grew within him, taking over all of his body's usual functions and sensations. It wasn't so much what was going to happen, though that was bad enough. Far worse was knowing he couldn't stop it no matter what he did.

Harry Mullins raised his voice, calling Etan's mind back into the room yet again.

"What I'm *saying* is we can't keep letting this go on. We're not talking about one lone scrawny woman anymore. She's stirring up shit with more than enough people to cause us real damage here."

"What exactly do you expect us to do, Harry?" Dana Chen said. "Just randomly round people up and hope we get the right ones?"

Etan turned to Dana, still the trusted leader of their security force. Her gleaming black hair showed a few streaks of silver, probably earlier than it would have if she hadn't taken on such a difficult job. But she showed no signs of wanting to step down.

A few people still weren't quite comfortable with the idea of any kind of organized protection, and that was one of the main things Mary used to cause unrest. Most of the residents of Wolf Branch seemed grateful.

Etan had never quite gotten comfortable with their gratitude.

"It won't have to be random, Dana, not at all," Harry said. "I know exactly who's working with Mary on this."

"How can you possibly know that?"

Etan didn't notice who spoke then, he was too busy watching Harry. The older man *did* know. That was the first thing Etan hadn't doubted throughout this whole awful day. His vision shifted, and he could have answered the question before Harry did.

"I recognize them, all of them. It started about a week ago. I can see it on their faces. Well, in *front* of their faces, more like. Something about their eyes – a cloud, maybe. They all look like Mary's eyes."

Etan watched everyone around the table, waiting to see the recognition. About half of them were scowled or shook their heads. Everyone else, though, either looked surprised or nodded.

He and Harry weren't the only ones.

"How long have you been able to see things like that?" Dana said.

"Oh, I always did," Harry said, his ears turning red. "That was one way I decided who to hire before everything went to hell. Who to invest with. There wasn't any secret research to it. That was how I knew who to fire, too."

"I understand, I can back that up," George said. "I saw something like that in my own congregation days. Has anyone else seen or felt this about people besides Mary?"

The same people Etan had noticed now held up their hands. Dana was unfortunately not among them. She took a deep breath, leaning back in her chair and crossing her arms.

"Even if this were reasonable, and even if every last one of you agrees on who they are, you still haven't said what I'm supposed to *do* about it. Even if I had enough officers to round up a bunch of people, which I don't, where would I put them? We don't exactly have a super max prison right next door."

"We don't need a prison," Harry said, a satisfied look on his face. "We just need them out of here. I was thinking we could ask Mary to be the leader of our next group of settlers. They'd be, what, lucky number nine or whatever such nonsense you want to call it. We can send their discontented asses out to find their own little paradise."

"Dad."

The repeated whisper finally broke through, and Etan looked over his shoulder at Caela. He turned his whole body when he saw her. Her blue eyes were wide and tears were streaming down her face.

"What's wrong?"

"Stop them," she said, loud enough that Alex turned around too. "You've got to *stop* this."

Chapter 34

Etan closed his eyes, his heart nearly bursting inside of him. He hadn't seen this moment coming, not the way their daughter surely had, but he knew this was why the dread was so awful.

This was what he couldn't stop.

Their little girl knowing so many people were going to die, knowing her fathers weren't going to be able to do anything about it. Facing the news of such a terrible loss would be nothing compared to facing Caela right now.

"No, sweetheart, it's going to be okay," he whispered, Alex nodding beside him.

"Don't *lie* to me!"

Her sobbing gasp was loud enough for everyone on their side of the room to look around. Protocol and pretense didn't matter anymore, and neither did people considering Caela to be an adult before she was ready.

Etan pushed his chair back and stood, and a beat later Alex did the same.

"Excuse us," Alex said, his voice rough.

Iris touched Etan's hand, and he leaned down to whisper in her ear. "I think she knows what's coming. We'll get her out of here."

Iris nodded, then turned to Gena.

"Come on," Alex said under his breath, holding out his hands. "Let's go outside for a while."

Caela's lovely face crumpled, and for a second Etan was certain she'd start crying louder. She opened her eyes and nodded, letting Alex pull her to her feet. The three of them walked into the small break room next door and sat together on the blue sofa. The same comfortable chairs and soft lighting, and the TV on the wall that hadn't been used in nearly two decades. Etan glanced over their daughter's head at Alex.

He knew his husband remembered sitting in the same room together almost twenty years ago, Etan finally agreeing to talk to the Council but still scared to death.

Long before they could have imagined such a beautiful creature in their lives.

"They're going to come back if they leave that way," she said, her tears falling again. "Come back and attack us. You have to go back in there and stop them!"

Etan blinked, drawing back.

Attack them? As far as he knew, no one had seen such a thing. He certainly hadn't.

"What did you see, Caela?" Alex said. "Did you have a Memory, like Iris does sometimes?"

Etan didn't want to say it or even think it, but his grandmother Anne often saw Memories, the waking Dreams of remembering things that hadn't happened yet. She'd suffered horribly because of that.

If Caela was having the same, he could only hope she inherited enough of Iris's stability to counteract Anne's struggles.

Caela took a few deep breaths, trying to stop the tears, then gave up.

"I know they'll cause trouble if they stay, I *know* that. I feel that too. But if they leave, they'll come back in a few months, maybe a year. They'll attack us, and security won't be able to stop them. They'll steal enough food and kill enough people that… We won't survive."

"You just saw that?" Alex said, every inch the Witness, even with his own daughter. "It feels solid and real, like we talked about? Not like a daydream?"

"Yes, it's real! It's every bit as real as Mary staying here and causing so much trouble that we don't survive that either. They *can't* stay, and they *can't* go. Have other people seen her causing trouble here if she stays?"

Alex nodded, brushing her hair back.

"Etan had that Dream, and Iris and many others have seen it too."

"But what are we supposed to *do*? Why do we have these goddamn Dreams if we can't do anything to stop this? If we're all going to die anyway, what the hell was the point?"

Etan's heart shattered at the terrible sound in their daughter's voice.

He hugged her, and he felt Alex's arms go around both of them. Their daughter's sobs were tearing him apart. Alex's grip on his shoulder told Etan he wasn't faring any better.

"I've been asking that question since I was eleven years old, sweetheart," Etan said. "Lots of times we can help, make a real difference. But I don't know why this kind of thing happens. I hate it too."

"*Fucking* Mary," Caela said, and the disgust in her voice made Etan wince. "If she'd never been here, none of this would happen."

"Maybe," Alex said, sitting back and wiping her tears. "But there could be some reason we don't know. Maybe if Mary had never been here, things would be even worse. Maybe even if we could stop things like this, that would be the *worst* thing we could do."

Caela scowled and shook her head, and tears filled Etan's eyes again. She was so much like Alex, almost as if Iris hadn't been involved in her making at all. Looking at their daughter, he couldn't imagine he'd thought he wouldn't love children who weren't a genetic mix of their fathers.

His love for her was so fierce partly because he saw Alex so clearly in her.

"Yeah, they keep telling us that in training," she said, brushing at her cheeks. "Hearing the words isn't the same as watching it happen, you know?"

"I know," Etan said. "Listen, you don't have to go back in. One of us can walk you back home, or you can wait out here. Alex and I can tell them what you've seen. There's no reason for you to go through this, love."

Caela rolled her eyes, then looked up at him under her eyebrows. That was a flash of Iris so clear Etan couldn't ignore it.

Of course she wouldn't take the easy way. The more either of them or anyone else suggested it, the more she'd resist.

"I'm the one who's seen it," she said, then took a shuddering breath. "I've never had a Memory this clear before. I feel like... I think I need to see it through or something. Do you understand?"

"I wish I didn't understand quite so well," Alex said, laughing under his breath. "I think both of us do."

"We do," Etan said, half-smiling at his husband. "Ready to go back in? It's fine if you need a little while longer."

Caela looked at the door, and the very air shifted around her. Etan saw it as clearly as ripples in water. Their daughter had come to some kind of decision, some kind of choice that was going to impact all of them far more than even the terrible Memory she'd just seen.

Etan had the strongest urge to pick her up and run. Pick her up just like the day she was born, when she wasn't any longer than his forearm. Just grab her and Alex and all of their children and get the hell away from here, away from this horrifying, empty world they'd been born into.

The remains of humanity would have to learn how to survive without them.

Without his family.

"They're not going to listen to some kid without their strongest Dreamer to back me up, are they?" Caela said. "Or their strongest Witness to those Dreams."

Before either of her fathers could answer, Caela stood, squared her shoulders, and walked toward the conference room.

All they could do was follow.

"She's never going to stop walking away from us, is she?" Alex said, reaching for Etan's hand.

"I just hope she looks back now and then."

By the time they opened the doors, Caela waited beside their empty seats, another chair pulled up behind her. Everyone else around the tables was moving closer together. She moved her chair into the space. When they were settled, Alex and Etan on either side of her, everyone looked at Harry.

"How are we going to get all of them to agree to leave?" Dana said.

Before Harry could answer, Alex stood, his hand on Caela's shoulder.

"Caela has seen a Memory she needs to share," he said. "A Memory about Mary and the others leaving."

Harry looked at them, his eyes narrow. He wasn't used to being interrupted, and he clearly didn't appreciate it.

"Your daughter is not a member of this Council, Alex."

"No, not yet. But only because of her age. She's been having the Dreams since she was eight years old. I'm not the only Witness to verify her Dreams. She knows what's at stake, and she knows when her Dreams and Memories are true as well as any of you do."

Harry pursed his lips, but he waved his hand and sat back. He had more than one child in the same training group as Caela. He couldn't deny her abilities without calling all of the other young people into question.

Alex looked down at Caela and nodded.

She turned to Etan, her eyes wide but no longer crying, then got to her feet. Etan stood beside his daughter and his husband.

"If they leave," Caela said in a weak voice, then she went on more clearly. "If Mary and the others leave, they'll return and attack us. Worse than the raiders from Maple Ridge who killed my grandfather. Worse than the attack that almost killed my father. They'll steal our supplies and kill many of us before we can defend ourselves. We won't... We won't survive long after the attack."

No one moved for several seconds, and Etan would have sworn

he was in a room full of mannequins. He felt the change before he heard sighs all around him.

The Memory had opened up for everyone else at Caela's words, Dana among them this time. She covered her face with one hand. Harry was pale, and George had tears in his eyes. Iris squeezed Etan's hand.

"Many of us have now seen the same Memory," George said in a low voice. "Etan, do you still see the trouble Mary and the other will cause if they stay?"

Before he could answer, Iris stood beside him.

"I've had this Dream as well, I and many others. It hasn't shifted for me, even with Caela's Memory."

Several people around the long tables nodded.

"So both paths lead to our damnation," George said, his tears spilling over.

No one spoke, and after a moment, Alex, Etan, and Iris sat down.

Caela remained standing.

"I believe I know another way," she said, and her quiet voice carried throughout the silent room.

Etan looked at Alex, but only he shrugged and shook his head.

"Your Memory has come to many of us, just like so many of your parents' Dreams have," George said, wiping his face. "Please tell us what you see, Caela."

"We know they can't stay here without causing trouble. And if they leave, they'll return and attack us." She took a deep breath. "We have to make sure they can *never* return."

Etan's mind reeled, trying to imagine what she was talking about. Then his eyes met Alex's, and he knew.

Too late to stop their daughter, too late to stop any of it.

He *knew*.

"My father Etan has had… He had a Dream of Laurel Gap, a town high in the mountains. I had the same Dream."

"No, Caela," Etan said. "Not this."

She raised her voice and kept talking.

"Laurel Gap looks safe and prosperous, with wood and game and coal. But the water there is bad. Something was buried there a long time ago. Something to do with the coal."

"I said no!" Etan reached for her hand, but she pulled away. "Why did you tell her, Alex? Why?"

"I didn't tell her a damn thing!" He looked as frightened as Etan felt.

"If they go to this town, they won't return to attack us," Caela said, nearly shouting now. "They won't *ever* return."

Etan stood, grabbing her shoulders and turning her to face him. She looked back without flinching, her face horribly strong, defiant, and beautiful.

"Who told you this?" he said, shaking her. "Where did you hear about this Dream? Was it Alex?"

Alex stood, glaring at Etan, his strong fingers trying to loosen Etan's grip on their daughter's shoulders.

"I said I didn't tell her," Alex said, his voice nearly a growl.

"He *didn't* tell me," Caela said, trying to pull both of their hands away. "I read it in his journal when he was teaching me about my own Dreams!"

Both men let go, leaving her to stand on her own.

"You did what?" Alex said, his voice soft and airy. "You read the journals of your father's Dreams?"

Caela clenched her fists and turned to Alex.

"I didn't read all of them, no. Of *course* not. But a long time ago, when I was first Dreaming, I heard you say I'd had the same as him one night. One I couldn't remember. You didn't write it in my journal, so I read the one in his."

"You shouldn't have done– " Alex started, but Caela cut him off, her face as red as his.

"It was *my* fucking Dream! You shouldn't have kept it from me!"

"Hold on, slow down," Etan said, desperate to stop the shouting in front of everyone else. "We can talk about this more at home. Was it the Dream about that town, Alex? Laurel Gap?"

Alex scowled, shaking his head. Etan knew he wasn't denying the Dream. He didn't want to acknowledge what it meant.

"Come on. Was it?"

"It was the same Dream," Alex said, looking down. "The town with the bad water."

Etan closed his eyes, cold nausea working through his whole body. He would have given almost anything if he could step backwards in time, just a few minutes. If he could be the one to bring up the necessary, terrible course they had to take.

If he could save their little girl from having to do such an awful thing before she was grown enough to even think about it.

"Alex, can you confirm you have Witnessed two Dreamers having this Dream?" George Light said, his deep voice as soothing as his words were damning. "I remember you sharing Etan's Dream several years ago."

"I confirm it," Alex said, his face strained and pale now. "Both Etan and Caela have had this Dream."

All three of them finally sat. Etan wondered if the other two had lost all strength in their legs as badly as he had.

"I know this is a difficult thing," Harry Mullins said, his voice as compassionate as the night Alex nearly died. "But Caela gives us a solution that sounds true to me. It *feels* true."

Etan clenched his jaw, trying to keep the nausea from getting worse. He'd made the terrible choice to end a human life when the drifter attacked Connor and wounded Alex nine years earlier.

None of that changed Etan's fundamental belief. With so dreadfully few people still living – only a few thousand outside of Wolf Branch that he knew of, with solid rumors of more farther away – sending any of them to death was almost the worst sin he could imagine.

The only worse sin was their daughter being the one to set it into motion.

"It feels true to me as well," Iris said.

Etan didn't have to look at her to know she was crying. He heard it in her voice.

"And to me," Dana Chen said, wiping at her own eyes.

One by one, everyone around the table either spoke or nodded. Not one person disagreed. When only Etan and Alex were left, they looked into each other's eyes. They joined hands behind their daughter without saying a word.

"We still haven't figured out…" Dana said, then she took a deep breath and shook her head sharply. "We don't have a way to get them all to leave."

"The idea I had before was a lottery," Harry said, looking at his hands clasped on the table. "A chance to leave and start fresh, for people besides the new settlers. We'd just have to rig the results. Simple as that."

Etan's nausea was only getting worse, but he knew even going outside and throwing up wouldn't make it go away. He had to say something. He had to try to stop this.

Even if it did lead to the end of all of them, he couldn't let Caela be responsible for murder.

"It's *not* simple, not one goddamn bit," he said through a tight throat. "We'll be choosing a bunch of people, when there are hardly any left, and sending them off to die. We'll be their judge, jury, and executioners."

"We're not choosing them," Gena said, reaching past Iris to touch his arm. "They're planning to hurt the rest of us, whether they stay or leave. It was *their* choice. We have to think about the bigger picture here."

"Fuck the bigger picture!" Etan said, trying not to wail like Caela had earlier. "This is too much, certainly too much for a fifteen year old girl!"

"No, Etan, no," Alex said. "Look at me."

Etan squeezed his eyes shut for a second, not wanting to hear what his husband had to say. For that one second, for the first time since he was barely older than Caela, he didn't care about *anything* Alex had to say.

He didn't care if every single person on the planet died either. He couldn't stand such damage to his own family.

He finally looked into Alex's eyes: the saddest, and the oldest, he'd ever seen them.

"I don't like this any more than you do, but she's not a child anymore. This was the Memory of an adult, and she made the choice of an adult. Her Dream was the same as yours. You both had it for a reason."

Alex looked at Caela for a second, then squeezed Etan's hand.

"Can't you feel it, E? Everything changed. We have a chance now. We all do."

Etan squeezed back, the nausea shifting to a deep ache inside of him. He did feel the difference, the lifting of the dread and the dead end they'd all been facing.

Caela had put their solution together when he hadn't been able, or willing.

She'd spoken it aloud and shown them the way.

Salvation or not, his whole body twisted in agony over what she'd done.

He and Alex moved their arms up to their daughter's shoulders. She didn't say a word, but she leaned into their support.

"We'll have to be so careful," Dana said. "The biggest danger is anyone else finding out what we've done here."

"No, that's not the biggest danger," Etan said. "Not even close. The biggest danger is we all have to live with it."

Chapter 35

Alex drumming his fingers on the ancient wooden desk was the only sound in the quiet apartment. He was careful to tap with the pads of his fingers rather than the nails to keep it that way, though he wasn't quite sure why.

The scarred and worn surface had stayed miraculously clear of clutter and toys and papers for days now. Alex was surprised to wish for a mess he could either grumble over or deal with.

Outside the open window, Wolf Branch was unusually still and silent as well. The soft breeze playing over his skin, promising rain later on, explained some of that. But he knew everyone else was preparing for the difficult day when the next group of so-called settlers would leave.

Etan and most of their kids and almost everyone else was out helping today, like they had for the last couple of weeks and would for the next few days.

Learning how to prepare food and belongings for the trip. Getting experience with maintenance on the trucks and ATVs, so everyone could keep them running for as long as possible. Working with Mary and her followers to explain and teach and share what they'd all figured out so far, to send all that knowledge out into a new community so it would thrive.

And Alex and Etan and it seemed like all the residents of Wolf Branch who weren't going with Mary knew all the effort was a cruel charade. A vicious and nasty lie. A sickening play they were all caught up in that would result only in death if they all played their parts well enough.

That wasn't the worst of it, though. Not as far as Alex was concerned.

The worst of it was Caela knew what was coming and how well she'd done *her* part, better than any fifteen-year-old ever should have.

Neither Etan nor Alex had said a word earlier, when Etan headed out with the rest of the kids. Off to learn what they could, sadly including how to put on a good face. They'd all pretended nothing was unusual about both Alex and Caela deciding to stay home.

These preparation days had long been one of Alex's favorite times, with Caela never far from his side. He loved the increasingly rare chance to practice and teach his Engineer Alex skills, to help expand the precarious number of people roaming the empty world. They'd both done their share even this sad time around, up until today.

As soon as he'd opened his eyes that morning, Alex had known without needing one of Etan's Dreams that he and Caela would be sitting this one out.

Maybe he'd had a rare Dream of his own.

More likely he'd known through his own ordinary magic.

He focused on the swirls and textures of the wood under his fingertips, both natural and caused by countless years of use. Darker and lighter wood grain. A scratch here, a stain or a faded water ring there.

All part of the patterns that shaped his life.

The way Caela turned her head away the night before when one of the little ones giggled. The way she twisted her fingers through her lovely red curls. The way she gradually stopped meeting anyone's eyes over the last few days.

That turn in her mood didn't take a genius or a fortune-teller to catch. Only someone who knew her so well, and loved her even more.

But…the play of dust motes through the morning light. The rise and fall of their children's voices over breakfast. Even the beat of Alex's own heart, heavy with worry for Caela.

All those ordinary things let him know she needed him to wait for her, today.

He pretended not to glance at his current stainless steel watch, and anyone else in Wolf Branch wouldn't have had anything to glance at.

Two and a half hours since Etan and the younger kids had headed out, and still not a sound from Caela.

Alex stared out the window at the empty street for a minute, then got up and walked slowly into the kitchen. Whenever she was ready, a cup of warm holly tea with Walt's honey certainly wouldn't hurt. He was busy distracting himself by planning the next maintenance round on the basement boiler – the source for winter heat and precious hot water year-round – when Caela finally spoke from behind him.

"Could you make me a cup, please?"

"Already thought of that, sweetheart. Get us a couple of mugs?"

Alex lifted the strainer full of steaming soaked leaves out of the tea, waiting for it to drain. Despite the somber mood between the two of them, he smiled when he turned and saw what she'd chosen. Both brown and vaguely mug-like, the outer surface covered with unbelievably small fingerprints under the patchy glaze. No handle, but the bottoms were more than thick enough to hold without risking a burn.

Caela's own efforts at pottery when she was first at school. Thankfully the teachers had taken the time to smooth and properly glaze the interiors.

Alex was certain every adult who'd received one of these treasures kept them as carefully as he and Etan did. A row of similar mugs made by each of their children's sweet tiny hands took up the whole top shelf above the sink.

Only Gwen and Eddie enjoyed pottery enough to practice well past that first class. Alex never tired of them bringing something new and beautiful home, nor of using the plates or bowls or cups or flower vases every day.

Caela flashed a quick smile as she added a generous amount of honey to each mug.

"I was quite the artist, huh?"

"Artist enough that we've been happy to use them for ten years."

She stood beside him, staring into her tea as she stirred it.

Perhaps watching the patterns in liquid and steam for herself.

Alex waited.

"None of them know what's coming, do they? Mary and her people, I mean."

"They don't seem to, no," Alex said. "That's probably for the best."

She nodded once, still focused on her mug.

"Do you think they know it was me?"

Her face was calm, but Alex caught the faint tremble in her voice loud and clear.

"I don't think they know anything besides getting to leave on their great adventure."

Caela grunted, leaning her head forward so Alex couldn't see her face through the fiery curtain of her hair.

"It's a grand adventure all right. A one way trip to the grave, courtesy of me. If anyone ever bothers to bury them."

Alex had learned through Caela's tempers and tantrums a few years ago that she might not want a hug from him or anyone else, much as his heart ached at the soft whisper of her crying.

"What kind of person would *do* that?" she whispered. "Tell the whole Council to send a bunch of people off to die. When you *both* tried to stop me."

"The kind of person who knows how important her Dreams are. How to be true to them. Etan had the Dream too, remember?"

"Yeah, I read all about it, didn't I? I'm sorry about that, I really am." Caela tilted her head back now, letting her hair fall out of the way, away from her tear-streaked face. "Dad E didn't get anybody killed, either."

"I'm sorry too, Caela. I shouldn't have kept your Dream from you. You were old enough to know about them for a long time before then. You're old enough now to know how true Etan is to what he Dreams. What he sees. Even when it's hard." Alex paused, waiting for Caela to look up at him. "Even when some might call it murder."

She scowled for a second, then looked down again to take sip of her tea. A clear sign that she wanted to know, but she didn't want to admit it.

"I know you remember the day I was attacked," Alex said. "Much as I wish you didn't. Did anyone ever tell you what happened to the person who did it?"

"The monster. I heard he died. I always wondered if it was the rocks everyone threw at him."

Alex tilted his head to the side.

"*She* did die that day, but not from a rock. Etan had a vision, one of the few times he's had a Memory like you and Iris do, and your great-grandmother Anne did. He saw himself at the jail, giving the monster a choice between poison and a gun. She didn't speak, but she drank the poison. He never needed the gun."

Caela's red-rimmed eyes widened. "So you're saying…"

"All I'm saying is sometimes good people have to do terrible things. *Good* people, Caela. Like Etan. And like you. You might not remember this part, but I was trying to kill her when she stabbed me."

"I do. Because she grabbed Connor."

Alex closed his eyes, nodding. He remembered the fury that boiled out of him that day, the worst he'd ever known. He hoped to never know it again.

"The thing is, I *would* have killed her if she hadn't stopped me," he said. "I would have later if I hadn't been flat on my back."

"That makes sense, though." Caela's brow again furrowed, the same way Alex knew his own did. He saw the evidence of that habit in the mirror every day. "She tried to hurt one of your kids, you know? What I did… I don't think it was the same."

"Wasn't it? You should ask Etan about that sometime. Don't you think he would have told the Council the same thing if he'd had the

Memory before you did? He acted on a Memory at the jail that day when I was in the hospital, and not an easy one."

Caela looked away, but she didn't disagree.

"You knew Mary and everyone with her were going to hurt *all* of us," Alex said. "You understood when none of the rest of us could. You saw the way through. I wish you hadn't been the one to do this, and Etan does, too. But doing the right thing, the hard thing, doesn't make you a bad person."

Caela took a long, deep breath, then finished her tea. She studied Alex's face the same way she had his and Etan's and everyone else's since before she made the precious mugs. Making sure he was telling the truth. Apparently finding what she needed, she leaned closer for a hug.

And Alex found that embrace was what *he* needed, even more than he needed to give it.

Chapter 36

Early on the day of Mary and her group's departure, Etan couldn't begin to manage the cheerful façade he knew he'd need. His relief that everything had proceeded so smoothly from idea to imminent murder only drove his guilt and despair deeper.

Harry's lottery had gone off without a hitch. Not one "winner" had declined, and no one in Wolf Branch argued about the result. Etan would have sworn people who were neither Dreamer nor Witness had taken on some of those traits as the days passed.

Or maybe it was the gloom and sadness that hovered over everyone, on the Council or not.

After a mostly silent morning, he'd finally taken the excuse to head back into the bedroom by himself. Both he and Alex often caught up on sleep in the afternoon, when they really needed it. Today more than a lack of sleep drove him to escape.

Watching their kids play or study or even argue only reminded him how many children would be heading out later in the day. Heading out to their deaths as surely as they would have later brought death to Wolf Branch, yes. But no less horrible to contemplate.

Etan and Alex had often talked about moving out into one of the larger bedrooms once they didn't need quite so much room for children. For the brief moments when Alex could manage to contemplate that oncoming reality, at least. After so many years, Etan wasn't sure he wanted to leave the cozy space.

They could walk around their bed, but not a whole lot more. Two windows on either side let in plenty of fresh air but no morning or afternoon sunlight. Perfect for such frequently interrupted sleep.

A small bookshelf held all the fiction books either of them wanted to read someday, either from Anne and Evan's collection or from the town library, still lovingly maintained decades after the world's last big fiction publications. A new corner of the library held hand-bound volumes of the heavy fiber and cloth paper everyone learned to make in school now.

The soft green comforter Etan was currently face down on had come from his own childhood bedroom. With his mother's careful mending and his ongoing attempts to learn how himself, he hoped it would outlive him and be passed on to one of their children.

Same for Iris's paintings hanging over the bed and on the opposite wall. She'd somehow managed to capture each of their children, and not with the nearly photographic realism she taught to kids and adults alike at the old school. Impressionistic shapes, colors, hints and suggestions. Even though only Gena usually understood the most stylized and odd of Iris's paintings right away, with Alex close behind her, Etan recognized each of their children at first glance.

Their children.

All the children of Wolf Branch and anywhere else in the empty world were precious.

All *humans* were.

And yet they were sending so many off to die today.

"What have we done?" Etan whispered.

He jumped when Alex spoke from right beside the bed.

"Only what we had to, E," Alex said, stretching out on the bed with his arm around Etan. He smelled of earth and growing things, and his own clean sweat. "Only what we had to."

Etan shook his head, but he curled against his husband.

"At such a cost."

"It isn't going to be easy, "Alex said. "They didn't give us any choice though. We couldn't let them put all of us at risk that way."

Etan raised up to look at Alex, at the circles under his eyes, the deeper lines on his face. He knew he looked older and more weary too.

And Caela seemed to have aged ten years in just a few weeks.

"I hate what she's having to go through," Etan said. "She's too young for any of this."

"I hate what you're going through, too." Alex leaned his forehead against Etan's. "You didn't do this. Neither did Caela. I wish you could *both* stop feeling guilty."

"Do we really have to go to this thing?"

Alex pulled him close again and stroked his hair, as if Etan were one of their children having a particularly moody bad day.

Etan knew he was acting younger than Caela, younger than almost all of their children, but he couldn't stop himself. Watching Mary and her followers walk off to their deaths was worse than the first day of school or going to the doctor, things he'd fought kicking and screaming before the old world ended.

Going to this with a smile on his face felt impossible to him, even with Alex by his side.

"I think George is right," Alex said. "We've seen every group off so far, every single one. If we skip this or send them away in the middle of the night, especially with all the trouble Mary's been in the middle of, it'll cause too much suspicion. We're all going to have to do our best."

"I don't think I can," Etan said, his throat tight and achy. "One look at me and everyone will know."

Alex hummed low and sweet, and Etan wished he could curl up in his lap and go to sleep. He'd often envied their kids that when they were babies, being so warm and safe and secure against Alex's body. He'd give just about anything to be able to do that now.

"Let me tell you a secret," Alex said, his lips close to Etan's ear. "If you marched right up to Mary, to her broken Witnesses and followers and shouted the truth, none of them would hear a word you said. There's something off about the way she Dreams, the way they all do. And the way they *feel* the Dreams. Something spoiled or corrupted, I think. Maybe that's the reason they all have to go, all at once like this."

"Why were they here in the first place though? Caela's right about that part, what was the point? Just to torment all of us and see if we could go through with murder?"

"Who knows? It could be they all needed to be in a group so whatever the problem is wouldn't spread. Did Caela tell you about Mary's children?"

Etan took a deep breath, trying to pull his lover's scent inside his own body, then sat up against the headboard and pillows. Alex moved beside him.

"No, she hasn't mentioned it. Not to me, at least."

"I don't think she talked to anyone but Gena about this," Alex said, a sad half-smile on his face. "We might be too close. Anyway, Mary had three kids in her training group, two boys and a girl. Caela said all three of them seemed to have Dreams, but they got…*lost* in them or something."

"Lost? I don't understand."

"I'm not sure I do either, or anyone else. It sounded like the Dreams were right once in a while, matching with other Dreams, and those felt true to all the Witnesses. But the kids had a hard time telling the Dreams from reality. Caela said it was pretty scary sometimes."

Etan groaned, covering his face. He'd heard both of his grandparents talk about how Anne's own grandmother often got lost in time, lost in what he was sure now were her Memories. Two generations before Anne had them, and two more before Etan and so many others finally started.

She'd ended up basically institutionalized because of her frequent breaks with reality. Etan sometimes wondered how many other early Dreamers or Witnesses had suffered the same or worse, with no way to know their seeming madness would eventually save the remnants of humanity.

"Just one more damn thing Caela's had to deal with over all of this," he said. "She shouldn't have had to see that."

Alex pulled Etan's hands away and held onto them.

"She's a tough kid, E. She's not falling apart. What I'm saying is whatever sort of gift Mary and those with her have, it doesn't seem true. It's too weak or too strong, or maybe it's just broken somehow. The same thing is showing up in all their kids, not just Mary's."

"So we're thinning the herd? Culling them out before they can breed more?"

Alex shrugged. "Yeah, maybe that's exactly it. Our herd is pretty thin now, but that's why they can do so much damage. And you keep forgetting *they're* making this choice, not us. Don't you think it's odd that not one person has complained about not winning the lottery to go with them? And not one of the winners has declined."

"That's the one thing that's getting me through all of this," Etan said. "No one who's staying or going seems to feel anything off about the whole thing. No one outside the Council, anyway."

"Has anyone told you about Mary's Dreams lately?"

Etan raised his eyebrows, waiting to see what he'd have to absorb next. He didn't think he had room for a whole lot more.

"She's been Dreaming about the new place they're going to," Alex said. "How they're going to thrive and be happy and powerful."

"Is anyone buying into that?"

"The Witnesses in her group believe it's true, and so do the other Dreamers. The strange thing is it feels true to Witnesses who *aren't* part of her circle. I felt the same when I heard one of them talking about it. Chilled me to the bone, but it felt as true as one of your Dreams. She's not making these up. It's like she's Dreaming what she needs to for them to go through with this."

Etan blew his breath out through his lips, looking out the window at the green and brown of trees on the hillside.

"I don't know if that reassures me at all, Alex. If it comforts them and makes this go as smoothly as it can, that can only be a good thing. But if these Dreams are true, and the Dreams Caela and I had about all of them dying are true, how can we ever be sure about our Dreams again? We could be Dreaming whatever we want to see at any time."

Alex nodded, and Etan's heart broke as he saw that uncertainty settle onto his face and body. The downturn of his mouth, the lowering of his shoulders and head. He'd last seen Alex fall apart like that when they first talked about the Dreams, long ago and far away in their sweet little shoebox apartment overlooking Lake Michigan.

"Not what you *want* to," Alex said. "I didn't say that. It could be what you *need* to. I wondered about that, too. Since all of this started back in Chicago, I've just accepted your Dreams were true, even when you didn't. I can't think too much about that, honestly. If I start doubting what got us this far, I'll probably lose my mind in a hurry."

Etan shivered, trying to push the guilt away before it could sink in and start gnawing at him. Even if the Dreams had always seemed to be driving him crazy, they somehow kept Alex sane. He wasn't willing to disrupt even that cold comfort.

Alex tilted his head then, squinting.

"The one thing we don't ask, any of us, is where these Dreams come from. We wonder if they're real, if they're true, but not why you have them in the first place. I used to think it was because we were all trying so hard to survive through the next day. That's not nearly as desperate as it used to be, and still, no one asks."

"There might be a reason for that," Etan said, surprised at the instant jump in his heart rate. "If we're all afraid to, that could be something that protects us. The same way we knew we had to head southeast before everyone started dying."

"I know, I guess. I feel that dread sometimes, and that draw. I've always wondered what it is we're following though. Haven't you?"

Etan was shaking his head before he spoke, cold chills running up and down his arms and legs now.

"It's not so much that I haven't wondered. It's more that I'm *afraid* to, you know? This has all been hard enough with some way to know what to do, some kind of guidance."

"Are you afraid the Dreams will stop if we ask too many questions?"

Etan was terribly afraid of losing the Dreams. He and the other Dreamers had felt horribly blind right after the attack that nearly took Alex away. He couldn't explain how he could miss something he rarely remembered, but that didn't make it any less true.

Etan sighed, wanting this conversation to disappear the way the Dreams had then.

"We don't know what made them start, so we can't know what might make them stop. I just don't want to piss off whatever gods are involved here."

Alex smiled, then kissed one of Etan's hands.

"You sound downright religious, my dear."

"Just call it paranoid."

Alex looked at his watch, a relic of their past lives he still refused to give up.

"We need to get down there. I don't want Caela to be in the middle of this without us. She still needs us, no matter what she and everyone else might think."

Etan reluctantly followed his husband downstairs into the courtyard between the buildings, full of flowers and fruit and children. As they had since the horrible day of the attack, the youngest among them gathered outside here in fair weather, in the basement when it was nasty out. At least a few adults stayed with the bunch all the time.

Their kids and several others swarmed around Alex the same way they did anytime he or they came home, as if they hadn't seen each other in a thousand years.

Etan knew their children all loved him, and he adored every one of them. The closeness and trust and silly playfulness he'd gained with them when Alex was so sick remained, but it was never quite the same.

The affection between their children and Alex was as natural as breathing, as joy and laughter. He transformed himself into a six foot tall kid without even trying.

"I fucking hate the idea of giving this up," Alex muttered as they walked away.

One of the many long and painful discussions among Council members since the night Caela shared her Dream – and Etan's – had been about how to train young Dreamers and Witnesses. The talk centered on routines and rituals, ways to prepare their children to pair up as smoothly as possible.

Ideas about separate living arrangements for older children bubbled under the surface, though. Too often.

No one had said a word about Alex doing anything wrong, least of all Etan.

But Etan knew how viciously Alex blamed himself for what Caela had put herself through. Mainly because Etan blamed himself every bit as harshly.

"We don't have to give anything up," Etan said. "Not yet. Maybe not at all."

Alex grunted. "What were we just saying about being a good example?"

Alex was trying to smile, but it only pointed out how hard he was trying not to cry. Etan caught his hand.

"Making sure the Council stands together today is a little different than letting someone else raise our kids, Alex. No one's suggesting that."

"Maybe not from the day they're born, no," Alex said. "We can make sure they feel secure for eight years, maybe eleven. But when they really get into growing up and need us the most, off they go to some kind of boarding school. 'Sorry, kids!'"

"That's *not* going to happen. We're just trying to figure out how to handle their training. That's all."

"Yeah, I know that. I'm the one who fucked up training Caela badly enough that we ended up here."

"Hey," Etan said, slowing down before they got to the crowded square, barely visible between two low brick buildings. "She's not fucked up by any means. She's not even sixteen years old and she saved our asses, remember? That's *not* because she was badly trained."

"I never should have kept that Dream from her. It never should have been her place to save us."

"Well, you didn't make any more mistakes than I did," Etan said, touching Alex's cheek. "You're right. None of us understand how this works. Maybe it *had* to be Caela. What you did was train her to be as strong and tough as she is. I'm damn proud of her, and of you, too."

Alex smiled, a real one, then stepped forward into Etan's arms.

"No one can expect any of us to just make a change this big overnight," Etan said. "Some kind of dorm might be good later on, but not now. That would be too much for everyone. Don't forget every single person wants you to be involved in figuring all of this out. I don't want them out of my sight either. Okay?"

"Okay. I just can't stand the thought of it, letting them go when they're still babies. Letting Caela go in a couple of years is going to tear my guts out."

Chapter 37

WHAT EVERYONE in Wolf Branch called the Square wasn't so much a typical four-sided space as an open, paved area on the far side of town. Etan vaguely remembered a few old, falling-down buildings finally getting demolished when he was a kid. The empty spot turned into a gathering place before anyone could decide what to build there.

Farmers markets, town celebrations for spring, summer, and fall. Birthday parties and family reunions. The town wisely decided to add a few facilities and grass and pavement rather than buildings, and the Square was born.

Maple and dogwood trees grew around the edges, and raised beds in between still held flowers like they had years ago. The addition of mulberry, cherry, and plum trees added color along with a harvest. No one had complained about the addition of strawberry beds and raspberry bushes, either. Or hops vines for a satisfying variety of beers and ales.

The Square still served as a gathering point, most importantly when one of the groups of settlers was ready to depart Wolf Branch and reestablish another human town. Once or twice a year over the past ten, groups who'd straggled in from the outside recovered, gathered their strength, and learned how to survive in the new world.

Then they walked out to one of the roads out of town to do just that.

Mary and her group would indeed be lucky number nine.

The supply of precious vehicles, from four-wheelers to Etan's old van to a couple of big four-wheel drive trucks, would be loaded and waiting, ready to haul supplies and people before locals brought them back.

The crowd gathered today looked about the same as when any of the new colonies had set off in the past, with almost everyone in their community there. A closer look showed Etan and Alex they weren't the only ones who'd decided to leave the younger ones at home.

The youngest were around Caela's age, and Etan didn't see anyone that age who hadn't been at the Council meeting that awful night. Their daughter stood in that group, not far from the rest of the Council.

No one said a word about only adults coming, but apparently no one had to.

"Took you long enough," Caela said, hugging both of them. "It's calm so far. I don't think anyone else knows what's happening."

"I wish *you* didn't," Etan said, getting exactly the rolled eyes he expected from their daughter. "None of Mary's group are here yet?"

Caela shook her head, glancing around the crowd. People were crowded around the edges, under the trees, with a space left open in the middle.

"Nope. They'll be just late enough to keep us all waiting and make some kind of grand entrance. And exit."

"You're in better shape than I am, sweetheart," Etan said, kissing the top of her head.

"No, not really. Just trying to maintain until this is over."

Before Etan could think up a way to try to make her feel better – a way that didn't feel hypocritical – Dana Chen walked up beside him. Her face was composed, but her eyes were red and puffy.

"That was the toughest security meeting I've ever had to lead."

"I'm sorry, Dana," Etan said. "Did they understand?"

"They'll do what I asked them to whether they understand or not."

When Dana glanced around to see who was close by, Alex moved closer and Caela walked away.

"What I didn't tell the whole Council is neither my team nor anyone else will understand how serious this is until the first ones try to come back," she said, tension showing on her face. "That will be bad enough to convince all of them. I didn't try too hard today."

Alex put an arm around the much smaller woman.

"You saw that in your Dream?"

She leaned against him for a few seconds, closing her eyes. When she looked at Etan again, they were more red but she still wasn't crying.

"I did, several times. They're not going to be… By the time they make it back here they'll be pretty far gone. Mentally and physically. Security will take care of itself after that."

Etan touched her shoulder, not sure what to say. This wasn't the first time he was relieved he hardly ever remembered his own Dreams, not by a long shot. He often felt guilty for waking Alex with such horrors after he read his journals the next morning.

"You did the right thing by having your people drive the vehicles and bring them back," Etan finally said. "It's going to be bad enough here already."

The noise level rose at the east end of the Square. The crowd parted like water, and Mary strode into the middle of the empty space. All the other lottery winners, mostly her followers to begin with, filled in the space around her. Everyone shifted until the Council members were gathered in a group, with Mary at the head of her much larger group just a few feet away from Etan.

Neither he nor Alex had ever even pretended they wanted to be in charge, and he knew no one would have told Mary where the Dream of their exile came from.

Somehow she knew to focus on him.

As long as she wasn't looking at Caela, a few feet away with her friends, he would take whatever came.

George Light moved beside Etan and Dana. Etan felt a small

hand slip into his, and he looked down into Gena's green eyes. Her delivery of their beautiful little boy two weeks ago had gone smoothly, but her face showed how tired she was. Iris stood by her side.

"Brothers and sisters," George said, his voice clear and strong. "We're gathered together to celebrate our survival and our strength. We are once again blessed to have enough people to see a group of explorers off and wish them well."

The crowd around them applauded and cheered, and Etan was sure they were all more subdued than usual. The group around him certainly was.

The Council members did well with the illusion of celebration, considering what they were facing.

But they all avoided each others' eyes.

"The journey will be difficult, to be sure," George went on, "but the rewards will be great. We offer you the gift of food so you may prosper in your new home."

George handed Mary a carefully wrapped bundle of seeds and cuttings, well-prepared for the journey.

Everyone on the Council seemed to feel the same way. They hated to waste the plants, especially the ones that didn't require hand-pollination. But just as with this ritual send-off, not giving the plants would have caused far too much suspicion.

Mary took the packet and bowed her head, following the same traditions George was. George held out his upturned hands, giving her the chance to speak. This too was tradition, but so much more risky than sacrificing part of their food supply.

Mary turned slowly, making eye contact with several people in the crowd. When she came back around to the Council members, she moved more slowly. Etan thought she hadn't missed a single person in their smaller group. Before he was ready, it was his turn.

He returned her gaze, hoping he wasn't hurting Alex's or Gena's hand but needing the support. The accusation or fear he was afraid of wasn't in Mary's eyes at all.

He was sure he saw defiance, though, and triumph.

She finally turned away before she spoke.

"We thank you all for your kindness and generosity. We won't forget those who supported and encouraged us as we set out on our journey. The land ahead of us is rich and fertile. We look forward to sharing the bounty we find with each and every one of you."

She turned to Etan again with her last words, and all the hair on his body tried to stand on end. He thought Alex was right, that her gift of Dreaming was broken somehow.

Her visions were closer to insanity.

Even so, that part had sounded like a *prophecy*.

George saved him right before he knew he'd scream with the weight of Mary's gaze.

"Good journey!" George cried, throwing his arms wide.

"Good journey!" everyone in the crowd responded.

The people at the far end of the Square parted, creating a path for the new settlers. No one in Mary's group moved for several seconds while she continued to stare at Etan. Iris stepped forward and took Mary's hand, distracting her at last.

"Good journey, Mary. I wish you luck and prosperity."

Without a word to anyone else or a backward glance, Mary turned and walked through the middle of her followers. Etan let out a breath he felt like he'd been holding for a hundred years as they fell into place behind her.

The number of people Caela's age and even younger hurt his heart, but he was sure the cost would be worth it in the end. He had to believe that if he was going to keep breathing.

"For fuck's sake, are you okay?" Alex said.

He reached up to touch Etan's face, and Etan caught his hand, holding tight, then kissing Alex's palm.

"I am now. I was afraid she was going to cut my heart out before she left and use it for fertilizer."

"I think she was trying to," Gena said.

Harry Mullins walked toward them, his eyes still on the last of the group leaving the Square. He wasn't his normal, confident self. His face looked pale and washed out except for the dark circles like bruises under his eyes.

"You all coming back to the town hall after this?"

Etan's brain chugged for a second, still trying to clear out the afterimage of Mary's burning gaze. The missing piece finally clicked into place when lanky Walt Colley ambled up behind Harry. Despite his own Dreams, Walt had managed the trick of avoiding permanently serving on the Council, although no one ever questioned that he belonged on those occasions he decided to join them.

Especially not when Walt's years of hard work building up the honeybee colonies and teaching others to do the same helped provide the sweetness they so badly needed right now.

Gena spoke up beside Etan.

"I wouldn't miss it. I spent the past few days and all morning pumping enough milk to get the baby through my hangover."

"Think you have enough non-milk beverages for all of us?" Alex said, smiling at Etan.

Etan didn't want to go, not at all. But isolation probably wasn't the best thing after they'd all had to do such a terrible thing as one.

"Well, thanks to science and the printed word," Harry said, "and very generous help from our fellow natives, we've got quite a nice little setup going. It's not far from where the two of you used to live, near Laura and Connor's old place. Might not be the most refined thing you've ever tasted, but it will definitely get the job done. Walt's honey cuts it like a charm."

"That's a real hard thing you had to do just now," Walt said, his words slower than a couple of years ago. "If I can help ease your minds, I'm gonna do just that."

The sound of motors revving up, then heading out of town made the decision easier.

"Count me in," Etan said. "Will the kids be okay?"

All of them turned toward Caela and her friends, still standing together. Their daughter was speaking at that moment, holding hands with another young woman and looking into her eyes.

For at least the thousandth time, Etan was thankful she was so much like Alex.

"We figured they could join us for one drink." George said. "One *watered down* drink. Sandy and Dennis don't drink, so they'll go upstairs and spend the night with our youngest members. The little ones at home will be fine overnight. It's all arranged."

The others turned toward the town hall, and within a few minutes the Square was nearly deserted. Alex put his arm around Etan's waist.

"No one's going to forget, E. No one wants to do this again. But I need to forget for at least a little while."

"Just make sure I make it home at some point. Make sure I'm wherever you are."

Five years would pass before another departure hit Alex or Etan as hard.

PART V

TOWARD THE NEW WORLD

Chapter 38

Everything in the apartment was in the right place. Dishes clean and put away. Books closed and on shelves, or at least in neat piles on the oak coffee table in the living room. Clothing and shoes clean, stowed in the correct drawers or closets for each child. Even the battered old desk everyone wanted to use was cleared and spotless.

Alex forced himself not to think about how long it had been since he or Etan had to pick up toys from the living room or anywhere else. He made another restless circuit of the tidy space instead.

Joining up two apartments years ago had made everything easier, more than even he expected. All their children had a room to themselves, or would later tonight.

Another thought Alex couldn't fit into his mind yet.

That empty bedroom.

He and Etan had their own space again instead of wedging a small bed into their bedroom. Whoever was starting to Dream slept in a tiny bedroom beside them now. That was about to change, too.

Their youngest showed signs of being a Witness, unerringly joining Alex either when Etan Dreamed or when one of the other children did. His long, nearly sleepless nights of sitting with several Dreamers would end long before he was ready.

After another circuit through the kitchen, brushing invisible crumbs off the tiled counter, Alex closed his eyes. He leaned back against the cool, sharp edge, tilting his head to the left, then the right.

He could walk in circles through their home for another few hours or another few days, and not a thing would change.

Caela was leaving. She was ready.

Alex had to be, too, even if he only pretended for her sake.

Leading a group up to Maple Ridge – the first group Wolf Branch had ever sent out from their own children – was a wonderful opportunity. An honor. He was thrilled for her when he stopped to consider how excited she was to be setting out on her own.

Alex didn't want her to stay forever. Not really. His mind knew it was time. That this was a good thing. He knew he and Etan and everyone else had done a wonderful job getting their community and their children to this point.

His heart was nowhere near ready, though.

He opened his eyes and walked slowly through the living room, down the hall, and through the open door of her bedroom.

Alex told himself he needed to make sure she hadn't forgotten anything. That fiction evaporated when he got a good look around.

The room might have been left empty since this building was built well over a hundred years ago. Walls stripped bare, no longer decorated with paintings by Iris, drawings by Caela. Dark hardwood floor spotless and gleaming. Drawers and closets as empty and barren as the single bed against one wall, the faded and careworn blue loveseat under a window

Alex sighed and shook his head. He'd done exactly the same when he left his parents' house at sixteen.

He hoped Caela would *want* to come home for visits, unlike his own dread of the yearly pilgrimage back to Wisconsin. He hadn't been back since he and Etan left Chicago twenty-five years ago, and only a handful of times before that.

He knew he was luckier than many parents back then, when most kids left home at eighteen, many moving away for college.

Caela seemed mostly happy to have waited until her twentieth year to strike out on her own.

She wasn't going hundreds of miles away to a big city for college like Alex had, either. Maple Ridge wasn't even twenty miles away. With no more airplanes or trains or even fast cars, that was a long journey. Still, closer than their daughter could have gone.

Alex knew he was lucky in that, too. He also knew the empty place in his heart, where Caela had been the first of their children to dwell, would feel better over time.

But it never would close up and heal all the way.

He'd done his part by getting the power set up in Maple Ridge. He'd considered trying to get himself included in the group joining them for the next few days, pretending he had more work to do. But it wasn't true.

He'd been training a bunch of modern-day engineers, eager to learn something besides farming, for a few years now. Five of them would be making this trip already. They'd all worked alongside Alex to set everything up. Each knew the systems as well as he did.

Now wasn't the time to keep pushing himself into their daughter's life.

Now was the time to trust Caela. To trust everyone with her, his own work, and everyone he'd trained.

Now was the time to stay here and let them all go.

Alex heard the apartment door open and wiped at his eyes. Whoever that was didn't need to deal with his weepy mood today.

"Dad?" Caela called.

"In here. In your room."

Thankfully their oldest smiled more than she scowled these days, and she walked in doing just that. Caela was as tall and slender as Iris, with her long curly red hair caught back in a loose ponytail. Alex knew he was miles away from impartial, but he remained convinced she grew more lovely every day.

"My *empty* room, you mean." She sat on the blue loveseat and patted the cushion beside her. "Measuring for Eddie's things?"

Alex joined her, making sure he didn't grunt. Turning fifty a couple of weeks ago didn't mean he had to sound like it. Not even on a day like this, when he felt every one of those years in his bones.

"Eddie will be in here the second you leave, measurements or not. I was just thinking."

"You've been doing a lot of that lately. All the Dreams around here should have been warning enough."

Alex laughed under his breath, then held out his arm. She leaned against him, head on his shoulder.

"Someday you'll understand. All the Dreams in the world can't prepare you for some things. Everything ready downstairs?"

"Mom Gena is in a lot worse shape than you are." Caela sat up, but she didn't shrug out from under his arm. "Mom Iris is excited about the trip, I think. Dad E seems to be holding it together so far."

"Trust me. He's just better at hiding it than I am. I expect it will hit Iris when she has to turn around and leave you up there. When are you heading out?"

"Pretty much when *you* get downstairs."

Her smile was back, big enough that Alex heard it in her voice.

"Sent to fetch the old man, huh? Another few minutes up here won't make this any easier. Another few days wouldn't."

Caela stood and held out both hands. Alex squeezed them as he got up, but he dropped them to pull her into a hug.

"I know you're ready. I'm the one who's not. I'm going to miss you, Caela."

"I'll miss you too, Dad. I'll be back more often than you think."

Alex kept his thoughts to himself as he followed her out and down the stairs.

She'd be home for a visit, sure.

Not home to stay.

Chapter 39

Seven groups of new settlers had departed Wolf Branch since the nightmare of Mary's exile. As always, a huge crowd filled the Square, happy and excited. Several families were sending their oldest children today, so Etan suspected he wasn't the only one feeling a bit melancholy under the joy.

The biggest four-wheel-drive truck still in reliable working order was packed full of tools, supplies, and the few belongings that hadn't already made the trip up the mountain. Several smaller vehicles that could traverse the damaged road to Maple Ridge waited behind it in a line along the road.

A few parents would join the new colony for the first few days, then bring most of the vehicles back down. Iris walked along the line of supplies and milling families, pretending to inspect or organize. She knew more about Maple Ridge and the resources there than anyone else.

And if Etan didn't know better, he would have guessed she was closer to Caela's age than into her forties. Her blue jeans, t-shirt, and long black hair had her looking the same as the first day he and Alex met her and Gena. She caught Etan watching and smiled with her hand over her heart, the green fire of Anne's stone flashing in the sunlight.

Dana Chen and most of her security crew stood close to the biggest truck. Neither Etan nor anyone else on the Council liked the idea of ten guards having to go along, at least for the first few months.

No one old enough to remember the fatal nighttime raid from Maple Ridge so long ago – or Alex nearly losing his life not far from where they stood – were willing to argue. Nor was anyone who remembered the threat of Mary's broken Dreams that Caela helped them face.

A desperate, pathetic handful of those who'd followed Mary had tried to return a couple of years ago. Their ravaged skin too covered with sores to be recognizable. Not much more than bones underneath. Raving from mental and physical illness. Probably deranged from Dreams and Memories no one else wanted to know.

Too far gone to survive for more than a day or so, much less stage any kind of attack. Dana let Etan know every time it happened. Sandy assured him they met a quick and merciful end, with the method Etan remembered all too well. They all agreed it was best if no one else found out.

And best to assume it could happen again.

A hand as warm as the April sun in a cloudless blue sky found his. Etan looked down into Gena's red-rimmed eyes. His mother Laura stood behind her, close beside Iris's parents. All of them hugged Etan, their eyes showing their own pride and sadness.

Gena nodded toward the right. Alex walked down the nearly empty street, his head lowered to focus on Caela. Their daughter gestured and smiled as she spoke, no doubt describing the great adventure unfolding before her.

"He looks better than he did this morning," Gena said. "We'll have our hands full tonight."

"You'll be surprised, I think. Caela had the right idea to go get him herself instead of me."

"She's the only one of us with any sense today," his mother said.

Her real goodbyes said earlier, Caela had a quick kiss for Etan and Gena and the rest before she was off toward the center of the square. The group of seventeen heading up the mountain today all turned when she joined them.

"You two did a wonderful job raising her," Gena said, watching Caela. "They're lucky to have her as their leader."

After so many years, Etan had to admit one of the biggest advantages of a town full of Dreamers and Witnesses was no arguments over things like this. They'd all Dreamed of Caela heading up the new community in Maple Ridge. Even if she hadn't been the strongest Dreamer among them, decisions like this were incredibly easy, at least on the surface.

"She's part of *their* group now," Alex said. For the first time all day, he sounded proud instead of sad. "Head of their Council."

"Hopefully she'll go easy on us when we have to decide things together," Etan said.

The chatter all around them quieted as George Light made his slow way toward the group of new departures. His tightly curled hair was nearly all gray now, and he moved carefully after the chill of the night before. Growing fruits and berries better suited for the high altitude, and better to help with common problems like arthritis, was high on the list for the new colony.

George spoke into the hush, his voice as full and rich as ever.

"Friends and family, we're gathered for a momentous and joyful occasion. I won't lie to you after so many years, though. More than a little sadness runs through my heart today. I suspect I'm not the only one feeling that way."

George's son Daniel, a boy as strong, tall, and every bit as charismatic as his father, stood close by Caela's side. Alex took his hand, and Etan knew he'd also noticed how often the two of them ended up together.

Etan couldn't imagine a better Witness match for their daughter.

"Many of us arrived here nearly twenty-five years ago," George said. "Worried and unsure, so afraid to leave the outside world we thought was so secure behind. And terrified of leaving it too late.

"I won't tell you it's all been easy. Some of our time here has seemed nearly as dark as the old world outside. But we've made it this far together. And today, the very best of what we've accomplished stands before us, ready to set out into this new world on their own."

Etan noticed most of the Council had joined his family, standing beside and behind them. Dana Chen, her face proud and excited. Harry Mullins, not bothering to hide his tears or his smile. Most of them had children or grandchildren surrounding Caela.

"So while we're sad to see them go," George continued, "to know we won't be waking up to their voices tomorrow, to their smiles and their frowns, take comfort, my friends. These young people are the hope and promise of what brought us all together nearly a quarter of a century ago. They are the life and vitality that will see humanity through into a better future."

As the crowd shifted to let Caela and the other colonists move toward George, Etan spotted Gwen, Connor, and the rest of their children in a group of their friends. All their children were well into their teens now, smart and strong and independent. So much so that he had no idea who would want to stay in Wolf Branch and who would want to follow Caela into communities of their own making.

He hoped they would tell him and Alex before the Dreams did.

Caela stepped up beside George, and Daniel stood on his other side. George held out the traditional packet of seeds and plants despite the amounts already loaded in the trucks. Caela closed her hands over his.

"You're the first group to leave made up of our own families," George said. "You truly carry the seeds of our future. And so we offer you the gift of food so you may prosper in your new home."

"I can't add much to that," she said, grinning up at George as she held the packet to her heart. "So I'll just say thank you. To George and to all of you for coming here to see us off. Thank you to everyone who helped us get ready by going up there to get an idea of what we'd need and setting up so many things for us. Thank you to everyone who's going with us today. And thank you for being willing to leave when the time comes, even if we beg you to stay."

Behind Caela, Iris joined in the gentle laughter, but she blotted her eyes with her sleeve.

"Thank you for trusting me to do my best to keep our new

community organized. That means everything to me. I'll do my best, and I promise to ask for help *before* I need it.

"More than anything, we want to thank all of you. Our parents, our families, *all* of you. Everyone in Wolf Branch who took in a bunch of dazed settlers from the outside. Everyone who made that uncertain journey here.

"If you hadn't been so brave, so strong, none of us would be here. You left your homes, your lives, your entire world behind to give us a chance. Thank you for sharing that past world with us as much as you can. And thank you for trusting us to help you build this new one."

George raised his arms more slowly than in years past, but his gesture still managed to embrace everyone who could see him.

"Good journey!"

At the crowd's thunderous response, everyone seemed to move at once. For the first time, Etan caught a pale glimpse of what Alex saw all the time.

Patterns in the shifting crowd, the wind through the faintly budding trees around the square. Patterns in the beat of his own heart. Patterns that drove him away from here when he was younger than Caela, then brought him back home again to a life more full and joyful than he ever could have Dreamed.

Patterns that led to the man beside him, always.

Etan turned and stepped into Alex's arms.

The only home that had ever mattered.

ABOUT KARI

Kari Kilgore's wanderlust and imagination lead her all over the world on grand adventures. Her heart and family bring her home to her native Appalachian Mountains of Virginia. From that solid base, she and her husband Jason A. Adams bring those adventures to life in fiction.

Kari writes science fiction, fantasy, horror, and contemporary fiction, and she's happiest when she surprises herself. She lives at the end of a long dirt road in the middle of the woods with Jason, various house critters, and wildlife they're better off not knowing more about.

The Confidential Adventure Club

For Kari's exclusive free After The End stories and deleted scenes (including from the Storms of Future Past Series), discounts, early pre-sale releases, adorable pet photos, and a whole lot more not available anywhere else, visit The Confidential Adventure Club at www.smarturl.it/sofp-welcome.

Hope to see you there!

www.karikilgore.com
www.spiralpublishing.net

ALSO BY KARI KILGORE

I hope you enjoyed reading *Storms of Future Past* as much as I enjoyed writing it. Check out more of my fiction at www.karikilgore.com.

The Confidential Adventure Club

Curious what happened to Connor, the baby born at the end of *Dreaming the Storm,* and before the beginning of *Joining the Storm*? Wonder what happened after The End of *Fighting the Storm*?

Want more fiction from Kari, including stories, discounts, and box sets not available anywhere else? Want to hear about locations, research, and other cool things that inspired this story and beyond? All that and adorable pet photos, too?

Join The Confidential Adventure Club and get a thank you gift of *In the Eye of the Storm,* an exclusive short story from after The End of *Dreaming the Storm,* and a whole lot more at www.smarturl.it/sofp-welcome.

Hope to see you there!

Novels:

Until Death

The Dream Thief

Joining the Storm: Book Two of the Storms of Future Past Series

Fighting the Storm: Book Four of the Storms of Future Past Series

Novellas:

Songs in the Mountain

Legacy of the Land

Restricted Species

The Becalmed

In the Pines

Into the Storm: Book Three of the Storms of Future Past Series

> "Kari Kilgore is an author to watch—her lyrical voice a siren song; her insight, conjured voodoo."
>
> —Richard Thomas, author of *Breaker* and *Tribulations*

ADDITIONAL COPYRIGHT
INFORMATION

Dreaming the Storm

Copyright © 2018 by Kari A. Kilgore

All rights reserved

Published 2018 by Spiral Publishing, Ltd.
www.spiralpublishing.net

Book and cover design copyright © 2018 by Spiral Publishing, Ltd.
Cover art copyright © 2018 by SÃ¸ren Sielemann | Isoga1 |Dreamstime.com

ISBN-13: 978-1-948890-07-6
Library of Congress Control Number: 2018910624

Joining the Storm

Copyright © 2018 by Kari A. Kilgore

All rights reserved

Published 2018 by Spiral Publishing, Ltd.
www.spiralpublishing.net

Book and cover design copyright © 2018 by Spiral Publishing, Ltd.
Cover art copyright © 2018 by Joyfull | Ig0rzh |Dreamstime.com

ISBN-13: 978-1-948890-08-3
Library of Congress Control Number: 2018913208

Into the Storm

Copyright © 2019 by Kari A. Kilgore

All rights reserved

Published 2019 by Spiral Publishing, Ltd.
www.spiralpublishing.net

Book and cover design copyright © 2019 by Spiral Publishing, Ltd.
Cover art copyright © 2019 by Ig0rzh | Denis Tevekov |Dreamstime.com

ISBN-13: 978-1-948890-09-0
Library of Congress Control Number: 2018913210

Fighting the Storm

Copyright © 2019 by Kari A. Kilgore

All rights reserved

Published 2019 by Spiral Publishing, Ltd.
www.spiralpublishing.net

Book and cover design copyright © 2019 by Spiral Publishing, Ltd.
Cover art copyright © 2019 by Denis Tevekov | Joyfull | Ig0rzh |Dreamstime.com

ISBN-13: 978-1-948890-12-0
Library of Congress Control Number: 2019942219

www.ingramcontent.com/pod-product-compliance
Lightning Source LLC
Chambersburg PA
CBHW031602180726
48284CB00005B/1359